THE RISE OF THE IKHOR

THE GUARDIANS OF THE ASPIS SERIES
BOOK TWO

SARAH L. ROSE

ISBN (Paperback): 978-1-7388454-3-9

ISBN (Hardcover): 978-1-7388454-4-6

ASIN: B0DSJSG2Y3

LIV'S JOURNAL

Liv

I had one goal given to me—to wake the Aspis.

In my previous life, I had never been given a chance to be somebody. When I was taken from my home and dumped in new lands, far away, I believed I had travelled worlds. I was given a task that could save everyone, and I had hoped it was within me to be a hero. My chest ached as I escaped the Guardian lands, following my enemy turned saviour, and I clutched at it when the Aethar wasn't looking. It's not an ache from heartbreak, but a rising pain—as if my chest is holding in something that doesn't belong.

The Aethar is always watching me. Is she

looking for signs of the evil, waiting for it to rise? She suggested I keep a journal and write down my emotions to keep myself in check. I used to write—secretly, of course—when I was young. My mother made me learn and practice. She would burn the paper immediately, so we weren't discovered. I used to pour my darkest thoughts onto the pages. And why not? Why not get those feelings out of my head and onto paper if they would be destroyed anyway?

I won't be burning what I write anymore, and I worry that keeping these thoughts in the world is as wrong as thinking them.

My chest pains have been keeping me up at night, as does my fear of the dreams. I'm haggard, growing thinner every day. I've lived like this before, back home when I was alone. It was the Guards who brought me back to health. Now I am running from them, growing weaker again.

My chest hurts the most because my heart has withered within it. I had kept a box hidden deep within, where I stuffed my most undesirable thoughts and emotions away. They festered, transforming into something so dark that the evil magic chose me as its host. The box had names carved on its side—those of all who had wronged

me. If it still exists, a new name will be added:
the name of my once closest friend. Nuo.

I hear his voice before I sleep, and then I
dream of flesh peeling from a child of Night
and rising to the sky before it turns to smoke
and ash. The dreams are more vivid than reality
these days.

I thought I had lost everything when I ran
from the burning field. But no one ever prepares
for what it feels like to lose yourself.

I can feel it. As I fade, something else
takes my place.

It is trying to take over.

And it enjoys my pain.

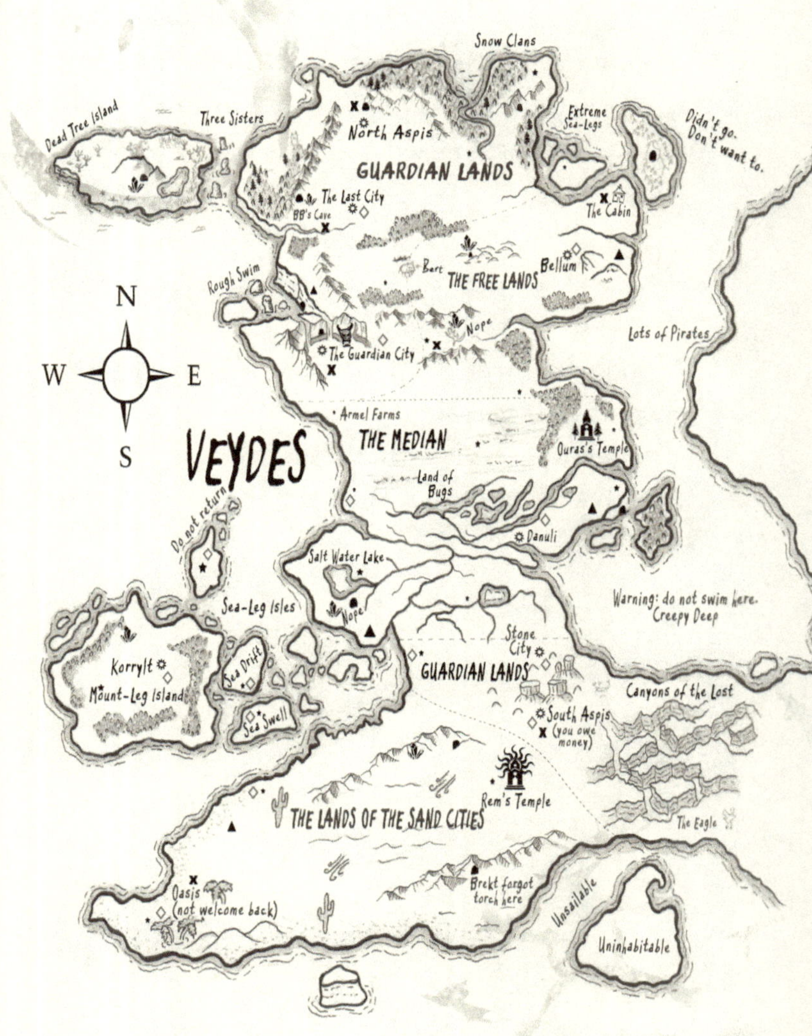

Snow Clans
Dead Tree Island
Three Sisters
North Aspis
GUARDIAN LANDS
Extreme Sea-Legs
Didn't go. Don't want to.
The Last City
BB's Cave
The Cabin
Bart
THE FREE LANDS
Bellum
Rough Swim
Nope
Lots of Pirates
The Guardian City
N
W
E
S
Armel Farms
THE MEDIAN
Ouras's Temple
VEYDES
Land of Bugs
Do not return
Danuli
Salt Water Lake
Warning: do not swim here. Creepy Deep
Sea-Leg Isles
Nope!
Stone City
Korrylt
Sea Drift
GUARDIAN LANDS
Canyons of the Lost
Mount-Leg Island
Sea Swell
South Aspis
(you owe money)
Rem's Temple
The Eagle
THE LANDS OF THE SAND CITIES
Brekt forgot torch here
Unsailable
Oasis
(not welcome back)
Uninhabitable

Nuo's
Map of
ARDE
★ Towns
● Cave
Crystal Cave
▲ Treasure
◇ Nuo's Faves
✖ Weapons
Aethar
Wastelands

PART ONE

Nuo

"Nuo," Liv cried out. "Stop this!"

I couldn't think. I couldn't process. My mind faltered over what was happening—what I had been trying to prepare for. Brekt was becoming the Aspis because the Ikhor had woken it.

And it was his *fucking* girl.

Everything was a lie. We had taken her in, healed her. Brekt had told me to trust her, as she was the girl he'd seen in his visions. He was in *love* with her.

Cursed Night, what had we done? The betrayal was carving a hole in my heart, while Brekt's dying was breaking it.

"I didn't know!" she pleaded. "I didn't understand."

A circle of dead earth, crusted black with ash and smoke, surrounded the Ikhor. Fire had erupted from her when Brekt was attacked, killing everyone around. The bodies closest to her smouldered, sending a terrible smell across the field toward us.

Yet Liv remained untouched, her clothing in perfect condition.

"How could you not know?" My hand shook as I thrust it towards Brekt. "He did!"

Brekt was fighting for control. His chest rose and fell, and his laboured breathing told me he couldn't pull air into his lungs. Blood poured from his heart while scales formed over other parts of his body. My chest was being ripped apart as if a blade had gone through mine as well.

"Don't speak to her, Nuo. It's not Liv," Brekt choked out.

The Ikhor had come and was already burning the earth. And the first one she punished was the man who fought to keep her safe.

I gripped one of my blades. "Already, it's trying to deceive us."

"It *is* me," Liv pleaded, her brows drawn together.

Brekt's skin flaked away, each piece equal to the horror choking the life out of me. They turned into smoke, churning and shredding like the embers of the fire, and I was helpless. I'd done everything to stop it. I'd searched for another way. There was no transferring the power to a new host. There was no bringing him back after he was gone.

What was I supposed to do now? I could fight, and I could kill … but I couldn't stop the will of the gods.

Brekt's lips curled back in a snarl—a sound I'd never heard, even when he threw himself at his enemies. Fangs grew from a mouth that was wider than it should be.

I turned to face the evil. We would fight now. If his last wish was to end the Ikhor, I would follow him to that death.

But my rage matched my growing fear.

"You liar!" I made it several feet on wobbling knees before I stopped.

"No, Nuo. I didn't know." The Ikhor trembled.

Was the magic wreaking havoc on the body of its host, just as the Aspis was wreaking havoc over Brekt?

How long had she known? Since the moment we met—that's why she was in that cave, so that we would find her.

The rage became a monster inside of me. It paired well with the horror of seeing Brekt withering. "You knew! You knew, and you said nothing. He's known for years, so don't lie to me."

Brekt had revealed his secret when we were younger. The dreams, the power—he knew he was the Aspis. It ruined his life, knowing he would barely live it.

Brekt's eyes shuttered. More skin flaked away to reveal scales.

"Nuo." Tears welled in Liv's eyes, her lower lip quivering.

No. Stop calling it *Liv.*

I searched its face for the lie. For the ghost of my friend ... but I couldn't see one from the other.

"Don't you come closer," I spat. "You don't get to touch him. You're going to kill him. You've already killed him." My voice broke, and I looked away from it, but the sight closer to me was worse. "You will never get to him, Ikhor." It was a promise I would make for Brekt.

"Stop, Nuo," Brekt moaned, hands coated red and holding his chest. "We knew this was coming. Control yourself, be ready to fight."

Even in his final moments, he remained demanding. He kept his composure as if it were a fight we would walk away from together.

We *always* walked away from a fight together.

"I'm not ready. How could I be ready for this?" He knew me. He knew I was not prepared. I suppressed the urge to vomit.

"You have to be."

"Why didn't you tell us?" Bastane's voice pierced through the night. I had forgotten the others—the Aether on the field and Falizha's horrid presence. "We could have helped. We could have figured out who she was."

"How?" I scoffed.

"I saw her react to magic when Rem was in the city. Only I thought she was the Aspis. You should have told us it was him." Bastane's face twisted.

How dare he feel pain. He thought he was tormented by Brekt dying? Bastane was the one who told Falizha about Liv. He brought us all here—he was the reason it was happening now.

"And give more reason for the world to cast me out?" Brekt growled, "Another way to be used as a pawn for the Days?"

Bastane knew the Council's hatred for Brekt. They made every attempt to stop us from becoming Guards. Legacies of Night weren't the only ones hated by the golden Council.

Brekt was losing his balance, trying to hide the pain, but I saw every one of his tells. "I chose to live with the little time I had in peace. It was bad enough I was chosen as a Guard, constantly controlled by the Council." Brekt leaned forward, spitting out blood, his mouth stained red. The fingers clutching his chest lengthened as claws curled from his fingertips.

Gods, how could I endure it?

Across the field, an Aethar, who was painted blue, approached the Ikhor, tugging on its sleeve. They spoke softly, so I couldn't hear.

"Olivia?" Even I heard the hate in my voice. How long had she been in league with the Aethar?

Liv paled when she met my gaze. "Nuo, no. It's not what it looks like."

"This whole time. You've been siding with those bastards this whole time!" The Aethar had killed my family, leaving me to be orphaned and raised in the worst, most unloving place to exist. And then I'd welcomed and made friends with Liv, one of them.

"I haven't. I promise." She was a good actress, fooling even me.

"Then why are you using the magic of their leader? Why are you standing with them? You've betrayed us. I lost my brother today!" Pain sharpened my words like blades. "This is your fault. You will pay for it."

The Ikhor searched for an ally, panicking. The other Guards held their positions. Kazhi watched Brekt with a horrified expression—she hadn't guessed he was the Aspis.

"Go, Olivia. You won't get far once the beast wakes," Brekt warned.

My mouth fell open. What was he doing?

"Brekt," Liv cried.

How could he let her go? We needed to stop her.

"She's not leaving this field. The Ikhor is ours," I said, "the rest of the Aethar too. They've killed everyone I loved. I will hunt down every last one of them tonight." I lifted my blade, but it was torment trying to hold the thing steady. "You know what I do to Aethar, Liv."

Brekt bent over again, groaning. Pieces of him kept flaking away, revealing more of the Aspis with every passing second.

My fingers trembled around my blade as I swallowed around the lump in my throat, my vision blurring. Not from tears, not from smoke. It was pure, uncontrollable pain taking over my senses.

"Nuo," Brekt said, barely above a whisper.

My attention shot to him, but it wasn't entirely him anymore, and I couldn't think of a thing to say.

His eyes shuttered, his throat moving as he struggled to speak. "You remember what I asked you?"

I flinched. "You can't be serious. Not after what we learned. You can't ask that of me."

"Use your head. It always worked better than mine. Don't make decisions from your pain. If it's her, please do as I asked."

I held my breath, refusing to let his words sink in because it was then that the last pieces of Brekt fell away. The last bit of skin turned to dust, revealing scales beneath. I reached out to the brother who was no longer there, and as Brekt faded, so did every shred of goodness within me.

The iridescence of his eyes flashed one last time, the fading brown winking out before it turned to yellow—to the eyes of the Aspis. Citrine eyes with sharp vertical pupils turned toward me and my body jolted. Brekt's face elongated, his nose transforming into slits as his ears drew back and twisted into spiralled horns. I recoiled from the man I had grown up with, who was transforming into a creation made by the gods themselves.

It was in pain. Its body stretched and curled like a wounded snake, chest rising and falling as it tried to catch its breath between hisses and whines. Then it collapsed, a black snake coiled and asleep.

Time stopped.

What do I do? What do I do? What do I do? I always had an answer, but this time, all of my insecurities came crashing down—*Weak-blooded Sea-leg. No real power*—I could do nothing to help. I dropped down beside it, feeling the heat of the Aspis's body, shaking it—but it had gone still.

I searched for help as the world spun ... and in the haze, Liv was there.

"Liv, come. Stop this." I held out a desperate, shaking hand—a final lifeline.

She had to be in there. She could stop it, right? Love fixed these things. A million tales told stories of lovers ending a curse. She hadn't lied. She was my friend. Brekt was falling in love with her.

I could forget what she'd become if she saved him.

She had to save him.

I held my hand in the air, waiting, urgent and insistent. She could—

"Nuo, I—" She stumbled away.

I grabbed the still form of the beast. "Liv? Liv, he needs you. We can find a way to stop this." I put my weight over it, trying to stop it from growing.

Liv *had* to come help. She was my last hope.

I couldn't catch my breath, knowing I was running out of time. I could fix it. I could fix anything. I hadn't fought all those years for Brekt to die this young.

"Don't be a fool, Nuo." Bastane stood behind me, and I battled the urge to stab him. He didn't understand—we needed to stop the change. "That's not her. Look what she's done. The dust around her."

I searched Liv's face and waited to see who would answer—my friend or my enemy.

"I'm sorry," she said, closing her eyes.

She stepped toward the blue woman.

Every. Fucking. Part. Of. Me. Raged.

Brekt was dying, right fucking here! She had the magic of the gods, she had the power to stop it!

She lied. Tricked us. Led us here!

The Ikhor must have been working with them from the start—Bellum, the villages in the jungle—it had the Aethar come to this field to help it end and kill Brekt.

I screamed. It was impossible to hold in the cracking, earth shattering hatred.

Brekt was gone, and his lover was the reason why.

"How could you! You side with the Aethar, and we are done. You are dead to me." I made a promise. To it. To myself.

"Nuo, I will find a way to fix this."

"You've already been corrupted. The lies began a long time before the evil possessed you. I will find you, Ikhor. I will find you and make you pay!" My hatred had such force it charged the air, poisoning it and making it impossible to breathe.

The blue Aethar grabbed the Ikhor and tugged it away from the burning corpses. I didn't blink, horrified and unbelieving, as they faded into the smoke and orange glow.

But I understood what I had to do.

As the faint outline of the Ikhor was engulfed in a cloud of fire, I shouted my promise for the world to hear. "You better run as fast as you can, Olivia, because I will follow the beast, and I will be there when it kills you!"

CHAPTER

TWO

Liv

"**G**reat, you just provoked a godsdamned Guard of the Aspis."

I couldn't keep up with the blue woman as we ran away from the burning field and into the black night ahead. I focused on her high leather boots. The world around me was a blur of smoke and ash.

I had lost everything. And he ... *he* was gone. This cursed world had ripped a hole in me *again*. A whirling storm of emotions threatened to tear me to pieces. Or was that the evil magic I carried inside me?

"Slow down. I can't keep up." I panted.

The purple casings of my twin swords bounced against my legs, tugging my belt lower, catching on my cloak as I hopped over rocks and brushed past trees.

Kazhi had tied my blades to my waist, telling me to escape with the strange Aethar girl knowing it was my safest way out. She had also lied about who she was. An Aethar—my enemy and the enemy of the Guard she was pretending to be.

"We need to get to my racer." The Aethar's delicate hand

8

gripped a tree as she maneuvered around it, her movements effortless compared to mine. Her skin, barely visible in the dark under her long flowing cloak, was a pale blue with navy markings. "It's not far. But I doubt we'll outrun the beast if you keep going this slow."

"I just lost the man I cared for." My voice shook, the words barely discernible. "You living through this is not my focus." I had to concentrate to avoid stumbling over every rock I passed. I was fumbling over pain ... and anger—both equal to the other.

Why did it have to be *him*?

Up ahead, the Aethar disappeared behind the few trees in the field. I wiped my tears, trying to clear my vision before I tripped over something. Although the sky was dark, the slight changes in the silhouettes told me the morning light was approaching.

"Don't be rude to me," she spat over her shoulder. "I'm risking my ass right now," she disappeared again, "... knee-deep in Guardian filth for weeks." Her dark cloak was all I saw slipping between trees. "... before they killed you."

Every step I took pulsated with pain, although it was nothing compared to my chest.

I should put an end to my escape and turn back to my friends.

They're not your friends anymore. You're the enemy now, I reminded myself.

I grabbed onto a tree and pulled myself forward with a trembling hand. The path ahead was on an incline, making it harder to avoid tripping. We were cresting a rocky hill when the skies above us vibrated with the roar of the beast. Its thunderous cry pounded against my chest until my heart threatened to stop beating. It invoked such fear I had no comparison.

The Aspis. The great black beast, foretold to return every millennium and save the people. It would hunt and kill its enemy, the Ikhor, and that was where my situation came in.

I was the great evil. The Ikhor. And the beast? It had been ... *no.*

By some divine curse, I was possessed by evil magic—magic

stolen an era ago and corrupted by every man and woman who had ever been its host.

The only problem with the whole "destined to be evil" thing was I didn't feel evil. But the events from tonight triggered emotions I had repressed for years—they had been the catalyst in letting the magic loose.

The blue woman stopped, and I finally caught up with her. She stared ahead, past the single tall tree next to her. We stood under a pale purple sky atop a hill that dropped into an open plain.

"What are you looking for?" I asked when she didn't move.

"A way forward. My racer is down this hill."

I saw nothing in the gloom. "What's holding you back?"

She tilted her hood up. "The open skies."

I couldn't distinguish the look on her face from the shadows cast by the night, but she was tall, and being looked down upon by a dark hooded figure made her appear like the evil one, not me.

"We are going to have to risk being spotted. I don't know how well that thing sees in the dark."

"I do," I said quietly. "The man whose body it stole was a pure-blooded legacy of Night. He would miss nothing in the dark."

"We must hope the traits don't pass to the beast. We make a run for it. Jump on behind me and hold on tight."

"Wait." I grabbed her arm as she moved to run. "What is a racer?"

"Please tell me you're joking." She whipped her hood back so I could make out the disbelief on her face. Her skin was smooth, though naturally marked by many navy blue lines and dashes. Straight, pale blue hair flowed over her shoulders and down to her waist. She was young like me.

I shook my head.

"Gods help me. Just sit behind me and hold on tight."

She didn't wait for my reply, sprinting down the side of a hill. Her pace was reckless, but the roar in the sky, louder than before, had me running as fast as she did.

"How do we escape a dragon that can fly?" I stumbled down

the hill behind her, trying to outrun my death. My flowing green pants swished around my legs, threatening to trip me.

"I don't know what a dragon is, but my plan of escape relies mostly on hope at the moment. Also, you are the Ikhor. I assume your magic will come in handy when we need it."

The Aethar assumed too much. She thought the evil possessed me and that I understood what I was.

"Once we get to my ship, I'm taking you to safety. And right now, that means leaving Guardian lands."

"Aren't we in the Median? It's neutral territory."

An uneven laugh came from her. "Nowhere in Veydes is neutral. It's all under the Council's thumb. We are heading to my home, where people want to help you."

"Won't the Aspis follow us?"

"I'm hoping that it will stick close to the Guards and that they will hold the Aspis back from crossing the borders. But, again, my plan is based on hope and your magic."

Her home would be in Aethar lands. The Aethars I had met before were horrifying, nothing like the woman ahead of me. They disfigured themselves from head to toe, hoping the self-inflicted pain would make them a suitable host for the magic of the Ikhor, because the magic always chose a host strong enough to contain the evil that it was.

Yet, the magic chose me.

The dark outline of what I assumed to be her racer grew closer as we neared the bottom of the hill. Pink tinged the horizon, increasing my hopes of escape. If crystals powered the thing, it would be our best chance of getting out of here alive.

As the Aethar reached the racer, she ripped off the weapon strapped to her back—the same one she had used to fire at Falizha, the Governor's daughter, almost killing the horrible woman. She strapped the weapon to the side of the racer before hopping on. The racer was the size of a small, thin cart, not as tall as a horse, but she sat atop it as if it was.

I maneuvered around the racer, pulling myself onto a cold seat, and wrapped my hands around her waist. The unease of touching a stranger would have stopped me in the past. The fact that she was my enemy made it worse.

"What now?" I asked as we sat there, unmoving.

"Give me a second to start it," she scolded, before a faint green-blue glow surrounded the Aethar. Something was lit between her hands at the front, but questions about the machine were wiped from my mind as the ground shook beneath us.

I sunk my fingers into her side. "What is that?" I asked, but I already knew.

"That is bad luck." She looked over her shoulder behind me, her face paling in the dark, so I followed her line of sight. "Don't look!" she yelled. "Hold tight to me!"

I barely had enough time to hold on before the force of the racer slammed my body back into the seat. I pressed my legs against the hard metal to keep from falling. The racer was silent as the wind whooshed past me, and the landscape tore away. Rocks passed underneath like shooting stars, blurring further as tears formed when I didn't blink. Terror constricted my muscles, and I worried I would lose my grip.

A shadow passed over us, and the wind carried away my scream.

High in the sky, the beast snaked its way through the waking morning. The black belly of the Aspis glowed a rose gold as the first rays of sunlight hit its smooth scales. It was flying ahead of us now. Had it not noticed us below?

My shoulders trembled as I bowed forward, hiding like a coward behind the Aethar.

The beast roared again, curling its body to descend and cut off our path. It dove for us like a bird of prey, and I clamped my eyes shut.

Once more, it roared, and my eyes snapped back open to find it landing on the ground before us, blocking the rising sun. Its black horns curled away from its snake-like face, its hungry appraisal glowing with murderous intent.

The woman skidded the racer to a halt, trying to spin us in the opposite direction. My knees were so tightly locked in place that I managed to stay on the racer but lost sight of the Aspis as we turned back around.

Out of the corner of my eye, the beast moved like liquid over the field, parting the grassy plain with an invisible force as it advanced, and in no time it blocked us once more, its head larger than the two of us and the racer combined. In the short time since it took *his* body, the thing had grown half as long as an airship.

Brekt.

To even think his name caused sharp pains of shock and sorrow to pierce my chest. My grip on the woman loosened as I held back the sob stuck in my throat.

In our short time together, I had grown closer to him than anyone—save my mother, whom I lost long ago. He had been the closest thing I had known to love since I was a child. Then destiny was called due. I became the Ikhor, which triggered the Aspis to wake, killing him in order to transform into the beast the gods had created to save the people.

The Aspis circled us, blocking any way of escape. Smoke curled around its body like a churning and shifting black inferno, and its yellow stare burned like the brightest fire. Its teeth—would those sharp fangs be how it killed me?

I couldn't tear my gaze away, rooted to the spot. My breath burned in my lungs as it continued to glide on an invisible wind. There was no recognition in its eyes. Nothing human. Another sharp pain tore at my chest.

He was truly gone.

I had been angry—so angry—when the magic took over, taking away my choices. Now, a current of pain washed the anger away, drowning me. A fog settled over my thoughts—my body's attempt to shut down from the anguish.

The beast's tail, shadowed in smoke, whipped around, taking the racer out from under us, and a scream came from the Aethar as we were thrown to the ground, rolling to a stop.

I spit grass from my mouth, my legs shaking as I got to my feet, bracing myself for the beast's next move, but everything was moving too quickly, the colours too bright. I couldn't see the Aethar through my panicked state, but I could see the black death before me, so I retreated, my knees buckling.

The sun highlighted every scale, every sharp tooth. My death was bathed in golden light as I shivered in fear before it, and I fumbled for one of my swords, my last defence. My sweaty palms slipped over the handle.

"Do something! Burn it," the Aethar yelled.

I paused, forgetting I could wield fire. How did I make it work? I shook, too cold to understand how to conjure the flames as I had before.

The woman reached for the weapon strapped to the side of the racer—the weapon that could shoot thick arrows. Everything slowed down and sped up all at once. In a blur, the beast lunged for her weapon, splintering it in its teeth before the Aethar could even touch it. She screamed, backing away again. The Aspis spat the weapon out, facing us, tensed to strike. Its thin, blade-like pupils darting back and forth between us, deciding.

This time, it chose me. Its teeth came together in a loud crack as it gave a warning shot mere feet away, showing me exactly how it planned to kill me. It shifted to the woman again, and I panicked. I didn't want the woman to get hurt, even if she was an Aethar.

"S-stop!" I screamed. Then, to the woman, I whispered, "You have to g-get out of here, once I di-distract it."

She gave no response.

The fear that froze me in place turned into a biting cold that claimed my body, crawling down my arms to my hands. My teeth chattered as I stared into my enemy's eyes.

I was no hero, but I hadn't thought I would be such a coward.

After another violent shake, a terrible itch clung to my palms.

"What is that?"

I didn't need to look at the woman to know what she was

seeing. Icicles had formed in my hand, and my sudden amazement when I held them up made them disappear.

The Ikhor could wield *more* than fire.

The beast shifted, preparing to strike again—this time, I didn't think it would be a warning. I lifted my hands, pushing them toward the beast. Nothing happened. I pushed them toward it again, holding them high in the air. *Why wasn't the magic working?*

The beast opened its mouth, and saliva dripped from its fangs onto the grass below. It coiled, its attention landing on the Aethar. Anticipating its movement, I stepped forward with my hands still raised.

Sharp, cold magic burst forth like blades seeking the roaring Aspis.

Icicles, sharp and deadly, tore its face, and its roar turned into one of pain. The beast's body curled around itself like a wounded animal, blood seeping from a gash that sliced through its left eye.

The woman ran for the racer. "Get on! Now's our chance."

I didn't question who or where she was taking me. She was all I had anymore.

The beast turned its head one last time to face me, its uninjured eye locking onto me.

It didn't move.

I shut myself down, ignoring the beast in pain because my heart wanted to believe that the look it was giving me was one of betrayal.

CHAPTER
THREE

Liv

What had I done?

I curled against the woman's back as she navigated her racer away. The fog soaked my mind, coating the pain, settling deep. I did everything I could not to think about *him*. To not think about what I was running from.

We passed groves of trees until there were none, crossing grassy plains until they were a blur of green. Far behind us, we had left the wounded Aspis.

I had half-blinded it. I bested the beast, untrained, in our first match. I should be celebrating. But instead, I was consumed with guilt. The feeling sat next to its close friend—grief. Gone was the anger for the gods, for this world and the curse. In its place was a leech, sucking the breath from my lungs.

I didn't know how the ice daggers erupted from my hands. Just as I didn't know how the fire was made when I transformed. The moment had come and gone so fast.

Now the Aspis was wounded—how long would it take to heal?

The sky ahead was clear as the racer drove toward the rising sun, and I steadied my nerves as green passed beneath us. How much time had passed? The Aethar paid no attention to me as she gripped the racer, taking us away from the family I had made after leaving my old home.

The Guards of the Aspis would search for me. Betrayals, secrets revealed, transformations. The death of the man I cared for and the loss of the closest friend I had ever had. My fingers clung to the woman's cloak. Drops of rain hit me as I stifled my cries.

"What in the cursed Night is that?" she yelled over the wind.

The sky opened above us, letting loose a torrent of rain like stones thrown from the gods. It forced the racer to the side, taking us off course.

"Dear gods, where did this come from?" I barely heard her over the wind that had picked up. "We have to find shelter. I can't navigate. Ollo better not be flying in this." The racer slowed, and the woman shifted in her seat and pointed to a small hill with a large tree growing from a rocky overhang. "We will wait under there until it passes and pray the Aspis can't find us in a storm."

She drove us toward the hill, stopping the racer near the overhang. The tree's thick branches whipped in the wind. Its roots wove over and around the rock, creating a small cave—the jutting overhang offering a dry shelter underneath, protected from the wind.

I jumped off the racer, standing at the rear, and for the first time, I noted it was made from the same ore the airships were. I had seen its replica in the Last City a lifetime ago.

"Come on. We need to keep hidden if we aren't moving," the Aethar said in a detached voice, moving the racer toward the rock.

The sky was a sheet of grey, with no sign of black smoke or beasts overhead. The wind whipped my dark blonde hair around my face as the rain soaked me through. I felt none of it. As water ran down my back, I wondered if the Aspis was okay.

"Are you serious?" the Aethar muttered, not intending for me to hear. She stomped back into the rain, the racer hidden in shadows. Her navy eyes met mine, heavy with disdain—they were the same colour as the lines running down and across her face. "Are you gonna keep me in the rain?"

"I don't keep you anywhere. Do what you want." My voice was hollow, even to me.

Her animated face didn't hide her disapproval, but she hesitated to say anything. "I know you must be disoriented right now. But I did save you. Please don't waste that effort." Her hands went to her hips. The blue markings travelled down her thin fingers.

"Are those tattoos?"

She glanced down. "You mean my skin?" She lifted her hand, and an eyebrow went up. I only nodded. "Wow. No. That's what I look like. Now, can you move?" Her expression changed as if remembering who she spoke to. "I mean, please come out of the rain. I am a friend. I am helping." Rain collected on her grey cloak, falling from the rim of her hood as she tried to hide her impatience.

I had never met anyone who spoke as this Aethar did. She had a light, feminine voice and would have been imprisoned back home for the sass in her tone. But she feared me—because I was the evil destined to rise.

As I moved toward the overhang, the colour of her wrist caught my eye. Her right arm was damaged. I reached for her, fearing what I saw.

"Don't!" she hissed. She pulled her arm back, cradling it against her chest and giving me a sour look. "Sorry. I mean, please don't touch it."

"Whatever." I left the torrent of rain and sat on a rock facing the racer. Drops of water fell from my hair, running down my back, and my clothing clung to me. It was damp under the overhang, and there wasn't much space to keep my distance from the Aethar.

"You almost grabbed my burn, is all," she explained. "I'm not *that* scared of you."

"So you are burnt. I thought that's what I saw."

She sat next to me under the roots, facing the rain that surrounded us. The sound would soothe most, but the grey only mirrored how I felt inside.

I turned to the woman, holding her arm to her chest, perched uncomfortably on the rock and grabbed the hem of her cloak.

"No." She pulled away.

But I saw enough to know the skin of her arm was a seeping wound of blueish-pink welts where it had been burnt away. I had burned so many of the Aethar. The scarred ones—who held me captive—I had burned so thoroughly they reduced to ash. And I had burned the woman's arm in the process.

Thunder cracked in the sky.

I was a monster.

I put my palm against my chest, feeling a sharp pull. I straightened my back to get a full breath in, though it didn't help.

I used to hide all of my emotions and trap them in a box inside. But that box shattered when I became the Ikhor. Now, I felt everything.

"What—" The woman stared as the grey darkened, a torrent descending on us. Though I had never seen a hurricane, I believed I was experiencing one.

I couldn't stop gawking at her arm.

I put my hands on my knees, concentrating on my breathing, holding in the sobs, afraid of what would happen if I let one loose.

"Your bracelet." She pointed to my crystal bracelet the Oracle had given me—it glowed, pulsing with a soft green-blue. It wasn't the first time it had done it. I locked eyes with her, worried about what she would say.

Why was I worrying? What was I hiding anymore—that magic

crystals glowed around me? That I could hear them humming sometimes? I was the Ikhor. I didn't have to worry about anyone mistrusting or hating me again. Everyone already did.

"Your earrings, too. Why would you wear a crystal full of magic? Miss ... Ikhor ... I don't know what you want me to call you. Are you okay?"

She was a weird woman. I bent over farther, dropping my head between my knees and counted to rid myself of the growing nausea, because the burn on her arm shone *wet*.

"Hey," she said. "Hey, look at me. This isn't your fault."

I protested, but she stopped me. "Okay, yes, my burns are your fault, but I saw how crazy it was back there. The burning field, I hadn't expected what I found either. Don't let it stress you. You have enough going on adjusting to your new body." Her focus shifted to the rain, then back to me. "My name is Maev, by the way." Her lips formed a nervous smile, distracting me.

I came from a world where everyone wore masks, hiding their thoughts and feelings lest they gain the Keepers' attention. No one was as open as Maev.

She had a pointed chin and a straight nose. Grey blue lips on her heart-shaped mouth should have made her look pale and sickly, but her features were ethereal. She was the prettiest woman I had ever seen.

"I am not possessed," I muttered.

Her round navy eyes were wide and untroubled—she wore her innocence with ease. We may be similar in age—she looked to be in her mid-twenties—but I sensed we would be hard-pressed to find anything in common.

"What do you mean? I saw you transform."

"The magic appeared ... I can feel it, kind of. But I'm still me. I can still remember my life before that moment."

"The legends say the Ikhor rises. Not just magic inside a girl."

"Well, the last time it rose was a thousand years ago. The legends have changed. Or something went wrong."

"Or you haven't fully transformed," Maev thought aloud, her

mouth popping open when she realized she shouldn't have said so. Thunder cracked again, and she held up her hands. "I'm sorry, I shouldn't scare you. I'm glad you're just a girl. Honestly, I was scared to travel with you. This will be much easier."

The sky lightened, and her brows shot up. She nodded as if the storm easing up would soften my mood. "Why don't you tell me where you're from? It was Olivia, right? That's what the Guard called you. I haven't visited many places in Veydes, but I have studied maps." She was distracting me.

I counted again, taking in a deep breath. I didn't know what she was trying to do. She was my enemy. Becoming the Ikhor didn't mean I would trust an Aethar so quickly.

"I am from the continent Rydavas." She pointed to herself. How long would the woman keep talking? "That's where I am taking you, the Northern Rydavian city."

"Huh?" Was there a city hidden in the Aethar wastelands?

Maev monitored the rain with a curious look. "We will meet up with my brother soon. He's with the airship, and we will get you away from danger."

"What do you mean, Rydavian city? And what is Rydavas?"

She rolled her eyes and slumped against the rock behind her. "I knew you Guardian folk were separated from the rest of the world, but this is just sad. You don't even know our continent's name?"

"First: I'm not a Guardian. Second: I'm not even from *this* continent."

She scoffed, "Uh huh. I know you aren't Rydavian."

"And how would you know that?" I asked because I wasn't certain I was right either.

"You look at me as a Guardian would. With hate," she huffed.

"Well, you're an Aethar. All your people do is kill."

Her lips parted at the insult. "I am *not*. The stupid name the Southlanders adore was gifted to them by the Guardians. And I would like to inform you that I've never killed in my life. I nearly did, with the golden Day-leg back there. A horrifying moment for me. On top of it all."

How did she lie so easily? She wasn't hiding her thoughts or feelings. She wasn't masking her emotions.

Who was this woman?

When I didn't reply, she added, "I'm nothing like the people here. I don't fight, kill, or even know how to use a sword. I learned how to use my crossbow a few months ago. And the Aspis destroyed it."

"That's stupid," I muttered.

"A little louder, please?" Maev's mouth twisted into a sneer.

How could she make me feel small with such a simple expression? I stammered before finally spitting out, "It's stupid. Not to know how to fight? This world is dangerous. How did you survive with the Aethar horde you travelled with?"

"Ugh, gods no." She folded her arms, wincing at the pain, then put them back softly on her lap. "I don't associate with that lot. Same continent, different worlds."

"They called out to you in the burning fields." They called her Blue One but had said nothing else.

"Well, that's true—I did run into a few who said they had information on the Ikhor's whereabouts and that a field was burning from its magic. I told them I would pay them to bring you to me. I was having a hard time pinpointing you on the field."

"Why were you looking for me?"

Thunder cracked in the sky once more, and Maev straightened, studying the new wave of rain. "Listen," she said, holding up her palms. "Just calm yourself a bit. I really don't mean you harm."

Liv

Rebeka left me to rot. Now the Guards have too. How do I feel about that? Thankful. Patterns are predictable. Lesson learned—no more friends.

—After writing that, I feel guilty. The Guards are not the same as Rebeka.

"Don't tell me to calm myself!" I yelled. "You understand nothing about me." I studied the dirt underneath me so she couldn't see the burning in my eyes.

My wet clothes stuck to my skin, making me itch, and I concentrated on that. Anything to stop the images of Nuo's face appearing or seeing the pieces of *him* fade away as the Aspis tore free from his body.

"I know. I know. I sometimes speak without thinking." She worried her hands in her lap. "And I want to get to know you, but right now, I'm pretty sure you're making the sky fall around us. We can't stay. We are in danger every second we stay in Guardian lands, so we need the rain to stop."

"You think I am doing this?" I thrust a hand toward the sky.

Maev flinched at the movement, afraid, and I jerked back, too. But not from her—from the sheet of rain.

A shadow passed outside. My hand that was pointing to the sky slapped over my mouth.

"What w-was that?" I leaned back, pressing my damp cloak against the root behind me.

Maev gave me a skeptical look. "What do you mean?"

"Didn't you see that shadow? Something is out there."

Maev jumped, scrambling back, and we watched, but nothing more passed by.

"Could the Aspis have found us?" My voice cracked.

She shook her head. "I don't think it's out there. Just the rain." She wasn't convincing when her attention continued to dart outside.

I closed my eyes, realizing how hard my chest was pounding as sweat clung to my back and my limbs ached. I shuddered as I told myself I wasn't losing my mind. I had just fought the legendary Aspis, and I was scared. Maev was right. I needed to calm down.

"Anyways," Maev said, keeping her voice low. "This rain, I think it's the gods' magic. They controlled the elements of the earth. All of the elements. If you are telling the truth and are still self-aware, at the very least, you have the Ikhor's magic and don't know how to control it."

The outside world mirrored the torrent of pain laying waste to my chest. Could she be right? I had made fire and ice. Was rain so hard to believe?

I eyed the grey outside. No more shadows passed the opening. "How did you figure that out? And so fast?"

She gave a shy smile. "It's my profession to figure things out. Anyways. Why don't we try again? Tell me where you are from. Concentrate on something easy."

A laugh escaped me. "Thinking about my home will make this storm worse." Lightning lit up the rain, the flash of light making Maev scream, and I bit down on my retort, watching again for anything lingering outside our hideaway.

"You said you weren't from this continent, but you definitely aren't from my side. You don't even know what my continent is called. So where are you from?"

She thought I was lying. Her expression said as much.

Nuo had warned me to keep my secrets to myself—where I was from would scare people. But she had crossed into enemy lands to capture the Ikhor, so maybe …

"I am from the Lost Lands." Why did I care what people knew anymore? "A place my people called the Endless Forest."

Maev blew out a breath. "Look, I want to ask you a question without making it rain harder."

"No promises."

How long would we be stuck here? If the rain was my doing, maybe forever.

"Well, I wonder if you hit your head or something when you transformed?"

I animated my face like the Aethar, tilting my head toward her, hoping to annoy her as she did me. It was unnatural and uncomfortable, showing how I felt. "I am not making this up. The Lost Lands are real. I also didn't know there was a world beyond our borders before I came here. The magic took me and brought me to the Guardian Lands. It was the Guards who first found me."

"Really?" Her face lit up. "My friend back home believes the Lost Lands are real. He has texts on the legends, but I always thought it was silly to believe in. What's it like there?"

"A nightmare. I was trying to escape before I was brought to Veydes."

"How were you brought here?"

"The Light found me, spoke of waking the Aspis and then the next thing I knew, I was lying in a damp cave thinking I was dead."

She blinked. "Interesting." Maev crossed her legs, resting an elbow on a knee. "If that's true, the magic must have some sentience to it." She reached into her cloak and pulled out a rectangular object. It was the same one she held on the field when she approached Falizha and me. She pressed on the front of it. "Perhaps over time, possessing multiple hosts, it has developed intention and thought."

"What are you doing?"

"Taking notes," she mumbled, ignoring me.

"What is that?" I said, nodding my head toward the object. It was made from metal, not the ore the strange objects in this world were usually made of.

"Oh, this is my little invention." She wiggled it in the air. "It's how I tracked you."

"How did that thing track me? Is it magic?"

"No," she chuckled. "*This* is science."

Maev was vibrant when she smiled. There was no question about it—she and I were nothing alike. She looked so youthful. Unburdened.

"What's science?" I had seen the word in forbidden books in a forbidden cottage long ago.

She stopped playing with her device. "Wow. I do believe you are from the Lost Lands now. Science is the study of, well, everything. How things work, how to make things work, and how to make things from nothing."

"I don't think I follow. That sounds like magic."

"Yes, magic, as we refer to it, is the earth's energy. Science is the study of the physical and natural world through observation, experimentation, and test—oh, never mind. The earth's magic is natural, while what I am holding is an invention. A human creation," she said before her face fell, seeing my confusion.

"So what does that thing do?"

Maev had a way of saying a lot while saying nothing at all. I had no clue what she was talking about. My attention kept wandering outside, and I was anxious to get as far away from the Aspis as I could.

"I technically borrowed the idea from my professor," she tried again. "I study the tech of the ancient world—ancient ore technologies—like airships and crystal-powered weapons. I also create new tech by taking apart AO tech and redesigning it. This device is a tracker. My professor's idea to track crystals."

"That thing can track crystals?"

My first instinct was to tell Nuo. The reminder that he was no longer at my side shot through my heart and undid the control I was gaining.

Thunder crashed.

You better run as fast as you can, Olivia, because I will follow the beast, and I will be there when it kills you.

"Our deposits are running low and creating a risk to our way of life," Maev continued. "His invention will help us find more and restore our numbers."

"You say *our* ..." I prompted, hoping she would keep talking. It was a good distraction.

"My people. Anyways, this device I created myself—the first of its kind. I tweaked it to search for elemental magic like that of the gods. Then I followed the biggest signal it could pick up." Maev gave me a tight smile, realizing she was rambling. "My device led me to Bellum, where I first saw you."

"You found me back then?"

"I saw you in the market with your Guard. The one who ..."

She was talking about *him*. She saw us together in the markets of Bellum, where he had bought me my swords.

My bracelet brightened again, and the rain tore across the sky. I wanted to be sick.

"I'm so sorry. I was caught up in my story and talking about my tracker. I didn't think about what I was saying."

I followed the steady drop of rain from a small root before me. *Drip, drip, drip.* Anything not to think of him.

"I can tell you cared deeply—"

"Stop," I demanded. "Please, stop."

"Sorry." She bit her lip, flinching when lightning lit the outside world.

"You hate the Guards. You're probably happy he's dead." I put my face in my hands so she wouldn't see how much it hurt.

One. Two. Three. My breathing was so ragged there was no hiding my grief.

"I didn't know him," she said softly. "I only hated what they represented. But you cared for them ..."

I bit down on my next comment, wishing I could make her stop.

She went to lay a hand on my arm, but I pulled away. I was not used to someone's touch and wouldn't get accustomed to an Aethar's.

"So what else does your tracker do?" My voice was hard.

Maev sat up and put the device away while she spoke. "I programmed it to take notes. I lose my train of thought quite easily with all that's going on up there." A blue finger tapped against her dotted temple. Her voice remained soft. Soothing.

She was quick to believe I was from the Endless Forest—could I trust she was not one of the scarred Aethar who had attacked so many times? Was she less of a threat?

"Why are you helping me? I get I'm the Ikhor, but why you, and what use do you have of me?"

Wincing as she moved her arm, Maev considered her answer. "I have reasons to help, but it's less about you and more about fixing things back home. Mostly, I came along because I have this tracker. And I am the only one who knows how to use it."

"What do you mean? You want to help me destroy the beast, right?" Her answer surprised me. I had expected a tale of ending the Aspis. "When the two rise, the battle will decide the fate of the people for the next era."

"Every *historiography* era, you mean. Not the *Alchemical* Era, which properly denotes a million years. The Guardians are far more negligent when calculating time frames ..." Maev blinked.

"Never mind. Clearly the Guardians have been giving you history lessons. And no. I don't want to help you destroy it."

"No? So you're going to let it kill me?"

"Let me explain first." Her eyes narrowed. "My brother was asked to locate you and bring you home—my only purpose was to track you. I am not even supposed to be here in Veydes. Events turned real fast on that field, though, and I had no choice but to get you out alone."

I rubbed my neck—it was going stiff.

"We were trying to get to you before the Guards did. Obviously, that failed. I have been tracking you for a while. We worried the Council would try to gain control over the magic and use it to further their war against us. This is kind of a secret mission."

"Secret from who?"

"Everyone," she shrugged.

So she was hoping to keep the magic for herself. She and her brother wanted to use the Ikhor. "And why do you want the magic? My guess is you two had different reasons apart from your mission."

She seemed surprised I had guessed as much. "Well, the reasons are piled high. But the biggest one, in the end, is you are our saviour, and the people need you." Maev spoke to the sky as she lied to me.

Everyone wanted to stop the Ikhor except the Aethar, who worshipped it. But why would only two Aethar, seemingly not warriors, come alone into enemy lands to capture me? The answers mattered, but for now, I had to follow her because I needed to get out of Veydes.

"Does that mean you don't believe I am evil?" I was relieved she wasn't saying she wanted to stop me from killing. That meant she didn't think I was a monster.

"No." She smiled. "The Ikhor is worshipped in my lands. It stops the beast from coming and eating the children while they sleep. It burns fires to keep the people warm. The first child to take it from the gods wanted those born without magic to have a fighting chance."

"That's what your people are taught?" It was nothing like the stories I had heard.

"You'll come to find, Olivia, that many things told in Veydes are wrong."

CHAPTER
FIVE

Liv

My mother had told me a story of a hero who sacrificed himself for the people. He died for those he didn't even know. It didn't make sense, but I had wanted to be him. Now that I'm older, I know—as a girl from the Endless Forest, I had wanted to be recognized. I've met more people in the world since then. People like Falizha exist. I'm not dying for her.

"So, all Aethar believe the Ikhor is good?" I asked.

The scarred Aethar, the Southlanders, wanted the Ikhor because they, too, were evil people. Right? I wanted to believe her if only for the hope that I wasn't becoming the evil destined to rise and burn the earth.

"May I remind you, once again, I am not an *Aethar*. And to answer your question, the first child fought for the people. He wanted us to have power like the gods."

"So you and your brother thought the magic was best protected in your hands? That your intentions are best? Because I won't kill my friends if that's what you wish in the end."

Maev's features tightened. Her damp, near-white hair stuck to her temple, which seemed paler than before. "Which friend were you referring to? Kazhi, who's an Aether herself? Or the Guard who let everyone hear his promise to find and kill you?"

I opened my mouth, but my retort fell flat—what could I say? She was right.

Thunder boomed again, and the rain came harder.

"Sorry," she said, reaching over to me and wincing from her burn. The colour drained from her cheeks. "I didn't mean to say it like that. I think we started off on the wrong foot. I am truly not your enemy, Olivia. And we need the rain to stop. The Aspis may come for you regardless of the storm, and I can't navigate in this. Not on a racer. We need my brother and our airship." She pulled back, holding her arm to her chest again.

Her attempt to comfort me failed when her eyes rolled, and I grabbed her shoulders to hold her up as she swayed. "We need to heal you." As reluctant as I was to do anything right now, let alone help my enemy, her arm sent my skin crawling. "Do you have any magycris?"

She shook her head. The healing liquid was valuable, and she was travelling light.

"Are you ok?" I asked stupidly. The blue markings on her skin were turning white.

"Sorry. The pain is really bad. Not to make you feel worse." She clenched her teeth.

"I don't know how to control the weather. We may have to go out in this." I wanted nothing more than to curl up and never leave the damp cave.

She put her head between her knees and spoke to the ground. "The rain comes down harder when you look sad like that. Try to think of something calming."

"How is magic affected by emotions?" I stared at the tree's roots and wondered what kind of thoughts would calm me. Not my old friends, not the family I left far behind. What part of my life was good?

"You need to find a way to shield yourself from it all."

"A shield ..."

"*This energy is an iron will.*" The Oracle's words floated back to me. The ones she spoke before I departed for the Guardian City. "*It surrounds you like the hardest metal and darkest storm. It is a beautiful essence and divine love. It is feminine energy. It will carry itself with you, Liv, into your darkest days. When you feel your heart is being ripped from your chest and your mind is split in two, don't let go. Do not rip away your shield. It will be all that can save you.*"

"I think I know how to calm a little. Can you drive your racer?" I asked as Maev attempted to sit up again.

"The Aspis ... there won't be many places to hide on the plains. We will have to go fast. I wish my brother were here." Maev gave me a worried look. "If I start the machine, can you hold onto it and direct us?"

I eyed the racer. "Is it like riding a horse?"

"Not at all." She closed her eyes.

"Okay, I will try. Point me in the right direction. Let's get this thing ready, and we'll make a run for it."

She rose on unsteady feet to start the racer, jolting when I screamed and grabbed her swollen arm. The shadow passed by our cave again, darkening Maev's figure before it disappeared.

"What is wrong with you?" Her face scrunched in pain.

"You didn't see that?" I yelped, a chill running down my back.

A roar drowned out her response as it shook dirt and stone loose from the roots.

We both stared at the rain. "It's not above us," she whispered. "But I bet this racer that was the Aspis flying overhead you saw. Which is bad news for us." She diverted her attention to the racer again, grimacing at the pain in her arm. She wobbled, struggling to stand through the pain. With a few presses of buttons and turns of metallic dials, a square-shaped area on the front glowed.

She jabbed the glowing square. "This display tells you how much power you are using and how much is left. We go max speed and find shelter again if it gets close to empty. This dot here is us, and this,"—she pointed to another spot on the square—"is where my brother is waiting with the airship."

I nodded as I sat on top of the racer, which was hovering off the ground. It shifted as Maev got on behind, her warmth cradling my back. Taller than me, she could easily see over my shoulder.

"Do whatever you need to slow the rain, and let's go."

The Oracle had told me I needed to keep my shield around me —the feminine energy of my mother. She was the one person in the world who brought me strength. I conjured her image—her wild brown hair, a halo around her face, and the warmth she always carried.

The rain slowed, and light peeked through the clouds.

A shadow passed over us, another roar ripping through the air.

"Are you kidding? How did it find us?" Maev said.

"What do we do?" A fresh wave of fear locked me in place.

"It's heading in the opposite direction we are facing. Go. Let's pray it doesn't notice right away."

The handles of the racer moved when I pushed, and we shot forward into the open field. The drizzling rain pelted my face, and I blinked against it to see ahead. I recounted memories shared with my mother as a child, keeping the rain at bay.

We were farther than I thought we would make it before I heard the next roar.

"All the way, Olivia. Max out the speed!"

Don't be afraid, I told myself while my arms shook so hard the racer veered to the side. *Think of your good memories.*

Maev's grip was painful around my middle. How she held on so hard with her burn, I didn't know.

The display showed our power was below half and going down steadily. Grass plains stretched before us. There was nowhere we could hide. To my right, a small collection of huts zoomed past, faces of those who lived there blurred. We passed over one river, then another, until the plains turned into a blend of swamps and streams.

"We are in the river lands now." Maev spoke into my ear. "Shift us to the left a bit."

My shift was a sudden plunge toward the left, but I righted us quickly enough. *Think of good things. Stop shaking so much.*

"How far is the ship?" I yelled over my shoulder, which was a big mistake. As I turned back around, a swarm of bugs collided with me, and I swallowed several, coughing and spitting them out.

"Oh, cursed Night! The bugs! I hate bugs," Maev cried. "The ship is not far now." There was a pause as I felt her turn in the seat. "Olivia, I don't think we are going to make it."

I pressed the racer forward as hard as possible, my stomach bottoming out as the power went below the quarter mark. "We are running out of power!"

"Ohhh noooo ..." she said in a low warning.

"What's going on back there?"

"It's not just the Aspis."

I closed my eyes briefly. "Out with it, Maev."

"A Guardian airship has found us."

Alarm rang through every vein in my body. There was only one ship that would travel with the Aspis. "Oh god." I clutched the racer with white knuckles, slowly turning, afraid to look over my shoulder.

The beast curled through the sky, cutting through the clouds. And passing it, gaining on us faster than the beast, was Falizha's ship.

They found me.

Was Nuo up there? Was Kazhi still masking as a Guard and pretending to follow the Aspis? Were Bastane and Falizha there, hungry to watch me fall? Or would they do as Maev suspected and try to take the magic to the Council?

I spun back around and focused on where we were going. The

racer shifted at the movement, and I steadied us so we didn't fall. The display flashed a warning that the power was nearly depleted. Maev's airship was close. So close.

"Do you have any other weapons?" I screamed over my shoulder.

"I told you, I am no fighter! I had my crossbow, and that was it. The Aspis ate it."

"We need a plan, Maev. The racer is almost done." As was my control over my emotions.

The racer bounced again as Maev said, "The airship is nearing us, and there's no shelter in sight. I can't think of a plan. I'm sorry."

The racer slowed, the wind dying down. Far ahead, I could make out the outline of Maev's ship.

"I have a reckless plan," I said over my shoulder. One that would cost me. "You're going to have to tough it out with your arm, Maev. We're going to have to run for it."

"Do what you have to do. They're nearly on us now."

I nodded, pushing the racer as far as it would go. I could see the rivers pass us in detail, no longer blurred colours but ripples reflecting the little daylight that came through the clouds.

"Recount what happened in the field for me," I told her, regretting the idea as soon as I said it. I didn't want to remember. Not yet.

"What? We just got over—oh!" she said, understanding. "Sorry in advance," she muttered before reminding me exactly why my heart was torn to pieces. "I tracked you on the field and found you being held captive by the golden Day-leg Guardian who thought you were the Aspis. She was giving you up, hoping you transformed so she could be named a hero. Then the Guards stopped her and tried to protect you against me and the horde advancing on you."

The downpour began quicker than I had expected, encouraging Maev as we continued to slow. "Then I put a bolt into the woman's middle, yet she ran away. The horde got a hold of you, and I lost you in the field. The next time I saw you, you were facing off with the Guards, who were outnumbered and losing. I was going to try to kill one of them before they got to you, but you screamed at me to stop. It was when the Shadow Guard moved to fight off the Aethars that everything changed."

I didn't hold it in—the sob that had been trapped. It exploded from me as the grief lashed out. I remembered the blade piercing his chest. It was so fresh in my mind.

"You weren't the only one to cry out. The other Guard, the Sea-leg, did too and took down the Aethar that killed his friend. That's when you turned into the Ikhor. You killed all the Aethar around you, burning me in the process."

The sky darkened, and the rain stung as the racer continued to slow.

"It's not enough, Maev. We need to hold them off until we reach your ship. They can't follow us. The storm needs to be bigger."

She paused behind me, taking in a breath and leaned back, before she said, "His name was Erebrekt of the North, the cursed child. He kept his eyes on you as he changed into the Aspis. I saw pieces of him fade away until he became the beast."

She didn't need to say it all. She only had to say his name.

I cried out a pain-filled howl to the sky, burning my throat.

The world turned dark. The sky became a nightmare as lightning tore across the horizon, illuminating the beast above, swirling in circles, searching for us below. I could no longer see the airship, and the racer came to a complete stop. They would never find us.

Maev was first to jump off, and she pulled me down with her as I wept. We both slipped on the wet ground. My feet sunk into the mud, and my knees nearly gave out. Any anger I harboured for being possessed by the magic vanished. There was only pain.

"I hate to say this, Olivia, but you can't hold your emotions in. Let them loose, girl. You're doing it." She looped an arm through mine, limping as she pulled me along.

We moved as fast as we could through the swampy ground. I

did as she said and felt it all. Everything from that field and from before it. It was no longer contained.

We were both choking on the rain—the downpour turned into a hurricane.

My hair stuck to my face, and I swiped at it, trying to see where I was stepping as I cried. My swords, strapped to my sides, thumped against my legs as my green billowing pants, soaked and heavy, slowed my pace.

"Keep going. Keep feeling it," Maev muttered.

The airship came into view. I could see the faint glow of the mesmerizing patterns around its edges, powered from the magycris. It was the ship I saw the night I was on the deck with *him*.

The ground sucked my feet in and I fell into the mud. Maev pulled me up.

My throat hurt from sobbing. My eyes burned.

Closer now, a buzzing was building ahead—a noise I couldn't place.

A roar came from behind us. I held onto that pain and let the storm continue. It was more than emotional pain now. My insides cramped, nausea threatening to pull me under.

The fog that was in my head grew heavier.

"Oh no, no, no," muttered Maev, pulling me forward. "The ship is surrounded by Southlanders! They've taken it!"

Holding my free arm over my head, I searched. A dark shape came into focus, surrounded by a group of fifty strong.

"My brother." Maev searched the area, but the rain made it impossible to see.

Aethars were tearing the ship apart from the inside—emptied and looted—commands shouted back and forth. Maev's ship was smaller than Falizha's. Its sleek body gave the impression that it would cut through the skies. Long, thin, glowing lines—powered by the magic crystals—pulsed across the side of the ship in neat, horizontal patterns.

"Over there." Maev pointed to a collection of bushes along a river. "We need to take shelter before the Guards see us."

Strange that it was the Guards she feared over the Aethar.

My world had turned upside down.

CHAPTER
SIX

Liv

I made a friend once when I was younger. We had a play battle with sticks, and I pushed her so hard that she fell. The look she gave me filled me with guilt. She never returned to play with me, and I was sure I had done something wrong.

I was too scared to tell my mother, afraid she would stop teaching me to fight. A week later, my mother pulled Rebeka and me out of the house and forced us into the woods. We weren't to return until dark. The Keepers were doing rounds.

The girl I had pushed, along with her entire family, disappeared. Rebeka was so angry as she pulled me into the woods away from our house. I was sure I had been the reason they were gone. When I gathered enough courage, I asked Rebeka why we were running, and she said Mother might not be home when we returned. I laughed, and that made Rebeka cry.

"Didn't you see Mother making a fire?" she said. "The eldest son from that family was caught making bows and arrows. They punished every member, including your little friend. Mother was burning things when we left. We are going to die too."

I had not understood then that Rebeka already hated Mother. After that day, she was adamant I follow the rules like her. Eyes down, don't react, blend in.

I now understand that our mother's choices shouldn't have been put on us. Just as my choices now should not affect others.

But they do.

Mud stuck to my boots as Maev clung to my shoulders. I blinked through the rain as we stumbled toward the bushes, fear and adrenaline pushing me along.

Eventually, Maev could stand with my support. She had a slight frame, but her height made her heavy to brace. "Not much farther," I told her.

The bushes were thick, with long, thin leaves drooping from the heavy rain. We were unlikely to be seen creeping along the river's edge, hidden from the Aethar and those in the sky.

I let go of Maev, steadying her before we both edged behind the brush. I ducked down, crawling underneath, my hands sinking into the cold, wet ground. I was covered in mud. Maev was close behind, paler than before.

We needed to get a view of the ship. I aimed for a dark rock between two bushes where there was a gap facing toward the field.

But it wasn't a rock. It moved.

A hand shot out, grabbing me by the neck and throwing me onto my back. A hard body pinned me to the ground, and within the next moment, a knife was held to my throat against the soft skin. "Don't move," came a low male voice.

The strength and the weight of the man were threatening. I blinked against the rain, looking up into the dark hood where blue-white hair flowed.

"Ollo!" Maev shoved the man off me, and the knife left my throat. "She's with me."

"Maev? Where have you been?"

The force of the wind flung his hood back. I paused, hand cradling my neck. It was ... the beautiful blue man from Bellum. His skin was pale, marked with navy dashes and lines, like Maev's. The patterns were similar, but different enough to note. The distrust lining his features disappeared at the sight of his sister.

Maev knelt beside me and placed a hand on her brother's shoulder. I lay awkwardly between the two while he patted her hand, pulling back to look her over.

"What's wrong? You look like you're going to—Maev!"

She collapsed over me, and I grunted when her dead weight landed on my stomach.

"What did you do to her?" he snarled at me, noticing her burned arm.

"She needs magycris. She fainted from the pain."

His nostrils flared as he reached into his pocket. Without moving Maev off me, he turned her over and tapped her cheek to wake her. "Stay awake long enough to drink. That's it. It's not enough to entirely heal you. It's the last of my supply."

"I can't breathe," I muttered, my words muffled under Maev's hood.

Maev's elbow dug into my ribcage as she pushed herself off me and sat on her knees, swaying as she regained strength.

"Thanks, Ol." She gave him a tight-lipped smile.

"I told you not to follow the Southlanders to that burning field. I thought you'd been killed."

They were so alike it was unnerving. Though both beautiful, Ollo was unmistakably male. His strong jaw set him apart, and his gaze was fiercer than Maev's. He had wide-set shoulders, and his body had felt lean and muscular while lying below him.

He put the empty bottle away, struggling with his wet cloak. His drenched hair stuck to his neck, his front covered in mud, like us. When I last saw him in Bellum, he was listening to a gold monk speak of the gods and the histories of the legacies—the gods' children. I had yet to learn what legacy these two were.

"You won't believe the story I have for you," Maev whispered. "But right now, we need to focus on the issue at hand."

Maev looked at her arm. It was no longer a seeping wound, but it was not well healed. The dashes that ran down the top of her arm were discoloured and deformed—mottled, like the other Aethar.

"Yes, our ship is compromised, as is our mission. It might be wise we call it a failure and return home." Ollo's voice was smooth and sure. He spoke with confidence, reminding me of the way Stephen had carried himself back home. "I have the Elder's request tucked away, but what good will a summons do if we are dead before delivering it?" His attention sharpened, taking in my face and neck.

I had dried blood caked under my jaw, which was Falizha's doing. Maev's brother had not broken the skin. I grunted, sitting up between the two, rubbing my throat.

"Our situation is a little worse than that." Maev pointed to the sky where Falizha's ship made its descent.

They were here. I could make out the shape of the glowing ship's wings, the gold railing visible on the top deck.

The Aspis flew overhead, and I cowered as it continued searching for me. It didn't yet land with the Guards.

"Who have you brought?" Maev's brother sat back, inching farther away from me.

"Ollo, this is Olivia. Our Ikhor."

He went still, save for his eyes, which darted to his sister as she nodded triumphantly, having delivered me.

"How?"

"My tracker. I told you it would work. I'll explain everything later." She settled on the ground, facing the field. "We need our ship. We need out of here. How did they swarm it?"

The scarred Aethar were all over Maev's ship, which sat fifty feet away from us on a flat patch of land. Their drab brown and grey clothing hung heavy from their scarred and deformed skin. They were all different legacies, though they were so scarred you could no longer tell who their god was. The Ikhor was all they worshipped.

I swallowed, tasting bile.

The Aethar spotted Falizha's airship now hovering on the ground beside them, and they scrambled, screaming about the Guards, unaware of the Aspis flying over their heads. Through the rain, I could faintly make out movement below her massive airship. Thunder crashed, and the rain came down harder.

The Guards were here. For the first time, I was scared instead of relieved.

"The Aethar happened upon our ship when I left in search of you. I only recently returned from the fields. They were razed to the ground." Ollo's eyes shifted to me, quickly looking away.

I didn't bother explaining that Falizha had lit fires all over Veydes, saying it was me. "How're we going to get out of here?" I asked. "We can't take on the Aethar and the Guards all at once."

"We can't?" Ollo sought the answers from Maev.

"Olivia is new to her powers. They haven't settled in yet."

Ollo's face fell as he glanced at the airship. His long hair fell in his face, dripping with rain, and he pushed it away. "My Elder is going to have my head, Mae. And that's before the others hear I've lost our fastest ship."

Mae? A nickname, perhaps.

"They're going to kill *us*," she added.

"The Guards are going to kill us sooner if we don't come up with a plan," I reminded them.

"Keep low," whispered Maev. "They've arrived."

Ollo and I joined her on our stomachs, lying flat on the soaked ground. His elbow bumped mine, and he jerked away. The three of us wore dark cloaks—the Guards would be hard-pressed to find us in the shadows under the bushes.

The rain grew colder as a wave of fear crashed over me.

Four black-clad, deadly and heavily armed Guards approached Maev's airship. Some of the Aethar fled into the storm as others hid on the ship. Only a daring few remained on the ground to face off with my old friends.

The Guards were fifty feet away, yet I could make out their faces. Blood streaked down Nuo's handsome face as he approached the group, swords in hand. The rain washed away the blood matted in his brushed-back chestnut hair, cleaning the slate for his new kill.

I expected to see anger, pain, remorse and suffering, but there was nothing to indicate a soul lived inside that body. He was emotionless—an empty vessel.

He was the last person alive attached to my heart.

"Where are they?" Nuo yelled to the waiting Aethar.

His voice was unrecognizable—raw and broken, as if he had been screaming for hours.

"Who do you seek?" a disfigured man replied, sounding confused, perhaps wondering why the Guards hadn't attacked.

"The Ikhor and its new pet," Falizha demanded, walking next to Nuo. He didn't even flinch at her proximity.

Falizha's long, golden hair was tied high on her head and

slicked down her back. She had almost been fatally injured on the burning field, yet she had cleaned and polished herself up prettily while the others were covered in grime and blood.

The Day-legs were all the same—made in the image of Rem. And the purebloods, like Falizha, had pure golden skin, hair and eyes.

She stood arrogantly next to Nuo, who looked like a ghost of himself—her priorities didn't match the bloodied Guards she walked with. It made me sick to see them working together.

She scanned past the Aethars to the ship, blinking through the rain. Maybe she thought we had boarded already.

"Do you want to die before or after you hand over the Ikhor?" Bastane spoke as if bored, holding back, waiting for the Aethar to make a move.

Although not a pureblood, he was nearly as golden as Falizha before him, with specks of gold that blended with his blue eyes. His jaw-length hair was stuck to his angered face. I couldn't see the metal rings in his brow and nose from here, but I could see the blood on his hands.

"They know they'd rather die sooner," Nuo said, eyeing his blade as if considering what side to use first.

"Which one is that?" Ollo whispered next to me.

"Nuo." My voice cracked because it wasn't the Nuo I knew. I hadn't seen my friend since that burning field.

"Ah. The mapper for the Guards. The Sea-leg orphaned as a child."

"Yeah."

"Also known as the Interrogator." Ollo eyed his sister on the other side of me, who paled at the mention of Nuo.

"What do you mean?" I asked, and Ollo searched my face. Was he looking for signs of the evil?

No. They thought I was a saviour. Possessed, but still a saviour. However, Ollo's reserved hostility toward me didn't make him appear happy to have the Ikhor close by.

A muscle ticked in his jaw. It was unnerving being so close to a stranger. And a man. And one so ... beautiful.

"It's known that the Interrogator is a well of information. Not only because he's well read and trained since childhood, but he's deadly once you're in his grasp. He questions and kills Rydavians, usually slowly, gaining information. He's a master of deception, clever and cunning."

The description was wrong. So wrong.

Was that how the world saw Nuo? What of his jovial nature? His dedication to his friends? Nuo was cunning, sure, but he used that to entertain a room, telling grand stories. He was the cleverest man I had met. The Aethar's depiction of him was backward.

"Don't worry," Ollo said, mistaking my concern. "All Guardians are our enemies. We are on your side. You'll be able to take them on when you're strong enough."

"What do they say about the others?" I asked, ignoring how Ollo assumed the Guardians were my enemy as well.

"Kazhi, legacy unknown."

Just as he spoke her name, Kazhi walked forward, her figure slight compared to the rest. Her body was covered in tattoos. The stripes along her face went up her chin, sideways across her cheeks and brow, leaving a white band around her black eyes. Scale-like patterns covered her torso and hands, while black covered her arms and legs. She had rings in her nose and ears like Bastane.

When we first met, Kazhi had known I wasn't from Veydes because I had no tattoos. I had not known she was an Aethar then, and I wondered if she ever thought I was one of her own people, lying about being from the Lost Lands.

Kazhi squatted low and braced her elbows against her knees. She scanned the field as Nuo continued to threaten the Aethar. Her dreaded hair blew around her face, though it seemed the torrent coming down did not bother her.

Ollo's voice went lower as if worried Kazhi would hear from across the field. "They say 'don't blink, or you'll be dead' when the female Guard is near."

They said right.

"Bastane?" I asked.

"The Council's golden Guard. He has strong ties to those who rule these lands and is Aethar enemy number one. As skilled in battle as the others, but his connections make him dangerous in other ways. We believe he will persuade the others to invade our lands with the Aspis in tow."

I used to think differently about Bastane—he was stern, but gentle. He had protected me those first few weeks. Until he turned me over to Falizha. I still couldn't understand how he had betrayed me.

"And ... what did they say about ... the Night-leg?"

"The Shadow Guard. All you will see is darkness before you die. Not much is known about him. He's close with Nuo, and they're a deadly pair. We call the duo *Shadow and Blood*. Rydavians that have returned to our lands have told stories of their brutality and accuracy in battle."

The rain came down harder.

I finally understood how he had felt all those years, knowing he was the Aspis and unable to control anything in his life. Lifeless. Even without knowing he was the Aspis, people didn't see who he really was.

That's how I was now—lifeless. He was gone, and I had to survive without him.

"The Shadow Guard was the host of the Aspis," Maev told Ollo. "The Guards are down one. But perhaps they've replaced him with the golden Day-leg woman."

"Good. One less to worry about," Ollo replied.

Maev's gaze darted to me, and she mouthed *Sorry*.

I shook my head. These two were Aethar—though it didn't hurt any less that he was gone and not missed. "They may take Falizha along with them, but she's not skilled enough to be a Guard. She has resources, however. And she's the daughter of Governor Yulen Ravin."

"The Councilman's daughter?" Ollo wondered.

"Oh dear." Maev worried her bottom lip. "That means the Guards have the Council's funds. We heard rumours that this generation of Guards were not in favour with the Council. If they are travelling with the Governor's daughter, we planned this all wrong. Our escape may not be as easy as we thought."

Maev's face pinched in concern, but her brother was quick to react.

"Listen." Ollo spun onto his back and motioned toward the river. He pointed to a lump covered by a tarp. "I have the one racer left. We can all fit, but at best, we may only make it to Danuli."

"Where is Danuli?" I asked.

His eyebrows met, and I didn't have the strength to explain he knew more about the continent than I did. We were still in Veydes, in the Median, but for how long?

"Never mind. What's your plan?"

Ollo turned back toward the Guards, grimacing. "The Guards will swarm the ship, taking whoever is inside. Next, they'll search the field. While they're in the ship, we make a run for it."

"Our equipment is in there, our supplies." Maev's hand smacked the mud, making a nasty squishing sound. "Ollo, you're jumping into these plans like you always do. Think about it—they'll have our ship. The *fast* one."

"We can replace it. We have the most important things."

The Guards advanced on the Aethar, who were just as ready for a fight. Kazhi was the first to strike down the Aethar—her own people. Did the others really not know? And how were they fighting next to Bastane and Falizha after what they had done? They kidnapped me and took me to that field to meet my death.

But I knew the answer—I was the Ikhor, enemy number one. That alone would bring them all together to work against me.

"Now's a good time. Let's go." Ollo pushed himself up.

Maev muttered a curse in his direction. We were all slick with mud and soaked through, but I was weighed down with something more as I took one last look at the Guards.

Following her brother, Maev reached the racer and jumped on

behind him. The racer was the same as hers—I would barely fit on the back.

She reached out a hand, but I stopped dead as a shadow passed across the river. I scanned the river's edge. Was it the Aspis? No, it hadn't been that large. So what was I seeing? Was I losing my mind?

"Come on!" Ollo hissed.

I reached for Maev, forgetting the darkness fading on the other side of the river.

Maev was kind enough not to mention my quivering lip as I said a final goodbye to the last piece of my heart left on the muddy ground, fifty feet from the family I thought I had made.

I tore away on that racer with one thing in mind—I was going to do whatever it took to get the magic out of me.

When the fog threatened to surround my thoughts again, I let it swallow me whole.

CHAPTER

SEVEN

Nuo

I stared at the Aethar dead at my feet. I hadn't remembered killing it. But the wounds showed it was my kill. Kazhi usually went for the throat. Bastane for the heart. Me? I let them bleed out. But it had died quickly. The state of the midsection told me that.

I was tempted to kick the dead body. I'd always kept my hatred in check, never allowing myself to tip over the edge into the monster I was capable of. The monster was the one who demanded the blade move, and I was the one who held it steady.

"Filth," I muttered to the body growing cold in the rain.

We'd flown far from the burning field where—

Where—

I forced myself to move again, cutting short the thoughts of what had happened.

Just keep going. Keep moving.

The Aethars we encountered were emptying an airship that curiously didn't belong to the Guardians. It was hard to believe the Aethar had an airship of quality—or had one at all. On top of that, the lying bastards said they knew nothing of the Ikhor or its whereabouts.

I could barely recall the fight or torturing them for information. I only remembered how the last one laughed seeing my hands shake.

For years, I'd been warned it would happen—that the time drew closer to when Brekt would be gone. But how could he have asked me to prepare for this? I was expected to hunt the Ikhor, pretending he hadn't ... flaked away to pieces.

"Nuo," Kazhi shouted, tearing me from the spiral I was headed down.

I looked in time to see her throwing one of my knives my way. Catching it, I stuck it in the sheath inside my vest. Blood stained the edges, but what did I care? I needed to pack up and move on, keep myself busy.

Passing the body at my feet, I kicked it in the leg. The cuts showed I had used my special blades to question the Aethar on the whereabouts of the Ikhor. She'd lied until I took her life, claiming they hadn't seen him.

Him. Ha!

The Ikhor wasn't a fucking him. It was Liv. Liv, who—

Stop. I grabbed a fistful of my hair, yanking it until the sharp pain on my scalp replaced the ache in my chest.

Trust had never been something I'd given easily. But Brekt had asked me to trust her, saying she needed us. Then he had the nerve to ask me to ensure she was safe when he was gone.

How could she have done that to him, betrayed him? He could have died not knowing. In his last moments, she showed us who she was. Why not spare him?

But now, *I* knew. I knew what she did—how she had made my brother feel before his death.

The Ikhor was going to pay.

"Nuo, get your shit together and get back on the ship." Falizha strode past, carrying crystals left by the Aethars. Soaked from the rain, her golden hair was pulled tight from her pinched face, sticking to the back of her cloak. Not a drop of blood touched her sword. She hadn't stepped in to fight.

"How in Mayra's forsaken seas are we supposed to follow the Ikhor without a crew?" I barked at her.

Falizha stopped, her eyes narrowing to vicious little slits. But I saw the lust there, too. Her attention wandered over my chest, my arms, my hands covered in Aethar blood. She wanted me, never stopped wanting me. Though she would spit how I was a disgusting Sea-leg, my refusal of her invitation to her bed irked her.

Falizha saw the power I had as a Guard, a rank far above her own. She wanted the power—to claim me and, in some way, take ownership of my strength and position. Right now she was taking in my weaknesses, thinking that in my saddened state, she'd find a crack and work her way in.

Like I'd ever touch her.

"I can run my own ship," she said, her voice taking on a sultry edge before sharpening like a blade. She was a confused one. "There's no one better to pilot her. And before you go accusing me, Nuo, remember who led the Ikhor around for weeks—bringing their *whore* into the Guardian City, where she could have killed everyone. Remind me, who was fucking her? I couldn't track who she was spreading her legs for."

Without realizing it, my special blades were in my hands, and Falizha backpedalled.

So easy. It would be quick. Or I could draw it out.

A tattooed hand wrapped around my wrist, stopping me.

"The Ikhor is no longer a she." Red streaks ran down Kazhi's neck, where the rain washed away blood. "That person is gone. We hunt an evil-possessed body. Our emotions about what happened on that field can be put away."

She spoke her last bit to me, and I couldn't argue. Time wasn't something we had. We needed to find the Ikhor before it caused more damage.

"I don't take orders from the Guards."

Falizha was asking for a death sentence, talking to Kaz that way. Kazhi's head tilted—just a fraction. My skin crawled when she looked at me like that, and knowing Falizha was a coward, I assumed she was shitting her pants.

"And yet, Falizha, you will get on your ship and take us to the Ikhor, like I said."

I savoured it when Kazhi spoke like that to others. Mostly because it kept her attention off me.

Falizha gave a frustrated huff before stalking off to her ship. "Come on, Armel. Let's get eyes on the Aspis."

Falizha passed Bas, who didn't answer. He was wiping off one of his swords and, in the next moment, dared to open his mouth to speak to me.

"Go on and follow your own kind, bastard."

Bastane was dead to me. More so than Brekt. Not that he and I had ever seen eye to eye, but I never thought he'd trust the Council over us.

Bastane's mouth set into a hard line before he sheathed his sword and stalked off toward the ship.

"How can we keep going like this?" I groaned.

My throat was raw from screaming. When we had first entered the gold bitch's ship after the burning field, I needed some time alone. *Had they all heard?* Of course they had. I'd trashed an entire room on the airship. Any other time, I would have been embarrassed at the show of weakness.

Kazhi searched my face, hers showing nothing of what she was thinking. "How will we get to the Ikhor on foot?" she asked. "How will we follow *it*?" She nodded to the sky, where the black shadow hid inside dark clouds.

A sickening wave came over me.

That black shadow used to be my closest friend. All I could see was his death—it had been brutal. And I stood by, making threats, not doing a godsdamned thing to save him.

Nothing was as I thought it would be. The honour, the glory, the pride I thought I would feel following the legend that would save us all.

I'd seen the faces on the Aethar when the beast roared above them. Pure fear. It wasn't much different from how I felt when the dark shadow crossed overtop. The idea that I had anything in common with the Aethar sickened me.

I pulled my hand from Kazhi's grip. "I need a minute." I stepped away, into the torrent of rain.

"I'll give you five. Then get your ass on the ship."

She hurt, too. Kazhi was always cruel with her words, but on Falizha's ship, she had a near meltdown when Falizha acted as though we'd all get over it and move on. On top of that, her fighting had been sloppy. Kazhi was never sloppy. It hinted she was distracted, too.

I moved away from the airship, the bodies, the blood. Several pairs of footprints appeared and faded from sight around the river nearby. The rain hid what lay in the distance. How many had I let slip away, lost in my bloodlust?

I sat down on a smooth rock, tipping my head to the sky. The rain washed away the blood, and a dark part of me wished it would stay. I felt dirty—I should look it, too.

Let the enemy see me covered in their blood. I wanted to cause them all so much pain.

I laid one of my blades across my lap. The water ran past me in the slow-moving river, unhurried, uncaring. The world went on while I watched mine fade like ashes in the wind—like Brekt's body had.

The man I was yesterday was dead. Dead like Brekt.

Did the Ikhor feel anything? Had it planned everything the entire time? Had it planned for us to find it in that cave, what felt like so long ago? Had it called the horde to that burning field and ordered them to take Brekt down?

One Guard down, another broken.

It took me too long to realize I'd been stroking the sharp edge of my sword. More blood was spread along the blade where my fingers had been cut.

I hadn't felt a thing.

I stared at that sharp blade.

Stared.

And stared.

The downpour cleaned it, and it shone. *I wonder what it would feel like to—*

I shot up, holding that thought in check—that was the monster taking over my thoughts. It wasn't like me to think those things.

But I continued to stare at the sharp edge.

I wiped a hand down my face. "This isn't you." I paced along the river, holding my breath. "This isn't you. You have shit to do. You have a goal. You're a Guard. Act like it."

A roar cut through the sky.

"I know!" I screamed toward the clouds. "I tried. I tried as hard as I could to find the answer. There wasn't one."

I'd let him down. The only skills I had were fighting and gathering information, and neither had saved him. Of course, there hadn't been answers on how to save him. There were no books on how to outrun fate.

"And how could you ask me to make those promises to you!" I threw my middle finger to the sky to feel less embarrassed at how my voice cracked. Then I let my hand drop because he wasn't in the sky.

He was fucking dead.

CHAPTER

EIGHT

Liv

As a child, I feared the night when terrifying sounds of the unknown would come from outside our home. As a young woman, I was afraid of what others saw—afraid of being an outcast and the punishment that came with it. Now I know what I should really have feared. Years of difficult lesson after difficult lesson led me to discover the biggest danger is myself—nothing has hurt me so much as my own mistakes.

I tipped my face to the sky, letting the mist hit my eyelashes, pretending—no wishing—I was alone.

I slumped on a wooden bench in a boat that didn't look as if it should be floating. Maev sat close, maneuvering a *rudder* with her good arm, directing the dilapidated thing. A roof over the benches was enough to keep some of the rain off.

Ollo sat across from me, pretending he wasn't staring when I looked away. But I caught the long, sweeping glances the beautiful blue man was giving me. Now that he knew I wasn't possessed, Ollo didn't sneer but instead studied.

I pulled my cloak tight. I wasn't used to men looking at me that way. Not strangers. And none had dared look at me like that when *he* had been around.

Ollo crossed his ankles, trying to get comfortable. "Maev, I can't take much more. The speed of this *thing* is aggravating. I should be in the skies, not some half-rotted boat."

The racer had died much sooner than he had predicted with the three of us. Luckily, the two Aethar were resourceful and found an abandoned boat on a muddy shore hidden amidst tall grass. We were all cold, soaked, hungry and scared. But, as Maev had pointed out, the rain kept the bugs away.

The mental fog enveloping me was a temporary shelter from a storm ravaging my heart, blinders keeping me focused on moving forward. It was a dirty bandage that did nothing but pretend to heal.

"Get over yourself, Ollo." Maev was losing patience, too, and taking it out on her brother. "I don't feel sorry that you have to move at the same speed as us ground-loving folk."

The way the two spoke was foreign. Not only the accent, but their vocabulary was thick with words I struggled to understand, words seldom used back home or with the Guards and not at all like the scarred Aethar. It solidified my belief that they were not aligned with those who attacked me on the burning field.

"I'm going to throw you overboard if you don't move this faster." Ollo sat tall, poised and confident. Yet his presence didn't indicate he was arrogant, which surprised me, given how he spoke.

Maev huffed. "I don't have control of the speed. And forget the Aerial Elder being pissed for losing that ship—Dad will kill you for losing me."

"How old are you two?" I cut in.

Two sets of blue, scathing looks turned my way, and I didn't get an answer.

From the little I had discovered about the siblings, they were two sides of the same coin. Ollo was bold and quick to have an answer, arguing any point Maev made with an air of sophistication. Maev was expressive and empathetic.

While I waited for an answer, I ran my hand over the top of the water, watching little waves form. My glowing bracelet lit up the ripples my fingers made, and I wondered again how the crystals had filled with magic.

"Careful the eels don't get your arm."

I jerked back so hard that the boat shook. Ollo was eyeing my arm over the edge, a slow grin transforming his face.

"Eels?"

A single nod. "River eels. They come up at night to feed."

I massaged my cold hand. "They'll eat me?"

"Ollo," Maev scolded. "Stop it. They may nibble at your hands, Olivia, mistaking you for something else. But I doubt they would eat you whole."

Ollo gave a quick shrug. "Don't fall in, or you'll find out."

I peeked over the edge of the boat, examining the water's surface but finding nothing.

"So ..." Ollo met my gaze for the first time, not looking away. "You're powerful."

I didn't have an answer, so I only shrugged. His scrutiny unnerved me. I had labelled him as *the beautiful blue man* when I first saw him in Bellum. But Ollo was showing he may be much more than his looks. His attention pushed the fog from my mind long enough that my cheeks warmed.

"You're doing this." He pointed to the rain. "With control over the skies, I'd surmise you have control over quite an amount of power."

"I don't."

His razor-sharp jaw tensed. "I can see you are not one for

talking. Well, here's the situation, *Saviour*—if you aren't leading us on our journey home, I am. Meaning if I say the word, you jump. We have a long way to go until we cross the borders. Especially if our means of transportation is this forsaken pile of scraps."

I gazed at the darkening sky, not responding. My hands shook in my lap.

Saviour. Is that what they saw when they looked at me? After what had happened? I was the reason ... I had caused the change in ...

The wind shifted us back and forth as we crept along the river. I only prayed nothing found us. We couldn't see far ahead, so every time the river made a turn, it took us by surprise.

The boat ran on crystals, and whoever owned it must not have expected someone to come upon it in the middle of nowhere—the boat started immediately when Maev fiddled with it. Ollo said it was common when Maev got her hands on equipment that they would start working. She was "a gifted mechanist". I had to ask what that meant.

Apparently, a *mechanist* was a more experienced alchemist, someone who worked on more than harnessing magic from crystals. Maev explained there were propellers in the back that moved us forward, and the rudder helped us turn. "I'm pretty handy with AO tech," she had told me. Like the weapons and the airships. But I couldn't recall the rest of her explanation.

Honestly, I couldn't remember reaching the boat. Or where we had left the racer. Or how long we had been on the river.

I checked the sky for the tenth time in the past hour. It was dark, making us impossible to find. Or so I hoped. If someone were to look down, the boat would blend with the dark colours of the water.

The day was almost gone. Having been on the run for most of it, it had flown by. *How many days has it been since I last saw* him?

I lay down across the bench and put my hands beneath my head.

"I found some food before we left shore. Would you like a bite?" Maev asked.

I shook my head and studied the moss-coated wood inside the ancient boat. Water was collecting in the boat, although I had already scooped it out several times and it gradually pooled beside my bench. Blades of grass floated in the water as the night sky reflected on its surface.

"Let me know when you're hungry. It could be a while until we reach the city."

The city of Danuli. We were still in the Median, in the river lands south of the burning field.

"We need supplies." Then in a lower voice, Maev said, "We need to get her food and a change of clothes. And some more magycris before we make our way home."

Home.

It wasn't my home, and I didn't want to follow these two if they continued talking about me like I wasn't even there. But where else could I go?

In the Endless Forest, people tried to imprison me. Now, here, the Guards and every Guardian on the continent wanted to kill me. It was scary that I was getting used to being hated.

Following them was my best option—my only option. Yet I didn't know the full scope of what they wanted from me.

The pool of water below my bench became deeper. I sat up to empty the boat when a black shadow passed over the surface. A jolt of fear went through me, my breath catching in my throat.

A dark form moved through the haze above us.

"How in Night's skies has it found us?" Maev asked.

But the shadow continued across the sky overtop of us and passed.

The beast was getting bigger.

"Maybe it doesn't know we are below it," I said back.

"Do you think it senses us?" she asked, gripping the side of the boat.

I smacked my palm on my forehead.

"Olivia?"

"When I was with—" I stopped, unable to say his name. "When I was with the Guards and first met *him*," I pointed to the sky, "I felt this pull toward him."

"Pull?"

I looked back to the growing puddle, ashamed to admit to myself and to Maev what I felt.

"I felt a pull and thought it meant something else. But it was the Aspis." I thought he had been my soul-bonded partner—something I would never admit to anybody.

"I see," she said, and I could hear the empathy in her tone. "So what do you think it means? Now that he's ... the Aspis."

Ollo shifted but made no mention of the Guards or my feelings toward them. Maev had warned him to keep his comments to himself. It made him watchful, and the look he gave me almost reminded me of the villagers back home. I hated that look.

"I think the Aspis can still feel the pull," I continued, ignoring the beautiful man. "It wasn't an exact thing, but I could feel the direction I needed to go to find him. I think it senses us here, in this area."

"Really? It worked like that?" she asked.

I nodded, searching the sky for its return. "Only the last time I followed the pull into the caves, Falizha found me first and took me to that burning field." What would have happened had I found *him* first?

"So we are never going to outrun the beast." Maev's face scrunched.

"We keep going, Maev. You'll get home," I tried to assure her.

"Me? What about you?"

"If it comes to it," I shrugged, "let the beast have me. I don't want this thing that's inside me." I lowered onto my side, ignoring the looks they gave me. A hint of shame spread through me for admitting such a thing aloud. I curled my arm around my waist to hold in all the pain. If what was inside me was to be let loose, Maev would have more than a burnt arm.

Because I could feel the Aspis, too—once I realized the pull was still there, I felt it, the need to reach the beast. And though the rain poured, it was a burning fire I felt deep down.

The world didn't know—*couldn't* know—the most feared magic was eating me alive. It was feeding off all my mistakes, and the Ikhor's magic liked the taste of regret the most.

Ollo's cloak shifted to the side when he folded muscled arms across his chest. His grey tunic underneath was clean-cut and tight to his form.

I thought of thick, chorded muscles. Tattooed arms crossed over a broad chest clad in black. A wolfish smile. A scar I wanted to trace with my fingertip.

"I could fight off twenty Aethars at once, but you? Wanting to know the feel of your lips ... fuck."

I pulled my legs up toward my chest.

Breathe.

Hold.

Breathe.

I focused solely on the sound of my breathing, ignoring the nausea building in the back of my throat.

Make it through the night and try again tomorrow.

CHAPTER

NINE

Liv

A breeze played at my neck, tickling my hair against my damp skin, rousing me from a hazy sleep. I sat up, finding a dark, empty boat. Maev and Ollo were nowhere to be found, and silence blanketed the night. Even the wind didn't want to be heard.

Over the past few days, they had made stops, going ashore for food, but someone always stayed to monitor me.

Past the boat and grassy shore lay only darkness. It must have been the middle of the night. Moonlight sparkled across the rippling river surrounding me, and the grass on the shore shone as it waved in the breeze. It was beautiful, yet terrifying.

"Hello?" I whispered. A chill ran down my back, and I was unable to shake the feeling of being watched.

It's all in your head. The heartache is messing with your logic.

Standing up, I put my arms out so I wouldn't tip the boat. My heart pounded, echoing. Why was it so loud?

Something was wrong.

I grabbed the rope that tied the boat to a worn-down dock and stepped onto the sodden wood. The moon only reflected the water and the grass nearby—everything beyond the shore was pitch black, as if cast in shadow. But there were no clouds in the sky. Checking the opposite shore of the river, I found the same thing—pure darkness.

The dock creaked as I shifted my weight, the thick darkness ahead pulling me in. I *needed* to reach it. An unsettling feeling crept along my skin, and I stepped closer to the shore, where the darkness lingered and seemed to pulse. Grabbing my neck, I sucked in a breath and paused. Waiting. Nothing happened.

The pounding grew louder, no longer coming from just my heart, the pulsing beat echoing in time with the night beyond.

Another step closer. The darkness receded like a rolling wave, revealing more shimmering grass. With each step I took, the darkness continued to pull away from *me* as if it was afraid, not the other way around. So what was pulling me in if it wasn't the dark?

I followed my instincts to head inland. Were Ollo and Maev in danger? Were my senses telling me to find them?

"Shit!" I jumped back as something slithered across the grass before me. It disappeared before I got a good look. When I stopped moving, I could hear more things slithering.

I swallowed my rising fear. Were we still in the Median? The fog creeping around the edges of my mind made me lose time— how many days had passed in the boat?

Night birds cooed in the distance, the sound haunting and familiar. I shook my head to rid myself of the feeling of being watched. Nightbirds terrified me.

As I travelled farther away from the river, the sounds of the animals grew louder, along with a ringing in my ear. The colours of the earth pounded in sync with my heartbeat. I squinted in the fading light, but only a small circle around me glowed in the moonlight.

Then everything went dark.

My ears popped as if my head were being squeezed. I slammed my palms against my ears, spinning in a circle, looking for the way back, for the shimmering grass, but no light found me.

Darkness. Darkness. Darkness.

"Help!" Would the two Aethar find me here?

"Help!" I screamed louder. *Why didn't I stay in the boat?*

I dropped my hands to my side, hoping to hear the river I left behind.

That's when I felt the tug. It was so powerful my chest heaved forward, pulling me farther inland on invisible strings. It wasn't a warning of danger. It wasn't instinct to help the two Aethar. It was magic—a kind I was familiar with.

The Aspis—the pull. No!

I stumbled ahead, unsure of my footing. Terrifying shapes formed—not a giant snake-like beast, but figures on two feet. They moved like ghosts, running back and forth in the dark. I wrapped my arms around myself, spinning as the shadows passed me. The sounds of battle grew—swords clashing and distant echoes of pain. Why wasn't I running back to the shore away from the horror?

My feet sank into the mud, slowing my progress. Why were my boots gone? And why was the mud so red?

"What is going *on*?"

I was tugged forward again as the chaos escalated. My feet dragged as I was forced to move. Shouts for mercy rang through the night, yet I saw none of it.

Agonizing screams filled the endless dark. Was someone being tortured?

Fingers brushed down my spine, so I spun, searching for the source. Nothing but more shapes ran in the gloom, screaming as if their lives were about to end. I backed away, limping in the dark, and ran into something hard behind me.

I stumbled as I whipped around, facing the towering figure. He stood as if he were made of stone, clad in scraps of black fabric, his head tipped to the sky. Curling horns sprouted from his matted hair as shadows crawled under his skin, warping his features from monster to man to monster again.

"No." I wrapped my hand around his forearm, around the

tattoos visible beneath the torn fabric. His skin was cold—freezing to the touch—hard. The shadows moved from his skin, up my fingers and sunk into my own, disappearing. I screamed, pulling my hand away.

I searched his misshapen, half-human face as the wind whipped his hair back and forth. Slits for a nose. Citrine yellow eyes staring upward.

I followed his line of sight. The sky above was dark, but it shimmered like millions of crystals scattered about in the vast darkness.

Something grabbed me from behind. A shrill scream tore from my chest as cold fingers wrapped around my forearms and yanked me back, gripping me tighter. They held me in place to watch the stone figure wince in pain.

The half-beast turned away from the sky, shaking and convulsing, a deep rattling building in his chest. He unleashed a roar, revealing sharp teeth, as the earth below shook.

The hands released me from their punishing grip, only to wrap around my waist, pinning me to a hard chest.

The half-beast turned into a cloud of shadows, *slithering* behind me. The cold arm around my waist grew warm as hot breath fanned my ear and sharp teeth scraped my neck. The rattling from before drummed against my back. The half-beast was now what held me, one hand snaking its way up the front of my chest to wrap around my neck.

It nibbled on my earlobe, licking up the side.

Something was wrong with me because whatever was behind me was dangerous, and yet the sensation of its teeth now scraping along the skin of my neck did something. It warmed a familiar part of me it shouldn't.

I inhaled a shaky breath, staying so very still.

The beast hummed its pleasure and, in a deep timbre, said, *"Mine."*

CHAPTER
TEN

Liv

What are dreams? I asked my mother once. She told me they were a place to escape the Endless Forest. In dreams, I could live a thousand lives, and sometimes I did. Until they felt too real ... like some place that I could step into—some place that could harm me.

I woke, screaming his name.

"Liv?" Maev shook my shoulders.

"He's alive," I shouted, tearing myself free from her grasp. I gripped the edge of the damp wood, searching the darkness.

"Who?"

"Him!" I couldn't bear to say his name again.

"I don't understand."

"The Guard. The Aspis—The Guard is still alive."

The pity etched on her face gutted me. "You were dreaming."

I pushed her off me. "It wasn't—it felt ..." I wasn't about to explain to her dreams involving *him* had once been very real.

It had *felt* real. And yet, the sky had been all wrong, the shadows, the shapes—those were not the kind of dreams we had met in before.

I used to be plagued with nightmares of my mother's brutal death. Was it *his* I would dream of now?

My heart sank as my mind cleared, and I inhaled the damp night air, shivering.

We were stopped at the edge of the river with the boat tied to an abandoned dock. Maev sat back on the bench across from me. Her hands knotted in her lap, attention darting to the shoreline. Ollo must have gone ashore while I slept.

Maev didn't say another word as I listened to the pattering of rain. I closed my burning eyes and lay down on the bench where I had first fallen asleep, letting the mist and rain collect on my lashes. The tears wouldn't stop.

Footsteps pounded on the dock, and Maev's whispering cut through the silence. "She's sleeping," she said to Ollo, the boat shifting as he stepped inside. "She's been having nightmares."

I rolled away from her voice and wondered what the Guards were doing. I asked myself, not for the first time, how Nuo could work with Falizha. He turned as fast as Bastane had.

"I couldn't locate a village or anyone to get directions," Ollo said. "I have no idea where we are. I was able to find a fruit tree with a few apples that hadn't spoiled."

"Save one for Olivia."

"She's not going to eat it, Mae. You need food, too. You can't afford to lose any more weight."

"Stop mothering me."

"I wouldn't have to if you took better care of yourself."

Maev's voice lowered. "If you'd stayed in touch these past few years, you would know I care for myself just fine."

"I did. I wrote on numerous occasions. You ignored me."

"I ignored your invitations to your parties because I can't stand even a minute with the idiots you spend time with."

There was a pause, and the boat swayed as Ollo took his seat before changing the subject. "When do you think she's going to snap out of it? She's miserable company, and I'm getting tired of the rain."

"Shhh. Don't be rude," she snapped.

"Rude? She hasn't spoken to us or offered help once. She's supposed to be our saviour." A moment of silence followed his remarks, then he said, "Do you think she's repressing it? Perhaps it's the Ikhor fighting her, needing to take control."

"Be more understanding, Ol. It's not because she's holding the Ikhor back. You can practically hear her heart grieving. Give her time."

I didn't have the energy to inform them their whispering could easily be heard in the small boat. Instead, I stared at the wooden plank I faced.

"Her attachments to the Guards could pose a problem, especially if she doesn't let the magic take over. She could use it against our people. She may be the reason this mission becomes more dangerous, not the Aspis."

"She deserves a chance first. She doesn't know us yet or what we are here for."

"Don't get attached to the girl, Maev. She will be gone soon enough. The Aspis grows bigger. Our saviour's magic will too. Either the Ikhor will take over, erasing her, or one of her many enemies will finally catch up."

"I am not making friends. And I'm not giving up on her yet. I believe she will help us. She just needs time."

"Time is something we no longer have. The Elders warn of our supplies running out. The Guardian Council's reach is farther into our lands. Strange things are happening. And, the Ikhor is not what we were foretold. She is supposed to bring safety to our people. Her magic was the reason I was chosen to enter these godsforsaken lands. Yet she's letting herself wither toward death.

You should see what it's like out there. She's making the Guardian's tales of the Ikhor sound more true than ours. I'm questioning the histories."

"You always question things," Maev whispered, and I could barely hear her. "We will take her home, as planned. Once we aren't running, we will push her to let the magic free."

"Let's hope by then it's not too late."

"Oh, you're awake, Olivia." Maev's smile grated on my nerves because she was trying to lift my mood. "I've been thinking."

It was hours later ... or had another day gone by? We were back in the boat after a short break on land—dark had already settled, and she was leaning sluggishly against the side. Ollo was asleep, breathing deeply—his head bent at a harsh angle as his body slumped in the seat.

"Why aren't you possessed?" she asked, as if pondering the idea rather than addressing me. "The beast is growing. Do you feel no signs of the Ikhor inside you?"

So much for her waiting until they had brought me to their lands.

"I thought you said the Aethar didn't believe the magic was evil."

"No, not evil. We believe the host becomes possessed by the magic and the spirit of the Ikhor—the warrior who challenges the beast the gods created."

"Why would you want the Ikhor to fight the beast? The Guardians say the Aspis fights for the freedom of the people."

"They do, huh?" Her nose crinkled. She clearly thought the Guardians were wrong. "The *Ikhor* fights for the people and their freedoms. The Aspis fights for the gods and their desire to have the magic returned. The gods created the Aspis, or did the Guardians say otherwise?"

"No, they said the gods created the Aspis."

"So it serves *them*. The first child wanted the magic for the people so that they could stand next to the gods in power."

It was a different tale than I had heard, but only by perspective.

"So the Aethar also believe the first child stole the magic from the gods? A child of Night?" I asked, trying not to think of the cursed child I once knew.

"Mmm-hmm." She kept her attention on the river ahead of us, removing her hood. Her long, silvery hair blew around her face. She fought a losing battle to keep it from her eyes, pursing her lips, clearly unimpressed. "The first child stole the magic to use it for the people. But he couldn't control it. In every era, the magic resurfaces along with the Aspis, and we hope that someone stronger will possess it. But it never stays. The Aspis, accompanied by its Guards, always win."

Meaning the gods always win. I inspected the sky, waiting to see another sign of the Aspis while she spoke. Her story continued while my mind faded—the fog blanketing me from reality made it hard to think and process her side of the tale.

Who was the bad guy? The line drawn between good and evil made it easier to know who the hero was.

Something caught my eye along the shore—a darkness that didn't fit in. I sat up straight, teetering the boat. Gripping the edge, I peered through the rain at the darkness creeping through tall grass, nearly indistinguishable from the night. Its movement was the only thing that gave it away.

The hairs on the back of my neck stood like I was being watched, and my breath caught when I thought I saw yellow eyes peering back at me. But when I blinked, there was nothing. I scanned the shoreline, keeping my breathing low while my pulse pounded in my ears. My heart wouldn't slow, even when my mind told me I was letting my sorrow see things that weren't there.

"So what I was saying was that you seem just like a regular girl to me."

I jumped as Maev's voice cut through the stillness and a

whoosh of air left me. "I am a regular girl," I said, leaning back against the side of the boat, focused on the shore, finding nothing.

"Exactly. So the stories aren't true. At least not entirely," she mused. "You have to grow into the power. That could prove the scrolls have the clues to what we aren't understanding."

"What scrolls?" I asked, finally giving her my full attention.

Maev shot a worried gaze at her sleeping brother. She played with the ends of her hair, trying to look innocent.

"What scrolls?" I tried again.

Maev sighed. "I'm not supposed to tell anyone, so please keep it between us. My friend has this scroll, and ... I can't tell you about it." She checked to make sure Ollo was asleep.

"I already know you're hiding things from me. But you're asking me to follow you away from safety. I deserve to know."

She nibbled her bottom lip. "There's a scroll written in the language of Night. No one can read the dead language, so it's of no importance to the Elders. It won't matter—they haven't seen it. Yet I think it is important. As does a friend of mine, which is why we hid it. I think there are missing truths to the stories of the Ikhor and Aspis."

"Why would you hide a scroll you couldn't read and think it had anything to do with me growing into my magic?"

"Well, I don't actually know. The reason we stole it was that there were images of the Aspis and Ikhor on it."

"There are paintings of the Aspis and the Ikhor on caves all over Veydes. I even saw one on the ceiling of an inn."

Maev's eyelids dropped, as if disappointed in my remark. "Something about the drawing is very different than any found in our current texts. Most images show a battle between the two legends. This one does not." She waved a finger in the air. "It makes me consider new angles. Alongside your perspective as the Ikhor, maybe there's more to the histories we don't know. I wonder why you feel the pull to the Aspis. It makes sense that the gods would give the Aspis the ability to find you, but why does it work in reverse if you were not created by the gods? Technically, *you* stole from them. Unless the scroll shows a different tale and what we know to be true is wrong."

There were already too many questions and variations of the story. The fog in my brain wasn't allowing me to follow.

"Would you let me see this scroll?" I asked, trying to hide my interest in the text.

She gave a half shrug. "I guess. You will be disappointed at all the scribbles."

There was more to the story—why she and her brother were here. Why was she hiding it from Ollo? Or did he forbid her from telling me?

I had an idea, and it went along with the plan that had already formed in my mind—I wanted to get rid of the magic.

She had no real answers about the scroll because they couldn't read the language of Night. What I had not told her was that I *could*. I had read the markings over the cave in the Guardian city when even *he* couldn't.

It made sense now when it hadn't before. The first child who had stolen the magic of the gods was a child of Night. The first Ikhor had been a Night-leg. Could that explain why I could read the dead language?

I needed to get my hands on the scroll.

"All I know is this," I said. "I feel the same, but something more is within me, and it's getting stronger. It feels like pain and suffering. And I think it wants control."

Maev was terrible at hiding her thoughts. Not for the first time, I saw fear. Fear of me.

"I don't have the desire to harm anyone, but I am not the saviour to the people, Maev. I thought I could be for the people of Veydes when I thought I was the Aspis, but now I'm expected to save those I've never met. I want the magic gone. I don't have the strength to fight it or the beast."

"But you have to. The beast will harm people as it tries to get to you."

"I-I won't let that happen. It can get to me. I won't let

innocents die. Not if I can help it. But I can't kill what used to be *him*."

"It's not him anymore. He's gone," she pleaded.

Thunder cracked in the sky.

I may have accepted the truth, but I would never recover from what happened in that field. As I never recovered from watching my mother die when I was thirteen. Though, I appreciated Maev not saying his name. It was a small kindness she gave me.

"It's pointless to argue. I am not going after the beast, but I also don't want to die. I will run as long as I can. But I'm finding another way out of this."

My bets were now on the scroll her friend had. I raised my palm to the rain and let it sting my skin.

"How can you get out of this?" Maev asked.

I wished I could see the constellations *he* had shown me. Night's Crown in the south—a way forward. The North Aspis—a way home. It had been those five stars in the north that connected *his* world to mine.

I turned back to Maev. "I'm going to find a way to return the magic to the gods."

ELEVEN

Liv

Eyes down. Don't react. Blend in. My old mantra is of no use to me anymore.

Breathe. Hold. Breathe. The constant distraction of the Aethar and talking myself out of pain is how I make it through these long days on the boat.

"Isn't this city beautiful?" Maev spun on the bench, taking it all in.

I couldn't recall how many days had gone by. I found no danger in the skies above us, and I wondered if the beast needed sleep as I did.

It took hours after seeing the tops of the massive trees before we finally reached Danuli, the river city in the Median of Veydes. High above us, the bottoms of massive branches swept over the river.

"From what I recall of Danuli, it's situated on a river that eventually reaches the sea." Ollo faced his sister with an arm slung over the boat's edge. "We could purchase a better boat to sail us to Rydavas. But, since neither of us are sailors, I'd say we need a clever way to find a new ship so I can fly us home."

Ollo's deep voice didn't match his softer features. He was not a rugged man like the Guards were. The patterned lines and dashes formed a downward crescent over his brow, straight nose and high cheekbones. His neck mirrored the pattern, with thicker lines running down between his collarbones and disappearing under his cloak.

The pitter-patter of rain stopped cascading off the top of the boat as we floated under the foliage high above. The reflection bouncing off the river was no longer a dull grey but a lush green, pulling us into a new world.

"The Danuli trees only grow along the rivers in the Median," Maev explained. The trees above highlighted her blue skin with a green tint. "If you swim in these rivers, you will taste the salt from the seas. This is because they connect the two seas east and west of Veydes."

"And the eels?"

Maev squinted sideways at her brother. "I'm sure the eels are scared away from the traffic of the city."

The city was not what I had pictured. I expected something like Bellum with streets and squares. But Danuli was a city built within a forest of the tallest trees I had ever seen—built *into* the trees.

"The other cities along the rivers are also built into the trees, but none so large as Danuli. Homes and pathways are built onto the branches, and the markets rest near the roots below," Maev added.

My grief ebbed long enough for the rain to ease for our arrival.

"Look, Olivia." Maev pointed ahead. "The trunks of the trees are wider than that Guardian airship."

Boats floated in and out of the massive rivers. Boardwalks interconnected the entire forest, with docks attached to the bottom of trees. The scope of Danuli was enormous, and I was reminded of how small I was. Next to the Danuli trees, I didn't feel powerful at all.

Maev rocked the boat as she pointed above. "Ohhh, look up. Wonderful. Look how high the homes go."

Citizens walked over bridges and along the paths set around giant roots. The river split into many paths, and for a time, we sailed in the city built entirely in trees and on water. The walkways multiplied as the trees grew denser, and soon enough, I found myself inside a sprawling city.

"What are those?" I pointed to the trees where massive shapes moved from limb to limb.

"You need to get out more, Saviour," Ollo said. "Those are Danuli tree lizards."

"Why are the lizards here the size of my shack?" I muttered. I had seen a cave lizard. It nearly killed Nuo. Now lizards in trees? "There's a person on it!" I faced Ollo, my mouth agape.

"The Danuli lizards have wings, unlike their cousins that live in caves or swim in the seas. They can't fly far, so they are used as transportation along the river cities. Danuli has the largest population so you'll likely encounter many." Ollo motioned to one gliding down from a tree. "They save a lot of travel time for those that can tame one. But they're temperamental. So don't get too close."

"How do you know this?" I asked.

"I read, Saviour."

I folded my arms, muttering, "I would have read too, Aethar, if I'd had the books."

Thunder rumbled in the distance, and Ollo's face hardened. It was the only sign that he had heard me.

If I had come here before, the sight would have lit me from within. I would've run through the trees, dipped my toes in the water, and tasted the food. But *he* wasn't here to show me around. Had he visited here before?

The wonder was wasted on me now.

"There is no loyalty in Danuli to the Guardians or the Council,"

Ollo said, scanning the streets from where he operated the boat. He was looking for Guardians, I imagined. "Here, people are motivated by sales and trade, and the crimes are often simple theft and bad bargains. It's a trading city and neutral. Sometimes, Southlanders come, though they aren't likely to stick around and mingle. Even though Danuli is neutral, no one here likes *Aethars*. Luckily, we don't look like everyone expects us to."

The large branches above supported buildings and walkways between them. People were walking in the skies on the sprawling paths that extended from tree to tree like a chaotic spider's web. I couldn't understand how they built it.

When I asked Maev, she said, "The trees were grown like that over time, moved and bent in specific ways so that, eventually, the walkways were formed. Paths were carved into them and fortified over the years. We were taught about Danuli in world geography back home.

"The buildings up high are not carved into the trees but built up around them, living and growing with the trees over time. The structures on the top are the oldest and least used. You can see they are darker wood, stained over time by the weather. I've read that's where the more questionable businesses operate."

The buildings closest to the bottom gleamed brightly with their glass windows and white siding. Had the sun been out, they would have sparkled like something out of a fairy tale.

"Let's stop and get information from one of the shops here," Ollo suggested.

"What information are you looking for?" I asked.

"We need to know if there is a boat crossing the sea. If not, we are in big trouble. I don't want to have to walk back to Rydavas. I'm worried we won't find a suitable airship for me to fly. Certainly not one as swift as my last."

The rivers were filled with boats stopped at shops built along the water. Maev explained that there was a high and low tide every day and that sometimes boats could pull right up to the shops.

Other times, the owners had to travel down to platforms that were currently under the water and out of sight.

Ollo stopped and tied the boat to a section of the river filled with market stalls. Legacies of all shapes and sizes mulled around, and the commotion made me dizzy after days alone in the rain.

Maev climbed out of the boat first, ignoring Ollo and me as she took in the street.

Ollo motioned for me to go next, and I stepped up onto the seat. The boat tipped with my weight, and my foot slipped on the wet wood. I fell backward, crashing against Ollo. His arms banded around my waist in an attempt to keep me from falling, but the boat rocked with the force, and he lost his balance, too, and fell back onto the seat behind us, pulling me with him. He grunted when we landed with me awkwardly on his lap.

I froze, embarrassed. "I'm so sorry."

His laughter vibrated against my back. The warmth of his body —his noticeably hard and well-defined body—reached me through my cloak, and my stomach dipped. I should not have noticed those things.

"Don't apologize," he said next to my ear. "I'm actually relieved."

"Relieved? That I'm squishing you?" I spun to face him, which was a mistake, as his face was now entirely too close to mine. I could make out each dark blue lash, framing his curious stare. How he looked at me carried none of the irritation it had on our journey here, and I wondered if all those looks before were more than just observations.

And for a moment, I pictured *him*, and imagined *him* looking at me like that. Then I realized I was still sitting on Ollo's lap, and I scrambled off.

He leaned back on the bench, sliding an arm over the edge, and gave me a new kind of smile I had not seen yet. I think he was laughing at me. "You're the embodiment of the gods. You possess their power. They say you can't even look upon the gods without trembling. I conjured the image of a tall, muscled warrior when we embarked on our search for the Ikhor. You are a surprise. I am relieved because you feel like a flesh and blood woman. Warm ...” His lips curved into a full-blown smile, then faltered.

I blinked. “Are you flirting with me?”

He coughed. ”No. I mean—Yes, I was. My apologies.”

“You’re bold.”

My balance threatened to send me back down onto his lap, and Ollo stood, holding my elbow to steady me. “Nothing is gained in life if we are not a little bold, Saviour.” He gave me an awkward yet polite smile and helped me out of the boat.

I stepped nervously onto a wide dirt path. Maev gave me a curious look, perhaps wondering why I was suddenly scarlet faced. Ollo set me off kilter with how he spoke so brazenly. I had thought the Guards had taken me out of my shell, showing me a new world and how to be brave. Ollo was ... a different kind of brave.

I didn’t meet his eye when he stepped onto the path next to me. Instead, I took in the shops along the side of the shoreline. Everything was basking in a green glow from the leaves overhead. The lights floating out from shop windows twinkled down the pathways. The city was inviting.

I spun in a circle, taking it all in, pausing when I caught pieces of a conversation.

“How long must we stay in the city?”

“Until the floods clear and the soils good to grow again.”

“The gods are angry with us.”

“Angry that the Ikhor lives.”

The couple who had passed were carrying bags over their shoulders and heading into the crowd and out of sight. What floods?

I turned to Maev, who was strolling ahead before coming to a halt between two stalls, and I nearly ran into her. I swore as I looked at what had stopped her. On a large board was a poster with a hand-drawn image of a person screaming. Underneath was a warning that said, *“Beware, the Ikhor has returned. Female. Legacy unknown. Extreme risk.”*

"Are you kidding me?" I groaned. Luckily, the screaming image under the words didn't look *that* much like me.

Maev scanned the crowd. "What do we do?" She turned to Ollo, who had crossed his arms, studying the poster.

His finger tapped his biceps. Shoppers shouldered past him, pushing him closer to me, and I bumped into his chest, getting a lungful of a clean, crisp, and very masculine scent.

Another memory slipped through. *He smelled like pine and leather.*

Ollo muttered an apology, lips twitching, and I stepped back too quickly to look casual.

"We need extra clothes for one," he said. "But our cloaks will do for now." He stepped closer. His hands came up toward my face, and I held my breath as he lifted the hood of my cloak and set it gently on my head. I was cast under his shadow as he said, "And for two, I am not going to harm you. No need to flinch in my proximity. Do I make you uncomfortable?"

The genuine way in which he asked caught me by surprise, and I shook my head. It was obvious Ollo was concerned for Maev, but him showing interest in my well-being when he hardly knew me was not something I had experienced back home.

Maybe only with ... with *him*. Even Nuo had been reckless with my safety.

Ollo's light grey tunic had ties that crossed over his chest, and a small image of wings decorated the fabric over his heart. His dark, slim-cut pants disappeared under tall leather boots, much like Maev's. He was leaner than the Guards, but no less strong looking. How many other details had I missed on our long journey while hiding inside the fog surrounding my thoughts?

"Thanks," I said. "Did you hear what those two said about the floods? It sounded like their farms were underwater."

Ollo ignored the question. It was Maev's clenching jaw that gave away she knew something.

"What is it?" I demanded.

"The lands have flooded from the rain. The rivers are so high that buildings have gone underwater. Even here, the river is over the path's edge."

I turned to see what she meant. Sure enough, part of a path was sunken and farther down a path was submerged.

"That quickly?" I gasped.

"Quickly?"

Maev's comment was lost in my panic. I had let the rain fall endlessly. I had destroyed homes and ruined farms. People's *livelihoods*. All to hide myself from the Aspis. "What have I done?"

"Nothing that others wouldn't have done to protect themselves," Ollo defended me. "You also saved *us*." He waved a finger between Maev and himself.

"But how many farms were ruined? How many people are fleeing their homes?"

A group of tattooed Guardians passed as I asked the question, and I ducked under my hood.

"First the fire of the Ikhor, now the floods," a man covered in piercings said. "The gods are punishing us. Unless the Aspis acts, war will come. Maybe even between the legacies of Veydes. Only a Sea-leg could be happy in this weather."

"What's taking the Aspis so long? The battle should have taken place by now," another replied.

Would they scream if they knew the Ikhor stood near, or would they aim to kill? I needed to get out of here. The city and its beauty faded from sight.

"It could be because they are down a Guard," the first Guardian replied before their voices trailed off.

"They don't realize the Ikhor caused the floods. They think the gods are punishing them." I looked at Maev, and her face softened.

"Don't get upset, Olivia. Stay focused. We should have told you sooner. Before we were in the city." Maev's eyes darted to her brother—they had discussed it before. But when? I had been with them the entire time. It was welling up—the guilt. Already, my actions could be argued as evil.

But the feeling shattered when a high-pitched humming rang

in my ears. I turned in a circle, searching for the source. The sound had been clear as day. But there was nothing out of place. The people shopping, Ollo and Maev ... no one reacted as if they had heard a thing.

I could have sworn I had heard the humming before. When it faded, I wondered if I had imagined it.

"Let's get going," Ollo said, putting an arm to my elbow, turning me and walking ahead. "There is an airship landing port on the opposite side of the city. And docks where passenger ships wait. I think we are all in agreement that we'd rather walk than sit in that boat any longer."

I wiggled my arm free from Ollo's grasp, disliking the familiarity of the contact.

A squat Sea-leg pointed us toward the landing site—a straight walk through the city's centre. "But I wouldn't be walking that way if I were you," the round greenish woman warned.

"Why's that?" Maev asked.

"I heard Aethar are in the city today, and more than usual."

Maev only nodded her thanks, rolling her eyes when she faced me. "Imagine if she knew who we were?" She smirked.

We. The Aethar and their Ikhor.

What was I doing?

CHAPTER
TWELVE

Liv

"Be brave, Liv, because no one else will be brave for you," my mother used to say when teaching me to survive. It wasn't until recently I considered maybe she wasn't as brave as she demanded I be. Every time I asked her about my father, she stayed silent. If the Guards taught me anything, it is that keeping secrets is a quiet betrayal.

My head craned back—I almost wished that dark figure would fly overhead.

Breathe. Hold. Breathe.

I had burned people alive and flooded homes. What else would I do before it was over?

"The Ikhor will destroy families, burn the earth and cause nothing but destruction until it is taken down," Kazhi had once said, *"We plan to find it and destroy it."*

I was proving them all right.

We walked over bridges and along boardwalks, passing the shops in the inner city. The sun was setting, creating shadows under the large leaves above, yet the city glowed under the canopy.

"Look, Olivia, all the lights in the shops up above!"

The trees glowed as if surrounded by lightning bugs. Magic-powered lanterns hung from homes in the sky, twinkling like ethereal stars under the trees.

We were at the apex of a bridge when a group of men caught my eye. They strolled toward me, wearing flowing green and brown fabrics, similar to the gold monk from the temple of Day. Their hair was thick, like vines hanging loose from a branch. They were so tree like that they blended in with the surrounding roots, save for their dark, hickory stare, which faced forward. They ignored the citizens around them as if they were of little importance.

Maev pulled me close, linking her arm with mine and whispering, "Monks of Ouras. They travel from the temple, which is a few days' journey from here, hoping to recruit new followers. They want servants, really. The temple worshippers are put to work tending the land. Not that that's a bad thing, only that the monks and the temple get all the reward."

A tingling sensation travelled down my back as they passed at the top of the bridge. These were pure-blooded monks from the temple of Mountain. They were direct descendants of the first children—rare bloodlines that carried magic and kept it a secret from everyone else.

The buzz and hum of their magic made me shiver.

The hum of magic—that was what I had heard before. I had forgotten what it felt like.

"Did you know true purebloods can sense magic in others?" I asked Maev quietly.

She turned to me, surprised. "I didn't think those bloodlines still existed. You know of this?"

I nodded.

"Have you met any? Magic is said to have died out, no longer carried down through the bloodlines."

I lowered my voice further. "They keep to themselves. But they can't hide from everybody. A magic user can sense another magic user."

"That's a very useful skill to have. And terrifying. The magical bloodlines were targeted in the wars of the past."

"Wouldn't your tracker work like that, finding the magic in bloodlines?" I asked.

"It can locate the frequencies and vibrations of magic. But it's not exact."

"I don't know what the first part meant, but you found yourself a more accurate tracker." I tapped a finger on my temple. "I can sense who it's coming from."

"Who?" She inched closer, wondering who I sensed.

"The monks."

While I had grown used to having a certain opinion of the pure-blooded legacies of Day, I didn't know what to make of the legacies of Mountain. They seemed suspicious of others around them, reminding me of villagers back home. But unlike the villagers, they didn't feel cruel. Instead, I suspected they used their quiet fortitude as a shield.

I recalled Nuo's map and remembered that the Temple of Ouras, the Mountain god, was to the east of the river city and in the Median as well. The Temple of Day had been even farther south in the desert. And, of course, nowhere on the map, Nuo's or others, did it show the missing temples of Night and Sea.

The monks passed me with no trouble. They didn't stop to inspect me as another magic user or scream at seeing the Ikhor. So they knew other magic users existed and kept it secret, too. Interesting.

"Let's stop here for something to eat." Maev pulled on Ollo's cloak.

"We should keep moving, Mae."

"We are hungry, aren't we, Olivia?" Maev raised a brow at me, waiting.

"Very hungry," I lied.

"Mmmhmm. You've had a real appetite, Saviour." Ollo lifted a hand to direct us onto the patio next to a river, with chairs and tables. Lights hung from wide-brimmed umbrellas, creating a warm glow around the patrons. With the afternoon fading to evening, the muted patio lights set me at ease as we found a table along the base of the tree the kitchen was built into. They forced me into a bench seat, Maev sitting next to me. I faced Ollo, who flicked his cloak to the side before he sat. Behind him was the river, where the people walked back and forth.

A thin man wearing an apron approached our table, and my back went stiff. "What'll it be for you?"

"Dinner, please, and three drinks," Maev said with a smile.

The man smiled back. "It'll be out real quick. Not many stopping by today with the commotion in town."

"We've heard." Ollo's tone was clipped. "We will eat and be on our way."

"No rush, good man. You folk must be from the Sea-leg Isles with that skin tone. I had a lady in here yesterday with the finest colour of blue I've seen on my patio. I'm a lover of the sea meself, though with my hooves and long tail, I find I sink more than swim."

Maev's face turned a funny shade of pink. It was strange to see on blue skin.

"We are from the north, not the Isles," Ollo replied.

"Ah." The waiter gave him a nod and headed to get our food.

Maev settled on the bench, watching people pass on the path. "It's so strange to sit here and have everyone think we are one of them." She kept her long hair hidden under her hood, but Ollo tore his off, settling back in his seat.

"It's not like we fit their description of Aethar," Ollo remarked in a low tone, relaxing in his seat and looking around. There were four Guardians at a table across the patio from us. They were drinking, talking amongst themselves, unaware of who and what sat so close.

I debated with the desire to get to know my enemy, fearing I would be swayed to see them as my friends. Because if they were my friends, that would make the Guards my enemies.

"What legacy are you, anyways?" It came out ruder than I intended, but I couldn't be bothered to repeat myself for politeness.

Maev pursed her lips, but it was Ollo who answered, his smooth voice surprisingly calming. "We are legacies of Rem." He showed no modesty when he looked me over, perhaps trying to see the Ikhor past the woman's skin.

"No, really," I said. "You must be children of Mountain." The darker lines and dashes across their skin had to resemble some animal they had on their continent.

The waiter cut in then, dropping three glasses in front of us. I sniffed it, worried it would be something strong, but it had a sweet smell. I glanced up at the siblings, wondering if they drank that sour drink the Guards had given me before. The drink that had come from the scarred Aethar's sack. I took a sip, realizing I was parched. When was the last time I had anything to drink? I tipped my glass, drinking more than I should and coughing when it burned my throat. At least the flavour was smooth.

"We are Day-legs," Maev said. "Are there really only the golden days in Veydes? I'd heard as much."

I went still. "I thought they were only gold?"

"Ah. Well, that answers my question," she huffed.

"We have been taught that our clan was regarded as lesser in Veydes," Ollo said. "And part of the *weeding out* the Council has done over the years."

"What do you mean?"

He rested an elbow on the table. "You'll no doubt have been taught the Day-legs are made in the image of Rem. That is incorrect. Our bloodlines are the temperaments of Day—we have the ability to survive harsh climates. The golden ones are children of the Sun," he told me. "They're impervious to the day's heat and resemble, as you could guess, the sun. My people are of Ice. We live best in cold weather. I could walk naked as I was born in the blistering cold and feel at ease."

Ollo gave me a lopsided grin, and I realized I was staring.

I glanced away, studying the glass in my hands, condensation rolling down the sides. I didn't want to picture him naked, but my mind was always overimaginative. Unfortunately for my warring emotions, it wasn't an unpleasant image.

"The last are the children of wind—pure white skin, black as night eyes. They travel with the wind. One of them could stand in a storm the likes of which you, the Ikhor, could make, and it wouldn't topple them over. We all tolerate the elements of the day well, but our bloodlines determine which we are strongest against."

My jaw dropped. I put a hand to my mouth and held in the dizzying realization. "Oh my god." My words were muffled behind my palm.

"That's a weird saying," Ollo said, "There's more than one god, you're aware."

"Yeah. I just realized—I think I know what Kazhi is."

Ollo rested both elbows on the table. "The Guard?"

"You be talking of the Guards now?" The waiter appeared again, setting down our food and making the three of us sit up straight.

My mouth watered from the smell of a fresh meal. But at the same time, my stomach rolled. How could I enjoy food at a time like this? My old friends were out there hunting me, and I was sitting with my enemy, enjoying a hot meal. Fields were being flooded, and I was sipping a cold drink.

"We were just mentioning them," Maev said, pulling her plate toward her.

The waiter rested a hand against the chair next to Ollo, throwing a towel over his shoulder. "Now, I haven't seen it myself, but many o'my customers here been saying they saw the Aspis. They sayin' it's not like the tales."

"What do you mean?" I asked, curious.

He nodded as he spoke. "They say it wanders in the sky, following the Guards. Tale says is the other ways around, ya see? Guards suppose ta follow the beast."

Ollo cocked his head. "And what do you think it means?"

"That somethin' fishy with the Ikhor. It be playing games this time around. You think?"

Ollo pretended to consider. "Could be. Is that what your customers think, too?"

"Customers been sayin' something wrong with the Guards too." The waiter glanced over his shoulder at the Guardians across the way. "Says they been fightin'. Says the big one abandoned. Only three of 'em left."

I clutched my glass, but it slipped in my grip, nearly tipping over.

Maev grabbed my arm, giving me a small smile, then she spoke to the waiter. "Likely, he didn't abandon. I bet the Aspis and the Ikhor aren't exactly what millennial old tales say they are."

The waiter stood straight. "Now hear you me, miss. Don't be saying such a thing round these parts. Danuli may be neutral, but we know the Ikhor is evil. Look what it's done so far."

"You're right." I ducked my head. "Thanks for the info. We will eat now." The waiter didn't seem to take offence to my tone and left the table.

"Why did they hide he was the Aspis?" I whispered, confused at what the waiter had revealed. They thought *he* had abandoned the Guards, his family.

"Not surprised." Ollo cut into his meat. It took me a moment to realize he meant how the people viewed the Ikhor. "They will never put the Aspis in a bad light. They aren't loyal to the

Guardians, being in neutral territory, but the Aspis is their saviour." He set his knife down. "I'm yet hung up on the Guard being a secret Day-leg."

I pushed the veggies on my plate around, too nervous to take a bite. "She has white skin, covered with black Guardian tattoos, and her eyes are so dark they look black. They remind me of the eyes of a lizard."

"Did you ever see her in a storm?"

A booming laugh made me jump. One of the Guardians had spilt a drink down their front.

I whispered, "More than that. I know she uses magic. She also hides her legacy from everyone."

Maev inched closer. "The Guard uses magic?"

"Magic doesn't exist in the bloodlines anymore." Ollo gave me a stern look, his tone sharp.

Maev set her fork down, giving me a triumphant smile, knowing something her brother didn't. "That's the magic user you knew, isn't it?" She asked me. When I confirmed she told her brother, "The Guard is a pureblood Day-leg. A descendant of the first children, no less. I didn't think the first children existed anymore. But Olivia has met them, can sense them even."

Ollo's face lit with interest. "I haven't met many from the wind clan. They stick to their mountains. But it would be understandable she hid her legacy in Veydes, where the golden Day-legs rule. Especially if she were indeed a first child."

Kazhi would kill me if she discovered I spilled her secret. "Please keep that to yourself. I didn't mean to tell you that."

Ollo took a deep breath. "That I can promise. That woman unnerved me. I don't want her to know I'm acquainted with her secret."

"So the first children are rare in Aethar lands, too?"

Ollo's face fell. "Rydavian lands. If you are to be a saviour to the people, address them accordingly. And to answer your question, yes, some yet think they are a myth. Me included."

Ollo's features were softened in the dim light of the patio, and his moon-bright hair flowed on a slight breeze. He reminded me of a shining knight in my mother's stories. They were always handsome. They always saved the girl.

My heart clenched.

He was not the knight I yearned for.

CHAPTER
THIRTEEN

Liv

The Keepers controlled us with strict rules and harsh punishments. It was predictable and easy to hate them, but when my neighbours and fellow townspeople turned on one another, that shocked me. We lived on the same streets, bought from the same baker, worked just to live, and then looked down on one another. That's how the Keepers won in the end. They broke us so fully that we became feral beasts, hungry to make others hurt as we did.

"Hey!"

We all looked up as a burly Guardian aimed for the table of four on the other side of the patio. They all waved him over, telling him to bring over a seat. "Have you been watching the skies? Aspis is a day's ride away. It's doing circles in the east. Kinda weird, right?"

"It must be looking for the Ikhor," another Guardian replied—a Mount-leg, based on their scaled skin.

"It's going to get away!" another said.

"The Ikhor isn't gonna win. The Aspis'll pinpoint the evil scum and tear it to pieces."

Everyone on the patio cheered, and I sank into my seat. Ollo wasn't shy about staring as the patio lit up with energy.

"Thought it would be over quicker than this," the burly Guardian said. "The lands can't take much more of this rain."

"It could be the Guard's fault." A Danuli citizen said, who had joined the patio with a group of two others. He was a Day-leg with a round belly. They sat a table away from the Guardians. "Everyone knows the Night-leg isn't with them."

The burly Guardian whirled on him. "Hey, that's one of our own. I've met Erebrekt of the North."

I shrunk farther into my seat, wishing I could close my ears.

"He was a loyal Guard and a fierce warrior. He wouldn't abandon. If he's missing, it's probably because he's gone ahead on his own, tracking for the others."

Maev tilted her head my way. "It's true then. They don't know who the host of the Aspis is."

I wiped my sleeve along my cheek, thankful Ollo wasn't looking my way. "Likely the Council's doing. Or Falizha's. Not giving him the credit. Maybe she never told her father it was—it was *him*."

A stabbing pain hit my lungs, but the Guardians weren't done. "Tracking would be left to Guard Kazhi. Erebrekt must be doing something else."

"What's more important than killing the Ikhor?" demanded one citizen.

"He's probably turned to shadows! I saw him do it once."

"I heard that the Ikhor was one of his whores. That woman on the poster? He dragged her around the Guardian City before the fires hit the Median. I bet he's seeking revenge."

"Would you like to leave, Saviour?" Ollo reached out a hand, putting it over my wrist.

I went still from the contact. The warmth he offered was kind, but ... foreign. I pulled away. "No."

The round Day-leg continued his complaints. "All I'm saying is the Aspis isn't what we thought. It's not protecting us. Look at our lands."

The big Guardian, drink in hand, walked right up to the table of citizens, getting into the face of the Day-leg. "You're sounding like an Aethar, friend."

Ollo turned fully in his seat, folded one leg over the other, and sipped as if watching a show.

The Day-leg stood, pushing his chair back. "Do I look scarred up to you? Friend?"

"Do *I* look scarred up to you?" Maev muttered to herself and sipped her drink. "Ew, it's sweet."

The Guardian swung, throwing the patio into a brawl, while the three of us watched the chaos. It was strange seeing how the people perceived the legends come to life, not knowing one was sharing a patio with them.

"Little do they know, most *Aethar* don't know how to fight." Maev smirked.

"We are too intelligent to be reduced to—" Ollo waved his hand toward the brawl. "This. They seem to know nothing of their own Guards. It now seems even I know more of Guard Kazhi than that lot."

Maev took another sip of her drink, wincing. "I much prefer our drinks back home."

Just then, a Danuli tree lizard landed on the path outside the patio, and the fighting stopped, attention fixed on the creature spreading its thin membranous wings. It was the colour of bark, with green spots running down its back. Much like the cave lizard, it had slits for pupils and a long tongue that darted out, tasting the air. It gave a long screech—a coarse sound like its voice travelled over rocks. Its long, thin body didn't have a rider, and it seemed uninterested in the people around it. It jumped high, landing on the tree I sat against, and I tipped my head all the way back to see it high above. Then it disappeared, soaring off to another pathway.

"Anyway, Saviour." Ollo twisted back toward the table, speaking low again as the brawl continued behind him. "The Aspis isn't what they expected, and neither are you. The legends are quite old. So don't let what they say bother you."

"Will your people fight like this? When they realize I'm just a girl?"

"Perhaps, but—"

The Guardian knocked the patron out, who landed with a thud on the ground.

Ollo continued, "It will not be so impressive. We do not have many trained in hand-to-hand combat."

"But you fly airships. Does that not make you a warrior?" The captain of the Guardian's airship was a supposed fighter.

"I am a pilot. I know airships and flying, not—" He peeked over his shoulder at the waiter bringing ice to the Day-leg. "That."

"Ollo is a boring pilot," Maev told me. "He does nothing else but show off and try to get others' attention."

Ollo's face fell, jaw tensing, but he quickly replaced it with a forced smile.

"I don't understand why you two thought to come to save me," I admitted. "The Guards couldn't protect me from danger. How can you?"

"We were counting on the power of the Ikhor to protect *us*," Ollo said, scratching the back of his neck. "We were the brains to get you out. I am the fastest flyer in our aerial defence unit. I got

Maev's help because her invention could track you down quicker than any method we came up with."

"How old are you two?" I realized they hadn't answered me the first time I had asked.

"Twenty-four," they said together.

So they were twins, as I had guessed. "A year younger than me."

Ollo finished his meal at the same time as Maev. I hadn't eaten half of mine and noticed Ollo eyeing my food, so I pushed my plate over to him. When he grabbed it, our fingers touched, and I quickly pulled away.

Humour flickered behind the once-over he gave me. He reached into his cloak and pulled out a rolled-up paper. "While we are on the subject of the Ikhor coming to our lands." He passed the scroll to me. "This is the official letter I was sent with. It's from the Elders to request your presence in our city."

I reached for the paper, swallowing my rising panic. What would they ask of me?

"I would have given it to you sooner, but the timing didn't seem right. Nor did you seem inclined to read it."

"Read it out to her," Maev said. "She will likely have difficulty seeing in this light, and we all know you've read it many times over by now."

Ollo pulled the paper back and unrolled it. He cleared his throat, winking at me before he began, and kept his voice low so only we could hear. "To the attention of the Ikhor. We, the Elders of Avenmae, Capital of Rydavas, welcome your return. As history suggests, you have been the saviour to the people, protecting us from harm caused by the gods' beast, the Aspis."

"Wait," I said, stopping him and causing his mouth to form a line. "I was told the Aspis always wins. Do your people say differently?"

Ollo shook his head. "In the end, the beast ends our time of prosperity. As it says in this next bit," he said, impatiently gesturing toward the paper. "Your original form took the power from the gods so that we may find peace in our lands during times of war."

"So you see, Saviour, the Ikhor does much for our people before the final battle." He cleared his throat to continue reading. "We fear that war is starting anew. We humbly request you be escorted to Avenmae, where we have provided you with every comfort you should need while you settle into your newest cycle of life. Our most trusted attendant and pilot of the first division—"

"That would be me, though I have wondered why they didn't call me by name," Ollo said, interrupting the reading, before he resumed, "has offered his aid in bringing you swiftly to our home where we will ensure you are kept from the ruthless advances of the Guardian armies. Yours sincerely, the Elders of Avenmae." Ollo rolled the scroll back up and passed it to me.

I set it on my lap and stared at it.

"It is signed by all members."

"Why did you bring Maev?" I asked. "She wasn't mentioned."

"They said I had to figure out how to locate you, and I did." He thrust a thumb in Maev's direction. "She's my locater."

"And you two are twins."

"Obviously." Maev gave me a deadpan look. "Just in looks, though. Ol was born before me. We share the same ambition for learning, but where I went the route of research and invention, he was pulled into using the machines I worked on. He studied under the city's best flight program. He is the youngest pilot to reach his rank in the program's history."

"I can speak for myself," he said. I saw their resemblance in more than looks when Ollo gave me a sarcastic roll of his eyes. His expressions were muted compared to Maev's, but they were there —still more apparent than the Guards. But I suppose the Guards were hiding secrets. These two surprisingly answered most of my questions.

"He's also stuffy. Boring most times," Maev added, leaning her temple on a fist and smirking. "And always quick to jump into action before thinking. Part of his show-off behaviour. Don't fall for it."

"And your people? You're Aethar. I've only met murderous people from across the borders. I will admit you two are not like the ones I have met, but I can see you come from a place far different than Veydes. I have never heard of universities or inventions. It sounds to me like you are from a powerful place. I worry what a powerful place wants with powerful magic."

The twins gave me withering looks. Identical indeed.

Maev was the first to be on the defensive. "My people are not the same as the ones you've met here." She nodded toward the patio, but I knew she meant all of Veydes. "We have a long history of suffering and have forgotten none of it. We lead with empathy and knowledge. Ollo does a lot for our city and considers everyone in his decision making. He always has since we were children. I may joke about his behaviours, but those are my dislikes, not for anyone else to look down upon."

Ollo was better at hiding his thoughts, but his tone hid none of his irritation. "Our people were shunned from these lands long ago and sent away to our continent. The southern lands are the wastelands you know of—barren deserts that are barely habitable. That's where the south clans have grown in numbers despite the harsh environment. They live near the crossing and are the ones you run into if you enter Rydavas on foot. But north are the civilized legacies. That's where Maev and I were born, in our largest city. It's not like you think, *Saviour*."

On the pathways in front of the river, Danuli citizens walked back and forth. I had a hard time seeing the twin's version of the Aethar lands when the one I was told of was cruel. What they described was unlike any place I had seen in my life.

"How come no Guardians know of your lands? They have airships to fly over there. They think it's barren."

"Our defence units take care of some," Ollo said. "They attack sometimes. But the last attack on my city was when I was young."

"But it doesn't make sense that no one knows you exist. Even the Guards believed the lands were destroyed."

"They've been lied to." Ollo shrugged.

The Council. Which meant that those who had seen the Aethar lands were either sworn to secrecy or …

"We have also learned while travelling Veydes that things are not what we were taught," Ollo admitted. "The citizens here are not like the Guardians we know of. Perhaps all of our eyes need to be opened."

I crossed my arms as I scolded myself. The way I had spoken to them, treated them, wasn't fair. I was so angry at the world for judging me before it knew me, and now I was doing the same. Maybe they weren't my enemy after all.

"You can call me Liv, by the way," I said tonelessly.

If they thought I was rude, they didn't show it. I would try because I didn't want to sink further and go back to being the girl I used to be—making choices out of fear. I had a goal—get the magic out of me and do it without harming anyone. Maybe these Aeth—*Rydavians* would help.

"There's an inn we passed a few trees back," Ollo said, leaving some coins on the table. "Let's spend a wasteful amount of my coin on a decent sleep for tonight and start tomorrow in a better mood."

FOURTEEN

Liv

The inn was cozy. We were put up in a spacious round wooden room on the ground floor with double doors that led to a romantically lit pathway. Four large beds lined the room, and I was dying to dive into mine. Instead, I sat on its edge, watching the twins move around the room, inspecting the Veydian decor.

I wasn't ready to sleep, so I brought up something I wished to know about Day-legs. "So the ice and wind clans were separated from the suns. Why?"

Ollo sat on his own bed, pulling off his boots and setting them neatly beside him. "I assume the reason is that the children of Sun resemble our god, Rem, the most. They were favoured. The Council likely has something to do with why only they remain in Veydes."

"Do you think they got rid of your bloodlines like they are trying to do with the Sea-legs?" Did Ollo have different views than Nuo on Sea-legs? My old friend told me they were not a desirable legacy.

Ollo's mouth set in a hard line. The low amber lighting glowed off the top of his white hair. "Sea-legs are not always treated well in Rydavas either."

"Why is that? What's so different about them?" I asked.

Maev opened the double doors and leaned on the frame, watching people pass outside, a slight smile on her face.

Ollo ignored his sister and continued. "Many legacies refuse to take the time required to understand each other—when they do, they can't accept their differences. I think it stems from jealousy. Sea-legs are made for two worlds. Above the ocean and below. Over time, those with power have turned jealousy into distaste and distaste into abasement."

I waited a moment, hoping he would explain more. My cheeks heated when I asked, "What's abasement?" Ollo's language was hard to understand at times, and I was not well read to begin with.

"Abasement is akin to dishonouring and shaming someone to lower their rank."

Another thing he and Maev had in common was that when they spoke, I understood half of what they said. "I see. Do you think of them like that?"

He failed to hide his irritation when he blinked twice. "I do not look down upon other legacies."

Ollo didn't bat an eye at my lack of knowledge. When he answered my questions, they weren't delivered with arrogance. That fact was not helping my goal to stay distant from these two. "I don't like that word. People should learn to like each other."

Ollo straightened himself, massaging his lower back. The chords in his neck stretched, giving me a view of his profile. It was a pleasant view. "It's not necessary to like others. You only need to accept they aren't like you and leave it be. In that space, hatred cannot exist."

I added to my mental list that he was smart—emotionally, as much as intellectually. I didn't like how I was starting to admire him, starting to notice more than his beauty.

"I wish everyone thought like you," I admitted, and he gave me a coy smile. Perhaps there *was* an ego in there.

"If everyone were like me, Olivia, the world would not have the wonders it does now. The world needs ambitious mechanists to make great inventions, like Maev."

She glanced over from the door, a smile plastered on her heart-shaped face.

"It needs artists to make music and beautiful things. It needs scholars to keep records. Pilots to fly airships." His hand landed on his chest. "We need strong bodies to protect the ones we love. The world cannot exist *without* the clashing of spirits. We must learn to fight for our differences and not against them. Something the Guardians could do to learn."

"I think that's the smartest thing I have ever heard." Damn him. If I were less stubborn, I might have admitted I was starting to look up to Ollo. He was unexpected, as much as his sister was. So much more than what the Guardians accused him of. Perhaps ... perhaps the Guards were wrong about the Aethar lands.

I heard a snicker come from the door. "You'll learn, Olivia, that Ollo is usually the second smartest person in the room."

"And I am guessing you see yourself as the first?" Ollo tsked. If her joke insulted him, he didn't show it.

"Find me someone smarter, and I'll change my mind."

There was a pang in my chest—the phrase reminded me of something Nuo would say.

"Maev isn't wrong. She's *usually* the smartest." Ollo smiled for the first time. His teeth were straight, and the corners of his eyes crinkled, lighting up his whole face. "That is until we share the same space."

A pleasant breeze came in through the doors as if the rain may have stopped. The lights twinkled above in the trees, and it made me want to walk the pathways. For the first time in days, I felt lighter. Instead, I lay down while the twins argued about the plan for tomorrow. As I watched the two bicker, I knew in my heart that neither would have sold the other out to the Keepers if they had come from the Endless Forest.

LATER, I stood under the twinkling lights after the rain had stopped. The dusty pathway muffled the sounds of my footsteps as the river beside me trickled past, rippling in the lantern's glow. I travelled over wide bridges and had stopped to watch strange-coloured fish as they came to the surface to eat.

The quiet soothed me, and I took a long, deep breath. I had wandered so long that I was completely alone. After years of hating my quiet solitude, I savoured the small moment.

I left the bridge and made my way back.

Behind me, the lamplight snuffed out. The shadows inched closer, then, one by one, the lights went dark.

Was there magic to the Danuli lanterns? Some trick I didn't understand?

"Hello?" My voice echoed over the river.

The remaining lantern light pulsed brighter, and my heart gave a thunderous beat. Something was here.

I turned to run but stopped, screaming.

The path before me was no longer Danuli.

I was in a long hallway made of black stone, white and gold banners hanging from the ceiling. The hallway wasn't lit, making it difficult to see, and I blinked several times, catching my breath, jarred by the sudden change in my surroundings.

I turned in circles, finding no traces of Danuli anywhere. Emerald green doors lined the moonlit hall. Each set of doors displayed a unique carving of the Aspis. Down the hall, banners flowed, catching moonlight that filtered in from large windows leading to a balcony.

I know this place. Its familiarity sent shivers down my spine. The last time I had walked these halls was a different time, a different life.

I kept still, listening for sounds coming from the rooms, but everything was quiet. I could *feel* that they were empty.

A loud roar shook the ground beneath me, coming up the stairs from a level below.

I reached for the wall to keep my balance, and the cold stone wall burned my fingertips. I bolted for the first set of doors, tripping over my own feet. If I remembered correctly, it was Kazhi's room. I was in the hallway belonging to the Guards' suites.

Locked.

I searched the dark stairs behind me, fearing the silence that followed the roar from below. Something was coming for me.

I ran down the hallway, sliding to a halt in front of Bastane's room, clinging to the carvings on the doors to stop myself.

Locked.

I shook the doors, throwing my shoulder against them, trying to use force. I pounded a fist against them. Nothing.

Next was Nuo's room. I darted toward it.

My head pounded, muscles seizing. The hallway was so cold it was getting harder to run.

I passed a wall of glass, and into the soft moonlight, its brightness blinding me. The plush carpet was a cushion on my bare feet, and I slipped before I skidded to a stop in front of Nuo's room.

Locked.

"Help!" Nothing. No one was inside.

It was coming. It was close.

The hall from where I had come was now bathed in darkness. Pulsing, living darkness.

Violent shivers shook me. I needed to find safety and fast.

There!

I turned for the last set of doors, the room I was most familiar with. The darkness closed in, but there was a sliver of hope ahead.

His doors were open.

I sensed the monster close behind, the darkness, wanting to devour me.

I pumped my arms, running into the last set of doors. They swung open on impact, and I went sprawling into the dimly lit room, landing on my hands and knees. The doors closed behind me on a phantom wind, shutting the danger out with an eerie, soft click.

I was alone in here. Warmth emanated from the fireplace to my left, cozy chairs situated around it. Past the living space, behind a divider, was the bedroom. Everything was the same. Bare, no visible signs of it being lived in—exactly how he had kept his room.

I got up from the floor, wiping my knees. The hallway behind me remained quiet. Why was I here? How was I here? My pounding heart, my burning lungs—it was real. My hands—they hurt. I rubbed a hand along my arms, watching the tiny hairs rise. The heat from the fireplace grew more intense as I approached it.

"What is this place?" I wasn't actually in the Guard's suite, and the ceiling confirmed it as I tilted my head back. "Woah."

The ceiling was gone, and high above stretched a dark sky made of black shimmering crystal, but the rest of the room was the same as I remembered. Shelves lined the wall, and among them was a small figurine made of sticks—the Aspis. I had made it for—

God, it hurt to see. It had been such a stupid thing, a small gift for someone I wanted to grow closer with.

I closed my eyes, shutting out the room, unable to handle it. A breeze came in from the patio past the dark bedroom, and my eyes flew back open.

Out on the patio was, "Bre—" I swallowed his name. Last time it had not been him. Not really.

I tiptoed to the divider separating the bedroom and hid behind it. I peered around, looking past the large bed and through the glass patio door.

A tall, dark figure, taller than *he* should be, faced the city below, and curling from its head were two spiralling horns.

I inched closer. The beast didn't move.

I hugged the wall close to the door, nearing the patio. It didn't know I was there.

Another roar shook the Guardian Palace from within. My

fingernails scraped the wall as I clung to it in fear as the beast on the patio roared in tune with the monster in the hall, covering the sound of my gasp.

I sank against the wall, afraid to move forward.

Smoke surrounded the half-beast. Its skin was a kaleidoscope of shadows, shifting from stark white to pitch black, as if it couldn't decide whether to be a beast or a man.

But it was not like the shadows I had seen before.

They were not like the magic *he* had. He could disappear from sight, become the shadows. These shadows were something else. These were churning smoke. Like the aftereffects of a fire where the embers were too dull to see.

It was the magic of the Aspis. Not the Night-leg.

Beyond the patio, the city below laid in ruins, nothing but buildings crumbled to ashes. Night birds filled the sky, flying in circles over what remained of the dark, silent city.

An ice-cold gust of wind blew back the half-beasts torn clothes to reveal a body wound with muscle, its skin swirling black and white. It rested its palms on the balcony rail, exposing its torn, burnt flesh.

A soft cry escaped me.

The half-beast whirled around.

Breathe. Hold. Breathe.

Citrine eyes locked onto me.

That's when I ran.

The glass patio doors shattered behind me as I darted through the bedroom, past the divider. I ran into the back of a chair and tumbled over it. The heat of the fire added to the sweat collecting on my brow as I landed on my ass and scurried back, bumping into the second chair behind me.

The half-beast prowled forward, slowly, patiently. It entered the fire's light, smoke swirling around the floor, reaching out into the room before the beast made its appearance.

I was frozen in place.

His face. This time, it was his face. No slits for a nose, but those weren't his eyes burning a bright yellow as vertical pupils held me in place. Its clawed hands reached for me, and its kaleidoscope skin reflected in the light as it entered the living room.

I scrambled back, heading to the main doors.

Which monster would kill me first? The half-beast before me or the one outside.

The beast cocked its head, horns tilting to one side.

"Please," I whispered.

My back hit the doors, and my foot slipped as I tried to stand. "Please don't hurt me."

The half-beast paused, giving me time to find my footing, scanning me from head to toe.

I held myself against that door, keeping as still as I could.

It took a step closer, the fire now behind it, and I could only make out those slits in its snake-like eyes, dilating and constricting.

The beast and I both flinched as another roar sounded from the hallway. The monster out there wanted in. It banged on the door behind me, shaking me and causing a whimper to break free.

The half-beast grabbed its head and shook it, its tattered clothing waving through the air. A rattling came from its chest.

Another loud crash came from behind me, and I screamed.

The half-beast roared in answer.

Then it lifted its head and whispered, "Run, Liv."

Just like *he* had on the burning field.

That's when the double doors opened. Ice-cold wind tore through the room, blowing my cloak wide open. The fire went out, casting the room in black.

I JUMPED, sitting up in bed. The room was dark, as were the pathways outside.

I was in Danuli with the Aethar twins asleep in their beds.

When had I fallen asleep? What had been real? Had I ever left the room to walk outside?

It took a few moments to locate my things in the dark. The twins didn't notice me slip from the inn. I wasn't following them to their home. They weren't the people I needed to help. They weren't the ones who would save me from the magic inside.

ONE FOOT in front of the other. The fog in my head inched in farther, and I lost track of the trees I passed. I had only been walking for an hour and I was losing my nerve.

I wiped my sleeve across my cheeks. I couldn't stop the tears.

Daylight crept slowly in as the city woke, and I jumped at every noise.

The dreams were too real. Was it part of becoming the Ikhor? Seeing things, feeling like they were really there? I had seen shadows by the riverside, monsters in my sleep.

A small voice in the back of my head asked, *what if the dreams mean something? What if I have been in that dream place before?*

I stuffed the thought away as a fist gripped my heart and squeezed. Thinking those kinds of things would only have me spiralling further.

The rain trickled down between the large Danuli trees. I couldn't let go of everything building up. The dreams, the floods, the fires.

I needed to find Nuo, make him listen.

I worried my sleeve between two fingers as I followed a group of drunk Danuli citizens down a large pathway. I was working up the nerve to ask them where the Guards were last seen or where I might find a group of Guardians.

And then what, idiot? They hate you.

I stopped. The Guardians were not my enemies. The Guards were my friends. Couldn't I try to explain to them what had happened? I could explain it to Nuo. I had to reach him. He was in pain, like me. He would understand.

Will he understand?

Kazhi had warned the only safe option for me was to flee, but whose side was she on? Who did she serve?

Maev and Ollo weren't my friends. They were using me. I didn't know their plans, but they had made them before we met. Were they any different from those who had hurt me before? They weren't like the Law Keepers. But were they like my sister, who had handed me over for profit? Or Stephen, who had closed the door in my face when he thought I might cause him trouble?

They weren't like Nuo. And they weren't like *him*.

With my nerves unravelling, I turned down a different path, losing myself in the crowd of merchants bringing in the morning supply.

The surrounding trees grew brighter in the morning light. The twins might be up by now. I needed to move, and fast. I crossed several more rivers, my pace slowing. But I couldn't stop, so I continued while hiding under my hood. It was a good idea, even if I felt a sliver of guilt for slipping away from the twins. I followed my gut, and it told me to continue in the direction I was going.

Finally, I spotted Guardians walking on the other side of the river from where I stood. I had been told the city was full of them. Was it from the Aethar presence the Sea-leg merchant had mentioned? Perhaps they were here to help those who had lost their homes from the floods.

Five Guardians stood at a stall across the water. The river that separated us had several boats floating past, packed with crates and barrels, blocking the warriors from sight before they reappeared again.

One of them—a tall, broad man with obsidian hair pulled behind his head—stopped in the middle of the path, pulling out his coin purse to purchase something from the closest shop. His dark eyes scanned his purse while he counted.

My heart cracked. He looked ... he looked like *him*.

The shopkeeper across the river stepped in beside him, breaking the fog building around my thoughts. Upon closer inspection, the resemblance faded until the man was an echo of the Guard I once knew. His height and hair colour, maybe, but he was missing the presence, the pull and the flash of iridescence.

He moved past his fellow Guardians, sidestepping around another tall man facing my way. When I focused on *that* man, I froze.

I nearly screamed when my eyes locked with Nuo.

CHAPTER

FIFTEEN

Liv

Certain memories return to me with stark clarity. They are the ones that changed me the most.

The world vanished. There was no city, no streets, no sounds of people or rain or boats on the river.

There was only Nuo and his warm eyes—though they were dull after the loss of *him*. They were pinned on me, wide in surprise, and his chest rose as he took in a sharp breath.

It had happened so fast I nearly missed it—my friend was in there, behind the mask he wore. For a moment, I was BB, and he was the leader showing me his world with no concern for the bad side effects. He was tied to my heart, and I welcomed it, missed it.

Then he remembered what I had become and an undeniable pain struck his face before hatred washed it away—the shift was a wave across his features.

I was his enemy.

The moment it happened, a weapon was in his hand, and the

bubble burst. A crashing of sounds and colour broke the barrier, and the city sprang to life again. His focus narrowed, his chin dipped, and he moved to cross the river.

All my plans to explain myself evaporated in the breeze. I bolted.

"Get back here!" he screamed from behind me.

It only made me run faster, and I was out of breath sooner than I should have been.

Nuo was crashing into citizens on the bridge, yelling at them to move out of his way. "Stop that woman!" he ordered.

Ahead, there was a large group of shops, and everyone had turned to watch. Their eyes lit up when they saw Nuo, recognizing him as a Guard.

My plan to return to the Guards was idiotic. I couldn't explain my side of things when he had a blade in his hand.

"It's the Ikhor!" he told the crowd. "Seize that woman!"

If Nuo had hoped to find help in the streets, his declaration had the opposite effect. A perfect storm of chaos and fear erupted as I sprinted over rivers and under roots. People ran from me, screaming that the Ikhor was in the city.

I pushed past women holding themselves in fear against market stalls, and men cursed me as I jumped over huddled children. No one was brave enough to reach out and grab the evil-possessed woman running from the Guard.

I stumbled past a wagon, its edge clipping my elbow, and I swore.

I ran past more posters of myself, screaming, with the warning written on the paper. People recognized me now.

Why wasn't Nuo gaining on me? He should be faster. I didn't dare look behind me as I darted around corners and took bends in the road. I made it as difficult as I could for him to keep up. Even if part of me wished I could turn and face my once friend.

God, I missed him.

A horrible humming rang in my ears, and I winced at the pain in my head. A nauseating wave of fear tore through me, and I stumbled, crashing into a railing alongside a bridge. The colours swam.

I had to keep moving. If I stopped, he would kill me, but the humming wouldn't relent, and I was afraid of what was causing the sound—the magic. It wasn't coming from someone else. It was mine.

The thing inside me ... was it growing stronger?

I held onto my head as it rose in pitch, darting down the path and elbowing people as I pushed past them.

Shadows darkened the edges of my vision—figures hiding in alleys, watching me pass. I ran from them, too.

I skidded to a halt when I came upon a large square that opened up inside a circle of impossibly tall trees. Stalls and crates zig-zagged through the open market, which was bustling with vendors and the morning shopping crowd.

Daring a look back, I found Nuo in the distance, racing toward me, having difficulty navigating the frenzy.

I sped into the market, keeping close to the exits, and found a large stack of crates at the base of a tree to hide behind. It was a stupid move, but I couldn't catch my breath. Squeezing my temples and squinting against the pain in my head, I dropped to the ground, huffing, choking on air. A large root behind me created an alleyway between the crates and the tree, and I peeked between two crates to watch the open pathways.

Nuo tore into the market and scanned the crowd. He stood thirty feet away, but I might as well have been right next to him for how safe I felt.

People ran about, unsure where the threat was, and any tracks I may have left were lost.

Nuo spun in a circle, stopping when three more dark figures stood around him.

Panic clawed its way into my chest. No wonder he had been so slow. He was gathering reinforcements. The Guards were here, flanked by one I hated more than any other—Falizha. Why were they keeping her around?

"Where is the evil bastard?" Nuo yelled.

Several shoppers turned at the sound, going wide-eyed at the sight of the Guards.

"Who are you seeking, Guard?" An older woman stepped in closer to the four.

"A hooded woman just came through here. Did you see where she went?"

The woman shook her head, turning to another behind her who said, "The market is crowded with many hooded shoppers, Master Nuo. Many who are running."

Nuo cursed, throwing his blade into the dirt, causing the people to jump back with a terrified cry. The blade swung from side to side with the vibrating force. He turned to the others. "We find the Ikhor, and you bring it to me. I get the first fucking hit."

"Nuo, clear your head, man," Bastane chastised. "We can't fight with emotion."

Fight with emotion? He was the bastard who gave me up because he cared more about his bloodline than his honour.

"I will hunt the whole godsdamned world to make that lying evil bitch pay. She betrayed me!"

Kazhi's glare was murderous before glancing at Bastane, and the two shared a knowing look.

Falizha seemed delighted to follow Nuo's plan.

A hand landed on my shoulder, and I covered my mouth as I spun around.

Maev kneeled next to me, and her mouth set in a hard line as she gave me a once-over. With a sigh, she leaned in close and followed my line of sight to the Guards.

"How did you find me?" I whispered.

She held up her device and waved it as if saying, *Duh*.

I was a fool. How had I thought I could ignore all that had happened on that burning field and return to how things had been? Nuo's promise to kill me was real.

Maev stuck her head close to mine so we could both peek between the crates.

Nuo was yelling at the others, but something was off about him. I hadn't fully taken stock of his appearance back at the river. Now I could see everything I had missed.

"What's wrong with him?" I kept my voice low so only Maev could hear.

"Who?" Light pouring through the cracks of the crates set a sharp line down the side of her face. It lit her blue skin, highlighting the lines and dashes across her cheekbone.

"Nuo. He looks awful. Sick."

Maev's face changed. Pitying. "You kinda look the same."

"I can't look like that." I pointed back to the Guards.

Dark circles framed Nuo's sunken eyes, and his skin was pale and tight to his bones. He had lost weight, even muscle. His hair was surprisingly long, nearly touching his shoulders.

"It's only been a few days." I gripped the side of the crate. "He looks like he's been tortured."

Nuo's clothing hung off his body. After chasing me down the streets, he was panting as hard as I was while the others had already caught their breath, and his movements were jerky as he searched around him.

"A few days?" Maev shifted position to get a better view. "Liv, it's been weeks."

A jagged breath escaped me. *What?*

"Weeks?" I sputtered.

She opened her mouth as if to say more, but only nodded and bit her lip, searching my face.

No. No! Weeks *couldn't* have passed. But it was there in plain sight, written over Nuo's face—the stress living under his skin, the wan colouring, his *long* hair. I touched my own to find it past my shoulders.

"How many weeks?" I croaked. How long had it been since I lost *him?*

"Nearly six."

I choked on my breath. Six weeks.

He's been gone six weeks.

My head pounded, humming with the magic. The sound was so powerful it blinded me, blurring my vision.

I tried and failed to recall all the time I had lost.

"It took us forever to cross the plains in the rain. The longest was that boat. We kept getting lost. We tried to get you to eat and to sleep. You were just quiet and staring at the sky most of the time."

I pressed my back against the crate, tucking my knees in and holding myself in one piece.

Breathe.

Hold.

Breathe.

"Is this the magic?" I trembled against the crate. Was it that thing inside me? Was it causing me to lose time?

"The magic has been consistent with your emotions," Maev explained. "The rains never stop. The thunderstorms start when you really disappear. I have thought it over many times, and I'm sure the magic responds to emotions. If you could control them, you may be able to stop any further flooding."

I turned to Maev, pleading, "I didn't mean to damage their lands. I didn't mean any of this. I want it to stop. I'm not evil."

Maev reached out to put an arm around my shoulder, and I flinched.

"Yeah, touching isn't really my thing either," she whispered, pulling back. "I'm just trying to offer comfort." She patted me on the shoulders, gave me a weak smile, and sat against the crate next to me.

"I've had this fog in my head, preventing me from thinking straight." I pulled at my hair, testing its length, to be sure. *Real.* It was real. Time had passed while I was unaware.

"The body and mind do amazing things to protect us from pain. You were mourning. Don't blame yourself for the floods. None of this is your fault. Just learn to control it now and prevent further harm."

Control my emotions. Control the magic.

I knew how to hide them, box them up, but control them? "I would have thought an Aethar would be happy these lands are drowning."

"I don't hate the people here. As a *Rydavian*."

"The magic is controlled by how I feel. That doesn't seem like how magic should work."

"I've never read or been told how the gods use their magic." Maev tapped her lower lip, not paying attention to the growing threat in the market. "I knew they controlled the elements, but not how. The pure bloodlines could control single elements, but I thought they died out. There's a lot we lesser legacies don't know. So much knowledge lost."

I turned back to the market. The Guards were gone, and in the distance, Bastane's retreating form disappeared into the crowd.

"They've left for now. We need to find a way out of the city. Ollo is waiting at the landing site. We can pay for passage on an airship and figure out the next step."

Six weeks. The more I let it settle in, the further his memory was. The further I felt from the possibility of reaching Nuo.

Did I trust Maev enough to tell her about my dreams? Would she believe me when I said I thought they might be real, that they may be trying to tell me something?

I took a deep breath. I had so few options. I could try to make it on my own, but that scared me even more than following the Aethar.

Not Aethar. Rydavians.

"Okay. Let's go."

I stood, brushing the dust from my borrowed cloak. A wind crept along the back of my neck. It hummed, just like the magic inside me, and dread pooled in my gut as I searched for its source.

SIXTEEN

Liv

"Kazhi." I whirled around to find the Guard standing behind us.

How did everyone find me so easily? I was supposedly the most powerful person alive, yet I was a walking victim.

What had she heard? Did she now know I wasn't the powerful Ikhor like they believed?

Kazhi's frame—shorter than mine by a couple of inches—paired with her stillness, made the hairs on my neck stand. Maev, who stood several inches taller than I, was also no match for the Guard's dominating presence. I don't think even the power of the Ikhor could stop Kazhi.

"The others search the city for you." Her black reptilian eyes didn't blink.

It was hard to focus on her. The stripes and lines across her face were dizzying. The metal in her nose and ears shone with the little light coming through the cracks in the crates—dark clothing and black tattooed arms and legs hid her well in the shadows, blending her into the roots behind her. Her thick, matted strands of hair fell down her back and shifted slightly as she turned her head.

"Do the other Guards know about you, *Aethar*?" I surprised myself with my tone. I was angry with Kazhi for many reasons. "Or what about the fact that you're a Day-leg?"

The corners of her mouth tightened, confirming the truth. It was a small victory to have some of the mystery surrounding Kazhi answered.

Maev rested her hand on my arm, trying to calm me. I couldn't feel calm in front of the female Guard—I had no idea whose side she was on.

"I am surprised you know so much," Kazhi replied. "More than those closest to me. My brothers hunt you, following the Aspis's trail. I gave you the best shot when I sent you with this one. And now here you are, back in our reach. I believed the Ikhor would burn the place down before it would skulk in alleyways."

I balled my fists. She believed I was no longer myself. Kazhi had never been warm to me before, but I thought she might be trying to help.

"Why did you send me away? Why bother? It sounds like you don't care if this place burns." I didn't let it show how much it hurt that I had lost more ties to the Guardian world.

"Because the snowflake here told me she was taking you back to lead their armies and stop the Council. You're supposed to be our biggest weapon." Kazhi pinned an icy glare on Maev.

Maev stood straight, holding her breath and not meeting my eye.

"Armies?"

Ollo's message had insinuated protecting their people from the Guardians. There was no mention they had armies of their own.

"You haven't even told the Ikhor what you're doing? Who are you? I thought the Elders were sending someone competent."

Maev sunk in on herself and didn't answer, scared, and rightfully so.

Kazhi directed her attention toward me. "I believe you have the power to stop the Council and what they are doing in the dark. But you're going to waste this opportunity." Kazhi sized Maev up, clearly unimpressed with our lack of a commanding presence. "I don't know what the Aethar have planned for the magic, but you know as well as I that every life is at risk, not from the Ikhor, but from the Council. Take the Ikhor, get out, and find a way to use the magic to stop them. That's your goal."

"You don't tell me what—"

There was a knife at Maev's throat, and the colour drained from her face. Neither of us had seen Kazhi move.

"I will tell you what to do, girl, because I have risked much more than you to get here. The magic is our best shot at stopping the golds in the Guardian City. Get her out of these lands and regroup. You're only saving grace is you've not started the final battle with the beast." Kazhi's irritation landed on me. "The Aspis grows daily, as I assume, so do your powers. Find a way to bring the Council down when you're strong enough. Do that before you take on the Aspis."

"Whose side are you on?" Damn Kazhi and her secrets.

Her smile was all sharp teeth. "Olivia would have withered at how you speak to me, Ikhor. I am on no one's side, as no one has been on mine for ages. My goal has been vengeance, and I will get it this time. The Council must fall." Her knife left Maev's throat as she backed away. "The Guards will rip this city apart looking for you. I will not stop them. I will not risk my advantage here. They are still my family, but I'm playing the long game with you."

"What of my brother's airship? The one the Guards found surrounded by Southlanders," Maev asked.

"Taken back to the Guardian City. It's a fast ship. The Councilman's daughter put in a request for it to be used by the Guards."

"And the beast? Is it ..." I was afraid to ask if she had seen signs of *him*.

"The beast is as told—a godly creation. It does not eat or sleep. It grows. Stay away until you take down the Council."

"And what of the man it once was?" Maev asked, her eyes meeting mine briefly before returning to Kazhi.

"The stories are true. There is nothing human left. In its gaze is only rage. It barely recognizes that the Guards are helping it. It nearly broke Nuo in half when he and Bastane were fighting. The altercation irritated the Aspis. Do you sense the beast, Ikhor? Because I have a suspicion it knows how to track you."

"I can feel it," I confirmed. I was being pulled far past the city to the east. The Aspis must be in the skies.

"That's unfortunate for you. The beast seems to be impervious to anything thrown at it. You may have a hard time defending yourself."

"Has it been attacked?" I gasped.

"Constantly. The Aethar haven't stopped coming for it—for us. Though they only use stolen airships and racers, they have a surprising amount of weapons at their disposal. Someone is helping them," Kazhi said, appraising Maev.

"It's not the Northerners. That I'm sure of."

"I've considered the Council but can't see their gain. They would keep weapons and racers for themselves. Something else you should consider on your travels. Keep an eye out for another threat."

I swallowed my growing panic. "I'm assuming the Guards and Falizha's crew have been able to protect the Aspis."

Kazhi's lip curled. "Her crew was left behind on the burning field. None have been heard from since. There is no one guarding the Aspis save for its Guards. If you think to test our might, Ikhor, I will ensure you fall before the beast does."

"You'd kill your chance at taking the Council down?" I met Kazhi's glare, giving her a *Maev look*.

"I would rather find another way to bring the Council down than have the beast destroyed and the earth burnt by your fury."

"But you're an Aethar. The Aethar worship me, the Ikhor."

Kazhi didn't blink. "I am as much an Aethar as I am a Guardian. And I am neither. It's been nearly one thousand years since you've last risen. The stories of your past may not hold the truth. I'm judging you from your actions. Tell me, what will you do to the earth before the beast is dead? You've already flooded half the Median."

I didn't answer.

"So I was right." Kazhi's head tilted. "You are the source of the rain, not the gods. Interesting."

"Leave her be." Maev stepped in to defend me. "She's done the best she could on our journey this far. And stop calling us Aethar. You know what you are. You are Rydavian, betraying your people by helping those who invade our lands."

Maev surprised me with her boldness. Even I couldn't speak to the Guards that way.

"You don't know anything." Kazhi tensed. "History and legends are all lies. I am a child of this earth, nothing more. I suggest you ignore those borders your leaders love to create."

I had thought the mystery surrounding Kazhi was diminishing, but it only seemed to deepen.

"How do you expect us to escape with all these Guardians watching the streets? They know we are here," Maev argued.

"I know exactly what you should do."

Shivers ran over my arms when Kazhi's mouth tilted up at the corners. What kind of idea made the terrifying woman smile?

CHAPTER
SEVENTEEN

Liv

We all have walls we build to keep ourselves safe. It matters how close you stand to yours and how hard it is to cross. Stepping over it is tough. Jumping usually results in injury. The best way to cross those boundaries is to fill yourself with determination and plow right through. Sometimes, the best fuel is fire. And anger makes you burn hot. I've accomplished a lot with my anger. I survived harsh climates, starvation, ridicule and death. Nuo, if you ever read this, know that I thought it was how you would choose to survive, too. Forgive me.

We slipped out of the market unnoticed. Kazhi had told us what to do, and it was a brilliant plan. After a quick discussion, she chased after the other Guards to lead them away from the landing site where we were headed.

"She's not a Rydavian. She's a Guardian and not to be trusted," Maev huffed, her pace too fast to keep up with. She was insulted, perhaps hoping for an ally on this side of the world.

"Which way is the landing site?" I said, pulling my hood tight around my head, and Maev did the same with hers.

The twins were taking me back to Rydavas to be used by their armies. Maev had known and acted like she was interested in ending the cycle.

The Guards would kill me, and so would the world if I tried to make it on my own.

What better choice did I have than to follow?

"We are at the central market. We have a bit of a walk."

We hurried over bridges and along boardwalks, making our way past the shops in the inner city. People were packing up their wares and making their way home. The streets were emptying for fear the rumours of the Ikhor were true.

I passed another poster of my screaming face and I flipped it off.

One foot in front of the other, I told myself.

Breathe. Hold.

Six weeks! The fog crept in, and I lost track of the trees we passed. Was it the reason I had missing time? Was the fog the Ikhor, or was it of my making?

I reached inside myself, searching for its presence. How did one find another sentient being inside themselves? I felt the magic and how much I wished I could use it to ease its hold on me, but no voice was attached. Many things were lingering under my skin, and I worried about what I would see if I looked too long. The very thing that drew in the Ikhor was hate in one's heart and a strong body that could survive its possession. Yet, it was in one of my weakest moments that the magic formed.

"Do you hear that?" Maev snapped me back to reality.

Distant shouting drowned my thoughts out. "I do, and it's coming from the direction of the landing site." With strength I didn't have, I picked up my pace to follow her.

She pushed through the growing crowd that was heading in the opposite direction from us. The citizens were whispering of Aethars, and Maev turned to me, mouthing at me to stick close.

"Is there a horde here?" I asked as we crested over a small hill built over a root.

"There may be. Many groups of the Southlanders came over when the rumours of the Ikhor's waking began to spread. Ollo got very little intel as we travelled, but he did discover that their numbers have increased."

"And apparently, even going so far as to attack the Aspis. Will they cause trouble for us? You are an Aethar your—" I sent her an apologetic look. "Nevermind. Sorry. A Rydavian. Maybe they won't be an issue."

Her mouth pressed into a thin line. "They don't have allegiance to anyone but their clans. Even the clans kill each other when they aren't unified in taking down the Guardians. They will kill me, only to get to you. They will offer you anything they can to get you to follow them home."

"Why would they want me?"

"Why everyone wants you. They either want you dead or to use you for your powers and kill the Veydian people."

Veydian people. I hadn't heard them referred to as that before.

The citizens shoved me, and the Aethar's presence corrupted the beauty of the city, just as everything else had been. It reminded me of what had happened in Bellum—I ran into danger and caused trouble for the Guards. It had been different then. Then I had been a liability, and had the Guards to protect me.

The rivers widened, and the giant trees spaced out, creating wider roads and larger shops. It became easier to run through the people, and judging by their expressions, we were getting closer to the Aethar. The paths were damp from the little rain that broke through the trees high above. Thunder crashed, muffled by the dense leaves. Trees parted to reveal the sky as we crossed over a large bridge.

Rain misted my face, and I blinked away the moisture.

I stopped at the top of the bridge, spotting the docks ahead. Boats of all sizes filled the wooden boardwalks along the rivers. The port was huge, and the river flowed out of the city into a vast open countryside.

The landing site could house ten, if not more, airships the size of Falizha's. Several were already there, including the golden bitch's ship.

Panic tore through me as I grabbed Maev's arm and stopped her.

"What are you doing? Ollo will be down there." She pulled out of my grasp. "This was the plan." Her face was flushed, and she was out of breath.

I only shook my head, unable to move on.

I wasn't afraid to face Falizha, who had plans to weed out the undesirable Legacies that weren't golden like her. I wasn't afraid of the horde of Aethar that surrounded the site, blocking our path. I was afraid of seeing my friend—the one who promised to kill me.

"Liv, you've gone pale. Wha—"

"I-KHOR!" The voice tore through the crowd, drowning out all others.

Maev and I turned to find Nuo running up the side of the river on the opposite side of the landing site. He was gaining on us quickly.

I spun back to the site, and not far from Falizha's ship, Ollo's flowing moon-bright hair caught my eye. "There." I pointed him out to Maev. "Go get Ollo and fill him in. I will race there in a moment."

"What will you do? You aren't trying to stay with them, are

you? They're going to kill you or at least try to stop you. We need you."

"I am going to stop them. We are getting away from here. I promise I'm not running again."

"I—"

"Go. I *can* do this." I said for myself more than for her.

Would I be willing to hurt my old friends for my new ones?

Maev nodded, looking apprehensively at the approaching Guards. "You'll have to fight them all. You might have to hurt them, Liv."

Bastane and Falizha had caught up, and Kazhi appeared from thin air. The Guards were closing in on the bridge.

Maev gave me one last worried look and pushed away, running toward the airship docks. She reached her brother just as the Guards reached the bridge.

Nuo was first to arrive as he skidded to a halt at the bottom of the bridge, sending dust flying past him.

I stood tall, chin raised, putting on a show of bravery.

He sneered up at me, chest rising and falling so fast, and it ached to see him with his frame diminished compared to the man he had been only six weeks ago.

I grew up in a forest, clouded and grey. Meeting Nuo had split the skies. He had shown me how vibrant a person could be and how exciting life was.

But Nuo, like me, had given up. The fog had reached him, too.

I had faced dark times when my mother died. I had cried for weeks and nearly starved. It had taken something strong to wake me out of that hell—something cold and unrelenting—my sister. Rebeka had urged me to smarten up, stating Mother's death would be for nothing if I let myself go. So I had snapped out of it. I had toughened up.

Anger and the fear of death had always motivated me to stay strong, and I needed to do that now for Nuo. He and I needed to survive. I knew my faults, and I had already promised myself I would be stronger, and goddammit, so would he.

I searched inside myself, feeling for that pain—the Ikhor's magic. It was a powerful force, a whirling torrent in my chest. My sorrow had flooded the plains of Veydes, and now, I would use it to stop the Guards from crossing the bridge.

The magic of the Ikhor always rushed to the surface like a current when I thought of *him*.

Yes, the magic hummed in response as I pictured his iridescent eyes and wolfish grin.

The sharp ripping in my chest travelled to my shoulders, stiffening my back and tingling the tips of my fingers. The water below the bridge responded as the river felt my sorrow and reached up to offer its aid.

It was like the world slowed so I could see it all unfold—so I could control the outcome. The Guards raised their weapons at a snail's pace. Shock lined their faces, seeing my power.

The water floated above the bridge as I turned my palms toward the sky.

Screeches that sounded like they dragged over gravel filled the city—Danuli tree lizards crying out.

Was it the magic? Could they feel the power of the Ikhor coming alive?

"The Ikhor wields more than fire." Falizha's voice resonated through the air, low and echoed.

"The rains. *It* was causing this flood. Not the gods." Bastane's words were sluggish, each syllable lingering.

Nuo's mouth opened slowly on a roar.

When I was in control of it all, I raised my hands in the air before me—the water knew what I needed.

I was powerful—the Ikhor's magic responded with vigour, needing to be let loose. The sensation was alleviating as much as it was terrifying.

As the Guards surged forward to attack, a deluge soared toward them, slamming into them as the rush of water also fell upon me.

I choked, blinking past the ache in my limbs.

Maybe I wasn't in *full* control.

The flowing rapid knocked the Guards back, and their limp forms rode the wave until they crashed into a large root.

The water crashed on the pathway, where it pooled and retreated to the river.

I didn't fully understand the Ikhor's powers and was bluffing my way through. Maev had been right to be concerned.

I pushed the wet hair from my face, standing tall once more, playing the part of the evil Ikhor. I demanded my sorrow to build, lifting my arms again and hoping the magic understood what I wanted. The river responded as a column of water rose and inched its way before me, becoming a moving thing—a cylindrical shape, like the Aspis. It coiled and slithered before the Guards, just as the Aspis had on the fields waiting to strike me.

Bastane was on his feet, sword in hand. He slashed at the water, only for his weapon to slide right through. The water forced him back, and he fell to the ground, sputtering.

Nuo's face fell as he just stared at me.

A lump in my throat turned to a knife in my heart.

Nuo belonged to me, as much as *he* had, as much as my mother. We belonged in each other's lives, yet he sat opposite me. Betrayal was evident—no mask could hide how much he hated me now. His hair was a mess of wet clumps stuck to his face as the others choked, coughing up water. But, of course, my Sea-leg friend breathed through it all.

While the others collected weapons and prepared to attack, I pulled the water back toward me. I commanded my heart to open, to feel it once more and control the river beneath. I lifted my palms to the Guards and spread my arms wide. The water rushed toward me, and right before it collided with me, it angled up and out, creating a wall taller than I stood. Only mist hit my face.

I was understanding how the magic worked—how to use my emotion to wield it. Water was sorrow—mist, rain and the steady flow of a river. I needed to use my emotions to tell the elements what I needed, what I wanted. I had to *feel* it.

Through my wall of water, I could make out the shapes of the others. I could see the rigid way Nuo held himself. He was dying from the inside out, and I could no longer let it go on. Six weeks of my life were gone without my permission. I had allowed that fog to erase it all, as had Nuo, because of our loss.

I knew what I had to do to bring him out of that fog.

I released the water, letting it smash below me, only to raise a single column. I made it form the Aspis again, knowing it would have the effect I desired. "Guard," I spat, eyes locking with Nuo.

Please let this work, I prayed.

He flinched, hearing my voice. Was he expecting the voice of evil?

"Look how weak you've become. Such an easy target." I smiled. It was a lie, a mask—one he should have seen right through. But the part of Nuo that knew me was locked away.

His face changed, no longer hiding what lay beneath, and he opened his mouth to speak. To damn me, I was sure.

"I know you," I cut him off and stared him down. I moved my hands, controlling the water-Aspis to move. Kazhi and Bastane were trying to attack, and I beat them back each time, not looking away from Nuo. "She's told me of you, as have my worshippers. 'Shadow and Blood' is what they call you and the other Guard."

Nuo's nostrils flared as he jumped to his feet, gripping his blades.

So he knew the nickname the Aethar had given him. It made it all the easier to bait him. "I'm coming for you first, *Interrogator.* You're easy prey. Weaker than the others. How you became a Guard, I will never know. When my followers are not at risk, I will come for you. The fight will be a disappointment, I'm sure." I looked him up and down, making it clear I found him lacking.

Nuo screamed, rising to jump toward the water Aspis, but Kazhi stopped him, wrapping an arm around his waist and holding him back. She gave me a concerned look, perhaps wondering why I was tormenting her brother.

"I'll kill you!" he shouted.

I smiled, and I hated doing it. "Try, Guard. You're too weak. What a pathetic excuse to defend the beast."

I prayed the hatred would work. I learned long ago that hate could be used as a driving force to make oneself hard. Hate taught me how to survive the forest and the endless loneliness. Hate fuelled my need to survive, to escape, and to be nothing like the rest of them.

Nuo would hate me more once he realized what Maev and I planned to do, what Kazhi had told us to do. We were stealing their only means of following the beast—Falizha's empty ship.

The water morphed into a wall again, and I struggled to concentrate on my sorrow while letting him watch my smile grow. "I like borrowing her body," I said, only for him. "I wonder what secrets I'll discover while living here."

Nuo had once trusted me when he trusted so few, and I promised myself I would return to him. We were going to survive this because he was the only one left in Arde I considered my family, and I would not lose him.

He was going to forgive me.

He had to.

Snow Clans
Dead Tree Island
Three Sisters
Extreme Sea-Legs
Didn't go. Don't want to.
North Aspis
GUARDIAN LANDS
The Last City
BB's Cave
The Cabin
Bert
THE FREE LANDS
Bellum
Rough Swim
Nope
The Guardian City
Lots of Pirates
N
W   E
S
VEYDES
Armel Farms
THE MEDIAN
Ouras's Temple
Land of Bugs
Do not return
Danuli
Salt Water Lake
Warning: do not swim here.
Creepy Deep
Sea-Leg Isles
Nope
Stone City
Korrylt
Sea Drift
GUARDIAN LANDS
Mount-Leg Island
Canyons of the Lost
Sea Swell
South Aspis
(you owe money)
(Completely useless)
Rem's Temple
THE LANDS OF THE SAND CITIES
The Eagle
Brekt forgot torch here
Oasis
(not welcome back)
Unsailable
Uninhabitable

Nuo's (Incorrect)
Map of
ARDE
★ Towns
● Cave
Crystal Cave
▲ Treasure
◇ Nuo's Faves
✕ Weapons
Aether
Wastelands

PART TWO

CHAPTER
EIGHTEEN

Liv

Maev says to think of happy memories and find a way to repeat those moments. After staring at this page for several long minutes, all I can think of is how my happy memories have left with the dead.

How often will I stand on this airship, promising never to return? Everywhere there were signs of the Guardians, the Council, and the Day-leg who captained it.

"You will steal the ship and take it as far as you can go," Kazhi had instructed.

"How could you work with Falizha after she let your friends die?" I had asked her.

Kazhi had known I meant her Guardian friends who died on the burning field. "I'm not using her for the ship, Ikhor. But for what's on the ship. There are books, records and journals. I can't easily get to *them. With Falizha gone, they'll be left waiting to be read. Find out what the Council has planned."*

Ollo and Maev had the ship ready to go before I reached the ladder floating near the ground. I had boarded, concentrating on holding the unstable wall of water on the bridge. But by the time I climbed the ladder, we were already rising in the sky.

I let go of the river, rushing through the metallic halls decorated with soft red carpets and gold hanging lights, easily remembering the way to the large war room where Falizha had commanded her crew.

Glass made up the front wall of the bridge, showing a complete view of what lay ahead. Green light cascaded across the floors, tinting the walls and tables full of books as we passed through the treetops. As we reached the sky, grey daylight flooded the bridge, washing out the colours before me.

The world beyond was so open, so vulnerable.

I felt for the beast. The pull told me it was still to the east but coming close, and fast.

"The Aspis will feel us departing, hurry!" I flew past the massive middle table, where maps and books were laid out to plan the Guardian's trips, running for the twins and searching for the pull.

I did my best to stomp down my emotions and cut off what I was feeling. It was a challenge since I had destroyed the box I had hidden my more painful memories and feelings in.

If I had built a box before, I could certainly do it again.

How I wished I could have reached the windows sooner to see the look on Falizha's face when her ship sailed away. Instead, I searched the skies for our death made of black scales.

It was there, in the eastern sky, circling the city, weaving through clouds of rain before changing course.

I reared back, my heart stopping as it came straight for us.

What tempted it to come for me now? The pull was there, so why, at times, did it linger in the distance?

"It's coming!" I bolted for the front window, passing Ollo, who focused on the sky as he pushed levers and pressed buttons on the panel in front of him.

"No need for concern." Ollo's jerky movements over the buttons said otherwise. "This airship, though not as fast as the one I lost to the Aethar, is built for impact. This is a battleship."

Impact?

Despite the situation, Ollo's face lit up. Of course, as a pilot, he fixated on the ship.

"Can it take the impact of a legendary beast?" I gave him the most withering look I could muster while my heart pounded in my chest, Maev's mannerisms rubbing off on me.

She wasn't looking as confident, and her face paled when the Aspis advanced.

"Well, if any ship could, it would be this one," Ollo replied. "It has a shield enforced by magic and weapons that can shoot long-range. However, from the ballistic readings here, few projectiles are left to throw at it. Our best bet is to escape."

"You said this ship was slower. Can it escape the Aspis?"

"This ship may not be as fast. But you have the best pilot in Rydavas steering it." Ollo was operating the ship with enough confidence that I didn't find the comment arrogant.

It was a strange moment to admit I was impressed. Intrigued even.

The thought vanished when I was suddenly thrown off my feet. I landed hard on my shoulder, facing the window to the outside. The ship moaned as it stabilized in the air once more. With shaking hands, I propped myself up.

The beast curled around us, blocking the daylight, and I stifled my scream. The magic barrier shimmered, deflecting the onslaught of the Aspis.

"To offer feedback on your inquiry, Liv—yes, the airship can sustain an impact from the beast."

I stood, ignoring Ollo's sarcasm. I was scared to death, and he was enjoying it.

"Head this way." Maev pointed to a spot on a display that was similar to the one on her racer.

I was behind her, grabbing her chair before the force knocked me off my feet again.

A loud boom shook the airship from above. What would happen if the Aspis broke through the barrier? Would it take down the entire ship?

I squeezed the back of Maev's seat.

A screen was lit up in front of her with the outlines of Veydes, similar to what Nuo had drawn. Yet there were no markings of Aethar lands.

"I want to go to Ouras's temple," I blurted without thinking.

The frantic button pushing and lever pulling stopped.

Maev whirled around in her seat. "What? We need to get out of Veydes."

"I want to go to see Ouras."

It would anger the twins, but while I ran from my old friends and boarded the ship, I had decided what I needed to do to end it all.

The room went dark again as the Aspis did another circle around the front windows.

"What's this about?" Ollo asked. "Was this part of Kazhi's plan?"

Maev's hands balled into fists as she spoke to her brother. "No, it wasn't. And we don't have time to be debating this right now. You said you would help us, Liv. Now you're giving up?"

"Giving up?" Ollo's focus trailed the beast, which was now doing lazy circles around the ship. Perhaps the shield would caution the beast from attacking.

"Liv said she wants to return the magic to the gods. Meaning we have risked our lives, lost the Elder's ship and planned this all for nothing."

"Is this true?" Ollo turned away from the controls to search my face for the truth.

"Yes."

"But why?" Ollo asked, and the twins' scathing looks had me pinned in place.

I lifted my chin. I would not back down to anyone. Ever again. "You two don't understand how it feels. This magic, the very one you see as an answer to your problems, is the reason for all of mine. It's killing me. It's taken time away from me. I control the magic by feeling *pain*. If the magic works by feeding off my emotions, it'll never stop. It's never going to get easier."

Anger flashed across Ollo's face. "We can help you—"

"No! I will *never* not feel the deaths of my mother or—" I swallowed, shaking my head. "I will *never* not feel their loss. I want it out of me. I want to see Ouras and ask him to take it back. It'll end the cycle. I'm sorry about whatever plans you had for the Ikhor, but at least future generations won't have to live in fear. Maybe this will even put an end to the wars."

"You think—"

Ollo stopped when Maev put a hand on his arm. Her face was void of emotion. "She's right, Ols. It's her choice. We came here to get the Ikhor, to take her home and fight. We can fight by ending the cycle. How far is the temple?"

Ollo turned to the map, his perfectly poised form stiff. "It's in the *wrong* direction. We don't have time for this."

"How many added days?" Maev asked.

"Two. If the visit is short."

"We go. And before you protest, imagine the glory you'll receive if you tell them it was you who piloted the Ikhor to the gods."

"That wasn't the instructions I was given. And this isn't merely about glory, Maev. Despite what you've come to think of me, I didn't come here for purely selfish reasons," he said, his glare filled with impatience.

"No part of this was my mission either."

"No one even knows you're here. Another reason to speed home."

They shot identical angry looks at me, but I stood my ground.

"Fine," Ollo said. "But after this, you follow my instructions. No changing course at the last second. We're on my schedule."

"Agreed." I didn't let my surprise show. I hadn't expected them to take me. It was another reason I could no longer see them as my enemy.

Ollo studied his sister, a million retorts in the fiery sheen of his eyes, and I envied his proud features. His calm acceptance of my request and his control over his anger were refreshing. He faced the front windows, where the Aspis stayed close, before finally returning to the controls.

The two moved the ship, aiming for the Temple of Mountain and the Aspis followed, hesitant to attack but not letting us out of its sight.

"Thank you," I said, but the twins ignored me. I understood—I was costing them a great deal by demanding we go to Ouras. They had plans for the Ikhor, which involved an army, and who knew what that army was planning to do?

So I stepped away.

"Maev, you keep an eye on power. I'm going to take us for a ride." Ollo spoke low, his words weren't for my ears.

The beast decided I wasn't worth the fight either as it languidly circled the ship, moving farther away with each pass. It was letting us go. But why?

I still felt the pull, did it not? What made it attack? What made it fall back?

I left the bridge, searching for supplies the Guards had left behind. I calmed myself to concentrate on rebuilding that box, piece by piece. When I had said I would never get over *his* death, that I wouldn't let the magic be in control, it was a promise I made myself. I would regain control of my life.

I didn't know whose legends I believed, the Rydavians or the Guardians, but I wasn't willing to risk the Ikhor taking over and becoming the evil that destroyed the world.

Any more than I already had.

AN EERIE SILENCE blanketed the ship without its crew inside, and the ghosts that haunted these halls sent shivers down my spine.

Falizha's crew of female Guardians had once manned the ship —before she led them to the burning fields and to their deaths. Now, these metal halls creaked and moaned—it sounded like cries of betrayal.

The worst ghosts were the memories.

The first room I visited was the cabin I had stayed in with the Guards. It was on this ship that *he* and I had opened up to each other.

Thinking of him led me to the dreams. The ones that felt all too real. I was almost afraid to fall asleep again, afraid to wake up and remember what had happened.

I stood in the open door of the cabin, holding onto the cold frame. The four sets of bunk beds were all made—there were no signs anyone had ever stayed here. There was no discarded clothing or leftover food trays from when Nuo and I had eaten alone, avoiding the crew.

Across the room was the bed Nuo had sat on while we talked. I could see him clear as day.

"I want you to show me it all. Show me your whole world. Let's live until we don't," I had said, realizing I had a genuine friend after so many years alone.

"You might regret telling me that, BB." His voice had been calming and sure. *"We live to the fullest."*

"No matter the bad side effects?"

The bad side effect was that we ran out of time.

I didn't go into the cabin, and continued retracing my time here on the airship.

I felt nothing when visiting the training room. It wasn't a place where I had built fond memories. The last time I was here, I had broken down and cried over my mother's death.

The storage room below was in shambles, as though something had happened, a fight maybe. Broken crates and bottles littered the floor, and the food was gone. The Guards had been chasing us for weeks. They must have depleted Falizha's supplies.

Working my way back to the higher levels, I ran my hand along the cool metal walls, trying to ignore my headache. The humming of the magic vibrated in my head, though it felt considerably less in the quiet. I was lost in thought when a loud crash came from down the hall and I froze.

Maev stepped into view, throwing a bag over her shoulder. Dressed as a Guardian, she wore all black. The dark clothing showed off her slim frame and made the blue of her skin and hair resemble a summer sea. She was so foreign and beautiful that I almost felt shy to look at her. She paused, giving me a weak smile, and pointed a thumb to her back. "I found Guardian clothing and thought it would be a good idea we all blend in once we reach Ouras's temple."

"What's in the bag?"

"Clothes, food, and other interesting finds amongst the Guard's belongings. Hope you don't mind I went through the Interrogator's stuff. Not that he had much, but I swiped his map too."

I swallowed the lump in my throat.

"What does that face mean?" she asked.

"A Guardians map is sacred to the maker." Nuo would be furious. It took a long time before he allowed even me to see it.

Maev grabbed a length of her hair and ran it between her fingers, chewing her lip.

"What does *that* face mean?" I asked, unable to help the small smile that broke free. I enjoyed how easy to read she was.

She scanned the hall. "It's well known the Interrogator is the most dangerous, the most ruthless. Will you tell him it was me who stole it?"

The humour of the situation vanished.

"I didn't know him to be like that—to be ruthless." Seeing her confusion, I continued, "Nuo was my friend. He was good to me. It's hard for me to see him so hated. That his reputation is surrounded with fear."

"His fame has reached our people, a world apart from this one. Guards are often talked of, and rumours spread. None have been talked of so well in my lifetime as Shadow and Blood."

"Hmmm. Well, I won't tell Nuo. Not that we talk anymore." I shrugged.

Maev approached, jerking her head to follow, and I didn't miss the sad look she gave me before passing. She appeared less animated than usual, and I got the feeling she didn't like to linger on negativity. Even though she was trying to be kind, I could sense she was still angry about my decision to seek Ouras.

Somehow, her kindness made me hate myself more.

We travelled the halls, peeking into rooms. Maev commented on everything she saw, distracting me. "That woman really liked to show off, didn't she? There's gold everywhere."

"Why did you have to bring Falizha up? If I get the chance, I am going to make a ball of fire and throw it in her face."

"Don't waste your fire. She's a Day-leg, a child of the Sun no less. You'll need to incinerate her to cause real damage. Make it an ice ball. Or better yet, drown her. Make her wish she was a Sea-leg for once."

There was an idea. "Where is this violence from?"

I had to walk faster than usual to keep up with Maev. Her legs were longer, and she seemed to be constantly vibrating, ready to go.

"I grew up around conniving women. I know what they're like."

"Were they golden Day-legs too?"

"No. The golds back home are not imperialists like here. The women I'm talking about were the ones who faked being my friend so they could get closer to my brother." Her mouth thinned into an unimpressed line.

I didn't know what to say, so I said nothing. I toyed with the hem of my cloak, ignoring the stabbing in my gut from being back on the ship.

"I'm sure you've noticed." She gave me a skeptical look, pretending she didn't see my discomfort. "Every one of them told me how handsome he is. I worry that makes me look like a man."

I almost laughed. "Well, you don't. And your brother is good-looking, but I wouldn't pretend to be your friend because of it."

Maev walked like nothing was amiss as we passed more cabins that looked like the one I had shared with the Guards. I thought no more of the dreams, wiping my cheeks dry and letting those thoughts go. Maev stared forward as she continued talking, and I was grateful.

"Uh-huh. I've invited friends to my home who ditched me to watch him study. Sighing at him when he had his nose in a book."

Maev's tone was too forced to be casual. Why was she being nice to me when she was mad about my decision to go to the temple?

As much as I could understand the motives of Maev's friends, I could tell it had hurt her at one time. "Have you not had men after you in the same way?"

Maev's blue skin turned a funny shade of pink. "No."

"I haven't had any female friends before," I admitted. "I don't know what's okay to ask."

"That's been made obvious."

"I was just trying to ask if you have had boyfriends."

She fixed the bag on her back so her hands could wave in the air as she spoke. "To tell you the truth, I haven't had many female friends either, not since I was a kid. And I haven't had any men in my life. I spend most of my time in my lab, not frolicking and going to parties. Not like Ollo does," she muttered.

With her heart-shaped mouth, straight nose and big blue eyes, Maev should have had a lineup of men. She looked me up and down, apprehensive. "There was this one guy."

"Oh?" I prompted, and for a moment, I wasn't thinking about

the airship or the look on Nuo's face when I threw a torrent of water at him and the Guards.

Maev raised a finger to the air and rambled, making me think she felt as awkward as me. "Nothing's happened between us. He and I used to attend classes together before he trained to be a city guard. All the girls in class admired him. But we were forced to be study partners, so I got to sit next to him for a full year."

She seemed proud of that fact, and it seemed strange to me that was something to brag about, sitting next to a guy.

She opened a door to an empty room, scanned it, and moved on, not finding anything of value. "Now, I see him once in a while when he comes to visit his uncle, who is my professor and lead alchemist at the university, by the way. But I don't think he notices me or has any interest."

"I'm sure he does. And not because he's trying to get to Ollo through you."

She was silent a moment before saying in a low voice. "So you do think he's good-looking."

"I would be stupid not to notice that both of you are." I wouldn't admit I used to call Ollo the beautiful blue man. Was it because I hoped Maev would be a friend? A real one?

She pointed a finger in my face, about to get angry with me, when I grabbed her finger and pulled it downward. "But he's not the Shadow Guard."

It hurt to say.

Her face fell. "I'm sorry. I was trying to get your mind off everything."

"I could tell. You aren't good at faking conversation." I dropped my hand.

We both stood woodenly, and with a huff, she placed her hands on her hips. "Let's keep searching the ship and pretend like we aren't terrible at conversation, okay?"

"Sure."

We continued down a hall I hadn't travelled. Maev halted, facing a large gold-inlaid door decorated with an image of the

Aspis. She tipped her head my way, giving me a deadpan look. "How much you wanna bet that behind this door is a room that makes you want to gag?"

I enjoyed how much Maev didn't like Falizha, even though she had never talked with her. "You know, you and your brother look alike, but you don't sound the same. You're much easier to communicate with."

"Ollo's always had an impressive vocabulary. My father tried to get us to present ourselves in a way that showed strength of mind. It didn't quite stick with me."

She tried the door. Surprisingly, it was unlocked.

"I'm guessing she wanted it open for any of the Guards who were willing to visit," I groaned. Would she be trying to win them over? A marriage for her image?

I remembered what Kazhi had told me after she had given us the plan of stealing the airship.

"I'm not using her for the ship, Ikhor. But for what's on the ship. There are books, records and journals. I can't easily get to them. With Falizha gone, they'll be left waiting to be read. Find out what the Council has planned."

"How come you haven't been able to discover those secrets?" I was familiar with Kazhi's magic and how it worked.

"There is a reason."

We knew why we were walking into Falizha's room, but neither of us knew what to expect.

CHAPTER
NINETEEN

Nuo

The long boughs of the Danuli trees shaded me as I tracked the commotion fifty feet away. My *team* was reloading our newest airship—now hovering next to the docks—brought to us by one of the many faithful Guardians from the city.

I was failing to keep my mind off what had happened the day before.

It had been there. In the city. Taunting me.

A Guardian was deep in conversation with Falizha, updating her on the Council's goings-on and passing the new orders to the *Captain*.

It made my stomach roll.

How could the other Guardians obey her? Falizha had led so many to their death and didn't lift a finger to help her crew. She let them all burn. It disgusted me that I was allowing her to live. But as Kazhi reminded me daily, I needed that ship because there was something else out there I hated more.

Kazhi had made me a promise—when the time is right, Falizha is done. I only had to wait for her nod.

In the meantime, I let all my hate for the Governor's daughter fester. It paired well with the hatred for the Aethar and the Ikhor ... how could I let it get under my skin the way it did? It called me *weak. Pathetic.*

I searched for the Aspis between the small cracks in the treetops, but the grey above was empty.

"The Aspis wasn't what we had anticipated."

I nearly flinched when Kazhi appeared at my side, following my line of sight. She smacked me on the back of the head. A surprising feat with our difference in height.

I rubbed the spot, scowling down at her.

"We were taught of a legend that saves the people," she continued. "But what we got was a mindless beast that doesn't recognize friend from foe."

I didn't respond. The Aspis had attacked the group of Guardians who brought us supplies.

It had attacked *me.* If there was a bigger sign that my brother was gone, I wasn't seeing it.

"Fortunately, the Guardians who witnessed the attack have stayed silent, so the citizens don't know. I've made sure to spread the tales of the Aspis attacking Aethar."

"But it was only because the Aethar had attacked it first."

And not for a second had I witnessed it go for the Ikhor. *What. The. Fuck. Everything is a mess.*

"This one is fast." Kazhi nodded to the new airship. "The woman who drove it here mentioned that they nearly crashed it during test flights." It was sleek and meant for speed.

"Think we should do as the Ikhor did and leave Falizha behind without her ship?" I asked, hoping Kazhi would agree. "We could watch her chase us, play a little cat and mouse."

Kazhi surprised me by considering it. "I hate that we need what they have. But the ships, the supplies, we can't do it on our own yet. We have to consider taking this fight into Aethar lands. We need more Guardians."

"And we won't get any supplies in a land void of life."

There was a slight shift in Kazhi, but I didn't meet her gaze, unwilling to see the disappointment or pity there.

"Those crates can go in the back," Falizha ordered, as Guardians loaded more supplies onto the ship—hopefully, more drink too.

I couldn't shake the nausea eating at me. No matter what I did or how many I killed, I couldn't escape it. I no longer slept, but faded off just long enough before my body would jerk me awake, reminding me of the pain, or about what had happened.

"What do you make of the Aethar the Ikhor follows?" I asked. "They hid their scars, making themselves look like they weren't worshipers."

"I don't know what to make of them." Kazhi squinted at the crates being moved around the airship. "But it's the ones from Bellum, where Bones first noticed the blue-skinned man."

Bones.

"Stop using that name." I tightened a fist, digging my nails into my palms as a distraction. "Makes me want to vomit. We know they're the same ones who the Ikhor ran into. Do you think it means there are more of them hiding in plain sight, forgoing their scars to blend in?"

Kazhi was quiet, and it pissed me off I couldn't tell what she was thinking.

"I don't know. The Aethar could be hiding things over the borders," she said.

"I guess we will find out."

Kazhi backhanded my chest, forcing the air from my lungs. "Let's head to the inn. We aren't leaving until tomorrow morning."

Right. We couldn't sleep on the airship. Not enough beds.

I followed Kazhi down the docks, passing the ship. We approached the rear doors and a female Guardian with light, shoulder-length hair appeared, grabbing a crate to load.

I jogged forward. "Let me get that," I said, winking at her.

I got the reaction I was hoping for—she blushed, giving me *the look*, and I gave her the smile I reserved for all the women whose attention I wanted. When she looked away, it told me I could still put it on. I'd have a distraction tonight.

"You don't have to do the work, Guard Nuo. I was sent here to assist." She smiled, and it was enough to forget what the Ikhor had said to me.

But only for a moment.

"I don't build these muscles up for nothing." I flexed, not really enjoying the attention as I should. "Let me show off a little."

I had never hated being seen, being recognized as the Guard that I was. I did now. The growing fear of failure fuelled the nausea eating away at me.

"Okay, but don't let Captain Ravin see me slacking. I don't want to have to face the Governor."

"I got you," I said. "If anyone says anything, you come find me. I'll be at the Red Door Inn tonight."

My smile faded as Falizha rounded a corner and opened her nasty mouth, barking orders. "Grab those bags inside there and leave those crates behind. We need to leave as much as we can." She caught sight of me standing next to the Guardian whose crate I had taken and eyed the girl up and down.

"Jealousy's not a good look on you, Captain," I said, hiking the crate up higher and walking toward the end of the ship.

I nodded to the Guardian, giving her a chance to walk away, and she took it, leaving me and Falizha to stare daggers at each other.

Falizha fixed the clasp on her shoulder that held her cloak in place. "Should have figured you would only stop to help if it would get you laid, Nuo. How many of my crew members did you go through the last time we flew together?"

"Why don't you ask them? Oh wait, you left them to burn." I hated using the dead to prove a point. The jab affected me more than it did the golden bitch in front of me.

Falizha was part of the reason I wanted to lose the contents of my stomach, part of the reason I wished I could remain unseen. The others looked at me differently now—with pity and concern, sometimes with skepticism. I'd received similar looks my entire life. *The poor orphan boy. The sad little Sea-leg whose blood was weak. No one to love me. No one to protect me.*

Did I look fucking weak? Had I ever? I was smarter, stronger and better than most of them. So what in the Endless Night were they seeing?

"Try, Guard. You're too weak. What a pathetic excuse to defend the beast," the Ikhor's voice echoed through my head.

Bastane appeared behind Falizha, and he stopped short when he stood before me.

I shoved the crate into his gut. "You look like you need something to do."

His mouth twisted, but he didn't argue with others in earshot. He grabbed the crate and left, taking it aboard.

Kazhi stood next to me, glaring. I had forgotten she was behind me.

"Nice, idiot," she muttered, leading us away from the airship, then surprised me by adding, "Why don't you go for a swim before we settle in?"

"So all the girls can see me topless?" I forced a charming smile, taking a peek over my shoulder to see where the Guardian girl had run off to.

"Not to feed your ego. To cool off."

I dropped the act. "I don't need to fucking cool off."

"You do. You need a lot of things, one of which is to smarten up and then pack. I'm not doing your work for you. And stop talking to me like that. Watch your mouth."

I looked past the airship to the horizon where the river lands ended. I hadn't gone in the water in weeks. Couldn't bring myself to go under the surface.

If I did, I wasn't sure if I'd bother to come back up.

My nighttime terrors were filled with sinking to the bottom of the darkest part of the sea, where my weak blood wouldn't allow me to survive. And Mayra—my goddess, my mother—would only look upon me with a frown.

"I do my share of work," I told Kazhi lightheartedly. "Not once have I slacked on my part. I'm the mapper. Very important." I patted my chest for show.

Then shame hit me—almost as hard as hearing the Ikhor use Olivia's voice to taunt me. The evil shit had called me *Interrogator.* The name the Aethar pinned me with. Not that I minded the fear that accompanied the name. That the Ikhor knew it meant the Aethar were in its ear.

My *friend,* Liv, had not been told what my enemies called me. She hadn't seen me as a deadly killer or the sad orphan boy.

But she wasn't your friend. It *had lied to you.* I reminded myself for the hundredth time.

When had the histories changed? Why hadn't the scribes mentioned the Ikhor's other powers? It wasn't only fire, as I had believed. The fucker could wield water magic, too.

We hit the bridge where the Ikhor had stared me down, and I said nothing to Kazhi as we crossed and made our way down one of the dirt pathways along the river. Her footsteps were silent. She didn't pay any attention to the citizens, but I offered warm smiles and friendly waves. The people always reacted when they saw the Guards. I'd loved the attention once.

"Falizha's intel confirms the Ikhor didn't head south," Kazhi said in a low voice. "With the ship, it shouldn't take us long to find them."

"The stories of the Aspis leading us to the final battle made us unprepared," I noted, and not for the first time. The Guards were convincing themselves as much as the public that they knew what in the goddess's blue seas was going on.

"The Aspis returned from the woods near Ouras's temple. Only to turn back and wind north again. We need to follow it," Kazhi said. "It's our only lead."

"This new airship, what's the defence system like? It's clearly not equipped with weapons."

We passed a group of elderly women who stopped to shake our hands and thank us for being in Danuli when the Ikhor was here. We saved them, and they trusted the floods would end soon. *Right.*

"Falizha will be told that information," Kazhi said as we left the women. "She's the best we have for a pilot now. But with the Aethar taking Falizha's old ship, we are at an advantage. They can't know how to fly it well."

"True," I nodded. "The blue fuckers grew up in a wasteland. We will get that ship back in our hands and end this."

Kazhi ignored the gaping mouths of a few young boys, who hugged the wall as she passed their front door. I clapped one on the shoulder, lowering my voice. "She's a prime example of why not to piss women off, boys. I keep my mouth shut around her when she's holding those knives."

The boys went pale.

Kazhi shot me an incredulous look. "My knives haven't done a thing to shut you up. Ever."

I shrugged at the three who were now gaping at me. "Nevertheless, Guard Kazhi is on your side. No need to fear her."

They nodded, but then all ran inside their home, which was built into the base of the tree, and slammed the door.

I caught up to Kazhi, dropping my forced smile. "Bastane sure looked cozy, working next to Falizha. Maybe next time the Aspis attacks, I'll let it chomp him to pieces."

"You won't. And it's time to get over it. He did what he thought was best for our people. Not for any alliance with the Council. We were instructed to find the Aspis, and he thought he had done so."

The first time she had defended him, I had raged. I'd heard all the excuses already. Bastane had tried on numerous occasions to corner me to talk. Every time, I shut that shit down. We were teammates in only one way that mattered: kill the Ikhor.

"How would you know any of that? That he's not working with the Council." I slowed my pace to walk alongside Kazhi. She hated it when I walked too fast. "He could be playing us, feeding the Council info, trying to get a seat with them."

"I know he isn't." She scanned the streets as she always did, on the lookout wherever we went.

I searched Kazhi's face and found no trace of a lie. "How?"

"Because I know—as I know many things. Do you doubt me now? After everything?"

"No, how could I? You control everything I think and do." I threw a weak grin, pointing to her knives. "I still don't forgive him. He went behind our backs."

"He did. But Bastane grew up privileged. Never had anything bad happen to him until his adult life. It didn't cross his mind that Falizha was as horrible as we all said. We can't condemn a man for believing the good in people, especially when, now, he has to face his failures. He knows he's to blame for how it all went down. He's putting himself through his own punishment."

"And yet working with Falizha?"

"Who do you think is feeding me info on what they talk about?" Kazhi smiled.

I would never get used to how unnerving it was to see her smile. I'd once considered Kazhi to be a secret god herself—the terror she could instil was godly in my eyes.

"So we trust him again?" My faith in Kazhi was my last lifeline.

"I do." There was no debate. She was giving an order, letting me know I needed to as well. It did very little.

"I don't know why I still trust *you*." I did my best to keep my tone light, to let her know I was teasing. Yet there was truth in what I admitted.

"You trust me because I keep saving your ass. You've been sloppy. Chin up. The end of it all is nearing, yet our goal is the same."

I stayed quiet.

Several people we passed tried to stop us and inquire about the Aspis. A group of women surrounded me, asking how long the Guards were in the city. One laid a hand on my arm, smiling up at me, but Kazhi yanked me away, muttering she was saving the citizens of Danuli in more ways than one.

A roar shook the ground, and a shadow was cast on the greenery above as the Aspis flew over the city. The beast had disappeared for a time, only reappearing above me now. Any hope that it had killed the Ikhor was a waste of time—the beast would be gone, too, no longer needed to destroy the evil. The gods would have called back their saviour.

I didn't admit out loud that I hated the Aspis—what it had done to my life. I had become a Guard for the beast, and yet when I saw it … well, it made the nausea worse.

I sometimes wished that I never wanted to become a fucking Guard of the Aspis. But Brekt was bigger than me when we were kids and forced me to train. As orphans and unwanted legacies, everyone was against us. Then, the Guardians chose me to be a *hero*.

Fuck that. I was a survivor. That's all. That's what no one saw.

"The attacks on Veydes have stopped. The Sea-leg villages have been left alone since the Ikhor's return," Kazhi said.

"What are you trying to say? The Ikhor isn't as evil as we thought? Look at the flooding." I kicked at a rock on the pathway, ignoring the boats passing by on the river and the stares of those steering.

The rock I kicked hit a post near the river, and it drew my attention.

Ugh. Another poster. Someone had added the two blue Aethar.

Posters of the Ikhor's face were everywhere, thanks to Falizha's description of Brekt's old lover. How many more times would I have to look at that screaming face? Or see citizens carrying the image around and posting it at their shops? Yet none had stopped them as the Ikhor ran through the streets.

They were afraid of her.

It. They were afraid of it.

It was exhausting to joke with other Guardians about how Erebrekt of the North was a fool for a pretty face, tricked by the Ikhor, and how he was now gone on his own mission for the Council. Falizha's father ordered us to keep quiet about who the

Aspis was. It killed me to lie about him, to be funny, to play the uncaring hero.

"The Aethar are in larger hordes," Kazhi said. "Growing. Bastane says Falizha confirmed the numbers. But the villages haven't been attacked since Falizha has been travelling with us. Flooding, yes. Deaths? No." She gave me a knowing look.

"Do we have any proof yet that she was involved in the attacks on the Sea-leg villages?"

"Nothing substantial. Once we do, we finally have a solid reason to cut ties with the Council and get others on our side."

I didn't reply. I didn't need to because Kazhi knew I wanted it as much as she did—to find a new future for the Guardians. There were too many put at risk and controlled for the Council's gain. When the war was over, if I survived, that would be how I spent the remainder of my life—ending them.

When the Council was gone? Well, maybe I would take that deep dive into the ocean.

"The Ikhor was wearing Olivia's things."

My attention left the path, and my jaw clenched. *Why did she use her name?* "What do you mean? What does that have to do with anything."

"It was wearing her swords. Why, when it can use magic."

I scoffed. "It likely doesn't care what it wears."

Kazhi thumbed the hilt of a knife at her hip. "And the Ikhor was wearing the bracelet the Oracle gave her. As well as the earrings Brekt gifted her."

"*It.* It's not a her, Kaz. And what are you trying to say?" My blood was boiling, hearing their names. How could Kazhi talk of them so easily? It was a stab to the fucking gut.

"It's odd," she whispered. "Did you see them glowing?"

It took me a moment to understand she meant the crystals in the jewellery. "Glowing? When would I have had time to notice those details."

"The details matter, *Guard*. Pay attention."

I lifted my hands, frustrated. "What does it mean then?"

"... I don't know. The crystals absorb magic. I'd seen them glowing in the Oracle's jungle."

Before the Guardian Palace. Before Brekt had confessed his feelings—his connection—to the traitor. "Why didn't you say anything."

"I didn't know what it meant. I guess it means I failed Brekt as much as Bastane."

Bastane, Kazhi, and I—we had all failed him. They didn't even know he was the Aspis until the end, and it was my job to stop it all from happening.

Kazhi slowed. The inn wasn't far now. "He's gone, and now we have to fix our mistakes. We have to find the truth in all this."

"You mean the Council? Because you can't be insinuating there's any lies surrounding the Ikhor."

"Why didn't it burn us?" Kazhi stopped us beside the river. Boats passed at a lazy pace below. Dim light passed through the green above us, turning Kazhi's black-and-white striped skin into an eerie tone. "It pushed us back with water and ran."

Her black eyes searched mine. She was being serious. She was questioning the Ikhor.

"It's a coward. It's too weak. That's the only explanation."

"No. Somethings wrong." She regarded me as if waiting for me to say something.

"Whose side are you on?" I hissed, making sure no one was around to see. "Are you seriously doubting the histories?"

In a flash, a knife was to my gut. The knife she always used to put me in my place. "You know what Nuo, you're sounding more like Falizha every day. Repetitive. Ignorant. Hateful. Things went wrong, but you're the one suffering in this cycle of hate. Get out of it." She pulled the knife back and spun it, returning it to her belt. "Bastane is asking questions too. You should start."

I forced a laugh, walking away. "I was the one searching the texts all those years, Kaz. I've read every book there is on the legends. I don't need to question anything. I need to kill the Ikhor and move on from this."

"You know, I never thought I would miss how annoying you were."

I turned back, jaw clenched. I was stunned at the surprising amount of emotion there. Kazhi never showed how she felt. About anything.

"I miss my brother. Bring him back," she said.

It was no longer raining, though the floods had already caused more destruction than the fires before that. I missed the rain. I wished it would return, so that I wasn't so visible to the world.

"Try, Guard. You're too weak. What a pathetic excuse to defend the beast."

"Are you admitting you care for me, Kaz?"

"Never." She spat at my feet, making me step back. "He'd be pissed at you if he saw you this way."

I couldn't look at her anymore, hating that she brought him up.

"He was always pissed at me," I reminded her.

She gave a rare laugh. "Ya, he was."

"Why are you smiling?"

"Because for the first time in weeks, you've acknowledged him. Not as the beast, but as the man he once was—as if he once really lived. If we don't speak our ghosts' names, they cease to exist."

Kazhi had stopped speaking her ghosts' names. I knew because I didn't know what those names were.

So when Kazhi left my side to find her room at the inn, I said my brother's name out loud, not wishing his memory to leave the world.

CHAPTER
TWENTY

Nuo

Sweat poured down my temples as I held onto the wide hips of the woman on her hands and knees in front of me—the very one I'd invited earlier today.

I pounded into her—hard, as she had begged for it—to distract myself.

It wasn't working. It hadn't worked for the past several weeks, and with the last few women, I had to fake my pleasure so that I wouldn't hurt their feelings.

Me—A Guard of the Aspis—faking my pleasure!

Again, I faked it and pretended to clean up a mess that wasn't there, all the while hating myself and what I'd become. I refastened my pants and grabbed my shirt from the floor, hoping she would do the same.

Instead, the woman sprawled out on the dark sheets in my room at the Red Door Inn. She laid the back of her hand against her forehead, panting. Her face was flushed, and her smile told me she was very pleased with herself.

"That was amazing," she said between gasps.

"You told me you wanted it hard, Lin. I am always down for

fulfilling a woman's desires." I smirked, giving her the show I'd given them all lately.

"Wow. I figured you were too important to remember a woman's name."

She was trying to be playful, but I could tell she believed it. She thought the Guard would feel like he was above her. I was a better fighter. That was all.

"I'm not heartless."

I was, but she thought I remembered her name because I cared. It was only that I had a fantastic memory. My heart had shredded to pieces when my brother died and *it* turned the world to ash. But my saving grace may be that I wasn't turning my pain onto others —the exception being the Aethar.

Lin was innocent.

Lin.

Lin.

So close to Liv.

Too close to Liv. How had I not thought of that earlier?

"I like your new look too," Lin said. "Last time I was training at the Guardian city, you didn't have the beard. And I like the long hair."

I forced a smile, my head reeling with the revelation that she was much too close to *looking* like Liv. Even the colour and length of her hair were similar.

Just in time, I ran from the room, losing the contents of my stomach in the adjoining bathing room. Lin was at the door in seconds, asking if I was okay. I couldn't look at her as I muttered an excuse about a bad dinner so she would leave.

I heaved again and again. I hadn't been eating much anyway, so it soon turned to choking on nothing, tasting bile at the back of my throat. It was nothing new. I'd lost so much weight because I couldn't keep anything down.

I was glad the Guardian woman listened and left my room. She wouldn't see the red rings around my eyes. She wouldn't know the Guard of the Aspis wept for those he lost. I tried to wipe Liv from my mind. Gods, when would I man up? My blood ran hot and cold just thinking of her.

Brekt and Liv—they had both become monsters. What did that make me—the wasted space the monsters left behind?

My stomach rolled as I got up and washed my face. I wiped a towel across my swollen eyes and leaned against the wall next to the sink. The dim lights made the room easier to bear. I slid to the floor, arms resting on my knees. The magic-powered light on the drab, peeling wall flickered as I fought the knot my stomach had curled into.

I jumped at a knock on the door. Before I could answer, it swung open.

Bastane stood in the doorway, wearing a pained expression. "I passed the Guardian woman in the hall. She told me you were sick. You look like shit."

Fuck him. "I don't want you here."

Bas didn't budge. He hovered at the threshold, pushing his golden hair back from his face.

I gave a hollow laugh. "Looking down on me, Bas? We have always butted heads. I didn't know you pitied me, too."

Bastane did well at hiding his emotions. I couldn't quite make out what he was thinking. Half the time, I didn't care. Or used not to care. Now? I constantly wondered if they all saw what I had become.

"You think I feel pity? Gods, man, I feel everything but. I understand."

"Sure you do. You must feel so sorry for my loss. You must feel bad about betraying your fellow Guards for Falizha. Does she let you fuck her? Is that why you did it?"

Bastane held his tongue, used to the berating, but I saw his battle not to lash back.

I would love to take it out on the mats, to move. To fight. It was the only way not to think so much.

"If you expect forgiveness—"

"Not forgiveness." Bastane's face hardened—he wasn't leaving as he usually did when I got mouthy. "No. I don't forgive myself. I was wrong. Not only the choice I made, but I was wrong about the reasons why I made it. I want you to listen to me, hear me when I say I know better. It's too little too late, but I see what's going on. They lied to me. The Council, Falizha … gods, maybe even my father. I want you to give me a chance to prove that I know I screwed up." Bastane moved from the doorway and mimicked me, sliding down the wall opposite and crossing his legs. He stared me down while I considered punching that apologetic look off his face.

He held his hand up, sensing it. "I won't stop you. But know, I won't hit back. You'll be on your own in that fight."

I deflated in an instant, denied the battle I longed for.

Bastane surprised me then by giving me the most raw, uncensored look I'd seen. "Falizha left them all on that field." He folded his hands in his lap. "She could have called them back, even if only to save a few. We barely made it out. Those were our people, and she saw them as nothing. I'm sorry I didn't understand before. How you all knew the Council and Falizha could do this … I should have trusted you above all else. I carry the weight of those lives on my shoulders every day."

"Had you made different choices, it wouldn't have changed Falizha. But what happened with Brekt? That was your fault. He died knowing his girl betrayed him and lied to him. He didn't need his last thoughts to be of that."

Bastane ducked his head, hiding his expression. But he kept talking. "They want control. Power. I was fooled into believing they were aiming for peace. It was all so wrong. And I'm sorry. It could have gone down differently."

I tilted my head back to look at the ceiling, knowing it didn't hide the fresh wave of tears. Gods. If it had gone differently …

"Wouldn't have made a difference. He was going to die. And our old pal Liv knew she was our enemy."

"I've told you my opinion," Bastane said in a low tone. "I don't think Olivia knew. She was not the best at hiding her true feelings. She didn't hate us."

"Whatever. End result was the same. They're both gone." Bastane had told me his opinion, but one thing Liv and I had in common was we were used to putting on a show for others. She was just better at it than I thought.

With no warning, Kazhi strolled into the bathing room and sat cross-legged in the doorway between the two of us. The low light made her striped face more terrifying.

I pounded my head against the wall, groaning. "This isn't a fucking party. I'd like some alone time once in a while."

Kazhi used her pinky nail to pick at her bottom teeth, trying to free whatever was caught there. She was wholly unaffected by the look I shot her or the disgust on Bastane's face as he watched her run a tongue along her teeth, inspecting them.

"I thought this was a meeting," she said after being satisfied with her cleaning.

"On the floor? Never mind. Just leave."

"Bas has updates." Kazhi put her hands on her knees.

I wiped a hand down my face, aware of what they were doing. They monitored me, gave me tasks, and kept me occupied. I wanted to scream at them and say unreasonably hurtful things. But I didn't have the energy. My stomach was threatening to heave.

"We need to be a team again," Bastane said to me. "The Guardians are collapsing. The Aethar are taking over the Land of the Sand Cities and driving the Day-leg villages out. Falizha says the Council has intel that the Aethar are planning a large attack. I think the Council has set their eyes on the Aethar borders and want the Guards on the ground to beat them to it."

"Do they expect us to cross the borders? That's unheard of. The battle should have ended by now." I dropped my hands to my lap, stretching my legs out. "Guardians don't go across the borders. They don't make it back."

"Well, this is what I've heard. Falizha is in charge of the

information coming at us. We are being called to the borders to stop the Ikhor from making it across."

"Obviously," I joked. "If the Guards are on it, it won't happen."

"Haven't caught it yet," Bastane argued.

"That's the beast's fault," Kazhi said. "It's leading us in every direction. North, south—it can't make up its mind."

"Watch it," I warned. Why was I always so sensitive about what others said of the Aspis? It was unreasonable to defend it. The thing hadn't led us to the Ikhor soon enough. The evil piece of shit was always one step ahead.

"I can't wait until we can kill her." Kazhi's mouth curled into a cruel smile. She wasn't talking of the Ikhor.

Bastane twisted his head to give Kazhi a bored look. "But how often will we have to stop to hunt crystals and find food if we're on our own? We've travelled like that for too long. It will be no faster without her. Slower, in fact, as we don't know what lies ahead. We would have gone to South Aspis to wait for the Ikhor to cross the canyons, only to find out it attacked Danuli."

"That piece of shit has caused so much damage already. We need to stop it." Kazhi said as she continued to pick her teeth, seeming uninterested in the conversation.

"We will stop it. Tomorrow morning, we fly north. I feel things will get much more serious—quickly and painfully." Bastane watched the flickering light, and silence fell in the bathing room.

Kazhi stared at the floor, her mouth set in a hard line. She rarely showed worry. I wasn't naïve enough to think she was afraid. She loved the thrill of facing death, thrived on it. But I knew she feared the pain her brothers were going through. Her heart was not in her own chest but given to a handful of people who probably no longer deserved it.

"While we were chasing the Aspis through the Median, the Ikhor somehow set fire to the south, tearing apart the Land of the Sand Cities." Bastane fidgeted with his shirt as he spoke. "Then it appears in Danuli, right at our feet, halfway up the continent, catching us off guard. The Aspis flies north now. I say we use caution when following it. We don't understand its methods yet. I don't dare discuss this with anyone other than you two—questioning the Aspis."

"Oh no? Not sending reports back to the Council?" I said. "The prince has been dethroned?"

Bastane ground his teeth, his face turning a light shade of pink. He got to his feet and stood over me, fighting against what he wanted to say.

"You know," he pushed his hair back again, making a fist when he dropped his hand. "For all the comments you've made about me being so devout to my legacy, you're no better when it comes to your hate. You lack forgiveness, Nuo. It's your biggest fault."

I had no response as he unclenched his hand and walked from the room, slamming the door shut. I rested my head back against the wall, glad he was gone. I just wanted quiet.

Kazhi was wise not to say anything as she, too, got up.

I stared at the empty doorframe, not hearing Kazhi leave the room. Then, I filled the silence with the screams I had been holding in.

Soon. I would unleash on the Ikhor.

Soon.

TWENTY-ONE

Liv

The day I told Rebeka about my visits with Stephen, my first lover, she struck me. She never trained with our mother like I had, so it didn't bruise. Not my skin, at least. Her resemblance to my mother always bothered me, how she wore her face. I always consoled myself that I had our mother's heart. But the looks Rebeka gave me with our mother's warm brown eyes were as cold as the Keepers she sold me out to.

Falizha's spacious bedroom was inviting and cozy, not what I had expected from the cold-hearted woman. It had a window for a wall opposite the door. The grey and stormy sky cast eerie shadows across the shaggy carpeted floor.

To the left was a wall of photos, and a dresser topped with weapons and discarded clothing. She was disorganized and had a surprising amount of keepsakes. I scanned the wall, seeing images of her standing next to her father with his arm wrapped around a man who had to be Falizha's older brother. The very one who was meant to be a Guard had Kazhi's assassination of *him* gone to plan. Falizha was not smiling, though her father and brother were, and I hated I understood how she came to be. I couldn't imagine being that man's daughter was easy. It was clear she was not the favoured child.

"Doesn't excuse you," I told the photo.

Awards hung next to photos of other Council members. I quickly lost interest, not wanting to know her any more than I did and turned to the other end of the room where Maev was combing through a large bookshelf. The bag she had slung over her shoulder sat near the door with a second bag next to it I hadn't noticed before.

"I found some Guardian clothes for you. And a pack to put your old clothing in. In case you wished to keep them."

"Thanks," I said, picking up the items she left out for me. "I think these may be too small."

It hit me for the first time that I had left my old pack in *his* room in the Guardian City. Meaning I had lost my beautiful crystal brush.

"Doubt it. Take a good look at yourself. You're half the size you were when we found you. Your green top is barely keeping on your shoulders."

She wasn't wrong. Not only my top, but my pants weren't fitting well either.

The humming, vibrating sound of magic filled my ears.

My fingers trembled, and I lost my grip on the clothing, as the familiar sound came back in waves, blocking out everything else.

Maev continued to explore the shelves, unaware of the magic's presence.

The Ikhor was growing stronger, reacting to every small emotion.

I picked up the dropped clothing, spotting my reflection in a standing mirror next to a large wardrobe. I straightened, holding my breath. The girl staring back was the one I had been running from, who I thought I had left behind in my old world—the weak girl who hid away in the Endless Forest, the one who had no friends and no loyalty to anyone.

Scared ... helpless, the perfect host for the Ikhor.

Everything the Guards had done to make me healthy and whole was gone. Any signs of the life they had revived had washed away in the weeks I had been hiding inside my grief.

"You okay?" Maev asked carefully, her hip against the edge of a desk close to the large bookshelf. She already had a pile of things stacked to go through.

The air rushed from my lungs. "No!"

"No need to get angry with me." Her lip curled as her arms crossed.

"What kind of joke is this?"

"Excuse me?"

"The gods—the ones that everyone worships—what kind of game are they playing? Look at me, Maev. I'm not a saviour. I'm a monster. I've killed without thinking. I've flooded I don't know how many homes. I've turned on my best friend."

My insecurities and weaknesses were stacked high, piled like a cage around me. I searched between the cracks for any kind of mettle that could push me—something that could lift me out of the catacombs and into the light. I demanded it from Nuo, so why couldn't I do it myself?

"You learn to move forward," Maev said softly.

"Move forward? How?"

"Just keep trying."

"Do you think you could? If you became something your friends hated?"

Maev softened, unfolding her arms. She took a step toward me but stopped when I flinched back. "I see you are in pain, but the rest of the world hasn't crumbled. You're missing the good parts still out there, worth fighting for."

"What would you know of my pain? What would you know of suffering?"

"Hello? Girl, it's called perspective." Maev pushed my argument away with a wave of her hand. "It's called empathy. I have eyes. I see the world around me and how it works. There are thousands of years of suffering and history shows us others beat it. If the past is any indication of the fortitude of men, then you should know you *can* get through this."

"And how am I to do that? If you're so wise, tell me."

Maev surprised me, showing her teeth for the first time. "You fight it. You're not fighting. You're drowning and not even raising a hand for help."

"You saw what happened. You remember what Nuo said to me. How am I supposed to get over that?"

"It's not fair to judge someone in their darkest hour. You haven't reached yours yet, the Oracle warned you. And there's a ton of bad you've said, too."

I took a step back. "How do you know about the Oracle?"

"You told me, Liv. On one of our many long days on the boat."

I had no memory of the conversation. What else had I revealed?

"Whatever. You couldn't understand anyway. I've lost everyone I care about. Who have you ever lost?"

"A brother. And a mother. In fact, I never had one. I grew up with a ghost and a few photos. Everyone has a story, so don't try to feel special because yours is hard right now."

I swallowed back the retort I had ready, and Maev frowned, tapping her finger against her biceps. Her words were as sharp as her expression. She was a tough friend to have—if I could consider my enemy my friend.

"I didn't know," I tried as an apology.

"Of course, you didn't. Cause you haven't tried for a moment to get to know me. Or my brother, who is quietly fuming while also doing as you asked, taking us away from the crossing to our lands and dodging the beast at every turn."

"What else have I told you?"

I was a coward, ignoring what she was making me feel. I had no memory of telling her about the Oracle or any conversation from our six weeks of fleeing the Guards. And she was right—they didn't need to help me, but they were against their own wishes.

"You told me many things in short, stuttered conversation—of your homelands, of your time with Nuo. You don't want to be angry with him any more than you want to be the Ikhor."

"Are you defending the Interrogator now?" I studied the black clothing in my arms, picking at lint.

"I'm defending your friend. Because you once believed in him. And if you don't give him the benefit of knowing he was in his own hell, who will forgive the Ikhor in the end?"

She was right. Who would forgive me? Yet I hadn't said the things Nuo had said.

"He promised to kill me." I choked on the swelling lump in my throat.

"Well, you'll know the truth next time you meet. I don't like the Aspisser. I don't like any of them, and honestly, Liv, I'm starting not to like you."

I stared at the shirt, concentrating on the colour that was fading on the fabric.

No one had ever said those words to me, though I saw it written on their faces time and again. I was too different, a risk to society, a terrible choice of friend. But Maev hid none of her feelings toward me. Either through words or her expressions, I knew exactly what she was thinking.

"Listen," she said, sighing and turning back to the bookshelf. "Let's go through these shelves and try again." She looked at me over her shoulder. The expression on her face was almost comical —judgemental, annoyed, yet hopeful all at once. "Maybe, if we push hard enough, we could still be friends."

"I thought you didn't like me." When had I become so pathetic? Perhaps I always was.

She smiled and fidgeted with the pile of books to her side. "Well, you haven't lost me yet. Get changed."

"The books Kazhi mentioned will have to be near the top." I quickly changed into the black Guardian clothes, hating how tight they were to my body. You could see bone more than muscle. "Or closer to the bridge where they're accessible."

I didn't feel right getting into Guardian gear. But my reflection showed I looked the part with crystals and bones in my ears. I was only missing the tattoos.

"I've never heard the word Aspisser," I said, grinning at the name. It was clever.

"You'll hear it often when we get to my city."

I stuffed my dirty clothing and my cloak in my new pack, reattached my belt, secured my useless swords, and joined Maev near the shelf.

"Journals, written in Day!" She lifted a book over her shoulder. Her face fell, remembering she was mad at me.

"Can you read them?" The script along my swords was written in the ancient language of Day, but I couldn't read them. It was the same with the journal as I peered at the words on the page—their meaning eluded me. It made me pause.

When I was brought to Veydes, I discovered I could speak their language—the common tongue. Weeks later, when I was at the Guardian City, I discovered I could read the language of Night, a dead language. So why, when I looked at the language of Day, did the writing feel like something I couldn't quite grasp?

"I can't read them quickly—it's an old language. But Ollo can decipher faster than I."

I scanned the room one last time, and just before leaving, I spotted a photo I had missed on the wall. A whimper escaped me, and I coughed to hide it, but Maev was too attentive to miss it. She found the framed image that stopped me—Falizha standing with the Guards.

He was there, standing stoically in his Guard's uniform.

He stood taller than the others, and the darkness I had always questioned lingering behind his eyes was visible even in the photo. I thought the weight of his goal, guarding the Aspis, caused him to lose sleep. Or perhaps the dark circles under his eyes were from worry. But no, it had always been because he was host to the Aspis. The beast had always been lingering beneath his skin.

I moved closer to the photo, setting the journals on the dresser below. Seeing the photo, seeing him as just a man, made me realize the dreams I'd been having were only that—dreams.

Nightmares.

I had been desperate to believe he might be alive, but a quick reminder of what he looked like as a man told me all I needed to know—there was no resemblance to what I was conjuring in my nightmares. He was gone.

I brushed some dust off the glass covering the image.

His hair was pulled back, revealing the tattoos inked above his ears—the Aspis tattoos. The scar running down the side of his face was faint but visible in the photo. No hint of the iridescence in his eyes showed the sign of his skill at seeing in the dark—the cursed child.

Maev approached, lifting the image off the wall and staring at it. Then, after a moment, she gave me a reluctant smile. "He *is* quite handsome."

"Was," I corrected.

Maev tapped the glass with her finger. "Is. Right here."

I sniffed, trying to hide the pain.

She turned the frame over and grabbed hold of the back covering. When Maev was in a bad mood, her movements were jerky.

"What are you doing?" I gasped as she ripped the back of the frame off.

Next, she removed the picture, tearing it apart, and throwing part of the photo to the ground. Falizha's face stared up at me from where it landed.

"I think this should belong to you. I'm heading back to my

brother. You can keep wandering or doing whatever it is you were doing," she said, passing me the photo.

I was almost too afraid to touch it.

"What about the other pile of journals?"

"I'll get Ollo's help. It's just he and I helping my people now."

She lifted a bag from the floor and shouldered it before walking from the room.

"Thank you," I choked out to an empty door frame, grateful and ashamed all at once.

CHAPTER
TWENTY-TWO

Liv

Was I ever afraid of the dark? No, the horrors of my past always happened in the light.

I sat on the edge of a bed, running a stone along the sharp edge of my blade, just as Bastane showed me on our travels to the Guardian city. I promised myself to practice through the movements every morning to calm my mind.

The stone scraped along metal, a grating sound that sent shivers down my spine. The sound transformed into a steady beating, echoing down the hallways of the empty airship. The halls didn't absorb any of the sound, heightening my sense of loneliness. It wasn't until sometime later that I heard a similar pounding coming from another room.

I returned my swords to their purple-dyed casings, and I left the room, heading through the halls in search of the sound, wondering what the twins were working on. The lights had dimmed, no longer golden. I had never noticed before how eerie the ship became at night.

The carpet muffled my steps as the banging intensified, and I followed the sound up the stairs leading to the top deck. I vividly remembered following Nuo up these steps one night to drink together while the others dined with the Captain.

I pushed open the heavy door, letting in a blast of frigid air, and my hair whipped back as I stepped into a large open room filled with candles and the smell of stale air.

"What the ..." Where was the deck?

The black walls were so smooth that they reflected the room back at me. Candles lining the walls and resting on a long wooden table flickered and mirrored on the stone.

I turned in a circle.

Gone was the door I had just come through. Gone was the Airship.

My breath came out in puffs of steam against the cold air, and I wiggled my toes. My shoes were gone.

High above, past the black walls, was a darkness that shone like a million black crystals.

I sucked in a breath. There was no ceiling.

The banging that led me here thrummed across the massive room. Five figures sat at a long table, fighting among themselves. One of them pounded a fist against the tabletop while he argued with the others.

This place made no sense. It felt real, but most certainly was not. If this was a dream like before, if the unending sound was luring me, it must mean *he* was here. I didn't care if my mind was fabricating this place or if he was half monster. A photo of him wasn't enough.

The air grew colder, and I was pulled to the group of people sitting at the far end of the room. "Please be here."

I passed grey and tattered banners on the wall. Some had fallen, lying in heaps on the floor. The table stretched endlessly in front of me, as if it were growing the farther I walked.

"I know this place ..." my voice echoed, matching the beat of the pounding fist.

The table, the room, I was in the Guardian Palace, just like in the last dream. Only now, I stood in the dining room where I had met the god Rem. It had been lavishly decorated, warm, inviting and full of Guardians. It had been alive.

Now, it was haunted, cold and dark.

I slowed, piecing together what I was seeing. Without a doubt this place wasn't real. This was a dream. A nightmare.

Over the high backs of the chairs, I could make out the curling horns of the half-beast at the far end of the table. As I neared, its citrine stare came into focus, its clawed hands splayed out on the table. It wasn't moving, as if in a trance while the other people spoke around it.

It was the same half-beast from the dream before. Dark, matted hair fell in its face. Slits for a nose and swirling dark shadows ran over its pale skin. It wore a black ripped cloak, and it didn't move an inch. Candlelight didn't light its face—it absorbed it.

No one paid me any attention as I approached, it wasn't until I was a few feet away that I understood who was speaking.

"I've searched every library in Veydes. I'm telling you, there is no answer."

Nuo sat to the left of the beast, dressed in Guardian black, his brown hair swept back from his face. He wore glasses and his vest with many pockets, and had a large piece of paper in his hand. On the other side of him sat a young boy with matching coloured hair, who had to be close to ten. The boy slumped in his seat, grinning at the others like he was scheming against them.

"No ..." I whispered.

The boy had honey-brown eyes that shone with mischief. The same as they had when I met him as an adult.

The boy spun toward the beast, his grin faltering. "I bet if he told us sooner, *I* would have figured out how to save him. But he kept it hidden from me until I was a teenager! He was just a bully, I guess, and never changed. I don't understand how we became best friends."

Another person spoke, and I ran around the end of the table, past the beast. A teenage boy sat to the beast's right. His brown eyes were jaded and rebellious as he reprimanded the young boy. "There's no way we failed him. No way! I'm the smartest Guardian there is. If there isn't an answer in these stupid books, I will find the gods and make them change his fate myself."

A pile of books appeared on the table between the arguing boys.

"He said he's old when he turns into the Aspis," the young Nuo said. Then he pointed to the eldest, the one in the vest. "It's your fault he doesn't survive. I'm just a kid. If my mom and dad were here, they would know how to save him."

"Your mom and dad are gone," the teenage Nuo said. "You need to grow up and get over it. The instructors will have you beaten if you keep crying about it. You don't need them or anyone."

They paid me no attention as they fought, and the beast never spoke. Instead, he lifted a clawed hand, growling and grabbing his head as if it hurt.

The Nuos all looked at him, some making faces, some laughing. All but one.

This Nuo didn't move at all, and I stepped closer, grabbing the back of a chair, my breaths coming faster as I stared at the final Nuo.

He was still, eyes facing forward, vacant and empty. His skin was a shade of blue, pale and ... this Nuo was dead.

"From the dream," I whispered. "*He* saw you die."

Each version of Nuo represented a time when *he* had known him—from when they had met as boys until the vision from his dream. He had always known what was going to happen in the end. *He* had seen Nuo die.

I squeezed the chair, holding back a sob. The dead Nuo looked not much older than he did now. His hair long, his beard shaven—

"Best not to look at him, BB," the teenage Nuo said. "It will haunt you as it did Brekt."

I pulled away, and two sets of honey-brown eyes and one set of empty, faded brown ones looked at me.

"You'll be next, Ikhor." The oldest Nuo turned in his seat. "I will find you, and I will kill you."

Warm breath hit my neck. The smell of leather and pine surrounded me, and a hum vibrated in my ears. At the head of the table ... the chair was empty.

I turned, catching a flash of yellow in my peripheral. The dark outline of curling horns and matted black hair blocked the room beyond. Pupils turned to slits as he whispered, "They are wrong. It'll be me that finds you first."

The massive doors blew open, and a roar tore down a long hall, shaking the room.

The Nuos scrambled from their chairs—even the cold, blue Nuo rose—disappearing like fading dreams.

"Time for you to go, Ikhor." The beast grabbed me with its massive claws and threw me across the room.

Before I was about to collide with the wall, I woke, screaming in the airship halls sitting with my back pressed against a metal door near one of the glowing lights. Drenched in sweat, I clutched the photo of the Guards to my chest. I didn't know what hall I was in.

My belt held my swords. Had I even sharpened them?

I checked the photo in my hand, checked down the hall— nothing was amiss. I wiped up my tears, pocketed the photo, and got up.

Perhaps carrying the photo with me wasn't doing me any favours.

I needed to walk, needed to keep myself awake. I was not falling asleep again because seeing any version of him ripped me apart.

TWENTY-THREE

Liv

One winter, while walking home after catching my first rabbit of the year, three keepers found me and took the rabbit as payment. Payment for what? For being caught with wire. Apparently, I could have used it to strangle someone. I kept that idea and tucked it away. I hadn't had meat in more than a month, and I went without food for another three days.

I needed to see the deck to know I was no longer dreaming. To know he wasn't really here somewhere. I opened the heavy door, and the wind kicked up my hair as the stars shone back at me in the night sky. It washed away the racket in the back of my mind—this was real.

The dream had left me in pieces.

Alongside it was the shame after what Maev had said. *"Honestly, Liv, I'm starting not to like you."*

I scoffed. "Get in line," I said, scraping a hand down my face. Catching the soft glow of my bracelet, I let out a long, deep sigh.

In the dark hours of the night, the faint edges of the magic barrier around the ship shimmered, shielding me from most of the wind. To my right, the distant horizon turned a soft pink.

The night was gone. I had spent it dreaming of the dead.

You've got to smarten up, I chastised myself. *The twins are trying to help you. You aren't alone.*

Something caught my attention—a sound, a vibration—I couldn't say what it was. It wasn't the humming of my magic.

I followed the sound to the front of the ship and gasped.

There was a mass of shadows, and I checked the sky to confirm the stars were still there, that this wasn't that dream place.

The shadow obscured the golden railing of the ship, swirling like water in a drain. It wasn't like smoke—it was too inviting, too warm, too soft. It moved like it wouldn't harm anything and made no sound.

I stepped toward it, and it whirled into a spinning storm before evaporating into the night air. The gold railing became visible again as if nothing had been there.

"Am I going crazy?" The night didn't answer back.

It was not the first time I had seen a shadow that wasn't there —the last time had been when I was in the boat, heading to Danuli. But ... I was in more control now, wasn't I?

I reached the front of the ship, vaguely recalling Nuo telling me it was called the brow. Or was it prow? I held onto the railing with weak hands.

Nothing. There were no shadows left on the ship, sky or trees below.

The faint colours of a forest came into view. Meaning we would soon reach the Temple of Mountain.

I closed my eyes, basking in the wind. *Breathe. Hold.* I wouldn't let one hallucination—or multiple too-real dreams—ruin the feeling of being up here.

I made a slow path around the deck, my fingers sliding over the metal, facing the coming sunrise.

My grip on the railing froze.

The Aspis floated on a silent wind, a hundred feet to the right, higher than where I stood. It moved in a circle, drifting lower, unhurriedly passing back. For a moment, it blocked the sunrise until rising higher, and the first rays of day hit my face.

Had it been there the entire time I had been lost in thought?

The Aspis continued its slow circle. Why did it stay close but not attack? And had the Guards finally found transport? They would easily see the Aspis in the sky.

I searched, but in the early morning hours, it was difficult to see any sign of pursuit.

For several seconds, I watched the legendary beast. My mother's stories taught me of dragons that were as large as mountains and could breathe fire and fly. Had the stories of the Ikhor and Aspis reached the Endless Forest and only changed over time?

It had been stupid not to reach out and sense the beast before coming out here. Concentrating now, I could feel it there—a slight tug in its direction.

I leaned toward the edge, and the Aspis turned, looking right at me. A chill ran through me. A deep-set scar ran down its left eye where I had attacked it with ice.

We stared each other down.

It moved again, worming its way closer to the ship, and the sky turned gold near the horizon as the Aspis stopped on the other side of the barrier. Ten feet away, it towered over me, making me feel like a tiny, breakable twig.

It was here. *We* were here. Two legends bathed in the glorious morning light.

"Why didn't you tell me?" I asked the beast, and it jerked with surprise. "All that time together. Had I known ..."

Would anything have been different?

The beast didn't blink.

"I guess nothing would have changed, except I would've been prepared. Or I wouldn't have assumed I was the Aspis. I would have tried harder with you."

Would I have guessed I was the Ikhor? Not likely since they taught me it was so evil.

I studied the Aspis, tracing the lines of scales over the beast's snout. "You've grown. I could stand on Maev's shoulders and not be able to reach the top of your head."

"I would say you were the first."

His voice filtered through the fog protecting my heart. His deep timbre rumbled through me even in memory. *"You are the first woman I've cared about. You could say that you were my first. Probably my last."*

I hadn't understood then what he was saying, how I would be his last of many things.

The Aspis regarded me, pupils dilating. Was it relaxed? Was it listening?

"Let me figure out where this threat is coming from and stop it. Then I'll make love to you in every way that you can imagine."

"Watching you fall to pieces like that was the worst thing I've ever seen. When you changed, it scarred a part of me. Something of me died with you that day. I watched my mother beaten to death. I watched the Keepers do awful things to people back home. But nothing hurts like seeing you as a beast every night in my dreams."

It wasn't him I was talking to. It was obvious now there was no humanity behind those eyes, yet I needed to speak to him. There was no grave, no place of worship to unburden myself—just a black beast who gave me its time.

The sun rose higher, the gold shining off its glossy scales. The Aspis's curled horns pointed sharp tips to the clouds above.

"I care for you, Liv. More than I should after so little time. It's suffocating, the need to have you. But there's something stronger beneath that, and that feeling controls everything."

"I miss you," I whispered, but it came out as a cry. "I wish I had told you how much I cared. I miss Nuo, too. I felt safe with you two and felt I had a place in the world."

A single tear left my eye. Or was it the rain?

I looked up to find clouds forming. Rain hit the magical barrier, streaking down it. The movement caused the Aspis to shift. Its head was so close, unmoving before me, as its body slithered side to side.

"Do you remember that night by the fire in the Oracle's village? It's my favourite memory with you. I know I could say the time we kissed or our time in the caves, but our walls came down that night. We said we would be friends. But a friend wouldn't have hidden what you did. I'm mad. I'm so mad. The fog in my head, the lack of control of the weather, is not only from missing you. I'm trying not to, but I really hate this world. I hate everything that's happened to me."

I peeked up at the Aspis, relieved that the beast didn't know how to judge me, and wiped away the moisture gathering on my cheek. "I am not going to live in my sadness anymore, though. I've done enough damage living inside my head. The twins hate me and are the only ones left willing to lend me a hand. And this magic ..." I looked to my wrist, where my bracelet glowed. "It responds to my emotions somehow. I can no longer keep them in. I think they've poured out of me and into this bracelet. I think the crystals are absorbing the magic I can't control. I don't know what that means."

"Go, Olivia. You won't get far once the beast wakes." Those were the last words Brekt spoke to me.

Ice-cold sorrow squeezed my heart, but I forced it away—put walls up against it. I built myself a stronger box to bury my unwanted feelings and emotions. I didn't care that the box had drawn in the Ikhor's magic. It was my only defence.

"I know you're not *him*. And I hate that you stole his body. But it may not be long until I join him. I'm losing my own battle. I feel it, growing stronger every day. It's alive inside me." I raised a hand

and placed it over my chest. "The magic. The pull to you to end this. It's consuming me. I can't breathe around it sometimes. And the pounding in my head is getting worse. The Ikhor wants to take over my body and mind. It searches for you. What I wanted to be love for *him* is instead a killing need. I will do everything I can to fight against becoming the Ikhor. But if it wins,"—I shrugged— "maybe it wouldn't be so bad to see him again. And my mother."

The beast inched closer to the ship. It was a few feet away, pushing against the magical barrier. The barrier shimmered above me in a rainbow wave, and the Aspis winced. But it pushed again, trying to move closer to me.

"Do you know that I don't want to kill you?"

I leaned forward, and the beast did the same. I could feel the heat of its breath now, see the saliva collecting where its fangs hung over its bottom jaw.

"Are the dreams ... *him*? Is he in there?"

The crystal in my bracelet pulsed with magic. Was it from the beast? From the pull? The bracelet glowed, bending *toward* the beast as if the light of the magic was reaching out for it.

"Do you feel the pull to me? It doesn't feel like hate." I lifted my hand.

The Aspis shifted back, sizing up my trembling fingers, then moved forward again, nudging against the barrier. It couldn't push past it, so I leaned over the railing a little farther. My hand slipped through the barrier, and I rested it against the beast's snout. "Hello, you," I smiled up at it.

That's when the Aspis changed.

Its eyes constricted, pupils turning to slits as it opened its giant maw, and before I could pull my hand away, the beast tore through the barrier. Its jaw closed with a sickening crunch, severing my arm from my shoulder.

TWENTY-FOUR

Liv

I screamed as blood dripped from the fangs of the Aspis.

My blood.

I fell to the deck, landing hard as the beast roared, thrown back by the ship's magic. The entire sky became a rippling wave of rainbows. Again and again, the Aspis attacked the barrier. My screams swallowed the deep moaning of the magic shield.

A blurry mess of flesh and blood lay next to me where my right arm should have been. Blood pooled faster than I could have imagined. I was going to die.

Colours swam—rainbows, black scales, and then blue swirls.

The roar of the beast rang in my ears over and over and over as the darkness crept in.

I snapped awake again as a blue-skinned figure pressed against me. The blue skin quickly stained red, and Maev lifted her hands before her. Her expression told me I was going to die.

Then she was gone.

I looked over my shoulder. I should have passed out by now.

Maev screamed for Ollo, pushing her voice until it cracked.

What could they do for me? I was growing weaker, dizzier. I could no longer feel my body. I needed to rest.

"No!" Maev slapped me across the face, and my eyes sprung open. "Stay with me, Liv. I am not done being angry with you."

"Get her arm and hold it in place. No, not at that angle," said a deeper voice.

"I'm going to be sick."

"You're not the only one. But if you begin, I will be helpless. Keep it under control."

"Oh gods, the arm is only holding on by a few tendons. I don't think magycris can save this Ollo."

"She may not need a lot. Can't you see what's happening?"

"She's ... healing. On her own."

"It must be the Ikhor's power. Hurry!"

"I don't think it'll work."

"We have to try. She'll lose the arm if we don't. Hold it there. Yes, like that."

Pain sliced through my shoulder, and I blissfully passed out.

THE FOG I lived in stayed with me, holding me under. It was silent. It was peace.

In the place between places, I found *him*. He was a pillar of strength, standing alone in the fog.

Was it a place of dreaming?

I didn't care and ran into his arms.

He wasn't warm. His body wasn't hard and strong. He didn't hold me, keep me safe or whisper any words of love.

He was a dream.

I came to shivering, and so cold. So very cold. The deck had seeped of all colour and warmth, the ship pale and wet. A mist hung in the air, so thick it blocked out the magic barrier. Strange crystal-like decorations hung from the railing.

The Aspis no longer attacked the barrier.

"What—"

"A little help, Liv." Maev's weak, broken voice sounded from the mist.

I sat up, discovering the airship covered in ice. The twins hadn't moved to help me because they were pinned in awkward positions to my right, several feet back from where they had been kneeling moments before. The ice had formed upwards as if a burst had escaped from me.

Reflections of gold and red shone through the glass-like walls. Blood.

"Oh my god, what happened?"

"You iced us." Ollo groaned, sending out puffs of hot breath. He shifted ever so slightly, trying to fight his way out.

The ice shone with the bit of light that made it through the mist, and I looked around the deck, amazed.

"Fear," I whispered.

Maev's eyes rolled, but I couldn't tell if it was from irritation.

"What?" Ollo's teeth were chattering.

"The elements respond to emotion. It's how I control it. I used fear for ice."

"That's great, Liv. Now … can you be … unafraid?" Maev whimpered.

"I am unafraid. How are you two not dead?"

The twins were part of the crystal-like towers. How had the ice not pierced their chests?

"We are … D-Day-legs … ice clan. U-usually cold … doesn't b-bother us at all," Maev said between clacking teeth. "But the Ikhor's ice … is something else. It's … painful, Liv."

I forced myself upright. The sight of my reattached arm, after remembering it was severed, caused a wave of dizziness to overtake me. They had put me back together. My sleeve was shredded, blood staining every inch of my skin. "How am I alive?" Horrible pink lines travelled over my shoulder where my arm met my torso.

"Ikhor's magic ..." Ollo whispered. "Explain later ..."

He attacked me. He tried to kill me.

No. I stuffed that pain inside my new box. I had to work on the current problem. How could I make the ice melt? Could I soak the magic back in?

I put my hands against the ice and pulled back immediately.

"It's so cold it burns."

"I noticed," Ollo added pointedly. Visible through the fading mist, ice covered his legs up to his torso, leaving his chest and neck exposed, but his hands frozen at his sides.

"Fire," I whispered and raised my hands, picturing the flames from the field.

Nothing happened.

What was I feeling in those moments? Sadness. I was heartbroken.

I remembered what it felt like watching him die, but still, nothing happened. No flames came.

"I don't know how to make the fire," I cried.

"Liv ..." Maev moaned. "I can't feel my body anymore." Crystallized shards surrounded her neck. Only her face had remained untouched from my attack.

"I don't know what to do." I panicked. How could I have let this happen?

"First, calm down," Ollo soothed, "Look at me, Liv." Though he watched me intently, his slight smile was reassuring. "Your panic will only create more ice. Slow your breathing and concentrate on me."

I did as Ollo said, and though the deck was freezing, a soothing warmth went through me. Ollo, even frozen at an awkward angle, was a pleasant sight. His blue lips, paler from the cold, were full and inviting.

"Concentrate," he continued. "Yes, like that."

My breathing slowed, and the panic eased.

"Now, you'll need to break the ice. Use something sharp to hit it with."

"Like a weapon?"

"Swords ... dammit." Maev's eyelids fluttered, her blue skin turning white.

I ran to Maev, fumbling for a sword at my waist. When I grabbed one, it fell to the ground. My arm ... I lifted it, testing. It ached, and the movement was stiff. I flexed my fist, but my fingers didn't close. I tried again. My thumb and pointer finger curled, and the middle twitched, but I could hardly move my last two fingers.

Using my working hand, I grabbed my sword from the ground and slashed at the ice near her feet, my movements clumsy. I added my damaged hand to my grip. Soon, my sword was stained red, blood dripping onto the ice at my feet. I slipped around, losing my balance.

"Harder, Liv," Ollo urged. "Use your body."

I hacked and slashed at the ice, panic rising. It chipped away slowly. Too slowly. "It must not be sharp enough," I cried out and dropped the sword, pulling the second one.

Kazhi had once told me the script on the blades was to encourage the wielder to remind themselves they held power. "*You can move an entire mountain, but one piece at a time.*"

I couldn't move mountains. I couldn't even save my friends. I was the reason they were in this situation.

"*A broken crystal still holds power.*"

I was past broken. I was shattered. I couldn't hold power any more than I could control my emotions.

With a frustrated cry, I smashed the sword against the ice, but lost my grip, and the thing fell to the floor, crashing into its matching blade.

What happened next confused me.

When my two blades connected, a wave of power erupted from them. It sent me flying across the deck toward the stairway as the surrounding ice shattered into an explosion of crystals.

TWENTY-FIVE

Liv

My head rang from the pain.

Maev landed in a heap near the railing, unconscious, surrounded by melting chunks of ice. She was close to the edge, and if she rolled back any farther, she would fall into the open air.

I reached out a hand. "Maev."

Ollo rushed for her, dropping to his knees and wrapping his arms around her. He held her to his chest while he rested against the gold metal railing.

"What did you do?" His tone was flat, angry.

"I don't know. It was the swords. They're magic."

"It's concerning to know you have ancient ore weapons and don't know how to use them."

"I never figured them out. I ..." I dropped my gaze, unable to look at him. "Is she okay? Would the barrier not have kept her on board?"

"The barrier keeps out danger. It senses attack, power and projectiles. It does not keep anything in."

"I thought the swords would help you—"

"I suppose I should be thanking you." Ollo sounded reluctant to say anything.

"It was my fault in the first place."

"Yes. It was. What's the matter with you? You could've died! Why did you take it on? I thought you wished to return the magic, not fight the beast."

His anger was jarring when, only moments ago, he was trying to soothe me. Now that we were all safe, I suppose it was time to let it all out.

"He wasn't attacking me, not until the last second."

"He?" Ollo's hair fell in wet strands, sticking to his clenched jaw. "Liv, it's a thing now. The Guard is gone."

I flinched. "You don't know that. I'm not gone! So he could still be in there." I didn't dare tell him about how I saw him in sleep.

He stayed quiet until a hint of compassion eased the heat in his glare. Then his nostrils flared, and he remembered his sister lying in his arms. "You're two sides of a coin. You bury the magic within. The Aspis is a beast without. You are magic taken from the gods. It's a creation to destroy you. The hosts, they never come back."

I ignored how his words stung. Ollo leaned his head against the railing, cradling his sister, trying to warm her, pulling her in tight. I was ashamed to note I was jealous. Ollo looked solid and warm.

"I'm not trying to hurt your feelings," he continued, brushing back the hair stuck to his brow. "Or to demand you get over your loss and love for the Guard. I'm merely trying to keep you alive. Despite our turbulent introduction, my sister has come to care about your well-being. As such, so must I. Let Maev and I protect you. Even if it's only until the temple. I want to make sure I get Maev home."

I shifted away, uncomfortable, and flexed my fist. My thumb and forefinger curled this time, and the middle moved, but the last two remained stiff. "You fixed me," I said in a low voice.

"Not so well. Your arm is attached, but the scarring—there wasn't enough magycris. You ... healed too fast on your own."

I tried my fist again, pushing my muscles. I healed myself ... but not well enough.

"We did our best," Ollo said. "I've never healed a severed limb."

My hand shook so violently it vibrated. I let it fall, studying the fingers that wouldn't bend as moisture dripped from the railing. "I should be protecting you. The Ikhor is the saviour of the Aethars— I mean Rydavians—is it not? You two should not be protecting me. I'm not that kind of girl anyways. I don't want a knight in shining armour."

"I am starting to see that. Then let me play advisor."

I lifted my head, covering my broken hand with the other. "Okay. What's your advice?"

"Smarten up, control yourself, embrace your situation and follow me. We must ensure Maev gets us to Ouras and then gets us home. We arrived close to the temple. I was coming up to get you two. Our bags are packed, and we are ready to go. After you change, of course."

For the first time, I noticed Ollo dressed in all black. The contrast to his pale blue skin and shining light hair was ... well, appealing. The clothing hugged his frame tightly, showing he was fitter than I had thought.

"Bags?" I asked as he shifted Maev so she was lying comfortably, her head resting on his chest.

"Maev found the Guard's room. We've taken their supplies. It's how we had magycris so close by when I heard Maev screaming."

"I'm glad you two were so close. Thank you." I tried to make a fist again. Still, the last two fingers barely moved.

"We have prepared ourselves this time in case the ship is compromised. Again."

Three packs laid discarded close to the door. I recognized them. One was Nuo's. I knew it well from gripping it as I followed him through a jungle.

"When Maev recovers, we will leave immediately. We have no idea how close the Guards could be. Not that they are a threat to you anymore."

"What do you mean?"

Ollo looked from my hand to my shoulder. "The Ikhor's magic seems to be keeping your body from fatal wounds. Though you are starving and growing physically weaker, I saw for myself how quickly you healed on your own. Had we not had your arm," he paused, squirming where he sat. "Had we not pushed your arm back toward your shoulder and aided with magycris, you would have healed anyway—if only one limb short."

"What does that have to do with the Guards?"

"They're trained to hunt and kill you alongside the beast. I don't think they would be able to. I think your only fear should be the beast itself."

It wasn't my only fear, but I didn't correct him. The Guards could harm me in other ways.

We waited for Maev to warm up, and I wondered how long I would be on the run. Was there nowhere in this world I wouldn't be chased down for who I was?

I hated that I was jealous of Ollo embracing Maev. My sister had never held me.

"What's that look you're giving me," Ollo asked, shaking me from my thoughts.

I should have considered not answering, but I was too tired and rattled to think before speaking. "Maev told me you had another brother."

Ollo's face changed so fast that I knew immediately it was the wrong thing to say. "Sorry," I backtracked. "I shouldn't have said anything. I had a sister, I do have a sister, but she's in the past now. She was not caring toward me as you two are."

I don't know why I thought mentioning Rebeka would improve the situation—like having a lousy sibling was better than a dead one.

"I'm surprised Maev mentioned our brother," he said after a moment. "We rarely speak of him."

"She didn't really tell me anything. She was yelling at me."

He laughed, breaking the tension, and my shoulders slumped in relief.

"She also doesn't get this aggressive towards people. You bring out a side of her I haven't seen in a long time. I thought I was the only one who received her caustic commentaries."

"That's not great to hear," I muttered.

"You are a strange woman, Saviour. Not bad, but strange." Ollo gazed down the length of my body, stopping at my hand in my lap. His expression hardened when he saw me playing with my stiff fingers.

Something stirred within me, held under his sharp gaze. Maybe it was the jealousy of Maev having someone close. Perhaps it was finally realizing the Aspis was not *him*. Maybe it was because I was lonely, but I liked how Ollo looked at me.

"Maev and I were inseparable once." He looked away too quickly to be casual. "When we began our studies several years ago, we parted for the first time. It was a thrill at first, the freedom."

"What happened? Maev commented that you two hadn't been keeping contact."

"She was surprised I asked her for help—asking how to locate you—because we hadn't spoken in months. I suppose I can admit now that when I was advancing in my studies and succeeding at every turn, I got a touch distant. No—arrogant. Maev tried calling me on my ego long ago, but I wouldn't listen."

"I got the impression you weren't full of ego."

A sadness made his shoulders sag. "It was another woman who made me see how my behaviour was unappealing. I was too embarrassed before to reach out to Maev and admit she had been right. This journey has been another lesson in many ways. I didn't know how much I missed my closest friend." He ducked his head, frowning down at Maev. "She knew me best, and yet, travelling with my twin these past few months, I realize I haven't known her in some time. She's changed. She's more fierce. This trip—and don't tell her I said this—it was also an excuse to have time with her so I could know more about the woman she's become. And now, I want to get her home so I'm not learning all of these things while we are in danger."

"What was she like before?"

The corner of his mouth lifted from whatever memory was brought to mind. "She was endlessly curious, always bothering someone to ask a million questions. I was more reserved at home, enjoying solitude. But when people were around, we were the opposite. Maev closed up, afraid of what others saw, while I enjoyed the attention. We were inseparable, however, and told each other everything. Now, I feel like we don't talk about what's underneath. She's surprised me with her displays of honesty regarding you. She was always overly polite when speaking to others."

"Glad to know I am bringing out the worst in her."

"You're bringing out the trueness of her. I think she intends to be your friend."

Guilt stabbed me—running from them, icing them, causing so much trouble. "I'm doing my best, you know. I'm not trying to make things harder for you two."

Ollo took a deep breath, checking Maev's temperature with a hand to her forehead.

"He was a mechanic. Our brother." Ollo glanced up at me through dark lashes, and the look sent a cool wave down my spine. It was hard to ignore the impact his attention had on me and the confidence he always carried. But behind that, he was kind, showing me something real.

"It was because of my brother I trained to become a pilot. He showed me his love for fixing machines, and I wanted to fly them. Maev saw what I was doing and decided she wanted to fix things too, like him."

"When did you lose him?"

"We were twelve. Too young to understand or properly deal with such heartache."

"I'm sorry."

Ollo adjusted his sister in his arms, trying to keep her comfortable. "Our mother died when we were born, so we only had my father to learn from."

"Magycris couldn't save them?"

The regret that passed over his face made me hesitant to ask more.

"We didn't come from wealth. Crystals are in short supply in Rydavas, so those that can't afford magycris don't have the safety net that comes with it. Being part of the aerial division, I have access to some supplies. It used to be a much more common thing. My mother's death would have been hard to avoid, even with magycris. My brother ... we didn't find him in time anyway."

This was not a conversation Ollo wanted to have—he was trying to be kind.

I changed the topic. "So what will happen in the future if the magycris runs out?"

"The future will look far different than the world does now."

I studied my bracelet, glowing through the drying blood. It never faded anymore. The crystals constantly reacted to my magic, pulsing with their strange light.

"It's why Maev came to get you," Ollo told me.

"What do you mean?"

"I was recruited to bring the Ikhor home—to fly fast. But Maev agreed to come so we could ask you for help before the armies did. She wants to make a change," he said, his smile crooked. "She thinks I am unaware of her other motives."

When I didn't reply, he said, "Maev told me you discovered our Elders want you not only for protection but to fight on our behalf. Yes, they wish to put you in the path of danger. Our people are running out of ways to defend themselves against the Guardians' numbers and their weapons. They have more crystals than our people and are better equipped to fight."

"But the Guardians don't even know you exist."

Ollo tilted his head to the side. "If that's what you are being taught, then it's a lie."

"Then the Guards are lied to. Because I know they were telling the truth when they said nothing civilized existed across the borders."

I considered it, wondering if the Guards had truly known. They couldn't have if they thought the Aethar came from wastelands. Not that I had proof that what they said about their lands was true.

"What could I have helped you with? If I wasn't taking the magic back?"

Ollo held my stare, searching for something in me before answering. "Maev believes the gods have the power to put magic into the crystals. Their magic connects to the lands. She believes the Ikhor would have been able to do this, too. Part of her studies was figuring out how the magic got into the crystals in the first place. I knew when I asked her to come, it would be part of her motivation. She believed she could plead with the Ikhor for help, replenishing our crystals so our people would have the resources we need so that when the armies leave, we aren't defenceless."

And so that families who were too poor to afford the healing liquid wouldn't lose loved ones as the twins had.

No magic burst forth when the guilt overtook my thoughts.

My decision to give the magic back would destroy the twins' hope for their people. Ollo would return, a failed mission. And Maev would lose her hope for the future.

"So why did you agree to take me to the Temple if you believe my magic can save your people?"

Ollo shrugged. "We don't believe in forcing anyone against their wishes. Our father raised us that way. I planned to talk you out of it. But not force you."

I searched his face. "People like you don't exist where I am from," I whispered.

I looked down at my bracelet, glowing strong, never fading, and knew then that Maev was right. The bracelet wasn't reacting to me. It was filling up with magic leaking from me. She had accused me of being foolish for wearing jewellery with magic crystals when they could be put to good use.

Maev moaned, lifting a hand to her face, and Ollo fussed, making sure she was okay.

"Ollo," she whimpered, "I want to go home."

I ground my teeth until it hurt. I balled the fabric of my pants in my good fist. How could I tell them Maev was right? The magic in my bracelet was from me.

I couldn't.

Because I still wanted to get this suffocating thing out of me.

CHAPTER
TWENTY-SIX

Liv

I have made several journal entries about shadows and dreams. One event blends into the next, and I'm no longer confident in my ability to distinguish reality from the fog clouding my mind. I have seen shadows twice now where there shouldn't be. My dreams feel too real. The magic is rattling inside me, begging to be used. Perhaps I'm mistaken, thinking his death broke my heart. Perhaps it was already broken. Maybe his death is what broke my mind.

I made a fist, once again checking how many fingers would bend. I had hoped mobility would come back, but after several hours and no change, I believed my hand would not recover.

"Should I be calling you two the Guards of the Ikhor?" I hid my hand behind my back as they joined me near the exit of the airship. The ladder that descended to the outside had already been lowered.

It was a weak attempt to ease the tension. Being surrounded by people who didn't like you wasn't something you ever grew used to. Ollo's words on the deck floated back to me. *"You're bringing out the trueness of her. I think she intends to be your friend."*

If Ollo was telling the truth, and that's how Maev felt ... it changed everything. My intentions had been to get rid of the magic, to save myself, but that resolve was cracking.

Maev and Ollo wore matching Guardian clothes—all shades of black and grey. Ollo had pulled his hair up in a knot at the back of his head, while Maev had braided hers down each side. Their tall, thin frames and blue-marked skin reminded me I was a world apart from anything I had ever known. Their expressions remained stony, glowing orange in the lamplight.

It would take more than a few jokes to earn their forgiveness. But I would.

I had bathed and changed into Guardian black, hiding the new scars lining my shoulder. Before coming to these lands, before becoming the Ikhor, I didn't have bones and crystals in my ears, and no scars marking my skin. Now? Now, I was showing signs that I had finally lived. I needed to toughen up, be braver, and try harder. Life could be quite adventurous if you let it. Losing an arm was a surprisingly effective lesson.

"What's the point of the backpacks if we aren't taking much?" I puffed the hair from my face as I readjusted the lightweight pack.

"Yours is a few essentials," Ollo said. "Ours are packed full in case we can't return to the ship and must make the long journey home on foot."

"Oh."

"I'm guessing you're staying in Veydes if you surv—" Ollo stopped abruptly.

"If I what?" I asked.

"If you survive," Maev snapped, her chin lifting, waiting for my reply.

Ollo rubbed his temples. "Mae, can you attempt at subtlety?"

"Why bother? This is her decision. She needs to face the consequences. We nearly died. If it's not the beast coming at us, it's the Guards cornering us. Now, we are going to pray to a *god* that isn't ours alongside the Ikhor, who doesn't know how to use her powers—powers that could have helped our people. You're a pilot, not a fighter, and I can barely hold a weapon. We are not even educated in negotiations."

"I'm equally as upset as you. We both had high hopes for Rydavas. But if Liv succeeds, she's ending it all. The whole world would win. Isn't that what you wanted?"

Maev looked away.

"I know why you came," Ollo said. "I know your intentions were not purely to help me deliver the Ikhor to the Elders."

Maev's weary gaze held her brothers as he gave her a knowing look and said, "I know you Mae, even if it's been some time. You are not one to risk so much unless it's to sate your curiosity."

She hesitated. "My research could have used her magic."

Ollo's head tilted. "And what about your conscience?"

"Obviously, I don't want to send Livy to her death." Maev's cheeks turned a shade darker.

"Livy?" Both Ollo and I questioned.

Ollo didn't meet my eye when my lips quirked.

"It may not seem like it," Maev continued, "because I am still so mad at you, Liv, for all the stupid decisions you keep making, but I consider you my friend. I am not only thinking of my people when I say I don't want to do this. I don't want you to die." She crossed her arms.

She was almost as frightening as Kazhi.

"But you are," I said, almost as a question. "Helping me, I mean."

I ignored the sting of her words because it was a novelty to have someone mad at me for reasons I *earned*. In my experience, people didn't like me for something I couldn't control. But another emotion replaced the harsh truth she lay on me. Something I had lost after Nuo's threats—a determination to live a life that was full. "I don't want to die either. I will do my best not to. If this doesn't work, I promise to help you two. I will help your research, Maev."

"And our people?" Maev said sharply.

"It's hard to want to risk everything for people I don't know. I am still learning how to do more than just survive." I held up my damaged hand before they argued. "I can't promise anything more. But I will go with you and see. I'll make a choice then."

"We take her to the temple to attempt to summon a god, or we get the next best option, and she helps our people," Ollo said to Maev.

Maev huffed, nodding. She pointed at me. "No more funny stuff."

I didn't know what funny stuff was, so I agreed. My situation continued to get more ridiculous as I went, from the moment I landed to now travelling with the enemy and facing another god ...

I gathered my courage, slapping the side of my face.

"What're you doing?" Ollo questioned.

"Getting ready. Convincing myself this is the best move."

Maev lifted her chin. "You mean we're about to leave the ship, potentially taking away our chance to reach home, and you're not even sure this is what you want to do? Do you ever think of others?"

I couldn't come up with a reasonable response.

"Why the hesitation?" Ollo stepped closer to me.

"As you keep reminding me, the process might kill me. When I stated I wanted to return the magic ... well, it's far easier to say it inside the airship."

"Then we should stay," Maev scolded.

I stopped, shaking my head. "I still want to go. I want to try."

"I will aim to help," Ollo said. "Though I can't fathom how we will take on a god."

"I'm surprised you're helping me at all. So I will take what I can get."

Ollo bumped his shoulder against mine. "I would never allow the saviour to take on the gods alone."

Maev's hands went to her hips as she faced him. "It's hard enough to keep my cool with everything going on. Please don't make the day worse by acting cocky. It isn't fooling either of us."

I stood awkwardly next to Ollo, unsure if I should interrupt.

"And you." Maev rounded on me. "You need to control yourself, too. You go from morose to angry to blushing in seconds. You need to present yourself differently if you're calling on a god. If you're too scared, we can wait."

"We can't. I've made my decision."

Ollo gave me a small smile. "My advice is to act like you're brave. Sometimes, if you try hard enough, the imitation can convince even yourself." Ollo went to descend the ladder, but I grabbed his shoulder, stopping him.

"You two can stay here. I can protect myself. You don't need to be put in any more danger."

Maev whipped a braid over her shoulder. "Unfortunately for you, Ikhor, we are coming with you. We are trying to help. As friends. No running away from it like a coward."

I bit the inside of my cheek.

"Since when do you make friends, Mae? I thought you liked being a loner." Ollo lowered a foot onto the first rung.

"You're one to talk," Maev replied. "All your fellow pilots are party animals that don't know a thing about you."

"Better than your overly enthusiastic hermit of a friend."

"What's wrong with Cal?" Maev bent over the hatch, her blue braids falling in front of her. "He is a great friend."

She held her hand toward the ladder, gesturing me to go next.

"I like the name Livy," I said quietly, thrown off by their bickering.

"Hmmm." She pressed her lips together, hiding a smile.

I made my way down the swaying rope ladder—a miraculous

feat with one working hand—and landed on a bed of soft needles. I studied the ground, inhaling a familiar scent. My five good fingers—and one stiff one—tightened on the rope as I raised my head to search the forest we had landed in.

"Liv?" Ollo stepped closer. "You're going pale."

"Are you sure we are near the temple?"

"Yes, Maev followed the directions from the map. You look like you've seen a ghost."

Maev climbed down the ladder as the world spun, and the temperature dropped.

Fear.

My magic surged, coming forth without my control. But I couldn't push the feeling down.

We stood in a small clearing, and the smell of damp cedar trees overtook my senses—it was identical to the Endless Forest, the home I never wanted to return to.

"What's going on?" Maev's feet thudded to the ground, which was now coated in ice.

"I don't know." Ollo exchanged a glance with his twin.

"Are you sure we are near the Mountain temple?" I spun on Maev, terrified she got it wrong. Was it possible they tricked me and returned me by airship? No one knew where my lands were.

"Where do you think we are?"

"This forest looks like my home. Did you lie to me?"

She turned in a circle. "The Lost Lands? This isn't exactly what I pictured a mythical place looking like."

I took a breath, really taking it in. Tall patches of grass pushed up through the layer of needles on the ground—the cold weather back home never retreated enough for the grasses to grow that tall.

"You know, it's kinda ridiculous you freak out over a forest, yet the Aspis nearly *killing* you was no problem," Maev muttered.

My breath came out in puffs before me. "Losing my arm was a consequence of my bad choices. It's another to live in fear of those controlling the choices for you."

"Well, you're not there. You're here, near the Temple of Mountain, about to summon a god."

I searched her face, finding every thought she didn't hide.

"It's not the forest you need to be scared of," she continued. "You're about to ask Ouras to rip the magic from you."

"I have to face the consequences. I want it gone."

Maev shrugged the pack off her back and pulled out a familiar looking rolled map.

"I forgot you stole Nuo's map," I said, distracting myself from my racing heart.

"Yeah. I stole a bunch of his stuff. There's a torch in here, too."

I couldn't contain the laughter that burst forth, and the twins eyed me like I had gone insane. "If he hated you for being an Aethar, it's not anything like the hate he would feel for stealing his most prized possession. You think I should be worried for *my* life."

I shook my head as she opened the map and searched for the best path to the temple.

"You've drawn on it!" I gasped.

Maev rolled it back up and motioned us forward. "His drawings are too simple, spaced out in a way that, while it will help us in the right direction, there's no indication of distance or proximity. I have been trying to correct his drawings." She was heading between two cedars, with Ollo and me trailing her.

I struggled to keep up with their long strides.

"The map is detailed when it comes to the locations he's been, but completely blank where Rydavas lays." She pushed branches as she went, diving into the forest. "He didn't even get our shoreline correct. There's an entire bay in the south he's missing. And the north shoreline is a joke."

I walked between the twins, who towered on either side of me. We may have seemed like a formidable group of Guardians to anyone we approached. When, in fact, none of us could use a weapon, and I lacked control over the most powerful magic a person could have.

"You don't make maps of your own?" I asked.

"We have maps integrated into our ships. Most are hypsometric maps detailed by our best cartographers and used by the aerial units, but our airship, the one we lost, was a simple navigational map—not so detailed," Maev said.

I checked to see if Ollo was as confused as I was, but he was listening, ignoring me.

"Rydavas has more airships at their disposal than the Guardian lands, and we work together," Maev explained. "There's no need for secret maps. The Guardians hide their treasures. As you can see from Nuo's drawings, he has treasures hidden all over Veydes."

I didn't mention to Maev that some of Nuo's *treasures* were past lovers. He'd also marked the places he couldn't return, and my guess was they were past lovers who were no longer welcoming.

Maev lifted her tracker and found a strong signal. "My guess is that way. If there are more monks who are purebloods, I'm likely picking up their signal."

"What if it's Ouras?" I asked.

"Not likely," Maev replied. "The gods are hardly ever seen by the people. We will have to call him."

Yet I had seen one. Rem had walked right into the dining hall in the Guardian City. Though, the Guardians at the dinner *had* all been stunned into silence.

I followed the twins as we passed between large cedars, listening to them bicker about what they would rather be doing back home. They seemed content to ignore me, and I didn't blame them since they hadn't wanted to take me to the Temple.

"Ah, dammit!" Maev shouted, coming to a stop under a large cedar. "My tracker died. Crystals have run out."

I continued walking, avoiding the truth, knowing it was cowardly not to admit I could fill their crystals. If I filled them with magic now, would the twins change their minds about helping me go to Ouras?

Maev twirled on her heel and walked backwards, facing me as we went. "So what's so bad in the Endless Forest that it scares you more than the Aspis? I'm still shaking from it." She lifted a hand in the air to show a slight tremor.

I thought about it for a moment. "A giant beast attacking me is so unreal I can't process it. But the forest I came from and the society that raised me? That was conditioning—a horrible way to live."

"Was it violent?"

"Oh no. The Law Keepers were, but there was no crime. Issues were quickly dealt with."

"That sounds like peace to me," Ollo commented. "The leaders used their control and gave the people a life with no worry."

I stopped walking. "I thought you were supposed to be smart."

"Pardon me?"

"When you are stripped of all choice, nothing is left of your soul. The suffering is in the lack of purpose or hope. It's a prison packaged as peace and prosperity. If you are fighting for your people, Ollo, I will warn you not to let your society become like that. I have seen what bad rulers can make of a home. I was dying every day. Eventually, my light would have been snuffed out."

Ollo dipped his head in apology as I continued past him, winding around a large cedar. "We had no gods to pray to. No stories to inspire us. We didn't have a saviour who would return to fight for our cause. I prefer having my arm ripped off to the suffering I went through living that way."

"I agree," Maev said up ahead. "You know, if you kept your magic, you could return there and show them what you think."

"I don't wish to have anything to do with them ever again. I would be stooping to their level. They killed my mother for speaking out."

"They killed her?"

I nodded. "Deciding what's best for other people is never the right answer. That's why I will never decide someone else's fate."

It occurred to me that it took weeks of knowing the Guards before I was brave enough to speak of my mother or the Law Keepers. I tucked away that realization—I was changing.

But something about Maev's idea to return to the Endless Forest with my magic roused something within me. It roared up, driving me forward, demanding to be used.

Revenge, it commanded. *I want revenge.*

The twins walked on, not noticing anything amiss. But it was clear as day. The Ikhor was getting stronger, and I didn't think the presence was made of anything good.

While they were walking ahead, I pulled out the photo I had hidden in my pocket. The picture of the Guards with one side ripped off. It ached to look at him. But at that moment, it brought me comfort, too. I pulled strength from the small piece of paper. He fought to the end, battling what was inside him, never letting it define who he was.

I was close to the temple, and I would beg Ouras to take it back. I may not be a saviour or a hero, but I could be *good*, and not become a product of hatred. I would not become the evil consuming me.

CHAPTER
TWENTY-SEVEN

Liv

The half-beast in my dream looks like the Aspis. It looks like him. Is my mind conjuring this image because I can't accept that one is not the other?

"Look over there." Maev pointed out two figures in the distance, moving between the trees. They were Mountain monks following a beaten-down path.

I felt nothing from them—they had no magic.

"They'll lead us in the right direction." Ollo clapped me on the back, making my spine straighten. His face lit with triumph.

We reached the path and trailed silently behind the monks far ahead.

Ouras's temple had been hard to find. We had searched the forest, going in circles. If Nuo's map was correct, we were walking over it.

An eternity later, we discovered why we couldn't find the temple. It was not what the three of us were looking for. We had expected a grand building, shining, drawing in its worshippers. Instead, a hill covered in roots and shrubs sat hidden, surrounded by three enormous trees—almost as big as Danuli's.

The monks we trailed moved toward a thick gathering of roots and travelled right through them.

A hidden entrance.

"Are all temples this way? So hard to find?" I asked Maev in a whisper.

"I couldn't tell you. I've only visited shrines."

"What's the difference?" I had never heard of a shrine.

Sunlight hit my lashes as I passed between the boughs of the cedar, heading for the entrance.

"In Rydavas, we have no temples. So, we built shrines where we could go and pray to our gods. They're holy structures sculpted in worship to their intended god. Our Day shrines—there's more than one—all bear symbols of Rem: the sun, the wind and the snow."

"What do other shrines look like?"

We followed under the branches of the cedar trees, and the twins' blue skin was a rich contrast to the browns and greens of the mountain forest. I soaked in the differences until we reached the hill, where we all stopped in unison before it.

"The only other shrine I have seen is a massive one by the sea. I flew overtop it once. Mayra's blue shrine is a day's flight from our city. The windows are rippled and tinted blue, so you feel like you are swimming in the ocean as you walk its floor."

"That sounds beautiful." I paused, searching the area. We had passed no other travellers in the forest or on the path to the temple. "It's very quiet. Do you think that's normal?"

"I don't know what to think. I wish my tracker was operational. We need more crystals." Maev spun toward her brother. "Who wants to go first? The bold and brave head of Aerial Division One?" She gave me a small smile. "How about the mighty Ikhor?"

"Funny," I muttered and walked through the vines.

I waited for darkness, damp air and the scent of mould, but things never turned out as I expected them. Behind the vines, a shining stone hall opened, tall and grand, with beautifully woven banners hanging from high on the walls. Light poured in between gaps in the roots, lighting a path forward.

"This is different." My voice carried through the long hall, bouncing back at me.

"Let's proceed with utmost caution. We may wear their black Guardians attire, but it won't take long for others to realize we exhibit none of their qualities. Not one of us can imitate a Mount-leg. Nor do we have Guardian tattoos." Ollo stepped in next to me, eyeing the end of the hall.

His proud stance gave me courage. Maybe having the head of an Aerial something or other wasn't a bad idea for a teammate.

We travelled the long hall made of polished stone. Our footsteps echoed, blending with the whispers coming from open doorways. Other passages led to grand libraries, dining rooms, lush sitting rooms and rooms I couldn't make out their use—all decorated in warm, earthy tones.

Maev was constantly lifting her hands to point and make comments, and Ollo would grab her wrist and lower her arm, shushing her.

We followed the largest halls that led deeper into the hill. Sometimes, the ceiling was so tall the light coming in didn't quite reach the floor. We passed a dimly lit corridor, light streaming in from the high ceiling, and I stopped at the sight of a massive painting that took up the entire wall.

The Aspis floated in the air, roaring in its rage, and across the great expanse of grey skies, a glowing figure floated, arms outstretched, with red eyes. Underneath the two legends, monsters with matching red eyes fought figures in black. Beneath them all was a red sea, bodies of all legacies floating in the dark, ruby depths.

"That's inspiring," Ollo whispered.

The Aspis had risen, true to the image. But it was the glowing figure I couldn't look away from. I swallowed the growing panic, kicking myself mentally.

So far, the legends had been mistaken. This painting was, too.

"Why are there never paintings of the gods?" I asked in a low voice. Not only did I look for an image of Ouras, but I wondered what Mayra and Erabas looked like, too.

"The gods are never depicted." Ollo checked to make sure no one was listening. "They're only spoken of, not painted. It isn't allowed."

"Sounds like home."

We passed more posters of the Ikhor screaming—two red-eyed Aethar with white hair were etched alongside it—as we went farther into the temple.

"Oh, please," Maev muttered at the deformed image of herself.

"I can feel magic here," I whispered to her.

"The monks?" she asked.

"Could be. It's strong."

"There would be many here. But that many purebloods with magic? I don't know how many still exist."

I caught glimpses of figures in grand rooms off the main hall, but none paid us any attention as we trekked farther.

A figure dressed in Guardian black leaned against the wall past a large open doorway, their face cloaked in darkness. When they lifted their head as we drew closer, a flash of iridescence stole my breath.

I stopped dead in my tracks.

A pale young female face with dark hair framing serious and haunted eyes latched onto me. Her expression hardened as I stared.

Several other Guardians emerged from the open door, one clapping her on the shoulder and telling her they were ready to leave.

I couldn't look away.

Kazhi had made it sound like *he* was the last of his legacy. Yet here was another.

The team of Guardians caught me staring, and they hurried their friend away and out of the temple.

Ollo grabbed my arm, turning me so that we were face to face. "It's not him, Saviour."

"How—" I didn't have the courage to look back at the Night-leg retreating with her friends.

"Night-legs are rare, even in Rydavas. There are few in Avenmae. They are not popular. Many are frightened of them—that they may be cruel like Erabas. I've heard that here, they are accused of harbouring the Ikhor. Either way, they're blamed and are not welcome. So they keep to themselves. That one's brave, being in the open."

"I knew it wasn't him. She was a woman."

Ollo searched past me at the group leaving. "I don't know what camp she trained at, but she must have kept her identity hidden as often as possible."

As we continued farther into the hill, the voices grew louder.

"I think the main chamber of worship is ahead." Maev pointed toward where the hall opened up into a large circular room.

It had to be where we would call to Ouras because the hum of magic was growing stronger, meaning the monks were there.

The room was the grandest of all. It was as tall as the hill outside, reaching the tops of the trees. The ceiling opened at the apex, leaving a full view of the midday sky. Banners and vines hung from above, where the sun shone down on the monks and the Guardians gathered.

A low baritone sang a hymn that echoed off the rounded walls, making it impossible to tell where the voice came from. The beautiful voice sang in tune with the hum of magic, enchanting me. I was being pulled, calmed, and excited by it.

Alcoves of all sizes decorated the outskirts of the chamber, where some sat with their eyes closed, praying, while others knelt on the floor before a giant statue.

A statue of Ouras.

The carved figure sat on a throne of shining stone, similar to the floors. The statue was crafted from copper, stained to blend with the earth and roots. But the veins in the statue had a striped pattern to them, like an animal. The statue towered over the room, the top of it hidden in shadow, obscuring how the sculptor depicted the god's face. Perhaps, like the painting, the gods weren't meant to be seen.

There were figures at its feet praying and some lazing on the dais. My face warmed when I realized the women worshipping at the statue's feet were partially nude. Some were petting it while touching themselves.

"Ummm." I stared for too long before I looked away, my face becoming hot, and I stupidly turned to Ollo.

And if the beautiful blue man's gaze didn't dart down to my mouth.

He went stiff before awkwardly stepping away.

Was Maev right? Was Ollo flirting with me before?

Maev had taken off, and I dashed to catch up with her as she approached the edge of the chamber. Luckily, those around us ignored us. Not so lucky was that she walked closer to the woman idolizing the statue.

I had been told the temples collected worshippers. I had no idea the ways in which they worshipped.

I blinked past the humming working its way into my chest— the hymn was getting louder. Or was I closer to the monks?

Many Guardians, all Mount-legs, were here. Monks and citizens mixed in with those sitting to the side, their eyes closed as their lips moved in prayer.

We reached the foot of the statue, and I craned my neck to look up. Still, I couldn't see into the shadows to make out the carved face of Ouras.

"It's huge," I said. "Do you think this is what he looks like?"

"I am unsure." Ollo stood next to me, staring up just as I was. "I have never been in the presence of a god, always wondering if they resembled the descriptions made of them."

"Well, Rem is tall and glows. And doesn't look human."

"You've seen him?" Ollo turned his head toward me. For some reason, I wasn't brave enough to look his way.

"He was visiting the Guardian city when I was there with the Guards."

"Why would he be visiting the city? Those who wish to see him would need to go to his temple."

I shrugged, facing the statue.

I didn't know where to begin, how to ask for a god to show themselves. So I closed my eyes, put my hands together and prayed.

"What are you doing?" Maev asked.

I peeked over at her while holding my hands in the air. "I am praying. Why are you laughing at me?"

"Because your hands don't do the praying. You call out to a god with your heart."

Ollo patted me on the head. "We have so much to teach you, Saviour."

I swatted his hand away as a few Guardians approached the dais, standing to the right of us.

"You three must be from South Aspis." A young man surprised me when he spoke to me. He had a long face with wide green eyes and pointed ears that protruded from the sides of his head.

"Why do you say that?" I asked.

"I haven't seen you three in the Guardian City. I just assumed since so many are coming north now. And you two,"—he pointed to the twins—"must be Mount-legs from Korrylt. So many of you guys head to South Aspis for training. Am I wrong?"

His tone was friendly. He was only a young Guardian trying to bond with those he thought were his fellow warriors.

"Why are so many coming north?" Maev asked.

"You haven't heard?" The young man looked to the other Guardians he travelled with, who were half paying attention and half praying to Ouras. "The Aethar have taken it down. The whole camp burnt to the ground, and survivors have been fleeing north."

"Burnt?"

His face fell, and he exchanged a sad look with his teammate. "Ya, the Ikhor is taking out the camps, trying to dwindle our numbers so we can't help the Aspis. Fucking evil doesn't know how strong we are. We will get him."

"It's not a him," interrupted one of his companions, a girl with two sets of eyes and antennae on her forehead. "The posters all show the Ikhor is a woman."

"Right. Same difference. Evil is evil."

Maev stepped towards the young man, but Ollo grabbed her shoulder, stopping her from saying anything. Was she going to stick up for me?

"You said the Aethar were down there." I played innocent. "Maybe it was them and not the Ikhor."

"The fire says it all."

The Guardians waved goodbye, discussing how no one wanted to train at the North camp, so the Guardian City was getting crowded. They lingered around the dais, seating themselves in a vacant alcove.

"Aspissers," Maev said under her breath.

I watched the Guardians, wondering about the fires and who was starting them. Would Falizha set fire to her camps?

Of course she would. That didn't mean it wasn't the Aethar who started the fires.

"What do we do now?" I worried about how I brought the twins here without a real plan. I grabbed my head, massaging my temples. A slow ache was forming.

"It's a good day for prayers," came a soft voice to our right. "How may I direct you in the Temple of Ouras? If you do not wish to ask for his blessing, is there something else you seek? Perhaps the library?"

All three of us faced the man to our left—one of the temple monks. He wore long robes that hung from him like vines. His face was long and gaunt, and two stubby horns protruded from his black hair.

The hum of magic grew. This was one of the first children.

"Why do you think we don't wish to ask his blessing?" I asked.

"Because his likeness sits before you, and you do not kneel."

"It's just a statue," Maev said. "We came to speak to Ouras himself."

"You think he speaks to any Guardian who appears in his temple?"

Our black clothes had easily fooled the monk, despite what Ollo had thought. His tone wasn't impolite, but his face suggested he thought we were out of line.

"We aren't just anyone. This is important," I explained.

"Everyone comes here for something important, child. What legacy are you? You don't have the look of any Mountain legacy I have come across."

Were any monks *not* condescending? This one was getting on my nerves as much as the Day-monk I met in Bellum.

I stood tall, remembering Ollo's advice to fake being brave until I believed it myself. But bravery was often one step away from stupidity, and I failed to think ahead before I blurted, "Tell your god he has a visit from the Ikhor."

In an attempt to show strength, my voice rose, echoing in the chamber. *Ikhor, Ikhor, Ikhor.*

Maev groaned.

"Smooth," Ollo commented, and I gave him a dirty look.

The silence that followed the echoing of my announcement was painful.

The monk stepped back, mouth popping open in shock. Screaming tore through the chamber as worshippers and monks fled the room. The one before us backed away with his hands raised. Guardians who had lingered silently on the outskirts raised weapons.

"Way to go, Liv," Maev said nervously.

I winced, realizing that while I thought it would highlight the importance of my visit, the monks and worshippers weren't aware I was here to return the magic.

I was evil, and they wanted me dead.

The women at the foot of the statue covered themselves, panicking as they ran between the Guardians who were closing in on us.

Enemies surrounded us, and now everyone knew who we were.

Screw them.

"I am the Ikhor." I raised my palms, appearing as the Ikhor had in the painting hanging on the temple wall, and it felt good when their looks changed from determination to fear. For once, the roles were reversed. "I wish to seek an audience with the god Ouras. I have the god's magic, and I want to return it."

No one answered. No one moved.

"They weren't expecting that." Ollo stood tall, waiting to see what others would do. "This is getting kind of fun."

Where did his bravery come from when he didn't know how to fight?

"Now is not the time to be a thrill seeker, Ol," Maev said through clenched teeth.

A booming roar echoed through the chamber, and everyone flinched, searching for the source. The ground moved as a great earthquake shook the temple.

Then, as suddenly as it started, it stopped.

I peered up at the sky visible through the roots, expecting the Aspis to be soaring overhead.

Movement out of the corner of my eye made me jerk away from the dais. The statue on the chair moved, groaning as if having been idle for too long. A low growl like churning stone echoed from the darkness as the figure in shadow bent forward, coming into the light.

Guardians before the statue cried out, clearly not having known it was more than stone.

I stumbled back when Ouras stepped forward, leaving the darkness behind—not because I was before a god, but because I was looking at the face of the Aspis.

Liv

I can't even write about how messed up I am after meeting Ouras. If I felt like I was losing my mind before, it's nothing compared to now.

Vines hung from shining black horns that curled away from a feral face made of copper and raven black stripes. Citrine-yellow eyes narrowed in on me, and the moving statue hissed as it stood high above us, bearing sharp fangs.

The light from above shone off Ouras's strange, reflective skin as he paused for us to take him in. More vines hung from his shoulders and arms, making him look as though carved from a tree. He was a true god of the earth, made from stone and wood.

"Do you see what I am seeing?" Maev's voice shook.

"He looks like the beast." Ollo stepped in beside me, trying to put me behind him.

What they didn't see was he reminded me of the half-beast. The one in my dreams.

Ouras's eyes were similar to Rem's—black where the white should be. Inhuman. But Ouras had slitted pupils surrounded by yellow iris—identical to the Aspis.

Black curling horns, fangs, claws—the gods had made the Aspis. Of course, it would look like them. But then, the Aspis bore no resemblance to Rem. What did that mean?

The magic that had enthralled me upon entering the Temple had been from a god, yet I hadn't crumbled from his power. My mind repeated that over and again as Ouras stood to his full height. The first time I met Rem, the magic caused me pain.

But I had grown used to that pain in the past weeks.

A deep groaning came from the god, his pupils thinning. He was much taller than Rem, who was already over ten feet.

The Guardians that surrounded us didn't know what to do. They hadn't known Ouras was here, and by the looks on the monk's faces, many of them hadn't either.

The sun from above cast us in a circle of light, while shadows fell on the Guardians and monks.

Ouras leaned over, blocking the sun from my eyes.

"I am the Ikhor."

Ouras didn't blink. He no longer moved, a statue once more, staring down at the evil incarnate.

"The stories say that the magic within me once belonged to you. I have come to give it back. I have come to end this war."

"Lies," a Guardian hissed from somewhere behind me.

Others echoed their disbelief. "You've torn villages to the ground. The south burns!"

A scuffle sounded behind me, and I found a Guardian with a blade in hand, being held back by his team. I didn't mention the floods or argue that it was one of their own burning the villages. Who would believe that the Governor's daughter caused as much destruction as the Ikhor?

I faced the god again, whose gaze was now tracing lines over my body, moving in unnatural ways. He cocked his head to the side, casting a reflection off his horns.

"Will you take it back?" My hands shook, but I didn't hide them behind me.

Still, the god said nothing.

The domed room was anything but silent—a humming echoed, getting louder and louder until it was a loud din. Magic saturated the air. Was it his or mine?

"Maybe he can't hear you," Maev said.

"I am the Ikhor," I shouted each word, making the Guardians raise their weapons higher.

A monk, younger than I, ran forward, stopping before the god and facing me. The woman had bird-like features, the feathers on her head pointing backward. She held her arms wide in front of Ouras in an impressive show of bravery. "What is it you seek from our god Ouras?" Her attention darted over her shoulder as if afraid of having him at her back.

Those snake-like eyes, so similar to the Aspis, never left my face. Why was he staring so hard yet not speaking?

"I want to return the Ikhor's magic."

The girl's mouth went round. "Why? You're evil. This must be a trick."

"Oh my god." I pinched the bridge of my nose, turning to Maev for help.

"Liv, you're in the presence of one. Don't curse them," she said through her teeth.

"He's heard curse words before. He probably created them."

"The revered god of Mountain doesn't speak the common tongue," the young monk shouted. Her nose, which came to a sharp point like a beak, clacked against her pointed lower lip. "Though he understands intentions. He wishes to hear your request."

Ouras hadn't moved. He looked ... unnerved.

Guardians all around were waiting, holding their breath, watching the god as much as they watched me.

"How do you know? He didn't say anything," I asked.

The young monk had a defiant gleam in her eye. "Of course he did. He's speaking now. The language of Mountain sounds like the whispering in the trees. The creaking of wood, the tumble of rock."

Over my heart pounding, I could make out a low rumbling. It was similar to the rattling of a snake. Similar to what the half-beast had done in those dreams. What did that mean?

"What's he saying?" I asked.

"That he thinks you look familiar."

I took a step back. "How so?"

Was this god in my dreams when I thought it had been *him*?

"He will not say."

I shook my head, not wanting to be given more riddles. "Never mind that. Will he accept the magic back? I'm trying to end this stupid cycle."

The monk listened to Ouras before saying, "You can't."

Guardians pressed in farther, and with them, Ollo. His arms pushed next to mine, keeping me close. He slid a hand to my swords, patting them to remind me they were there.

I stepped around him. "What do you mean? Tell him to take the magic back."

"He can't," she repeated.

"Why the *fuck* not?" My words echoed in the chamber.

I had once been terrified of uttering such a word. Now it was being thrown back in my face from a tall domed ceiling.

"Mind your tongue, Ikhor. He said he can't, not that he won't. The magic won't go to him. Find another way."

"Tell him he's useless."

Several Guardians gasped, along with Maev, who wrapped a hand around my arm, squeezing.

"I will not." The young monk paused, looking over her shoulder.

"What did he say?" I demanded.

"He says you're a good host." She craned her neck. "But the magic is corrupt, Father. Why do you compliment it?"

"What makes a good host?"

The god's scrutiny was dizzying. The longer I looked into those yellow eyes—the eyes of the beast—the more I thought the god might be insane.

"Ouras says the magic that you stole suits you. Your emotions are wild. Ouras loves wild things."

"I thought the magic was his?"

"No." Her shoulders relaxed as she put her hands behind her back. The monk raised her chin, and I was impressed how this one, so little compared to the others, showed me no fear. "The magic belongs to all of them."

"Right. So, who do I need to ask? How do I give it back?"

I exchanged a look with Maev, who shrugged.

A Guardian stepped forward in the growing circle around Ouras and my small group. "The magic will not be returned until evil is vanquished from the hearts of men. Until then, you must die, Ikhor."

Several more stepped forward, and the bird monk raised her hand to stop them, unafraid of the many weapons held close. But it didn't stop the Guardians from advancing.

I flinched when several ran for me. My hand landed on my blades.

Ouras roared, shaking the temple and causing the Guardians to stumble back in fear.

The young monk fell to a knee but held her hand raised to keep the Guardians away. "Stop," she said. "Our punishment is to be righted by the Aspis. Our saviour is the one to make the kill. Call the Guards."

The Guardian, who had spoken earlier, gave a quick nod and fled from the temple. Several Guardians broke the line and left to follow.

"Shit, if the Guards are close, we may not make it back to our ship." Maev went stiff as Ollo put a hand on her shoulder.

"We packed just in case. But Liv still has the power to get us out of here."

"If she uses the magic, it will only call the Aspis to our location," Maev replied.

As if in answer, a loud rumble came from above, shaking the room from outside.

"Too late," Ollo said.

Rock and dirt crumbled from the gaping hole in the ceiling, and those who weren't Guardians cowered against the walls.

Ouras rattled the room in reply. He seemed unhappy.

"But Father, that goes against your teachings." The monk blanched.

"What did he say?" A Guardian asked. "Does Ouras not want us to attack?"

The monk levelled her hate-filled glare at me. "He says if you find the others, he may change his position on the matter."

"The other gods?" I asked, surprised. Why wasn't the god striking me down? Shouldn't he hate me too? I represented what had been taken from him, but the monk said I impressed him.

"The two *missing* gods?" Maev asked.

Frustrated, I put my hands on my hips. "What if I go to Rem? Can he not help me? It's said he loves his children. Surely, he would use magic to save them."

The monk shook her head. "He says find the others and ask." She looked from her god to me, and her face displayed the confusion in my heart. "But if you go to Rem, you will be forfeiting your life."

"How so? Why would Rem not want the magic back?"

"After you've turned their magic evil? Why would any of them? I suggest you do the world a favour and see the god of Day, Ikhor. Rid us of your evil. You are nothing but destruction. You are the end of everything."

Ouras growled, showing his displeasure, and the monk bowed deeply, her hands shaking.

Maev squeezed my elbow. She was looking at me hard, and it hit me.

The Oracle's warning, "*You will be the end of everything.*"

She was right. I would be. "I *will* be the end of everything, monk. Tell your god I will find the others and end everything on *my* terms."

Maybe what the Oracle said could hold a different meaning if I took the prophecies into my own hands and moulded them into something new. I would end everything—end the cycle.

When I looked back at Maev, she had a smile on her face and seemed excited. Shouldn't she be mad? I wasn't offering to return home with her.

"Don't let them escape!" A Guardian shouted up at Ouras.

The god backed away and lowered himself to his chair. He hid his upper half in the shadows of his temple, ending his conversation with us.

I'd had enough. Because of the being before me, I was forced into this world. I had made friends, a new family, and fallen for a man who died to protect the people from what the gods had put inside me. I had forgotten my anger when *he* had died. I had forgotten how this had been done to me. The magic was put inside me without my permission. The reminder that this was not my doing—that stronger forces had controlled my life—raged through me.

Smoke gathered as the floor hissed.

"Saviour." Ollo warned, "You're steaming."

"You're lying!" I screamed at Ouras.

He had gone so still he looked like a statue once more.

"You can take it back. You did this to me. You brought me here. I want to know why. What is the point?"

"Brought you here?" The monk asked, who stood her ground before us. She took a step toward me, taking in my face, skin, and lack of noticeable markers of a legacy. "Where are you from? Ouras would like to know."

The Oracle's warning rang clear in my mind, *"Do not speak of where you are from, even if it's the gods asking."*

Smoke and ash gathered when I could no longer contain my anger. I looked toward the twins, who, though unaffected by the heat, looked worried.

The Guardians were getting ready to attack, even without the god's blessing.

"Take her down! The Ikhor is attacking our god!"

"The magic will kill us!"

"The two blue ones! They must be Aethar," another said.

"Dear gods," Ollo swore, stepping back.

"They've hidden their scars so they could be spies!" The Guardians seemed to forget all about the Ikhor after the monk's declaration that the Aspis owned my death. Instead, they zeroed in on the twins.

"We gotta go." Maev pulled on my elbow again, trying to back me away from the angry mob. "Liv, we have no way of protecting ourselves. You need to use the magic."

"But the Aspis."

"Then burn it too. Anything, please." Her voice shook.

My body jerked at the sudden tug to my ankles and wrists. Vines thicker than rope curled around my limbs, holding me tight and pinning me in place. I scanned the crowd to find Mountain Legacies with their hands raised, controlling the earth to hold me hostage.

"Purebloods?" whispered the Guardians.

"Magic users!" shouted another. "They aren't supposed to exist."

The monks of the Mountain temple were using their magic, giving away their secrets to capture the Ikhor.

The Guardians went still—their teachings told them that magic was meant for the gods, not the children.

"I wasn't attacking!" I shouted. "I am not going to hurt you!"

Guardians stared at the display of magic.

Maev and Ollo, having seen mine, were only shocked that the monks no longer hid it.

"You can control magic?" a Guardian asked the monks. "But how? Did Ouras grant you this power?"

"Look not at us, Guardians. Look to the enemy. It attacks."

The Guardians were now nervous. Some even scowled.

Another divide was happening between the legacies, and I was witnessing it.

"You don't fool us, Ikhor," an older monk covered in scales and spikes said. "You're not here to give the magic back. You're here to destroy the gods so you can keep it for yourself."

The temperature in the room soared, as flames burst in a circle around me, catching the vines alight and turning them to dust.

Guardians and monks jumped back, running for the walls, running from the room as the flames fanned out.

Everything glowed red.

My attention jumped to the twins, who were untouched by the flame.

My control was improving.

I was improving. This power, it was exhilarating.

Maev and Ollo stuck to my sides, where a circle of safe ground surrounded me.

Ouras remained on his dais, uncaring of the heat, and through the flames, I could see yellow irises fixed on me. He didn't lift a finger to stop me.

Ollo bowed with a hand resting over his heart. "Ouras, father and protector of Mountain," he shouted over the roaring flames, "I am Ollo Pretruq, child of Day. I beg you to forgive the Ikhor. She has lost a lot in these past weeks. She wished to change the fate of our people, and we have travelled with her today to do as she wished. End this. Please tell us how we can end the cycle. Surely, you must know."

I silently thanked Ollo for his interference because Ouras fidgeted, seeming to listen.

Maev wrapped her arm around my shoulder, calming my racing heart and pulling me close.

"I hadn't asked for your family name," I said to Maev in a low voice.

"I'll add it to the long list of things that have slipped your mind when it comes to us."

I smiled despite her cutting words. "You really aren't afraid of me anymore, are you?"

"You're mistaken about that as well."

Ouras raised a hand in the air, pointing to me.

The young monk raced to the god's side, dodging the flames creeping along the floor. "He does not lie to you, Ikhor. He can't take it back."

"Then get the others," I demanded. "I will give it back to all of you."

"That is not possible." The monk faked a sad smile, so exaggerated I wanted to laugh. "He has been unable to find his sister Mayra, who has hidden away in the depths of her seas. And his brother Erabas has not been seen for millennia. He can barely recall the time of his leaving or his reasons for doing so."

"Then what can I do? There must be something," I cried.

"You must atone. If the legacies cannot fix their greed, then they are doomed. Your other option is to find the other two yourself. But I fear you will not live long enough to take on such a task, for in thousands of years, he has been unable to do so himself."

Maev squeezed my shoulder tighter, a warning.

"No," I spat.

"No?" another monk asked.

"No," I repeated. "I don't accept that answer. I will get rid of the magic. I won't die from it. If you need the other two, then I will find them."

Movement grabbed my attention in the shadows of Ouras's throne. The god sat forward, coming into the light once more. The eyes of the Aspis held mine. The god actually fought to hide a smile. He shifted that gaze to the twins, clearly interested in my resolve.

Ouras seemed to like this plan. Now, I only had to figure out how to find two missing gods.

"You cannot mean to allow the Ikhor to escape," a Guardian asked, trapped behind a wall of fire.

I let the fire spread, protecting the twins and me from any attack.

The young monk, now hidden behind the vines growing from Ouras, stepped forward. "You know how this goes. The Aspis was created to destroy the Ikhor. It is the only thing that can. The gods cannot kill one of their children."

"Ikhhhorrr."

The ground shook. I stumbled, catching myself before I hit the ground. Some of the fire snuffed out, creating holes in my defence.

The god's booming voice echoed low and rocked the temple. Everyone turned to face the statue in the shadows.

"I thought he couldn't speak the common tongue," Maev said.

"Probably because he shakes the entire earth when he does," I replied.

"Do nnnnot returnnn to mmmy temmmple again."

Because I was already near the ground, I only had to spread my hands out to stay upright.

Other Guardians fell this time when the temple shook. One landed in the fire and rolled away, patting their arm where their shirt was lit.

"But what if I can bring the other gods? Return the magic? I'll have to come back!" I could no longer see his face in the shadows, but he was watching me.

"Youuu will nnnnot make it through mmmmy doors. It wwwwill cost you yourrrr life."

Why did it seem like the gods didn't want the magic back?

When the dust settled after Ouras spoke, the Guardians surrounding me jumped to their feet, faces stripped of fear and settling on hate.

"If you can't stop her, we will," shouted a Guardian with wings like a butterfly.

Others nodded in agreement, eyeing the gaps in my fire.

But nobody moved to attack because, at that moment, the temple shook with a roar.

The Aspis. It had sensed my magic and was coming for me.

"Looks like we don't have to lift a finger," a Guardian shouted, cowering against the wall.

I was getting really tired of all this. Running, fear, the blame being cast on me. Every place I went, there was conflict. I missed being on the road with the Guards. Somehow, they avoided conflict much better than me.

It was easy to call the fire and set the rest of Ouras's temple ablaze. It was even easier to escape.

What confused me was the god's smile.

As I left, running to keep up with the twins, I thought how, once more, the earth would burn, and only hatred would rise from the ashes.

Liv

The first time I entered Stephen's cottage was to ask for his help to repair my boots. It was his friendly smile that enticed me to go back, and I made up some excuse to see him again. The third time, he knew I ripped the hole in my shirt on purpose to have a reason to visit. When my pants had a sudden tear, he invited me to stay. Walking through that door, leaving the suffocating silence of the forest to the still serenity of his company, was like the heavens opening up for a lost, weary soul. So when I suspected the Keepers were coming for me, I ran to that same door for help, but it was slammed in my face, and the protective bubble burst. I didn't think I would have the heart to trust anyone ever again. That day I cast aside my naivety and built that box in my chest to be a little stronger.

We entered the forest, running as fast as we could toward the airship.

"If that ship has been taken, I swear to the gods I will kill someone," Maev yelled ahead of me.

"We will get there. Don't worry," I panted. I was not made for running.

"They are on our trail." Ollo was a few steps behind Maev. "The fear has abated, and now they're primed for attack. If we can outrun them, we will be fine."

Sweat clung to the twins' black clothes, sticking to their slim builds. My Guardian clothing hugged me, making it much easier to run.

"I don't know how we outrun legacies with wings," Maev said.

"Well, you two have the Ikhor protecting you, don't you?" I gave a harsh, laboured laugh.

"Now is not the time to be funny, Saviour," came Ollo's broken reply.

"Forget about the Guardians. We have to watch out for the big black thing in the sky." The light that shone through the boughs showed no sign of the Aspis, but I knew it was close.

My shoulder burned where it had been severed, and my fingers still refused to close.

"The magic is drawing it in." I swiped the damp hair from my face. "But using it once more may be the key to getting the Guardians off our trail. I don't know what call to make."

Another loud roar filled the forest, and needles fell from the trees, showering us as we bolted down the narrow path.

"You two keep running. Don't stop. Get that airship moving."

"What're you going to do?" Maev turned to look at me, her eyes widening from what she saw, what I was hearing—a crashing and splintering of trees behind us.

The Aspis was plowing through the forest. A great boom cracked the earth each time a tree snapped in two. The crashing was growing closer.

"Stop using the magic," Ollo yelled.

"What do you mean? We have to get out of here!"

"The magic attracts it and, at the same time, eats you alive. It's the reason we are in this mess. Let go of it and run."

"The beast won't stop, Ollo!"

"If it doesn't sense you, it won't be able to follow."

"He's right, Livy. Hide the magic." Maev had not stopped running, and they were getting farther ahead of me.

If I was far enough behind, using the magic wouldn't matter—they would make it to safety.

Build your box. Build your box, I told myself. *If there's one thing you've done well in your life, it's hiding what you really feel.*

Rebeka's lessons all those years would pay off.

Eyes down. Don't react. Blend in. Don't feel.

Either I had to hide the magic or use more, and there was no time to change my mind. It had been easy once before—turn it all off, become nothing inside. I hollowed myself out and stuffed everything into that small box. Using my resolve, I fortified the box.

I wasn't worth much in this world—I was no warrior. But I was a survivor, and if the people of this world thought they could take me down, they could go fuck themselves.

"Okay, Liv. Ground yourself. Control the magic. Control your own thoughts," I said to myself, but it wasn't working. I was too distracted with trying to keep up with the twins, so I slowed, the twins disappearing into the sea of green ahead.

I had to stop the beast, or at least get it off our trail. If using the magic drew it near, stifling it may make the Aspis leave us alone.

"Ground yourself. Let the fear and anger go."

I concentrated on my breathing, repeating the mantra in my

head as the crashing of trees grew louder. "Ground yourself," I said soothingly, and my heart slowed.

An itch on my ankle distracted me. I shook my head, focusing on my breathing, inhaling a fresh breath of air and calming my racing heart. Another itch pulled me from my thoughts, so I looked down and cursed when I found vines crawling up my legs. Roots sprouted from the ground and held me in place.

"No, no, no. Not literally ground yourself!" The vines wrapped around my calves and up to my knees, thickening and rooting me in place. "Stupid magic. Listen to me. I don't want you!" I swatted at my legs, trying to push the growing vines off.

A tree broke ahead of me, and splinters tore the fabric of my shirt as the forest was cast in shadow.

I screamed as the Aspis roared above.

The magic was in control—I had never been close to stuffing it away.

I lifted my hands, my last effort to defend myself, as the Aspis's monstrous form broke through the trees and stopped before me. Cold like I had never felt left me, turning the world blue. Ice exploded all around, more than I had ever made.

The Aspis was frozen from its scaled head past its shoulders, which was no small feat, considering its head was now nearly the size of Ollo's old airship. Steam billowed from its body where heat met cold, and I lowered shaking hands as the steam around the beast evaporated.

Through the ice, I felt it marking me for its next meal.

I shivered, my breath sending plumes of mist. Taking my chance, I conjured more vines, grounding myself, feeling them in the earth, and pulling them to the surface. They crept around the Aspis's body and pulled it to the ground with a loud thud. It shifted uselessly, scraping against the needles on the ground, trapped under the thick layers of ice holding it in place.

"You bit my fucking arm off, you asshole!"

I used to be terrified of the consequences of disobeying the rules of home, like swearing and fighting, but now I was let loose and had *magic*. Fuck the rules.

"I'm done letting everyone push me around. That includes gods and stupid beasts they created." I pulled more roots, loosening the ones tied around my ankles, wrapping as many as I could around the black scales.

There was no kindness, no knowing behind those eyes.

"Damn you." I grunted as I strained to pull more magic. My bracelet glowed vibrantly as I struggled to stay grounded. "Damn you. Damn you. Damn you."

Damn you for not being him.

The strain numbed me—my voice was shaking, my threats growing weaker. I let go of the vines, praying they held the Aspis long enough for the ship to fly away.

I stumbled as the Aspis writhed on the ground, pulling at the vines and fighting against the ice that held its head and upper body. "And fuck the gods for taking *him*. Making it so I can't even kill you. You bastard dragon."

Smoke that hadn't been there before churned around it. Black tendrils snaked through the air, circling its scales. It resembled a Guardian's tattoos—the giant beast with smoke and script. Something about the beast was changing—

Talons sliced through the air, narrowly missing me.

The temperature dropped as I fell against a tree. "Where did that arm come from?" I squeaked.

Long, thin fingers, tipped with sharp-as-knives claws dug into the ground, shredding grass and dirt as the Aspis tried to escape. The smoke swirling around its body vanished, revealing a tail that lashed out with razor-sharp spikes on the tip, aiming for my head.

It missed, smashing into a tree, and pieces of bark flew past me. I put my hands up in defence and, once more, sent a wave of ice over the beast, locking the vines I had put in place.

A dizzy spell hit me as my vision blurred. The magic—I was using too much. But the Aspis was down and slowing. I had to keep trying.

I lifted my hands to conjure more vines, to pin its tail in place, but when I stood, the forest shifted, and I lost my balance. Strong arms caught me before I hit the ground, and I didn't need to look behind me to know it was Ollo holding me up. My head was pressed against his hard chest, while one arm gripped my waist, holding me tight, and the other held my elbow, keeping me from falling sideways.

His jaw scraped against my temple. "Give it a bit more, Saviour. I will keep you up." His voice was low. Confident. Brave when he shouldn't be.

His body became a brace, warming me, holding me high, and I leaned into his strength to gather my own. "Why'd you come back? You can't fight it." My voice was so weak, but I pushed myself to use the magic.

"I'm not fighting. You are. Hurry up and restrain it. I'll ensure you get safely to the ship."

Ollo. My new friend. Maev was wrong about him—he was kind and thoughtful of others.

I conjured more ice, encasing the beast, halting its movements before I stopped. Panting, I took in the dark marbled sculpture twitching beneath my well-made cage.

Then I flipped it off.

Nuo

"We have one of the fastest ships that Guardians have ever laid their hands on," Falizha said. "So why are you telling me we still haven't located the Ikhor? It's going to cross the borders and get into Aethar hands."

She was piloting the airship, and I had the unfortunate job of sitting next to her, mapping the way *north*. What the fuck was going on?

We had been following the Aspis while it ambled through the sky when suddenly it took off. That was an hour ago. We tracked it as far as we could. I could only assume it had reached Ouras's temple. I'd come to that conclusion because of the smoke rising far ahead.

It had clearly fought the Ikhor while the Council tried to convince us the evil shit was setting fires to South Aspis.

Falizha's lip curled, showing her straight row of teeth. She was sending continuous reports to her father, and when the replies came, she unleashed her father's anger on us. But with every reply, the Governor sent crystals, food and spare clothing. And honestly, I couldn't be bothered to locate those things on my own. It gave me more time to think of a clever way to kill her.

"If one of your letters has a better idea, we would be happy to hear it." Bastane sat behind Falizha on a bench against the wall, flipping a knife in his hand and staring daggers at the woman's back.

Bastane had admitted that he was done with the Council. I was reluctantly believing him. Forgiving him? Gods fucking no.

He had questioned Falizha on her crew, and when she admitted abandoning them, he became suspicious. When she pushed the Guards forward those first few weeks, scared the Ikhor would cross the borders, Bas became angry. When Bastane finally caved and snooped through her letters on the ship, he gave up.

"I used to believe my family was honourable," he'd told me. *"My father trusts the Council's decisions. But what I see here, the fact that Guardians are expendable, and they are demanding no one cross the borders, all I can see are lies."*

"What's the problem with crossing the borders?" Kazhi asked.

Bastane told us what he'd read—the Council gave Falizha strict orders not to let us go into Aethar lands. But why?

"We lose the advantage." Falizha looked back at Kazhi as if she were too stupid to understand. Big mistake. "What are you people not understanding? What did your training teach you? The Aethar have large numbers across the borders. Who knows if they've stolen our ships over the years."

"But they wouldn't have the crystals to fly them, right?" Bastane continued to flip his knife, locking eyes with me briefly before landing on Falizha again. "And how was it that the ship we stole from the Aethar is the fastest the Guardians have ever seen? What else might be across those borders?"

"Watch yourself, Armel," Falizha warned. "What the Council demands is all we need to know. Now, we need to find that stupid beast. We wouldn't have been so far behind if you three didn't need *ground time.* What in the Endless Night does that even mean?"

"It means time away from this airship and the noise that comes out of your mouth," I said. "The temple is there. Let's land and ask questions. The Aspis isn't in the skies, and we are flying aimlessly."

"I will ask the questions," Falizha spat. "I don't want you running your mouth and making the rest of the Guardians think you can't keep up with the Aspis. Like you were supposedly trained to do. Gods, if you three didn't have me, you'd be still in the plains with the Aspis long gone."

I spun my seat to face her, and she went still. I gave her one of my charming smiles with an elbow on the front panel while crossing an ankle over my knee, loving how it pissed her off. "We are Guards of the Aspis. Not Guards of the Whiney Little Prude. You're here because we are using you, LP."

"LP?" Kazhi asked, ignoring Falizha's look of rage.

"Little Prude," Bastane clarified. "Nuo's being clever."

Talking about her like she wasn't there gave me a sliver of pleasure. With a bit of charm and a fake smile, I was closer to being in control of the monster raging in my head, demanding I kill her.

Falizha pretended she hadn't heard and landed us in a small clearing.

The scent of cedars hit me as I walked down the rear plank, entering the forest. Smoke enveloped me, and I coughed, waving a hand in my face. "Could have picked a landing spot farther away," I said, pulling my shirt up to my mouth. "But maybe pre-emptive planning is a skill left to more seasoned pilots."

Bastane grabbed my shoulder, pointing to a group of five Mount-leg Guardians running our way.

"The Ikhor!" one of them shouted, halting in front of Bastane. "It was here."

Bastane laid a hand on the hilt of his sword. "Where?"

"Gone now. It was here an hour ago. Challenged Ouras. And then set fires. It took off in the woods, and the Aspis looked like it was chasing it, but—well ..."

"Well, what?" Falizha demanded. "We don't have all day."

The Guardians looked from her back to Bastane, and I hid my smile.

"Let the Guards handle this," I said in her direction. "You can go back to the ship and wait for us to investigate."

Falizha's eyes burned. Ohhhh, I loved it.

"I will follow you. Collect intel," she said through clenched teeth.

"So professional," I said back. Then I asked the Guardian, "What direction?"

"That way. You can't miss it."

"Is it not in the air?" Kazhi moved in the direction the Guardian pointed.

"No, it's been held down. The Ikhor has strange powers. Not like we thought."

"What powers?" Falizha walked faster, trying to get to the head of the group.

I passed under large boughs. The sun peeked through to the needle-covered ground. The broken trees ahead, the work of the Aspis, carved a path through the woods.

The Guardians followed us, and the same one spoke again. "The Ikhor can wield more than fire. We all saw it. The monks can use magic, too."

Falizha stopped dead in her tracks and spun to face the Guardian. "What did you say?"

"I saw it too, Captain Ravin," said a female Guardian. "They had vines coming from their robes."

"That's not possible." Falizha turned a darker shade of red.

"We saw it." The Guardians exchanged a glance, seemingly unsure of how to explain.

She stepped closer. "Do you understand the kind of accusations you are making of the monks? Do you realize you could cause panic by saying such things?"

"We—"

"That's enough," she ordered. "You won't speak of what you saw again."

Bastane and I shared a look and tucked that away for later.

We reached an area where something had broken the trees in half and torn the ground to pieces to find the Aspis with hundreds of thick vines tieing it down. Vines that weren't growing anywhere in the surrounding area.

It was true then. The Ikhor could control all elements.

What in the Endless Night did that mean?

"It hasn't moved in some time." None of the Guardians approached the beast. They stayed far from it. Even Falizha kept a good distance.

Kazhi and Bastane walked next to me as we approached the Aspis, cast into its shadow when we reached its side. Its eyes were closed, and it was breathing deeply.

"It's sleeping?" Bastane whispered.

Yellow eyes snapped open, and Kazhi reached for a knife. Only our years of training kept us all from flinching back.

"Nope," I replied. "It's waiting."

"For what?" Kazhi asked, easing her hand away from her belt.

"Directions? How should I know." I approached the beast, its hot breath hitting my face. "It should be able to get out of these vines, no problem."

The Aspis went back to sleeping.

I dared another step closer. I'd never gotten this close to the beast, not since the night of the transformation. If you didn't count the time it tried to attack me. I passed its massive head, aiming for the vines, when its eye popped open again.

"Hey, just helping." I held my hands up, moving cautiously. A long pupil the size of my arm followed me. "Not the best time for a nap."

I swallowed my disgust. I was being nice to it when I wanted to yell, *Get the fuck up! Kill the Ikhor, so I never have to see you again.*

I reached the first vine and pulled. It wouldn't budge, not even a fraction. It was like a metal bar, stiff and unyielding. "Okay, maybe you can't get out on your own."

A low rumbling from the beast told me to keep my mouth shut. Did it understand me?

Bastane was at my side moments later, helping me chop at the vines.

Falizha inched forward but, of course, didn't offer to help. She sighed as her haughty stare trailed the beast. "God, he's even useless as the Aspis."

I shot toward her so fast I didn't know I'd moved. Bastane had his arm around my waist just as my blade was inches from Falizha's heart.

Damn Bastane.

Falizha backed away, sputtering, nearly tripping on her purple cape.

The Aspis thrashed, spurred into action, a rumbling coming from its throat.

I shook with anger—fuck my control. Let her see what lay underneath, why I was chosen as a Guard. I was the Interrogator for a reason.

"Not yet," Bastane whispered, for only me to hear. "There are others watching."

"You three better remember who I am." Falizha kept her voice low. "Word gets to my father I have been harmed—it will be your lives." Her voice shook.

Coward. Gods, I wish I could send her to Mayra's black depths.

No. She deserved so much worse.

"And who will they send to take out the Guards?" I spat. "Who could your father find to end us?"

The Aspis growled behind me.

"Last time the Council tried to take out a Guard, it didn't go so well," Kazhi reminded her.

Kazhi, hired by someone high up in the Council, had failed because Brekt saw her coming, but Falizha didn't know that.

I finally felt like I was part of a team again. Having my family on my side was a small blessing in this huge fucked up world.

"Just remember how this mission is funded. If you three are

going through the canyons, I am not going with you. The Council has ordered me back. If you don't stop the Ikhor before it crosses the borders, you are done with your supplies. You are on your own. And you'll be dead."

"Interesting." Bastane lifted a brow.

We had already talked about this several times. The canyon was the next stop, and after that, Falizha was going home. We might finally get some answers as to why we had to stop the Ikhor before then. It was a tricky game following the Aspis and taking down Aethar while spying on our leaders.

"How I hope the Ikhor reaches the Aethar wastelands, and we will be rid of you," I said, making Falizha grit her teeth and stomp back through the woods toward the airship.

"I'm this fucking close." I jabbed my knife to where Falizha last stood, tugging myself free of Bastane's grip.

The other Guardians turned their heads away, pretending not to see me. They filtered out of the clearing, disappearing back into the woods.

"Get in line," Kazhi said. "There will be a fight to decide who kills her once it's time."

Bastane sat on a rock several feet from the Aspis, putting his hands on his knees. "So the Ikhor went to see Ouras. It's visiting temples."

"So why is the Council telling us the Ikhor is south?" Kazhi's face contorted into rage.

Bastane rubbed a calloused hand against his chin. "I think she's playing games with me now, too. She says one thing to me, then another in front of you. I think she's trying to discover if I am telling you two everything or if I'm still a pawn of the Councils."

"Either way, we can't believe everything," I said. "We know it's true the Ikhor has visited Ouras. They're getting sloppy with their lies. Do you think it's planning to bypass the Aspis to kill the gods?"

"The Ikhor did leave it here. If it killed the Aspis, then we would enter an era of suffering. Maybe it needs something before that happens. Let's consider that maybe the Ikhor will try to steal more power," Bastane mused. "The forests around the temple are burning, so my guess is it failed with Ouras and it's going to try Rem next."

"Fuck that." I returned to the vines, hacking at them.

That's when the beast woke and growled, fighting against the vines.

I jumped back as the vines snapped.

The Aspis twisted its head and faced us—its Guards—pupils narrowing into fine slits. Hot breath fanned my face, blowing my long hair back. It opened its mouth and roared, shaking the surrounding forest, and I clapped my hands over my ears, wincing at the sound.

The Aspis shot in the air, vines and needles spraying the forest floor.

I covered my head as debris landed over me.

Its tail end disappeared behind the tree line as it vanished from sight, and we wasted no time running back to the airship.

"We need to make sure we don't lose it this time," Kazhi yelled from behind me.

"Hopefully, our useless captain has the ship ready to go." I huffed, out of shape.

I would make sure I didn't stay that way. My little run in with the Ikhor in Danuli was a wake-up call. I'd been training every day since.

We reached the airship, entering it up the metallic plank to where Falizha was waiting. She took a step back as I stopped to face her.

"If you say one more thing about Brekt—if you mention his name—I will carve you up like an Aethar."

Falizha turned pale before her face reddened with anger.

I headed toward the front. "You know, when your face blushes like that, you look like an orange fruit. Not a great colour, Falizha." I sat near the front window, looking out toward the distance, ignoring her stomping around behind me.

We got into the air in time to catch the Aspis ambling through the sky with no direction in mind.

The smoke from South Aspis turned the far horizon a strange colour. It would have to be miles high to see it from here. Our intel had told us the structures were burnt down, and any survivors had fled the camp. The Council said it was the Ikhor. But the Ikhor had been at Ouras's temple.

I was terrified of the small voice in my head that questioned if the Ikhor had caused *any* of the damage.

CHAPTER
THIRTY-ONE

Liv

Rebeka's wedding day was a turning point in my adulthood. It was a small ceremony in town with her new husband's family. She asked me not to attend, then demanded that if I didn't listen —because I never did—that I didn't talk to her or her new family. She knew I couldn't hide how I really felt in front of others. The Keepers were in attendance to watch the crowd who gathered to see the sad display of false affection. When her husband leaned in to kiss her, her spine went stiffer than it usually was. She didn't love him. She was playing along because it was safe. I had to bite my tongue from yelling out when he touched her. But her fake smile told me that was how she wanted it.

She didn't speak to me the entire day. Her husband looked my way a single time, lip curling as if I was a stain on Rebeka's makeshift dress, given to her by his mother. They walked right past me to their home, the one I had been kicked out of. She had never even asked if I found a place to live. I ran into the woods after, found a stick and beat it against a tree until my palms bled. Then I screamed to the stars, promising I would never marry. I would never let a man touch me that I didn't love. That had been before the true loneliness set in.

It took me several long minutes to stretch my body enough to sit up. The magic drained me, taking a heavy toll on my body and giving me more reason to stifle it.

Ollo had saved me, and I was running out of fingers to count how many times the twins had put themselves in harm's way with no way to defend themselves. They had their own motives to get me to their lands, but I had a suspicion those reasons weren't why they put their necks on the line.

I think they were just good people.

Which destroyed my last wall of defence against becoming friends with the Guardians' enemy.

Ollo had half dragged me to the spare cabins of the airship, and I slept until the next evening. Thankfully, my sleep had been dreamless.

The twins had taken over the front of the bridge. Maev had found every useful tool on the ship and set them near the front windows. The middle table had maps and books piled twice as high as before with reading materials on the Guardians' missions, which Ollo studied to report back home. They had brought clothing and food there for convenience, and when I asked why they moved everything, Maev had said, "*I don't like walking the halls. I don't like being in their rooms. The Guardians are terrifying to us, so I am using as few rooms as possible.*" That night, we stripped three beds, dragged the mattresses to the bridge and made camp.

When I tried to sleep, I woke to dreams of *him*. Not the half-beast, but him. Perhaps he had always been in my dreams, and the fog had shielded me from it, only allowing me to see the terrifying place. Perhaps that was why I saw shadows when there weren't any, even when awake.

Over the next two weeks, one of them would shake me awake before I started screaming. Someone was always awake, on the lookout for an airship ferrying the Guards.

During the daytime, we got to know each other, talking about our past—many times this led to the twins bickering. Ollo grew bolder, not glancing away when I caught him looking at me over a book or tracking me across a room. Maev ignored it and stayed at my side. She would do my hair in the morning to match hers, and we would talk about all the things she would show me in Rydavas.

I would sit by the front window, watching the river lands pass below, slowly turning to grasslands and then to rock and sand. And I practiced my swords—never letting them touch. I was glad I finally knew what they could do once powered with crystals, but I wouldn't take the kind of power they released for granted. They were dangerous weapons.

One night, while dreaming of the caves below the Guardian city and a large black cave lizard, Maev hadn't been quick enough to wake me. My flames had woken her, creeping over to her mattress beside me. I was losing the battle against the Ikhor. It had a voice now, controlling, demanding the magic be used. By suppressing it, I had only made it worse. Maev and Ollo started sleeping on the opposite side of the room after that. The books we were combing through stayed with them.

One sleepless night, I clutched my small photo of the Guards close. I searched the photo for his character—the teasing humour, the serious moments when he remembered his path in life. The darkness under his skin. His unwavering love for his family. But the photo showed me only a still image. I just saw those things because I knew him.

Had been falling in love with him.

It occurred to me I had known him for less time than I had been running as the Ikhor. He'd been dead for longer than he was in my life. Wiping away tears, I got up and walked to the control panel where Ollo sat reading. I decided it might be best that I didn't bother sleeping tonight.

It surprised me how unfazed I was at being alone with Ollo. When I first met the Guards, I was terrified to be alone in a room with a man. So many unwanted layers of myself had shed off, and I didn't miss them. But these past weeks with him taught me that Ollo was respectable and caring. I was curious to meet his father and see the kind of man that raised him. I had never known a father figure and had nothing to compare a good one to.

Ollo leaned back in a chair, resting his legs on a second chair in front of him, feet crossed at the ankles. He held a book in his lap, his hair pulled back behind his head. The moon cast a dreamlike glow over his pale blue skin. He fit in the night as well as he did the day.

"You look like a Guardian." I stopped at the pile of books at his side.

"Please don't say that." He looked up at me through his lashes. "That's hardly a compliment."

My chest tightened. His ethereal beauty was captivating, and his calm demeanour was welcoming. He could have been mean or had some major flaw, and the fact that he didn't was irritating. It meant my imagination was free to roam. Though any time it did, *his* face swam in my thoughts.

"Can I see?" He held out his hand for the photo I gripped at my side.

I passed it to him, curious about what he would say. He surprised me by laughing. "What's so funny?"

"What's funny is the differences in what we see. Your fingerprints cover this photo completely, and the edges are frayed from how often you hold it."

"And that's funny?"

"What's funny is when I study this, I see my enemy—people I have hated and feared my whole life. I see killers, murderers and symbols of the Council. What's funny is the perspective."

"Perspective?"

"Yes. Humanity is an interesting thing when you consider perspective. One single photo can make *you* weep while it makes *me* scared."

"They scare you? Even now, Nuo, Kazhi and Bas scare you?"

"Yes. When we saw them in Danuli, I don't think I have ever been more afraid." He pulled out a chair and patted it. I sat next to him, and he held the photo so I could look at it, too. "I have flown ships high into the sky at speeds others have never experienced. That's when I learned about perspective. We are so small and insignificant compared to the vastness of Arde, but from above, you can see what we do to level the earth below. I gained a new understanding of perspective in Danuli when I saw the Guards. I realized that I would rather soar high in the clouds, risking falling from the sky, than face one man in black clothing. I've been called a risk-taker by many. But I would not risk standing in their path."

Ollo eyed the photo, memorizing their faces. "And yet they loved you, and I am growing to like you too, so how many degrees of separation does it take for the hate to disappear? Because for myself, even one degree doesn't do it."

"You still hate them, even after all I've told of them."

He gave me a hard look, a sad look. "Yes. I do. And I'm sorry if that hurts your memory of him. But too often were crimes committed in my home that were done by the Guardians. Maybe not the Guards you know, but can you say if they landed on our shores, they wouldn't have killed my people?"

I considered the answer. "No, I can't. But they would have stopped to notice your people weren't like the scarred ones. They stopped to give me a chance when they thought I was a stranger in their lands."

"Or was that because the Shadow Guard saw something he wanted?"

My back stiffened, immediately defensive. "I don't know. But I knew they had love and honour. Maybe they would've hesitated."

Ollo held up his hands. "I don't mean to offend. I'm only telling you what I think. I don't blame the man for wanting you, Saviour. Any man would. And I would much rather you didn't give me that look."

"What look?"

"The Ikhor look. You're all emotion right now. And I have been on the icy end of your emotions before."

I sunk into my chair. "I wish I could be like you."

Ollo tilted his head. "What do you mean?"

"You are exactly what I want to be like—brave, talented, smart and kind. You say what you want. You do what you want. And you're in control of yourself."

"Why do you not see yourself that way?"

"I don't know. I think I'm too angry inside. I could have been like you, but my old home ... they took some of the good parts away." I stared at my photo in his hands.

"I met him once, you know," Ollo said.

"Brekt?" A sharp pain stole my breath, having said his name aloud. I hadn't spoken it in so long. It was almost foreign on my tongue.

"In Bellum. During the big attack, we came head-to-head. I was quite terrified in that moment."

It was hard to imagine Ollo being scared. He sat tall beside me, his posture strong.

"What happened?"

"Nothing. He looked me over, decided I wasn't his enemy, and we both moved on. I didn't know what to think of it then. I still don't."

"He was good, Ollo."

"So you say. Was he kind to you?" Ollo was staring at the photo, not meeting my eye.

"He was thoughtful, not always kind, but respectful and wanted to make things better for me. He had a playful side, too. Liked to play games and tease—"

"I get the picture." Ollo elbowed my arm, making me shift in my seat. "No need for rhapsodizing." He put a hand behind his head and dropped the photo in his lap. "I don't see it, but if you say so. Hard to picture this guy being playful."

"It's funny—you're very open and good-hearted, yet he was the more sentimental one. He didn't mind me ... rapo-da-zing."

Ollo laughed, smooth like honey. The way my heart sped was like a knife in my gut—like a betrayal to the photo he held.

"Well, we men come in all shapes and sizes." Ollo winked to drive home his meaning. "Some are teasing, and some are to the point, world-class flyers like me." He held my gaze, turning serious, his smile fading. "I am sorry. For what happened—for losing him. I can see it's not easy."

"Now, who's rapodizing?" I teased.

He returned my picture, and I stuffed it away in my pocket.

"When this is all over, I will personally give you a lesson in vocabulary," he said. "Luckily, you can distract others from your lack of knowledge with a good fireball to the face. Or some of your other more appealing qualities."

I studied him. Was he planning on me being around after the magic was returned? It was ... sweet.

"You're not going to prove to Maev that you've controlled your ego. Not if you're offering lessons in how to talk as good as you."

His face fell. "Do you think I am arrogant, too?"

He waited for my answer as if it meant something to him—not what I expected from my teasing.

"No. Actually, far from it."

He nodded slowly.

"Why? You seem bothered."

He made a face. "I've had more than one woman calling me

arrogant. The last one that did so hasn't spoken a word to me since. I suppose I can admit Maev has a point, and I had let my accomplishments get to my head."

"Was she someone important to you?"

"Unfortunately." Ollo pretended to be distracted by his book again and fidgeted with it in his lap.

"What're you reading?" I asked.

This wasn't the first time he had mentioned a woman. It sounded like an old wound that he didn't want to be reopened.

"A journal of all things, written in the language of Day."

"Can I see?"

He passed me the book, and I was stricken once more by the scribbling. Even though I couldn't read it, the script looked arrogant, like the woman herself. There was no question in my mind that this belonged to Falizha.

"This writing, I've seen it before," I said.

"It's not common to see the language of Day, but it's easily found in old texts."

"No, I mean, I've seen Nuo with a paper written like this. It wasn't this person's writing, but the words were formed the same."

Had Nuo copied something he'd seen in this book? I flipped the pages, looking for something that would stand out. I found a page with underlines and a star next to an entry.

"What does this say?" I returned the book to Ollo, who read it slowly, taking time to translate.

"He has told my father to be warned of the new Guards chosen. They will work against our plan. Father and I are working on ways to remove the Guards from their position. But hidden members of the Council have beaten us to it. When I brought this up, he was angry with father. All the while, Aeden has not returned from the island, and I have not been told what he's doing there."

"Well, that tells me nothing." I slumped in a seat next to Ollo, letting the moonlight pour over my tight Guardian clothing. I made a fist, and like before, two fingers refused to close as my bracelet glowed in front of me, the magic never fading from it.

"I think this tells us that the Council is being run by someone behind the scenes. Not by the Governor."

Ollo read the following entries before he said, "Nothing here suggests who it might be, but I get the impression the Councilman's daughter was afraid of them. She mentions Rem visiting the City and being displeased with the Council. But why would our god care about the politics of the Guardian city?"

Ollo put down the book, searching my face for an answer I didn't know. I wasn't a fan of the gods or the Council. "Rem met with the Council while I was there. Everyone seemed terrified and surprised by his presence." I didn't care why they were involved in each other's business. Not unless it interfered with them taking the magic back.

"Why did you help me go to Ouras when your mission was to bring me to your home? To your army." I hadn't asked before now, but it had been bothering me since he'd saved me in the forest.

Ollo's jaw clenched. "I'll admit, I thought of forcing you to come with me at first. But knowing it was impossible and coming up with no other ideas, I agreed out of necessity."

"Oh."

"It was after the carnage on the deck of the ship that I realized I should be helping you. You were scared and hurt and had no one but us for help in all this. It's become … I can't help seeing the woman behind the magic. I know I can't force your help to fight in our war, Liv. I won't."

I shifted in my seat. "Why?"

"Why indeed." His attention snagged on my wrist, where I was fiddling with my bracelet. "Why do you wear crystals with magic? They're rare, you know."

"They weren't filled with magic when they were given to me. My earrings, too. Something happened to them."

I stopped breathing. Why did I say that? I just didn't want him to think I wasted precious crystals and flaunted them.

When I peeked over at him, Ollo's eyes went wide—darting from my wrist to my ears before his mouth popped open.

"What?" I covered my wrist, wondering if I had done something, when a smile broke out on his face.

Shit.

He had figured it out.

HE TORE his feet off the chair before him and set them down as he faced me. "There's a tale of how the magic crystals were formed, how the earth couldn't hold all the magic, so it stored it in the crystals. Seeing how the earth did this, the gods tried it as well, to ease the strain of bearing so much power, and drained the magic into the crystals. But when the Ikhor took their magic, that all stopped, and the legacies' power supply dwindled."

"Let me guess, as part of their punishment?"

He nodded. "Think about it. You have magic you can't control. Perhaps subconsciously, you have been easing yourself of the strain by putting it into the crystals."

I realized why the Oracle might have given the bracelet to me. "She knew. She knew it would help me."

"Who?"

"No one. Ollo, what will you do with this information?"

He went still. "What do you mean? This is good news. This was the answer Maev was looking for. And it means we can remove some of the strain of magic on you."

"You mean, you're happy for my sake and not for what benefits you?"

"Well, yes," he said carefully. Then, his face smoothed out. "Because you thought I would find a way to use you. Come on, Saviour. Have you gotten to know us at all?"

Apparently not well enough. Why was I still expecting betrayal?

"We should find more empty crystals. Test your theory out." I glanced away.

I had thought they would use the information against me. After all this time away from home, I still expected the worst in people.

"Come on, look at me. I do see the benefit this could have. I won't lie. But my first thought was not selfish. Maev will be happy it helps you, too." I nodded, making him grin. "How long have you been holding this information in?" he asked.

I scrunched my face, embarrassed. "Since before the Aspis bit my arm off."

He let out a long breath. "Nothing ever gets accomplished if you don't tell the truth and ask for help."

Didn't I know that—the Guards kept so many secrets and look what happened to them.

Ollo grabbed my shoulders, leaning closer. "Do you realize what this information could lead to? Our people would have a chance at a future. Our armies could have powerful weapons to protect us from the Guardians. And you could ease the strain on your body, giving you time to find the gods."

I pulled back, and Ollo grabbed my chin. I went to swat his hand away, but his expression stopped me, his navy eyes scanning mine. "Liv?"

"What?" I tried to pull away, but he held me tight, so close I could feel the warmth of his breath.

"Are you feeling okay? Something is off about you."

He leaned in closer, and I shivered from the proximity. I inhaled a pleasantly male scent that was smooth and inviting.

"Your eyes," he said. "Are no longer grey."

I swatted his hand away this time, startled that he knew the colour of my eyes. "What? What colour are they?" I stood, making him look up from his chair, and his forehead creased as he scanned me over, searching for more signs of change.

"They're pink. It's as if they're being stained somehow. And your hair—it's lighter. You've been growing skinni—Liv!"

I ran from the room to a cabin where there was a mirror. In moments, I was standing before myself, but it wasn't me. I was a shadow, a warped reflection—I was looking closer to the image painted on the wall of the temple—*the Ikhor.*

Red rims around my irises bled into the grey. My skin was so pale it seemed to shimmer in the light, and my hair looked like the logs on the cliffs at the edge of the endless forest—bleached from the sun.

I spun to the doorway where Ollo stood, the corner of his mouth pulled down. "Do you really believe the Aethar's legends of the Ikhor? That it's not evil? Look at me. Look at the things I've done. I'm starting to believe the Guardians were right."

"What things have you done?"

"You've seen it. I've flooded people from their homes. I've burned a god's temple and possibly the people within it."

Ollo stepped into the room, crossing his arms, back against the wall. "And is it evil to defend oneself? Or to feel pain? I don't see your intentions as evil, Saviour. I see a woman who is trying her best."

"I have done everything for selfish reasons," I argued.

"That still doesn't define evil. Being selfish isn't bad. Sometimes it's very healthy. Greed and intentional harm are bad. I don't see you doing either of those things."

I huffed the hair out of my face and looked back at the pink eyes, the sunken cheeks. "I look terrifying. Like a monster."

"I disagree. There's a beautiful woman standing before me."

I glared at him, but he didn't cower when the Ikhor stared him down, and it calmed my rising panic as his words sunk in.

"There's a beautiful woman standing before me."

Could Ollo really find me beautiful? Surely not when he must get the attention of any woman around him.

"Here." Ollo held out a piece of dried fruit, stepping closer.

"What's this for?" I took it, wondering why he was passing me food at a time like this.

"A snack."

"Why a snack?"

"Oh, I don't actually know the why of it. I bring Maev snacks when she's upset. It almost always turns her mood for the better. I had that one in my pocket." He pointed at the dried fruit. "Situation control is what I call it."

Despite my anger and concern, a small laugh escaped me. "Situation control." I took a bite. It was delicious. "I suppose you're right. I am distracted."

A strange smile played on his lips. "See? Women are absurd, but a manageable relationship is possible if you meet them on their level."

I threw the fruit at his head, and he caught it, taking a bite. "Guess not all of you are the same."

He gave me a half-cocked smile, and the butterflies tossing around in my stomach caught me off guard. Ollo was clearly unfazed by female anger, and I was grateful.

There was another look on his face before he wiped it away. "What's that look of worry?" I asked.

"Nothing, Saviour. Ignore me and my musings."

"What does that mean? Please tell me."

He hesitated as if considering how I would react. "I worry about the tales of the Ikhor. The ones that say the host never returns. I worry about how this ends for you."

"I see. I worry about that, too."

"I—I don't wish to see you succumb to that fate."

"I am going to stop this. And I am a selfish person. I will make sure I live."

The corner of his mouth lifted half-heartedly. "Please, do. In the meantime, I would be happy to take up your time. We will not talk of 'could-be' unless you wish it."

"Is this your way of offering a shoulder to cry on?" I gave him a shy smile, the best I could muster up. Next to this man, I didn't feel as confident as I did with *him,* but I was certainly at ease. Ollo was like a warm blanket.

"A shoulder? How boring, Saviour." Ollo pouted. "I'd offer you a bit more than my shoulder."

His quick change of subject shocked me, leaving me rooted to the spot. "Are you flirting with me?" It wasn't the first time it had happened or the first time I had asked him that.

Ollo laughed, his entire face lighting, kind and teasing. "I'm not in love with you, Saviour. I'm only having fun."

Bold. Risk-taker.

My heart pounded loud enough that I was sure he could hear. "I don't know how to flirt for fun."

"Sure you do." Ollo winked, sending a strange thrill through me. "You banter, tease, push buttons and then back off. Don't worry. I know your heart is in the sky with the beast. I only meant to be playful. Flirting can be healthy." Ollo fidgeted.

Suddenly, my body was alive, wishing for more. I wanted him to flirt with me. Should that make me feel shame? Because it did.

I was at war with myself—Liv versus the Ikhor, loss versus desire. I craved touch, love and acceptance. If I asked, Ollo might even offer those things.

His arms fell to his sides, his face falling. "Maev is going to have my head when she finds out I was being cocky again."

And wasn't that how Nuo treated me? How did I tell him I enjoyed his company offering nothing more in return? "You're more scared of Maev than the Ikhor? I could burn you where you stand."

He leaned closer, face shifting into a clever grin. "I love the risk, Saviour."

"I've noticed. You're quite the thrill seeker."

"And what a thrill it is that the Ikhor isn't a hulking warrior but a lovely, curious woman with a perspective on life from which we could all learn something."

"You see me that way?"

"I may live up in the clouds sometimes. But I tend to come down occasionally and study the little people." He patted the top of my head before turning to leave. "And this little person is quickly becoming a favourite friend of mine."

CHAPTER
THIRTY-TWO

Liv

The streets of Bellum while under attack had been loud. The roaring fires of the burning field had been loud. But the years I spent alone in the Endless Forest, day after day, with the song of birds and trees ... that kind of silence was deafening. My heart still bleeds from the impact of that solitude. I never want to be alone another minute of my life.

Ollo had done his best to distract me from my eyes changing colour, but soon after he left, the fear crept back in. I was changing. The fog in my head, the dreams, the swirling shadows and now my eyes ... they all had to be connected.

I opened the door to the deck of the ship, needing the fresh night air. A storm met me, and I didn't question the flashes of light in the sky or the ferocity of the wind—the tempest inside me whirled and mirrored the storm ripping apart the night sky. I pushed toward the front of the deck as the ends of the ropes holding down the many crates left by the Guardians snapped in the breeze.

I stared upward, wondering why in The Endless Night I was looking like that painting after weeks of the magic waking inside me.

The magical barrier glowed as it protected the deck from the onslaught of the static-charged wind. The Guardian clothing I wore clung too tight, offering little warmth.

I closed my eyes. Lost. Broken. Even my mind continuously betrayed me.

"You're not lost," I said in a low but determined voice, clenching my fists. I had a new focus—find the gods. Get rid of the magic. Not die. "You can do this," I lied to myself.

When I opened my eyes, I cried out in alarm.

In the distance, on a fast wind, a shadow travelled through dark clouds. Lightning lit up the sky, dancing off the scales of the Aspis as it flew directly for me.

I had used magic without thinking, and there was nowhere to run.

The Aspis cut through the air, travelling faster than I had ever seen. It closed in on the airship, carrying the storm with it. A sea of smoke and shadows followed its trail.

Lightning lit up the ground below, and the Aspis cast shadows over the deck. Its roar woke me from my frozen state of fear, and I ran, slipping on the deck as I bolted for the door.

The magical barrier hadn't kept the Aspis out before, and at that speed, I wasn't sure it would now. I had to warn Ollo to get moving and outmaneuver the beast.

The metal walls of the airship were the only protection I would have.

If I just reached that door.

The wind picked up, knocking me off course, and slammed the door closed. My muscles seized as another roar shook the sky. I yanked at the door, and with the wind and the fact only seven and a half of my fingers were working, I couldn't get the damned thing open. I was running out of time as the pure black figure in the sky closed in.

Lightning struck, highlighting my death and casting my shadow against the metal. I wrenched the door again, and it opened a fraction of an inch before slamming shut. My hair whipped around, blocking my sight as I yanked and yanked and yanked, but it didn't budge.

I did the only thing I could think of—I raced to the higher landing of the deck to the same platform where Nuo and I had hidden, drinking and laughing. Crates, stacked high, swayed in motion with the wind. The ropes tying them down danced in the storm, nearly whacking me in the face when I ducked behind them. Piles of crates surrounded me on all sides, creating a little room of sorts. I moved away from the gap I had come through, hitting another crate and collapsing to the deck. I pushed my back against a wooden surface and hugged my knees to my chest.

There was a pathetic barrier between me and the outside, and I prayed it would suffice as I waited, hearing no bang, no crack, no sound of any kind. Had the Aspis stopped? Or had it simply broken through the barrier silently?

Was this one of those nightmares? I looked up—just a starry sky. Nothing out of the ordinary, no black crystalline night. This was real.

Flashes of light lit up the deck, filtering between two large crates, and I kept my eyes on that crack. Waiting. I shook as if the ground beneath me was moving.

I screamed when a thunderous crash echoed throughout the sky. The wind whistled, widening the gap in the crates, testing their restraints. I couldn't breathe, the fear suffocating me. Mist crowded the small hideout.

I'm not using my magic! I can't control it.

But the beast didn't attack ...

There were more flashes of lightning. My back ached, muscles wound tight. Would I have to attack the beast again?

What was I doing—I was the Ikhor! I had my own power. Through my fear, I had forgotten that I wasn't *weak*. I was as dangerous as the monster outside, and I no longer had to worry about calling it to my location.

I pulled myself up, using a crate to stand as my knees threatened to give out. My body didn't agree with my mind's resolve. I checked that my swords were belted to my hip and nodded to myself.

Be brave. I stepped toward the gap in the crates to peer through.

A shadow moved between the crack, gone in a flash. I covered my mouth and swallowed my scream. It was too small to be the Aspis.

I grabbed the crate, remembering the nightmares I had experienced while awake—shadows in the rain, by the river, on the deck.

The thing moved again—this time, slow enough for me to catch sight of it.

It wasn't the swirling blackness I had seen on the deck.

"No ..."

A tall figure prowled the deck, their tattered clothes a mess in the wind.

The half-beast, the one that used to be *him*. But I wasn't dreaming!

Yet, it moved the same—but where was the Aspis? Had the half-beast scared it away?

The crates flew apart, pushed by two massive, tattooed arms. A scream tore from my chest as the creature stood tall in the opening.

The wind blew in from the storm, sending me stumbling back.

It was more defined than before, taking on the look of a man standing there in dark clothing.

It was here to kill me. I could feel it.

The powerful wind whipped the ropes around, and the beast's clothes did the same, dancing on the breeze and slapping against a body packed with muscle.

Wait.

There was no tattered cloak, no horns, no glowing citrine eyes.

Wisps of shadows curled around its body, but its chest and arms were solid. There was … tanned skin. Was it changing? Growing in power?

I backed away, raising a hand to use whatever magic would be called forth, stupidly waiting for it to attack. My movements must have triggered its awareness, and its head snapped toward me. I waited to hear its rumbling, the humming, the roar of anger. But when its attention landed on me, a flash of iridescence told me it was more than just a shadow.

A man stood at the entrance to my sanctuary.

A flash of iridescence.

Black clothing.

Muscled arms.

"No." I took another step back.

I couldn't breathe as the man dropped his arms and took a menacing step forward.

"This isn't real." I tripped over my feet, using a broken crate to hold myself up. Splinters tore at my fingertips.

The man didn't speak. Long, dark hair fell past his shoulders, his clothing loose around his chest. There was a hole ripped in right where *he* had been stabbed before transforming into the beast.

I couldn't gather myself to speak, my legs shaking. I didn't blink.

Lightning flashed again, throwing the figure into darkness as he took another step.

A feral, predatory step. Shit.

I screamed, backing away as he swallowed up the distance between us. He reached for me, and his fingers traced a line across my skin as I climbed over the crates to escape. The crates cracked under my weight, collapsing. I fell, spinning around and pressing my back into a solid piece of wood.

He was near invisible in the darkness.

Lightning flashed again, and I caught his hands going to a long plank of wood—the one I was standing on.

He yanked the piece out from under me, and I cursed as my head hit a loose board on the ground, stunning me long enough to give him the upper hand. He grabbed my ankles, pulling me across the debris toward him.

I yelped as more splinters tore through my cloak, and as soon as he let go, I kicked him square in the chest, throwing him off balance.

With a grunt and a thud, he hit the deck.

"Shit. Shit. Shit." I turned onto my stomach and crawled over the debris, putting a solid pile of scraps between us.

What was happening? This was all so wrong. I must have mistaken what I saw. It couldn't be *him*.

He was dead.

I scrambled to my feet, spinning back to search the other side. The space was empty. I stood on tiptoes to see over the pile. The deck was clear.

Darkness moved out of the corner of my eye, and I threw myself backward, narrowly avoiding his attempt to grab me again. I got tangled in a flyaway rope, falling to the ground. I fumbled with the rope, loosening its hold on my leg.

My swords ... were tied up at my hip. I threw the rope to the side and crawled behind a small pile of boxes.

Moments later, they were airborne, crashing against the railing, exposing me, and I took off running.

A growl behind me told me my attacker was close behind. I jumped down the small flight of stairs to the lower part of the deck, where there were even fewer places to hide.

I needed to get to the door.

I kicked out when an arm banded around my waist and lifted me off the ground, pulling me against a hard chest.

The magic flared to life, and the temperature dropped. Mist surrounded the ship, blocking out the dark sky beyond.

I flailed against his arm, and the man growled. The sound vibrated through my chest. "Stop. Using. The magic."

It was *his* deep timbre.

My body went limp.

My blood ran cold from shock.

No, Liv. Fight. This is a trick.

I thrashed harder this time, and the arm around my waist tightened, making it difficult to breathe. It was a lie! He would never harm me. He would've stopped by now, given me a chance to talk.

"Let me go!" I twisted, forcing his grip loose and pushed away from him, crashing into the wall outside the door and landing hard on the deck. A sharp cry left me, the air forced from my lungs.

The attacker didn't stop. Another crate went flying across the deck, and he stood over me, chest heaving.

I looked up, hoping to find some recognition, but the deck was too dark, too misty.

"Please, don't hurt me," I choked.

The man paused.

I took that chance to move, grateful my mother's lessons hadn't gone to waste. Years of her training to fight, to defend myself, kicking in. I rolled to the side, finding my feet fast enough that he couldn't grab me and ran away across the deck. Not the most brilliant move, since the wind was strong enough that I couldn't open that door.

I made the mistake of forgetting the ropes that were flying wild from the wind. One snapped on the breeze, smacking me in the face, and I bent over, moaning, dazed, as blood pooled and dripped from my nose.

When the attacker reached me, he pinned me to the railing, spinning me so my back was to the open air. His thighs trapped me between them, holding me against the cold metal. A hand wrapped around my neck, pushing my back at a terrifying angle over the ledge.

I remembered with sharp clarity how Ollo said the magic barrier didn't keep things from falling overboard, and I grabbed onto his wrist—a solid, warm and very real wrist—as I stared into a misty black sky, growing clearer as the wind blew the cold air away from the deck.

He was choking me.

No, no, no! It's not *him*. He wouldn't harm me.

Lightning flashed again, revealing iridescent eyes roaming over my face and a strong jaw covered in dark stubble. A scar ran from his temple to his jaw—the one I wanted to trace with my fingers so many times.

It was when his pine and leather scent hit me that I believed.

He's alive.

CHAPTER
THIRTY-THREE

Liv

My heart warred against my mind. I wanted the man overtop of me to be *him*, even if it was the last thing I saw. If his appearance wasn't enough to alert me that it was not a hallucination, it was the cords in my chest pulling tight—to *him*.

His smell enveloped me as he leaned in, pressing his hand farther into my airway.

I forgot I couldn't breathe. He blurred as tears streamed down my face, and I wasn't sure it was the air being cut off or the relief that caused them. He was so close now I could see him, even in the darkness, but what I saw was sculpted with hate—his expression promised death.

Fear pierced me like a knife, and the temperature plummeted.

His lips parted as the hand around my throat shook. "I curse the magic for choosing her." His voice was smokey, cracking with pain.

Who? Me?

My mind spun, but at the sound of his voice, I lost it. My heart shattered, hearing the sound I had longed for—that I had not even dared hope to hear again. Nothing had ever sounded sweeter.

I held his dark stare, never wanting to look away.

He was alive.

He shook his head as if fighting off a bad thought, and when his attention flew back to me, I caught a faint glow. Citrine eyes flashed. He growled, guttural and full of pain, revealing sharp fangs protruding from his top row of teeth. "I'll rip your head off before you can use the magic. So. Cut. It. Off."

What did that mean?

I swatted at his hand as the world spun, and his eyes widened before he released my neck. He held me in place with a hand banded around each of my arms.

I blinked away the tears, my head lolling to the side, and I gasped down at the long fall below. "Don't drop me!" I thrashed in his hold, grabbing a piece of his torn shirt and looking up at him, unbelieving. "Is this real?"

His skin swirled with shadows, nearly disappearing before me. Brekt growled over fangs, distorting his words. "Oh, it's very fucking real. And if you don't give her back, I will kill you now."

What? Her?

"Don't give me that look. You can go willingly, or I can kill you both and free her from this hell."

He thought I was possessed.

"I—"

"Stay silent, Ikhor. I see what you stole from me. I know what I must do."

Brekt was going to kill me. My death would not come from the Aspis. Not the Aethar. Not the gods ...

"Brekt." It came out as a whisper—half question, half plea.

Please let this be real. Please don't be a dream.

He went still, focusing on my mouth. "Interesting." A warm shiver travelled through me at the deep tone of his voice. "She's given you her memories."

I struggled against his grip. Wiggling my way from between his knees. If I could just get …

His fingers dug in harder, and my back arched over the rail.

"It's me," I cried.

Don't look down. Don't look down!

He pulled back, his features shadowed. His hand curled back around my throat as he pressed into me, and I didn't fight him. I couldn't.

"You stole. What is. *Mine!*" Brekt's large frame shook as his fingers dug into soft skin.

God, he was strong. The deck grew colder when I couldn't mask my fear. "Brekt, *please,* it's me."

"Do not speak!" His body leaned into mine, forcing me to see what was written on his face.

Hate. Loathing. Distrust.

This wasn't who I remembered. The Aspis had changed him.

But his hand had not tightened. He held me, pressed into me, and I savoured the pleasure of it—fear mixed with longing. He was here. He was alive.

Moisture hit my cheek, and for a moment, I thought it was raining. The shadows cast around his features made them too dark to see, but a tear had fallen from his cheek to mine. I wanted to see him, feel him, so I lifted a trembling hand to his face. It was warm. Real.

"She was mine," he whispered. The words cracked and broke around an emotion I understood. "The gods have stolen everything."

"I told you once before. I belong to me."

He went still. Deathly still.

Quiet.

A flash of iridescence told me he was searching for the truth. His attention stopped on the earrings he'd given me, and his eyes flared with surprise. It gave me the chance to push at his chest.

Lightning lit the space, illuminating the shock etched across his features.

The main door crashed open, and someone gasped before running to where we stood.

Maev slammed into Brekt. Her fists flew, pounding against his arm, screaming to let me go.

Brekt didn't move an inch, Maev's attack going unnoticed.

Time slowed as we tried to grasp the truth. That soul-deep pull tugged at me, drawing me closer to him.

Ollo was there, too, a rope in his hands. He wrapped it around Brekt, tying his arms to his sides and releasing me from his hold.

"Stop! Let go," Maev yelled as she continued to pummel him. "Don't hurt her."

Brekt's face changed. He became the Guard, the god of Death I once saw before. His obsidian gaze turned to Maev.

"Don't you dare touch her," I demanded, grabbing his jaw and turning it back to me. Surprise flickered, part of him knowing it was not the Ikhor demanding him to listen.

Maev stepped back. "It's him. Liv, is that him?"

Ollo pulled the rope tight, yanking Brekt from my grasp.

"Do something, Saviour. This won't hold the Guard for long."

I shook my head. "You two need to leave," I said to the twins, pointing at the door.

Brekt didn't take his eyes off me as he grabbed the rope banded across his upper arms, yanking it out of Ollo's grasp with little effort, and threw the rope to the ground. Then he spun to Ollo, who reared back, his long hair blowing away from his face.

"Don't hurt him!" I tried to grab Brekt, but he was too quick to act.

Fuck.

Ollo flew across the deck when Brekt kicked him in the gut.

Maev screamed, and Brekt grabbed her by the hair, dragging her toward her brother, who was pushing himself back up.

Shadows swirled around Brekt like they had the night he transformed. His skin darkened, horns flickering in and out of sight, as if he couldn't hold his form.

I ran for them, knocking a shoulder into Brekt and skidding to a stop in front of the Guard, pushing against his chest as Maev batted at his arms. "They're protecting me! Brekt, they are my friends."

Brekt glared down at me, not letting Maev go.

"He's not getting it, Saviour." Ollo was on his feet behind me. "That's not him. Not the man you once knew."

"Sure looks like him," I said over my shoulder.

"I don't appreciate the tone directed at me," Ollo spat back. "I am trying to protect you from your asshole boyfriend."

Brekt growled, teeth growing sharp as he took a menacing step forward.

"No!" I stood in front of Ollo, raising my hands in the air. "Let Maev go, please. She's not attacking you."

Brekt studied Maev. Did he see the differences?

She grabbed his arm, snapping him back to the present, and he let her go. She rushed to Ollo's side, tears streaking down her face.

A strong wind gusted across the landing, wrapping itself around Brekt. The torn pieces of his shirt showed me a glimpse of hard muscle. His chest was a kaleidoscope of shadows.

The twins backed away.

Brekt cursed as he grabbed his head in both hands, shaking it and wincing.

Panic seized me. I didn't know what was happening. Everything was so wrong. He faded in and out of sight as smoke curled around his legs and his skin darkened. He was transforming again.

"Stop it," Brekt groaned. "Stop using the magic. I feel it. It's tearing my mind apart."

Shit. I tried to stuff my fear away. What would happen if the Aspis appeared now inside the magic barrier? How had he come through in the first place?

Brekt gasped for air, his face pulled tight in pain.

The eyes of the Aspis opened.

He grew darker by the second, blending into the shadows of the night. His long hair fell in his face, floating around his shoulders, lifted by the breeze. He'd never looked more deadly, and something about his ferocity was more beautiful than anything I had ever seen. Wild, dangerous, fighting for control, and right now he was facing three enemies and looked very much like he wanted to kill us all.

His focus landed on me.

If he expected the nervous girl, the one scared to show her teeth, the one who let the Keepers instil fear into her, he was in for another truth. I had wished every day that I hadn't lost him, but this was not how I wanted him back. I would not be the pathetic girl he remembered. I had fought across burning fields, flooded rivers and set fire to a god's temple to live.

I stood straight, brushing the hair back from my face, and Brekt reacted, taking a fighter's stance and keeping us all in his line of sight. He wore no weapons, but I knew how deadly he was with his bare hands.

"Are you sure this is the Shadow Guard, Saviour?" Ollo whispered, and Brekt's head whipped his way, pinning him with a deathly stare.

The yellow was fading back to obsidian. He was gaining control.

"You know it's him," I said. "You've seen his photo. You met him in Bellum."

"How?" Ollo cautiously reached for Maev and pushed her so that she was standing behind him.

"I know your face, too, Aethar," Brekt growled—a cornered animal.

I pointed a finger at Brekt, marching forward. "If you don't listen here, so help me god, I will throw you over that railing."

Brekt flinched, and the smoke stopped swirling at his feet.

I swallowed around the pain of all these weeks without him. "I have mourned you every day." My words came out cracked and broken. "I begged every god my mother told me of to have you returned to me."

I had lost my friends. I had two enemies turned allies for help. I had gods to find and magic to get rid of, and something in me finally snapped.

I was angry—not sad, not lost—angry.

I swiped the hair from my eyes again, hating that it kept stealing my view of him. "If you want a fight, you can leave. And only when you smarten the fuck up can you come back. You're not harming me or them. I am not possessed or evil or whatever other name you want to call me. I've heard it all, and I'm sick of it."

Brekt was a statue, watching. Was I really asking him to leave?

I took a daring step closer, wanting to be nearer. "I am Liv. I am —" *Yours.*

He took a sharp breath.

His attention roamed over me, seeing my changed hair and pale skin.

Maybe I wasn't exactly as he remembered. I put a hand over my heart. "You can feel it here. The pull."

That wasn't the right thing to say.

His skin shredded, scales taking its place, and his hair fell to pieces on the deck as horns solidified. Slits formed in his eye.

The Aspis sprang for the sky, tearing apart the magic shield, roaring so loud we had to cover our ears.

Running to where he last stood, I reached to the sky, trying to grab onto something, anything to bring him back.

THIRTY-FOUR

Liv

When I asked Maev if she'd ever heard of two minds sharing a dream, she snorted, saying I had read too many stories. I corrected her, stating I hadn't read the stories in my childhood —they were told through my mother. Brekt and I unquestionably shared the dream. I had entered his dream world before; he said he'd known me for years. Since leaving the Guards, since becoming the Ikhor, my dreams have turned dark and haunted. What if this place is real? What if Brekt and I met somewhere outside our understanding? If it were true, this place is terrifying and houses something sinister looking for me. I felt it when I travelled to the dark and

quiet place. I was being hunted; I was being
watched, and I was about to feel pain.

Maev paced around the main table. She had circled it ten
times while I waited for her to speak. My attention
darted to the door, waiting for Ollo. He was
somewhere on the ship, looking for empty crystals to see if I could
fill them.

I fidgeted, testing my hand and trying to force my fingers into
working again. My leg bounced as I held it all in, slamming
everything into my box.

I was close to exploding.

I hadn't stopped crying since the Aspis flew off an hour ago.

He is alive. I need to find him.

The thought overruled the desire to find the gods.

I had removed several splinters from my arms and legs from
crashing into the crates. There were still some lodged in my back
from being pulled across broken wood, but Maev was too
preoccupied, so I hadn't asked for help.

It was pitch black beyond the glass wall at the front of the
bridge—the sun wouldn't be up for another hour or so. Crystal
powered torches set the room alight, throwing it into a golden
glow.

He is alive!

Maev halted, her hand going to the air before she paced again,
braiding her long, silvery hair as she thought.

"What are you trying to figure out?" I asked. "I could really use
a distraction right about now."

"What am I trying to figure out? Are you kidding? We found
out several days ago we need to find the actual *gods* for you to
return the magic. Meaning we had to change our plans. Then I
find out it's possible you can fill crystals, changing plans again
because we could do so much for the people before you return
the magic. And then the Guard returns. The actual Shadow

Guard—the host of the Aspis. Meaning the legends are all wrong."

I bent over my knees. My tears had run dry, and now my stomach threatened to heave.

He is alive.

"Liv?"

"I'm okay. Just panicking. I got this."

Maev was at my side, rubbing my back, and I winced when she hit a sliver. "Oh, your back is torn up, Livy!" She lifted my shirt. "Let me get these out." She sat behind me with a small tool and began plucking wood, starting near the base of my spine.

I sucked in a breath."Let's go back to the gods and the crystals. I'm not ready to talk about ... anything else right now."

A few weeks ago, I would have argued that it wasn't my job to help her people, but the twins were rubbing off on me. For the first time, I considered saving my magic to help the people in need. The twins had gone against their own wishes to help me—teaching me about sacrifice. They were kind, brave and intelligent. Because of the twins, I believed there were people out there worth helping.

"On one hand, you could save a lot of people," Maev said. "But on the other hand, the magic is hurting you, and part of me thinks we need to get rid of it fast." She moved up my spine, carefully plucking as she went. "Ollo has to report back to the Aerial Elder, explain the missing ship, and we need to sneak back into the city without people knowing you are with us."

"Why do we have to sneak?" I focused on my feet. Pushing the toes of my boots together.

"Oh." She stopped again. "Well, his mission was a secret. My being here is a secret to those who made the mission. If it got out the Ikhor was in the city, the Elders would parade you in front of everyone."

"Not that I want that, but is that bad?"

"Rydavians have waited a long time for the magic to return to them. You will have to face people begging for your help and need to understand their reactions when you say that you can't. When they find out you plan to return the magic, you will have people after you. Especially the defence units."

"Okay. So, we keep my identity a secret for as long as possible. What about the crystals?"

I may be willing to help innocent people, but if they asked me to fight for them? No. I would not fight the Guardians.

Guilt settled in as I realized I would fight for *him*.

He is alive! My whole body shook.

"Well, that's another thing. I am trying to figure out if there is a reason to test the theory in my lab or if we search for the gods first." Maev's usual excitement about her experiments fell flat. Her tone was low with worry. "Having a supply of magic crystals could really help the people and help our journey. I'd love to test how many you can produce and how often."

I flexed my hand out of habit. "Because the supply is running low. Meaning people can't get medicines and power their weapons."

"Exactly. But Livy, you're changing. I've noticed it but didn't want to alarm you. Ollo likely surprised you with it."

I snorted. "Not the biggest surprise I faced tonight. But you're right. I hadn't looked at myself lately, and I feel it. I'm changing within, too."

Maev set her tool down and came around to stand in front of me, tilting her head. "How so?"

I hesitated to admit how crazy I had gone. "I hear things, see things, dream of awful things. I am angrier than I have ever been."

Maev didn't respond, but I knew what she was thinking—how I felt resembled the Guardians' version of the Ikhor more than it did the Aethars' hero.

"You dreamt of him." She folded her arms when I nodded. "What things do you see?"

"I've seen shadows while awake. And monsters when I sleep. I don't know where I go, but I find him there. I didn't think it was real until I saw him on the deck. It's the version of him I've been seeing while asleep."

"And what about these shadows while awake?"

"I don't know. It's something else. Do you think I can do more than control the elements?" I had been wondering about that for several days now.

"What do you mean?"

"What if the Ikhor's powers can do more than manipulate the elements? Like, what if I could fly or read minds? What if I am seeing into places that aren't … *here* … this place?" I waved around the room. "What if I'm conjuring monsters into this world?"

Maybe that would explain why I sometimes felt like I was hearing things.

"Where have you heard such ideas?"

"My mother would tell me stories like that."

Maev blinked. "Who did she know that could fly? I thought there were no legacies in the lost lands."

"They weren't stories of real people."

"Ah. Well, the gods can only manipulate the elements. They work in tandem with the magic of the earth. The pure-blooded legacies could only work with a single element that passed through their bloodline. Or rather, they can, since I just found out they still exist." She tapped a finger to her mouth. "Like the Shadow Guard becoming shadow."

"Do you think the shadows I've been seeing are him?"

Why could I not say his name? Why was I shaking, feeling so cold, when I should be happy?

"Maybe. You two are connected. And now, he's alive …"

Ollo returned then, carrying a handful of empty crystals. Our gazes met briefly, his hardening. He had come to my rescue before being thrown across the deck, while their enemy—a Guard of the Aspis—held his sister.

A man I had defended as being good.

Had I lost Ollo's trust?

"Stashed in the storerooms." Ollo held up the pile of empty crystals. "There aren't many, but we can stuff your pockets and see if you fill these too. I would be interested to see how many you can fill and how fast."

He strode up to me and stuffed crystals in my pockets, and all the while, I held my breath, so he didn't hear it hitch. He bent down on a knee before me, his hand around my ankle as he put more in my boots, but he wouldn't look at me. Then he went to my mattress and put more under my pillow. "We will check on them every day and see if it works."

He turned around, finally meeting my eye, and the look that passed through them confused me. "In the meantime, try to concentrate on the crystals and see if you can fill them."

"Okay."

"You alright?" His tone was clipped.

I nodded, but he didn't seem convinced.

He took a breath, searching the room before saying, "I apologize for my words above deck. The moment got away from me. I should not have made comments."

My shoulders slumped, and I bit my lip to stop my smile. The twins always surprised me. Ollo was not mad at me, but embarrassed for insulting Brekt.

"He's not an asshole," I said. "Not to me. Not usually."

Ollo held back his next thought, but I could tell he disagreed.

"And ... and how do you feel about what happened?" Maev asked. "We should talk about it. As far as our next move goes."

My head snapped up.

Maev was staring at me, unblinking, and Ollo made himself busy, fooling around with papers on the table.

"I don't know," I whispered. "I—I don't know what to feel, what to think."

"He's alive," Maev said calmly, like she was talking to a child.

Ollo cleared his throat. "He changed back into a man. This doesn't confirm it is him."

"Liv won't see it that way," Maev argued. "He spoke to her, recognized her."

She didn't bring up the dreams, and I was thankful.

"And was he always physically violent? Saviour?" Ollo had both hands on the edge of the table. "You told me he was good to you. The display above was not what I would define as good."

I wiped at my cheeks, and couldn't stop shaking.

"Ollo, be understanding," Maev whispered.

"I'm being cautious. For our sake, for the world's sake and Liv's. This situation just got more dangerous."

Maev mouthed me an apology, and I shook my head. "Ollo is right. It wasn't exactly him. But then, I am not the woman he last saw, either."

I raised my hands, flexing my working fingers, seeing the physical evidence of change. My eyes and hair, my magic, it all spoke volumes. "We are enemies now," I whispered.

The room was eerily silent. Neither of the twins had any advice or wise words, so I said. "We make a plan, forge on ahead. Find the gods. Get rid of the magic."

What I didn't say was that I had a new resolve.

I was going to save him, too.

"Ollo and I mapped out our journey home." Maev directed me to the table.

"You've drawn even more on it!" I exclaimed, noticing more of Nuo's map filled in on the Aethar side.

"Yes. The Interrogator doesn't like detail, it seems. It shows impatience. He didn't even try with the canyons. There's no useful information about them or the path through."

"He wouldn't have travelled them. Are we going through?"

Would the Aspis follow? Panic seized me at the thought of missing the chance to see him again. Would he be lost to me if I travelled away from Veydes?

"Over them," Ollo interrupted. "They're safer to fly over than the seas. The seas have pirates and Guardian ships in every direction, but the canyons aren't frequented by pirates as often because there are far fewer travellers. We may find trouble if they spot our ship, but we will move fast and not stop."

"Why would pirate ships bother us if we fly over the canyons?"

"Pirate ships travel by sea and in the air. They have the advantage. The Guardian airships have a hard time taking them down, let alone a crew of three. Well, one, since the two of you can't pilot as well as I."

Pirates in the sky. I wanted to see it, yet I was glad we were avoiding them.

"Canyons it is. Is that how you flew here? Over the canyons?"

"Yes, and nothing got in our way," Ollo replied.

"Doesn't the Desert Eagle live down there?"

Maev covered her mouth to hide her laughter. "How do you know so little of this world and yet know of the Desert Eagle?"

I looked down at the small drawing of the Eagle that Nuo had sketched on his map. "It's one of Nuo's favourite stories."

Did Nuo know *he* was alive?

Maev dropped her hand, and her smile vanished with her distaste. "It was Ollo's too. I had to read it to him a million times as a kid. The Eagle was one of the reasons he wanted to learn to fly."

"I am *not* like the Interrogator." Ollo pointed a finger in my face, and I didn't mention that standing in this airship, wearing Guardian black and mapping our trip, made him look very much like Nuo.

"Bastane told me many young boys liked the story. So you are like many young boys. Stop getting so offended that they were my friends."

Ollo's skin paled.

His earlier comments about the *asshole* came back to me.

"I'm not offended," he said. "Only, I don't wish to be compared to murderers. If we were similar as young boys, it was simply because stories like the Eagle made us want to grow up to be heroes."

"Depending on what people they were saving," I said.

"Well, the Eagle didn't save anyone. He took down his entire bloodline—the Feathers. They were an ancient Mount-leg bloodline that controlled the island south of the canyons. The Eagle's mother was their matron. She was cruel, took Sea-legs as slaves and controlled the passage from Veydes to Rydavas. Eventually, the Eagle saw her cruelty for what it was and, in secret, helped free the slaves. In the end, the best thing he could do was destroy his entire clan."

"He killed his whole family?"

"Yes, the later part of his story isn't so savoury. He burned the entire island to the ground. That was a few hundred years ago. That's why he's not a concern, because he isn't even alive anymore. If he was ever real at all. Anyway," Ollo said, giving his sister a look, "I think we should hit up Mayra's shrines on the way north to Avenmae."

I was stuck on the viciousness of the Eagle's tale, the part I had never heard, before I clued into what Ollo was saying. "Avenmae?" The name was familiar.

The twins both nodded. "Our home," they said together.

"It's a grand city, with structures built in the golden era of the gods." Maev's face lit up. "There are schools and shrines and all kinds of business. It's the capital city of Rydavas and one of the oldest standing cities in all of Arde."

"Is it bigger than the Guardian City? Or Danuli?"

"About twice the size." Maev nodded. "It's a beautiful place."

It was still hard to believe there were more than wastelands on the other side of the border.

"You said we are going to Mayra's shrine, but we also need to go to one of the Night god's. Where is Erabas's shrine?"

The twins gave me identical sympathetic glances. Likely, they knew I was avoiding the biggest topic of conversation.

I took my shaking hands off the table and hid them at my sides, playing with the fabric of my sleeve.

Ollo bent over the map, searching it. "Unfortunately, there are none. Many have searched for his lost temple but haven't found that either."

"I could go see Cal," Maev suggested.

Ollo gave her a deadpan look. "That guy is a quack, Mae. Better to scour the library."

"He's not a quack. He's brilliant. Cal's ideas are strange, not wrong."

"Who is this guy?" I asked. They had mentioned him before.

"Her *friend*. He's asinine." Ollo's mouth twisted in distaste. "He's also in love with Maev, but she won't admit that."

"He's just friendly," she said, her cheeks turning pink.

I wondered if there wasn't more to the story.

"If you're taking Liv to meet him, count me out."

Maev rolled her eyes as her hands went to her hips and her mouth went into a flat line—her most impressive show of irritation yet. "I think he may be able to help us with the theory on the crystals, as well as ideas about the missing gods. He comes up with all sorts of brilliant ideas."

"And what about Rem's temple?" Ollo cut in.

"I want to skip Rem. For now," I said.

"And why is that?" Ollo's mouth tipped up at the edges. "Could you be nervous about taking on another god?"

"Don't egg her on, Ol. For once, I'm happy she shows caution." Maev's attention roamed over the map, smug about her comment.

"Something feels off about Rem," I admitted, ignoring her.

The trembling in my hands reached my shoulders. The force with which I held myself still made my back ache. The two exchanged a look, and Ollo leaned closer toward me. "Be careful what you say of the gods out loud, Liv. And our father Rem is good to his children. He's kept us safe for generations where others have abandoned the legacies."

But something bothered me. It wasn't something I could get into with the twins. It felt more important to find the missing gods first. However, they agreed to leave Rem for the last visit.

"So we head for the canyons," I said, trying to understand the plan. "Then the shrines, and all the while, find crystals to fill for you two to take home."

"Yes. And try to avoid the Guards and the Aspis in the meantime. Can you handle that, Liv?" Maev waited for me to answer, actually asking me.

If I said I wasn't ready, would they agree to let me run from all of this? I think they would. I let out a long breath. "I can keep the magic locked down."

"It hurts you." Ollo said. "Tell me if this is too much for you."

"What else can I do?"

Ollo and Maev exchanged a look.

I huffed the hair from my face and studied the map. Maev had filled out the bottom half of Rydavas, and the Southern clans took up a huge part of the map. "I'm glad we are flying over that." I pointed to the clans.

"We wouldn't make it past a single village," Maev said, shivering.

"Even you two?"

"They don't consider themselves one of us. We also don't call ourselves Aethar. We are Rydavian."

"You, on the other hand, Saviour,"—Ollo smiled, turning toward me—"the Southlanders would put you on a pedestal. They'd probably do awful things to you, thinking you'd like it."

"How did they become so twisted?" I asked.

"Who knows," Ollo replied. "How did the world become so divided? The Lost Lands so lost? Our histories are ripe with secrets."

"Secrets are the reason nothing ever changes. An alchemist told me that. Maev, does your friend have any books written in the language of Night?"

"I'm not sure. But if he does, they won't be of any use. He can't read them. No one can."

"I can."

I hadn't told them yet—I could read the scrolls she had mentioned once before.

Maev drew back. "It's a language that's been dead for a very long time. There are no records of it."

"There was something written in the Guardian city, in the language of Night. I could read it."

"How?"

"The ability came with the magic. As did speaking the common tongue. It comes to me easily."

"Can you read the other old languages?"

"I tried reading the language of Day, and the understanding is just out of reach. I recognize the lettering, but the words don't form."

Maev paced again. "You said the magic glowed, like Rem, when it found you?"

"Yes. And when it spoke, it sounded so similar to him with a multilayered voice."

Maev nodded as if her thought process was making sense.

"And Ouras looked like the Aspis."

"Yes, although Ouras wasn't black like the Aspis. But the horns, the eyes, certain features were the same."

"And you can read the language of Night."

"What are you getting at Maev? Sum it up," Ollo said impatiently.

"They're parts of each god. I wonder if the first Ikhor, the first child, stole more than just the god's magic. What if it stole an essence of their being?"

Ollo thought for a moment. "If that were true, and Liv is part of each god, we could figure out how to use that to find the others."

"Or what if Erabas created the Ikhor," I asked. "It's said the first child who stole the magic was a child of Night, making their legacy disliked, but what if Erabas made it himself? Are the Rydavian stories of the first child—the cursed child—are they the same?"

Both twins were speechless. "The stories are the same," Maev said slowly. "If it were Erabas that created this whole mess, that would change our entire history."

"Think about it," I continued. "He's hated. He's been erased from history. Rem went to war with him. It would make sense if this were all his mess."

"It's known that Rem is good." Ollo turned to Maev to see her reaction. "What if the other gods helped make the Aspis because of

Erabas? That would also mean they would not want us to find him."

"Maybe there was no first child." Maev nodded and then quickly shook her head in denial. She waved her hands as if wiping away the conversation. "These theories have no proof. We have anecdotal evidence. And besides, why would Ouras tell us we must find all the gods to return the magic? Let's focus on what we know. The facts: you are changing Liv. It makes me wonder if more will happen to you. The Aspis is also growing and changing. What if it —he—whatever, will become more powerful?"

Ollo stood. "We need to get to Rydavas. Fast. Maybe it isn't such a bad idea you visit your weird friend."

Maev scowled at her brother before leaning over the map, forming a plan and an exact route home.

"By tomorrow, we will be flying over South Aspis," Ollo said. "Then the canyons. Your tracker can be refilled with crystals, thanks to Liv, and we won't run out of power to get ourselves home. And Saviour," Ollo turned to me, chewing on his words before he said, "Keep close to us. It would be best if you didn't have more run-ins like what happened on deck without us there. We may not be able to protect you as Guards, but I don't want you to face this alone."

I gave him a single nod. "I'll keep close."

He patted me on the shoulder, easing some of the tremors in my spine.

"Another thing I found while reading late last night," Maev started, and we both waited while she chewed her lower lip. "After going through the journals and logs from the Councilman's daughter, I've compiled some disturbing information. She is aware of attacks on Rydavas. She knows there are more than the Southlanders living there. And she marked several coastal cities to be attacked once they stop the Ikhor."

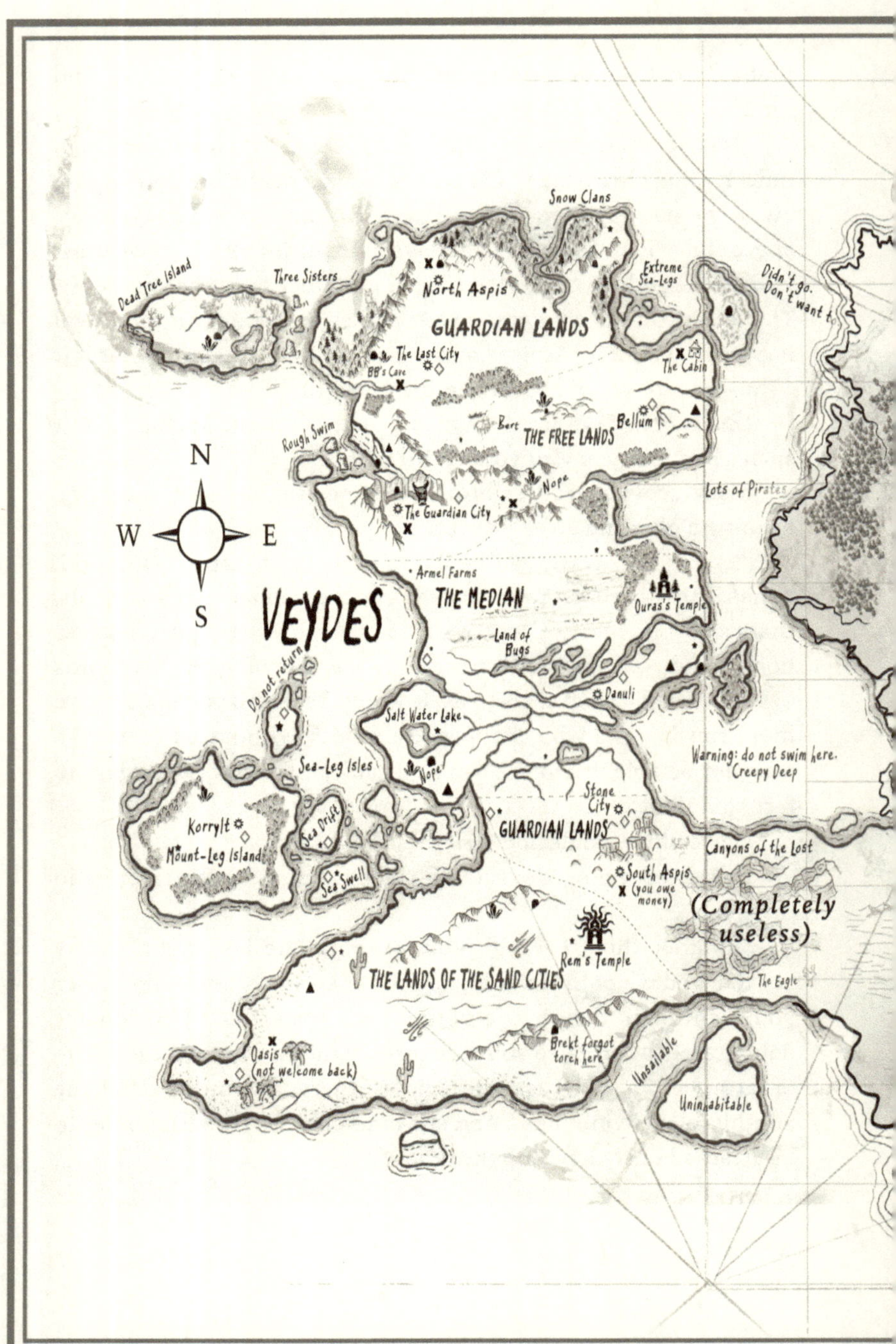

Snow Clans
Dead Tree Island
Three Sisters
North Aspis
GUARDIAN LANDS
Extreme Sea-Legs
Didn't go. Don't want to
The Last City
BB's Cave
The Cabin
Rough Swim
Bert
THE FREE LANDS
Bellum
N
W   E
S
The Guardian City
Nope
Lots of Pirates
Armel Farms
THE MEDIAN
VEYDES
Ouras's Temple
Land of Bugs
Danuli
Do not return
Salt Water Lake
Warning: do not swim here. Creepy Deep
Sea-Leg Isles
Nope
Stone City
GUARDIAN LANDS
Canyons of the Lost
Korrylt
Mount-Leg Island
Sea Drift
South Aspis (you owe money)
Sea Swell
(Completely useless)
Rem's Temple
THE LANDS OF THE SAND CITIES
The Eagle
Brekt forgot torch here
Oasis (not welcome back)
Unsailable
Uninhabitable

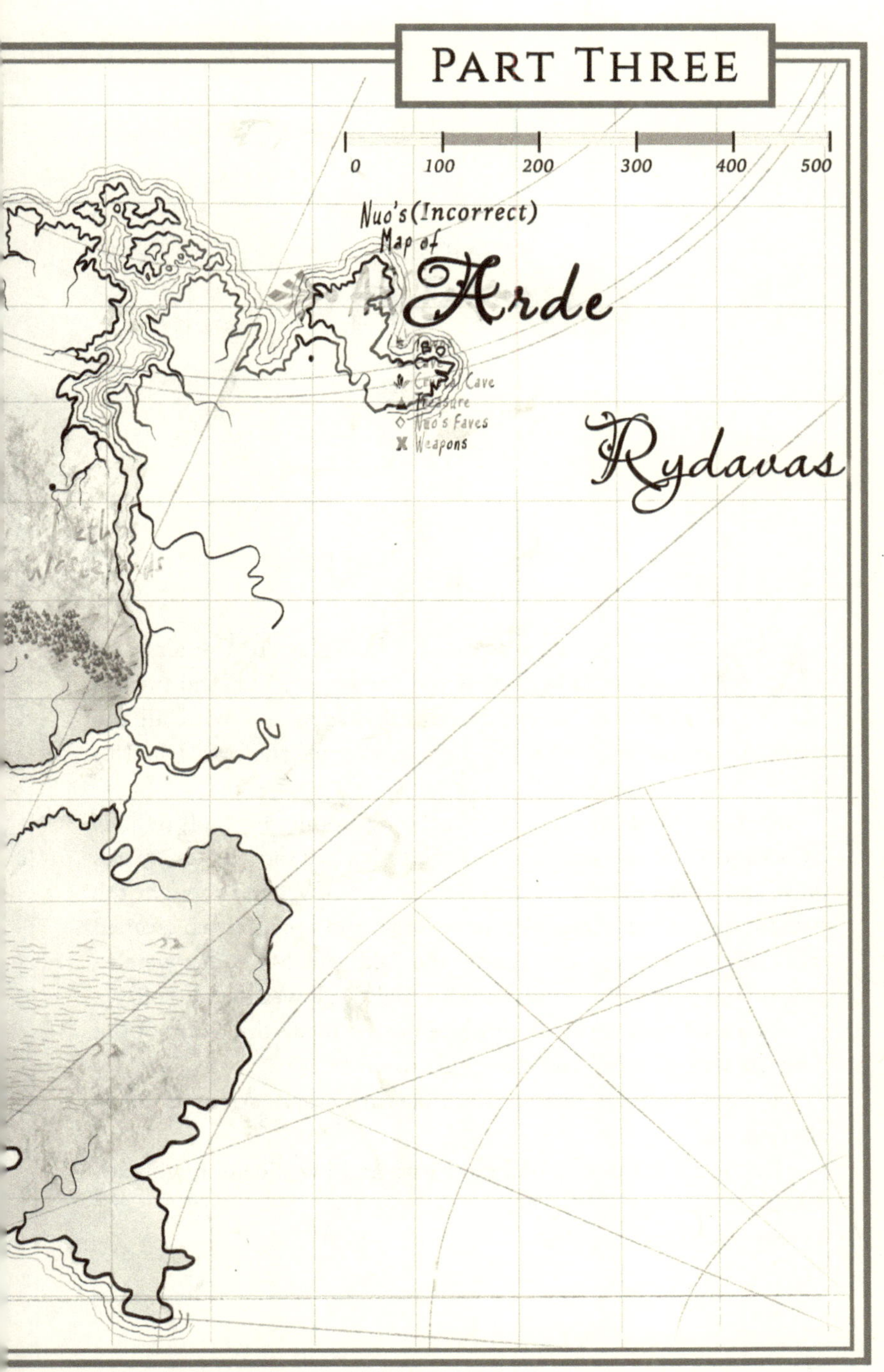
0   100   200   300   400   500
Nuo's (Incorrect)
Map of
Arde
Rydavas
Crystal Cave
Treasure
Nuo's Faves
Weapons

PART THREE

THIRTY-FIVE

Liv

My palm rested against the cold glass of the airship's front window. It was too dark to see the land turn to desert as we neared South Aspis, and with all the emotions screaming to be let loose from my little box, I had to move.

My heart thudded in my chest, echoing around the dimly lit halls as I escaped the suffocating silence the twins had settled into. *He was alive*, and I didn't know how to see him again. When I thought the twins were out of earshot, I let the tears go, and a painful sob escaped me. I held myself together against the cold wall. My hands were so pale—fading to white—and in the low light, I glowed ever so softly.

I allowed myself the tears while boxing away the worst of the pain. He was alive, so why did it hurt so much?

A slight tug on my chest made me stand straight, focus sharpening.

The lights in the hall had gone out, and I was cold, my breath misting before me.

My body jerked again.

The hall grew darker, and I stepped forward as the darkness behind me moved in, pushing me almost gently. I didn't have to look up to understand what was happening, and my steps quickened with excitement. Sure enough, the dark crystalline sky, sparkling like a million stars, stretched overhead. The night sky had never made me feel small, but the crystals floating around endlessly made me feel like if I stared too long, I might become lost in them with my mind fractured.

Wasn't that already the case? I was seeing things, walking in a dream world, knowing it wasn't real.

I was vaguely aware I wasn't wearing boots. The floor had a layer of dust over the stone—no one had travelled this place in a very long time.

An archway marked the end of the hall, darkness behind it. I stopped there, where the airship walls disappeared, becoming black stone. In the ancient language of Night, there was a warning carved above my head. I didn't need to read it again. I had seen it before.

To descend here is to embrace all that lies in darkness.

It was the same warning written above the caves in the Guardians City, but where that archway led to a staircase going down, this one led to a wall of black liquid. Lifting a hand, I touched the blackness. My fingertips disappeared, the black rippling like the surface of a lake. It didn't hurt, and it didn't push or pull or deny me entry, so I walked right through.

Nothingness met me. I didn't feel cold, hurt, or any sensation at all. It was a sad, lonely place, and I knew if I stayed too long, I would lose my sense of self—lose my way home.

But I was not the only one lost to it.

A presence watched me from somewhere in the dark, making no sound.

I emitted a soft glow, but there was nothing around me to light. Even the surface I walked on didn't light up, but whatever else was in here—it could see me.

"Please come out," I whispered. Would he recognize me this time? Or see the Ikhor.

A rattling resounded in the endless space, turning into a low growl. Deep. But not threatening.

It was behind me.

A vibrant, warm energy travelled the length of my body, making every nerve end come alive. It was a warning, but I wasn't scared. The presence behind me was testing me, probing me, seeing who and what I was.

The deep growl echoed behind my right ear, then my left. Chilling fingertips traced a line down the length of my back. There was a deep breath, and the hand was gone.

Then a whisper made me jump. "You feel it, don't you little evil?"

I swallowed the wave of heat coursing through me. That deep timber was next to me. I couldn't see him. But the warmth gathering in my core, the way my body reacted—it was *him*.

"Feel what?" I turned to track him, but I saw nothing.

"You felt the pulsing energy between us."

Behind me again. I turned a second time, and the glow from my skin caught a small section of black fabric before it was out of sight. "Let me see you."

He circled me.

There was a faint view of a muscled arm. A reflection of a curling horn. Citrine eyes glowing and disappearing before he was the half-beast once more.

"Ikhor."

My heart sank.

The rumble of his voice was more powerful than it should be for just a man. It was powered by godly magic—by strength and death. Perhaps it was him, but he was something *more* now.

Closing a fist, I dug my nails into my skin. "Did you forget my name?"

There was a pause.

"I've forgotten nothing."

The power of that voice racked my body, controlling the beat of my heart. I huffed the hair out of my face, holding that fist tight and not letting my irritation rise. "Then you remember you used to call me 'love'."

There was a smile in his voice when he said, "I remember."

I followed the deep timber, not turning my back on him as he circled me, his steps slow and deliberate, his breathing hard as if he had been running. Fingers ran through my hair, scraping along my scalp before his palm landed on the back of my neck. He continued circling, keeping me still until he was behind me, teasing the soft skin of my neck with a gentle touch. "What a situation we've found ourselves in." He held me in place. "I'm torn on my own desires."

My chest rose and fell, but I kept my breathing quiet. "What desires are those?"

Skimming his fingers along my neck, he walked around in front. The slight glow from my skin reflected off his arm next to my head. Swirling shadows crept underneath his skin, making me dizzy, but those yellow eyes were gone as he stood before me. I could make out the line of his strong jaw and caught a faint glimpse of his wolfish smile. Iridescence flashed as his gaze wandered down the length of my body. Strands of his dark hair fell past his shoulders, but I could see little else.

He was controlling it, controlling the Aspis.

Hope soared as I realized what that could mean.

"What are those desires, Brekt?" I asked again, my heart skipping as I said his name.

"So bold, Ikhor." He leaned in closer, enveloping me with pine and leather. "Tempting me. I want to devour you, to take you. I want to kill you yet warn you and make you run far away from me."

None of those answers were what I had expected. Not even close to what I had hoped for. "Try any of that, and I will show you the power of my magic."

"And if I wanted to kiss you?" he said seductively.

I shuddered, not sure I was strong enough to resist him. "No."

He went still, and it should have been a warning, but something about his posture suggested intrigue. "No? Why fight me?" His words were like velvet, dangerous and taunting. Not like an enemy, but a lover. "I don't believe she would fight me."

Everyone dreams of reuniting with those they lost. In a desperate attempt to soothe the pain, we picture those miracles. Finding them in a crowd, discovering their death was a lie or maybe one of our prayers actually worked, and a god gave them back.

But his return? This dream place? It's not what I imagined.

I pictured tears and kisses and words of love. But this? This was violent and messy, and the anger rose.

Brekt was not playing along with my fantasies.

"It would be different if you were Brekt," I whispered. "Not a beast."

I shivered in fear, and I swallowed the feeling—it was a surprising taste, sweet and tempting. A delicious mix of longing and instinct to do as he said—to run. Or maybe to kiss him. The extent to which my body was under his control should have been alarming. "What desire do you feel most?"

Brekt's head tilted unnaturally to the side. The citrine glow returned, pupils thinning to slits. "I've known you for years. Finding you in this place. Wanting what was a figment of my imagination. You were a tender relief from the pain of knowing what future was to come." His hand fisted my hair, fingers curling around the strands and holding. I winced, but didn't pull away. His breath was hot against my cheek. "Then I discovered you were real."

I grabbed his ice-cold wrist, trying to pull his hand away. He was too strong. "I am real. You choked me over the railing on the deck, remember?"

A low growl escaped him, sharp and warning.

He was here, but so was the Aspis. It crawled under his skin, watching me through his eyes. It was there in the way he squeezed my hair, making it hurt, bending my head to the side. "Turn the magic off."

"You really are possessed by the beast," I spat. "You were never this much of an asshole."

Ollo's earlier words slammed into me, but I did as the half-beast asked. I stuffed my anger and disappointment away. I could process it later.

Brekt's nostrils flared. "Was always an asshole, just gave you the nice version." The hold on my hair loosened, and his arm dropped. But he stayed where he was, inclining his head toward mine. "Then I finally discovered why I dreamt of you bathed in flames. You were sent to destroy me. You were my salvation in my dreams before you became my damnation in the flesh." Brekt's eyes returned to obsidian, not warm like they once were. Instead, they were as cold as a winter night. "I have kept my sense of self, living inside this place, knowing I am the beast but remembering everything before. Tell me, Ikhor, is it Liv inside that pretty head of yours?"

"Yes."

His lip curled, showing those sharp fangs. "Then I have one question for you, Liv. And answer me honestly." He grabbed me by the chin, tilting my face up so I looked him dead in the eye. "When I found you in that cave, did you know what you were?"

Brekt expected a lie—I could tell by the set of his jaw. He was giving me the look the Keepers had, like Rebeka always had. Even Nuo had called me a liar. But I never earned the mistrust people placed on me. And this time—*for the first time*—Brekt was asking for the truth when no other had before him.

I shoved his hand away, grabbing his face instead, and his dark eyes went wide.

"I didn't know. And that's the truth. Nothing between us was a lie."

"Is that so?" He turned his head into my palm and kissed it. "So we are enemies by fate, not by choice."

I held my breath, wanting to feel more of those lips, wishing in some twisted way that he was still holding me hostage. "So, what does that make you feel now?"

Brekt went eerily still, turning his gaze back to me. The rattling in his chest returned, filling the dark. "I want to kill you as much as I want to fuck you."

My mouth hung open.

Brekt gave a quick shake of his head, and the curling horns appeared and disappeared. "I am no longer just a man. I no longer have a single urge."

"Then you can leave me be."

I stepped back, and he vanished, all but those glowing slitted eyes. The beast was back. His chest rattled, echoing in the silence that followed my request. "Leave? Where is the simpering girl I found in the cave? You want to command me now, Ikhor? No longer feel the pull, love? You've moved on to your pretty replacement?"

Did he mean Ollo?

I sucked in a breath and clamped my muscles tight, holding my fists at my side, resisting the urge to slap him across his stupid face.

"Never start a fight you can't finish," he'd once warned me. I wasn't sure I could use my magic to protect myself from the beast —not in this place.

"So you believe it's me all of a sudden?" My anger flared. We were and had always been hot and cold. One second yearning, the next ready to spit fire. "You die on me, then come back to be a real pain in the ass. More so than before." I shook my head. *Unbelievable.* "I didn't move on. I mourned your death. I flooded the lands, missing you. But this before me? This was not what I wanted to come back. If you're not the same man I cared for, then I don't know you anymore."

He prowled again, and this time, I didn't spin with him. He was at my back when he replied. "I am, and I am not."

That was my biggest fear after seeing him alive on the deck, that it wasn't the same man I had once known. "Then leave. And return when you are."

Brekt placed a hand on my hip, sliding it over my waist, stopping when he held my stomach. He pulled me back, so I was flush to his chest, and pressed into me, lips brushing my ear. My body melted against him as a fire raged through me that had nothing to do with magic.

"And what of my desires? Should I not demand the woman I knew? You are not the same woman from my dreams. Do I tell you to leave and return when you are what I want?"

It was hard to ignore the inferno raging through my body. I never needed so badly as I did around this man, but this wasn't how I wanted him.

We had fought before. He'd always pushed me and welcomed it when I pushed back. I raised my chin, not backing down. "I accepted you as you were before the Aspis rose. You were a cranky bastard who barely ever spoke his true feelings. You shielded yourself away from people. But you were thoughtful, teasing in surprising moments. You were not an easy man to lo—"

I shook my head, dislodging those words from my tongue, "I wanted you then. If you aren't that man, then I don't know you anymore."

The chest against my back vibrated—the Aspis was angry. Or was it Brekt?

"I am not that man anymore."

"Then I don't know where that leaves us."

"Enemies, it sounds like." His mouth pressed against my neck, and I knew only that spot where his kiss marked me.

I hid my hurt, not letting my breathing hitch or the tears run. This was a battle between two legends, only it wasn't violent—it was a test of wills.

Brekt's fingers dug into my stomach, and his face buried into my neck. "Turn. It. Off." His voice was guttural like he was talking around those fangs.

I shoved my emotions down and calmed my mind.

His jaw travelled the length of my neck. "You go with the Aethar now."

I leaned into him, feeling the hard length of him against my lower back, suppressing a moan. "Two of them. Not the Aethar you know. These people are different."

Brekt seemed to consider my words, adding a second hand to his embrace. His arm encircled me, holding both of mine pinned down, his hand squeezing below the scar on my shoulder. "You are not from my world. You wouldn't understand what Aethar I know. What they have done to my people."

"Well, you're a new man now," I said, using a tone I picked up from Maev. "Get a new perspective."

Brekt smiled against my neck. "Vicious as always. Your words sting like the point of a knife. Does your pretty boy get this kind of treatment? Does he get off on your anger like I do?"

He rubbed himself against me, and this time, I couldn't hold my whimper in. My head fell to the side, allowing him to bury his face farther, and his lips brushed my collarbone.

"He doesn't force it from me," I said.

He let go of my arm, grabbing my chin and moving my face so our mouths were a whisper apart. "Oh love, I have never forced you." He let go of me, and a chill rushed to every spot he had been touching. He was out of sight when I spun around, but his voice drifted to me. "Even as a beast, I don't force. Your anger is beautiful. Likely, the pretty boy doesn't know it was always a part of you. Your fire has always been your own making."

I squeezed my fists tight. "I haven't decided to forgive you for wasting the time we had before. And I don't know if I'll forgive you for coming back to me like this. If you're leaving now, you *will* come back."

Darkness pressed in, and a deep voice echoed from far away, "That's a promise."

He didn't push. He didn't beg. He was right that he forced nothing from me.

Dear god. It really *was* him.

Eyes flashed in the shadows. It was terrifying, and yet … I couldn't help the burning desire to rush to him. I liked the attention, even if it felt like it wasn't him—liked that I was his prey.

I hated pushing him away, and a moment later, my heart broke when I sensed the room was empty. I hadn't even asked what would happen next. I reached out in the dark, regretting letting my anger speak for me. "Please come back."

I waited.

But there was no response.

CHAPTER

THIRTY-SIX

Liv

The days that followed his return were a fog, much like the days after his death. I lost myself in the disbelief and the fear of too much hope. Back in the Endless Forest, I learned that if something good happened, you would be punished for it later.

My cheek stung as I rolled my head on my pillow. A crystal unstuck itself from where it had lodged into my face and dropped onto the padded fabric, glowing and full of magic. I stretched, my body feeling less burdened than it had in weeks, and I checked the crystals stuffed around my bed to find a glow emanating from them all.

In a single night, I had filled every crystal.

I stuffed them in my pockets excitedly. I got up to tell Ollo, but before I reached him, my steps slowed, seeing what was outside the large window. All my excitement from the dream and crystals vanished. A dull yellow hue bathed the bridge, muting the reflections and casting shadows behind every structure.

"The world is burning." I stopped behind the control panel, and Ollo looked over his shoulder at me.

The ship had landed in sand, yellow desert stretching out before us. In the distance, large rock formations jutted from the earth, round and nearly hidden in haze.

Maev sat near the front window, putting her hair into braids. "It was hard to tell it was daytime at first due to the smoke," she said, voice muffled against the glass.

"What's going on?"

"Like the Guardian in the temple said, South Aspis has burned. We are landing for a bit before we fly through the smoke. It's spread far, and Ollo made a good point that we don't want to get caught by anyone and need to land where it's difficult to breathe."

"This is all from South Aspis?"

"From surrounding villages, too."

"The Guards told me South Aspis was where the veteran Guardians trained and guarded Veydes from the Aethar that crossed the canyons. I wonder how many were lost? And those villages …"

The destruction was unimaginable. The lives lost. Who could do this?

"They will blame you, Saviour." Ollo turned in his seat to face me.

"Based on the maps, it was a large camp." Maev finished with her hair, standing. She was peering at the dark sky. "It was built out over a distance, rather than tall buildings like the Guardian City." Maev's faded reflection in the window showed her face pulled down in concern. "How are you feeling today, Liv?"

"I feel really good today. The crystals are taking some of the magic, easing the stress." I approached the front window and stood next to Maev.

She didn't seem as excited about the news as I thought she would.

"What's wrong?" I asked.

"Your hair is lighter, near white. You could almost pass for a Day-Leg, from our bloodline."

Ollo approached the window too, his reflection to my left, Maev's on my right. The strange colour of the sky had turned the twins' skin a pale green. We were silent for several moments, watching the smoke swirl outside the ship.

Past the smoke were the canyons, and I remembered what Nuo had said about them. *"Those who have gone to Aethar lands do not return. The land is as scarred as their faces, and the southern borders of our lands are a maze of canyons, impossible to travel through. If somehow you make it through the maze and the long desert, you won't go much farther from the violent nature of the Aethars waiting for intruders."*

Yet, that's exactly where I was going.

"Any more dreams?" Maev asked quietly. When I turned to her, she added. "Ollo overheard you speaking of them last night. He knows."

Heat rushed to my face, but his slight smile told me he would not ask me about them.

"Yes. I saw him again," I said.

"Your boyfriend is chasing you down in every reality," she said, not teasing. She was worried.

"Are we calling the beast her boyfriend now?" Ollo asked, a shade too dark to be casual.

"We are not," I replied, ignoring their stares and watching the smoke in the distance.

Ollo put his hands behind his head, peeking over at me. "You know, before this mission, I was leading a life of peace. I was making handfuls of friends, had achieved an early high ranking in the aerial division, women were giving me attention, and I was worrying less about Maev, who spent too much time alone."

Maev frowned. "What does any of that have to do with today?"

"I always knew my life was good. I will better appreciate it when I am home. I will appreciate the good days after seeing the worst."

We were quiet again, perhaps all thinking about our own mortalities.

How fast had the fires burned through South Aspis? How could the Guardians fight against an enemy capable of causing that kind of damage?

"What you'll appreciate when your home is the welcome party where everyone will sing your praises," Maev muttered.

Ollo took a deep breath. "I admit, Mae, I enjoy the friends I've made and the attention I get." He clenched his jaw, eyes flashing with regret. "But this trip with you ... it's shown me I've neglected my family. That I must change a few things."

Maev's mouth popped open. "How very observant of you."

I should have left them to have this conversation alone, but it was captivating to see siblings who cared—who tried.

"I have observed that you have changed since before we left for the city and went our separate ways." He gave his sister a thoughtful look. "You're different than you used to be. When we get home, Mae, I want to make sure we spend more time together."

"All of our lives have changed," I added before thinking. I had become so comfortable around these two that my thoughts spilled so easily. "I would like to spend time with you guys, too."

Maev toyed with the end of her braid. "I am glad of your change of heart, Livy, and that you are not feeling sorry for yourself today, but that doesn't make this situation any better. You're infatuated with your enemy."

"I'm not infatuated," I muttered.

"Mae,"—Ollo returned to his seat at the control panel—"did you pack the bags as I asked?"

"Bags for what?" I tore myself away from the window.

"Ollo thinks South Aspis is a bad sign. Since you obviously didn't start the fires, and if the Governor's daughter is with the Guards, then who caused that much damage? The Southlanders couldn't overtake that many Guardians."

"The Guards were always worried a war would start once the Aspis rose. I think it has," I said.

"But a war between who? No plans were made for South Aspis from the Aerial defences," Ollo mused.

"It's why we've packed emergency exit bags. We may need to abandon the ship at some point." Maev moved behind a seat near the panel and patted it for me to sit. When I did, she braided my hair like hers.

"But maybe not if Liv is filling crystals for us. Nice job, by the way." Ollo winked at me, and I didn't feel guilty for the attention. Ollo gave it to me freely, asking nothing in return. He made me feel bold. Was that so bad?

Maev dropped the first braid. My hair had grown long enough that it fell over my shoulder, and I looked out into the desert landscape while she worked on the other. I sat in silence, thinking how scary it was out there, yet how safe I felt right now—uncertain of myself, perhaps, but safe.

Was ... *Brekt* out there somewhere? Was he returning as himself and seeing what had become of his lands?

The ache in my chest took my breath away. I wanted to find him, to see him again.

"I'm going to go and make sure I have everything we need packed." Maev patted my shoulder, dropping my second braid.

Ollo surprised me by turning in his chair toward me. "When we return to Avenmae, I would also like to spend time with you, Saviour."

"With me?" My voice cracked. "Doing what?"

"Worried I am trying to ask you on a date?" His eyes glittered with mirth. "I want to spend time getting to know each other when we aren't on the run."

He held me trapped in his navy-blue gaze. Yet, I didn't fear Ollo. I had shed my fears. I had become bold, too.

"I want to take you out," he continued, taking a quick peek behind me to make sure Maev wasn't listening. "Show you my home. Show you me. I want to get to know you, and ... I want to be better."

"Better?"

Ollo looked down while a hand lifted to the back of his neck. It was the most unsure I had seen him. A crease formed between his brows as he took a deep breath. "I want to be someone who is missed. I want someone to fray the edges of a photo of me while I am gone. I want to earn that affection, not because I can do great things. I want someone to miss me because I was good. And all the other things you've said about your Guard." Ollo placed his hands on his knees. "Maybe it's strange that I ask such a thing of you. But after his return—I—I think you understand what love is. Something I have yet to fully figure out."

"Why do you say that?"

"You don't mince words with him. Or with the Interrogator. Just as Maev doesn't with me. You are a strong woman who loves deeply. I want to know how to fill that role in someone's life."

Ollo was talking of a specific woman. I bent forward, laying a hand over his, and it tensed beneath my touch. "I think you are already in the hearts of the most important people. You don't have to improve."

His jaw clenched, about to argue.

"You don't. I know something was said to you once. I'm guessing from an old lover. Maybe she was right in the moment. But from what I see, you are a really good man."

Ollo's grim demeanour changed, growing soft. "Are you flirting with me, Saviour?"

My neck grew warm. "No, I was telling you what I think. Maybe you have an ego, but it's not in the way of you being good."

"I plan to save you, Liv. They say the host dies ... between Maev and I, we will make sure to save you."

I couldn't control the overwhelming gratitude. "I don't know what my future holds, but I intend to save myself. And now that I know the Shadow Guard isn't dead ..." I wrung my hands together. "I plan to save him, too."

"Are you telling me I am aiding in this quest to save your past lover, who happens to be my enemy?"

"Depending on your perspective."

Ollo barked a laugh. "I like your form of manipulation, Saviour. I will help you. If the Shadow Guard is saved, well, that's not something I will stop you from doing."

"Because you are a good man."

"The bags are all ready to go." Maev returned to the bridge, taking a seat next to me.

Ollo stood, taking one last look out the window. "I'm going to get changed for the day, and then we will head through the cloud. It's getting quite hot, too hot for these long-sleeved Guardian shirts. I think they have some lighter ones here somewhere."

"Your hair has gotten very long." Maev grabbed a length of braid and tugged on it as Ollo left.

I admired how intricate the weaving was. "You're very good with styling it." And then, I asked before thinking, "Does Ollo have a girlfriend?"

Maev scrunched her nose at me. "Why? Are you asking for your own sake?"

My face fell. "You think the day after the Shadow Guard returns is when I will go after your brother?"

"There are constantly women asking about him. You could be, too." Maev pursed her lips and stared.

"Does Ollo get mad when his friends flirt with you?"

Maev quickly changed her features, looking away shyly. "They haven't. No, they—they wouldn't."

"Does Ollo get pissed about the guy you went to school with?"

Her cheeks went pink. "You remember him? He's too busy for me, but ..."

"But what?"

"I'm not good at this girl talk." Her shoulder slumped. "We had a night together. But we didn't ... Have you ever, umm ..."

"Had sex?" I asked bluntly.

Instead of blushing, she gave me a terse nod. "I don't have girl friends. Have you—um—were you and the Guard together like that?"

Somehow, she sat stubbornly, angry that she had to ask, but I could tell she was trying to get to know me better, and I shook my head.

"Only with one man, and it wasn't him. I think if I had been with the Guard, with Brekt, he would have ruined all men for me." I checked to see if Ollo was back yet, embarrassed at where the conversation had gone. "So tell me about this guy," I said, hoping such a simple topic as men would be enough to distract myself from the one I was desperate to find.

"You're not talking of Hanold, are you?" I jumped.

Ollo had returned wearing lighter clothing, still in black.

Maev's irritation was immediate. "So what if I am?"

"He's too dumb for you."

Ollo's flippant remark sent Maev into a fluster. "We were in the same tech class. He can't be that much dumber than me."

"Cause his uncle was a professor. He had the lowest grades and spent more time on his hair than his studies."

"Whatever," Maev huffed. "Yes, I like him. He *is* smart, and he's interested in the same things as me." She turned to me and said in a low voice, "And a fantastic kisser."

Ollo stopped in his tracks, a look of disgust coming over him.

"Seriously?" Maev's hands shot to her hips as she stood. "I'm supposed to say nothing when you make eyes at the Ikhor, but you can't deal with the fact I *kissed* a guy?"

"Are there any men you do approve of?" I asked Ollo, trying to end their bickering.

He shrugged. "What can I say? I actually care for my sister's future."

"Well, you don't have to worry about Hanold out here." She spun in a circle, motioning to the mess we'd made on the bridge. "I'm quite safe."

I wondered about Maev's men and what they were like while

trying to ignore the emotional mess I was in. I thought of spending time with Ollo in his city, alone.

Without realizing it, my fingers stroked the picture in my pocket. I let go, standing and heading to the front window for a better view of the sand-covered horizon. I reached the glass, gazing out into the smoke-filled desert. It was a scene I had never imagined back home in my cold and bleak forest. This place, though desolate, made me feel bigger, part of something important.

The desert seemed to stretch endlessly, and I was sure, through the cloud of smoke, it went on until it disappeared behind the horizon. To the left, massive rock formations rose towards the sky. On the right, shapes hid in the smoke. I inched closer to the window, squinting. One shape, in particular, moved in the dark cloud.

It wasn't the swirling shadow I had been hallucinating these past few weeks, and my cheek pressed against the cold glass to see better. "Safe isn't the word I would use, Maev. We are all dead meat."

"What do you mean?" She looked to where I was pointing.

"The Guards have caught up."

THIRTY-SEVEN

Liv

"Get to the weapons panel, Liv. Do as I instruct." Ollo hurried to the captain's seat.

Maev raced to another panel, braids flying behind her as I ran to where Ollo instructed, finding a slew of buttons and levers in front of me that made no sense.

"The short lever on the far left, with that circular symbol. Get ready for that one," he shouted.

"The one marked B2?"

"Yes. Ballistic number two. The others are empty. That's our one shot if we need to get anything out of our path."

"Great," I muttered.

The smoke-filled sky made it difficult to see, but in the distance, travelling fast around the outskirts of the smoke cloud, I could make out the Guard's ship.

Ollo leaned over the control panel. "Those Aspissers stole my fucking ship!"

It was the first time I had heard Ollo swear, seeing his old ship being flown toward us. "We will need to fly into that cloud to lose them. Otherwise, they'll catch up in no time. Get ready with that lever, Saviour."

"I thought your ship didn't have weapons. Why does it matter if they catch up?"

"All they have to do is jump on board, and we are done. If they take us, you become our only defence. Will you kill the Guards to save us?" He shot a knowing look at me as the ship rose in the air.

I didn't answer. Instead, I asked, "But the magic barrier, won't that keep them off?"

"Depending on speed." He was intent on the panel before him. "If it's an attack, the magic will push back. If they hop on board, the magic won't push them away. It reacts to speed and force, meaning—"

"Look out!" I pointed outside just as the Aspis flew past, casting us in its shadow—my earlier question, of where *he* was, answered.

Ollo swerved, taking us out of its path. "Blessed Rem," he said as he got us righted again, aiming for the smoke, pushing the airship faster.

"The Aspis will be able to sense me in that cloud, Ollo," I warned. "I don't have control right now. And we won't be able to see it!"

"I'm going to line us up. One shot to slow it down. Let's aim for the beast and get in that cloud."

"You want me to fire at him?"

"It, Saviour. *It.* There's no man flying through the sky."

Was I really going to aim for the beast and fire at it?

Brekt—

We were moments from entering the cover of smoke when I felt the Aspis. It was on our tail. I hadn't used magic, but it was coming for me. My fear must have triggered it.

Before we reached the cloud, Ollo spun the ship toward the Aspis, piloting the airship in reverse, and I righted myself after being tossed sideways. The move would have impressed me if I weren't shaking so badly.

The beast was hard to track as it slid through the sky like a snake in water. It was fast, feral, as it zeroed in on us. The sun shone off its long fangs, ready to strike.

"Its movements are too wild," Ollo shouted. "Scratch that plan. We head for the smoke."

He turned us again, aiming away from the beast, and I grabbed the panel as the entire ship tilted. We dove into the smoke cloud, the room growing darker, and the time seemed closer to dusk than midmorning. I couldn't see a thing outside the window except swirls of grey pushing past it.

"My ship has a better navigation system," Ollo complained. "So the Guards, if any know how to read it, will find us easily in this. The Aspis, however, will be searching for Liv. We need to keep our eyes peeled for shadows, and Liv, keep your inner detector open for the Aspis."

"It's behind," I said. "Gaining on us. I can feel its hunger."

Could it feel my fear? Was Brekt aware? Did he know what was going on?

"Get ready. When it's close enough, you need to pull. Tell me when it's close, and I'll face us in the right direction."

"I'm ready." My trembling hands hovered over the lever as Maev held onto the edge of the panel, watching her brother with tears threatening to spill.

"It's close, Ollo, real close." My voice shook with anticipation.

"You tell me when to spin us around, Liv. We are trusting your instincts here."

"The cloud is thinning. I think we are near the other side!" Maev shouted.

I felt it, the excitement, the killing need.

"It's here!" I yelled.

Ollo spun us toward the Aspis. "Now, Liv!"

I held onto the panel as the room plummeted into darkness, facing a black shadow that rivalled the night sky. The beast's jaws opened wide, its yellow eyes brimming with animalistic rage.

I grabbed onto the lever and yanked.

Only I forgot.

Two of my fingers weren't working because the beast that was aiming for us had torn my arm off.

Ice coated the entire panel before me.

My hand slipped off the lever, and the Aspis collided with the ship, sending a rainbow of light waves across the front window when its teeth clashed with the magic barrier.

The crash sent us all flying, and I fell forward onto the frozen panel, my body pushing against the lever, engaging it and sending a projectile into the smoke.

The ship spiralled in the air, and I flew sideways, smashing against the wall.

Ollo had the good sense to hold on to his seat and was now dangling from it, trying to hoist himself back into place as Maev landed on top of me with a loud crunch. Somehow, Ollo got himself back into his seat, grunting with pain. "Maev, Plan B. Get out now."

"Plan B?" I muttered.

"Now?" Maev screamed, "No. We can still get away."

Ollo righted the ship, and the grimace on his face told me he was injured. "Get the godsdamned bags, Maev, now."

"Ollo—"

"Get. The. Bags." Ollo didn't look over his shoulder. I had never heard him use such a tone before, and Maev stiffened next to me as he continued, "Shields are gone. You have three minutes. I will level us with the ground. The canyons are within sight. You can get there on foot."

"Come on." Maev grabbed my wrist and pulled me along.

"What are we doing?" I got to my feet and followed Maev, who wasn't answering me. She grabbed a bag that had flown to the back of the room and passed it to me as a tear streaked down her face.

I looked back to Ollo, who was ignoring us, pressing buttons and turning the nose of the ship downward.

Maev slung a pack over her shoulders and marched from the room.

"Maev, what's Plan B?"

"We go on foot."

"What about Ollo?"

"Ollo is distracting them while we escape. He knew we would get to this point. They're desperate because we are about to leave Guardian lands."

"Isn't this a little dramatic? Why risk your life, Ollo?" I turned around, rushing into the control room when Maev grabbed my arm, stopping me.

The twins exchanged a look, and Ollo nodded, making Maev turn to me. "Ollo was tasked to bring you back to the Elders to lead their armies to invade Veydes. We hoped to find a different answer to end this, but it's our people's last hope. They plan to strike the Guardian City."

Maev held my stare, waiting to hear my answer.

"You lied to me. You said I wouldn't have to fight."

"Argue about it when you're off this ship!" Ollo shouted.

I searched Maev's angry gaze. "I'll follow you."

What I didn't say was there was no way I was leading an army to kill any more Guardians.

"I don't think this is worth you dying over," I said to Ollo. "Not for me."

"Don't worry, Saviour." Ollo's mouth pulled tight, and it wasn't his usual cocky smile. "I'm not bragging when I say I am the best pilot in Rydavas. I will show these Guards what to expect from my people if they plan to attack. I'll find you on the other side."

"The other side of what?"

Ollo looked at his sister, and an emotion that I rarely saw flashed across his face—love. Ollo loved his sister, as I had never felt with my own. "I'll see you at home," he said, voice shaking.

With that, Ollo turned, and Maev pulled me away from the bridge.

I focused on Maev, and only Maev, as we ran through the halls. She was wiping at her eyes, stumbling around corners. When we reached the hatch, she ripped open the door as the ship approached the ground fast. "We jump when he hovers." Her voice cracked with pain.

"He'll be okay, Maev." I tried to reassure her.

"He will not," she spat.

A roar came from outside just before the Aspis slammed into the ship, hurling Maev and me through the hatch and into the open air.

My stomach bottomed out as we fell ten feet to the sand.

I landed on the ground, and the wind knocked out of me on impact. Sand burst into a cloud of dust as I choked on dry, hot air.

The ship sped away as Ollo shot straight into the air, aiming for the sun. The Aspis followed, and my braids whipped around me as a smaller ship flew by, following the beast into the sky.

Maev watched Ollo go, climbing high, heading toward the canyons ahead. "Stupid. Idiot. He thinks he's brave." Maev was facing away from me, wiping her sleeve across her face. "You're not brave!" Her voice cracked, breaking from her pain. "You're just a stupid show-off!"

I didn't know how to comfort her. I couldn't lie again and say that he'd be okay. "We need to make use of his plan, Maev. We can do this. The Guards are following him."

Maev spun, eyes red and glistening. She nodded anyway, and with one last glance at the sky, she rose and removed Nuo's map from the bag. "The map shows only the beginnings of the canyons. We have to use luck to make it through. After that, I have a fairly good idea of the road we need to take north." She stumbled over her words, trying to pretend she wasn't crying.

"He said he'd find us on the other side."

Her eyes closed, and she shook her head before opening them again.

"How long will the journey take?"

I brushed the sand from my pants. It was a horrible, scratchy feeling. The air was no better.

"If we don't find a horse or another airship? On foot, it will take us months."

"We don't have time for that."

"We best get started. We won't find help on this side of the canyons."

It was when we began to walk that we heard it.

An explosion, loud and damning, echoed across the open sands, and in the distance, a plume of black smoke rose above the canyons.

Flying away from the explosion was the smaller ship piloted by the Guards.

THIRTY-EIGHT

Liv

When my mother died, I hid for weeks and barely ate. Rebeka was a constant nag, warning that we couldn't slack. Work had to be done. The world continued to move. When I finally braved walking the streets of our small village, no one said a thing to me. My mother had been the one to make a scene, but the echoes of her protests affected our lives long after she was gone. Rebeka became meaner. Keepers laughed when we passed. Some even spat at our feet. I think that's when I first built the box in my chest, and carved names into the edge.

He wasn't dead. He couldn't be dead.

I felt numb as we headed for the canyons—present but not present. It was my fault. Ollo was—no. Ollo wasn't stupid. He wouldn't have given his life up that easily.

Maev walked ahead, silent like a spectre gliding across the sand. She hadn't spoken to me since the airship was destroyed.

I didn't blame her. None of this would have happened if I had pulled that lever. I squeezed my fist, and only two fingers closed. I lifted my arm but could only get it to shoulder height before the pain struck. I was the most powerful being in the world, and I was useless.

Maev stared at the sky for what felt like an eternity, trembling, mumbling to herself, before she walked away toward the canyons. She had already lost one brother. A mother. Now she had to go home and tell her father that his second son was gone.

Perhaps what we saw was wrong, I wanted to say, but didn't.

If I hadn't made them go to Ouras's temple, would we have made it across?

How many more mistakes would I make in my life to ruin others?

I was a liability. The Guards hadn't wanted to bring me along for that reason. It was because of me we were on that burning field when *he* died. Now, I had an entire world of people who hated me or craved a power that wasn't mine.

Would I ever be just Liv? *He* saw me that way, and now I was the thing meant to kill what remained of him.

Behind us, on the horizon, was a hazy mirage of a smouldering ruined city. South Aspis had been a large camp for the Guardians. Now it lay lifeless. Could I be capable of that kind of damage? Were any of the Ikhor before me powerful enough to do something like that?

It didn't go unnoticed that while Maev was being torn apart inside, I thought of myself—maybe I *was* the perfect host for the magic.

We walked in silence for several hours until we reached the edge of the canyons. I was hot, sweat-drenched and sore when the sand gradually gave way to light-coloured rock, which became boulders, then towering cliffs.

The black smoke from the crashed ship had turned grey. It would be difficult to find in a day or two ... if there was anything left to find.

Our path dipped between stone walls that rose higher than the Danuli trees, and I imagined great rivers ran between the winding pathways once upon a time. Horizontal red and orange rock with thin veins formed the canyons. It was beautiful, if not confining. Unless you counted the bones littering the pathways—in some places, there were so many you couldn't see the ground.

Maev didn't comment on them as she stepped over countless skulls shaped exactly like a human head.

Birds screeched in the distance, echoing off the walls.

The dry heat tore at my lungs and parched my already sore throat.

Maev still didn't speak to me. She had never been quiet for that long.

My chest hurt. For Ollo. For Maev.

Every so often, she stopped to check the map, scribbling on it. It wasn't until the light was fading from the sky that she turned to look at me, but her eyes were empty. She wasn't seeing me at all.

We stopped for the night in a tight crevice between high rock walls, and she didn't say a word. The towering rock swallowed any light cast by the moon and stars as the sky turned black. Everything became dark shadows. The glowing crystals from my earrings and bracelet gave off enough light that we could situate ourselves between two boulders. Maev sobbed in her sleep, and I nudged myself closer to her, offering any comfort I could.

I reached a hand into my pocket, where the photo of the Guards lay tucked away. I didn't pull it out—it was too dark to see, but I held it with the three fingers that worked on my right hand. I tried and tried to close the other two, but they wouldn't budge.

"I'm sorry, Ollo." I leaned my head back toward the sky.

How could he sacrifice his life for me—for the mission he was on? It made me wonder how bad things were to push the twins to do all this.

But I wouldn't go to war. I wouldn't kill those who didn't know the secrets being kept from them. It was all a lie—what the Guardians thought of the Aethar, what the Aethar saw in the Guardians. The people on each side had nothing to do with the games played by those in power.

This was the Council's doing.

Would anyone see it my way? I think that's what Ollo was trying to explain to me about perspective. Who else had it when it came to beliefs?

Millions of stars moved across the sliver of sky between the black walls of the canyon. The wind whistled between the cracks, blocking out any sounds of the night that would surely haunt me. After an endless amount of time, when my mind was fading to dreaming, the sounds of the wind changed—whistling turned to humming.

I bolted upright, peering toward the edge of the crevice, and stifled a gasp. I slapped my cheek. "This isn't a dream."

The stars above sparkled as I had seen them thousands of nights before—no sign of the strange crystalline sky from that nightmarish place.

But there was a monster here.

A swirling darkness, almost invisible in the already black night, moved like water in a drain. It was a pillar in the dark, blocking our way out of the tight gap in the canyon rock.

It edged closer.

I jumped to my feet, fumbling with my swords, getting one into my hands. The glow from my crystals only reached a few short feet past me, but I didn't need light to see and feel the shadow. "Stop right there," I said in the most confident voice I could muster.

Be brave and fake it if you must. That's what Ollo taught me.

The shadow didn't listen. It glided toward me, swirling and whirling as it transformed into the shape of a figure. Arms. Legs. A head. It took steps now as it slunk forward, hunched, as if scared to approach.

I couldn't keep track of the things that haunted me, but the shadow was one I couldn't explain. "Wha—what are you?" I tightened my already painful grip on my sword, and I slid my foot outward, scraping on the rock to find flat ground.

The shadow rose higher, its height impossible for a man. Arms that shouldn't have been there reached out. It was so close now.

I lifted my sword, only a foot away from the shadow. "Stay back."

It glided closer, sliding past my sword, through it, unaffected by the sharp point.

I tilted my chin up as it towered above me.

A shadowed hand appeared beside my face, and a touch as cold as ice traced a line down my cheek.

I shook violently, my breath coming in short gasps as the blackness swirling inches from my face absorbed the glow from my earrings. My back was flush against the canyon rock as I blinked in the darkness, straining to see better.

A low rumbling came from the shadow as it loomed over me, pinning me against the wall. I jumped when the shadow held me by the hip like a lover, and its ice-cold touch cupped the back of my head.

"Who are you?" I hated what my subconscious wanted to believe. "Brekt?" My voice cracked with his name on my lips, and I felt like a fool. He hadn't appeared like this before, but nothing was normal about what he was—what we both had become.

The rumbling intensified. It was a growl—a warning. The shadow stopped moving—no more spinning blackness. The cold hand on my hip tightened, freezing me, as two eyes cracked open. Glowing. Deadly. Hungry.

The creature roared in my face, and I closed my eyes to hide from it, whimpering. The hand left my body, and my eyes shot open.

The shadow swirled again. Gone was the human form. It was a churning whirlwind, blocking out the world beyond.

I waited, afraid of what it would do. But it only turned into smoke and rose toward the sky.

I remained there. Shaking and still holding my blade.

No. It can't be him. Was something happening to him—changing him? He had been a man the last time ... nearly.

"Liv?"

I spun, my feet sliding out from under me, and I fell hard on my ass, dropping my sword.

The sky was turning lighter, outlining Maev's form sitting up and staring.

"You heard that?" I asked.

"Heard what?" She rubbed at her eyes.

"W-what woke you?" I grabbed hold of the rocks, kneeling to retrieve my sword.

"I only heard you talking. I have been awake for hours."

I put my sword back into its casing, and it settled in place. That's when I realized what she was saying. "You were awake? And you didn't hear anything? Did you see anything just now?"

"No." Maev's voice was raw like she had been crying most of the night. "Not until I looked over and saw you standing against the rock holding your sword."

I had been hallucinating. The shadows I continued to see—it wasn't him. It wasn't *real*—I had lost my mind.

Unless the shadow was something else ...

Was the shadow monster connected to Brekt and the Aspis? Something about the swirling smoke was the same.

"Let's get moving if we can't sleep." I retrieved my pack with shaking hands.

I needed to get out of here, to get away from all of this and to find those gods. Maev hadn't seen the shadows. Did that mean—

"Maev," I choked. "On the deck of the airship. I wasn't making it up, right? I saw him?"

"What are you talking about?" Maev stood, yawning.

My next words were a plea. "Did you see the Shadow Guard? What's real—I don't know anymore."

Maev was silent for a moment. "I saw him, Livy. He was real. What's going on?"

The crystals Ollo had stuffed in my pockets were full, no longer easing the strain from the magic. Every bone, every nerve vibrated and shook from the power within, longing to be unleashed. My erratic change of emotions triggered it. I was losing control, and I needed to stop *feeling*. "Nothing's going on. Let's get moving, okay?"

When we left the crevice and the morning light reached us, Maev made a face. "How are you doing now?" she asked, eyes roaming over me.

I looked worse than before. I felt everything, and none of it was good. My shoulders sagged, and the weight of it all came crashing down. "Everything is my fault. Nuo, Brekt, Ollo. The floods. The fires. I—I ..."

Maev stared, and the dark circles under her eyes said everything she was not.

"It's going to get worse, Maev. I'm losing control over everything. I should've known a long time ago I would hurt them all," I continued.

"How should you have known?" Maev walked next to me, wrapping her arms around herself.

She was holding herself together as we continued along the thin stretch of the canyon. We aimed for the dark cloud of smoke we could no longer see.

"I felt the power in me. I noticed strange things. I should've known."

The morning sun peeked over the cliff edge creating a beam of golden light, which hit the other side.

"No one could've guessed they were the Ikhor," she said,

surprising me. I didn't expect her to understand. "Half the time, I thought it was just a fable everyone believed in, that I would find nothing when I followed Ollo here."

"The Shadow Guard knew what he was. I was stupid enough to believe I was the Aspis—what the Guards were looking for. I thought I would be the hero."

"You think you're not?" Maev held herself a little tighter.

"I haven't done a single thing to save anyone. And I won't be able to save anyone once the magic is returned."

Her face pinched.

"I'm sorry." I placed a hand on her arm. "I will help you. I made a promise that I would. But I need to fill your crystals and get this magic out." I dropped my voice. "I need to save Brekt, too."

She faced forward, hugging herself as she walked.

"Why did you follow Ollo if you weren't sure I was real?" I asked.

Her steps slowed. "Hope, I suppose. So much was going wrong. Crystals were becoming scarce. Hate was festering in my people. Every day life looked the same unless you paid attention. No one was doing anything positive about it. So I decided to follow Ollo to find you. I knew my tracker would give him an advantage he wouldn't have on his own. I hoped the Ikhor would change people —that maybe ... maybe we didn't need to go to war with Veydes. I wanted you to solve everyone's problems." She gave me a weak smile.

When I laughed, her face fell. I think she remembered Ollo was dead, and that we were both trudging through danger alone and afraid.

"But this *is* your fault," she said. "That we are here without him."

Her words were a sharp knife in the heart, and the way Maev looked away from me reminded me so much of Rebeka—the deep-rooted disappointment that I was in her life.

Maev's attention shifted back to me. "No." She shook her head. "No, I didn't mean that, Liv. I don't mean it. I'm sorry I said that."

I didn't reply because she had meant it, and she wasn't wrong.

I brushed the lingering sand off my clothes and fixed the straps of my bag. "Let's focus on finding the crash site and getting out of the canyons."

We walked in silence once more, stepping over bones and sticking to the shade when the sun was high.

"Liv ..." Maev stopped, and when I searched ahead, I saw what made her pause.

They weren't the first we had come across. Bodies—bloody bodies. There had been decaying bodies guiding our path, but these were *fresh*.

I gagged and covered my nose to stop myself from throwing up. The smell was ... indescribable.

A shadow passed overhead, blocking the sun.

"You saw that right?" I asked. We exchanged a look and picked up our pace, sticking close to the rock walls. "I'm not imagining this, am I?" I stepped over a pile of bones and avoided a body face down in the dirt, lying in a pool of dried blood.

"The dead, stinking bodies? No, Liv, you aren't imagining this. Stop freaking me out."

"I'm only making sure I'm not lost in another nightmare."

"Well, unfortunately for me, I am here in this nightmare with you. And *ugh*—" Maev gagged, swallowing and holding the back of her hand to her mouth. "Stop flinching at every sound. I'm supposed to be the one scared, not the all-powerful saviour. This isn't a good look for us."

"I can't be all-powerful when it's that power that calls the Aspis."

"It's probably what keeps blocking out the sun. And I doubt if you called it, it could squeeze its head in this section of the canyon. It's too tight."

If the path forward hadn't been so narrow, we might not have had to step over bodies—some of which were bent in grotesque ways, like they had fallen from above. The next one I passed over had its arm bent underneath its back. An Aethar, easy to see from the scars.

"This one hasn't been dead long." I stopped before Maev passed, reaching a hand out to stop her. "Don't touch it, Maev. Look at that one."

The body hadn't been dead for long, and there were rashes around its neck. Dark, red veins protruded from their throat, arms and temples.

"Disease, I think." Maev did her best to avoid touching the Aethar.

We agreed to walk in silence after that, and stuck close to overhangs and large rocks, listening for any sound of danger. Somehow, the red-coloured canyons had become far scarier than the nightmares with the half-beast.

Another day of travelling in the canyons led nowhere, with no signs of the airship. Maev swore she was tracking the sun's patterns and taking us in the right direction, and I had no option but to trust her. It was awkward travelling like this. With someone you knew was angry with you. Sleeping side by side was even worse.

On the third day of walking, red became my least favourite colour, the lines of the canyon walls dizzying and blurring as I passed them. At least I hadn't seen that shadow again.

Maev said we would search one more day for the ship before giving up. She had packed our bags with dried food and water, but we needed it to last. It was late in the afternoon, and the sun disappeared behind the cliff when she rolled up the stolen map, having scribbled some more lines below the canyons, and stopped me to shove it in my pack. The sweat that gathered on my brow dried to salt before it dripped into my eyes.

"I'm too hot to remove my bag," she said. "You can carry it for me. Easier to grab."

"Don't squish it in like that," I argued, wiping my hand across my grime-covered forehead.

She snorted. "As if you plan to return it to the Guard one day?"

"Are you sure you know your directions?" I dragged my feet, holding onto the straps of my pack to keep myself upright. At least the pack was getting lighter since we had eaten some of the supplies I carried.

"Liv, the canyons will take days to cross. This is day three, and we have been searching for the ship, barely making any headway."

"I'm getting anxious. Maybe it's from the hundredth decaying body I just stepped over."

"We have to find that ship."

"I know we do," I said, swallowing around a dry tongue, dizzy. "Just be prepared for what you'll find."

Maev stopped and pinned me with a scowl. "He's alive."

That wasn't the first time she had said it. "I know. We will find him."

"You don't believe me. But I know it." She stomped forward, eyes darting back and forth, searching.

"How do you know?" I tripped over a rock, then kicked it, mumbling a curse.

"It's a twin thing. We are connected. I know. I would feel him gone from this world. He's alive."

I was connected to someone, too. I was too lost in my grief to understand it before, but I think ... I had known he wasn't truly gone. "If you feel it, Maev, then he is alive."

I wasn't sure if I was trying to convince her or myself.

"When do you think we will come across the first shrine of Mayra?" I asked an hour later, the sun gone from the trail.

When I first arrived in Veydes, I loved being in the sunlight. Now? Now, I almost wished to be under the canopy of the Endless Forest.

"The one I know of is far north. But there must be many along the coast. We will exit the canyons and follow the sea."

"Will we pass any Southlanders?"

"Very likely, yes. They've taken over much of South Rydavas. I can't say how close they settle to the sea, but we will find out."

I hopped down off a large slab of rock. The pathway we were in was tight, and Maev had complained of something called claustrophobia, which I learned was a fear of small spaces. I wanted to know how she would have felt living in my old shack.

"Let's sleep under this overhang." She motioned to a small space where we could hide from anything coming from above. We dragged some rocks from around the pathway ahead to block anyone seeing us from the ground, and sat against our packs, side by side.

Without saying another word, we waited for the long night to pass.

THIRTY-NINE

Liv

Maev thinks I don't react properly to danger, and perhaps I don't. I figured Death would have come for me long ago. But that was before I had hope—before I met the Guards and began a new life. Now that I have discovered Brekt's alive, I can save him. Danger isn't scary—hope is. It puts danger into a sharper perspective and shows you everything you could lose.

S creams.
A loud roar.
Someone shook me.

Terrible echoes bounced across the canyon walls until they reached where Maev and I slept, and it took me several long seconds of blinking away sleep before reality set in.

"It's coming from all sides," Maev said as she strapped on her pack, searching the far reaches of the pass we were trapped in. The look she sent me told me to smarten up and get moving.

The sun was up, the heat already reaching us in the overhang's shadow, but my blood ran cold. The bellows were getting closer now. There was a scream of death before silence, then another took its place as Maev and I moved out into the sun and stuck to the rock wall, continuing toward the crashed airship. My heart pounded with each step.

The canyon walls were high, and there weren't many places to hide past the overhang.

"We need to move fast, get out of this passage and away from the voices," Maev whispered behind me.

A dark shadow passed overhead, and we both threw ourselves against the rock wall and glanced up.

"Is it the Aspis?" Maev asked, a tremor in her voice.

"I ... don't know." I felt the beast, but it was faint, as if it were far away. Had something dulled the pull?

The screaming stopped.

"This is worse than the nightmares." I coughed as dry air hit my lungs, and my tongue stuck to the roof of my mouth.

"This place is like a death trap from a horror story," Maev added. "All night, I thought the jagged rocks looked like teeth that would chomp and squish us."

Dirt scuffed at the end of the passage in the direction we'd come from. My fingers trembled violently when I pressed a hand to my mouth.

A stranger's voice echoed, "Run. This way. They're close."

Were they coming for us? Maev and I exchanged a terrified look before bolting for the other end of the passage.

"Run, Maev, don't stop for anything." My foot slid on dirt as I took off, and Maev cursed behind me as she followed. With the little strength we had, we vaulted over rock and dried bones. One snapped under my feet as I landed on it.

The shadow blocked out the sun again, and a loud scream tore from the sky.

"Liv, what is that? Is it the Aspis?" Maev panted. "Those screams are from people in the air." A loud thud hit the ground behind us. "Don't look!" Maev shouted as I turned.

There was screaming again, this time from around the bend, and we skidded to a halt. I grabbed Maev's arm, pulling her towards a boulder to hide behind. "We are surrounded, Maev."

We ducked down when more footsteps came around the corner.

Several Aethar in drab clothing and scarred skin raced past, heading in the direction we came from. They kept their attention on the sky as they ran. Blood soaked their clothes, as sweat poured down their marbled skin.

"He's getting closer," a gravelly voice warned the group. "He's killing everything that moves."

"Then we should stop moving." It was a woman leading the group. She was climbing over a rock when a loud scream came from the distance. She paused before running again.

The others followed, leaving a trail of blood behind them.

"Enemies at our back, enemies in the sky. The Ikhor will be proud of what we survived when we reach him," the gravelly-voiced man said before he disappeared.

So the Aethar coming from Rydavas didn't know who the Ikhor was.

Maev and I wasted no time getting out of the small passage. Around the next bend was a round opening in the canyon, several paths leading off it, and we spun in a circle, each taking in the pathways until we faced each other.

Maev's face was a mix of dirt and sweat, the lines and dashes of her skin were peeling from days in the sun. "What do we—" Another scream silenced her, and we looked back to the turn we had come from. "I'm scared, Livy."

"I'll use the magic if I have to."

"And call the Aspis to us? If that's what's in the sky, let it focus on the Southlanders. We keep running."

Footprints in the sand surrounded us, leading in every direction. I pointed to my right, where there were fewer steps. "Let's try that way."

Rock scuffled behind us, and we whirled around.

My blood went cold.

An Aethar, over six feet tall with blood dripping from his temple, stood behind us. "It seems I've found more little Guardians to play with." He reached out a hand and wrapped it around my neck, squeezing. "You have seconds until you are dead."

I batted at his hand to no effect, staring into his blood-red eyes.

"My lucky day. The Canyons are full of little tattooed pests scurrying about." His voice choked around fluid in his mouth. Blood. He'd been in a recent fight.

The veins on the Aethar's neck were swollen and pulsing, infected perhaps. The veins in his arm, the one holding me in place, had red lines running up and down that stood out in stark contrast to his marred skin. He was more than burned. He was turning rotten.

Behind him, two more Aethar crept in on silent feet, surrounding Maev and me. They looked the same. Red-eyed, sickly, panting like rabid, diseased animals. One of them reached out and grabbed Maev by the arms. She gave a weak cry of pain.

I grabbed the wrist of the monster holding me, trying to shake him off. It was useless. He was one of the largest men I had ever seen. A Sea-leg, too, I could tell from his neck.

He looked up above us. "Keep an eye on the sky, fellas. We don't want any more visits."

Blackness edged my vision, and I choked to get air.

It's time I start playing the Ikhor, I guess. I gathered my courage.

I raised my hands to the air to call on my magic, and a biting cold gathered in my palms as I seized the Aethar's arm that held me.

He screamed, letting go, and I choked on the fresh wave of dry, sandy air scraping its way down my throat. I stumbled toward Maev, slamming my hand into the face of the one holding her. We scrambled away, putting ourselves back-to-back, moving in a circle together so I could keep them away from Maev.

I held out my palm to the shocked faces of the Aethar. We had to run—but which way was the right path?

The big Sea-leg was kneeling on the ground, holding blackened arms to his chest. The cold had burned him. I had seen the effects before, in the Lost Lands. There was no repairing damage like that. His breathing laboured as he looked up at me, his face lit with joy. "What do we have here?"

Maev and I stumbled back, putting more distance between us and them. At least we would have a running chance before they tried to grab us again.

The big Sea-leg on the ground spoke again, his liquid voice making me cringe. "These are no Guardians. We have found the Ikhor. Look at my arms." He raised his frostbitten arms proudly, shocking the other Aethar, and all three turned their attention back to me.

I kept my attention on the Sea-leg, who eyed my black clothing.

Another Aethar spoke, revealing herself to be female, her face red and peeling from where I had frozen her. "Are you certain? Look at them. They reek of Guardians."

"I am who he says." I lifted my palms, shimmering with frost. I didn't mention it was them who reeked after days of travel in this heat.

The Aethar stayed silent as uncertainty settled on the group.

The man on his knees gave a curdled laugh. "We will deliver the Ikhor to Veydes. We will take their lands."

"We need to run, Liv." Maev's voice was surprisingly steady as she inched away from the Aethar. "Ice them all. We need to run."

"Show us your magic," one of the Aethar demanded. "Show us the truth."

A sliver of hope—I could convince them not to attack.

I took a deep breath, and looked down at my palms, dripping water, no longer frosted. What was I feeling at that moment? Scared, angry, and hopeful that I wouldn't die.

I had no idea what would happen next as I raised my palms, sensing what magic I could pull from the earth. I was hot and cold at once—flame and ice battling to form.

Neither did.

Shit.

Everyone flinched when the light above us winked out, and we all turned to the sky as it brightened—empty.

"It comes. We must go now." The Sea-leg on the ground stood.

The other Aethar reached for weapons—bows strapped to their back, and I strained harder for my magic, the wind whistling through the canyon.

"Hurry it up, Liv. Once they've taken you, I am dead."

"You're already dead, Aethar," came a deep voice from behind us—one so familiar it should be soothing, instead, it sent chills down my spine.

I twisted as an arrow flew past my head, nearly missing Nuo as he stared me down.

The Canyon disappeared. The Aethar meant nothing.

All of my focus narrowed to that searing hatred set deep into his honey-brown eyes. He nearly blended into the pathway's shadows behind him. He had come on silent footsteps, following his prey.

"The Guards! They lied to us! She is not the Ikhor," shouted the Aethar behind us. "Kill them all!"

That explained all the footsteps in the sand. They had been cornering the Aethar, herding them like cattle. The screams had been the Guards taking down their enemy, and the shadow was the Aspis overhead.

Bastane and Kazhi appeared silently behind Nuo, the light of the sun beating down on the flat rock and shining off their swords.

Guards at our front, Aethars at our back.

Maev fled for the canyon wall as I stayed frozen, paralyzed in fear.

My magic. I needed to use my magic!

Nuo's attention flickered toward the Aethar behind me. I think he was deciding whether he had time to kill me before they reached him. His mouth drew a hard line, and his posture shifted. He shot forward, aiming for me, Bastane and Kazhi closing in behind.

Falizha was nowhere in sight.

More arrows shot past my head. "Shit." I had no time. Nowhere to go. Maev was running away, disappearing down a path, and I was standing in the middle of a fight, unsure what side to take on. Once again, my cowardice reared its pathetic head, and I ducked, holding myself to the ground as ice surrounded me, blocking everything out.

The wall stopped Nuo in his tracks. He slammed his fists against it, the crystallized vibration echoing. *Boom boom boom.* His distorted form stilled, turning.

I followed his line of sight.

Shame hit me—I had protected myself and left Maev out in the open.

"No!" I screamed.

I watched with horror as Nuo disappeared down the same path Maev had just fled. I scrambled for my swords, remembering the trick I had used before to break the ice, but it shattered before I could get my swords in my hands.

The Aethar had reached me first. A gnarled hand wrapped around my arm, pulling me into the open, and I swore. Pain shot down my shoulder where the Aspis had severed my arm as the big Sea-leg's scarred face filled my vision.

A knife embedded itself in the Aethar's neck, spraying blood.

He made a face before he collapsed, taking me to the ground with him. I hit my side hard, eating dirt. I stared into his blank face —eyes empty, soul gone. Blood pooled, and I scrambled away from the river of red that cut through the dirt toward me.

A shadow blocked out the sun, and I jerked away when I found Kazhi overtop me.

"Go after your friend," she said in a low voice. "Nuo is the biggest danger to you two now. Nothing else. He wants blood."

I groaned as I stood. My entire side would be bruised.

Kazhi's smile was wicked as she turned back to the attacking Aethar.

I flew past her as she took on the last ones standing, not stopping to question her motives. I didn't see Bastane. I only ran.

"Please, Nuo," I cried to the canyons before me. "Don't kill her."

CHAPTER
FORTY

Nuo

I abandoned the ice barrier and the scarred fuckers, letting Bas and Kazhi finish the remaining Aethar while the Ikhor cowered. It would be an easy win for the two of them. The Ikhor was protecting itself in its little ice cage and letting its worshippers die for its own safety.

What was I going to do with the blue Aethar? Get answers. Then, spill more blood. The blue girl was going to tell me everything about the Ikhor and lure it right to me. I would avenge my brother and my family from long ago, and make the Aethar pay. I would end this.

The Aethar hadn't made it far after making several bad turns. I followed her footprints. She'd fallen, bled, and now was running in a wide-open pass along the canyon wall, heading for a space between some rocks, unaware I was following her.

I threw the blade I was holding, and it landed on the ground in front of her. She tripped over her feet, screaming.

The sounds of death rang out from behind—the Guards were ending the Aethar—but all I could hear was the blue one whimpering.

The sun beat down on her, shining off the strange tones of her hair as she surveyed her surroundings frantically, trying to find a way out. Then she saw me. Her eyes, red-rimmed and glossy, grew wide as she collapsed against the rock, shaking.

Aethar usually loved the fight. I wasn't sure I enjoyed this one's fear.

Dust kicked up around my feet as I stalked forward, hiding none of the monster within—the one that loved ending their lives. I was faster, stronger and smarter. There was no escaping, though I gave her credit, she still tried.

The Aethar surprised me by jumping up and running again. I caught up quickly and grabbed her around the waist, throwing her to the ground. "Nowhere to go, Blue. You've trapped yourself against a wall. Wasn't very smart of you, was it?"

She cried out and backed up against the stone. Tearing at the rocks, she tried to climb over them, only to fall hard as I stood over her.

I reached down, fisting her braided hair and pulled her up to face me. Her legacy was as difficult to pinpoint as Kazhi's. Tears streamed down her face, streaking the sand caked onto her cheeks.

This one was strange. They usually smiled at the pain.

"Please," she sobbed, barely able to speak, grabbing at her hair.

Scarred burns covered one of her arms. She kept a pretty face to blend in, but she was one of them.

"Aren't you pathetic," I said. "Your kind usually laughs when they face death."

"I know you will torture me first." Something in her snapped, and she pounded a fist against my arms, twisting, hoping to dislodge herself. "You bastard. I know who you are. You're a monster!"

I pulled her closer, and her face paled to a soft blue as I held her near eye level. She was tall. I only had to duck slightly. "I will be worse than a monster if you don't tell me everything I need to know."

"How could she ever love you?" She grunted as she thrashed. "She told me you were her closest friend. You're horrible."

I went still. "Who?"

"Liv!"

The woman screamed as my fist tightened in her hair, and she grabbed my hand, trying to ease the pain.

Her tricks wouldn't work on me. "Don't fuck with me, Blue. Tell me, where were you taking the Ikhor."

"Nuo!"

Bastane's voice cut through my anger. He came up beside the blue woman, gaze raking over her. "Something's off here, man. The Aethar are showing up already bloody. We need to grab her and go."

I noticed the woman bleeding from when she had fallen. Blood streaked down her face, and ran along the side of her slender, very breakable neck.

Bastane laid a hand on my shoulder, for some-fucking-reason, trying to stop me.

"What are you doing?" I shrugged his hand off. "She's an Aethar. Get out of here. You know what I'm about to do."

Bastane didn't leave. He stared at the girl, whose whole body was trembling.

"Don't let a pretty face stop you, Bas. And don't you dare stop *me*."

"Something's not right. Use your head. Look at her. The Aethar were pointing their weapons at them. They weren't travelling together. The bodies we found were broken, not burned."

We had been waiting days by the crash site for the Ikhor to show up for its ship. Then we searched the canyons for it, only to find dead Aethar everywhere.

The girl I held was muttering to herself, holding onto her hair to stop the pain.

I grabbed her arm, the scarred one, and held it up for Bas to see. "She's pissing herself 'cause she knows she's caught. I'm sick of your hero attitude, trying to save every lost girl."

Bastane gave me a look before nodding to the blue Aethar. "They never act like that. They love the fight, the pain. This one isn't scarred up. A single burn doesn't signify."

"Please," she said, latching on to Bastane's hesitation.

She was wearing Guardian clothing, strapped with one of our packs ... *fucker!*

If I was angry before, I was seeing red now.

"Is that my fucking bag?" I let go of her head and tore at the straps. They stole our ship, raided my belongings and dodged us at every turn. I was getting tired of that shit.

She struggled against me, long blue fingers tugging the straps, pulling the bag back toward her.

"This belongs to me." I jerked it out of her grip and plucked a knife from my belt, levelling it with her face, and she froze, forgetting the bag.

I reached in, searching, and stifled the sigh of relief. I found my glasses and pocketed them, surprised she hadn't left them behind. I couldn't admit to the other Guards how difficult it was to read the reports sent from the Council.

"Please, I need what's in that bag," she pleaded.

"Like I give a shit what an Aethar needs. You didn't care what I needed when you stole everything belonging to the Guards." I rummaged through the pack, but I didn't find the thing I wanted most, and I raised my eyes to the girl, letting her see the face of the Interrogator.

She sunk back, shoulders bowing.

"Where. Is. My. Map."

That map got us around without the Council's help, and more than that, it had the locations of crystals we desperately needed.

Her lips moved, but no words came out.

"Where is it?" I screamed in her face.

When I pulled out a strange device, she changed. She clawed at me, trying to get the thing back. It was made of metal, unlike the ancient ore from which some of our weapons were crafted. This metal was strange to me.

I pushed the girl away, and she stumbled back like a leaf in the wind.

Bastane put an arm in front of me, and I swear I was ready to turn my monster on him, too.

I pocketed the device and flung the bag at her feet. It was useless to me now.

"Are you being forced to follow the Ikhor?" Bastane asked her.

She stared at my vest pocket, where I stored her device. "No!" she cried, "The Ikhor is *good*. Listen to me."

It was the wrong thing to say.

Bastane took a step back. He shook his head once, debating his next move.

"Enough of this," I said.

The girl flinched and backed up as far as she could.

"Leave, Bas, I am going to find out—"

Something collided with me, and I crashed into the rock wall, falling over the blue woman as a heavy weight took me to the ground. Hard.

"You stupid Bastard!"

In a blur of motion, a fist was in my face, stinging my cheek. My chest was being hit. Over and over. However, the strength wasn't that of a man.

"She's bleeding! How dare you hurt her!"

I recognized the voice.

So quickly, my hand was around its neck. I was back on my feet, and I slammed it into the wall next to the blue one. I stared down into the strange, tainted grey eyes of my old friend. Brekt's old lover—the one who had lied, who had given her body to the evil. The signs already showed.

Her eyes had changed colour, and her skin was pale and gaunt, sticking to her bones. Her braided hair was longer, turning white. Colour had seeped from her, fading to this pale, evil creature I held by the neck.

I used to think she was sweet—a soft-hearted contrast to my brother's rough exterior. I used to think she and I were so similar—

hurt by the world, yet woke everyday hopeful for the next adventure.

I was wrong.

It didn't fight me. It just waited, anger obvious by the set of its mouth.

I couldn't take it. The betrayal was a living thing inside my chest, ripping and tearing at my flesh to be free, and I finally had my hands on the Ikhor.

I wanted to hurt it. I wanted this *thing* dead.

"You have taken *everything* from me!" I screamed into its face.

CHAPTER

FORTY-ONE

Liv

You have taken everything from me.

Nuo's words echoed off the canyon walls as they buried deep inside my heart.

He let go of me, and it stung more than his screaming in my face. "Nuo ..."

Sweat beaded on his forehead, the dry wind blowing his long hair around. He didn't blink, waiting.

I just gaped at him. My attempts to force his anger before seemed to have worked—he was here, stronger, angrier.

"I'm sorry. I should've stayed to explain ..."

His face contorted, changing from rage to sorrow to bewilderment, then quickly back to rage.

Maev scrambled away as I faced off with my closest friend, and Bastane stayed near.

"Stop it!" Nuo took a step forward, thrusting a knife in my face. "What's your goal? What's on the other side of these canyons? Are you after the gods for more magic?" A single tear streaked down his cheek, past a clenched jaw. He gave a violent shake of his head.

I put my hands up, making him jerk his blade higher. "I didn't know what I was—I didn't know. I panicked and left." I couldn't look away from him. "I didn't know what was inside me. I didn't know what would happen to *him*."

He flinched back. "Him?" His eyes narrowed, lips pulling back in a sneer. "You can't even say his name? He took you with us, protected you. Defended you. *Died* because of you, and you don't even say his name." Nuo grabbed the front of my shirt, pulling me close, his teeth flashing. "*Say* it."

"Stop," I cried, wishing I could shield myself from his hate.

"Say his fucking name!"

"Nuo," Bastane interrupted. "Let's listen—"

Nuo lifted the knife above his head, its sharp edge aimed at me, and I cowered as his knife shot forward.

A sickening crunch rang in my ears, and darkness surrounded me.

But there was no pain.

I inhaled a cloud of dust as rocks fell around me.

Nuo leaned over me, his hand wrapped around his knife that was embedded in the canyon wall next to my head.

"Why?" I didn't know exactly what I was asking.

His head was so close it was nearly touching mine. His chestnut hair fell around his face, hiding him from me. "You were supposed to be there," he whispered, his voice cracking. He let go of my shirt, letting his hand fall.

"What?"

"When he died. You fucking left. You betrayed me. You were supposed to be there." I reached for him, but he pulled back. "Don't touch me." He stepped away, looking down at Maev, who was shaking against a rock.

The tales she had heard of his cruelty weren't entirely untrue. This version of Nuo was not the one I had known.

"He's alive, Nuo." My whisper was so small. But somehow, he heard it.

He inched back, unblinking. "What did you say?" His tone was deadly. A warning.

"I've seen him. Brekt is alive."

Nuo's skin paled, and Bastane couldn't pick who to stare at.

My knees threatened to give out as I waited for him to say something.

"How dare you say such a thing to me." His face contorted, the knife coming up between us again.

I had not expected more anger. "It killed me, too, when he died. I wouldn't say such a thing to you if I didn't know it to be true."

Disbelief creased his forehead. "You knew him what? A couple of months? He'd been at my side my entire life! You have no such claim to the type of pain his *fucking* death caused me." He turned his head away, hiding his hurt. "You're evil knows no limits."

"What are we doing here?" Bastane raised his hands in frustration. "If you haven't noticed, something is hunting us all, and Kazhi is having a damned time on her own back there. The Aethar are scattered around every corner. Can we catch up after they're dead?"

What we were going to do didn't matter, because that was the moment Kazhi appeared bloody and beaten, panting as she stopped next to Bastane and grabbed onto him for support.

"More Aethar are entering from the west. This open pass is a death trap for them. And the Aspis is flying overhead, looking agitated."

We were cast into shadows as the Aspis passed, disappearing behind the rock wall.

Bastane grabbed his hair, pushing it from his face. The heat covered the others in sweat, but not Bastane. A Day-leg—one from the sun clan—would be unaffected. His only discomfort was the war he seemed to fight in his own mind. "We need a clear path out of here. We head back to our airship."

I stood straight, pulling my swords from their casings.

In a flash, the Guards had weapons in their hands, thinking I was attacking.

"Where is my friend, Ollo? He was in the Airship you took down." I glanced at each of them, my chest slicing in two when I looked at Nuo.

"Gone," Kazhi said. "We came upon the ship too late. It was being ransacked by a large crew of pirates. We saw them carrying away all manner of things. We lingered another two days waiting for you to come. There were no signs of your friend."

Maev gave a startled cry at the news, and when she turned to me her face didn't show sorrow, but hope. *Ollo is alive,* I imagined her thinking. She had known it, and I would bet he was out there somewhere, needing our help.

"I am getting her out of here." I pointed a blade toward Maev, who flinched.

"With swords?" Bastane lifted a brow, eyeing my blades. "Not with fire?"

The sword slipped in the weak grip of my right hand, and I winced, knowing the Guards saw. "I can't control the magic. I never know what will happen."

Bastane's other brow went in the air, and he turned his look on Nuo as if to say, *See?*

"Maev," I said. She was crouching against a rock, her attention on the Guards. Dust and blood coated the side of her face. "We need to go find Ollo."

It was the least I could do for all the trouble I had caused her. As much as my heart cried out to stay here with the Guards, I had to help Maev. After everything he had done for me—and as much as I wanted to find Brekt—Ollo had to be first.

She wrapped her arms around her legs, burrowing into herself, but nodded.

A dozen Aethar flooded into the pass, yelling commands to attack.

Kazhi ran forward and took two down while Nuo glared at Maev. "This is who the Ikhor travels with?" His mouth twisted in distaste before his scowl was on me. "Guess it doesn't matter how you burn the world. Only that it burns, right? Did it feel good to kill all those Guardians? South Aspis was like a home to me."

"That wasn't me."

"And Ouras's temple? Do you know how many were injured?"

My face heated. "*That* wasn't on purpose."

Bastane's sword was in the air, clashing with an Aethar's as he defended us. He and Kazhi pushed them back, and I was happy to note their weapons weren't pointed at me—for now.

My heart pounded, knowing the Aether were running at us, but unable to concentrate on them, not when Nuo was standing there.

"So you admit to the Temple of Mountain. But South Aspis wasn't you? Who else would cause that much destruction?" Nuo stood toe to toe, towering over me.

"I don't know," I said, heavy on the sarcasm. I stumbled as Bastane backed into me, sword against an Aethar's. "Can we think of anyone who might like setting fire to their own people for the sake of ridding weak bloodlines?" I waited, knowing he understood who I meant. "I notice Falizha isn't here fighting with you, protecting her people."

Bastane ducked as the next Aethar swung at him. "She's got a point there. Falizha said she'd be leaving us here in the canyons. Is it really you, Bones?"

"It is." Bastane and I shared a moment, where he took me in.

Kazhi was behind Nuo, knives in hand, looking me over. "Perhaps it's you, but you are not the girl we found in the caves all those months ago." Kazhi was taking an Aethar to the ground, a knife in their throat.

"No kidding," I muttered.

I had vowed to never be that girl again. Little did I know I would become the painted image of evil.

"And I am not lying about what I saw. Brekt, he—"

"Enough!" Nuo raised his sword, facing the Aethar surrounding us, even though Kazhi and Bas were handling them just fine. His wide shoulders, covered in dirt, blocked most of the battle from sight. "Your followers are coming to collect you."

"They come to kill me as much as you."

Nuo scoffed but didn't reply. Why was he not taking me down if he thought I was evil?

Part of him believes me. My heart swelled with the realization.

"Maybe you don't fully believe me," I said, walking to his side but not facing him. "But one day you will. I made a promise when I left that burning field that I would come back for you. And that is still my goal."

"Come back for *me*?" He spat, "Like I need you saving me."

"Not for your sake. For mine. Because despite what you're going to say next, we were friends."

There was silence beside me, and everything in me screamed to look at him. To see what was on his face. But I wouldn't be able to handle it if I saw hatred.

Nuo's swords lowered, ignoring the fight. "Friends? You stood on that bridge, threatening to kill your friend? You left when Brekt died, because what? You were scared of your *friend*? How dare you call me that."

I lifted a finger, still holding my sword, and pointed it in his face. "You weren't listening to me as he was changing." I had never spoken to someone with so much anger before. "You didn't listen to me when he was changing on that burning field, and yes, I can't say his name sometimes—it hurts. But I know he's in there. Just as I am still in here." I tapped my chest. "I tried to tell you it was me back then and that I didn't know. You went nuts. And in Danuli? You were chasing me down, saying you were going to kill me again. What was I supposed to do? So I lied. You needed to hear that. You were looking as bad as I was."

I stepped in closer to him, but he didn't budge. My heart raced as I got in his face. I had only been this forward with one other before, and he was the Aspis now.

"I said those things to wake you up, knowing you were hurting. I may not have grown up with friends or loving family, but goddammit, Nuo, you *were* my friend! The bad side effects, remember?"

Nuo's mouth popped open as if to say something, but he closed it, his jaw clenching.

Was that voice in his head getting stronger? Telling him to look and see that it was me?

More Aether flooded the pass, but the biggest part of the horde hadn't reached us yet.

The Aspis roared somewhere past the cliff edge, birds screeching in reply.

Kazhi and Bastane were managing the battle but giving us looks as if to say, *Hurry the fuck up and let's get out of here.*

Nuo finally lifted his blades, taking down an Aethar a little too close to Maev, who cried out in horror as the body landed at her side.

Sweat gathered at my back, soaking into my black Guardian clothes, which attracted the heat in an ungodly manner.

"I don't believe you," Nuo grunted while dodging a knife. "It's not possible. You expect me to believe a girl I knew for several weeks over histories going back hundreds of years? You're possessed. You want us destroyed." Nuo pointed his weapons at me. "I am done arguing with my enemy. You're pretending to stand against the Aethar. What is it you want? To get us distracted, to get access to the Aspis?"

A shadow passed overhead, and the Aethar stopped their attack, screaming and pointing to the sky. Some of the scarred faces blanched and fled the pass.

I didn't care about the danger in front of me. All I cared about was convincing Nuo. "I want the magic out of me. I'm going to find the gods to make them take it back. And I am going to save Brekt."

He stiffened. "Liar."

"That's why I was at Ouras's temple. That's why I am going to search for the others."

Doubt glazed those honey eyes.

Bastane stepped between us and shoved Nuo back. "You're

arguing like a child. Look around you, man. The Ikhor isn't attacking us. The Aethar are. Fight the current enemy."

Blood streamed down Bastane's temple.

Kazhi overreached when she threw her knife and missed her target, and a large Aethar with red veins in his neck tackled her to the ground.

Maev screamed, and my attention darted to where she was staring.

Nuo.

He was gawking down at his chest. An arrow protruded from it, close to his shoulder. He grunted, pulling the arrow free and stumbled back. An Aethar came from behind him and wrapped an arm around his neck, holding a knife to his throat.

"Nuo!" I screamed, but the Aethar yanked him back, and the blade pressed into the skin, drawing blood.

Kazhi yelled for help, and Bastane ran to her. I waited, terrified as another Aethar grabbed him and held him back from rescuing Kaz.

The Guards were overrun.

I had been squabbling, thinking it was okay, that the Guards were undefeatable. I tested my right hand. I could barely hold on to my sword, and I couldn't lift it very high. I would have one shot to drive the Aethar back. And when I did, would I stay, or would I run?

The Aethar behind Nuo spoke up. She was a large woman, her dark skin shining with sweat. "This was a pathetic fight. Give yourselves up, and we will let you live. Maybe the Ikhor will spare you."

A few of the Aethar laughed, and Nuo, whose throat was pressed against the blade, looked confused.

"What do you mean? You are here with the Ikhor." Kazhi grunted, struggling under the Aethar, pinning her to the ground.

"The Ikhor is burning the Guardian lands. We go to join him."

Bastane fought against the one holding him, three spears

digging into his sides, pinning him in place. "They don't know it's her."

"Come on, they're Aethar," Nuo warned. "It's a trick." The one holding Nuo looked ready to end this.

Nuo nodded once toward Bas and Kazhi, and the three of them, with speed I couldn't track, pivoted, slashed and pushed their attackers away, taking them down with deadly precision.

Instantly, Nuo was at my side, a hand banded around my arm and a knife in my face.

I leaned away, staring down at the blade. "If you believe I'm lying, then why am I not dead already?" I prepared my own swords, knowing their power would come in handy if need be.

The rest of the Aethar charged, but a large roar overhead drowned out their war cries.

Nuo gave me one last scathing look before he let go of my arm and ran.

"Maev, stay behind me." I held my swords, afraid to bring them together with the Guards so close by.

Bastane took on the horde to the right as Nuo went straight ahead, but several Aethar met him head-on. His blade made quick work of the first one, but the second one dodged, and the third rounded behind him.

Bastane took down the one at Nuo's back, and Maev turned her head as blood poured from the gut of Nuo's attacker.

Before long, the Guards were pushed backward, fighting closer to Maev and me.

They were losing.

I closed my eyes, blocking out the sight, searching for what I felt.

Fear. Anticipation. Worry.

I was too wrapped up in the fact that Nuo was here.

"They're going to lose," Maev said from behind me.

Bastane pulled an arrow from his arm, shouting something at Kazhi, who threw a blade at an archer and got them in the neck.

"They're trained to fight like this. They'll win." I tried to convince myself, but my hands shook so violently that I couldn't hold my swords steady.

The magic felt further and further out of my control—because my emotions were out of control.

Nuo yelled in pain, slashing at an Aethar, and when he backed away from a group of swordsmen, I caught sight of a large hole in the front of his vest.

Another Aethar aimed for him.

I screamed, running forward without thinking, and brought my swords together. Like before, a blast of energy pushed back the Aethar, causing blood to pool out of his eye sockets.

The impact threw me back, and I stumbled into Nuo. I glanced down at the hilt of the swords where the crystals sat, the magic fading from them.

"What the fuck was that," Nuo said behind me.

"Me saving your ass." I put the swords back in their leathers, having no use for them now.

"Kazhi," Nuo shouted, pushing me away from him. "Group back."

Kazhi sliced open the neck of an Aethar coming for her side before she ran back to where Nuo and Bastane stood. "Looks like those swords were a good find, Bones."

I swallowed hard, hearing my old nickname. "Little help they are. We are going to need a lot more to get out of here."

"We can run, Liv." Maev, pale and shaking behind me, threw a thumb over her shoulder. "This way."

Leave the Guards? I couldn't. "It's the wrong way. We need to get you home."

"We don't have much choice right now."

I looked across the clearing. More Aethar poured in through a narrow passage on the far end, no more than two at a time, but they were never-ending.

Nuo held the hole in his chest with red fingers. "Run, Liv. You're good at that."

Bastane wiped blood from his eyes, muttering something about Nuo's stubbornness as Kazhi gasped for breath.

A shadow passed over us, and I braced myself to face the beast, waiting for its thunderous roar. Once it arrived, the fight would be over. We were going to die.

But instead of a roar, a loud screech echoed off the walls of the clearing. What was above was an entirely new threat.

The shadow swooped over us again, and a booming sound blocked out the shouts of the horde as it descended upon us, slamming into the ground between the Guards and the Aethar, kicking up a cloud of dust.

A sweeping wind knocked me off my feet.

The Guards backed away, Kazhi standing close to my side as we watched the cloud, waiting to see what would happen.

The horde stopped to watch, too.

My heart lurched—a towering, broad-shouldered figure as dark as night appeared, and for a moment, I thought it could be the swirling shadow.

I was wrong.

A man—I think it was a man—stood in the dissipating dust cloud. His arms hung at his sides, his stance casual, as two massive wings tucked against his back. Even bent, the wingtips brushed the earth beneath his feet. The dark figure looked over his shoulder to where we stood, amber eyes appraising the Guards. His nose was curved, and his skin was so brown it blended into his black wings.

A few Aethar ran forward, screaming, "Attack!"

The man, looking toward my group, opened his wings, pointing them wide like a great black horizon, and spun so fast he became a dark blur.

Despite the heat, the surrounding air turned cold as I suddenly realized why there were so many bodies and broken bones throughout the canyon.

Thuds sounded as severed heads hit the ground, the bodies collapsing around them in a pool of blood. The man stopped spinning, flicked the tips of his feathers and sent blood flying into the dirt below.

"Did he just cut their heads off with his wings?" Maev asked behind me.

"Oh my god. Is that him?" I faced Nuo, whose sweat-drenched face had drained of colour.

Nuo's favourite legend was real.

"That's the Desert Eagle."

CHAPTER
FORTY-TWO

Liv

I used to lay on the forest floor for hours, waiting for one of my traps to spring and watching the sky between the long boughs of the cedars. I would make shapes out of the trees, count the clouds that passed, and I would pretend someone would come find me lying there and save me. The only thing that ever found me in that forest, after twenty-five years of lying still, was the Light.

Bastane levelled his sword, and the movement triggered the winged man into action. He became a black blur, and the next thing I knew, Bastane's sword was clanging on the ground as he clawed at the hand now cutting off his air supply.

The man flapped his wings once, twice, and was in the air with a single jump, dangling the Guard ten feet off the ground. Bas's feet swung as he fought, but the winged man hovered as if he weren't holding a full-grown man in midair.

I didn't know what to do. The Guards had always been the most fierce—there was no one their equal. But this man lifted Bastane like a toy as his powerful body moved and rippled with each beat of his wings. He was sculpted with one thing in mind—power.

"None pass through my lands and live!" His voice echoed, and the canyon full of Aethar quieted to hear him speak.

Held by the neck with a single clawed hand, Bastane's eyes went wide with shock, his face turning blue as the claws of the Eagle sunk into his flesh, drawing blood. It ran down his neck, soaking into his black clothing.

He was going to kill him. Despite everything that had happened between Bas and me, the harsh words, the betrayal, I knew at that moment I didn't want him dead.

Kazhi ran past me. "Eagle! Don't drop him. He is with me."

"Kazhi, you know him?" Nuo asked, bewildered as I felt.

The Eagle's intense, amber stare levelled Kazhi, but he didn't let Bastane go as he struggled for air, holding on to the Eagle's arm. "Kazhi. You're aware that anyone who passes through my canyons uninvited forfeits their life. Why have you brought them here?"

"I thought he saved people," Maev whispered behind me. "It can't be him."

Kazhi put her knives away so that she could point back at me.

"The two women need to cross safely to the other side. The Guards stay with me. I will return them to Guardian lands. You can handle the rest as you usually do. This is a misunderstanding, is all."

This was the shadow killing everything in sight.

"Are you making demands of me?" His nostrils flared, glaring down his hooked nose at the female Guard—*not friends then*.

"A request. A favour if you must."

"And why are the lives of these two women worth me risking

them on my lands?" His wings beat like a drum, dust kicking up from the ground with every pulse, as he held onto Bastane, who was turning dark purple.

"One is the Ikhor, and the other is her guide."

The Eagle slammed to the ground, releasing Bas, who landed on his knees, coughing. Kazhi ran to him, lifting him to his feet as the Eagle watched them, expressionless.

There had been so many bones littering the canyons. *None pass through my lands and live.* Luckily, the Aethar were no longer attacking, knowing they now faced a bigger threat.

The Eagle turned his eyes on me, taking me in, seeing the signs of the magic weakening me. "Five lives may leave my canyon. The rest are mine. I am owed a favour, Kazhi. And I can think of a few to torture you with," the Eagle commanded in a voice not deep, not loud, but controlled.

"Why are you helping me?" I asked Kazhi.

"I want to see what happens next, Bones. What you can make of this world." She peered at me with her black eyes, and I knew she had more secrets she was hiding from us all.

Bastane stumbled, holding a bloodied hand to his neck, and he stopped before me. He grabbed my shoulder and swallowed before he spoke, his voice like gravel. "I didn't trust my instincts before, and I'm sorry. But I am trusting my instincts now. You two get out of here. We won't follow."

"You're apologizing? You believe me."

His hand squeezed my shoulder, and I could *feel* Nuo's stare damning us all.

"You still need to train with those swords. If you're heading into Aethar lands,"—his focus shifted to Maev, suspicious—"you'll need to keep yourself safe. Practice what I showed you. Every morning. But don't forget that you are better with your fists. Stop trying to use sharp blades when you have a keener sense of your own defences."

I hesitated. "I want to hate you for what you did."

"And you should," he said, and I heard the remorse. "I'm sorry for thinking I knew what was right. I won't make that mistake again. Perhaps someday, I can earn your forgiveness."

The Eagle made us all jump as he burst into the air and aimed for the horde.

"The Eagle will finish the Aethar off," Kazhi said, standing next to me, holding her knives as the horde prepared to attack again. "We cannot follow you past the canyons, Bones."

"We still obey the Aspis," Nuo said. He turned from Kazhi to Bastane, searching for an ally. "Our mission is to stop the Ikhor."

Screams tore through the sky as the Eagle laid waste to the Aethar.

"I'm not attacking again until I know for certain Liv isn't inside there," Bastane said, studying my face for a hint of a lie.

Even with all the changes in my appearance, it was Bastane who saw through to me.

The air left my lungs in disbelief. "I'm inside here, Bas."

He was skeptical, I could tell, but it gave me a small amount of hope.

Nuo, however, seemed outraged.

"I don't know what to believe." Bastane turned toward the horde. "Just go. We will make sure your path is clear."

"No!" Nuo stood in front of me, blocking our way.

"Nuo, we can't get through the canyons anyway. We will be stopped." Kazhi nodded to the Eagle, who was taking Aethar down with ease.

He didn't even have weapons. He used his wings and sliced his enemies in half. He carried them into the air and dropped them. It was horrifying. Efficient. Dizzying.

"Wait." Maev had something in her hand, and she jumped when the Guards of the Aspis spun on her. She hesitated, then skirted a wide circle around Nuo, stopping beside Bastane and passing him a book.

"This is information I have been collecting on the Governor's daughter's texts. She hides important information in the ancient language of Day." Maev glanced to Kazhi, who had been the one to ask us to collect this information. "If what you say is true, and pirates came upon the downed airship, they likely took all the books on board."

Kazhi dipped her head in confirmation, and Bas took the book carefully, as if expecting it to be poisoned.

"Maev, we need that," I said.

"No, we don't. I have it memorized." Maev let go of the book, now in Bastane's care. "The Council is planning on attacking my people. Innocent villages along the coasts. They want to tempt us into war to gain access to our city. They're stealing ships and crystals from our shores to use them on us so they can then steal our more useful supplies in Avenmae. You need to decide if you're going to support them—if you're going to fight against us—citizens who don't know how to fight."

"Who is us?" Bastane thought she was talking of the scarred hordes. "You're not with them?" He nodded his head to the dead Aethar around us.

Maev made a face. "No. I am not like the Aethar you know."

Bastane was deep in thought, inspecting the journal. "Is this why we have been ordered to stop you before crossing over? Is there something over there we are not allowed to see?"

Maev shrugged, blushing when Bastane held her stare. "It's not so different than here. There are villages, cities, and legacies like anywhere else. I don't know what you've been told or ordered. But that book says the Council has planned attacks and has been there in the past. If you don't know what you're fighting, they do, and they are hiding it from you."

"Bas, come on," Nuo groaned. "We can't take their word for it. They have everything to gain by keeping us at arm's length."

Bastane continued to regard Maev with curiosity. "And what do you plan to do with the Ikhor? If we let her live."

"Liv is fighting her own battle." Maev's voice shook. "Finding a way to return the magic to the gods. She will get those answers by going to the shrines in Rydavas."

"Rydavas?"

Everyone went silent, making it possible to hear Nuo mutter, "I'm surrounded by idiots."

Maev went rigid, but she didn't turn her irritation on Nuo. Instead, she drew up to her full height. "My brother was on the ship you shot down. I don't need to be helping my enemy. I could easily ask Liv to turn her magic on you. I am helping because things need to change."

Bastane's jaw clenched. Swallowing, he bowed his head in apology. "I'm sorry."

Maev didn't back down. "My brother never harmed your people. But he will if they come to our lands—know that. Even though we have been hated, attacked and *ridiculed,*" Maev sneered in Nuo's direction, "Ollo has been helping Liv in hopes of saving everyone. Including the Shadow Guard, his enemy."

"Brekt?" Bastane grabbed Maev's shoulder, making her flinch. "You know something about Brekt? This isn't a lie?"

"I saw him, as did my brother. He's still a part of the Aspis." Maev stepped away from Bastane. "You have the truth in your hands. It's up to you what you do with it."

My heart swelled. Maev, who was never as brave as Ollo, was more like her twin than she realized. I was proud they were my friends. She was no fighter, but she was brilliant, and she would help her people with her mind.

"Guards!" The Eagle shouted.

We all turned to where he was taking off into the sky, an Aethar in each hand.

I put my hand over my mouth as he dropped them from an impossible height. Their screams lasted an eternity as they fell from the sky, and I looked away before they hit the ground with a sickening thud.

The Eagle came down for two more as the Aethar scattered, some running, others now coming for us.

He had ordered us to leave his lands, and I wasn't about to linger. His brutality was something I hadn't seen even in the Aethar.

"Get out of here." Bastane pointed toward the other side of the canyon.

"But—"

"We'll distract the Aethar on the ground." Kazhi pushed away from us, following Eagle's lead.

Nuo joined the Guards, giving me one last scathing look.

Maev stepped back. "I'm sorry to say Liv, they're much scarier than I thought. Worse now that I've met them. And the Interrogator is a horrible man."

"Let's go." I ignored her comment, nodding to the edge of the clearing where we could skirt around the battle. I was beginning to think she was right.

The Eagle continued dropping Aethar from the air, and the Guards were blurs of black clothing fighting through sand coated with blood.

My steps were unsteady. I was growing used to being afraid, but new fears continued to pile up. Maev and I were halfway across the open space, almost past the horde, when the Aspis joined the fight. It landed on the hard ground, slithering over dust and bones, aiming right for me.

The next scream to tear through the canyons was my own.

THE CANYONS HAD PROVIDED safety before—too narrow for the beast to descend, too winding to keep track of our movements. That was not the case in the open, flat span of rock.

The Aspis moved like a snake, lowering its head, blocking our way out.

The temperature plummeted. I would never get used to how terrifying the beast was. It was carved by a cruel hand, menacing and lethal.

Maev and I skidded to a halt. She grabbed my shirt, pulling me back.

I used magic when the Aethar arrived.

Its citrine eyes held me captive, pinning me in place.

My breath misted the air, blending with Maev's as we stared at our death.

The Aethar were stuck between the Aspis and the Eagle, each blocking one end of the pass, and the Aethar chose to risk facing the Eagle.

Kazhi shouted at the sky, and the Desert Eagle took to finishing off the remaining enemies.

The Aspis's head hovered a dozen feet above the ground, nearly as large as Ollo's airship. Smoke churned around its body, and the talons it tried to slice me with hid in the churning black depths. It shot forward, slithering across sand and rock, fangs at the ready.

I stumbled back, crashing into Maev, and held onto her to keep myself up.

We were going to die.

The Aspis slowed when we stood twenty feet apart.

What would it do next? I had no choice but to battle it, to get it away from here so Maev and I could escape. I still had my swords, though Bastane was right—I could hardly use them in a fight.

The Aspis roared, sending my braids flying back as I reached for my twin blades. I pulled them from their casings, shaking as I lifted them, my right hand aching. I slammed them together, sending a shockwave at the Aspis. It turned its head in irritation, but the energy coming out of my swords was weak, the crystals in the blades going dull. I had run out of magic.

Maev screamed as the Aspis came at me, snapping its jaw. Its fangs reflected the sunlight, shining from the saliva running off the curved teeth. The scar over its eye, where I had first attacked it over two months ago, had faded to a dark pink.

Our only chance of escaping was through my magic. I had to use it, even if it drained me. I dropped my swords. They clanked together, powerless, on the ground as I lifted my hands to the beast. I pushed my hands forward, screaming as I sent a wave of ice-cold fear toward it.

But when the magic left my hands, it didn't transform into ice.

"What the—"

There was no fire, no vines—nothing like what I had done before.

What left my palms, what leaked from every inch of my body, was pure magic—golden, glowing, vibrating.

The Aspis opened its mouth, not to roar, but to breathe my magic in.

It's sucking the magic out of me ...

It hadn't been waiting all these weeks to be stronger for the fight. Instead, it had been waiting to take the magic for itself.

It's sucking the magic out of me!

The gods sent the Aspis to kill the Ikhor and reclaim what was stolen.

CHAPTER
FORTY-THREE

Liv

I think my mother was heartbroken, too. For years. She never spoke of my father, yet she swallowed that pain and raised two girls. She kept us alive on her own without letting that pain seep into our childhood. It was time to be like my mother, now more than ever.

My magic was beautiful. Golden and shimmering, it reminded me of the sunbeams that would peak through the boughs of the giant cedars back home and hit the snowy ground, sparkling like a million tiny crystals. It shone like the Light that found me dying in my old homelands. It poured away from me, coming from my chest and floating through the air toward the Aspis, who absorbed it.

The Aspis opened its mouth wider, pulled harder, and the magic flowed past its long sharp teeth, over a forked tongue and down its throat.

The magic hummed, as it usually did, but it vibrated my body, burning hotter than the sun. It was like a fire was being set to every nerve.

The air changed, and I was lifted off the ground as I strained against an intense pain that felt like flesh tearing from my body. I tried pulling myself away, twisting, thrashing, but I only bowed my back and gave the Aspis more access to the magic. It was draining me. I felt weak, my breathing shallow.

So this is how the Aspis defeated the Ikhor. It stole the magic, killing the host.

But was it taking the magic to return to the gods?

"Help!" Maev screamed, but her voice muffled, as if she were in a different room.

She ran up to me, hand outstretched, but the closer she got, the more her face contorted in pain. "The magic, Liv. It's taking it. It's killing you! Do something."

The magic pushed her back.

Like the barriers that surrounded the airships, it vibrated like a living rainbow, turning Maev hazy. I reached for her, lifting my heavy arm. So weak. I couldn't get to her. The bracelet on my wrist was no longer glowing, fading back to a clear, empty stone.

"Help!" her voice echoed, terrified.

She hadn't given up on me, and was here, standing before the Aspis, trying to help me.

Thank you. I tried to say. *Sorry,* got stuck in my throat, and never made it to my lips.

The cycle of hate would continue. Her people would go to war against the Guardians without the Ikhor's help. At least the Aspis would return to its slumber before the Guardians could use it against more of her people.

I looked up into the empty, hate-filled eyes of my enemy. It would be the last thing I saw. Never in a million years did I think this was how I would die. I always thought I would die starving and alone in the Endless Forest. Or by the hands of the Law Keepers, like my mother.

My breathing became laboured, my magic not glowing as bright.

A jerking motion around my waist caused the last bit of air to leave my lungs.

It happened again. And again. Was I convulsing?

No—hands bound around my waist, painfully yanking on me.

The pain intensified as I was knocked from the air, and the magic came crashing back into my chest. Like a whip, it hit me, pushing me back. I sucked in a large breath, coughing. I landed hard on the ground—no, not the ground—a hard body.

Arms pulled me from the beast, dragging me across sand.

The Aspis wailed, rearing back, angered.

Maev was lying on the ground ahead of me, trembling with fear, staring at whoever held me.

Bastane stood in front of Maev, blocking us from the beast.

The Aspis shook its head, roaring as if in pain, spittle flying around us.

Us. Me, and the one who saved me.

I turned slowly as the person pushed me off them.

"Fuck. Fuck fuck fuck." Nuo stood, putting himself in front of me, blocking the Aspis.

I was too shocked, too weak to speak, but I asked, "Why?"

It was the second time I had asked him the question today.

He pushed the hair from his face, sweat dripping off his jaw. He lifted his sword and aimed at the beast. His hand was red and swollen, like a sunburn, likely from the magic when he pulled me free—when he saved me.

Kazhi skidded to a halt beside us as a loud screech filled the air, and the Aspis roared when the Eagle swooped down and grabbed its horns, pulling the beast's head back at a dangerous angle.

The Eagle's roar filled the canyon pass with his anger. "I want no part of this battle, Kazhi. Get your men off my lands."

Enraged, the Aspis curled in on itself, snapping at the Eagle, who was too fast in the air for the beast to catch. He soared high, faster than the Aspis could track, coming down again and clawing at black scales and curling horns.

"Why!" I said louder, Nuo standing over me. I had to know.

He finally looked down, masking his emotions, lowering his sword to his side. "I made a promise to Brekt."

"Liv." Maev landed on her knees before me, but I didn't acknowledge her, not breaking eye contact with Nuo.

His warm eyes searched mine. And Searched. His mouth worked around words he didn't say.

But he was here.

"You two need to get away before it comes back," Bastane said above us. "The Eagle won't be able to distract it for long."

"I don't understand," Maev said as Bastane reached out a hand to help her up.

"You and me both, Aethar." Bastane appraised Nuo, looking concerned.

Nuo offered me his hand, and I couldn't blink. I couldn't speak as my throat worked around something lodged in it. I took hold of his warm, calloused hand, and he pulled me to my feet.

Tears ran down my cheeks, and his face changed back to that cold, cruel man. "This doesn't mean I won't continue hunting you." He stood so close I could feel his warmth. I could see the lines of his gills along his neck. "I need time to think about what to do when I find you next, now that I have fulfilled my promise. He never said anything about saving you twice."

It was no real threat. That voice of the Interrogator was gone. There was meaning behind his words, emotion. It was Nuo, not the Guard, talking to me now.

My heart swelled. "I'll take it. And I'll prove that you don't need to kill me—like you promised."

I jumped when Bastane put a hand on my shoulder. "Bones ... I hope whatever is on the other side of these canyons doesn't kill you."

"From what I've faced, I think the only thing that could kill me is the—"

I didn't finish that thought, realizing how quiet it was. The Guards, Maev and I, all turned to where the Eagle had been fighting the Aspis, where now, only a cloud of dust remained.

A screech echoed, bouncing off the canyon walls as a shadow shot toward the sky. The Eagle flapped his wings high in the air. Blood dripped off his hands, his feet, and fell the fifty or more feet to the ground, disappearing into the dust cloud that was too small to hide the Aspis.

"What did he do?" Bastane asked.

We searched the cloud, which was dispersing from the dry breeze. The beast was nowhere to be found.

I stifled a gasp when something moved in the cloud of dirt.

A tall, dark figure stepped forward, appearing out of the shadows. Citrine yellow eyes found me through the haze. Curling horns pulled away from a handsome, angered face.

Brekt had returned—a snarling, bloodied version of him.

The Eagle landed behind him, looking past the half-beast to where Kazhi stood frozen. "I promised you five lives could leave these canyons, Kazhi. I wanted no part in this fight."

The Eagle grabbed Brekt's head and twisted.

My scream echoed through the canyons, likely heard a world away.

FORTY-FOUR

Nuo

The Ikhor's scream was one of agony. Of fear. Of heartbreak.

It wasn't the sound evil would make when its enemy was dying. There was a truth in that wailing cry that snapped my reality into sharp focus.

The Ikhor wasn't possessing Liv.

The Aspis had become a half-man creature.

The Eagle was real, twisting this creature's neck, and it was *not breaking*.

He yanked its horns back and forth, using his wings, pulling the creature's head sharply to the side. Only the half-man wouldn't succumb to it. It fought, roaring in outrage, and wouldn't go down.

My jaw hung open, trying to understand what I was seeing. Part of me knew, deep down, though I wouldn't accept it.

A growl ripped from the creature's chest as he fought against the Eagle, but its yellow, slitted eyes were pinned on the Ikhor.

Liv, she—she stared back, unsurprised it was here, scared for it even.

How? A voice asked, and it couldn't have been mine.

What I saw didn't make sense. *She'd been telling the truth, that's how*. This whole time—about Brekt, about the Ikhor's magic, about her intentions to return it to the gods ...

"Ikhor!" The creature yanked its head, trying to loosen the Eagle's grip.

That voice.

The Eagle's face contorted in anger when his victim's neck didn't break. Even the famed legacy of Mountain couldn't stand against the divine creation—the dark creature carried the power of the gods.

I couldn't understand who it was. Dark hair covered his face.

You fucking idiot. You know who it is.

"It can't be." Bastane's words cracked as he backed up, blocking the blue woman cowering on the ground.

The hair on the back of my neck stood, my instincts rising to defend the others. Something was off. The creature's voice was too familiar.

"Bas—"

"We need to stay back. His eyes! They're yellow. He's not himself," Liv said. "Kazhi, can you get the Eagle to back off?"

Kazhi crouched into a fighting position. "Not likely. He follows orders from no one. We are going to have to intervene."

Was this a hallucination?

The wind picked up, blowing the hair away from the stranger, his tattered clothing revealing skin swirling with shadows.

But he wasn't a stranger. He was a ghost.

His dark hair. The tattoos. His stance, his build, the way he fought off the Mount-leg ... I stopped breathing.

"Brekt!" Liv shouted, running for him.

I grabbed her around the waist, stopping her. "That thing will kill you." I grunted when she pushed me, stumbling away to my side, but she stayed put.

"How is this possible?" Bastane stepped toward the half-man, but I remained frozen, my chest squeezing so tight I couldn't get air into my lungs.

"Bas, stop," Liv tried. "He's not himself. Don't hurt him."

"Doesn't look like anything's going to stop him, Bones," Kazhi said. "Even the Eagle can't contain him."

Did they believe this? Whatever this was?

It had to be a game. Some kind of magic of the Ikhor's.

My heart told me it was my dead brother throwing the Eagle over his shoulder, slamming the famed legend onto the rocky ground below.

"Eagle! Don't harm him. He's one of my own!" Kazhi screamed.

The Eagle, held down by the towering figure, screeched, his wings coming upward and together. He slammed his wings against both sides of the creature's head.

It roared in pain, stumbling back, but didn't fall.

The sound of their battle was like thunder on the darkest night. They came together like hammers—explosive power reverberated around them when they landed a hit.

"How?" Bastane asked, now within reaching distance of the half-man.

A sickening blow to the gut threw Bastane off his feet.

The creature's clawed hands dripped blood as he breathed heavily, growling at Bastane's limp body before turning his yellow gaze on Liv. "Ikhor!"

The colours of the canyons swam, bright and fuzzy. I needed a slap to the face. Someone needed to wake me up. I was breathing too hard, losing blood, losing my fucking reality. "He's alive," I said stupidly.

"You need to protect Liv."

The voice came from the blue woman, who was crouched low to the ground. "Last time he appeared, he wasn't like this. I think he's going to hurt her. Protect her, please. You're the only one who can."

Liv skidded to a halt over Bas, who was clutching his gut, blood pouring from his hands.

The sight of the blood, the Ikhor bending over a Guard to *help* him, had me snapping out of it real-damn-fast. I ran up to them just in time and raised my sword to hold off the creature. He was fucking strong, roaring as the flat side of my blade connected with his arm.

Those snake-like eyes, glowing like magic, turned on me, and the changes that stole his features weren't enough to hide who he was. I'd known him longer than anyone.

But my lost brother had never looked at me like that—like he was about to kill me.

"Wait," Liv shouted. "That's not him. Not right now. He'll hurt you, Nuo."

"He's not aiming for me, Ikhor." I snapped, "Maybe a fucking thank you for saving you?"

I pushed the blade, landing a straight kick to the creature's gut and sending him back several paces. Enough to balance myself, ready for the next charge. But then the Ikhor made a stupid move, pushing me away and standing in front of *me*.

Kazhi was at Bastane's side in a flash, inspecting the wounds. "You'll live. You only need to get some magycris in you." She knocked him in the chest with her knuckles, and Bastane closed his eyes, cursing her for her lack of affection. She fished out his magycris and passed it to him.

He smeared some across his stomach, wincing at the pain, before he staggered to his feet. Reaching for the blue girl, he passed her the bottle of magycris. "Use the rest."

She grabbed the bottle, mouth hanging open.

Liv wavered, stumbling back into me. The loss of her magic weakened her. "The horns. The eyes. They're still yellow. That's the Aspis," she repeated, her chest rising and falling. "Let me hold him back. Go."

I gave a short laugh. "Hate to break it to ya, Ikhor, but you're not exactly winning any fights right now."

I pushed her behind me once more, seeing exactly what she

meant. Brekt—he was there behind the twisted, dark features. "I don't understand this," I said.

Liv struggled against my hold, but I grabbed her by the arm, keeping her in place. She winced and hissed up at me, "The Aspis controls him. I haven't seen Brekt outside that dream place, not for long, but he's in there."

Dream place.

I stared at her. The canyons went quiet. Time froze.

Though her features had been stolen, I finally saw her—Liv was in there.

She wasn't possessed, and she knew about the dream place, the one that Brekt had been subjected to since he was young. She had seen it?

Creature-Brekt ran for her, and again, I stepped in to stop him. Guess I was keeping my fucking promise. "Bastard," I muttered as I spun, kicking him from behind so he stumbled past us.

He rounded on me, snarling.

Liv stepped in front of me again. "I can heal, idiot. You can't." She raised her hands to defend me. "The magic of the Ikhor heals me like magycris. Let me hold him back."

"He just took your fucking magic, Liv!" I yelled in frustration. "So I don't think your special powers are going to save you. Now get the fuck behind—"

Thrown off my feet, I landed hard on my back, my head slamming into rock.

The horned creature prowled forward, towering over me. It roared as I moaned in pain.

Two figures appeared beside him—Kazhi on his left and Bas on his right. They grabbed his arms and pulled him to a stop. He flailed in their grip, dragging them across the dirt, and I rose, the world spinning, grabbing his horns to stop those sharp teeth from sinking in.

Whatever shit was running through his veins was powerful. Brekt had never been this much of a force before.

He's alive. I held onto my brother's snarling head, my heart breaking at his tortured face. Any recognition of his family was stolen by the beast that possessed him.

"Get out of here, Bones!" Kazhi shouted over her shoulder at Liv, who was helping her friend to her feet.

I looked past the creature, eyes locking with her. "Go."

"Nuo—"

For the first time since they'd both changed, I felt some of the pain inside me—my own monster made by the fates—slip away. There was a sliver of hope. "Go. I will hunt you down after this little reunion."

She shook her head, tears spilling down her cheeks. "He'll hurt you. He doesn't know. You can't hold him off."

My smile showed teeth. "Of course I can. I'm a fucking Guard. Now, get out of here before I let my better judgment take hold. The Aspis is supposed to kill the Ikhor. I can't believe I'm stopping him."

She grabbed her friend, pulling her through the sand and over rock. Liv stopped to look back over her shoulder, and the expression mirrored a feeling I wasn't ready to admit to. An unpleasant feeling quickly replaced it when she turned to run away with the Aethar.

The Eagle, who still hovered overhead, watched them leave and then took off over the cliffs, disappearing.

The beast roared, thrashing and pulling as his Guards held him down.

The citrine eyes of the beast I had come to despise met mine, and something about the way its pupils constricted and dilated told me he was somewhere in there—Brekt.

"Oh hey, buddy." I grunted, holding tight to his horns. "Nice to see you again. Grumpy as ever. Your long nap didn't brighten your mood?"

"Are you taunting the Aspis?" Kazhi asked, struggling to hold on to Brekt's arm, her eyes bright with unshed tears.

Bastane tightened his grip. "Yup. That's Nuo. The dumbest smart man you'll ever meet."

Kazhi made a face at the comment, and I missed what she said next because the beast grew, skin turning to ash, smoke churning around his body.

"No, no, no." I panicked. "Not again."

I held tight to him—tighter than I'd ever held onto anything. I lost sight of the canyon. Of the others.

I wasn't done. I needed more time. There were things I had to say!

"Hold him!" I yelled, not wanting to relive that moment on the burning field, my brother fading to ash.

It happened anyway. Beneath Kazhi's hands, his arm flaked away. Bastane's grip slipped as ash coated his fingers, and the horns grew until I could no longer hold on. And I relived every horrifying moment from the field. Relived every nightmare I'd had of watching Brekt die.

"Please, don't."

But he never fucking listened to me.

We were thrown back, forced away from the swirling darkness. The man transformed, and the Beast shot high into the sky, its scales glinting in the fading light.

FORTY-FIVE

Liv

Hope is dangerous. I learned that long ago. It was much easier to be angry. Because when someone inevitably disappointed or betrayed you, you half expected it. I had been hopeful with Stephen. I had been hopeful following the Guards and with him. I was hopeful with the twins and with Nuo's change of heart. What good did that hope do for me?

Maev and I wasted no time leaving the flat lands in the canyon. It was harder than I thought, watching the Guards hold Brekt down, knowing I wouldn't see them for a long time.

"Why are you smiling?" Maev gave me a sour look. "It's creepy after what just happened. You were aware, right? The Southlanders, the Guards, then the Desert Eagle. I am in shock, Livy. Speechless. Did you see the magic coming out of you?" Her hands flew through the air, reenacting the Eagle swooping down and taking on the beast.

"I would hardly say you're speechless." I checked around the bend we had reached to make sure we didn't run into any more Aethar, but only walls of red and white rock lay ahead.

Bones littered the ground. Why did the Eagle kill everyone who came here? And how did so many Aethar make it across to Veydes?

"So why the smile?" Maev asked again. "I swear, you need to fear death more than you do."

"He saved me."

Apparently, I wasn't listening to my own advice because hope was precisely what was tangled around my stupid heart.

"The Interrogator? Did you miss the part where he said that he'll still hunt you when he's done back there?"

I shook my head. "It's a lie. Nuo is great at lying. Not a trait to brag about, but I learned to see it. He was putting up a front. He's doubting himself."

"Well, lucky you. Must be nice to have a bully as a friend."

I rounded on her. "He's not a bully. He's a good man who said a lot of bad things. He was hurt after his closest friend died. I know he's killed a lot of people, but he didn't kill you."

"Um, hello." Maev pointed to the blood running down her neck. Dirt covered her, muddying her blue skin and matting her hair, and I imagined I looked much the same. "He stole my tracker. I have worked years on that tech. I had entered it into a competition back home. My professor said I was likely to win first prize. My work will have meant nothing now since my prototype is in the vest of the Interrogator."

I bit my tongue. She was right to be upset.

As for the blood, I remembered the magycris Bastane passed her. "Use the medicine on your neck. The one Bas gave you."

"Bas," she said, snorting. Then, she blushed. "He wasn't so bad, I guess. A golden Day-leg, but still. He was kinda sweet."

I lifted my head to the sky, a laugh escaping. "Oh, no."

"I'm not saying anything." She held up her hands. "Other than, you know, he's really good-looking."

"Better than your guy from home?"

She considered it. "Would I be a traitor to my people if I said yes?" She failed at hiding her smile.

"You're giving me shit about not being afraid that we almost died, and you're blushing from being attracted to a *Guard*. Ollo was right—women are kind of crazy."

Maev's face fell.

"Sorry. I shouldn't have brought him up." I fidgeted with my pack, trying to keep my hands busy. "We will still look for him. Find answers on where he may have been taken. But I also have a question to ask ... I want you to explain why you never mentioned the planned attack on the Guardian City. You knew that Ollo was going to lead me back to the people who would want me to be a part of that. Not only that, I have a feeling you are hiding information about the scrolls your friend has."

Maev bit her lip, applying the magycris to her head where she had hit it against the rock. "You must be angry with me."

"I would say we are equally angry. I wanted to ask you before but knew you were worried about Ollo."

"I'm still worried."

The heat of the day dissipated as we trudged through the canyons, making it easier to keep going after losing so much energy. Maev was re-braiding her hair as we walked. "The scrolls talked of how the Guardian City used to be where a ruler once sat. Veydes used to be a kingdom, much like Rydavas was before our matriarchy disappeared over two hundred years ago. The scrolls show a map, and a crown sits where the Guardian city is now."

"Why is that important to me?"

"It's important because the Council sits there now. How and why? It could mean there's a royal family missing. Ollo believes that's where the Rydavian aerial units will be sent to attack. If an attack is properly planned. He thinks that's what the Elders will ask you to help with."

And now all the Guardians from South Aspis were heading to the Guardian City.

"No. Is it possible the fires at the south camp were started by the Elders? To send them north where they plan to attack."

Maev's eyes went wide with fury. "No. I do not think that." She blew a breath out through her nose. "But that's not all."

She gave me a sideways glance, and I gestured for her to continue.

She smirked. "I think I've been rubbing off on you. Anyways. Another scroll my friend uncovered, which was badly damaged, talked of the gods and possibly how to bring them together. I think it tells how to get Erabas to return." She frowned, expecting my anger.

"What?" My heart pounded with this information. "You've been hiding this from me while knowing I wanted to find the gods?"

"I don't know if that's exactly what the scrolls say. My friend hadn't translated everything before I left. I didn't tell you because I wasn't sure what you were trying to accomplish, and why bother risking my friend's safety if ..." Her cheeks turned pink.

"If I was unstable?"

She tied off one of her braids, sighing. "Yes."

"Well, you *are* risking your friend. I have been unstable. So what's your plan now?"

"I can confidently warn him of the risks. Like the possibility that you might spontaneously combust."

"I what now?"

Maev was about to reply when a black blur of wings landed hard on the ground before us. I screamed and grabbed her arm, and Maev held out the bottle of magycris as defence.

The Desert Eagle went still, statuesque like the rock around us, and I realized the black hair pulled back from his cruel face was more like feathers. "The Ikhor doesn't use magic, and the Northerner defends herself with a tiny glass bottle. This is not promising."

"Are you going to kill us? Kazhi said to let us free." Maev's voice shook.

The Eagle's feathers were the only thing that moved when a light breeze passed between us. It was intimidating. Lethal. "Kazhi doesn't control these lands. I do. No one escapes without my say."

"And what is your say?" I itched to grab my swords but didn't dare.

Maev was shaking under my grip.

"I say you follow me."

"Why?"

The Eagle walked ahead without another word, leading us off the path and toward a narrow gap in the canyon walls. Maev pushed me forward, making a face like I shouldn't argue. Not that I was going to.

He didn't speak as he led us through bones and rock, silent as a ghost.

The man was a legend. According to Maev, he killed his entire clan hundreds of years ago. Seeing him and the terror he invoked on those who passed through his canyons ... I believed the legacy before me capable of murdering his family.

It was also possible this wasn't the same man from Nuo's story. But then I remembered the Alchemist I met in Bellum who told me he was over three hundred years old. Perhaps the Eagle was a descendant of the first children. Maybe his tale transformed over time, moulding it into something legendary—much like the tales of the Aspis and Ikhor.

Some time later, Maev asked, "Can't you fly us there?" Her feet dragged against the ground as the sun lowered in the sky, but still he ignored us.

The farther we went, the more my feet hurt and the more my irritation grew. "I need to take a break."

Silence.

He marched on, wings tight to his back, his clawed feet making no sound as he moved over the rocks. This man before us had taken on the Aspis, then the half-beast, and remained standing. It had taken three Guards to hold Brekt, yet the Eagle had done it single-handedly.

I checked to see if Maev was as afraid as I was, then I decided I no longer cared if I angered the Eagle. I was in pain, and I was going to stop.

I set my bag down, plopping myself on a rock.

The Eagle didn't stop walking. He didn't wait, disappearing around a bend.

"Are you kidding me?" Maev gaped after him. "Do we follow?"

I sighed, anger rising. "Yes." I sprung up, running over the uneven rocky land, angry for not standing my ground more often.

We rounded the same corner and found him walking up a slope that led to the top of the canyon walls. We hurried to catch up. I tripped on a stone and cursed as the gravel dug into my knee through my pants. When I stood, the Eagle was in front of me, looking down his curved nose, and I nearly shrieked.

"Put that anger away, Ikhor. I will not have you use magic while behind my back."

I took a step back. "You can feel it?"

So he was one of the first children.

"Though the Aspis stole some of it, what remains within you is vibrating violently. I do not care if you are angry with me. I don't care if you bleed, if you live, or if you escape my canyons. I am doing this for a favour in return," he said and continued to walk.

The orange rays of the setting sun hit my face as we reached the top of the canyon walls. This high up, the wind threatened to blow me off the side.

The Eagle continued to where a fire burned far ahead in a small alcove.

Maev reached the top, stood beside me and whistled. "This is quite the view. Look to the distance there, Liv, the southern sea. That's where the Eagle's island was. The old Feather territory."

The horizon sparkled when the setting sun hit the vast expanse of water. The wind tousled my braids, and some of the anger that had been building in my chest dissipated.

"What does the wind feel like to you?" I asked Maev.

"The wind? What do you mean?"

"What emotion do you feel when it gusts around you?" I closed my eyes, savouring the sun on my face.

"I don't know. Adventurous maybe. What do you feel?"

I held my hands to the wind, letting it flow through my fingers. "Freedom."

The wind hummed, answering my heart's call. It was a feeling I had always wanted a taste of. And here I was, transformed from the girl who was alone, hiding in her woods. I stood on top of the world, basking in the sunlight as if nothing could touch me here.

Hope soared through me, breaking me free of the heavy chains that were made by *his* death and Nuo's promise. Things were changing. Healing. I had hope, and I was going to save them. Though the road ahead was dangerous, it would be worth it. My friends were waiting at the end of this journey.

I made a mental note of the moment so that I could capture the feeling in the future.

I had another element I could control.

Fire had been easy, with the anger I carried from my past. Water, too, when I thought of *him*. Vines were nearly impossible, as I never felt grounded or in touch with the earth below.

Could I easily feel freedom? Would the wind answer my heart's call when I needed it?

A huge gust of air told me yes.

I may be angry.

I may be sad.

But I was free, and no one would take that from me.

Ever.

FORTY-SIX

Liv

"Kazhi?" I couldn't believe my eyes.

The Eagle had led us along the top of the canyon cliffs, and as darkness set in, we approached the fire I had spotted earlier to find the Guard drinking from a bottle. She sat on a rock before the fire, which was sheltered from the wind by a large overhang. Past her were shelves built along the rock and a bed roll tucked to the side. I hadn't seen her earlier, hiding in the shadows.

The Eagle prowled closer to the fire. "I almost didn't recognize you, covering yourself with Guardian tattoos."

Were they friends?

His tone suggested they may not be. "The last time I saw you—"

"Enough," Kazhi stopped him, nodding in my direction.

"Who said you could drink that?" He tore the drink from her hands.

I froze, waiting for Kazhi to plunge a knife into his chest. Instead, she gave him a warm smile. Her teeth were red from the drink and looked too much like blood. "You left the good stuff sitting around. And you took too long."

"I don't enjoy that you know where my various perches are located."

Kazhi was a startling contrast to the red rock behind her as she sat against the overhang, the fire casting shadows over her features, dancing across the white and black striped tattoos on her face. She reminded me again of a lizard, this time one that belonged in the desert.

"Why didn't you fly here?" Kazhi asked, uncaring of Eagle's threatening stance before her. "I can't risk staying too long."

The Eagle's stare was as terrifying as hers. "I took my time and enjoyed watching the Ikhor suffer. Punishment for coming through my canyons without permission."

Heat rose to my face.

He turned in my direction just as my hands fisted. "And keep that anger to yourself. You've already had one warning."

The Eagle strode back and circled me, his attention sharp, clear and intelligent.

I took a deep breath, calming my racing heart.

He was a powerful, pure-blooded legacy of Mountain. The vibration of his magic floated around us.

"You're a magic user yourself. Why should I be careful?" I asked.

He stopped, piercing me with a glare. "You will do well not to reveal a magic user lest you find yourself dead."

"And yet you've brought my magic up twice?" I glared back.

"Liv," Maev warned.

The Eagle continued to circle around me, while Kazhi and Maev watched. Muscle packed his broad shoulders and slim waist. If it didn't look like he was ready to kill me, I would have found him sexy.

"Why does your body look so plain? Did the possession of the body strip it of its legacy?"

"I am not an it," I spat back at him. "And although the magic is affecting me, I never had signs of a legacy."

"It's rather ... exotic," he said in an appreciative tone, his gaze roaming over my body.

"Don't bother Eagle," Kazhi said. "The Shadow Guard claimed her already."

My jaw clenched. She spoke as if Brekt had never left. She saw what he was now. Did she have hope, too, that he could be saved?

"I never had the pleasure of meeting this generation of Guards," the Eagle turned for the fire, moving past me. "Until today. Not sure what I think about them. Where was the fourth?"

Kazhi toed the dirt. "You met him—a version of him, anyway. He became the Aspis. A surprise even to me. I always felt magic stirring within him and thought it was his legacy."

"The other one reminded me of one of your boys," the Eagle said, poking the fire, and the flames rose.

Kazhi shot me a look when I opened my mouth to ask.

What did he mean one of her boys?

"Is that why you travel with them?" The Eagle asked.

"I don't particularly enjoy talking about my past." She raised her chin, stopping him from whatever he was about to say.

"I suppose things have changed since we last fought together. You have joined a new team."

She peered up at him. "You haven't changed a bit. Still ignoring the rest of the world while you defend the passage. One would think your skills could be used elsewhere."

"I am where I wish to be." His voice was low. A warning.

Kazhi seemed excited by his threats. "I appreciate you bringing the Ikhor to me. You could have been a little faster. The others are waiting for me to come back from scouting."

The Eagle's attention went over my shoulder to the canyon we left behind, scanning the cliff edge. "I took my time because I wanted to know what followed the Ikhor."

Maev, who was about to sit by the fire, froze, looking at where the Eagle was watching.

"Followed?" I couldn't see anything in the growing dark as the shadows of the canyons blended. "Is it the Aethar?"

"Pirates?" Maev asked.

Kazhi got up from the fire, swiping the drink from Eagle while he was distracted, and stood next to me, looking in the same direction as the rest of us. Her knotted hair moved with the wind, but she otherwise was as still as the others.

"I don't know what it is," I said. "I can't feel it ..."

"It's not magic." The Eagle was like a statue, waiting for whatever it was out of sight to reveal itself.

"I feel nothing." Kazhi seemed on edge for the first time since I met her. "Is it the Aspis? I can't sense it as I can the Ikhor."

"You can't feel the Aspis?" I asked. "But you can feel me?"

Kazhi nodded. "Magic users sense magic, which you are. The beast is something else."

What did that mean? This pull between the Aspis and me wasn't the tug of magic?

"I saw no sign of the beast trailing us." The Eagle continued to watch the darkness past the small fire.

"How does the Aspis not have magic?" I asked, but he ignored me.

Instead, Kazhi answered. "Whatever it is made of is not something we can sense."

"So what followed you, Ikhor? During our walk here, you continued to look behind you as if seeing something there."

Piercing, wild eyes ensnared me.

The fire cracked behind me, making me jump.

Maev gave out a small cry of alarm before she sat back on the rock, attention glued to the dark.

My heart was in my throat. Ever since the swirling shadow started visiting me, I always felt like something was close, watching. "Did you see anything?" I whispered.

"I saw nothing." Suspicion lingered beneath the Eagle's tone.

Kazhi returned to the rock, giving Maev a look of ridicule before sitting.

My heart sank—was it too much to hope I wasn't going insane? Was I the only one who could sense it? See it?

Kazhi said she sensed no magic from the Aspis. It was the same with the shadow ... did my imagination conjure more than the shadow?

"You all saw the half-beast, right?"

Everyone around the fire turned my way, but only Maev nodded.

Not completely insane then.

People I didn't trust surrounded me, as it had been while travelling with the Guards. But this time, I understood the ramifications of what happened when you hid secrets. Nothing ever changed. And I *wanted* things to change.

"There has been a shadow I've seen countless times. It's followed me since I became the Ikhor."

"Did it look human? Did it have a face?" The Eagle sat on a squat rock, his wings blowing dirt across the fire as he readjusted them.

"No, it was only shadow," I said, settling myself closer to Maev. "Parts were darker where a face might be. But I saw nothing that resembled a person. It had arms at one point. But no face."

"That's what you were talking to the other night?" Maev took off her pack and set it at her feet, eyes darting to the cliff every few seconds.

"Shadows belong to the Night-legs," Kazhi said.

"Do you think Erabas could still be alive?" Maev asked. "Maybe he's trying to reach Liv, knowing she's looking for him. Maybe he sent this shadow to find her."

"Everyone knows he's gone." Eagle's tone suggested he was certain.

"Gone? Not dead?" I asked.

"Gone. The first children know the old stories. He left these lands a long time ago. It's why there are so few of his children. No more are born, only bred. He has not blessed a child in millennia. He hated what this world had become. Erabas was a fickle creature. Some say, however, that he lives in the shadows of the night. When it's truly dark and no signs of his brethren can be found, he will lurk. So, if you're looking for Erabas, you must search for pure darkness. No day, no water and no ground."

"That is impossible. Such a place doesn't exist," I scoffed.

Eagle tilted his head. His piercing gaze tore into me.

"You're from the Lost Lands, Bones." Kazhi took a drink. "Have you not learned that many things exist beyond what you imagined? Be more creative."

I sat straight. "Interesting. I guess we don't keep each other's secrets."

She stopped drinking to take in what I meant. "And what secrets of mine do you think you can get away with telling?"

I crossed my legs, holding her gaze. "I suppose you have suggestions for such a place? Where to look for the God of Night?"

Kazhi smiled. "Your new teeth are sharp Bones. I like them."

"The gods don't wish to be found," the Eagle said, answering my question. "Nor do I care ever to meet one of those temperamental beings. I have my own problems. Which I will be getting back to when the sun rises."

"So why am I here?" I waved a hand at the fire where we sat.

"You are looking for those temperamental beings." Kazhi rested her elbow on her knees, the drink dangling between her legs. "We wish to speak on that."

"Fine. A trade," I dared.

"A trade for what?" the Eagle asked.

"Tell me how to find the pirates that stole Ollo. Then I will tell you what I have planned regarding the gods."

Maev reached for me, grabbing my hand and squeezing.

"Pirates?" Eagle asked.

Kazhi's face lit with interest. "I would have expected you to run hiding at the mention of pirates, Bones. You want to go search for them?"

"Yes."

"Don't bother," the Eagle replied. "If they've taken someone you know, it's for ransom. Otherwise, they'd be dead."

"Ransom?" Maev's voice rose.

The Eagle nodded. "The pirate's goal is always profit. If this person is a Northerner like you, you'll hear of their request for a sum in a port city. Look there. Now tell me of the gods."

"We will look for Mayra first," Maev said, unbraiding her hair and running her fingers through the waves, brushing the debris from the long strands.

The Eagle scoffed. "She won't answer. Don't waste your breath."

"What do you mean? You've tried?" My stomach growled, and I searched around the fire for food, just realizing I hadn't eaten today.

"No. But many have, for many years. She only answers to those of her first children, her direct bloodline, who are able to descend to her dark depths. And the pure-blooded Sea-legs that live in her domain haven't come to the surface for many decades."

"How do you know this?"

"I knew one. Once." The shift in Eagle's demeanour made me think he had been close to this person. "There is a shrine of hers at the edge of my canyons by the north coast. It used to be that when a true child was born, they were to come to shore when they reached the right age and test their lungs in the air above. It became dangerous and eventually fatal for them to come ashore. They were hunted and killed, so they stopped coming, and the tradition ended. They cut away from the rest of the legacies, as well as their half-blood siblings who remained on land."

"So Mayra abandoned the others of her legacy?" I asked. "My friend is a Sea-leg."

Kazhi's brow went into the air, knowing who I meant.

Did she think Nuo would laugh at me, calling him my friend?

"She doesn't answer anymore. She stays hidden in the deepest parts of her seas." The Eagle put his hands on his knees, sitting with his back straight. His posture showed arrogance, ego and a confidence that rivalled Kazhi's.

"Then we look for Erabas? We need a direction," Maev said.

Kazhi took another drink. "I want to know what you plan to do, Bones. Before you return the magic."

"What do you mean?" I asked.

"What're your intentions with the magic? If you do not find the gods, will you go to war against the Guardians?"

I went cold. "You tell me what you plan to do. And how you two know each other? Why did you never say anything when Nuo talked of the Eagle's tale? What are you hiding from everyone?"

"I will say nothing. You may have more magic, but I have the power. I need to know what your intentions are."

"The truth is the only way forward," the Eagle added.

These two demanded a lot in return for nothing.

I let out a long breath. The man was right. I had no strength to lie about my plans. Maev would be the one upset with my answer. "I do not plan to fight the Guardians. I plan to return the magic or die trying. I will not go against either side. And I will not do others bidding."

Our small circle went quiet.

Maev fidgeted but said nothing after hearing I wouldn't help her people.

The Eagle stood and brushed past Kazhi to where a pile of belongings sat undisturbed beneath the overhang. He bent down, and close to her ear, he said, "I am sorry about Erebrekt. I was happy for you that you found a new place in this world. I hope he can return when this is all over."

Kazhi turned away from us, murmuring something in response.

I couldn't contain my sorrow when I saw the emotion on her face. She never showed how she felt, but with the mention of his name, pain tore away that stony expression, mixed with a fraction of hope.

The Eagle set a clawed hand on her shoulder. "It was him that made you change your path. Everything's changed since then." He returned to the fire, where he set a pot over the flames, suspended on three poles.

"There is another option for you, Bones." Kazhi examined me, taking a deep breath, seemingly uncomfortable with what she was about to say. "There are others you could fight alongside."

"You?" I asked. "The Guards don't trust me, even after what I witnessed back in the pass. And I have a feeling you plan to travel to Rydavas, which means you plan to put my friend here in danger."

"I'm not talking of the Guards."

"The cryptic speech isn't working for me anymore." I crossed my arms. "We've danced around like this before. I am not interested in being caught in lies and games. If you want something, ask me plainly."

The corner of Kazhi's mouth twitched.

"I do not approve of this, Kazhi," Eagle said, giving me a sour look as he stoked the fire.

"I've known her long enough. I trust her."

"Never felt that way," I muttered.

Kazhi's lips turned up into a smile this time. "It was Bastane who convinced me it was you and not an evil spirit. He is right— you were never a good liar. You hid a lot, but you were a fool with your emotions and clumsy."

"You still aren't convincing me, Kaz," the Eagle said as he made a soup that smelled mouthwateringly delicious.

I stayed focused on Kazhi, wanting to know where she was going with this.

"You come from a world that is controlled, and you have learned that it is the same here," she said.

I nodded. "Though I would say the canyons are a lawless land. Far different than any I have seen before."

The Eagle scoffed. "That only means its crimes are out in the open. My lands are just honest. A civilized society hides its crimes behind closed doors—behind a fabrication of security and peace.

Here, you see the face of the one backstabbing you or stealing your things. There's a truth behind this place. It's reliable."

"And it is a safe haven for those unwelcome on Guardian or Aethar lands," Kazhi added.

"What do you mean?" Maev sat up. "Who else is there? We haven't come across anyone in the canyons except those you killed."

"Know that I will have you killed if the information I am about to give you is repeated." Kazhi looked at Maev and me, and we both nodded. "There are those of us who are pure-blooded legacies, who have lived a good number of years. Long enough to put together lies that are centuries deep. And over time, us purebloods have come together and decided to make a new world, a new people."

Maev's eyes lit up. "The rebellion is real."

The Eagle was the one to react. "How do you know of this?"

Maev smiled at me. "I have a friend who hears stories on his travels. Whispers have reached him, where there are those who go against the gods."

A deep chuckle came from the Eagle's chest. "Not against the gods. Only those playing at one."

"What is the rebellion?" I asked.

"It has no name." Kazhi took out one of her knives, weaving it between her fingers. "It will never have a name, and those in it will never say. But it is a series of connections where pure-blooded legacies know the truth—that there is some hidden force controlling our world and changing it for the worse. That bloodlines are being thinned, and war is a growing threat. Hate is purposely spread between the continents. The Guardian lands are controlled with lies, and the Rydavians are controlled through fear. Those who seek the truth fight for neither side and for both."

"It is uncertain the gods are aware of the power struggle between their children," the Eagle said. "They may not know of the Council blaming everything on the Aethar or that the Elders blame the Veydians for the lack of resources."

Maev stiffened at the mention of her own people at fault.

"Rem is often seen at the Guardian city, as you've seen, Bones." Kazhi reminded me. "I believe he is beginning to piece together someone is hurting the legacies, someone trying to take control."

"So what do you want from me?" I asked. "What can I do with my magic? I said I wouldn't fight either side. Who are you fighting against?"

Kazhi leaned forward. "I want to know what's going on. I no longer have eyes in Avenmae. Several of my contacts have gone missing over the years."

"If I did see something or knew anything, how would I tell you?" I asked. "What am I looking for?"

"If you hear anything of this hidden leader, who I believe is hiding behind the guise of the Council, I want to know about it. I want to know if the Elders of Avenmae are aware that this person is setting fires to Veydes. I want to know if they are part of it themselves. I want to know why there are more of the scarred Southlanders than ever and why, now, they are attacking Veydes as if someone has instructed them to do so. The Council will say it is you instructing them. They are organized. They never were before. I will find you from time to time or send someone in my stead to hear anything you have discovered."

"The Governor's daughter mentioned she was taking orders from someone," Maev said. "Her journals spoke of it, though she never said their name. Only that it was a male."

Kazhi was spinning her knife on the tip of a finger, focusing on the blade. "The journal you passed Bastane will be useful. Your translations are good, though inaccurate at times."

"You can read the language of Day." Kazhi had told me what the script on my swords said. "Why didn't you know what was in her journals?"

"There was no access to them before you stole the ship. The opportunity was a blessing I never saw coming. I can't risk anyone questioning my loyalties. It will ruin years of work on my part."

"And how come you haven't discovered the secrets at the Guardian City when you've been there so many times?"

Kazhi could pull secrets to her using magic. She should have heard something.

"Magic users can sense magic users. I do not use my skills in populated areas. I have been discovered before, and it cost me a great deal."

"And if we find who is controlling the Council?" I asked. "What then? Do you turn on the Guards? Do you expect something from me?"

"My brothers will be told when they are ready. Nuo is too hot-headed, and Bastane has been too loyal to his bloodline, but he is quickly changing. Those who know of my allegiance know that no harm is to ever come to my fellow Guards. They are protected."

She shot a warning look at the Eagle, but he made no move to acknowledge it or to apologize for nearly killing Brekt.

"And me?" I asked.

"I can not help you, Bones, on your search for the gods. Nor control where you point your magic. But if you survive and have the desire to make a change, I would ask that you destroy whatever is hurting all of the legacies."

"Your secrets run much deeper than I thought," I mused.

Kazhi only shrugged. "The Guards thought I killed for the Council," she said, eyes downcast. "I never corrected them. I did get rid of those the Council wanted out of the way. But those people always found their way to the canyons, where a certain friend kept a clear path to safety. I've killed far fewer people than the Guards believe."

I inhaled sharply. Did that mean she had never meant to kill Brekt, even when he saw her coming to assassinate him?

She'd been the one who had given him the long scar down the side of his face. If she hadn't meant to kill him, she made it believable enough.

I turned to the Eagle. "You kill anyone that comes onto your lands ... to keep it safe for those the Council wants dead, for those Kazhi sends to find safety?"

The Eagle held my stare. "The passage is safe for those who agree to join our cause. And I ferry them to a safe haven. An open pathway exists from the north coast to the south, and those who exist above land and below seas may travel it if they have my approval."

"That's why they call you the Ferryman," Maev said.

He nodded. "Every tale has an origin of truth."

Though I knew nothing of the two purebloods sitting at the fire, I knew they were part of something big. They may be deadly— killers even—but what they represented didn't feel that way. I think they were trying to make a change for the better.

Something deep within my soul shifted, and a new kind of fire was lit that had nothing to do with the magic. It called to me, the cause. I wasn't being asked to fight the Aethar, or the Guardians or the Council—those things asked of me never sat right. Now, I was being asked to save people on both sides of the sea. Defending those who needed help, regardless of their legacy, the lands they came from or their beliefs.

To be a hero meant you might have to defend those you didn't align with. It meant saving those you might not think deserved to be saved. That was something the power of the Ikhor could do.

That was the fight my mother trained me for—protector, not killer.

"I will help you," I said to Kazhi.

She didn't seem surprised as she stood to leave. "You've had your eyes open to the world for a long time, Bones. I know the magic chose you for a reason. Whether the reason is because it needed a strong host or because it latches on to those who are angry, I hope you know that doesn't matter now. What matters is that you use that as a strength. Hone that anger and hate into a sharp blade to take down those that create more of it. Previous Ikhors may have been evil bastards, but lead by example and show the world that anyone can break the cycle by simply choosing to do so."

CHAPTER
FORTY-SEVEN

Liv

I've come to resent my power. It isn't stable. It's not good. It's poisonous. If someone drinks poison long enough, they no longer feel its effects. But they aren't healthy. They are just more comfortable with dying. That's what's happening. I'm dying. I have three choices: get rid of the magic, let the dark voices in my head take over or die and take it down with me.

—Coming back to this entry, I've changed my mind. Fuck that. I'm not dying. I'm fighting.

The next morning, the Eagle led us to the north-west coast of the canyons, and I was dragging my feet by the time we reached the cliff edge at midday.
The walk, high above the world, had given me too much time

to think. Too much time to mourn. I missed Brekt. I hadn't dreamt of him in a while, and I wanted to turn around to find him, but I knew we had to search for Ollo.

I would save Brekt by finding the gods. And I would search for him in my sleep.

I needed to avoid the Aspis because it wanted my magic. And what would happen if it succeeded?

I can't let that happen. I have to find the gods first.

The wind tore some of my worries away as I reached the edge of the canyons. The smell of the sea hit me before I saw it, similar to the waters off the cliffs of the Endless Forest. The birds flew in dizzying patterns over the shore, shining when the sunlight hit their bright-coloured feathers. Inland was a sea of sand, rising and falling like waves themselves. Dark patches on the land showed the nearby Aethar villages.

"We've reached Rydavas," Maev said, coming to stand at my left. The sun complemented her blue skin.

"You will want to follow the shore." The Eagle stood to my right, his dark feathered complexion a stark contrast to the sea behind him. "You will avoid the larger Aethar settlements."

"The people of the Endless Forest, the Lost Lands, believe everywhere else is a wasteland," I said. "Where once was a technological society, war and greed destroyed everything. The Veydians believe that of Rydavas. But this doesn't look like a wasteland."

"Live in it for several weeks, and you will think differently. Make your way quickly along the shore until you reach rocky hills. Then watch out for reclusive Mount-legs. They don't like trespassers to the same degree as me."

With a solemn expression, he looked out over the waves, staying quiet for several long minutes.

"What do you fight for, Ikhor?" The Eagle's focus stayed forward with his hands clasped behind his back. He searched the rough waters, looking for something that wasn't there.

"I don't—I mean—I haven't fought for anything but survival."

"You are self-possessed. You could help others, yet you would return the magic."

"I want to find peace. I've never had it."

The Eagle's attention flickered over me, unimpressed. "I have heard many tales of the Ikhor. Some told with horror, some told in reverence. It all started millennia ago with a child of the gods who wanted more. But the power was given to a girl who wants nothing?"

Without warning, he shot a hand out to grab Maev and brought her to his chest. "And now?" he asked, holding a struggling Maev by her neck.

"Let her go," I demanded, grabbing his arm and fighting him off.

He shoved me away with his other hand. "You can't make me without your powers, especially if you give them back to the gods. And why should you care? You want to be left in peace."

"She's my friend. Let her go."

He wasn't hurting her, not really.

Maev struggled in his grip before the Eagle let her go, and she stumbled away over the rocky path.

"So you would fight for a friend. You're capable of thinking of others outside of yourself. You easily agreed to relay information to Kazhi when you heard of all those in need, when you heard Kazhi wanted information on the Council. You would help the rebellion but say you wish to be left alone. So what's the truth?"

"What's your point?" I ground my teeth, feeling the heat rise in me, the magic responding to my growing anger.

"You speak from fear. Words may seem weak, but they have power. Eventually, you are going to believe it. I have experienced being raised in a world I did not like. I know the person it can make you become—exactly like those who made it bad in the first place."

The temperature grew as my hands fisted at my sides. "I was

told you killed everyone to be left alone. Your family included. I would hardly say you are one to hand out advice."

The Eagle was before me in a blink—his golden, hawk-like eyes boring into mine. "I freed hundreds of slaves. I ferry the Council's victims to safety. I don't do it kindly, but I do it, so that kinder souls may have the safety they deserve."

"Don't I deserve that?"

"You are not a kind soul. You are not prey. Though, I see that is the lie you've told yourself. You can conjure fire, Ikhor, but I feel it was in your heart long before the magic touched you. It's people like you who change the world. You could be *the end of everything*."

I sucked in a sharp breath as the Oracle's words swam through my mind.

Could he be right? Could I be like that?

"Where do you get the strength to help if the world was so cruel to you?"

A pitying look replaced the Eagle's sneer. "You will find it." He regarded Maev behind me. "When you have a purpose, it becomes your strength."

Somewhere in his life, someone had given this Mount-leg a purpose.

He turned back to me. "Stop the negative commentary. Stop trying to be something you are not. You are self-possessed? Then own yourself. Be a fighter. A good fighter has a strong body and a calm mind."

I gave a humourless laugh. "A calm mind was never what I was blessed with."

The Eagle's wings snapped together in irritation. "Stop being pathetic. You hold the power of the gods. Fate has blessed you with choice. Use it."

With a single jump and a loud gust of wind, the eagle soared into the air.

THE SUN BEAT down on us as we made the terrifying descent from the canyon cliffs, and my first day in Rydavas was gruelling, but I would have many to come. It would go from hot to damp to cold as I travelled those long weeks.

On our third day, I found myself by the sea, having avoided any encounter with Aethar—their villages empty. The seawater battered the edge of the platform I stood on, soaking me through, and by the time the sun disappeared across the water's horizon, I was shivering, cursing the gods, and feeling completely lost.

The Desert Eagle was a harsh teacher. But he was right. The way I spoke, the way I thought, had to change. I had the ability to make a difference.

Was finding the gods the best option for the people of Arde? Or for me?

I had spent years being broken down, but now I had a taste of freedom—a taste of life—and everything I enjoyed about it was being taken, tainted by what everyone else wanted.

What did I want?

I wanted to help the innocent people, as Kazhi's secret rebellion claimed to do, but I didn't want the magic to kill me in the process. There was a constant battle in my heart. I was two people—the beaten-down girl I had been and the one I was capable of becoming. But what would I become?

I didn't want to be pathetic, as the Eagle had accused me of. He was Nuo's favourite story and quickly became mine, too.

I stood with my toes at the edge of the platform, on the edge of land and sea, facing the North Aspis, the constellation that showed the way home. It was barely visible in the fading evening light.

I thought of all those forces working against me.

I would not be pathetic.

I flung two middle fingers to the sky, cursing when the mangled mess that was my right hand didn't work. My bracelet pulsed with magic as it refilled—the magic inside me growing stronger.

I thought of the gods who didn't show up for their children

when they called. I thought of the Keepers, Rebeka, the Council, the Guardians, the Aethar and the Elders I hadn't yet met.

"Fuck you!" I screamed for the whole world to hear.

I was going to save them all. Even the ones who didn't deserve it.

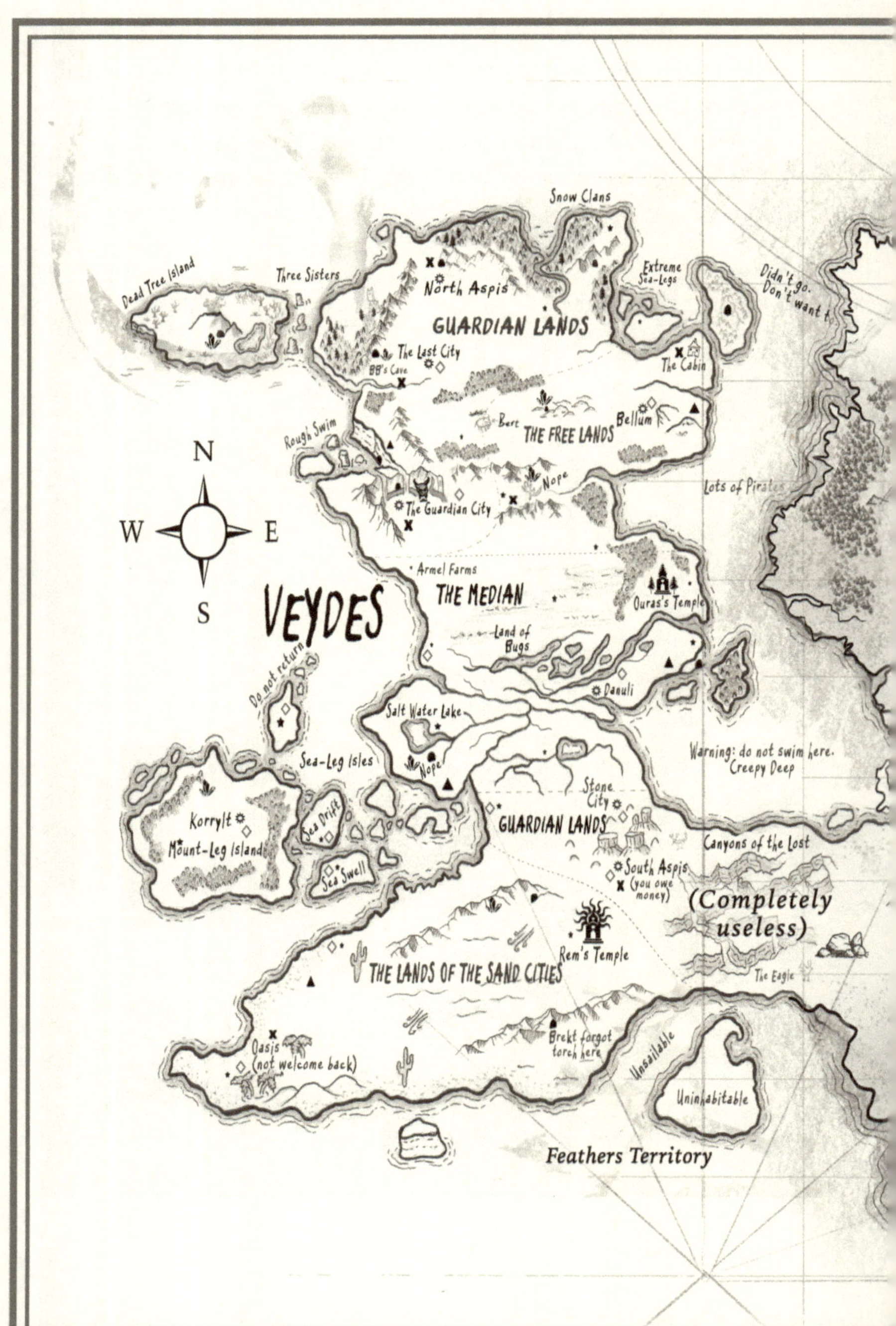

Snow Clans
Dead Tree Island
Three Sisters
Extreme Sea-Legs
Didn't go. Don't want to.
North Aspis
GUARDIAN LANDS
The Last City
BB's Cave
The Cabin
Bert
THE FREE LANDS
Bellum
Rough Swim
Lots of Pirates
N
W E
S
The Guardian City
Nope
VEYDES
Armel Farms
THE MEDIAN
Land of Bugs
Ouras's Temple
Do not return
Danuli
Salt Water Lake
Warning: do not swim here. Creepy Deep
Sea-Leg Isles
Nope!
Stone City
Korrylt
Mount-Leg Island
Sea Drift
GUARDIAN LANDS
Canyons of the Lost
Sea Swell
South Aspis (you owe money)
(Completely useless)
Rem's Temple
THE LANDS OF THE SAND CITIES
The Eagle
Brekt forgot torch here
Oasis (not welcome back)
Unsailable
Uninhabitable
Feathers Territory

PART FOUR
Northern Sea of Mayra
Bay of Avenmae
Nuo's (Incorrect) Map of
Arde
Rydavas
Avenmae
Kalitazarhi Sea
Southlander Camps
South Rydavas
Sevarina Sea
0   100   200   300   400   500

FORTY-EIGHT

Nuo

"Assassins?"

Kazhi was quick to react after I rolled the dead body at my feet. Long grass stuck to the black clothing and well-made weapons—the first giveaway that our attackers weren't Aethar.

The day was only beginning as the sun peeked over the horizon. I'd been leading Kazhi and Bastane across the southern river lands toward Danuli. With each passing day in the two weeks since we left the confinement of those canyons, we put miles between us and all the shit that was revealed. We stopped for nothing because we couldn't explain why we were headed north without the Aspis because fuck me, everything was fucked.

"They aren't Aethar," I said, pulling up an assassin's shirt and revealing his back.

"Guardian tattoos? One of our own attacked us?" Bastane ripped the shirt open, showing me an Aspis tattoo on leather-like skin—a Mount-leg.

We hadn't seen an Aethar since leaving the desert and passing what remained of South Aspis.

"The question is, did the Council order this? Or is Falizha working alone?" I wiped off my knives, regretting that I didn't get a chance to interrogate them. However, turning my blades on my own sickened me.

"My guess is Falizha's covering her mistakes. She failed to deliver the Guards to the final battle and then left us for dead." Kazhi was pulling her knives from several dead Guardians. "I bet she's had them watch the roads for us to exit the canyons."

Bastane pulled the bodies off the road and hid them in the long grass. "Do we go back to the Guardian lands if we have hired killers after us? This is unbelievable," he grunted, lifting the legs of a particularly large man and dragging him off the road. "They are our own people."

"We go back." Kazhi checked the assassin's pockets, taking crystals and weapons, and scored some dried meat. "We're taking the Council down. Let's not forget the Council has hired assassins before to kill our own. I was one of them." She brought several bundles of food to my horse and added them to the bags I already carried.

I snatched one from her hand. "Why am I stuck with all the bags again? I can barely fit my seat." My ass was sore from something digging into it for several hours straight.

"You're bag boy." Kazhi took the bag back, tying it to my horse.

"I am not the bag boy. I am the mapper, the Interrogator, the best-looking one among us that makes me the fucking leader of this operation."

"The biggest pain in the ass gets stuck with the bags," Bastane added, wiping his forehead. "Guess who takes that title? Every time."

"You two never learned to respect me. When Brekt finds out—"

Kazhi snorted. "He's going to knock out your teeth when he finds out what a shit you've been these past months."

I busied myself with my horse. It was my own godsdamned fault for bringing him up. I avoided discussing what we saw in the canyons. The others ... it was like everything was back to how it was before he became the Aspis.

I shook my head. "He doesn't need to hear everything. That is if we ever see him again without having to calm his rage."

Liv said she'd seen him, not as that dark creature but as a man —as himself. I wasn't sure I believed her. Fuck—I wasn't ready to believe anything.

I clutched the strap on my horse, holding my breath. Only when my vision blurred, and the pain eased from my chest did I exhale.

"Haven't seen the beast since we left it circling in the canyons." Bastane walked behind his own horse, making it difficult to hear him.

The beast took off several days after the Ikhor ... after Liv left. It flew south over a cliff and hadn't reappeared since, and I waited for the skies to go red, the sun to go out, or the ground to break open. Some sign he was dead. But every day I woke, the world went on, and nothing changed—the final battle hadn't taken place.

The Guards were useless. We couldn't kill the Ikhor, as Liv had said, because she healed from the magic that possessed her, and we couldn't follow the Aspis because we had no airship.

So we fell back on our other plan—to discover the secrets of the Council.

"We've discussed this every day. Regretted the decision to abandon the Aspis," I said, waving my hand in the air. "I'm over it. He can take care of himself."

After the canyons, we'd found a small village in the desert where we bought sand angulas to ride until we reached the river lands and traded for horses. In a few days, we would need to hire a boat and sail for the Guardian city and find Guardians to ally to our side.

The assassins put a dent in those plans.

I lifted a foot and set it on a broken, damp log. "I agree with Kaz. Being on the run does nothing for my beauty sleep. We go back to the city, have a nice meal, let the people see we are still alive and badass, and start getting others on our side. I'll do the sweet talking."

Bastane muttered something about my mood improving, then added, "Hopefully, the Aspis shows up so we don't look like fools."

He was fixing his hair—the poor prince worried about his image while surrounded by miles of nothing.

Kazhi's dark stare swept over the clouds. "I wonder if that's why it followed us before—somewhere inside, he knew."

I scoffed, turning back to my horse, pushing the bags around to figure out what had been poking me in the ass. "Well then, the bastard hasn't changed. He still does whatever he wants while I suffer and carry all your shit."

"Keep your mouth shut, and I'll carry them. Until then, you suffer." Kazhi's mocking smile dropped when her attention went to something behind me.

I followed her line of sight to find a dark figure tearing through the sky. "Fucking finally," I muttered, though my heart rate didn't match the tone of my words. It sped with anticipation as I went over all the things I was going to say when he showed his face again.

"Think Brekt will show up at some point?" Kazhi asked.

The Aspis glowed golden on one side where the morning light hit its scales.

I was about to answer when the Aspis dove for the ground.

"What in the Endless Night?" Bastane yelled.

It didn't slow as it wound in circles, aiming for a flat patch of land twenty feet from where we stood.

I sucked in a breath, taking several steps back. "It's going to nose dive—"

The Aspis disappeared into black smoke as a whirlwind of darkness replaced the beast and blew away on a breeze, leaving a lone figure standing in the grass.

Morning light shone off the dark head of hair—a head that was void of curling horns. He dusted himself off, spotting us gaping like fools, and regarded us with obsidian, normal, annoyingly casual eyes.

Then, he waved as if he'd seen us only yesterday.

My mouth hung open for several seconds before I could speak. "A fucking wave?"

Kazhi raced toward him, but I couldn't bring myself to move. Otherwise, I might fall apart.

It's a trick, I told myself, even though I'd seen him a few weeks ago.

He let out a grunt when she collided with him and wrapped her arms around his neck.

No horns, no fangs. Was this a hallucination?

Bastane was on the move.

I was—*no.* I wasn't scared. *You're a fucking Guard.*

Bastane clapped Brekt on the shoulder while Kazhi remained wrapped around him.

His gaunt face broke into a grin as he looked my way. "Get your fucking ass over here." His arms went out as if to welcome me.

My brother's voice. My *dead* brother's voice.

I tried to move forward but couldn't. I fell onto my knees, and the image of Brekt blurred.

It couldn't be him. He was dead. I watched him fade away. I watched pieces of him float into the sky and vanish. I watched the blood gush from his chest after the Aethar stabbed him. I held him as his eyes closed for the last time.

I watched him return as a beast and then fade to the Aspis again. Now, as if all I had suffered was a dream, he was before me, grabbing me by the shoulders and pulling me to my feet.

I stared into a face more familiar than my own—one I'd known since we were boys, though there was a new scar on his face, over his left eye. I'd seen every expression that face could make. I'd seen it battered and bruised and seen it lit with joy, even if only briefly. Nothing could fake this. No magic could conjure that look he was giving me.

"Always knew you were a sap," Brekt said, drawing me in for a hug.

I couldn't speak. *What the fuck.* I yanked him close, and if the cursed bastard wasn't as rigid as he'd always been.

Then my sister was there, and my second brother—my family. And I fucking wept. I wept because the gods had never blessed anyone as well as they had me in that moment. I had not loved many. In fact, they were all right here. The only ones I would ever let into my damaged, rotten little heart.

Brekt pulled away, his face streaked with tears. All our faces were. Then he backhanded me in the gut.

"Cursed Night." I coughed around a laugh. "Did you have to come back?"

"We've got a lot to catch up on. Stop whining." Brekt wiped a hand down his face. And I shook off the tremor running through me. "Pull yourself together, team. The fucking Guards are back in business."

Kazhi tilted her head back and howled like an animal, making the birds screech high above. She jumped on Brekt's back, swatting him in the head. "Lead on, you handsome bastard." Her hands were in his hair, messing it around his face.

"What in the Endless Night happened to Kaz?" Brekt sent a look at Bastane, who shrugged.

"Miracles can change a person. And we've all unloaded a little baggage since you've been gone." Bastane wiped at his face and pushed his hair back, standing straight. "It's disturbing to see, to say the least."

"You got that right." Brekt grabbed Kazhi by the wrist, trying to smooth his hair from his face.

I swallowed the sob that threatened to escape. "How? Last time, you were not yourself."

Brekt stilled, taking in my beard, my long hair, my gaunt frame and what was lacking. "I don't know how. Not yet. But I intend to find out. None of the legends can be trusted."

He was living, walking, breathing proof.

"The Ikhor?" I asked.

"We've seen each other, in a sense. It took some time for me to understand I was a man, to recall who I was. But she knows."

"She knows what exactly? You spoke with her?"

"Yes. She's as much herself as I—battling what's inside. Between the magic and the beast ... we are both still here."

I stared at the ground, biting my tongue.

"I'm sorry I was not here sooner. I didn't mean to leave you waiting." Brekt put a hand on my shoulder. "I wouldn't have chosen to come back this late or to have spoken with you after her. You are equally as important."

I nodded, shaking off his arm. "I know. I know. It's not that." I clenched my fists, keeping still to hide my shaking hands. "What was she like?" I finally asked.

Brekt crossed his arms. Like always, he looked like he was about to lecture me. "She was different. But it was her."

"Different how?" *I* could even hear the anger in my voice, and I knew I wasn't hiding it well.

"I think she's been suffering the Endless Night and come out stronger for it. I think I know who's been causing some of that suffering."

"Don't give me that look." I shoved that monster down, crossing my arms so I wouldn't do anything stupid, like hit him for defending her. "She became the fucking Ikhor. She left us and followed the Aethar. What was I supposed to think?"

"You were always the most hot-headed of us," Brekt grumbled. "I told you to watch over her. Keep her safe."

"Might I remind you that she is the one with *magic*. What was I keeping her safe from?"

"From me!" Brekt shouted, then he pulled himself together, his nostrils flaring.

"Nuo did save her from you." Bastane came to stand at my side. "Even though he didn't believe it was really her. He did that for you, man. Give him a break. We all crumbled after you died."

Brekt hid his anger. "Ya, well, I'm not dead."

Bastane grabbed his face. "We can't even celebrate for a moment. Just for once, I would like to enjoy myself."

Kazhi kicked the back of my knees, making me drop to the ground. Her gaze darted between Brekt and I. "Are you done now?"

"Still mothering us, I see," Brekt said with a hint of amusement.

"Still acting like children." Kazhi rested a hand on her belt. It was a warning. Her knives were close by. "We are on our way back to the Guardian City to give the Council a talking to. You coming?" She asked Brekt.

He chewed the inside of his cheek. "No."

"Why not?" Bastane demanded while I got to my feet. "The Guardians need hope. All of Veydes needs hope. Seeing us reunited would give them that."

"They have the Aspis to give them that. In the few moments I am a man, I'd like to be left alone."

"Just like old times, I see," Bastane muttered. "Things could have been different had you not kept this to yourself. You being the Aspis. I wandered for years, dreading we'd never find it."

"Well, when you unwillingly get a millennia-old legend shoved inside you, you can decide how you live with it," Brekt growled. "Things could have been different had you not gone to Falizha and told her Liv was the Aspis."

Bastane's face flushed with shame. He'd spent months trying to earn my forgiveness. I was interested in how he was going to convince Brekt.

"I was wrong to think Falizha was on our side. I am going to take the Council down with you. I will make sure she pays for what she did. Then, you can punish me any way you like. I have a feeling I will yet pay for the mistakes I made. But right now, you need me, and you know it. Kazhi knows it. Nuo's been too hot-headed to think straight, but he hasn't stopped me yet."

"Don't include me in this." I waved a hand between my brothers. "I'm enjoying myself. Keep going, shadow man."

Brekt turned skyward, sighing. "I think I was less stressed when I was stuck in that dark place."

"And how did you become unstuck?" I asked. "Why now?"

Brekt shook his head. "I can't say. Only when I feel something outside that place, something I am connected to ... I latch onto it, and I ... I don't know. Even now, I feel it trying to pull me back in. Or, the Aspis is trying to get back out. It doesn't want me in control."

"So what now?" Kazhi asked him. "You hide? Go back to whatever *dark place* you linger in, while the Aspis does nothing?"

Brekt had the good sense to think about his answer while Kazhi glared. "Yes. Falizha made it known that the Ravins want to use the Aspis for their own gain. If she finds out I'm alive, she won't stop coming for me."

"So we go on as usual?" Kazhi's shoulders slumped. The most defeated I'd seen her in weeks. "Hunt the Ikhor. Hope the Aspis doesn't kill her. Take down the Council with no real plan."

"Is that what we were doing?" I asked.

Kazhi threw me a look to shut up.

"The Ikhor can't win. It must be stopped," Brekt said in a low voice, and I drew back.

What did that mean?

He was debating something, his jaw clenched tight. He pushed the hair from his face, cursing. "Not to kill. To stop. Liv must survive this. But the evil can't win."

"You still think it's evil?" Kazhi studied Brekt, taking in his subtle movements.

"Some parts of the tales have to be true. Last time I saw her, it looked like it was killing her from the inside. It can't be good."

"And will you be able to go against her?" I asked. I couldn't believe he would hurt her. "If she goes against our people?"

"When I'm the beast, I don't even recognize it's her. I only feel the need to reach the Ikhor and devour. It doesn't care who lives or dies. I will do everything in my power to stifle that urge. But I don't know how long I can go on for." Brekt paced. "How long has it been since I've changed? Since I last saw her?"

Bastane dropped down to sit on a decaying stump, resting his elbows on his knees. "Nearly three months since you've changed. A few weeks ago, we were in the canyons and saw you for the first time."

"I vaguely remember it." Brekt took several breaths. "I haven't felt Liv since then. I haven't seen her. I don't feel the pull." He shot his worried gaze my way. "I have to find her."

"Bones is off to find the gods, to end the cycle. She's going to give the magic back." Kazhi said, causing us all to pause.

I lifted my hands. "We are trusting what the blue Aethar girl claims now. She could have been lying."

"When did you hear this?" Brekt asked.

"In the canyons. That's what they said the plan was," she said.

Brekt considered this. "And you are heading to the city?"

Each one of us mumbled an affirmation. We didn't have much of a plan, but that was it.

"Good. Find out what you can. The Aspis will be drawn to Liv. I'll try to get intel from the other side."

"We should follow you," Bastane said finally. "Find the Ikhor and end it. The Council will still be there when it's over. And we will make peace for the next generation."

Kazhi scoffed. "And then in a thousand years, it happens again. Bone's has a better plan."

Brekt sighed, speaking to Bastane. "I can't enter that final battle and let the Aspis kill her. But I will stop her if she starts a war with our people. Let me find out what she plans on doing. She and I need to sit down and have a talk. I only have to find her first."

Kazhi squeezed Brekt's arm. "I think you'll find the woman she's becoming is something a warrior can be proud of."

We all went silent, hearing Kazhi praise the Ikhor.

Brekt paled, swallowing before he turned away, walking north along the path he'd come from.

Bas and I exchanged a glance and followed, Kazhi trailing behind.

"So what will you do about these assassins?" Brekt asked. "There may be more." He'd kept mostly quiet as we walked, admiring the horizon while he ambled alongside Kazhi's horse. He was in no hurry to get anywhere. I wondered if he was soaking it all up, enjoying walking on his own two feet.

"We are no longer untouchable, it seems." Kazhi was petting her horse, her eyes glazed over, staring at nothing. "The Council isn't concerned with their image. Something is happening if they are willing to let go of the Guards. We were the symbol of power to our people."

"What is that symbol now?" I asked, and no one had an answer.

I took a long breath as the three of them waited for me to come up with something. I hated that they put me in this position. "We head back to the Guardian City," I lifted a shoulder. "The best defence is a full-on attack."

Bastane drew up short. "Attack the Guardian City?"

Brekt's dark gaze appraised us as we argued. Did he see how united we were, how our truths were being laid bare?

I shook my head. "Attack the Council."

"We won't have back-up," Kazhi argued. "But we need to know what's happening and send a message—they can't take us down, and we aren't abandoning the people. It's a message to the citizens and those who align with the Council's orders."

"You have any ideas on how we should make our triumphant return?" I asked.

Bastane swore, kicking the dirt when Kazhi smiled. It was never a good sign.

Brekt was there as she told us her plan, adding in his own thoughts. He was always preparing backup plans to make sure his team was safe. I didn't miss how his plans excluded him.

I couldn't take my eyes off him as we walked, waiting, knowing it would soon happen again. The smoke, the ash, the fading image of my brother when the legendary beast took him from us once more.

Time was cruel.

It didn't take long, a few hours, and the beast claimed Brekt. I turned my head, like a coward would, so I wouldn't have to relive it, and when I finally dared raise my face to the sky, he was far above us, heading south again.

"I couldn't have asked for a better afternoon," Kazhi smiled, pulling the reins of her horse and setting a faster pace north.

CHAPTER
FORTY-NINE

Liv

"Liv, what are you doing now?" Maev finished burying the night's fire under a mound of earth and dusted off her hands, looking down a dirt-smeared nose to where I was lying.

The sky was turning pink, just coming over the horizon, and the air was crisp, with puffs of steam billowing out every time I exhaled.

"Can you hear it?" I reached out a hand and brought her to the rock my ear was pressed to.

The damp earth seeped through my thin layers of clothing while I listened to the hum. The smell of dirt, the cold bite of the morning, and the sounds of the ground singing its serene melody put me into a trance.

Maev pressed her ear to the ground, giving me a funny look. "I don't hear anything." She grabbed a piece of my near-white hair and pushed it away from my face. "We need to keep moving. We need more crystals for you. You are fading further and further."

We were in a beautiful, flat, wooded area. The trees, wrapped in a creamy white bark, were tall and slender, shooting straight into the sky. You could see everything on the ground because the bulk of its yellow leaves were high in the air.

"The earth is speaking, Maev. It hums like the magic does. It's soft, like a mother's voice."

"Oh-kay." Maev clapped her hands, and her voice became steel. "Time to get up and go. That's enough of that. It's been nearly a month since our last crystal was filled. You're overflowing. We have lucked out so far, not being stopped by anyone on our journey north. I was worried someone would see you, say a mean comment, and you'd accidentally blow them up. Instead, I get tree-hugging Liv. I can't predict you anymore."

I rose, letting her pull me to my feet. The forest spun around me as I collected my strength. Bearing the weight of the magic meant I had to stay calm and move unhurried—otherwise, I would lose control. My slow pace made our travels drag on, but if I continued to cut off the magic, the Aspis couldn't find us.

The Rydavians would wage war if the Guardians came this way.

"It's not luck that no one has stopped us," I said. "It's that we haven't been travelling on roads. My feet are proof of that."

Some days were easier than others, and I knew it had to do with my self-control. The box in my chest wasn't always so solid, and those were the days I reverted to my old self. I had severed my only connection with Brekt, and I was desperate to see him, but I had to stay strong.

"What do you mean it's not luck? We passed through the Southlands, and all the villages were empty. We've followed the coast north around the large bay and over rivers, and no one has guessed you're the Ikhor. That is luck," Maev argued.

Except there was no sign of Ollo. Maev swore he was alive, and we would continue to ask about him on our way north.

I shook my head. "It's not luck. I think we have a guardian keeping us safe," I whispered. Even with cutting off the magic, the shadow continued to appear—it had to mean the shadow had nothing to do with Brekt or the Aspis.

Maev's face fell. "Your shadow isn't a protector. The thing follows you, not us. And it has done nothing but cause you nightmares. I can't find you when you wander off in the dark. How is that a good thing?"

I took a deep breath and held it before releasing—a practice Maev had shown me to calm my mind. I pictured myself in a pond, playing in the water with my friends. I was safe there. The pressure in my head, the buzzing headache, the humming earth—I tuned it all out.

"They aren't nightmares." I followed Maev's lead and grabbed my things.

The wastelands to the south had been a nightmare. It had been nearly two weeks of travelling on the edge of the barren earth. South Rydavas resembled the stories my mother told Rebeka and me—that past the shores of the Endless Forest lay nothing but empty wastelands.

The Aethar built villages using dead trees atop scorched earth. It was all in the worship of the Ikhor and its godly powers. Why would the gods or anything they created want worshipers who maimed and destroyed?

We abandoned our Guardian's clothes once we passed the first Aethar village, and we stole clothing from their huts. A week later, we threw away the scratchy material after finding an abandoned cottage near the coast. There, we stole loose fabrics that clearly belonged to a man. I had to tie the clothing to keep it on me, and Maev's pants didn't reach her ankles.

The strangest parts of our journey were the airships. We caught several flying from the sea over the wastelands. Maev said it was pirates. So anytime we saw a ship, we hid, watching and hoping for them to land and for Ollo to come running. But he never did.

"They are absolutely nightmares," Maev said as we moved through the trees. "Because you scream every time you see the shadow thing. It haunts you. That's not protecting you. It doesn't do anything but chase you in your sleep."

It was not the first time we had argued about the shadow.

"I have seen it while awake." I held onto the thin trees as I walked, swinging around them.

Maev's mood was almost always sour, but she was perfect company. She talked when I needed it and was quiet when she understood I needed to box my emotions up, even though she didn't believe it to be healthy.

My refusal to use the magic left us unprotected. Neither of us said it out loud—we were scared. Though Ollo had not been skilled in fighting, he had offered security. His absence had been difficult, and Maev didn't speak of him much, which was something I understood. She continued to believe he was alive and that the pirates were keeping him for ransom.

"*He's too smart,*" she had said. "*And he's not the type to sacrifice himself. He will use every advantage and get off that pirate ship. He's probably already waiting for us at home.*"

I twirled around a tree, letting my long white hair flow in the breeze. "I still think the shadow has something to do with the god of Night." I had dreamt of the shadow creature many times. But the dreams were never that place with the crystalline sky. And Brekt never came to me in sleep anymore.

"I know you do. But if it is Erabas, why would he not reveal himself?"

"I think it's his ghost." I saw a lot of ghosts.

Maev was obviously concerned about my well-being, but she was not in great condition either. We were both dirty, losing weight and tired. Though my years in the Endless Forest gave me enough skill to make fires and scavenge food, neither of us was physically strong.

I only had to hold on, have hope, and pretend like everything wasn't falling apart.

CHAPTER
FIFTY

Nuo

The Council stood atop the stairs leading to the Guardian Palace, facing the crowd below, and I squinted against the sun, impatient to get this over with. Liars and murderers who all wore false smiles surrounded me, dressed in clean-cut golden clothes, saying well-delivered lines to the people, telling them exactly what they wished to hear.

The Council meeting was no meeting at all, but a trap. Set for who, I couldn't tell—but they never appeared before the public like this.

Kaz and Bas stood beside me in the crowd gathered before the Palace. A sea of Guardians surrounded us, their black uniforms scattered across every visible street and balcony. We had our hoods drawn, as did many others, blending in and staying hidden.

We had lucked out on our travels back to the city. Some poor Guardians with a small airship stationed in Danuli gave us a free ride back. A trip that should have taken us four weeks took two.

There was no word from Brekt, meaning we had no updates on what happened to the Ikhor after the canyons. The Guardians we'd run into said the citizens were getting worried that the Aspis hadn't entered the final battle. Apparently, many went directly to the Council to demand answers. And there I was, standing amongst the crowd.

The cloak I wore was too heavy with the sun beating down on us. I tried not to fidget, but several times, I caught myself forgetting where I was and trying to get Bastane's attention. I had already stolen four of Kazhi's knives without her noticing. The Governor's droning speech was putting me to sleep.

Falizha stood next to her father at the top of the stairs, the head of the Aspis carved into the mountainous rock behind them, and I realized the carving wasn't precise. The horns were wrong.

The beast loomed over the Governor as he delivered his lines. "The Guards will be made anew, stronger than ever before. The trials will begin soon, after a period of mourning for the tragic loss of our fellow warriors. We will honour the lives of Erebrekt of the North, Nuo, Kazhi and Bastane Armel, who died in battle against the Aethar in the Southern region of Veydes."

"Fucker," I muttered, earning an elbow from Bas.

The Guards killed in a battle with the Aethar? Hah—fighting them was like practicing with swords.

"In one week's time," the Governor went on, "we will begin the age-old trial by combat to decide the next set of Guards and who goes forth to battle alongside the Aspis."

I crossed my arms, leaning toward Kazhi, and she placed her hands on her remaining throwing knives, sheathed at her side. She pierced me with a sideways glance—she had known I took the others. Damn.

Falizha's brother stepped forward—a tall, broad-shouldered golden Day-leg dressed in Guardian black rather than gold like his pompous father.

"My son, Aeden Ravin, will take one of the vacant positions in the Guards, as he was a runner-up in previous years—"

I tuned the rest out. I wanted to puke.

The trial of the Guards was sacred. And the Governor's son had never been a runner-up, though no one in the crowd argued it. The

Ravins would pay for every one of their lies, but we couldn't kill them and end the Council. The smiling faces and cheers of the people below said as much. If we took them down without proof, we would be the villains, and nothing would change. A new Council would step up, and the control would continue.

No. We needed solid proof and a plan to end the Council's tyranny. Kazhi's plan was going to help us achieve that. We went over it many times on the way north. I only had to wait.

Aeden Ravin was passed a long sword—ancient ore powered by crystals—and turned to face the crowd. The women cheered louder than the men. He smiled, warm and welcoming. The sun reflected off his hair and piercing golden eyes.

"I think it's time." Kazhi tapped my arm, moving forward through the crowd.

I turned to a hooded figure several feet away and nodded. The hood dipped in understanding and signalled to the other thirteen who had come at our request—the only others who knew what we had planned.

They would be witnesses.

We worked our way through the crowd as Aeden gave a nonsense speech filled with empty promises—how he would be the new hero everyone was waiting for. My heart thumped with excitement. I'd waited days to reach the Guardian City, hoping we'd get this chance. I had my sights on Falizha, waiting for the moment when she noticed the three Guards walking up the stairs and destroying their plans.

I reached the bottom step, pausing only a moment, waiting for Bastane to catch up. Kazhi was ready, and her smile was pure venom, her sights set on the Governor. The three of us ascended the stairs, pulling back our hoods so that the entire crowd could see who had returned to the city.

No thanks to *Captain* Falizha Ravin.

The crowd gasped and then went silent.

Everyone would know Falizha was a liar and betrayer. Her reaction was what we needed for the next step.

I heard only our footsteps hitting the stone as we took our time ascending. And those fourteen survivors saw what passed the faces of the Council. The Council members looked to Falizha with disbelief—she was the one to blame for the lies of our death. She was a coward and hadn't bothered finishing us herself. Not that she could.

Our witnesses had proof that she had left us there to die, and the Council was not on our side.

Based on the reaction, not all of the Council members were involved in our "deaths". Interesting. It meant Bastane's father, who had a seat on the Council, may not be a traitor to the people.

Aeden Ravin had the good sense to look nervously at his father. Was he part of the plan?

It was the Governor's and Falizha's expressions that showed what we had all expected—rage. It was the final piece to the fucking fantastic puzzle. *Gods*, it felt good to piss her off.

Kazhi had planned it well. She had so many secrets hidden up her little sleeves that I was amazed. In the crowd were fourteen survivors of the burning field. Fourteen of Falizha's crew, whom she'd abandoned to the flames. Fourteen warriors who had bided their time, hiding in the Oracle's jungle waiting for Kazhi's orders, and now they had further proof that members of the Council were working to control everything.

Not a single member of the Council had smiled when they saw we lived. They had left the Guards for dead and were shocked that we returned.

Tonight, when Guardians went to eat and drink together around the city, mingling with the visiting citizens of Veydes, the surviving women would tell their stories, share their proof and win more to our side. Things would finally change, and the Council members would be replaced.

I reached the final step, walking to Falizha, who was furious, judging by her stiff posture. I stopped beside her, inching closer to whisper, "That's called a power move, hun. I thought I would point it out since you're shit at them."

Her nostrils flared. "How did you make it out of there? I thought for sure—"

I clicked my tongue, stopping her. "Don't think, Falizha. It never works out for you."

Kazhi walked past the Council, past the Governor, then Aeden, to the far end of the group. Bastane halted past Kazhi, facing the crowd, and I turned to join them, but Aeden stopped me, giving a warm and open smile, and reached a hand out to shake mine. The move caught me so off guard that it took me several seconds before I accepted his outstretched greeting.

"Happy to see you've returned. I am sorry for what happened to Erebrekt of the North," he said with a solemn smile.

He was golden-skinned like his father and sister, his hair pin-strait like Falizha's. Pieces fell from where he'd tied it behind his head.

Great. Another prince, I thought. *One likely without a conscience.*

"I know I am not a replacement for what you lost, but I hope we can fight together as you did with him. I heard many tales of your skill, Guard Nuo. I am honoured to follow the Aspis with you."

I nodded, aware of what his people thought of Sea-legs and those with weak blood. I knew a liar when I saw one. "Glad to have an extra sword," I lied right back, not saying any more. He would hear the disdain in my voice if I did.

Next, he broke away from his sister's side to greet Bastane and then Kazhi, who I noticed had a full belt of knives once more. I dug into my pockets to find the ones I'd taken were gone.

A hint of triumph lit her striped face as she shook Ravin Jr.'s hand.

Bastane shook Aeden's hand with familiarity. Bastane's older brother was the same age as Aeden. The Ravin and the Armel family had close ties, but Bas didn't smile as Aeden offered the pleasantries that fooled everyone around us. It was an act for those at the bottom of the stairs.

I knew a thing or two about lying. I had pretended my whole

life to be a lighthearted idiot to make others laugh. Aeden Ravin was a liar, too—maybe one of the best.

Joyous cheers spread through the crowd, seeing us return and Aeden joining our ranks. I played my part and waved to those who were below. Aeden took his place next to me, standing as a barrier between me and Falizha, who gave me a mocking grin over his shoulder.

Aeden was poised, serious, not at all like her. He gave his sister a nod and patted her on the back—she went stiff, forcing a smile that looked more like a wince as she pulled away from him.

Interesting.

She glanced back, her eyes narrowing on Aeden's neck. He was scratching a large red spot. A rash, perhaps. The cords in his neck were taught, the veins distended. Was he sick?

"Several teams are being put together to follow the Guards, now returned from the south," Governor Ravin said as if not believing we were there. "For the first time in known history, the Guardians will work as one to defeat the Ikhor. As the Aspis and Guards have been unable to finish it on their own, we will send our best. The Ikhor is now across the borders, in the Aethar wastelands, building its army."

I exchanged a look with Kaz. The Ikhor was with a *single* Aethar who couldn't fight.

"We will send units overseas to infiltrate this gathering horde and bring the Ikhor down," Governor Ravin continued, facing the Guards and addressing us. "The Aethar are vile creatures. Dangerous. Any you meet must be dealt with swiftly. They can disguise themselves and trick you into thinking they aren't vicious. We don't know what the Ikhor has done since it woke, what magic it has used to sway so many to its side. Some may still look like us before shedding their legacy to their cause. Do not hesitate to kill."

So this was it. We were heading into enemy lands. It wasn't the first time the Council had sent teams over. We'd learned this from the information in Falizha's journals.

The Governor admitted they knew some would look like us—

did that mean what the blue woman claimed was true? Were there cities full of citizens, just like Veydes, across the border?

"Before we adjourn for a celebratory dinner, my son has a special demonstration for the Guardians here today."

I exchanged a wary glance with the others, and Bastane's jaw tensed as Aeden stepped to his father's side with a warrior's grace. He folded his hands behind his back as his father continued to address the crowd. "You will be first to witness the hard work my son has been doing these long years."

Several Guardians dragged someone out of the Palace with a woven sack tied over their head. Muffled shouts came from the person as they struggled and kicked out, their arms tied behind them.

"What do they have planned?" Kazhi whispered.

The crowd below the stairs quieted, and the sun beat down on us as we waited for the prisoner to be shoved to their knees on the edge of the high platform.

The person, their black clothing ripped and bloodied, was on display for the entire crowd below. They squirmed against their ties. Muffled curses came from the hood, where they fought with the Guardians holding them down.

Aeden nodded to a Guardian who had a long weapon slung over his back, and the Guardian brought the weapon over to him. The thing was made of fabricated metal, not Ancient Ore. It had complicated parts, though it was obvious where the weapon was meant to be held. Aeden tested its weight and then placed the weapon against his shoulder.

The device I stole from the blue one sat heavy in my vest pocket. Aeden had access to these strange metals, the ones so unlike the Ancient Ore used for our weapons and airships.

"This device was invented by our most prized alchemists. They have altered magycris to be used not for healing but as a conduit for power. In this device is a small projectile, like the cannons we use on our airships. Its small size may not seem as threatening, but powered by the magycris, it can shoot at undetectable speeds. The small missile can pierce armour, and when it passes through the body of an enemy, the magycris becomes harmful to the system."

The prisoner inside the hood squirmed harder, his shouting muffled. Most likely by a gag hidden under the fabric.

"I have a bad feeling about this." Bastane lowered his chin, keeping track of Aeden's every move.

"This is a power play," I said. "Not only for us, but for the crowd. The Council usually doesn't show their cards."

I had marched into the city, thinking the Guards finally had the upper hand. That we were a step ahead of the Council, but something in my gut told me I was wrong.

"This could mean they finally believe we are on their side," Kazhi added, "Or they no longer believe we are a threat and don't care what we witness."

The crowd below went silent as the Governor and Falizha backed away and came to stand close to my side. Falizha gave me a mocking smile, proud she was a part of this show. "If only the Ikhor were here to see its worshippers fall," Falizha said in a low voice.

Aeden tucked the weapon closer to his shoulder. "The Aethar have harmed our people. They have burned our homes. They aided the Ikhor in burning South Aspis to the ground, along with many of our Veteran Guardians—some of whom were previous Guards. The Council promises to avenge our fallen brothers. Starting today."

Aeden nodded to the captors, and the prisoner's hood was removed, revealing an Aethar, causing the crowd to gasp.

"What is this?" Kazhi demanded, taking a step forward.

I recognized him, though I only saw glimpses of the man. I had seen his image on the posters throughout Veydes. I had been feet away from his sister, who had nearly identical features.

"That's one of the Aethar Liv—" Bastane coughed. "He was leading the Ikhor away from Veydes."

"The pilot we shot down," I agreed. "How did he get here?"

"Falizha," Kazhi whispered, full of menace. "She went back to her fallen airship. I thought pirates had taken him when they raided the wreckage."

The Aethar's face was torn up—one eye swollen shut, his lip split open, and his nose bent. But there was no mistaking the white hair, his blue skin, and the dark patterns down his bruised neck. Skin was missing along his cheek, along with patches of hair from a bloodied scalp.

"He's been tortured," I whispered.

The man turned to the crowd, shouting through a bloody gag. He was missing part of his ear, and blood stained his clothes from head to toe. Although he must have been in pain, he showed no signs of injury when he tried to stand and run.

The Guardians above him shoved his shoulders, slamming him back down onto his knees. The crowd below remained silent. They were seeing a beaten man, not a scarred-up Aethar.

"The Aethar have learned to forgo their scars, to blend in with us," Aeden explained to the silent crowd.

"He looks like one of us," said a woman from below.

Falizha stepped away from her father and addressed the crowd. She held up a poster—an image of Liv and her two companions—one of the many pinned around the Guardian city. "You've all seen this man before. He was personally responsible for taking the Ikhor to South Aspis."

I couldn't help myself. I looked back to the Aethar, and his wide eyes were on me. I had to give it to the man. A sea of his enemies surrounded him, but he showed not an ounce of fear. He was not begging. He was demanding.

He yelled something indistinguishable through his gag at me as his brow creased in anger. The words sounded a lot like *They're liars. Help ... Liv ...*

A sharp and quick bang silenced him.

I jumped, having not expected the sound.

Aeden lowered the weapon in his hand.

Several moments passed before the Aethar's eyes rolled. Pain twisted his face as he tried one more muffled plea at me, and I thought I heard him mention Liv again. Then his head fell forward, and he collapsed.

"I wouldn't touch it, Nuo," Falizha said from somewhere behind me. "Who knows what they catch in the wastelands."

The Guardians holding him let go, and he dropped to the ground with a thud, blood pooling under his unmoving body, the sun reflecting off the dark liquid.

I hadn't even tracked how he had died. What was this weapon Aeden held?

A hand on my arm yanked me back, and I turned to find Kazhi, bright eyed and furious, pulling me back to stand next to her.

"Kazhi, what's happening," I said stupidly.

Why did it feel like I just witnessed a murder? I'd killed many of their kind.

"It's nothing like I'd ever seen," Bastane said in a low voice. "Look at the wound in his back. It went right through his body."

"Liv will be devastated," Kazhi said. She had gone still. So very still. "Now more than ever, we must find ways to bring them down."

I scanned the people below, finding the horrified faces of several of the women who had come to our aid.

The Council crimes were leaking out in the open—pouring, not trickling.

The sun continued to shine down on the crowd of silent Guardians. Why did I feel like I was stuck in a torrential storm? This didn't sit right with me. Why did I react to my enemy's death with remorse?

Perhaps because the man on the ground had been keeping Liv alive when that was the task that Brekt had left for me.

I caught Falizha grinning, turning her sneer toward the Guards as if she was thinking of using the weapon on us. Little did she know, the crowd she thought she was impressing would soon be turning against her.

The Guardians below had remained silent, waiting for the Aethar to rise, and the Ravins seemed to be waiting for a reaction from the Guards. So many faces turned in our direction, and as always, the Guards were a symbol. If we showed remorse for the Aethar, we may never get the people on our side.

I felt sick as I slid my mask back on and winked at Falizha, trying to ease any suspicion the Aethar's death affected the Guards. "We are still the best looking Kaz," I said half-heartedly for those in earshot. "I count that as a win. Aeden's neck looks like he's caught something from one of the snake ladies."

Bas sent me a dry look. "This is serious."

"Don't bother, Bas," Kazhi cut in, then she whispered, "Keep it up, Nuo. They are playing a game, but so are we."

I thought Falizha was waiting for a reaction, but when her arrogant grin didn't fade, I wondered what else she was waiting for.

That's when Aeden addressed the silent crowd.

"We have been able to duplicate this weapon enough times that we have a full arsenal. Every Guardian called forward is to join our mission to the Aethar lands."

Another Guardian stepped to Aeden's side, holding a list of names.

Aeden stood tall as he held up his weapon. "And each of you will be armed with your very own Deathmaker."

Nuo

We followed the Council back into the Palace, where there would be a dinner honouring Aeden's new position. I walked as if amused, making jokes with Kazhi, and as we cut past the still form of the Aethar, his hand twitched. Both Kazhi and I caught it, but looked forward as if we had seen nothing.

The Ravins ignored the man on the ground as they brushed past us.

"Congratulations," Falizha said sarcastically, veering to walk next to her brother as they stepped in the shade cast by the gigantic Aspis head.

"Chin up, little sis. Father will give you some role to play, I'm sure. Too bad the Guards returned. You almost had a spot in their ranks." Aeden elbowed his sister, who scowled at him.

"I am going with you across the border, don't you forget. You might have been given a fancy title, but I will be leading the teams."

"Whatever you need to tell yourself. It's cute seeing you weasel your way into becoming captain of an airship."

I walked behind the two, enjoying the fury that crossed Falizha's face. Maybe I'd enjoy having Aeden around, after all.

Falizha's sneer was audible as she said, "And what, may I ask, have you been doing while away?"

Aeden wiped the posturing from his face, voice going flat, turning cruel. "That is none of your fucking business, brat."

Falizha's fists clenched at her side, but she continued walking as if nothing happened. Aeden might be a worse bastard than his sister, but he hid it twice as well.

We entered the dining hall, where the two sat next to each other.

The black stone walls were polished so smooth each member of the dinner was reflected back at us. Even in the low lighting, I could see everything going on around me without having to look down the long table.

Bastane took a seat next to me. No one searched for Kazhi. There wasn't a council meeting she attended all the way through, if at all.

Falizha and her brother took up the two seats across from me, their father several chairs down at the head of the table. I noted Aeden didn't join his fellow Guards. No matter. He was a new pawn in our game. It felt like fate was knocking at my door. Soon, things would be brought into the light, and the masks would fall off.

"First," the Governor said, lifting his glass, his cold scowl on his daughter. "A toast to our returning Guards. We bless Rem with this luck."

Sullen mumbles came from the table, and I coughed to cover my laugh. I lifted my glass, bringing it to my lips.

"While the Guards were vacationing in the south, I was able to get rid of the last Sea-leg from the caves, Father." Falizha's grating voice was usually enough to send me into a rage, but nothing worked faster than those who put my people down. "They had been living off our generosity for far too long. I was happy to see that last family leave our gates, off to wherever they would go.”

Another Councilman sitting next to Falizha dipped his golden head toward her, lifting his glass. “It took some time to find them homes, far too long if you ask me.”

“Blessed Rem,”—Falizha poured herself a large cup, the first one already gone—“I couldn’t stand to look at them another day.” The corners of her mouth lifted, knowing that I was listening.

Pure, unbridled hatred coursed through my veins.

Aeden leaned toward his sister, placing a hand on her arm. “Perhaps you should go slow with the drink, dear Falizha, lest you embarrass us all with your hateful comments.”

Aeden’s remark was loud enough that Falizha flushed with anger before he turned away, nodding to me and ignoring her.

“Well said, Aeden,” the Governor interrupted. Aeden took a slow sip of his drink, not turning his attention down the table to where he was being addressed. “Falizha, take after your brother here and drink slowly, lest you say things you don’t mean.”

She turned a bright orange and slammed her drink down. “What do I have to hide, Father? We are winning against our enemies. We should be proud. I brought home the very Aethar who was leading the Ikhor.”

“I would have been proud had it been the Ikhor you shot down, not a no-name legacy from the wastelands. Did your interrogation at least gain us new information about the Ikhor’s plans?”

Falizha said no more. Instead, Aeden rested his glass on the table and addressed the question. “He was tough to break. As we all know, the Aethar have a high tolerance to pain. None of our methods worked.”

I didn’t know the blue Aethar, and I had already threatened his sister, but openly speaking about his torture didn’t feel right.

Falizha turned her malicious tongue on me. “That’s what happens to those that don’t cooperate. That’s why he was used to demonstrate our new weapon.”

"*My* new weapon, Lizha," Aeden said in a tone that suggested she quit talking.

"So Aeden." Bastane relaxed in his seat. "Tell me of this Deathmaker. It's quite the advancement. May I ask who designed it?"

Falizha spoke first, drowning her brother out. "Aeden has been making all sorts of things on behalf of the Council to use against the Ikhor. Since the Aspis hasn't done a godsdamned thing to save our people."

"I believe the Guard asked me," Aeden said, shutting his sister down once more. "I have not invented a thing. The Alchemist under my hire has. He is a genius."

"I would be honoured to meet this Alchemist," Bastane probed, swirling the liquid around in his glass.

"Alas, he is in his facilities in the far north. He is a Mount-leg of the northern tribes. I helped to build him a lab in his preferred working conditions—that is as much credit as I can take for the invention. I have asked him to make one for each of the Guards. I would like to present them to you before we head out together on our next mission."

"And what is our next mission?" I asked, remembering the Governor saying we were crossing the borders.

Aeden bent forward, resting his elbows on the table. "There is a horde of Aethar spotted on the northern borders of the wastelands. We will attack. I worry they will be using ships to cross next, forgoing the canyon pass."

A plate of steaming vegetables and a chunk of meat was set before me, and my mouth watered at the meal. "What makes you think they could use ships? And how do you know of this horde when none can cross the seas to witness those borders."

"Though it will upset my father to hear,"—Aeden shot a look down the table, pausing a moment too long—"I have made use of the pirates that patrol the air above the seas. I pay them for information of who crosses and what they see on the borders."

The Governor grunted his disapproval of his son's tactics. "This is how we receive information about the Aethar hordes?"

Aeden gave his father a single nod.

The Governor thought on this a moment and said to the Councilman at his right, "My son keeps me informed while creating weapons in the north. Very useful boy."

Aeden's face hardened at the comment. It flashed so quickly across his face I nearly missed it—the way the corner of his eyes pinched a fraction, his mouth going tight—he was irritated.

"He does me proud. I send requests his way, and he's always so quick to deliver, never failing his father, are you son?"

Aeden blinked, wiping clear any traces he was affected by what his father said.

Could it be that the son doesn't favour the father? The dinner just got a lot more interesting.

"But we do have to worry about the Aethar flying, don't we now?" Another council member said, a golden Day-leg sitting a few chairs down from me. "This one who was leading the Ikhor was piloting an airship, was he not?"

"He stole Falizha's ship in Danuli," Aeden told the councilman. "Isn't that what happened, Lizha? How was it he was able to take it from you?"

"The Guards were busy running around in the streets." Falizha held her glass so tightly I thought it would break. "I was rounding them up to chase the Ikhor. Instead, my ship was stolen, and they let the Ikhor slip away."

"You took them down in the end, Ms. Ravin," said the same councilman. "And you were able to apprehend the pilot."

"It's what I do to those that get in my way."

I snorted when she held my gaze, thinking it was a threat. *I'm counting the minutes.*

Bastane nodded to Kazhi's empty seat. "Where is she?"

I wiped my chin, where a drop of grease had made a path. "I asked her to go to the library. I need more books on the history of the Ikhor."

An audible whoosh of air passed, and someone sat in the chair next to me, the hairs rising on the back of my neck as the smell of drink wafted my way.

"What do you want?" I muttered.

Falizha rested her arm on my chair, her slimy gaze raking me up and down.

I shivered, my stomach rolling. With her desire for power, she was missing how many mistakes she made—how much information she let slip. I had to control my desire to lash out at her and remember that she was the key to finding the truth about what the Council was doing. They were hiding the truth about what was across the border and lied about who was burning the villages and the South Guardian camp.

Falizha spoke in a low tone so no one else would hear. "My brother is taking your brother's place. Doesn't it bother you that you left him flying aimlessly in the sky? You abandoned him in the south."

"Interesting that you mention abandoning one of my own." I licked the spoon in my hand, savouring the flavour of the meat, wishing I could tell her who was in the crowd today. "So when did your brother come back from his super secret mission?"

Falizha was dressed in her tight-fitted Guardian black and wore that hideous purple cape that she pinned to one shoulder with a crystal to remind everyone she was the Captain of a ship. "Someone needs to do the work the Guards are not. The Council wants to replace you. You might be out of a job, Nuo. And with that goes any value you have. No suite, no weapons, no home. What will an orphan boy do then?"

There was a wicked gleam in her eye, so I tilted back in my chair, balancing on the back two legs, turning my smile up a few degrees. "They decide who earns the position of Guard through combat. Wanna test me yourself?"

Falizha straightened, and I tracked the slight movement in her throat as she swallowed. That thin layer of skin held no protection from my blade.

She blanched, noticing where my attention was caught.

"I was chosen for my skill," I reminded her. "Everyone in the Council knows you can't defeat me. No one could defeat me. The same goes for Kazhi and Bas. You'll have to show them you're better to be able to take my place, and we both know you can't."

"I suppose you're right. What else is there for a waste of life like you, anyways? Filthy Sea-leg."

My knife landed between two of her fingers, where her hand splayed on the table, the blade vibrating from the force.

"Damn, I missed." I rested my arm on the back of my chair, savouring her scowl. "I have never once in my life called a woman a cunt, but none have ever deserved the title as much as you."

"This is my home," Falizha seethed, dropping her voice even lower. "You disrespect *me*, and you are out."

"No, no, no." I waved a finger, turning up the charm. "It's the Guardian's home. Your father just sat his rather wide ass on the head seat of the table. You, Falizha, have no claims to anything here." I let the chair legs fall back to the ground, turning away from her. "But this conversation is boring me. I feel like I have repeated this to you endlessly. Why are you sitting here?"

She was silent a moment before she said, "I came to tell you the details of the Council's next mission. But you know what? I'd rather you die, Nuo."

I smiled, playing with the veggies on my plate. It was difficult not to throw another knife her way, but I had gained control over the past few weeks—my monster was on its leash again.

"Your life is ended once I get the nod, Falizha. That's all it will take. One nod," I said in a low voice.

She leaned away from me. "Who—"

"Your life is no longer your own. You lost the right to be in this world when you left all those Guardians to die on the burning field. We all saw it. We need you only for one more piece of proof. You've been sloppy. We know."

"Know what?" Her face was turning a darker colour, but it wasn't enough for me anymore to see her squirm.

"What you and your golden assholes have been doing." It was a half lie.

She fidgeted with her cape, scoffing at me. "You know nothing. The Guards have been playing games without even knowing the players. My brother is joining your ranks. And you'll be brought to heel, Nuo." Falizha wobbled in her seat, taking another sip of her drink. "Where is your other team member? Does Kazhi think she is too good for us? Or is she snooping where she doesn't belong?"

I ignored her, but Falizha inched closer. "I would have loved to send the body overseas for the Ikhor to witness what we plan to do to all of its followers."

I didn't take the bait, but tucked away the information she was letting slip. It sounded like Aeden was being sent to watch us, since Falizha failed. "I look forward to being on the road with your brother."

Her eyes lit with delight. "But not alone. You heard how the Council is ordering a full team to accompany the Guards. You failed to understand those orders extend to every one of your missions. And I'll be captaining the ship. "

Why were they sending teams? That was too many witnesses for their plans.

I raised my glass, took a sip, and noticed she was eyeing me. "You tried to come into my suite once before Falizha, and I knew what you wanted then. I know when you look at me, you hate what you see but still desire to have me."

"How dare—"

"It's the power." I lifted my hands while I shrugged. "It's wanting what you've been denied. But I will never give it to you, no matter how much you try to prove yourself." I drew closer, backing her away in her seat. "Your daddy will never see you as a strong warrior like your brother. Others will not respect you no matter how hard you try to gain the favour of the powerful men around you." I gripped my glass so tightly that I was surprised it didn't smash. "You could have been your own woman. You could have been powerful in your own right. But you never will be if you seek to steal it from others."

She stumbled out of her seat, fuming as she stormed back to her side of the table, and sat herself back down beside her brother, who was smirking over at me. Weird.

She would retaliate for what I had said, and I was looking forward to it.

Things had changed in the canyons when Liv knocked me to the ground, screaming to let her little Aethar friend go. A part of me had snapped, waking back up. The Ikhor could have flayed me for touching its follower, but instead, it had taken a fist and tried to beat me off the blue woman. Not fire, not ice, but a fist that barely made a bruise.

When Brekt had reappeared, I could finally admit the legends were wrong. But whether or not Liv was still my friend? Different story. One thing I needed to get straight was how in the Endless Night it all could end. I needed to search through those texts and read every account of history and see the information in a new light. If I was going to have to admit I was wrong, which I was nowhere near doing, I had to have solid proof to refill my mind with what was right.

The device I had stolen from the blue Aethar—I had taken it apart and reassembled it to see how it worked. It was genius— meaning the Ikhor wasn't following crazed worshippers. Meaning Liv left me on that field by choice.

I pushed my hair out of my face and blew out a frustrated breath. I hated her for leaving, for lying, for abandoning Brekt when he was dying in my arms. I was still angry and ready to do what I must if I saw signs of the Ikhor taking over and destroying the world around it.

But it had been nearly four months since the two legends had risen. The Aspis wasn't saving the people, and the Ikhor wasn't burning the lands.

Everything I trained my whole life to become meant nothing anymore.

What was I if I wasn't a Guard?

CHAPTER

FIFTY-TWO

Nuo

"So, Kaz, where did you head off to?" Bastane stood against the railing of the Guard's balcony—the open space between the suites, where only we had access. "Nuo and I barely escaped that dinner when they brought out the snake ladies. They did their best to keep us from leaving."

Kazhi had determined the balcony was the only safe place to speak, where the wind would cover our words—not that anyone could hear us way up here.

I dropped a book I'd been reading on the lounge chair next to me and stood straight, pressing my back against the glass wall behind me. There was a pile of them to go through. I'd checked the publication dates in several books to understand what I was reading. None were older than two hundred years.

"I searched for the body." Kazhi was facing the Guardian city, aglow with lamp-lit paths. Businesses were still open for those seeking entertainment after training, and I wondered how the women from the burning field were doing, if anyone was believing their tale. "That's why I missed dinner," she said to Bastane. "I went to confirm the man was dead."

"And?" Bastane asked.

Kazhi turned around, her elbows resting against the railing. Next to Bas, her slight frame appeared smaller.

"I couldn't find him. However, I overheard a shipment is being sent north on Aeden's behalf for '*his work*.' I learned nothing more."

"Do you think the Aethar could have survived that kind of wound?" I asked.

Bastane held the journal the blue woman had given him. We had all read it by now. "Aeden said the ballistic is infused with magycris. But not the healing liquid. He made it sound as if he's found a way to make magycris a poison."

"Didn't know you two would get so bent out of shape for an Aethar," Kazhi said mockingly. "Admitting you're opening your eyes?"

I flicked some lint off my arm in her direction.

"It was me that shot down that airship." Bastane set the journal down next to my pile, nodding to it. "It was her brother we shot down. The Ikhor wasn't even on the ship."

"After this mission to the Aethar lands ..." Kazhi gave us a troubled look. "I want to follow Aeden if he returns north or catch one of these shipments and follow. I want to see this secret place he scurries off to and what he does there."

"You? Not us?" I asked.

"No. I would be gone for a short time, and I will keep myself hidden."

"I don't like the sounds of this. You would be on your own far from any backup." Bastane gave Kazhi a stern look.

"I survived many years on my own. I can handle it."

"Many years, huh?" I said. "How many is that?"

She had called out to the Desert Eagle in that canyon with no fear. In fact, she called to him with familiarity. When we questioned her later, she said we were hearing things, and that she was desperate for him to let Bastane go. I knew she was lying and not just of her past. She had some plan of her own when it came to all this.

"Kaz—" I started.

She tapped her boot, waiting. "Something on your mind, Gills?"

"Don't call me that." I drew a knife from my belt and toyed with it to keep my hands busy. "Brekt hid what he was from you two," I said finally.

Kazhi stopped bouncing her foot, and Bastane unfolded his arms. They stood in the fading glow, waiting to hear where I was going with this. We hadn't talked about it since he'd changed— likely because I had not been clear-headed and because none of us openly discussed our feelings about losing him. We had fought about Bastane's fuck-ups, but not Brekt's.

"Brekt asked me to keep his secret from you because he didn't want to be the Aspis. He didn't want people to know what he was or watch him waiting for it to appear. He considered you two his family and liked that you saw him as just a man."

"I wasn't waiting for you to apologize for Brekt," Bastane said in the kindest manner he'd ever spoken to me.

I waved off his comment. "I'm not. I am apologizing to you for my part. I made a promise to him before I ever met you, but I'm sorry for the anger I know you must feel from being left in the dark. If you can't forgive me for that, then I have another favour to ask of you."

Bastane slid his attention to Kazhi, who was chewing on a fingernail. He shivered, blinking away his disgust before facing me. "I'm listening."

We all jumped when a pair of boots slammed to the ground. One of the lounge chairs flew backward, screeching across the balcony as a loud curse interrupted what I was about to say.

The swirling shadows that shielded him from sight vanished on the wind. Brekt was holding the railing, face pale. "I wasn't sure I landed where I intended to. It's ... unnerving to come back to myself."

"How do you do that?" I clutched my chest to catch my breath. "You scared the shit out of me. I didn't see you in the sky."

"I've been travelling at night to remain hidden. I've been more myself lately. More than before." Brekt's wild hair blew around his face.

"Why do you think you feel more yourself? Are things changing?"

"What of Bones?" Kazhi asked before Brekt could answer, going to his side. "Did you find her?" She inspected him. For what, I wasn't sure.

"No," he grunted, pushing Kazhi away. "I can only think of one explanation as to why I can control the Aspis, why I can't feel her."

I held my breath. It couldn't mean what I thought, no way.

"She's repressing it," Brekt said, and I let my shoulders fall.

The stupid bastard saw my relief and grinned. Fucker.

"I think she's holding the magic back, meaning I can't sense her. And she's severed our connection. I don't see her in the dreams, either," he said to me.

"Dreams?" Bastane asked. "How many frigging secrets are we spilling tonight."

"You should be used to spilling secrets. Isn't that your specialty?" Brekt snapped.

Bastane tapped his chest, mocking the pain delivered there. "I can take it, Beastman. I deserve it."

"I was about to get into the spilling of secrets before your abrupt and unasked-for arrival," I said to Brekt. "Since you barged into our meeting, I suppose we can let you in on the conversation."

Brekt didn't seem amused. "Don't let me interrupt then. Do go on."

"No, no. You were talking about your dreams." I waved a hand, realizing I was still holding a knife, and put it away.

"Can't even catch my breath. Interrogated as soon as I land," he muttered before resting his hands against the railing and looking out over the city. "I've had dreams my whole life—things that were to come. I knew of you all before I met you."

Kazhi threw me a look, and I shrugged, admitting I already knew this.

"I had dreamt of Liv before I met her," he continued. "I dreamt of her bathed in fire and thought it meant she would be victim to the Ikhor. I don't know why I never put it together."

"Likely because she was too innocent," Bastane said. "Liv didn't seem the evil type."

Brekt nodded. "But I don't see her anymore. Not since I was in those canyons. Though I wasn't in control, I vaguely remember her amongst the rock and sand, as well as you three trying to hold me down."

"So you have to wait until you feel the magic to find her?"

He dipped his head in affirmation. "Until then, she could be anywhere."

I thought about what happened in the canyons, which led me to question everything. "You tried to take the magic from her. You were absorbing it."

Brekt went still. "Don't confuse me with the Aspis. I have no control. I wouldn't harm Liv."

"Semantics. The Aspis tried to take the Ikhor's magic. It wasn't trying to kill." I'd forgotten to discuss that the last time we saw him, too shaken by his return.

Brekt was transfixed on the mountains beyond. "Yes, it's drawn to it. When the Ikhor's magic is used, it's a call for the beast. When Liv refrains from using it, I gain control."

I held my hands out. "So that's how this could all end. The Aspis takes the magic and returns it to the gods."

Brekt peered over at me, angered. "And based on what you saw, would taking the magic have killed Liv?"

I opened my mouth to argue when Kazhi cut me off. "Nuo saved her from it, so yes, he thought it was killing her."

The look that crossed his face disappeared before I could understand. "I will not risk killing Liv. I want to find another way. Have there been no reports on the Ikhor's whereabouts or her guides?"

"No word on Liv," Bastane said to Brekt. "But her companions ... the Ravins killed the pilot leading Liv away from Veydes. We shot down their airship and didn't think he survived. Falizha must have returned for him. Liv will want to know."

Brekt paused, staring at the sky before speaking. "She considers the two Aethar her friends. I vaguely remember her saying so. He's dead?"

"I don't know that he's dead," Kazhi said. "If you want to wait to tell her."

"I won't hide such a thing from her," Brekt said. "Not if she considered the pilot her friend."

The night grew colder, the sounds of the waterfalls around the city soothing against the darker turn of our conversation. Kazhi took her place beside Brekt, both staring at the stars lit high above. "Have the gods spoken to you, their champion, to give any instructions on how to end this?"

I had wondered about that, too. "Maybe a helpful hand or 'Fuck you! Do what you're told'?"

Brekt shook his head. "Not a word. I don't sense the gods. I don't know what their plan is, but it's clear they want no part in the battle."

"Lazy bastards," Kazhi said, and we all looked at her with surprise. "I'm getting tired of defending our gods."

"Me too," Bastane added, then regarded Brekt over Kazhi's head. "Sometimes you don't seem yourself. Last time we saw you ..."

Shadows under Brekt's skin moved as he faded in and out of sight, clearly uncomfortable with the questions. "I apologize for what I do and say when I lose control. I—I am stuck inside this place. It ... it's like a nightmare, but sometimes the nightmare shifts, and I can see the real world, but I can't tell if it's an illusion."

"If they're yellow, he'll kill a fellow," I said toward Kazhi.

"What?" Brekt asked.

"If they're black, Brekt is back." Kazhi rhymed.

Bastane groaned. "Their little song—to determine if you're dangerous or not."

Brekt wasn't catching on.

"Your eyes, bud," I said, smirking. "If women were scared of your creepy Night-leg orbs before, it's nothing like the slitted snake eyes you've been sporting lately. You're not invited to the taverns with me. Bad for my image."

"I should have known that even following the fucking Aspis, you'd still find time for women and drink."

Bastane snorted while I mocked offence. "How else am I supposed to get over the gruesome death of my fellow Guard?"

"A mind healer?" Bastane suggested.

I barked a laugh. "Mind healers? I'm smarter than anyone you'd stick in front of me. Wouldn't work."

"How about training?" Bas said, his mouth forming a flat line. "You used to do that a lot more often."

"I'm fine with women and drinking. The final battle always claims the lives of the Guards. Let me have my fun."

The three shared a look, and it pissed me off that they weren't falling for my flippant remarks.

We remained silent for a moment, unsure of what topic to dive into.

"So, what conversation did I really interrupt?" Brekt asked.

I nodded, taking the cue to get back to it. Brekt was ready to be open. Were the others? "As I was about to say before Beastman returned—we need to go all in. Nothing left behind closed doors. All trust on the table. As it should have been from the beginning."

Kazhi spat, and I was about to argue my case further when she said, "Agreed."

Bastane coughed, "Agreed? You? Finally going to admit you're some dark creation by the god of Night himself?"

"She wishes," Brekt muttered.

Kazhi fixed her hair, tucking pieces of it behind her ear. "I am no such thing. But I do have a past I wish not to speak of." She pointed at me. "Before you push me, my past has nothing to do with being a Guard or affects anything about what we are heading into. There are pains I don't wish to speak of."

"Then what secrets are you hiding that matter? Who are you, Kaz? Tell us something that unifies us. I want to believe we are in it together until the end."

Kazhi's shoulders slumped. I would've dared to say she looked hurt. "I am your closest friend—one you can trust until your dying breath. I will never let any of you be hurt. Not by anyone on any side of the battle. My ambitions are the same as yours. I only know other players involved."

"Other players?" Bastane asked.

Kazhi nodded, regarding each of us. "You should sit. This will take some explaining."

"I am fine standing," I said, trying to hold in my impatience.

"I don't get to use my feet enough," Brekt grumbled. "I'll stand, too."

The wind kicked up, making it hard to hear her when she said, "I have hidden from you that I am a pure-blooded legacy."

I didn't hide my irritation. "That's not a shocking revelation." She wasn't taking this seriously. "That explains nothing about you."

"Our team hasn't cared about that," Brekt said. "You never batted an eye that I was one."

Kazhi frowned at Brekt. "I've hidden that you and I could both use magic."

He shook his head, disagreeing. "I never had magic."

Bastane backed away from the other two, and Kazhi scowled at him. "Don't make me regret telling you."

"So you are a legacy of Night?" I asked.

Kazhi could use *magic*. Magic users were a myth. Magic was supposed to be used by only the gods.

"I am a pure-blooded legacy of Day." She waited, perhaps wondering how we would react.

Bastane's face fell. "Kaz, don't mess around. There's not a speck of gold on you."

"You have been lied to your whole life." She pushed more hair from her face as the breeze picked up. "The golden Day-legs aren't the only clans in the bloodline. The Guardian lands have been controlled for years, far longer than you know. I am a pure-blooded legacy and have magic of my own. And I don't know how you never pieced it together, Erebrekt."

Bastane's chest rose and fell like he had been training. "That's a bold statement to make. Day-legs don't have *clans*. And magic doesn't exist outside the gods and the magic the Ikhor stole from them."

Kazhi gave Bastane a sad look. "It used to exist a lot more. As did the magical bloodlines. Brekt was never told—he didn't understand that his ability to shift light and shape himself to it was magic." She searched Brekt's face. "You were taught they were a gift, like Nuo's second set of lungs, but it is magic, like the god of Night, Erabas. You never understood what you were sensing when I used my own. I have magic, too. I can use the wind and make sound travel back to me."

I clapped my hands together. "No wonder you know everything. I thought you read minds. You're just a snoop." Though I had a hard time wrapping my mind around the new information, it made so much sense it could only be the truth.

"A very powerful snoop." Her expression darkened, and I stopped laughing.

"So this is the secret you've kept? That doesn't seem to help us much." Bastane looked pale. It would be harder for him than anyone to accept that Kazhi could use magic. "Aside from your own safety, I don't know why you kept it from us."

She shrugged. "It would mean you asking questions about where I came from, which I still won't talk of. It means I know a lot more than I've let on. I knew Liv could feel magic." Kazhi raised a hand when I opened my mouth to argue. "I thought she was a descendant, like me, hiding her identity. I promise I didn't know what she was. However, I have met many other purebloods along my journeys and know there are others hidden in the world. We were hunted and killed for our magic, and eventually, the world was taught that it didn't exist in the legacies so that we would be hated and feared if discovered. Possibly even labelled as the Ikhor."

I thought about what she was admitting. It was true. I already feared the power she spoke of, even though I knew who she was. "You're right. Several months ago, that's exactly what I would have accused you of."

"A Day-leg, huh?" Bastane said dazedly. "How's that possible?"

"The golden ones have been exterminating the undesirables for a long time. Not just Sea-legs and Night-legs. Their own people, too. They believe they're in the image of Rem, and the rest were unworthy of his name." Kazhi went to the lounge chair and sat, folding her legs beneath her.

It amazed me—like I was seeing her for the first time. She was always there, following us like a ghost. I trusted my life with her, but I had never felt like I truly knew her.

"Can the golden Day-legs use the power of the wind too?" Bastane shifted uncomfortably. Was he upset that he didn't know everything about his people? Or had he seen something already with the Day-legs?

"There are three lines. Golden, blue, and white—or the sun, ice and wind clans," she said, fixed on his reaction. "My people were Day-legs who harnessed the power of the wind. We often lived in open plains or high on the mountain tops. The wind powered us, and we never toppled from its force. The blues were masters of wielding ice, frost and even the changing of the season. They would control the cold to bring on spring flowers. *If* any purebloods are left, they can survive extreme cold and manipulate water. But I have not met a pure-blooded Day-leg from the ice clans in a very long time."

"They were Day-legs Liv was travelling with?" I asked,

stunned. The markings on their skin were something I'd never seen on a legacy.

"Yes, they were," Kazhi confirmed. "The blue ones told Bones what they were, and Bones was quick to call me out as a Day-leg in Danuli, understanding what my features meant."

"She's observant," Brekt said with pride.

"And the golden ones?" Bastane's voice lowered. "You know I am asking about my own people. *Clan.* Whatever."

"The golden bloodlines have always survived well in harsh climates. The heat never bothered them. And they had their own element they controlled. Dangerous. They were always the ones to fear. Your bloodline has a vicious history, Bas."

"What powers did they have, Kaz?" I asked, afraid I was making connections to what she was going to say.

Her expression told me I was correct. "The pure-blooded Day-legs from your line, Bastane, could wield fire. And if one might be so ambitious, could convince an entire world the Ikhor was alive by setting fires to the earth."

Neither of my brothers spoke, and I couldn't find the words.

I'd blamed Liv for it all, yet it was ...

"Falizha ..." Bastane said for me.

"I have never been close to the Ravins when magic was used, so I can't say for certain it's them." Kazhi was staring skyward.

Was she thinking of the burning fields as I was?

"Falizha was at the burning fields that night. Did you feel magic then?" I asked.

Kazhi dipped her chin. "But Brekt and Liv were there, too. So many times, I have felt close to finding the truth. But I was one against many." Her black eyes glazed with excitement. "Now we are four, and we all agree the Ravins have committed evil, more so than the famed Ikhor."

"The fires that were set before Liv became the Ikhor, I hadn't questioned them." I stared at the books next to me. So many things were beginning to make sense.

"There are too many things to question," Kazhi replied. "And I am partly to blame for keeping you in the dark."

Bastane threw me a look. He was angry, and I suppose part of me was, too.

"Who else have you met on your journeys?" he asked Kazhi. "You said there were other purebloods."

"Many who know old truths, and they do not trust the Council. They would be on our side if we made a move. The Eagle was one. An Alchemist in Bellum. Others who wish to remain unknown. Many are waiting for me to bring you two in and join us." She turned to Brekt. "If you're okay that people know who and what you are and that you are alive, I will bring you in, too."

He nodded. It was the Council he was hiding from.

"Why have you waited so long?" Bastane threw his hands up in irritation.

Kazhi pointed an accusing finger at him. "Because you were a slave to your bloodline." She turned to Brekt. "You were afraid of what you were." Her finger swivelled to me. "And you were a slave to your hate. Don't deny it. I know what that is like, as I was once, too. But now? Now, things are different. I think a certain evil someone is changing minds—changing the course of the future."

"You think the Ikhor has changed my mind? Please." I let my mask fall into place, hiding what I didn't want them to see. "She's just a selfish girl."

"Watch it," Brekt growled.

"The Ikhor is a girl now?" Bastane said. "Not an *it*?"

"Semantics, Bas. The Ikhor is our enemy."

He made a sound in the back of his throat. "Is that why you saved her?"

I shrugged the comment off. "You aren't the only one who's a gallant hero when a woman is watching."

Kazhi was on her feet and smacked Bas on the back of the head before he could reply.

I threw him a middle finger before Kazhi could turn her scolding on me, and then flopped onto a chair, moving some books aside to sit back. "I have found nothing in the texts. I believe these were all written by a one-sided narrative."

"What will you do with that knowledge? Admitting your wrong, Nuo?" Brekt's smile was smug.

I scoffed at the idea. "Never. What I will do now is find a new library. In a new world. Just so happens we are being shipped to one."

Brekt straightened. "You're going to the Aethar lands?"

I waved a hand. "Catch him up, Kaz. He needs to know where we are at."

She smacked me on the back of the head next, and I rubbed it, cursing her as she retold everything that had happened. "And now you three know as much as I do, as Liv does, and you can join the people who fight for freedom for all legacies."

"These purebloods," Brekt said skeptically. "They are part of this so-called rebellion. I'd heard the stories in passing, thinking it was some silly rumour."

And the Eagle was part of it. I couldn't wrap my head around it. I thought the hidden players were in the Council, but it seemed like we had some on our side as well. And Liv was going to help them? What the fuck.

"We are unified, more of a family than we ever were," she said, ending the story in a serious nature. "We are no longer Guards. We only wear their clothes. You all want in on my secrets, then you are no longer even Guardians."

Brekt whistled. "I can use magic, eh?" He swivelled his annoying head my way. "Hear that? I'm even more important and powerful now."

I fiddled with a book at my side. "If only your pure blood could have made you better looking."

"Please, concentrate," Kazhi pleaded. "Did you hear what I said?"

My chest gave several hard beats before it sunk in what she meant. Kazhi was suggesting we abandon who we were—betray our training—our identities.

"What are we then?" Bastane looked as surprised as I felt.

"Besides fucking legends." I pushed my hair back, faking calm. I hadn't expected the conversation to go this way—she was asking us to give up everything we knew, and I could admit, I was ... uncomfortable. But I wouldn't show it.

"I will tell you what I know of the past, our history, that hasn't been told in the open for a long time. But I can't risk that conversation, even here."

"Where then?" I asked.

"As far away from any others as possible. A remote location."

"I suppose you won't wait for me to return to be a part of that conversation?" Brekt asked.

"Not if it takes you several more weeks to return."

What would his thoughts be? What were my own? Would we abandon what it was to be a Guardian to join a cause we knew nothing of?

"That's a lot to ask without giving us much more information," I said.

Kazhi didn't blink. "I can only say so much for now, but don't forget Nuo—I am not your enemy."

I let my head fall as I thought. I would never have thought Kazhi was my enemy. Just as I never thought I would fight on the same side as the Ikhor.

Not long after, I collected several bottles of drink for us to pass around. The four of us settled in, bringing the lounge chairs together. The cold night warmed as we drank and fell into easy laughter and constant bickering, just as it had always been. Nothing about the night differed from the hundreds we shared before, but I would remember every moment. I would hold on to every second with my family.

Brekt left much later, under the cover of night, once again hoping for a sign of the Ikhor. Of Liv. We were all reeling from what Kazhi had told us, wishing she would elaborate on these other pure-blooded legacies who wanted our help. What was this rebellion, and where was its base?

So in the coming days, we trained, waiting to hear from Brekt and waiting to hear the orders that we were to leave for Aethar lands.

Another week passed, and still, no books in the library hinted that the powers stolen from the gods were anything other than evil.

Brekt did not return, and there was no news of the Ikhor.

CHAPTER
FIFTY-THREE

Liv

"Kazhi once told me that everyone on Arde marks their skin in some manner."

The fire cracked, sending sparks across the grass, and Maev stomped at the one that landed near her feet. She sat on a log she had pulled toward the pile of sticks I had just lit without the ease of my magic.

I warmed my hands while the night settled.

"Well, it's true that most people do. My father forbade Ollo and me from marking ourselves. He made us study, work hard and show the world with our minds how we were different."

We had to abandon the coastline when it no longer led us north—we crossed a large river and began our journey inland. We gave up hope of finding Ollo ourselves, and I understood Maev's desperation to reach her city, hoping there was news. The twins had a strong connection, even after the wedge driven between them in recent years. Maev said she could always feel Ollo out there. She would know if he were gone. So we continued to hope that he would be waiting in Avenmae when we arrived.

We travelled from sun-up to sundown, and had traded some

crystals for horses while we passed over grassy plains. We then traded them in a village the day before yesterday and had a full sack of dried food and a change of clothing. The horses wouldn't travel well through the mountain pass that would take us to Avenmae.

"What do the northern Rydavians tattoo themselves with?" I asked around a mouthful.

"Markings of their gods. Suns, mountains, seas, or night. Some like the symbols of the elements to worship the Ikhor. Ollo wanted one when we were fifteen, but Dad said no."

"Your dad didn't want to celebrate your legacy?"

Maev's hair fell around her shoulders as she combed through it with her fingers. "He wants us to be defined by our character, not bloodline. Because there are always bad people in every legacy, it's not always a thing to be proud of. Look at the sun clan in Veydes. I am somewhat glad not to be of that bloodline right now. At one time, however, I bet many were very proud."

Rydavas hadn't shocked me as my first trip through Veydes had. The two continents were so alike. The lands we passed through coming north looked identical to the lands I travelled with the Guards. Maev had led me through plains and forests and within a week's time, we would be passing through mountains. Past the mountains was her city.

"*Day-legs control those mountains,*" she had told me as we walked. "*The wind clan. White skin and black eyes, like the Guard, Kazhi. They used to have cities built into the tall cliffside. Guardians destroyed the cities before my time. Some records say the Aspis destroyed their homes the last time it rose a thousand years ago. So now, the Days of Wind hide in the ruins.*"

I wasn't likely to see them unless we climbed the mountain, and my sore feet were reason enough to avoid that visit.

A soft and ethereal cooing came from the dark woods beyond. A sound I recognized.

"A night bird," Maev muttered, thinking I wouldn't know what it was.

I pictured the large black bird with pointed ears, a long curved beak and round eyes. "They usually only appear for Night-legs," I said, searching the surrounding forest for it.

Could that mean *he* was here?

Maev was munching on fruit when it cooed again, getting closer. "I heard them outside my window when I was a girl. Terrifying creatures." She was watching the fire.

I was transfixed by the woods where a particular spot between trees was darker than the rest.

Something shifted in the air.

"Ollo pretended he wasn't afraid ..."

The shadow moved, and I scanned the forest, hoping for a flash of iridescence.

The swirling darkness grew, edging past the trees and closer to where the firelight met the forest like it was testing how close it could get.

Maev lifted a brow in question, lowering the apple in her hand as she looked behind her. "Do you see something?"

I shook my head. She couldn't see the swirling shadows, and it usually came when she was asleep.

Everything glowed as if a full moon had risen, bathing the forest in an ethereal light. It shone off the white bark, blades of grass glimmering as they swayed.

A low rumble from deep in the woods made me jump, and I spun back to see it there—the shadow. Standing tall between two trees.

It watched me.

Womannn.

The voice echoed in my head as the forest pulsed brighter, like a heartbeat. Waves of light reflected all around like they were coming from me. Or maybe from it.

Ever since the canyons, it approached me in the form of a man —arms, legs, broad shoulders, a head—but it didn't reveal a face, and it had never spoken.

It stood watching me. Waiting.

"What do you want from me?" I got to my feet and took a step toward the shadow, and it ducked like it was afraid.

Its shadows swirled on a silent breeze. No sounds came from the forest except for the rustling of leaves as the wind brushed them together.

"What do you want? Who are you?"

Ret-t-turnnn.

"Return? To where?"

The rumbling grew louder, reverberating in my chest.

That same voice rang out, like a cry in a long empty hall.

Returrrn.

The fire faded until the only source of light came from the forest. I turned to Maev, but she was nowhere to be found. The fire, the logs we sat on ... gone.

I stumbled backward. The ground shimmered as a wave of light rippled across black sand. My bare feet sank into it, the air turning damp. The forest was gone, replaced by a cave.

My stomach dropped like I was falling, but it was only my mind racing over how the forest was no longer there.

Then a roar shook the ground beneath my feet.

Behind me, the monster crouched amongst the rock and sand, moving its head from side to side. My heart pounded as I realized what its stance showed. Years of training with my mother only taught me the basics of hand-to-hand combat, but I knew what that stance meant—attack.

I turned and ran through rock tunnels that glowed blueish green from worms overhead. These caves were familiar—so beautiful, so deadly. The rock walls grew impossibly taller, and the sand turned ice-cold against my feet. I whipped past stalagmites and through tunnels that led to more cavernous rooms.

The shadow followed me, keeping the same distance but never missing a step. It stalked me, moving like liquid, like water, unnatural.

I picked up the pace, though my body was weaker than ever. I looked back again, and the shadow was closer, crawling over rock and sand. It was impossibly tall and looked more like the Aspis, with curling horns protruding from its head.

It was mocking me, changing forms to scare me.

I tripped over something and landed hard on the ground.

The shadow pounced, towering over me, blocking the light of the worms. It held me in place, its touch cold as shadow hands pinned my arms above my head. Its knees pressed against my thighs as it straddled me.

It lowered its head, swaying back and forth. One dark hand let go of my arms, its second hand strong enough to keep me restrained. Its shadowy fingers touched my cheek, running down my neck and over my collarbone. A steady growl hummed low in its chest.

The cave glowed, turning the shadow above me darker, and when I looked above, I found the crystalline sky. I was in the dream place—the shadow had followed me into it!

"Brekt!" I screamed. "Brekt, I'm here!"

The monster trailed a line between my breasts, and I inhaled the icy air, arching my back. It was painful, so cold it was almost like fire. My magic hummed in response.

The box inside my chest shook, wanting to let my fear and anger take over, wanting the magic to be released.

The shadow's finger pressed against my skin, pushing *into* me, and I thrashed against it. Its hand came back up to my neck, and when I twisted my head to the side, anticipating, the shadow wrapped its icy fingers around my throat and tightened.

"Brekt," I said weakly against the pressure on my neck.

Another roar shook the cavern, and the shadow let go, spinning around.

I gulped for air when it released me.

The shadow monster vanished in an explosion of darkness, and when the last of the dark tendrils disappeared, citrine eyes found me, sending my heart into a frenzy.

Strong hands lifted me to my feet.

My fist flew against a hard chest, and the half-beast twisted me in his grip, turning me so my back was to his chest.

A palm banded around my mouth, stifling my scream. "You called for me, little evil. Now you attack me?"

Let me go, I tried to say, squirming in his grip.

"Shhhh." His voice was low, warning me to keep quiet.

I scanned the area. Rocks, stalactites, black sand ... I was back in the dream place, in the caves below the Guardian Palace, and the roaring seconds ago was from a monster, but not the shadow that followed me. This monster followed—

"You woke it up," the half-beast said in my ear. "Now we must run."

He surprised me by letting me go, his other hand wrapped around mine, pulling me in a different direction. His hair was damp, sticking to his muscular build. The curling horns on his head reached high above me as he padded silently through the black sand, nearly pulling me off my feet.

He stopped to peer around a corner.

He held a finger to his mouth, turning just enough for me to see him—just enough to give me a quick glimpse of his face. There were deep shadows under his citrine eyes. He wasn't himself, but he was helping me.

He scanned behind me. When he was sure nothing was there, he leaned down. "Turn the magic off. I feel your fear. This place will feed off it, and I will lose any control I've been gaining."

"What's here? What's the danger?" I shivered, cold terror running along my spine.

"Not now." He continued to monitor the caves behind me. "Just concentrate on me." He squeezed my hand before turning and pulling me forward.

I held onto my cloak with my free arm and did as he said. I went from admiring his back to huffing from the ache in my legs as they burned. These caves were endless, the black sand harsh on my feet. My chest tightened when I focused on the hole in the back of his tattered shirt, where the Aethar had run their sword through. It had been what woke the magic in me and started this whole mess.

We reached a large cave, and a low rumbling stopped him dead in his tracks. "Fuck." He grabbed a hold of me, shoving me behind him and pushing us against a wall. "Don't breathe."

I hid my face in his back, taking a breath and holding, inhaling the smell of him. His back was damp and hard as stone.

The cave grew darker, near black, as a shadow passed us. It was slow, lethargic, rattling like a snake. When the light crept back into my hiding spot behind Brekt, he took off again, yanking me along with him.

My heart soared even amid the nightmare, with danger coming for us. Brekt's warm, calloused hand enveloped mine and pulled me through the caves, away from the monster that haunted this dream place, until he found a small cavern. He pulled me behind a large stalagmite and pushed me against the rock.

He held me by the shoulders, staring at me with those shockingly bright eyes. I took in every detail of his face—a face that was entirely his despite the eyes. Scrapes and wounds, the shadows under his skin. Brekt was alive and standing before me. My only complaint was that it wasn't real—it wasn't entirely him.

A shy smile lifted one side of his mouth as his gaze held mine.

"It's you," I whispered, lifting a hand to touch his scar and stopping when his snake-like pupils constricted.

Brekt frowned. "I wish you weren't here, Liv. Though I am relieved to see you alive."

"The last time I saw you, you tried to kill me. And your friends."

After all these months, I finally had him before me—I finally reached the dream place, only to see a look of remorse come over him. "I'm sorry. I've been learning to find myself again, but it's never easy. It's taken a great amount of time, and I have to concentrate—to remember—my life outside here. The more I remember myself the easier it is to return. I assume withholding your magic has helped."

"You can tell?" I was surprised. I held myself still against the rock. This connection between the legends was so strange that it felt good to understand it—or at least understand how to find each other.

"What is that thing that attacked me?" I asked. "You saw it. The shadow monster." No one else had seen it before.

"I don't know what it was. It's not the same as what lives in this place."

"It follows me everywhere, even outside of here. I used to think it was you."

His gaze hardened. "Could parts of this place be leaking to the outside world?"

"You and I exist in both. Perhaps the monsters do, too," I said in a low voice.

Brekt lifted a hand to my hair, putting a strand between two fingers. "It's changing you—the magic." His jaw flexed. "I didn't feel you for a long time." Creases formed around his mouth. There was more he wasn't saying.

"Something has happened." I grabbed his arm. "Is it the others? You attacked them last—"

"The others are fine." His magic flickered, causing him to vanish. Then he was back again, frowning. Darkness floated beneath his skin. The pull tugged on me, and I knew the Aspis was hovering below the surface. "You cut me off. You hid your magic."

"Did you think I was doing it to separate myself from you?"

He cocked his head. It was so animalistic that I shivered. "You ran into enemy lands. You still carry the magic after all this time, yet you told the others you were going to return it to the gods." Brekt searched my face.

I did the same, memorizing all the pieces of him so I would never forget. "What aren't you asking?"

He cursed, shaking his head. "Are you turning against us?"

I squeezed my hands into fists. "No! I have been trying to survive. It's taken time to travel north, where Maev and I will get help. I'm still going to search for the gods. I asked Ouras already, and he wouldn't take it. I am looking for the others next."

Brekt gave a single nod. "Why haven't you visited me in the dreaming place? I've been needing to talk."

He was serious. He thought I was choosing not to go.

"I cut off the magic so the Aspis wouldn't follow me into the Aethar lands. I cut it off so there wouldn't be a war. You would have been attacked if you were floating around the sky. They have aerial units and airships with weapons."

"You did it to save me?"

His lip twitched, and I recalled a lifetime ago when we were travelling on the road—no beast, no magic. Just two people.

I relaxed my shoulders, which had wound too tight. "I told you I was going to save you."

"My little hero," he said with a hint of amusement.

"I am not going to be the evil everyone expects me to be."

The cave shook with a roar, and Brekt put his hand behind my head, holding me in place. His claws scraped the soft skin there. He spoke faster, though he kept his voice low. "Where are you now? How far into their lands have you gone?"

If I didn't know him better, the ferocity with which he held me would have been frightening. "I've only seen the map Maev has drawn. I am south of a mountain range—past that is her city, Avenmae."

"I am coming to find you. Outside of this place. I will search for the pull." Brekt drew closer. The Aspis was drawing his features, making pieces of his skin darken and flake away. "Don't cut me off completely. The world may think we are enemies, and the things possessing us might feel that way. But Liv ... that's not what we are." He squeezed the back of my neck, and I winced from the pain. "What existed before this fate ..."

I held back the tears threatening to form. "I'm not cutting you out. I promise. I never did. Come find me."

More skin flaked away, and his chest rose and fell. Just like before, it was as though there was something he wasn't saying.

"What is it?" I asked.

Brekt checked over his shoulder. Did he sense the other monster coming closer?

"There is something I must tell you," he said, turning back to me. "Something the others witnessed."

I waited, watching him struggle to find the words.

"Your friend," he said carefully. "The pilot."

I didn't move, not daring to breathe, dreading what he would say next.

"The Ravins got ahold of him."

The breath I was holding left me all at once. I clutched onto Brekt, shaking my head. "Ollo—" My voice broke. "Is he—"

Brekt shook his head, pain twisting the sides of his mouth, fighting the Aspis. "The Ravins made an example of him. Kazhi never found the body."

I lost hold of Brekt and nearly fell, but Brekt grabbed me again.

"He can't be," I said.

"I'm sorry, Liv." He held me so I was standing, and I covered my mouth. I couldn't let that monster hear me.

"Ollo was my friend."

"Liv." Brekt's voice had changed.

I pulled back, and through my tears, I could see black scales on his cheek. My emotions were out of control. I couldn't box them in, and the magic was reacting. "I'm sorry. I can't hold it in. I don't know how I am going to tell Maev."

The cave shook again, and when the beast roared, it was different. It was angered.

"It comes," Brekt said around growing fangs. "You have to leave."

"I don't want to. There's so much to say."

Brekt grabbed the wall, flinching. "I will find you. The Guards are coming to the Aethar lands with a whole crew of Guardians. I will find you before they do."

The cave shook, debris falling from above. "Wake up now, Liv." *Wake up!*

"Wake up." Hands grabbed my face, holding me still while a high-pitched voice yelled at me to settle down. Then, a sharp pain on my cheek snapped me back to reality, and the forest came back into view. It was not shimmering. It was not pulsing. There were no monsters.

The fire was several feet away, and Maev was above me with a bloody lip, holding me down.

I was crying, covered in dirt, and desperately trying to hold the magic in.

How was I going to tell my friend that her brother was dead?

"It's not true!" Maev was on her knees, her hands banded around my arms, shaking me. "It's not! I know it's not."

"The Guards saw it happen."

She sprang to her feet. Tears made a mess of her cheeks. "Listen to me. I've told you, I feel him." She slammed a palm to her chest. "I don't care what they saw. I don't care what the Shadow Guard claimed. Ollo. Is. Alive."

I wiped my tears away, searching the woods for the truth. I had seen horrible things. I had seen miracles, too. I came from a world where no magic existed, but I always believed there was more. I knew it in my heart. Magic was powerful. But if the people I had met taught me anything, it's that love is more powerful than it all. "If you say Ollo is alive, then I believe you."

Her lip trembled violently, and I would have done anything to make it stop.

"I'm so sorry, Maev."

She shook her head, wiping her tears. "None of that. No sorrys or condolences. Ollo is alive. He may be in danger, but he's alive. It only means we can't linger when we get to Avenmae. We have to do something."

"What will we do?"

She paced around the fire. The same one I had thought vanished from the woods. "The Guardians are coming to our lands. I knew it was only a matter of time. The Guards are coming with them?"

"That's what Brekt said."

"We will make a plan to meet them and get their help. They might be able to figure out where he is."

"They will help. I know they will."

Maev stopped. "That doesn't mean we quit looking for the gods either. You are in trouble too, Liv."

My face crumpled. How could she think of me after hearing about Ollo? "I was supposed to be your saviour."

She frowned. "The Council and their spawn are to blame for this one."

I watched ashes from the flames float to the sky on a breeze, touching the stars. I had watched Brekt fade to dust, and yet he was alive. Maev had to be right. This world had powers I could never understand.

Nights Crown was visible from here, the stars gleaming in the south. A group of tree hid North Aspis. A way forward and a way home. Brekt had given those stars to me, so that I never felt lost in his world.

"You know, I don't think there's anything I am actually good at." I toyed with the hem of my sleeves. "I can't hunt, I can't make inventions, I can't fly airships. I can barely fight. I can't manage my emotions, and I can't keep friends safe."

Maev bit her bottom lip before a laugh broke free, her eyes swimming with tears. "You're right. You're not very good at being the Ikhor."

Something about the stinging remark made me laugh.

Maev turned to the fire, hugging herself. "I don't know how to explain it, Liv. But I know I will find him."

"*We* will, Maev."

She reached over and grabbed my hand. My heart swelled as much as it hurt for her. Maev was brilliant and vibrant, so much like my mother. She was sunshine and a beacon of light. I would do everything to keep her safe.

I had experienced so few moments of joy. Of peace. Of love.

I blinked back the gathering tears.

Maev hadn't left me through any of it, even when I was terrible—even if I could easily be blamed for Ollo being taken from her.

I glanced down at our hands.

I loved this girl.

She was the first person I loved from whom I wanted nothing in return. I wanted my mother's lessons. I wanted Rebeka's approval. I wanted Brekt's heart. I wanted Nuo's thirst for life.

I wanted nothing from Maev. She was peace. She was humour. She was a sister.

Home.

After years of not feeling like I belonged anywhere in the world, here in these strange lands, with tears in both our eyes, I finally found my home.

I squeezed her hand. Not used to being forward with my feelings, I wasn't sure how to express how grateful I was for her.

She squeezed my hand back, and I knew she understood.

CHAPTER
FIFTY-FOUR

Liv

Following the Eagle's advice, I wake each morning with determination, choosing to not be pathetic. I'm determined to be strong and resist the magic. In doing so, I have severed the cord I had to him.

"Can you walk in there and pretend you are the Ikhor and in control?" Maev fixed my bright white hair outside a large set of doors made of aged and dried wood. We were in grungy clothes and standing in a castle. In the biggest city I had ever seen.

After nearly two months of travel, we'd finally reached Avenmae, only to be stopped outside the borders by city patrol—so much for sneaking in undetected. Because the Elders had no word from Ollo in the months since the airship last sent a signal home, the Aerial Elder had ordered patrols for either an attack or the Ikhor's return.

We were ushered immediately through massive white wood gates, through a city that shone with bright white stone buildings and led to the grandest building of them all—Avenmae Castle.

I held onto the wall outside the large doors—I could barely stand. The march through the city had been dizzying, and I remembered little of it. Weeks of travel had turned me into something I didn't recognize. It would take a lot more than Maev's fiddling to make me presentable.

"Of course I can." I gave Maev one of her own looks, my new favourite thing to do. "I spent my whole life pretending to be something I am not. Why would now be any different?"

"Dramatic much?" Maev scolded me. "It's only for a few minutes. They will be too scared of you to push you into anything if they see you as powerful. Pretend to be bad and scary." Her hand waved in the air between us. "Or whatever it is you're supposed to be these days."

"I can do scary." I smiled. I *was* scary. I had been repressing the magic since the canyons, boxing up every emotion I could, and it was taking a toll on my body and mind.

Someone had recognized Maev immediately upon her arrival —to her great confusion—and she informed the men at the gates she'd returned with the Ikhor. I noted more than a hint of disappointment when Maev introduced me—a city guard had muttered, *"A woman?"*

"Once we get a good night's sleep, we will meet up with Cal, get the info we need, and get supplies together. We should be out of the city in a week and off to visit the shrines. The hardest part will be convincing them to lend us an airship."

"Because they won't want me leaving?" I asked.

"Yes. If my Mechanist professor won't let me use the ship I've been doing tests on, we may have to resort to theft."

My jaw dropped. "You would do that? Steal from your own people?"

"I'm not so bold as Ollo, but when desperate, I can be quite creative."

"We both have to be bold now."

My two fingers still refused to close, the scar over my shoulder ugly and jagged. Maev's arm was burnt and scarred where I had marred her skin during my transformation. We both wore markers of our long journey here.

I stared at my feet, hoping Maev's instincts were right, and Ollo was okay. Brekt hadn't visited me again, though I watched for him every day. Maev and I were waiting, hoping to hear if the Guards had learned any more about Ollo's whereabouts.

She snapped her fingers in my face. "You are the Ikhor. You can burn the whole place down to the ground with a thought. Don't forget that when you walk in there."

"What are you preparing me for?" She was making me more nervous. "I thought you argued your Elders were fair people?"

"I don't know what they will ask you. But you're shaking, and it doesn't line up with the image you've taken on. If you don't want to be forced into fighting against the Guardians, don't let the people in there tell you what to do."

Maev had promised me a mountain of empty crystals to release the magic and ease the stress on my body. I only hoped she could locate them before the end of the day.

We decided to hold off telling the Elders that the Guardians were coming to Rydavas. We wanted to speak with the Guards before the aerial units scared them away. Maev explained Avenmae had the manpower to overrun the Guardians. It wouldn't matter when the units discovered their enemy had come to their shores.

This begged the question—why would the Council send their people here in the first place? Did they really not know Avenmae existed?

"Ollo risked his life for this moment. For me to bring you before the Elders." Maev stared at the door and I wasn't sure she was speaking to me. "But things could change now for our people if we find the gods instead of following an army. I pray to Rem that Ollo's sacrifice was worth it—that spying for the rebellion and lying to the Elders about our plans was worth it. Otherwise, he died so I could betray him and fail anyway."

"His sacrifice was to make sure *you* got home," I said. "You didn't betray him. You're here, after all. He'd care more about that than following the mission given to him by his Elders."

I held my breath. Maev told me she would let nothing bad happen to me, but I was on edge.

"But for the sake of getting along," Maev continued, "try not to burn the place down. We don't need a repeat of Ouras's temple. We need to have a discussion with the Elders, and then you can rest. I promise I won't let them ask anything of you today."

"Okay. Let's go then."

Maev pushed the doors open and strode into the massive room.

Avenmae was a new kind of beauty. Light streamed in at sharp angles from large windows on both sides of me. Pale grey stone made up the room, and the furnishings were bleached wood, like the doors we had just come through. The blue rug below my feet muffled my footsteps.

I tilted my head back to take in the mural painting on the high, arched ceiling. It was strikingly familiar, and it took me a moment to remember the painting at Ouras's temple and the inn in the Last City.

Yet here, the Aspis was painted as a terrifying beast—jaws open wide with blood pouring from its teeth. Bodies lay on the ground below where it hovered, surrounded by warriors dressed in black. The next section over showed a glowing being, arms spread as it hovered over the body of the beast, now lying dead at its feet. People on their knees surrounded the being, praying to him while he shone his light on their hunched forms. How different from the terrifying way the Ikhor was painted in Veydes.

It made my blood thrum as I walked toward the front. Everyone had an opinion about me. In the Guardian lands, they feared I would be their death. Here, they worshiped me as their saviour, and I understood now what Brekt had meant when he said he felt empty, because if he had told the world that he was the Aspis, then he would have no longer existed. Just as I felt in this room—Liv no longer existed here. I wasn't a person to them, but a symbol.

The only person who knew I was real was at my side, and I truly hoped she only ever saw me as Liv.

Ahead sat a group of intimidating figures. Twelve, I counted, in wooden chairs in a half circle. Their heads swivelled our way when we entered. Several of them stood, and I noticed one stoney-faced man, grey at the temples, wearing clothes similar to Ollo's—the Elder of the Aerial Division. He didn't smile like the others.

One woman held a hand over her mouth as I stopped a short distance away.

Maev halted at my side.

"Where is Ollo Pretruq? He was to deliver the Ikhor to the Elders." The Aerial Elder was stiff in every manner. He had near-white skin and pitch-black eyes—a Day-leg like Kazhi, from the wind clan.

Maev cleared her throat. "He was shot down in the Canyons of the Lost. We were being chased by Guardians, and he distracted them to help us get away." Maev delivered the news with a surprisingly steady voice.

Several Elders exchanged looks.

The Aerial Elder sat straight, looking down his nose at Maev. "I was made aware that Pretruq had compromised the mission by taking his *sister* to Veydes to locate the Ikhor. Your father visited my division many times to demand the whereabouts of his children. I would be glad to end those visits with an explanation of why a student alchemist was on a mission strictly designed for a Senior Pilot."

"I am a graduated alchemist and a studying mechanist, nearly done my program. I had a device that was able to locate the Ikhor. We succeeded in finding her much faster than Ollo had planned. It was our return that caused the delay. And when we lost Ollo ... we returned on foot."

"Pretruq knew the risks when he went on this mission," the Aerial Elder said. "Your father will be proud of his son, who located the Saviour for our people. His sacrifice will not go unnoticed."

My jaw slammed closed with an audible clack at the lack of concern for Ollo, for what had happened to him. I squeezed my fists to stop myself from shouting at the man. Ollo had risked everything for these people.

"Please introduce us," said a woman with golden hair.

"You can call me Olivia," I said to the Elders, not waiting for Maev. Only my friends could call me anything less formal.

Several whispered, and again, I heard their surprise I was a woman.

"Olivia." The golden woman—a Day-leg—bowed her head, her long strands of hair falling from her shoulders as her hand covered her heart. When she straightened, tears welled in her eyes. "I am Cloudine, Elder of the Crafters. I speak for the artistic souls of our people. I have been restless waiting for your return when I finally heard the pilot Pretruq had located you. I was worried you were lost to the Aspis."

I glanced at Maev.

"They must have thought I was Ollo when we were spotted approaching the city," she whispered.

I stood straight, falsely brave. Behind my back, my hands shook, and my knees were threatening to buckle. So many eyes on me. My old mantra reared its controlling head. *Eyes down. Blend in.* Hah! For once, I wished to go back to my old ways and hide.

Another man stood, using the chair to push himself up. He had dark brown hair, frizzed and greying, tied behind his head. His skin was the colour of pale sand, and he wore a white dress of sorts with a tight, short jacket buttoned up to his neck. Three gills rested above his collar. "Please. Our Saviour, I am Pellon, Elder of Medicine. I ask that you show us."

Maev didn't move, staring ahead to where Ollo's Elder was eyeing her with a stern glare.

"W-what are you asking?" I said.

Pellon's curious gaze roamed over me. "Most of us have never seen magic. It is all but gone from our lands. The gods never make their presence known in Rydavas. I would like to see magic. As I am sure my fellow Elders would."

I shifted. "I'm sorry. I won't."

"Won't?" The Aerial Elder said. "Or can't?"

"Can't?" I repeated.

Did he know I was struggling with the magic? Was it obvious?

The Aerial Elder's knuckles went white as he gripped his chair. "Is this some game, Pretruq? Are you and your brother scheming by bringing us a false saviour? Perhaps trying to advance your place in the mechanists department?"

Maev stifled her curse.

My nails bit into my palms. "Why am I here? Is it just to show you magic, or is there something you want from me?"

The Elders went silent, their focus on me. Not exactly what I had wanted, but I was glad the attention was off Maev.

"Want from you?" Cloudine looked around the half-circle. "Have you not returned to give the power to the people? To share your magic until you defeat the Aspis?"

I stayed silent, having forgotten this is what Maev's people believed—the Ikhor stole the magic to give power to the people, to equal them to the gods. They didn't see me as a threat. I was a tool, a saviour and their hope for the future. I relaxed a fraction, realizing the position I held.

"My magic is powerful. Too powerful to display for a game of show." I stood taller, moving my body the way Ollo had when he was making a point. "I would not aim to put anyone at risk."

If I told them my magic called the Aspis, would it work against me? Something in my gut told me to keep that kind of information to myself.

"I see." Cloudine sat back down, looking at the Aerial Elder, whose brow was in the air.

"I wish to rest and come back at a time when my head is clearer to discuss what I may offer the people here."

The Elders stayed silent, several visibly upset.

"It's not up to them what you do, Liv," Maev whispered.

She was right. I bowed my head like I had seen the gold woman do and made to leave.

The Aerial Elder stood. "You *must* show us something. Prove you are who you say you are."

I turned slowly, my nerves being tested.

"As I explained—"

"I don't believe you." His lips pulled back into a sneer. "You are from enemy lands. I've lost one of my Senior Pilots because we had to locate you amongst the Guardians. There is nothing displayed here that makes me trust you." He appraised me as if I was weak.

Had he expected a tough, hardened warrior to be the host of the magic like what was displayed in their painting over our heads?

"Audel, please, sit down. Remember who you speak to," said a woman beside him, who appeared to be the oldest of the Elders. She had bright white hair and pale green skin, with eyes like spring grass. A mount-leg, I guessed.

"I know with whom I speak. Our saviour. The mighty Ikhor appears as a weakened woman. We have waited nearly one thousand years for its return, and it wishes to *rest*. This is no display of power that we expected."

"First off," I said, my heart pounding. "I will not be referred to as *it*."

That was how Nuo saw me. A thing. A creature. Something I was looking more like every day.

My anger only rose as the man stared back at me with disbelief.

"Second, I assume you can see what I look like from where you stand. Do I resemble any legacy you have seen before? Do you really believe I am lying about what I am?"

"She looks like the gods," Cloudine said, raising her hand to the ceiling where a glowing figure was painted, as Audel studied my glowing skin.

"Third." I didn't wait to hear any more from the Aerial Elder. "I am not anyone's puppet. I am not anyone's toy. I won't do as you say, ask your permission or wait for instructions. If you think I am a weak woman, then test me, and I will show you how weak my magic is."

"Liv," Maev warned. "The temperature is getting warm in here."

I found smoke rising from my hands, and several of the Elders gasped. Good. They should know not to test me.

I looked up through my lashes at them, showing them the woman I was becoming—the one who was brave, strong and full of power. "I am not someone you wish to upset. I will not be controlled."

The box in my chest rattled, demanding my anger be let loose. Months of bottling my emotions had me ready to explode. My box was testing the strength of the lid, and it would not let these people control me. Never again. I would carve their names into it like I did the others who had caused me pain.

The Aerial Elder sat back in his chair, folding his hands on his lap. "I suppose it's not the right time to mention we had planned on announcing your arrival to the citizens at today's festivities."

Daring man.

Maev rested a hand on my shoulder, calming the storm in my chest. "I will take Olivia to her quarters and return in time with her answer."

"Don't waste any more time than you already have. The people need hope. They need a symbol that times are going to change."

Did he mean he needed a new weapon? Wanted the magic at his disposal?

Maev bowed, nodding at me to take my leave, and I followed her from the room, fuming.

Having the Elders look at me the way they did reminded me way too much of the Keepers back home. A disobedient Ikhor would go against the Elder's promises to the people. To them, I was a risk to their neatly structured plans.

The Eagle told me not to be pathetic. I held the power here. And now, no one could push me around.

CHAPTER
FIFTY-FIVE

Liv

Sadness used to be a heavy weight tugging on my arms and legs while I dragged myself from place to place. It had seeped into the cracks of my skin and burrowed into my flesh, making a home. I allowed myself to be weak, selfish and terrified. But now I wear my sadness more efficiently. I walk with surer steps and I'm learning control. I don't think I need this stupid diary anymore.

—Afterthought: Perhaps the diary is partially to thank. I won't throw it away just yet.

"This used to be the home of the royal family," Maev said, walking stiffly away from the Elders sitting behind us.

The castle was not what I assumed a royal family would live in. It was warm and inviting—like a home. The bottom floor was for public use, while above housed personal suites.

Maev explained it was a collection of several rectangular buildings with sloping rooftops. Balconies lined every window and door. Elegantly decorated, the open space inside was inviting despite its dark history.

Maev was practically running toward the large staircase to the second level. I hadn't noticed the stairs when we first entered the room. "They have anticipated your return in recent years. Not all floors have been dusted and cleaned, but the top floors have been prepared for your stay. The lower level is where the Elders meet. The rest of Avenmae Castle is empty."

"No one lives here now?" The walls were white stone with massive windows, allowing the natural light to shine off every polished surface. The white velvet curtains matched the wall, and the carpets were intricately woven with blue patterns. Gold crystal-powered chandeliers hung from above.

"Parties are held here." Maev's voice echoed around the massive hall on the second story.

"And no one else is here. In this entire castle?" I asked. It could house dozens of families.

"No one. Just the staff who will serve you. It's been deserted since the royal family was killed. The last royal family that ruled was two hundred and thirty-one years ago."

I stopped. "I don't understand. I have to stay in this place alone?"

"You're bigger than royalty, Liv." Maev grabbed my hand, pulling me to a large blue-carpeted staircase leading to the third floor. "But I am going to steal a room here too. So you won't be completely alone."

I was worried about the trail of dirt we left on the carpeted staircase as we passed a member of the staff, who bowed.

How ridiculous. I was in tattered, dirty clothes, and I had red eyes with black around the iris. I was skin and bones and not a towering warrior. I had done nothing to deserve this respect.

Yet, it felt good. For the first time in my life, I was welcomed. Wanted.

"The festival the Elders mentioned ..."

Mave gave a curt nod. "The Festival of the Arts is taking place over the next several days. There's a competition too. I had planned to enter my tracker in it."

"You can still enter. We aren't leaving right away, correct? You should do it."

"The stupid Interrogator stole my tracker. I have nothing to enter. All my work is wasted." Maev banged her hand against the railing as she let out an exasperated breath.

There was a pang in my chest. I hadn't known at the time it had been taken from her. Otherwise, I would have demanded Nuo give it back.

"Just another reason that man is horrible," she said. "Although, I could try entering my blueprints. But that won't win me first place. I need a demonstration."

"So, this festival of arts," I interrupted. "What does it have to do with me?"

"Today is the parade. I'm guessing the Elders wanted to send the Ikhor through the streets for everyone to see. A big start to a week of celebrating."

Sent through the streets? How many people would be looking at me? "Do I have to do or say anything?"

"You don't have to. You don't even have to go."

I thought about it. "It would give me a chance to see your city. And I don't mind making the people feel better if I don't have to do anything. It's already known I've arrived. If I know how people talk, the entire city probably knows I am here."

"Probably," Maev agreed.

I was out of breath when we reached the top of the last flight of stairs, having lost track of how many we had ascended. The landing opened to a short hall before a gold set of doors.

"You need more crystals, Livy. You're getting weaker. If you're going to agree to meet the people, at least let me get you some crystals."

"Thank you. Then I agree to do it. We can tell the Elders after I clean up."

"I will run to my lab before we go." Maev stopped at the top of the final step, lifting a hand to the door before us. "Your suites."

We were first met by a small room with cozy chairs and several doors leading off. I followed Maev around the luxurious cushioned seating area.

"These rooms belonged to the last queen. She lived in this home with her three children, who had quarters on the floors below." Maev opened the first door, peering inside before moving on to the next. "She lost her children in an attack from Veydes. The princes were nearing adulthood, in which they would marry. The first daughter born would be in line for the throne."

"What happened to the queen?" I asked.

"It is believed she was captured and died on enemy lands, refusing to betray her people."

"You don't know what happened to her?"

"Her body was never recovered. The princes' deaths were bloody. They fought but were outnumbered and executed in front of the Queen. There was a trail of blood, indicating the queen had been taken. After that, the remains of the city were so bad that the decision to have the Elders run things took effect. The Queen was never found. Over the years, so many false ransoms were sent that our people gave up hope for her return. Our forces had no power to retaliate. So we stayed as such—weakened, with no rulers. It became our fate. We've rebuilt since then, as we always do, and now our city is functioning well. But supplies are difficult to maintain, and magic crystals become rarer and rarer."

I pulled the few from my pockets that were glowing, having long ago eased the tension in my body. "Here's a start."

Maev tucked them away before opening a new set of doors into a spacious bedroom. To my left was a canopied bed nearly as large as my old shack back home. To my right, arched doors opened to a stone balcony that wrapped around my entire suite.

My suite. I couldn't stifle the laugh that bubbled out of me.

"Life is crazy," I said to Maev when she gave me a look.

It reminded me of the Guard's suites back at the Guardian City and made my chest ache, but I pushed that thought aside as I went to the balcony.

From nine stories up, I looked down to the streets below. Avenmae had the tallest buildings I had ever laid eyes on. The sun was out, shining brightly over the tiled roofs, and in the distance, the giant outline of a mountain range—the same one we had passed on our way here—stretched across the horizon. A great river flowed through the city, trees and flowers lining the streets. The city was loud but peaceful.

It was nothing like I could have imagined back home, and it made the Guardian City look like it belonged in a time from hundreds of years ago. Avenmae was fresh, energetic, and modern.

Airships flew by in the distance, silent on the wind. The clouds high above floated by, not caring at all about what was happening below. For a moment, I forgot I was a saviour or a great evil. I was just a speck in a massive city.

Until I saw citizens waving their hands in my direction. I backed away immediately, my earlier fears confirmed—the citizens knew I had arrived.

I ducked back inside.

"You're going to have to be braver than that if you expect to be paraded." Maev chuckled.

I ignored her, taking in the dark navy walls in the suite. The space was cozy and private. Opposite the door we entered was a seating area and fireplace that was so large I could walk in it. Next to the bed was a door going into a room lined with shelves.

"The closet."

I turned to where Maev stood at the end of the bed, watching me.

"This is a whole room for clothing?" I asked.

"Yes?"

"This room is bigger than the shack I lived in back home."

Her face fell. "Well, there's nothing funny about that. Even our most poor residents have homes bigger than this closet."

"The difference is almost too much." I took a seat in a cushioned chair near the fireplace. "The people who are in the Endless Forest suffer, while places like this exist where a room for clothing is bigger than some homes." I picked at the chair's fabric, tapping my foot on the carpeted floor. "I don't know if I can stay here, Maev."

"Not staying here won't change things. You're being offered comfort. Take it, Livy. You need rest before you go search for the gods." She sat in the chair next to me before the fireplace. "You have a good conscience. It's one of the reasons I like you so much. Even if you have a shorter temper than I do."

"Short temper and godly powers is not a good mix."

Her mouth went taut. "Nope."

She showed me the clothing supplied for me in the closet, and then left to find crystals, while I made use of a bath already drawn up in *another* room. When she returned in a new set of clean clothes, she helped me into a long-sleeved gown that sunk low on my chest. She tied my hair up off my shoulders and wrapped a belt of silver around my waist. It was simple, but beautiful.

The fact that I looked like a colour-leeched version of a god took away my love for the gown. It made me want to be sick. I dressed well in the Guardian City. But *his* reaction and presence at my side had distracted me.

Now? Now, I could see the staggering difference between the girl I used to be and the one I was becoming. I was no longer scared or broken. But one thing that was the same was knowing how cruel the world was.

What would I have thought when I was dying beside the

frozen river if I had seen into the future to me standing in this room?

I didn't deserve nice things just because I had power, and I didn't deserve them more than the lonely girl alone in her shack. I got them because others wanted something from me.

Maev squeezed my arm. "It matches the pale skin and white hair. You look like a star." She smiled at her work when she finished my hair.

"A red-eyed star?"

She blinked and pursed her lips. "Well, I guess we all have flaws."

FIFTY-SIX

Liv

I hate the feeling of the in-between—the moment between change. Like when I was dying by the river, just waiting to be found by the Keepers, or worse, to be found by the god of death. Avenmae has become the in-between. I'm waiting every day for something to happen, and I fear what that something will be.

Despite my conviction, I did let people boss me around. I couldn't recall Maev's city because I had been in a state of panic. Fear tunnelled my vision until there was no street, only the two large horses pulling an elegant white carriage displaying me before hundreds, maybe thousands of people shouting and celebrating.

The Festival of the Arts spanned the entire city. The crowd was endless as I was carried along. I recalled flashes of colourful streamers in the air as the sun shone off them, waving on a breeze.

Triumphant cheers and screams for the saviour had my blood running cold, and the demands for protection twisted my gut.

I had been attacked by Aethar, yelled at by a god, and come face to face with a giant black dragon who sucked up my magic, but I had never felt more fear than I had in that carriage, sitting ramrod straight and looking from one horse's ass to the other because I couldn't meet the eyes of the people.

I was not what they had waited thousands of years for. But then again, neither was the Aspis. It hadn't killed me like the Guardians had hoped.

After being paraded through the city, Maev found me a cloak to cover my hair and looped her arm through mine to drag me through the markets. The Festival of the Arts brought vendors selling all kinds of well-made crafts and foods. Large squares had towers where musicians played, and crystal-powered devices amplified the sound. People danced below in brightly coloured clothing and painted faces.

I came alive in the streets, no longer seized by fear when the citizens weren't watching, able to enjoy the city for what it was.

Maev found a vendor selling jewellery. They were all in sets of two, and she bought us a matching pair of blue necklaces and tied one around my neck. "*Friendship necklaces*," she had told me. There were crystals woven into them, mine now glowing to match my bracelet and earrings. Maev then lent me coin so I could buy two sets of bracelets.

When the sun went down, lights exploded in the sky, and we joined the people to dance and drink. It was freeing. My face hurt from all the smiling.

Maev called it when she grew too tired to continue, and she walked me back to the castle. "I am exhausted," she said. "My feet hurt worse than when we had to climb those rocky hills."

"I will sleep like the dead tonight," I agreed.

"Tomorrow, I'll send word to Cal that we will meet him in two days' time." Maev yawned, stopping at the floor beneath my suite.

"I need another day to collect crystals for you and to make arrangements for an airship and supplies."

"In the meantime, I plan to hide from the Elders. I can't handle another day of being dragged in front of a city of strangers."

Maev waved goodbye, agreeing to avoid the Elders as much as possible.

I pulled myself up the stairs, ready to discard the dress and slippers. I needed a bath and was grateful when I found fresh water hot and ready in my bathing room. The staff here made themselves invisible.

I took my time in the hot water. Like the rest of the castle, the massive bathroom was made of white stone, with the softest blue carpets. A lightweight nightgown provided for me shone like an opal in the candlelight.

I was drying my hair, about to go to bed, when a crash came from outside.

Someone was in my suite.

I tiptoed into the bedroom to find the doors to the balcony standing wide open.

I had closed them after I entered.

"Maev?" I whispered.

The breeze from outside sent the door crashing against the wall, and I jerked back. I covered my mouth to stifle my scream, catching a glimpse of a tall figure moving past the window outside.

I padded silently past the bed, terrified that the shadow monster was prowling outside the doors. I held the thin fabric of my nightgown as I peeked outside.

My jaw went slack.

Brekt was there with his arms braced on the railing, looking out over the city. Hair tied back, he looked exactly like he had in my worn-out photo.

I didn't make a sound, scared the dream would end, and I would wake to find I was alone. A quick glance at the sky lit with a million stars told me this was no dream.

He was here.

His black clothing hugged his muscular frame, showing off his powerful body. I sighed in awe of him, and he turned in my direction. A shy smile lifted one side of his mouth as his gaze collided with mine, warm and inviting.

Did I dare go to him? Was I safe?

I checked to make sure my swords were beside my bed where I left them.

Brekt's shoulders dropped, but he didn't say anything.

"It's been over two weeks since you said you'd visit." I wrapped my arms around myself and stayed partially behind the doors. My mind, my body and my heart warred with each other.

He was checking me over—looking for signs of the Ikhor?

That's when I realized what I was wearing—a sheer nightgown that covered very little.

I did the same and took in every detail of him. I was ashamed when I noticed the new scar over his left eye. A mark I had made when he was the beast.

"I would have thought you were just another dream," he said in a low voice, "wearing that thing. But the hair, the eyes—this is real. This place beyond the railing is unlike anything I've seen. I'm in the Aethar lands?"

"Yes. In the city of Avenmae."

"Amongst the people who worship the Ikhor."

Moonlight played over the balcony, lighting up the polished stone. But Brekt? He absorbed the light and turned it to shadow. Parts of him disappeared, hiding from sight.

He was hiding from *me*.

"Don't call me that." My jaw clenched, and I shook myself to stop the growing irritation.

"What should I call you, love? Little evil upset you, too."

"So you were aware of what you said as the half-beast?"

His gaze sharpened on my mouth. "I was aware, though not fully in control. But if I recall, I believe you enjoyed my company."

"I haven't said I've forgiven you. I can barely accept that it *is* you."

The damned man grinned. "Don't blush when I call you names like that, and I'll stop saying it. And forgive me for what? What have I done to anger the Ikhor?"

He was baiting me—testing me—which meant he still wasn't sure where we stood.

"I don't know. Lying to me the entire time and hiding that you were the Aspis?"

He scratched the back of his neck. "You're right about that one … love." His lips twitched.

Fucker. I gathered my sanity. It was like trying to gather sand through loose fingers, I was a mess, but I decided to join him on the balcony.

He faded farther into the shadows, blending with the night.

The last time we stood together like this—with no signs of the Aspis or the magic—had been on the deck of the airship. When he had tried to kill me.

I walked cautiously, my arms falling to my sides, toying with the fabric of my nightgown. My bare feet padded on the smooth stone. The soft wind was cool on my legs, which were bare from my thighs down. My silvery hair blew over my shoulder, exposing the mangled scarring around the arm I almost lost.

I pulled a strand of hair, chewing my lip. I was suddenly shy. Unsure of myself. Would he run when he got closer and saw the terrifying colour of my eyes?

But he was hiding, too. We were both unsure of the other.

What were we to each other after everything?

Brekt rested a hip on the railing, folding his arms across his chest. The sight of him standing there casually made my breathing hitch. The desire to jump into his arms was overwhelming.

It was the hole in his shirt that pulled me away from uncertainty and soothed it to a calm desire to reconnect with him. We were changed, but not enough to let a rift separate us.

"I apologize," his voice dropped even lower. "For the time we spoke in the dark place. I didn't know whether to trust it was you."

"And what about the deck of the airship? You nearly threw me into the open air, almost killed my new friends."

Brekt shrugged. "I suppose I got a little forward with the blue one."

The reminder that Ollo was in danger, or worse, dead, hit me hard. I had to stuff down the pain before my magic reacted. "Is there no word on him? Have the Guards seen him?"

Brekt shook his head. "I haven't seen the Guards since I saw you in the caves."

"Maev, his twin, swears he's alive. We have to find him. We need your help."

His form darkened, and I could feel his desire to ask me something, yet he remained silent.

"Ask me," I said, because I knew where his thoughts had taken him. Of course, I knew. He had met Ollo. He had heard me call him "the beautiful blue man" a long time ago. He knew I had travelled with said beautiful man and saw me crumble when I discovered the Ravins had taken him.

"Is he your lover?" The words came out in a growl.

I let out a breath of frustration, unsure of what to say and deciding on the truth. "We became close. And he promised to help me save you. So no, we were not lovers."

A single nod and Brekt disappeared.

I held myself back from reaching for him. Did he hide on purpose, or was he unable to control himself, like me, when emotions were too strong?

My next words were shaky. "What will you do with the information?"

The iridescence in his eyes flickered as he reappeared. An unnamed emotion swam through them. "Make up my mind."

If I had never found that photo of him, it wouldn't have made a difference—I would never have forgotten a single detail about his strong jaw, the scar running past his temple, or the way his dark gaze entrapped me.

"Whether to kill me?"

He inched closer. Even with all the power I held, I was so small next to him.

He shook his head. "Whether to fight for you."

"You want to start a fight with a man who may be dead." The thought shouldn't have thrilled me as it did.

Brekt smiled, and seeing those full lips shaped into a wolfish grin, I stopped thinking. He bent forward to level his obsidian gaze with mine. "That wouldn't be a fight, love. I know my capabilities. I know how to size up an enemy."

"His name is Ollo."

"Dickhead sounds better to me." Brekt faced the city as if ending the conversation.

And I suddenly wanted to hit him.

"Ollo is hardly the dickhead. I think you earned that title."

"Don't hold back what you really think." Brekt pushed dark strands of hair out of his face.

"Like you didn't hold back your viciousness every time before?"

He winced. "I apologize for that more than anything. I am doing my best and gaining more control. I haven't been thinking clearly." His nostrils flared as he glanced sideways at me. His back was rigid, wound tight. "What happened to your shoulder?"

"That was your fault, too."

He faded further from sight, but a shift in his shadows told me he turned to face me. "How so?"

I puffed the hair from my face, walking up to the balcony and standing next to him. I leaned my forearms against the railing and looked down, regretting it. We were towering over the city below. "I guess I can admit that one was the Aspis. You bit my arm off. I still can't bend two fingers."

I held my hand in the air over the railing. I made a fist to demonstrate.

"Liv, I ... *fuck*."

I peeked over at him. He was visible again, his mouth open, gaping at my shoulder.

"It's not the worst thing I've been through. Hardly makes the cut."

His death had been. I forced my attention away from him before I unravelled from what I had been through—what I was *going* through.

"What happened on that field?" His voice was low, pained.

"The burning field?" That was so long ago.

Brekt was taking in the buildings past the balcony as if looking for answers in the night. "I remember very little after the Aethar got my heart. I haven't asked anyone about it."

"How much of it did you feel?" My chest constricted, remembering his transformation into the Aspis.

"All of it. The sword wound, the skin peeling away, my body stretching and growing. But my consciousness began changing. Pieces of myself fell away until I didn't exist."

"I had hoped you were spared from feeling it."

He was silent for several moments, captured by the city beyond.

"I had dreamt of darkness before." He threaded his fingers together in front of him, now gazing at his hands. "I thought it was my death. But it was my time as the Aspis. Now, I wonder how much I understand my dreams. I thought you died from the Ikhor's flame." He sent a smirk my way. "Was pretty wrong about that one."

I couldn't think about that night without feeling the pain of it all over again. "After you faded, I ran. Nuo hates me because of it. They've chased me ever since."

"They didn't stop you. Some part of them had to know. They believe you now."

I wasn't sure what he wanted to know or what I should admit. "I've only run into them a couple of times. I've stayed out of reach."

"And did you attack them?" His unguarded look hurt to see.

I realized too slowly what he had asked, and the feeling quickly turned to anger.

"I didn't harm them." I stepped away. "You want to know how

much harm I have caused. You asked me what happened since you became the Aspis, but what you really mean to ask is what I have done."

Brekt cursed. "I don't know what's happened. That's why I am asking. I am waiting to hear it from you."

I pounded a fist against the railing. "I didn't harm anyone." That wasn't true. "Well, I accidentally killed the Aethar that night on the field. I didn't understand then. I flooded most of Veydes. I set fire to Ouras's temple—"

"What?"

"But none of it was on purpose. The most I used my magic was fighting you—the Aspis."

His head dropped into his hands. "I'm having a difficult time with willpower. It's not my own will controlling me. Not my body. Not my choices." His fingers ran through his hair, squeezing. "It's hard to keep things straight, and I—sometimes, I don't remember what I'm fighting for."

I made to step closer, but he flinched, forcing me to back away. "The reasons you fight are a short list of names, I think."

Brekt's eyes flashed as they collided with mine, waiting to hear what I meant.

"Nuo, Kazhi, Bastane. Me if I'm being so bold."

I wasn't sure if I should have added myself.

"And what do you fight for, Ikhor?"

"An even shorter list of names."

Disappointment was evident in the way Brekt dropped his shoulders. "Ah. These Aethar, the blue ones."

"Yes, they saved me every step of the way. They had been looking for me when I was with the Guards, with you. They were tasked to bring me to their home, Rydavas. This Aethar continent."

Brekt skimmed over the city, at the modern buildings and streets, and I could tell he was fighting against something in his head. "I could have never pictured this existing. Do the scarred Aethar live here too?"

"No, they live only in the south, near the canyons. Most of Rydavas is inhabited by legacies like you. Like the Veydians."

"How?" Brekt was already pale and beat up, but the shadows under his eyes deepened as he searched my face. I knew how it felt to have too many truths thrown at you while believing none of it.

"Don't pass out," I teased. "It took me weeks to believe it. And I'm new to every part of this world."

"How could there be legacies hidden from us? How could we not have known?"

"The Rydavians hate the Guardians. They keep themselves safe." Brekt's brows came together as I continued. "They are told stories that make them hate the Guardians when they should hate the Council. Both sides are wrong, in my opinion."

"Well, it seems that we agree on something, these Aethar and me."

Liv

"How did you find me in this city? What brought you here now?"

Brekt leaned a hip against the stone rail, his focus drawn to my mouth. "I think of you. Always. And sometimes, I can feel you out in the world. I sense where you are. And when the Aspis feels the pull of the magic, I can find you much easier."

"You can feel me?"

"It must be some power from the Aspis. I felt the magic earlier. So I came."

I used magic in front of the Elders.

There was something else I had wondered ever since becoming the Ikhor.

"I was dropped in that cave for you to find. Right at your feet," I said. "You were always meant to find me. The dreams, the light sending me to you. The Aspis knowing where I am. Some of the legends are true. The beast was made to hunt down the Ikhor."

Brekt had known me before we met—had seen me many times.

"So the magic possessed me and took me to my death. Why?" I asked, knowing he didn't have an answer.

"Perhaps part of it wants to defeat the Aspis as well, and it took its host to the source." He raked his gaze up my body as we spoke, and my face heated.

"How're you feeling, really?" I checked him over for new scars.

His attention snagged on my nightgown, where it dipped low on my chest. He followed a path down to where the cold breeze hardened my nipples. Or was it his presence that made my body react?

I pulled on my nightgown, trying to cover more of my legs. The ache deep inside me took me back to when things were simpler between us. We had always been connected. I was afraid to touch him then. I was afraid to now.

"How am I feeling?" He repeated the question. "Despite the confusion of it all, right now, with you here, I feel like a king. On top of the world." The sensuous curve of his mouth stole my breath.

My sanity ditched me on the balcony to figure it out on my own. "Why are you smiling? We've spent months trying to kill each other, you know."

The mirth fell from his face. "It felt like years with how I've lived the same nightmare over and again. At the moment, however, life's good."

I grabbed onto the railing to keep my hands busy. Everything in me wanted to touch him because I still couldn't believe he was real. And we were talking. Why were we talking?

I could think of a few other things I would rather be doing with him.

"How is it good? We have been at war with each other. I've been running from you, and nearly died several times."

He was closer, unabashedly drinking in my bare legs. "Right now, my mind is my own, and I have the most ... temping vision before me, bathed in moonlight. And I don't know if you saw, but I can turn into the Aspis—a literal legend."

"I've seen." Heat rushed to my face with every inch he gained.

"What more could a man want?"

God, he was everything I missed. Yet he had never been this forward before, this at ease. He had always held back.

"Did I mention the part about being with the most beautiful woman I have ever seen?"

My face fell, and I stepped back. "In case the moonlight isn't highlighting the changes, I don't look beautiful. I don't look anything like myself."

Brekt didn't let me step away. He followed me, coming forward and leaning in closer. The pine and leather scent of him surrounded me. "I don't care about the colour of your hair, love. The way you look at me, speak to me ... I see you in there, Liv."

Time stopped when his hand palmed my cheek, and I could have wept for how much it felt like home. "And there's the blush that always made me hard as a rock. As wild as I know your mind is, I love it when you get shy about it."

The soft wind stole my breath, and I looked up into those warm obsidian eyes, impossibly darker in the night. His strong jaw was shadowed, dusted with the hint of a beard. I couldn't remember where we were or why we were here. He was touching me. There was a pathetic piece of fabric separating his warmth from my skin. I wanted it gone.

"Time has been taken from us. But no more. No more gods, no more fate, no more enemies. You want the Guards to help you find your friend. I want to help you find the gods and end this. I want us ..." Brekt swallowed. "Before, when we were in the Guardian Palace ... I asked you to be my first. To be mine. I haven't changed how I feel."

"Even seeing me now, standing amongst your enemies."

Brekt's thumb brushed my cheek. "I see only you—the brave woman from the cave who wanted to live until she didn't. The one who promised her friends to find the gods and save them all. Who promised to save me. My little hero. I dreamt of you like this. Bold. Brave. And so fierce that it makes others afraid."

"Brekt," I whispered.

Had anyone ever seen me as he had?

"Do you feel differently about me now? After I've nearly torn your arm off and chased you across the world."

"I flooded that world, mourning you. If anything, I feel stronger than before."

He was closer still. "Tell me I can kiss you."

My heart beat once, twice.

Hesitation and uncertainty etched his face.

"Do you need my permission?" I asked. "You'd still hold back? The big bad Aspis can't take what he wants? You didn't mind acting like a territorial beast before."

His gaze darkened, his attention snagging on my lips. "I've been gone for weeks, as you say. I no longer know what you desire, love."

Brekt traced a line along my jaw, down my neck and up again, sending waves of pleasure to my core. His palm cupped my cheek, and I leaned into it.

There were a million things we needed to talk about. To figure out. For the life of me, I couldn't gather a single sentence to stop myself from what I wanted.

"You know what I desire. You knew before you met me." I reached for his torn shirt, still a mess from the last battle he fought on that burning field. I pulled myself closer, and his eyes flared. The hand on my face moved to my neck while his other hand reached for the small of my back.

Like magnets, we were pulled together.

"Don't ever hold yourself back from me again. If we only meet for moments at a time, I don't want to waste them fighting."

I didn't even see him move.

His lips were on mine, violently claiming. We came together like a storm. Like we always did.

But this time, there was no hesitation.

Brekt pulled me against his body with an animalistic groan as his tongue found mine, and my arms banded around the back of his head, my fingers sliding into his hair and pulling.

He tasted like life. Like water would taste to someone dying of thirst. He tasted like sin. Like power. Like sex. Like *mine*.

He gripped my thighs hard and pulled up, wrapping them around his waist. The feel of his warm body rubbing against mine was ecstasy. I ran my fingers through his hair, ran my tongue over his, and squeezed my legs tighter to *feel* him.

He was moving us. My back hit a hard surface, and his whole body pushed against mine. I arched, pressing my breasts tight against his chest, moaning into his mouth. He fit like he was a part of me. Every hard angle of his chest. His abdomen. The thick length that was confined and yet toyed at my entrance.

Had anyone ever succumbed to their desires so easily? Had anyone climaxed just from the feel of a body pressed tight to theirs? I was close.

Brekt's lips explored my neck, teeth nipping at the soft skin below my jaw, and all I could do was squeeze him, pulling him closer. I arched my neck, giving him access, rubbing my hand along the back of his head as his tongue ran a line up, up and up to my jaw. I moved against him, forcing out a growl as his hands found my ass and squeezed, pushing his hips closer, digging in. He rolled into me, and I could feel every inch of his hard cock through his pants.

Because I had nothing on under my nightgown.

A storm grew, tearing apart the city beyond with its ferocity as Brekt's mouth returned to mine. Our lips melded. Our tongues explored hot and wet. I wanted every part of me wet with the evidence of what this man did to me. We were messy, and I loved it. It wasn't enough. I wanted. I needed. I couldn't live without this.

His hand left my ass and travelled up my side, exploring my curves until he found my breast and squeezed, moaning with me, playing, toying with me as I unravelled. His thumb found my nipple, brushing it, and he pinched the rough peak as I caught his lower lip between my teeth. Not in punishment, in demand for more.

He knew.

I was on fire for this man. No. I was becoming a storm of my own for him. A current ran through me as I ground myself against him. Electric. Powerful.

I was vibrating with energy.

Literally.

Crackling energy filled the balcony, competing with the sounds of our kisses, our moans.

My eyes flew open. I was glowing, shocking veins of light emanating from me, spreading into the air. The balcony lit up as if lanterns had been placed all around.

Brekt's face contorted in pain as he pulled back. He set me down, eyes squeezed shut, as streaks of light licked his hands, up his arms and travelled down to his feet.

"No, Brekt. Oh my god. I'm sorry. I lost control."

He clenched his jaw where two elongated fangs grew, lowering his head to hide the sting of betrayal. But I saw it there. For a moment, his belief slipped. He thought I had used the magic on purpose.

He cracked open his eyes long enough to look at me, and then he screamed in pain.

Horns grew, and shadows crawled across his body. The Aspis was trying to break free.

He dropped to his knees, his back bending. "It's true, then ... you wield ... more than fire magic." He held his head.

He didn't know all the truths I had learned since his death. Part of him would always be the Guard of the Aspis—seeing magic as strictly for the gods. His goal had always been to kill the evil that came back.

"No, please. Stay."

Yellow fought with obsidian, and a new wave of pain must have come over him because he dropped to the ground, landing on his side while his back continued to arch at that unnatural angle. Scales formed along his arms and neck, and the shadows swirled around his legs.

"Everything has changed," he could barely form the words. His eyes snapped open, searching the sky for something.

Answers? The gods? They wouldn't help.

He winced, fighting a losing battle against the Aspis, and I wrapped my arms around myself, shaking. Was I going to lose him again? I couldn't touch him, I couldn't help.

"Some things haven't."

Could he hear the pleading in my voice? How could I make this stop?

Our gazes locked, and his lip drew back in a scowl. "Run," he said around sharp teeth.

Brekt was holding a hand against his chest. I was hurting him with the magic.

"Don't make me leave. Please."

Brekt rolled onto his hands and knees. The shadows on his skin churned, going darker as he fought. "Run. Now. Shut. It. Off."

I backed away toward the door.

"The parts of us ... ugh ... that belong to the gods," he whispered around the pain, "are made to kill each other. I can hardly hold it off ... we have to be careful ... I won't hurt you ..."

"Careful?"

Of course. The gods had sent him to kill me.

It all came crashing down—if I used the magic, he became the Aspis.

If I didn't use the magic, I would slowly kill myself by holding it in.

"Because until we are dead, we are the worst of enemies," I whispered as he turned into smoke and scales.

Before I could run, the force of his transformation shoved me back into my room, and I landed in a heap, alone on the cold floor.

CHAPTER

FIFTY-EIGHT

Liv

I spent the night awake going over the things Brekt and I argued about. Somewhere in my anger, I remembered the sound of Stephen's door slamming in my face when my life was in danger. Every day, I learn more about the world and the people in it. Words often mask emotion, hiding the reason they were said in the first place. Every action tells a truth, and in Brekt's actions, I've only ever been loved.

I sprung from my bed, grabbing the wooden frame and curling against it.

I had been floating past consciousness when a knock at my door ripped me from my dreams. I had slept for nearly two days. After months of travel, meeting the Elders, being paraded around the city, shopping in the markets with Maev and then Brekt's visit—I fell into the large bed in my suite and slept.

And slept.

At some point, Maev came to my room, and I told her of Brekt's visit and that he hadn't heard any more of Ollo. She had brought me a full bucket of empty crystals, which now sat glowing next to the bed. I felt a million times lighter than I had in weeks.

The knocking at my door continued, and I scanned the room, finding no shadows crawling in the corners or hiding behind curtains. "I'm coming."

Maev had been searching for more empty crystals and supplies for our journey. When she was done, we would see her friend Cal. I was getting anxious. After all the time it took trying to reach her city, I was ready to leave it just as quickly.

I opened the heavy doors to find a staff member with fresh linens and food. He set them down on a table after I thanked him and informed me the Elders would be downstairs in an hour and requested my presence.

I swung the door of my suite closed.

My anxiety spiked. I skipped the food, my gut twisting as I got dressed inside the massive closet. Lifting the hem of my new dress —today a colour close to the sky—I tied the laces of my boots. No, they didn't match the dress, but they were for comfort. I would need every ounce of bravery I could muster.

And I had learned from a wise friend to fake it if I must.

An hour later, I approached the seated Elders, dressed as they had been two days prior. The sun cascaded across the floor where my boots landed, warming me every time I passed a window.

Cloudine, the Elder of Crafters, smiled as I stopped before them. "I hope you've rested well, Olivia. I trust the suite has provided you with every comfort?"

"It's been nice. Thank you."

Where was Maev? I assumed she had received an invitation as well.

"We wished to discuss with you our plans for the city. Plans that we have long debated well before your arrival."

I waited for her to continue. Every Elder was watching me, and I clasped my hands behind my back, toying with the hem of my sleeve.

The Aerial Elder wasted no time with courtesies. "You are the Ikhor who has returned to give the power to the people. That power is much needed to protect this city."

"Audel," a man said next to him. This Elder had wild, knotted hair that grew from his head like vines, flowing away from his face. He resembled the monks at Ouras's temple. "This is not the way we speak to those we wish to ask for help. Slow down." His tone suggested he wasn't one for nonsense. "Saviour, I am Xandar, the Elder of the Mechanists."

"Are you Maev's professor?"

His eyes crinkled at the question. "I used to teach, but no longer, as my duties became much more complicated. I work closely with the university where Ms. Pretruq studies."

"Are we not here to discuss our plans? There is no need for formalities," Audel argued.

The oldest of them, the white-haired Elder with green skin and eyes, shook her head. "I am the Elder of Alchemists, Esthar. I work with the distribution of magycris to our people who need it most. However, we are in short supply. Legends have told us the Ikhor will return power to the earth, where it has run dry. Can you do this, Saviour?"

I squeezed my hands together. Attention was all on me.

Pellon, Elder of Medicines, stood. "The Hospitals need magycris first, Saviour."

"The airships need crystals for defence," Audel said, standing too.

"Agriculture needs healthy soils." An Elder with bright red hair and scaled skin rose to argue with the others.

Cloudine frowned at me. "We have long discussed our plans and have never come to a conclusion about which area of the city the Ikhor should help first. We discovered too late that the Aerial Elder had sent a letter to you, Saviour. He requested help with defences and an attack on the Guardian City—plans he made in private. War is not *my* first concern."

"We must show them our strength," Audel argued. "The Guardians have never stopped. Our borders are uninhabited because the people are afraid. And now we discover our returned saviour is one of them!"

"I am not," I stopped him.

"You came from Veydes. Don't lie about not retaining your identity. The magic possessed you, but you remember who you are. You were raised as our enemy."

I shook my head. "I am not a Guardian. I am a free citizen. I am friends with Maev and Ollo and promised them I would help your people as best as I could. My magic is strong, but it is wild. It belongs to the gods, not people. It doesn't always listen to what I say."

"You can't control it?" Cloudine asked.

I shook my head. "It can be manipulated. Not controlled."

"You mean to say you can't do anything for our people?" Audel's white skin darkened with anger.

"I won't start a war." I gave him a hard stare. "If I can find a way to heal the magic of the earth, I will. To help the people. But it's important that I return the magic to the gods in the end."

I prayed that telling them the truth was the right move.

Audel slammed a fist down in anger. "The gods haven't bothered with our people in thousands of years, yet you would give the power back to them. You would let the suffering continue."

The temperature in the room soared.

"I have seen suffering. I have seen villages wasted away from starvation and lack of medicines. Do not tell me what happens to those left unprotected and weakened."

The Elders sat wide-eyed and nervous.

"Your people may be worse off than they were years ago, but

they have homes, they have food, and they have hope. There is no one kicking down their doors and dragging away their mothers for speaking out against their rulers. There is no one telling them to line up for food or work. There is no one with a fist in their face to keep them quiet. So before you make one more demand of me, let me make myself perfectly clear. I am not your hero. I am not your enemy. I am not Veydian, Rydavian or any such citizen trapped by borders. I am a free woman who is possessed with magic that belongs to the gods. I will return it to them. And when things are set right, and the cycle is ended, you can argue then about how hard you have it. But you won't get sympathy from me."

Hate had always buried itself deep inside me, but now I hated something new—people who couldn't see their own privilege. Who whined and blamed someone else. Who begged and threatened instead of fought.

I hated the weak-minded people who thought controlling someone else would make their life easier.

"I promised to help those in need. To end the cycle and bring down those who try to control others. If you are leaders who force, coerce or manipulate, I will add your names to the list. There will be no attack on Guardian lands. And certainly not one with me in the lead."

The Elder of Mechanists, Xander, stood and walked away from the others, stopping before me. He didn't speak for several long seconds, studying me like a problem that needed fixing.

Only I didn't need fixing.

"Saving every person, rather than a few. It sounds like a challenging quest, Saviour. You will have enemies wherever you go."

"So nothing will be new."

His mouth twitched. "You have made enemies here, I am afraid. Watch where you go in the city. There will be eyes around every corner."

With that, he passed me and left the room, effectively ending their meeting.

"My apologies, Saviour," Cloudine said, also standing. "It seems we were out of line to demand so much from you so quickly. Perhaps we could meet another day."

I said nothing as she, too, left.

The Elder of Agriculture stepped away to follow Xander. "A crowd of citizens has gathered outside the castle, Saviour. They wait to meet you."

I took a step back. "What will they ask of me?"

Audel stood. "Everything. As it was expected for the last thousand years." He left his chair, passed me, and headed outside.

"Will you join us, Saviour?" Esthar asked. "We will ask no more of you, only that the citizens may look upon you while we assure them we are taking steps to receive your aid."

I felt like I really had no choice.

ESTHAR USHERED me to a stage where an entire city waited to see me on display. The crowd was alive with voices yelling, asking favours of me. I concentrated on the sting of my nails digging into my palms, and I squeezed harder. Where was Maev?

The sun shone brightly overhead, but where the city glowed before, it was now muted. They forced me onstage, and the citizens of Avenmae cheered and waved.

I relaxed, knowing I was in no danger.

Until I saw a man in the crowd I had never seen before, but I recognized the look he gave me—distrust and dislike.

I scanned the many faces and found another. Then another, until it was all I could see.

What was happening?

The Elders smiled and waved at the people. Audel stood next to me, wearing a scowl. He eyed me as the Keepers had.

I swallowed my anger, stuffed it away, and shut the lid tight on my box, which was rattling viciously.

Audel bent closer. His grey tunic matched the hair at his temples. "You see it, don't you—the dichotomy of a legend. They love you for your power, and they hate you for it."

He was right. There were as many happy faces as there were angered.

"Why? I've been told the people wanted my return." I couldn't bring myself to say more. All I could focus on were the looks of disdain. My stomach rolled as the force of the magic tried to break free.

"The ones who look at you with loathing—they are starving. They are sick. They know magycris is in short supply. They know crystals are not being excavated, and their homes and vehicles will not be powered."

"And how is that my fault?"

"It is your fault that it's not fixed, Saviour. You've been here for two days and not lifted a finger to help them."

"Two days isn't enough to undo all that's gone wrong."

"The city heard of your awakening months ago. They knew you were coming. And since you've got here, not a word has been said to them. They don't trust you can help them."

Cloudine raised a hand to quiet the crowd. If she thought I would give a speech, she'd see the side of the Ikhor that the Guardians feared.

"The Ikhor has returned, as you have seen. We have come here today to promise the people that she is working with the Elders to implement changes to our city."

"When will our supplies come back!" an angered man screamed.

The crowd waited for a reply that didn't come.

Farther back, someone else yelled, "My children are sick. There isn't enough magycris to heal them."

The crowd shouted complaints at the stage. I jumped when something smacked against my leg. A rotted piece of fruit landed at my feet, staining my dress. The yelling in the crowd stopped.

I held myself composed while my ears pounded.

Eyes down. Don't react ...

"The farms can't run without our AO tools. I can't afford to grow anymore."

"Why do they think I can fix these things?" I asked Audel.

"The legends say the land will be fruitful with your return."

Another rotted fruit hit the stage, and the Elders tried to calm the crowd.

My jaw clenched hard enough that it made my teeth hurt. I pulled at the skirts of my dress, but nothing could distract me from the faces in the crowd. The ones who were angry were fighting with those who were cheering for my return.

The Eagle had convinced me I could be a hero. I thought I was being given a chance when I came to this city. Things had been changing—I had listened to Ollo's advice to be brave and the Eagle's advice not to be pathetic. But heroism had to come with a desire to help people. That desire was quickly fading. Not everyone deserved it.

A putrid smell assaulted me when a fruit hit my cheek.

I froze.

My vision tunnelled.

"Saviour, are you hurt?" Coudine was at my side, but she backed away when she looked down at the wooden boards we stood on.

"Get off the stage! Get off the stage," she warned, moving away from me. Flames erupted at my feet, sending shocked cries through the street.

"There are rumours that Guardians are on our shores!" a woman yelled.

"You said the Ikhor would replenish the lands!"

The Elders fled the stage as more fruit was thrown, and the flames spread farther.

My hitched breathing was difficult to hear over the growing roar of the raging heat. A glowing light leaked from my skin, illuminating the stage where I stood alone. I met the shocked stares of the people. "Send one more piece of fruit my way," I warned, "and I will show you something to fear."

Some backed away at my display of magic, running from the stage.

It wasn't even a fraction of my magic—they didn't know fear. They were lucky I had a strong grasp on my little box inside. The hardest emotion to control had always been my anger.

"Livy!" Maev came rushing past retreating citizens. She stopped before the stage, eyeing the flames creeping toward the crowd. "I have something that'll help you." Maev held her hand out to me. "Please. Come with me."

"Maev." Her voice had burst the bubble I was trapped in—my box stopped rattling, the flames died down, and my mind cleared enough to realize I had been losing myself in the magic.

It was her worried, navy-blue stare and the friendship necklace wrapped around her neck that calmed me down and doused the flames.

"That was a lovely visit with your people," I spat.

Maev had returned me to my room after I had taken one last look at the crowd, none of them smiling or cheering, and walked away. They were lucky I was strong enough to control the magic, and that Maev interfered.

And that was a revelation in itself—I controlled it now. I could call it forth when I wanted. I owned the power.

Maev pulled open the golden doors, entering my rooms. "You have to understand, Livy, those were not the best representation of our citizens."

"You mean the ones who threw rotten fruit in my face?"

"Peaceful citizens don't attend these demonstrations. They're out shopping, not interested in conflict. You stood before those who like to push buttons and demand actions. Of course, a crowd of angry people will show you the dark side of a society."

"What's in that bag?" I gestured to the tan-coloured bag slung over a shoulder.

"Oh!" She pulled it forward. "More crystals. I have located a storage room with buckets full of them to be sent to a waste centre. I filled my bag and will go back later for more. Here." She passed some to me. "I saw you already filled the ones I brought yesterday."

"Maev, the Elders demanded to know what I would do with the magic. I—I told them I plan to give it back to the gods."

Her face fell. "I suppose that's better than telling them you can fill the crystals. You will be paraded around the land for the rest of your life." Maev reached into the bag, adding crystals to my pockets. "I've already started preparing for us to leave. I just need more time to get the airship. I don't want us rushing off to the shrines unprepared." She played with the straps of the bag, toying with a loose string. "There have been reports of Guardians on the borders again. The Elders may ask you to protect the city. And if the Guardians are on the borders—"

"The Guards could be there." Meaning they might have word on Ollo. But it also meant they were here to attack. "I am not fighting the Guardians. I've said this before."

"And how about defending innocent people?" Maev argued.

"I never chose this role." The temperature rose. "How can you ask me to defend people who threw rotten fruit at my face? I didn't promise to come here and play hero."

"You wouldn't have to play. You can *be* a hero. You have magic."

"This isn't even my city. These aren't my people. It's not any of your business who I defend or why. It's my choice. I am the one with power! I am the one who decides. If they so desperately want my power, I can go back there and show them what it's really capable of."

"Liv," Maev interrupted, moving away from me. "Something's off—"

"No. Maev, I won't listen to it. I don't care what the excuses are.

I am being used." I walked to the bucket of crystals, lifting several in my palm. "I deserve to choose who I protect. Do I think I need to stay in your city? No. Do I have any allegiance to you? No. I am the Ikhor. I go and do as I please. I saw how people treated me in the streets. I am practically a god to them. They fear me."

Maev took a breath. "I know you Liv, and this isn't you." She grabbed me by the arms, pushing the hair from my temple. She scanned my face. "The whites of your eyes have nearly gone black. You're letting your anger win. Don't let your anger corrupt you."

I pulled away from her. "What do you know of my anger? You haven't been there to watch the Keepers trample over me, silence me, chase me to my death. I have been tormented and controlled until I was a shell of a person. I won't be used and controlled for my magic."

"You didn't let the bad stuff that happened before change who you were. But this? You're letting it get to your head."

I let out a strange laugh. "And why shouldn't I? I could have given them hope. They can fuck off if they think I will give them anything now."

"Excuse me?" Maev stepped in front of me. "I get that you never had people accept you back home. I get that you've been through a lot in the Guardian lands and on our journey here. But now you're getting pretentious. You're acting like your powers are something to be proud of. They aren't yours, I'll remind you. You're taking credit for something that took over your body, that you've endlessly reminded us that you want to be rid of."

The back of my neck burned, sweat gathering there. "So that's what this is now? Putting me in my place? Wanting my power and then not wanting me to use it. You parade me in front of your people to display to them what I can offer. Then, show me that people don't actually like me. You need my magic, and I'm supposed to suck it up?"

"I am your friend, Liv! I like you, and not because you have power. I like you because we get each other. Because you listen to me, and you don't shut me out like everyone else. So listen to me now. You're losing it. You're losing the battle against yourself. If you don't pull back now, you're going to turn into the evil that everyone believes you are. And then? You won't have any friends. Not even real ones."

Maev was right.

But did I admit it to her? No.

She took the bag from her shoulder and flung it at me. "I have stuff to do. To help *you*. I am going to be at my lab tomorrow. If you aren't going to cower in your room, you can find me there."

I blinked several times, taking a breath. Maev was right. Where had that anger come from?

"Maev, I—"

"You're a real piece of work, Liv," Maev yelled from down the hall. Then she was out of sight.

Liv

My mother used to tell me stories of gods and monsters, great tales of heroes and evil. I knew what dragons, witches and demons were, but I had to learn on my own that my biggest fear should be someone who looked like me. I wish she had told me stories of mankind.

This time, when I wandered alone in the streets, it was shame that sat heavy on my shoulders. Maev hadn't returned for me. After a night of hiding in my room and denying the summons of the Elders in the morning, I snuck out to find her.

The Elders were having me followed. Even though I had my cloak on and hood up in a crowd of celebrators, eyes were always on me.

My first goal was to locate Maev's university. It was time for us to see her friend and read those scrolls written in the language of

Night. I was going to find a way to summon Mayra and Erabas before I lost all control of the magic consuming me.

The streets were so full of life, yet a dark cloud hung over me as I pushed through. The dark cloud was poisonous, reaching into my lungs and stealing my breath. I felt …

Alone.

I came to an open area amid the towering buildings with a circular garden and a fountain in the centre. The pouring water blocked the sounds of the festival beyond. Flowers made pathways around the fountain, and intricate wooden benches laid artfully under arches of bright-coloured blossoms.

I found a bench near the fountain and sat with my back to a large square building, watching how the sun reflected off the water, creating little explosions of colour where the mist hit the air. I thought about all I had done, how my friends were hurting and how the whole world was waiting for the Aspis and the Ikhor to end their battle.

A young girl passed in front of me, running to the fountain and throwing a coin into the water. She wiped tears from her cheeks before she turned and found me behind her. Even with my hood up, she somehow recognized what my white hair meant. Her mouth hung open. "You're—"

"Shhh," I said, leaning forward. "I am hiding today."

She covered her mouth, and I waved my hand for her to come closer.

"You're the Ikhor," she whispered. She was at an awkward age between childhood and teen.

"Yes, my name is Olivia."

The girl looked around the fountain and then back to me. "Dad said you were our saviour with the magic of the gods. Can you make magic?"

"I can. But it's dangerous stuff. I have to be careful."

Her face lit up as she drew nearer. "Wow. Your eyes are red and black."

I snorted. "Yes. They are. Do they scare you?"

"No. My teacher at school has black eyes. She's a Mount-leg. I'm a Sea-leg, see?" She leaned her head to show me her neck. "What are you?"

I checked the park to make sure we weren't being watched. "I don't know what I am."

Her face scrunched. "How do you not know?"

"I come from somewhere far away where we don't have gods."

The light reflecting off the water behind her danced over her dark green hair. "Does that make you scared? To be away from home?"

"I was before. But not anymore."

She was brave, hopping up on the bench beside me. "Why not anymore?"

Were children always this chatty?

"I made friends. Though they're mad at me right now."

She nodded. "My brother is my friend. We used to fight a lot." Her smile faded, and her attention fell to her shoes.

"Used to?" I asked. I checked the park for the girl's parents. "Are you here alone?"

She shook her head. "Mom and Dad are in the hospital behind us."

I looked over my shoulder at the large stone building several stories tall. "Are they sick?" I asked.

"No, that's a hospital for children. My brother is in there. My parents asked me to leave while they talked to the healer. They always ask me to leave when the healer comes."

I stared at the building. *A children's hospital.* And this girl had a brother in there.

"What's wrong with your brother?" Would it upset her to ask?

"Mom and Dad think I don't understand. But I do. He is sick. He told me he has bad blood. And with bad blood, you die."

I held my breath. The child, who seemed innocent yet brave, was living through a nightmare.

The dark cloud following me sparked with lightning and thunder, and I scoffed.

The little girl's brows drew together.

"I was here feeling bad for myself," I said. "And I realized just now that I had no right to do so."

The girl swung her legs, holding the edge of the bench. "My brother says it's okay to be sad when someone else is the one who is hurting. He says my tears are okay, and that my sadness is just as important. So yours is too, Ms. Ikhor."

"Olivia," I reminded her. "Call me Olivia."

Her cheeks went red. "Why are your friends mad at you?"

I leaned back against the bench. "Because sometimes I say things I shouldn't. Sometimes, I don't even mean them—I just can't contain the hurt parts inside."

"I yell at my parents sometimes. I don't know why I get so angry."

"We are alike then."

Her face lit up, but I found it disheartening that she was happy to be like me. In her eyes, I was the saviour, yet I didn't feel like I deserved that look of adoration.

"But I bet you aren't as selfish as I am," I said, finding an unusual camaraderie with this girl. Maybe it was because life had given both of us difficult situations we couldn't control. "I can't help thinking about myself now that this magic is inside me. And I shouldn't be that way because the Desert Eagle told me to stop being pathetic."

Her eyes went round. "The Desert Eagle? The legendary Mount-leg with wings?"

I nodded, pulling a pink blossom from the arch overtop our bench. "I met him." I toyed with the soft petals between my finger and thumb.

"Wow. You should listen to him. He's a protector. I sent a prayer to the gods to find a protector for my brother. His favourite legend is the Desert Eagle. But I don't think the Eagle knows how to fix blood disease."

My heart sank, and my dark cloud grew a little bigger. I stared at the child, understanding the harsh realities of her life more than she did.

She chewed her lip. "My brother said that he won't have to go away if the Ikhor came back. That the hospitals would have medicine again. Is that true?"

I swallowed a hard lump in my throat and grabbed her hand, making her gasp. Mustering a kind smile, I said. "I made a promise to the Eagle to be better. And that I would fight for those that needed my help. For people like your brother."

"Can you save him?"

Her eyes filled with tears, and I blinked away my own. She didn't need to see the Saviour cry, not when she needed strength.

"I can try. I suppose I haven't been trying, not well enough."

"Your friends should know you are a kind person, too, Ms. Ikhor."

A shadow blocked the sun as someone towered over us, making the girl and I both spin toward the intruder.

A dark hood blocked the man's face, but when iridescence flashed, my heart soared.

"Olivia's friends know the unique type of kindness she carries," he said in his deep timbre.

The girl drew back on the bench, and I patted her shoulder. "That is one of my friends."

"You're friends with the Desert Eagle *and* a Night-leg?" she said in awe.

I stared up into the hood, my heart racing with joy, fear, nerves. "This is Brekt, and Brekt, this is my new friend ..." I turned to the girl.

"Kat." She swung down from the bench.

My skin prickled, and I was too stunned to speak.

"I should go see if the healer is done." She gave me one last hopeful look. "I think you are nice, Ms. Ikhor. I don't think the Desert Eagle would be friends with a bad person."

She ran off, and it took me a moment to collect myself.

"Why did you make that face when she gave you her name?" Brekt asked.

On the steps of the hospital, young Kat was bounding up the stairs to the main doors.

"Because that was my mother's name."

"You're here," I said stupidly, unbelieving that Brekt was casually standing in the garden with me.

"I've been following you for the past hour." His head dipped down. "The pull led me here."

I tucked my messy hair behind my ear, and raised my hood that had fallen when I stood. I didn't want any attention on the Ikhor.

Brekt stood rigidly, taking me in. "Are you upset I've come back?"

"No!" I shouted too quickly. "But I didn't feel the pull. I didn't sense you at all before you appeared."

We stared at each other awkwardly. Unsure. We had kissed, and then I had hurt him with the Ikhor's magic.

I couldn't see enough of him. He wore an oversized green jacket with a large hood, and it did too good of a job of hiding his face. He wore black pants and boots, but it didn't give him away as a Guardian.

"I thought it would take you a while to come back." I played with the ends of my hair, embarrassed by how it was white and how my eyes had gone red and black.

Brekt grabbed my hand, stopping me. "You look beautiful, Liv. Don't fuss." He dropped my hand. "I didn't make it far, and the Aspis calmed. You're controlling the magic, controlling how strong the pull is from the beast." He held himself back from me, and I got the sense he was going to pull away. "And I'm sorry for the other night. It was selfish of me, and then I left, unable to explain myself. I hope I haven't done anything to push you away."

I twisted my hands together behind my back. "I wasn't complaining. There are moments when you've been ... more ... demanding. But on the balcony wasn't one of them."

"Demanding?" Warmth gathered behind his shy smile. "Telling you how I've wanted you?"

"You said something along those lines. Maybe with more colourful words."

"What colourful words were those?" Brekt folded his arms, waiting.

"I believe you once said, 'I want to kill you as much as I want to fuck you.'"

Brekt coughed, and I wanted to laugh as he turned a dark shade of red. "As I said, when the Aspis feels you near, I am not fully in control."

"So it wasn't true."

"I don't want to kill you."

Delicious heat travelled to my centre when I realized he wasn't denying he wanted me.

"Kissing you makes the evil come out in me," I said in a low voice.

Brekt drew closer, the shadows under his hood deepening. "Should we continue our battle, mortal enemy? Here on the streets of the Aethar city?"

The way he said it was pure seduction.

"Yes."

He took a step back.

Be bold, I thought, and followed. I reached for him, placing a hand on his chest, warm and hard. His hands came to my sides. "I want you to fight me against a wall again, with my legs wrapped around your waist."

My chest squeezed, unsure about being so forward.

His fingers tightened, and his grip was almost painful. "Liv, say the word, and I will burn to kiss you again. I don't care what magic you throw at me."

I stood on tiptoes to kiss his cheek, pulling a shocked breath from him. "I wouldn't risk hurting you. Not after everything. Not after seeing you fade on that field. I need to learn how to control the magic better."

"You're doing a fine job, Ikhor. I am here. I am thankful for that." He grabbed the edge of his hood to pull it off, but I stopped him.

"Don't. You're recognizable. They will see your tattoos, and people would run screaming. Walk with me. Talk. I have a million questions."

The hood dipped in a nod, and I wished I could rip the thing off to see his face. I was sick of seeing him only in shadows.

"Did you go see the others again?" I navigated us through the streets toward the university—I hoped.

"No. Last I reached them, they were in the Guardian City."

Brekt walked close to me but kept space between us. His eyes darted around the street, tense energy pouring off of him.

Be bold, I thought again.

Brekt was here, and I prayed his discomfort was because he was walking in an Aether city and not because of me. I wrapped a hand around his, slowing him to walk next to me.

He jerked to a stop, staring at where our hands were joined. "Is this okay?" His thumb rubbed across my fingers. "To touch. I don't know what's too much, what triggers your magic."

I studied my feet, the tips of my boots peeking from under my dress. "I connect a feeling to elements and use that to call forward the magic. I am shit at it. I have no control."

"The magic chose an interesting host if that's how all magic works," he teased.

"It chose the most emotionally illiterate person in existence."

His thumb continued to rub my hand. "That's not true. You were just never allowed to display your emotions safely. You were already changing that when we first met. My being here means you're learning to control it."

I ignored the lump in my throat. Even after everything that happened—like becoming god-like enemies—he believed in me.

His hood turned in my direction. "You're different, you know."

I put a hand on my hair, hanging over my shoulder.

"Not because of the way you look. You used to hide what you thought and felt. You hesitated before every conversation. Now you wear it all on your face."

I smiled. "You can thank Maev for that. She's been influencing me. Ollo too, I guess." I frowned, thinking of him.

He squeezed my hand. "You remind me of the dreams I used to have of you—of the strong-willed woman who kept me company while I slept."

We turned down an open street. There were no racers on the ground here. The airships drifted past overhead, and as Brekt looked up at them, his hood fell away.

My heart ached, finally seeing him in clear light with the sun high in the sky. His sharp jaw was clean shaven, his skin void of any shadows. When he looked down at me, full lips lifted in a smile. His dark eyes had so much warmth in them.

"The fire hasn't changed between us," he whispered, bending closer. His hand came to my face, and I leaned into the touch. His thumb swiped a tear away from my cheek.

Voices behind us had me reaching for his hood, drawing it back up. "I don't want to be interrupted right now. So keep this on."

"You've also become bossy, I might add."

"And is that a problem?"

"Oh no." His grin turned wicked. "I liked the woman who was wild, fiery and knew what she wanted. She was bossy, too," he continued. "My dreams failed me when it came to understanding what the fires meant, but I think they were right in showing me who I would care for one day."

People passed as we stood staring at each other.

"I wondered, after you died, how all your dreams came true except the ones of us together."

Brekt leaned closer. "Because they haven't happened yet. I will make sure to relive every one with you so you don't miss a thing. Once we figure out how to stop you from incinerating me when I touch you, of course."

My heart skipped a beat. "I'm not incinerating you now."

"There is a current running through you, just like on the balcony. Only it hasn't turned painful yet."

I pulled my hand from him, but his grip tightened, stopping me.

A group of young women passed, shouting and laughing. It snapped me out of it. I needed to get Brekt off the streets.

"I am going to take you to see someone," I said, hiding my red face in my hood.

He let go of my hand, only to run a finger over my cheek, down my neck to my collar. "Who are you taking me to if you don't want my presence known? Am I going to have to fight someone?"

I made a face at him. "Not everything has to be solved with violence. No, I am taking you to find Maev. Then we are going to see her friend. I have questions for him that pertain to the legends of the Aspis and the Ikhor. I thought you might want to hear what he has to say."

His delicious mouth curved again. "You want me to show myself to an Aethar? They will tell you the Ikhor must kill me."

"Not if we hide who you are."

"Are you okay, Liv?" He grabbed my hand to inspect it. "Your skin looks like it's glowing, just like the painted images. Does the magic hurt you?"

I sighed. "I guess we should catch up. Walk with me. And I'll tell you everything that's happened."

CHAPTER
SIXTY

Liv

"The Elders here assume I am Veydian, and some don't trust me." I waved my hands in the air as I told Brekt of my travels.

We took our time searching for the University as if we were in no hurry to get these godly powers out of us. God—*gods*, my senses were on fire with his presence next to me. The force with which I wanted him was painful, but there were answers I needed, and I had come all this way to Maev's city to get them.

I pulled on Brekt's arm, stopping him when a man with vine-like hair approached me. The Elder of Mechanists—Xandar. He had been the one who warned me I would have enemies wherever I went.

"Are you following me?" I stepped toward him before he spoke.

Eyes the colour of bark lit with surprise. "Everyone is watching you, Saviour. You are a millennia old legend."

He spoke with a calm, sure tone, and I was relieved when I didn't detect hostility like I had from the Aerial Elder.

"May I ask who your friend is?" The Elder eyed Brekt. "You

seem familiar with him, yet he was not with you when you arrived."

"A Guard," Brekt warned.

A chill went through me, waiting for the Elder to scream, but he just raised a brow in question. "Do you feel so much in danger in our city that you travel with a guard? I am sorry for the way the other Elders have treated you, Saviour. We only wish the best for our people."

I wanted to smack Brekt. The Elder of the Mechanists seemed genuine—worried and offended that I would feel in danger. I was relieved he hadn't assumed Brekt was one of *the* Guards.

"I am the Ikhor, Elder. I don't feel in danger. But some that I am close to can feel overprotective." I gave a warning look to Brekt, who didn't seem to be the least bit sorry. In fact, he seemed to enjoy my anger. "I am looking for the University to find my friend Maev."

"Ah. Madam, welcome to the University of Alchemy and Mechanists," the Elder said, pointing to a large domed building behind him. "There are many buildings that make up the school. Your friend has a lab down that way."

"Thank you." I pulled on Brekt's hand, but the Elder held his own up to stop me with a kind smile.

"I do believe the other Elders are skeptical, Madam. So I tell you this in secret. I'm privy to rumours."

"What rumours?" I held my breath.

"Colleagues have informed me of a supply of crystals that arrived with Ms. Pretruq. A massive supply. Filled with potent magic." He gave me a knowing look.

I blinked, failing to come up with a response.

"The source is unknown," he said in a low voice. "The timing, however, interests me."

"And I'm guessing you will tell the others what I can do?"

"No, Madam. I will not."

I pulled back. "Why?"

"Because, although I wish to request testing of your magics, I do not believe men or women should be used as tools like they are in the aerial units. People are complex and layered. And I also prefer to have facts over rumours."

"Thank you," I said, surprised.

Brekt was appraising the Elder with similar confusion.

"Will some of those crystals be made into magycris?" I asked.

"I believe it is already being processed. Why do you ask?"

I stood up straight, acting brave even though I didn't feel it. "As the saviour, I demand it to be sent to the children's hospital. I want them to fix a child with a blood disease, as well as the other children in dire need."

The smile that lit the Elder's face told me a truth I had been wondering since I arrived—the Elders were not like the Council.

"I believe that is a wise and most thoughtful choice. It warms me to know this is the first request of our saviour. I will do this for you."

Relief flooded through me, thinking of the young girl and hoping the magycris helped. "Thank you. And thank you for your help today."

"Our Elders are chosen to represent the people. The fact that we disagree is a great benefit to our city as long as we can come to a conclusion that suits the citizens. This request, though not discussed with the group, would please them. I know this. I hope you will forgive their temperaments the other day." He tipped his head in apology.

"If such rumours are true," he continued, "and the stories of the Ikhor's power returning magic to the earth's crystals are fact and not fiction, I think you have made the right choice to help the sick first, Madam. Yes, our city's defences need help, but as we aren't currently being attacked, the hospitals and the crops are what I would aid first."

"Not the Mechanist's school?"

"Ah, a curious mind never goes away. I am a patient study. I do wish to test the magic of the gods. However, I will wait, and after this meeting, I am most eager to see you again, Madam. You are a delight." His vine-like hair fell over his shoulder as he bowed with his hand across his chest. "A Mechanist professor has told me there is an airship being loaned to a student for an extended period of time—though they didn't give the student's name. I am told this student has put hours into upgrading the navigation system and that she is top of her class." He nodded as if in deep thought. "I am glad you are not what the Aerial Elder was hoping for." He winked. "And the building you are looking for is that one. Ms. Pretruq is in there."

Past a domed building was a square structure with large windows and a sloping, tiled roof. I thanked him and hurried to find Maev.

"Saviour ..." Brekt mused. "To see the other side of the legends is no easy thing. It puts me on edge." He stopped before the large doors of Maev's building. "I can't wrap my head around this city."

"Avenmae? Why? The differences between this city and the Guardians City are far less than the difference between your cities and the Endless Forest."

"This place isn't even supposed to exist. I'm—I'm angry, Liv. And confused at what the point is, hiding this from the Guardians."

"The Council?"

Brekt closed his eyes and inhaled. I wanted to reach out and smooth the lines creasing his forehead. "It's been hidden from my people for far longer than the current Council has existed. The corruption and control goes back much further."

"Let's go inside. Let's keep searching for the answers."

A flash of iridescence rewarded me when he faced me again, lifting a hand for me to lead the way. We entered the square building made of dark stone. Sound didn't echo in the dimly lit hallway. Doors lined the hall, but I headed for the open one at the end, which revealed a large room lit with natural light.

"I've never seen such a place," Brekt remarked.

Neither had I.

Long desks lined the room, covered in contraptions with glass bottles and metal arms.

"It reminds me of the Alchemist's shop in Bellum," I told him.

"I wonder if the old man had been from the Aethar's side of the world. Though he didn't have as much equipment, nor was it this advanced. Veydes isn't ... like this part of the world."

Well, we *were* on the other side of it.

Brekt followed me into the room.

We passed stacks of books, contraptions like Maev's tracker, and things that I couldn't understand. I stopped when I heard voices ahead, and Brekt bumped into my back. I held up my hand, listening.

"You travelled all the way here with the Ikhor, Pretruq. That's pretty badass."

"Ugh, thanks. My tracker was what found her," Maev said, her voice pitched.

"She's really a girl, eh? I pictured a hulking dude if I'm being honest. Would have set a cooler picture."

Brekt leaned into me as my hackles went up, hearing the man's tone as he spoke about me. "Easy, little evil," Brekt whispered next to my ear. "I feel your magic pulsing."

Why did this mystery man think it disappointing that I was a woman? Who was Maev talking to? I didn't recognize the voice, and I missed her reply.

"I came in to find my uncle, but I am glad I found you instead. Wanted to see when you were free."

"Free?" Maev's voice had risen impossibly further. I peeked through a large glass container suspended in the air.

A man stood next to where Maev was seated at a corner desk covered in pieces of metal, ore, wires and knobs at the far end of the room. I couldn't tell what the other things were, but I guessed some of them were tools.

"I heard you were back in town, and I had been meaning to ask you out before you left."

Was this the guy she had been talking about? Hanold, the city guard—the one she liked? He was not much taller than Maev, but he made up all his size in muscle. His shoulders and arms were packed—different than how the Guardians carried themselves—and his white shirt was snug on his chest. He had light brown curls that fell in his face, and I couldn't tell his legacy. He was handsome—and I got the impression he thought so, too.

"Who's the guy?" Brekt asked, keeping his voice low.

"I don't know," I whispered back. "Are you gossiping?"

"No. I'm spying. Following your lead."

I stifled a laugh.

"Liv?" Maev said when she caught me spying.

She sat on a stool with her hair braided down her back and goggles on her head. A dark smudge covered the natural lines and dashes on her cheek. She wore a long-sleeved white shirt that was protected by a black apron. Her black-gloved hands held something that resembled her tracker, forgotten with her current distraction.

Her mouth popped open when she saw who I was standing next to.

The guy she was with tapped her desk. "Come get me when you're free. We will head to dinner tonight."

"Okay." Her eyes were like glass, watching him go.

Oh no. That was definitely the guy she was into.

He passed Brekt, giving him a nod and ignoring me. Clearly, he didn't know what the Ikhor looked like. Or maybe I was too unimpressive of a woman to notice.

I pushed the hair from my face and made my way to Maev's desk. "You remember Brekt." I gestured behind me, trying to clear my irritation away.

How did Maev not think that guy was insufferable?

I glanced back at Brekt, who was facing Maev, wondering what he would do. This was his enemy, according to everything he'd known growing up, but after telling him about my journey, would he be willing to hear her out?

Brekt lowered his hood, and Maev's attention flickered over his

Aspis tattoos, including the one visible on his neck that disappeared under his shirt. She dropped her device, and it crashed at my feet.

Brekt bent down to retrieve it, and flipped it over a few times, confused. When he couldn't figure out what it was, he returned it to her shaking hands.

"Say something, Maev." I looked between the two. Would I have to pull Brekt away?

He surprised me with a small smile. "I'm sorry for how we first met. As much as Liv is possessed by the magic, I carry the beast. It's not easy to control at times. I wanted to thank you for everything you've done for Liv. I can tell she thinks of you as a real friend. And I've only seen her that way with one other."

A pang shot through me.

"As I told Liv before," Brekt continued. "My team will do their best to locate your brother. I'm sorry I don't have any better news than that."

Maev nodded, her eyes darting to me, then back to Brekt. But she wasn't seeing Brekt. She was facing the Guard, Erebrekt of the North—part of *Shadow and Blood*. That's who she knew. I went to her, standing between her and Brekt, grabbing her device and putting it on the table. "Now. This is the situation, Maev."

Her entire frame shook.

I had been right. She was terrified. I glanced back, trying to see what she saw. Brekt was tall and heavily built, unlike the men here. That was the difference between him and the man who had just left. Brekt's muscles were developed from combat, from fighting for his life and surviving North Aspis. They were tight to his large body, and every inch of him was deadly. The man who had left was bulky, likely from working out and never using his body the way a warrior would.

Brekt was also covered in tattoos, representing Maev's enemy. He was the Aspis—he didn't often come off as approachable.

I faced Maev. "The first batch of crystals are being sent to a hospital here. I want to leave instructions for the Elder of Mechanists so he will send more to the places that need it."

"More crystals will be in your rooms tonight," she whispered.

"Brekt and I want to see your friend, Cal, and pick his brain," I said.

"Cal?" She removed the goggles, which had left dents in her forehead, and set them on her desk.

"Cal," I said, unable to contain my smile. "He had those scrolls you mentioned. Right?"

That snapped her out of it. It was the reason she had brought me home with her. "Blessed Rem, I completely forgot. I've been preoccupied with preparing our airship." She leaned over her desk and pulled out several glowing crystals. "My professor has given us the airship I've been using to test my inventions. I was updating it and other inventions earlier today. And I've been testing old prototypes of my tracker, trying to get this one up to standard. Like the one the Interrogator stole."

Maev squeaked when Brekt moved, folding his arms across his chest.

"Is this one working?" I asked to distract her.

"Not at all." She spun on her chair. "I can take you to Cal now. And we can see what he says about the Ikhor. I'll come back later to finish my work. I promise, only a few more days." Maev didn't move, however. She was watching the man over my shoulder.

He pinned her with his obsidian glare. "Just so we are clear, I am not okay with Liv being used in anyone's plan to battle the Guardians. I am here because she asked me to be."

Maev swallowed her fear and got to her feet, removing her apron. "I never wanted war. And Cal doesn't believe either side is right. So she is safe with us."

"I was told your brother was sent to bring Liv to your Elders. You're telling me you didn't agree with him?" Brekt didn't move.

The Guard of the Aspis was glaring down the Aethar, assessing the threat.

Maev was taller than me, and still, Brekt towered over her. But she didn't back away. "I can't speak for him. You are clearly aware of what my brother's job entailed. He was—no is—part of the aerial division that protects our borders. But he's also Liv's friend. He decided to save her with his own life."

"Brekt knows Ollo is someone I care for, and he is going to make sure we find him." My tone dared him to argue. "But he's also used to everyone being an enemy. Might take him some time to warm up."

"Liv's goal is to get rid of the magic," Brekt said. "If she is on a mission to find the gods, then so am I."

"Okay." Maev grabbed a bag from her desk and threw it over her shoulders. "Let's go ask Cal. He will pass out when we tell him who we've brought to visit."

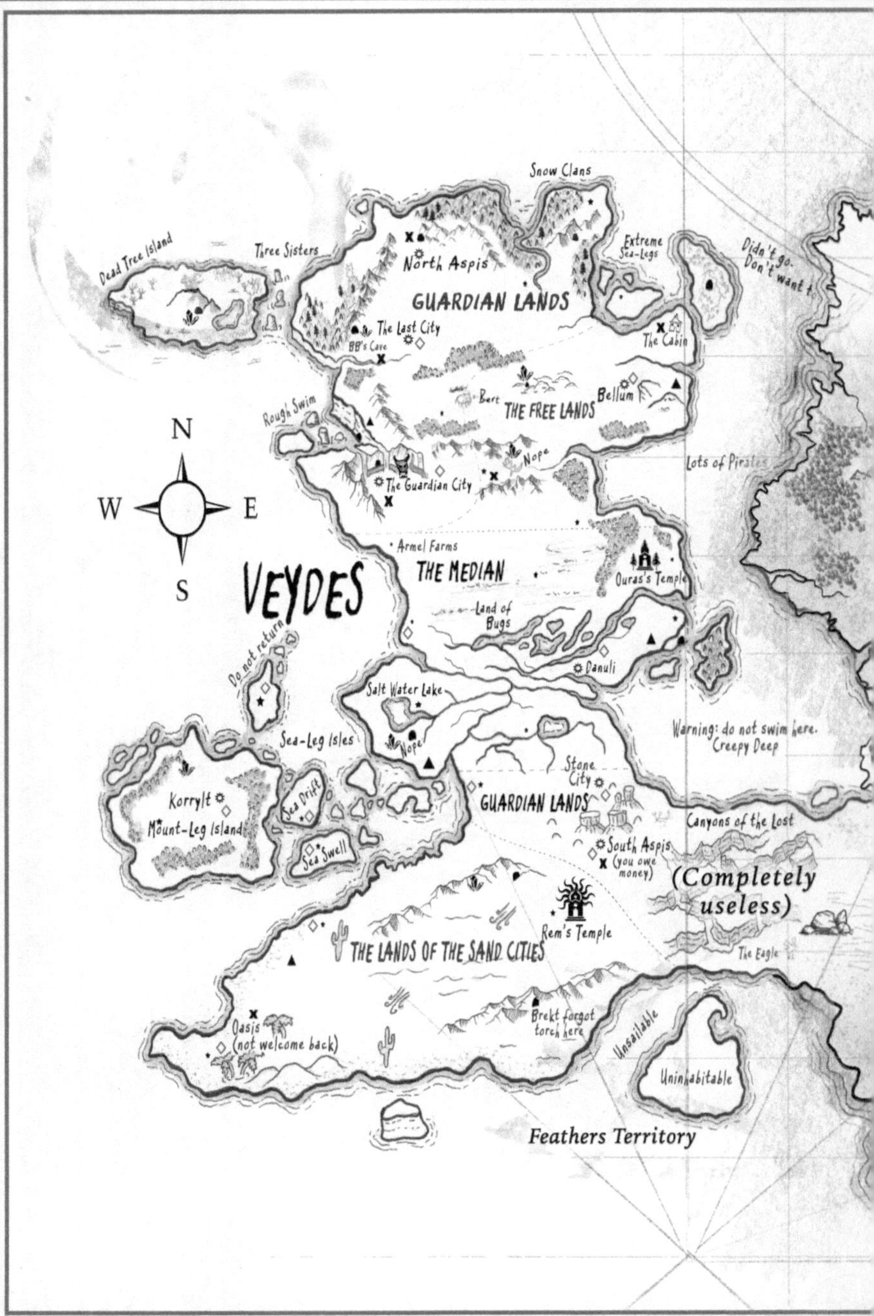

Snow Clans
Dead Tree Island
Three Sisters
North Aspis
GUARDIAN LANDS
Extreme Sea-Legs
Didn't go. Don't want t.
The Last City
BB's Cave
The Cabin
Rough Swim
Bert
THE FREE LANDS
Bellum
N
W
E
S
Nope
The Guardian City
Lots of Pirates
VEYDES
Armel Farms
THE MEDIAN
Ouras's Temple
Land of Bugs
Danuli
Do not return
Salt Water Lake
Warning: do not swim here. Creepy Deep
Sea-Leg Isles
Nope
Stone City
GUARDIAN LANDS
Canyons of the Lost
Korrylt
Sea Drift
Mount-Leg Island
South Aspis (you owe money)
(Completely useless)
Sea Swell
Rem's Temple
The Eagle
THE LANDS OF THE SAND CITIES
Brekt forgot torch here
Unsailable
Oasis (not welcome back)
Uninhabitable
Feathers Territory

PART FIVE
Northern Sea of Mayra
Bay of Avenmae
Nuo's (Incorrect) Map of
Arde
Rydavas
Mayranton
Avenmae
Rydav
Kalitazarhi Sea
North Rydavas
Khetar
Gahruh
Khaevyn
Uenn
Southlander Camps
Roemm
Rosaam
South Rydavas
Sevarina Sea
Tseana
Konmin
0   100   200   300   400   500

CHAPTER

SIXTY-ONE

Liv

"So Erebrekt …" Maev walked next to me, twirling her braid around her finger, trying to act normal. It was the tremor in her voice that gave her away. "When did you become a Guardian?"

I peeked over at Brekt, who was on my other side, to watch him as he spoke to an Aethar. His mouth pulled into a tight line as we left the busy area, heading toward the outskirts of the city. Well-maintained wood-planked homes were spaced out with yards full of flowers and large trees.

"I was always a Guardian," he replied, focusing on the road, constantly checking who was around us.

"Even when you were a child?" Maev asked him. Her face turned red, and she straightened, twirling her hair faster.

"There was no other choice. I was brought up in a Guardian camp."

"And did you want to become a Guard?"

I didn't want to laugh at how hard Maev tried to kill the silence with her awkward questions.

"No," Brekt replied, and I elbowed him when he didn't

continue. "I knew I would become a Guard. There was no one better."

"If you weren't raised at the camp, what would you have done?"

"I would have lived alone somewhere where it was quiet."

I snorted.

Maev asked no more questions after that, and I was thankful. A half hour later when we left the city behind, she pointed to a rocky cliffside, saying that we arrived at Cal's place.

"Where is it?" I asked, not seeing a house.

"Underground."

Brekt stopped me. "This is not wise. I don't wish you to be led underground to meet someone you don't know."

Maev huffed but said nothing as she continued to the wall of rock.

"I trust Maev with my life. I've travelled with her for months, and she's become one of my closest friends, which means this Cal will be my friend as well. So please, don't make them uncomfortable."

"Uncomfortable?"

I rolled my eyes. "Clearly, you don't know how grumpy you are."

Brekt blinked, and I stuck out my tongue, enjoying how it threw him off to see me so animated. We followed Maev, and as we approached the cliff, a grey door was revealed, built into the rocks.

Maev knocked several times, then sighed when there was no answer. "He's going to be pissed when I go down with strangers uninvited. Follow me."

I stepped behind Maev, climbing down a dimly lit stone stairwell. She was quiet as she walked us into a dark dungeon of a home. I jerked back when a door at the bottom of the stairs flew open, revealing a tall, strange man pointing a weapon at us.

Brekt wrapped an arm around my waist, pulling me away as Maev shouted. "It's me!" She raised her hands in the air.

"Maev?"

It was difficult to see what the man looked like in such little lighting, but I could tell he was tall with wild hair. I pushed Brekt's arm off me.

"I don't enjoy this, Liv." He said in a low voice behind me. "Escape will be difficult."

I shushed him with a finger to my lips, and he grabbed that finger, pulling it away from my face, glowering at me.

"What are you doing with a weapon, Cal?" Maev stepped down toward the door.

"I heard several pairs of footsteps. No one ever visits me. At least no one other than you. So I grabbed this tube. It has a bunch of scrolls in it."

"A tube?" Brekt muttered.

I turned to whisper, "Cal is not a threat."

"Obviously not." I could see the tension in Brekt's shoulders recede.

Cal opened the door farther, and we followed him inside.

We collected in a confined room lit by magic-powered torches. They gave off a warm, golden glow, hanging low from the ceiling, making the space cozy.

I played with the fabric of my skirts to ward off my building nerves. I didn't like meeting new people any more than Brekt did. Brekt noticed my worrying, and I shoved my hands behind my back before he said anything.

Cal sat back against the edge of a desk in the centre of the space, staring nervously at me.

Brekt was against the wall close to the door. He'd put his hood in place, hiding his tattoos.

"Cal, this is my friend Olivia." Maev waved a hand toward me.

Cal forced a smile. "Hi—"

"She's the Ikhor," she finished.

"Cursed Night!" He tore away from the desk, stumbling backwards.

I jumped, knocking my head against a shelf. Suddenly, years of fear and distrust roared through my head.

Eyes down. Don't react. Blend in.

"Whoa." His hands went up. He moved around the desk to put it between us. "Don't hurt me."

What?

Right. I was the Ikhor. I was not the one in danger. I *was* the danger.

"I'm not going to hurt you. You just surprised me." I didn't move from the wall. "I thought Rydavians weren't scared of the Ikhor."

Cal had a fair complexion with green undertones to his skin. Dark hair was tousled around his face in waves that, despite being messy, looked good on him. He was tall, thin-waisted and broad-shouldered, but he bore no muscle. He wasn't a fighter. A nervous smile crinkled the corners of his deep green eyes, and two sharp teeth hung from the top row. When he moved his head, he revealed three slashes along his neck.

Gills. Sea-leg.

"Maev, you are sure we are all friends here?" He snatched a pair of large, round glasses from the desk and backed up again, hitting an over-packed shelf behind him.

"I wouldn't bring anyone I didn't trust."

"And the other guy?" Cal asked nervously.

Maev avoided looking Brekt's way when she answered. "He's —ugh—Livy's Guard. Bodyguard."

Maev shrugged at me.

Good enough.

"If you say I will be okay underground, with the most erratic and powerful magic aside from the gods ... no, you must not be of sound mind." He fixed his glasses on his nose, and his attention focused on me. "Are you?"

"Am I what?" Puffs of steam billowed before my face as the room grew colder.

Brekt tensed by the door, the tendons in his neck stretched tight, holding the Aspis in.

I shut my emotions down, worried I would cause the transformation.

"Are you of sound mind?" Cal didn't move from where he hugged the wall.

I looked around the room. There were books, dark shelves crammed with more books, rolled-up papers, maps on the walls and images with pins and strings tied from one pin to the next. To my right, there was a desk, a chair, a tall worktable, and a bed.

No weapons.

"You're a scholar?" This was the man Ollo thought was weird.

"Yup."

"Friend?"

"One-word sentences—got it. Yes. Me. Friend." He patted his chest with both hands.

"Are you making fun of me?" I asked.

His back straightened. "Gods. No. Just trying to figure out how you speak to an all-powerful being."

He wore a plain white long-sleeved top. His tan-coloured pants were loose, belted around the waist. He wouldn't have survived well back home. He seemed sweet, if not a little rude, and he acted nothing like Ollo, which explained why Ollo thought Cal was weird.

"One way might be not mocking them when they are confused," I added.

Cal eyed the closed door on his left, blocked by Brekt. Was he thinking of escape? Not that I blamed him since I was thinking the same.

He was Maev's friend, I reminded myself. She trusted him. "I am not going to hurt you. Just so you know."

"If anyone in this city—no, in this world—knows more of the

legends and the gods than I do, I would like to meet them. Meaning, I know what you are capable of."

I blew out a long breath. "I bet you I know more." Crystals had eased the strain of magic, so my skin wasn't faded, and my body didn't hurt. When my hair fell before my face, it was silvery, not white. "I am certainly capable of setting all of your books on fire."

"And me."

"And you." I nodded, suppressing a smile.

There was something about Cal that put me at ease. Perhaps it was his nervous behaviour, but I think it was that he spoke freely with me, with little hesitation.

"I am well aware you can use all the elements to end me. So what can I do to make that not happen?"

His nostrils flared as I moved away from the wall, so I stopped, not going any closer. A laugh escaped me. The fear of strangers, of what people saw in me, wasn't as strong as it once was. And for once, it was someone else backing against a wall, not me. "I am not going to do anything to you. Maev said you were her friend. So I am your friend."

"Yeah?" He scratched his head, making more of a mess of his dark waves.

"Yeah."

"Well, don't crisp me if I don't warm up to you immediately. I'm not typically a people person." He made a face of disgust, as if the idea of people bothered him.

Cal's back hunched slightly as he returned to his desk and his open book. He pushed his glasses back and read. Only he wasn't reading. His eyes were darting to me every time I moved.

"What is this place?" I wandered the small room.

Maev approached his desk, picking up a book to read, but she watched me too, her face lit with humour. She was laughing at me.

"My home." He glanced away. "My office."

"Underground?"

"I like being away from the sun. Sea-leg. Prefer the dark."

I stopped in front of a bookshelf and turned back to face him.

"Is that the case for all Sea-legs? My friend is one, but I always saw him outside." I couldn't tell what Brekt made of the comment.

"Most prefer to be underwater. I spend about half my time on land. I have another spot I live the rest of the time."

"I suppose books don't do well underwater."

Cal cracked a smile at my comment. "You would be correct."

"And my friend was not a full-blooded Sea-leg. A weak line, I remember someone saying."

Brekt's expression dulled. Was he bored? And here I thought he enjoyed not having to be the one to talk.

I snooped through Cal's shelves. He had a massive collection of strange items and papers. There were gadgets made of ancient ore and some made of different metals like Maev's device.

"Cal," Maev said. "I've brought Livy here to talk about the legends of the gods. She wants to find them. When we were in Veydes, she spoke with Ouras—"

"Directly?" Cal asked, sitting straighter.

I nodded. "He is terrifying. Looks like the Aspis."

Brekt tensed, I'd forgot to mention that part earlier. I knew he would ask me about it later, since, apparently, he would not speak at all while he was here.

"We discovered that for the Ikhor to return the magic, *all* gods need to be there. We need help," Maev said.

"You've been on quite the adventure." Cal grabbed a hold of his desk, leaning back and grinning at her. It was cute. Sweet.

"I have been." Maev's face fell. "And ... Ollo was with me."

"Something happened." Cal sat straight. "Is he okay?"

Maev shook her head, swallowing. "He was taken by the members of the Guardian Council. But I've been told the Guards saw him, and they are going to help me find him."

"You think he is still ..." Cal looked from me to Maev.

"Maev knows he's alive," I said for her. "She can feel it."

"Maev is too smart to give into forced sentimentalities. If she says so, then he's alive." Cal leaned an elbow on the desk, turning to Maev. "So you met the Guards?"

I was thankful Cal changed the subject. I think he saw how it was bothering her.

"Liv travelled with them for a while." She gave a dismissive wave of her hand, pretending it was nothing.

Cal's attention shot to me. "You mentioned a Sea-leg," he said excitedly, flipping a page in his book. His mess of hair fell in front of his face.

Was he talking to me? "Yes?"

"You travelled with the Guards. You knew them."

"Yes."

He lifted his head from his desk. "Was the Sea-leg the Guard Nuo? The Interrogator?"

I braced myself, ready to hear how awful it must have been for me to travel with such a horrible man.

Brekt dropped his hands and stood away from the wall as I nodded to Cal.

"Is it true he fights with two short swords and seven deadly sharp knives? And that he is the mapper of the four?" Cal grabbed a notebook in the middle of a pile of books. Others crashed to the ground as he pulled the leather-bound book from the stack.

"What?" I asked.

Brekt rubbed at his temples, losing his patience.

Cal flipped a few pages and stopped. "Two short swords for close combat, seven knives for range. Nuo is not as fast as Kazhi or as fluid as Bastane but is the cleverest fighter in the Guards. Raised in the harsh climate of the North camp, he is argued to be the cruellest to the Southlanders, second to the Shadow Guard, Erebrekt, who fights with brute force."

The *Shadow Guard* glared at Cal with an unusual expression, and I put a hand over my mouth as Brekt's boredom washed away, replaced with that dumbfounded look. I bet he never expected admirers of the Guards across the border.

Cal kept reading. "Nuo has long lines of script tattoos down his entire back, which is an ancient Sea-leg poem of two soul-bonded lovers who spent a lifetime apart, fighting for the freedom of being together. He also has a full leg tattoo on the right, dedicated to the Aspis with smoke and scales." Cal lifted curious eyes to mine. "Are my notes correct?"

"A poem?" Maev asked, surprised.

That's what was on his back? "What are your notes for?" I asked.

Cal left his notebook open and pushed his hair back from his face, only for it to fall again. "I've been fascinated by the history of the Guards since I was a kid." He wiggled his book in the air. "These are my notes from the information I've gathered about them, along with previous generations."

"Why? They are your enemy."

"For fun." He shrugged.

"For fun? How is that fun?"

Cal leaned back in his chair, somehow still hunched over. "Knowing stuff is fun. Every little boy likes stories of warriors."

"It doesn't sound like you hate them."

Brekt was sizing up Cal curiously. I could see that, already, he was deciding his teachings about the Aethar were wrong. Brekt was mad that he'd been lied to about the city. What would he make of Cal, who knew so much about his people and didn't hate them?

Cal waved a hand. "I don't get caught up in who hates who and who attacks who. Everyone is to blame in war. We have just as many idiots here who want titles and accolades. I am not a fan of fighting or politics, and I certainly don't believe in borders or being a slave to your country."

Was he talking of Ollo?

"You don't support Rydavas?" I asked.

"I support no one, really. I don't wish ill on any innocent people, but I'm not about to bother others because I don't like their way of life. The Guards believe they're protecting their people, just as much as our aerial and ground units believe the same."

Brekt listened while Cal talked about war and politics, and

though Brekt was a fighter, I believed that deep down he didn't like it either.

Cal reminded me of the rebellion Kazhi had spoken of, that fights for all people. The rebellion I wanted to help—because I believed the same.

"And what do you think of the Council, ordering the Guards? You think they're just doing their duty to the people?" I asked Cal.

"No. It is usually those in power that fight for more power. Believe me, if you meet our Elders, which I'm guessing by the look on your face you have, you will see striking similarities."

"I had the impression the Elders here care for the people."

Cal was surprisingly open with his opinions. Had I said anything negative about the Keepers back home, I would have disappeared instantly. Was it possible that if others heard his opinions, he would be taken away?

Cal scratched his chin. "They do things that end up being good for the people, but they hold positions of power and make decisions for lives that are not their own. Some don't agree with those decisions. I'm not a fan. I don't follow anyone. I do things my way." Cal returned his attention to his desk, grabbed a different book, and wrote in it.

Perhaps Avenmae was a place where you could state openly your dislike for those in power.

"Where are you from?" he asked abruptly.

"The Lost Lands." I waited for him to scoff at me.

"You're going to drop that on me and not explain further?"

I turned to find him sitting straight, brows raised, and I smiled. Something was charming about Cal.

"I was brought here by the magic of the Ikhor. Somehow."

"That would mean it has sentience. It was able to take you from your lands to here."

"How would that work?" I asked. "I haven't seen any magic that can transport people."

Cal bit his lip—a small, sharp tooth stuck out as he thought. "It's the god's magic. The gods have powers no legacy has ever possessed. I have it on record that Rem can travel great distances with a thought, though I have not spoken directly to eyewitnesses. Perhaps the magic has part of his essence and an understanding the Ikhor needed to be on these lands and not the lost ones."

Rem? I had already considered once that it was him who brought me here, when I saw him in the Guardian City.

"It's all too much for me," I said. "I guess I don't fully understand the magic I carry."

"Tell me about the Lost Lands."

"What do you know of them?"

Cal pulled another notebook from the pile. "From what I've read and heard on my travels, the Lost Lands are a myth. The tales are that it is the place of our creation. And—"

"What? What do you mean, creation?" My heart sped at the new information.

Cal held up a hand. "Theories, remember. Some think that before the legacies existed, we came from the Lost Lands. Our people arrived on the continents of Veydes and Rydavas, where they first came in contact with the gods. Only after that were the first children born. But originally, our ancestors came from the Lost Lands."

That was too romantic of a story for my homeland. "I doubt that's the case. The Lost Lands are behind the advancements of Veydes."

"And Veydes behind Rydavas," he argued. "Which I don't believe was always the case. It may be true, as I see you don't carry any legacy yourself."

"How do you know I'm not of weak blood?"

Cal shrugged. "I don't know. Guessed."

"So, do you know how to get to the Lost Lands? Not that I want to return."

"I don't."

I continued to look through his shelves, disappointed for some reason.

"But I could guess where they are."

I whipped back around. "How?"

Cal lit up, enjoying my reaction. Not because he wanted to show off—that wasn't what it seemed like, anyway. I think he enjoyed my curiosity. "I have taken an interest now and then. I studied maps and flying routes the aerial division has used for training purposes in the past. Then I acquired similar maps of the routes the Guardians use."

"And you saw someone had flown there?"

"No, the opposite. There is an area, far north, where *no one* flies."

"I don't get it." Though he was right, I knew the Lost Lands were north.

"I believe there's a reason no one has visited your home. I believe the location is where no one can fly."

I waited, still not understanding.

"It's hidden by magic."

Magic? It made perfect sense, even without knowing why. Hidden by who?

"Why, though? Why was my home hidden?"

Cal shrugged. "There could be something there that is meant to be hidden."

Everything in me went still. "Could it be a missing god?"

His smile brightened. "I like your thinking. I never considered it. I wonder ..."

I was nearly bouncing with excitement. "Maev said you could help me find answers. She said if anyone could, it would be you."

"I will look again for books referencing the Lost Lands and see what comes up. Why are you interested in missing gods? You mentioned something earlier."

I tucked my hair behind my ear, nervous. "I want to return the magic. I've been told I need all of them to accept the magic back."

"Oh, right. I'd forgotten why you'd come here." Cal rested his elbows on his desk. "I don't envy you that job."

"I feel worse for Maev, who has offered to help me do it." Maev pursed her lips at the comment. "She's smart enough. She'd be the best help."

"Even though she's not a fighter?" Cal asked. "I would have thought the Guards would have been a better help. And you mentioned they were your friends. I've heard the Interrogator is intelligent. Is he more so than Maev? Wait, let me get my book."

"Nuo is a fighter. And when he's not being a jerk, he's very clever and funny."

Brekt's face fell, and when he shifted uncomfortably, I could tell he wanted to say something.

Cal paused his writing. "He's your friend."

"Was."

"Why?"

"We had a falling out."

"Were you lovers?"

My jaw dropped, my face turning red.

"Sorry," he blurted. "None of my business. I won't write that down."

"They were not lovers," Brekt growled, glaring at Cal, making the poor man flinch.

"Oh." Cal scribbled some more in his book, avoiding the hostility coming from Brekt. "So the Shadow Guard—" He looked over his glasses at me.

"Is the host of the Aspis." Brekt stepped away from the wall, dropping his hood and coming to stand at my side. "And he's curious why you need to know so much about the Guards."

Cal's eyes grew wide. "Tall, powerfully built, with tattoos of the Aspis past his temples across his skull. The Shadow Guard is the deadliest of them all. Having the abilities blessed by Erabas, he can disappear from sight. You won't see your death coming." He moved to write more but paused, as if sensing the tension in the room.

Brekt lowered his voice further. "You would be wise to explain why you know so much about me."

CHAPTER

SIXTY-TWO

Liv

Cal's eyes rolled into the back of his head, and he fell from his stool. He was out cold on the floor, and Maev was overtop him, waving one of his notebooks over his face. Brekt stayed against the far wall.

"He's not bad looking, Maev," I whispered, eyeing Cal on the ground. His glasses were askew, his mouth slightly parted, showing his two sharp teeth. The green tint to his skin went well with his dark waves. "You sure you don't like him? He's smart like you." I grabbed Cal's glasses and fixed them. The angle of his head exposed the gills on his neck.

It sent a pang of guilt through me. I missed my old friend.

"I like Cal, he's great. But just not like that. He never leaves his dungeon."

Cal moaned, going pink when he saw Maev over him. "Mae— you're actually here. Please tell me I was hearing things. Did your friend, the Ikhor, bring a Guard into my home?"

I laughed, and Cal's head tilted my way. "You."

"Me," I said.

"I wasn't dreaming."

"No."

"The Guard is here," he whispered, pointing to the door.

I nodded. "On the other side of that desk." I grabbed Cal by the arm, hoisting him up with Maev's help. "Best get your notebook out now and get the questions over with."

Cal sprung to his feet, and Maev and I fell backwards. "Right, my notes." He stopped at the sight of Brekt and fixed the glasses on his face.

Brekt had taken off the jacket and had it thrown over his arm, which was crossed with the other over his chest. His nostrils flared when we all stood staring at him. "I'm not a fucking show," he grumbled.

I hid my smile. I guess the grouchy demeanour wasn't just because he was secretly the host of the Aspis—it was just him.

Cal sat on his stool and found the same notebook he'd written about Nuo, opening it to a different page. "I have been collecting information on the Guards for years. I am hoping I can get you to clear a few things up for me."

"Why?" Brekt's brows lowered. "Don't assume I will pass the Aethar our secrets. Even if you are a friend of Liv's."

Cal looked close to passing out again. "I, um, well, I enjoy the stories of the Guards."

"I'm your enemy."

"I'm not one to draw lines in the sand."

Brekt didn't appear convinced.

"Wait," Cal said quickly, "Did you say before you're the Aspis?"

Brekt growled while Cal looked back and forth between us.

"The Aspis and the Ikhor. You're both here and not killing each other."

How could I even begin to explain Brekt and me?

Cal chuckled. "I see. *You* two are the lovers." He cleared his throat. "This may cause a problem for you two. History says only one survives."

Brekt stepped away from the wall. "Well then, I suggest you do your part and help us find a different way."

I grabbed Brekt's arm. "Cal is helping us," I reminded him.

"He's been obsessed with you warrior lot since I met him," Maev said, sending Cal an apologetic look. "I mean obsessed in the nicest way possible."

Cal fidgeted with his notes, taking quick peeks at Brekt. "Now, I have mixed accounts of how you came to be at the North camp. Sources have said you were born from shadows and were brought to the world unnaturally—explaining your skill in combat."

Cal lifted his attention to Brekt, who wore a tired expression.

I failed at holding back my laughter. "And is that how you were born?"

His eyes narrowed on me. I was thoroughly enjoying this. I went and sat on Cal's cot tucked on the opposite wall, and enjoyed the view.

"Others have said your parents left you on the steps of the North camp, terrified to raise a shadow-wielding demon," Cal added.

"Let's go with shadow demon. Whatever that is."

Cal scribbled in his notes. "Born of natural causes, left as a demon baby," he said slowly. "Next question. You fight with a long sword, three short swords, and ten throwing knives. You avoid the long-range weapons like the bow because you never mastered the skill."

Brekt looked ready to fight. "Want to test me on that?"

Cal shook his head and smoothed out the paper from his book, waiting.

"Bastane had the best skill with the bow. I didn't have the patience to watch the target and aim. Any more questions?"

"Oh yes—"

"Liv, why am I giving my enemy information on our fighting styles? Is this being passed to the Aethar defence units? The ones the pretty boy was part of."

I frowned at Brekt for bringing Ollo up, and waited for Cal to answer.

He waved a hand around his room. "I collect information,

which most times goes through one ear and out the other when it comes to the Rydavian aerial units. The *pretty boy* doesn't visit me here." Something about the way Cal referred to Ollo made it sound like a sore wound. "I wouldn't expect anyone to knock on my door except for Maev, who is a curious person herself. And well, now, the Aspis and the Ikhor. Best day of my life."

I didn't miss how Cal went pink when he talked of the twins.

Maev sat patiently at the edge of his desk.

"You called Brekt a demon," I said.

"I didn't." Cal pointed at his notes. "These are words from others."

"I've never heard anyone use that term. My mother told me stories of demons and witches and even dragons."

Cal whistled. "It's ancient lore. Stories that have been long forgotten and are no longer talked of. Maev, you never told me the Ikhor was more well read than you."

"How dare you." She put her hands flat on the desk, her tone teasing.

"It's refreshing to hear someone speak my language. Most times, I'm called a weirdo."

Brekt wasn't listening to the conversation anymore. His attention lingered on where the dress was tight around my ribs, showing every curve. I refrained from moving. The urge to go to him, to touch him, was sudden and overwhelming.

"So what *does* bring you here? It doesn't seem like Erebrekt of the North is one for talking." At that, Cal added the extra information to his notes. "Silent type."

I couldn't help the laugh that escaped.

Maev explained, "I told Liv on our journey back to Avenmae that I originally went after her because of the scrolls you found. I want to show her the scripts and the maps."

"I thought you laughed at my theories after I showed you those."

Maev's face scrunched up. "I don't laugh at you. And it was about the origins of the Ikhor and the Aspis. And the shrines."

"Let's hear it then," Brekt said. "Liv told me how the Aethar are taught about the Ikhor and Aspis. I'm interested in what you have to say, Cal."

Cal paled, hearing Brekt say his name. He stood and walked, with a slight hunch to his neck, over to a tall shelf with rolled papers. He shuffled a few around until he found what he was looking for. "I had to trade twelve ancient texts for this one scroll. There are other collectors like me. One in particular boasted about *this*."

Maev waited for Cal to unroll the scroll from a large tube. "We've already made copies of the maps he found and magic-protected them from bleeding."

"Bleeding?" I asked.

"The ink," she clarified.

Cal unrolled the parchment carefully, using books and weights to hold down the edges.

"It looks to be protected with magic as well," Maev explained, coming to stand over Cal's shoulder. "Which told me it was the real deal when Cal first showed me."

Brekt and I joined them behind the desk.

The text was long, written in the language of Night, but much of it had faded and flaked away.

"There's a drawing of the Aspis and the Ikhor," Brekt noted, "And what is that drawn between them?"

"I haven't been able to figure it out." Cal nodded at the image that was half faded, the ink run off the page. The edge looked like a stone of some kind. "I have slowly been working on the text, written in the ancient language of Night, but haven't translated much. There are no written records to go off, except for artifacts like this that I can compare scribblings."

"I can read it," I said, turning every head in my direction.

"Since when?" Brekt asked.

Shit.

"I forgot to mention on the way here. There is likely a lot we still have to learn about each other. When the Light brought me here, do you remember my shock when I discovered I knew your language?"

He nodded. "You assumed the magic was responsible."

"I think the same thing happened with the language of Night. I could read the script over the archway leading down to the caves in the Guardian City."

Brekt's face fell. "Why didn't you tell me?"

I fiddle with the hem of my sleeve. "I was scared that what I felt inside of me was the Aspis. You had told me most times throughout history that the host was a child of Night. I told you that I didn't know what I was. So I thought if I admitted I could read the script, you would know, and you would ask me to become the beast and find the Ikhor. I didn't want to at the time."

He ignored the other two watching and leaned in, pulling me into his arms and kissing me on the forehead, and I wrapped my arms around him, melting into his touch. I would never get used to touching someone so freely.

"There were too many things unsaid between us. Between all of us."

When he pulled away, I caught Maev's look of surprise. She was seeing the man I had told her of—the warrior who had a good heart.

"So what does it say?" I could hear the impatience in Cal's tone.

I leaned over the paper, studying the words. "There's so much faded that no sentence is complete. There are words like gods, sister, war, children, blessed children."

I trailed my finger under the beginning of a sentence, reading slowly. "Rem never wanted to admit he was afraid ..." My eyes traced the aged writing. "Then, more words like crystals, gods again, legacies, crystals. Oh! This line." I pointed to the edge of the parchment. "When the three unite, he will return."

I stared at the faded script, hoping it would transform and explain more.

"What does that mean?" asked Maev.

"It means Ouras was telling the truth," I sagged in defeat. I was no closer to finding Erabas. "The gods need to be brought together."

"You think it means the gods? But there's four of them." Cal pointed to the image. "And what do these drawings have to do with it?"

"What if this scroll isn't about returning the magic?" I asked, "What if this was a clue on how to find Erabas? It's written in Night, likely left for his children. It has something to do with the other three."

"It sounds like they need to agree to bring him back," Brekt suggested.

"This just got so much more difficult. How are we supposed to make three gods agree?" I leaned my head against Brekt's shoulder and sighed. He went still, and I looked up.

He was watching me with a curious expression.

We had never been fully open before, or at least, I had never been bold enough to touch him casually. When I travelled with them, we always had a wall between us, caused by our secrets and my insecurities, my fears. I wasn't like that anymore. Becoming the Ikhor had shown me how easily you could lose so much. Becoming friends with the twins showed me how brave I could be.

Cal was looking at the text. "I don't feel like we've figured it out. I feel like something major is missing. There's a mention of crystals above here. You think the decline in crystals has to do with Erabas?"

"Maybe we can convince the gods that bringing Erabas back will be a good idea. Good for Arde." Maev faced Cal. "The maps we found mark the shrines all over Rydavas, even Veydes. Let's show them."

I put my head back on Brekt's arm, savouring him not turning me away. "What if the gods can't convince Erabas to take the magic back? What if when he returns, things get worse?"

"Worse than an endless cycle of war?" Brekt's deep timbre vibrated through me.

Maev nodded her head, clearly thinking about something. "You're glowing, like Rem," she said to me. "The Aspis has physical similarities to Ouras. And the other gods are missing, not part of anything anymore."

"What're you getting at?" Brekt asked.

Cal unfolded the new maps while Maev continued. "What if the histories are wrong about why you were made? What if the Ikhor never stole the magic, and you're actually both creations of the only gods that are left? What if Mayra is gone too?"

"That's a bold question to ask Maev," Cal said, smiling. "What would Rem and Ouras want by creating the two legends?"

"Maybe to replace the old gods?" I asked.

"These questions are hurting my head," Brekt complained.

"Me too," I whispered to him. "But I think they're doing a good job of seeing different angles."

Brekt answered with a grunt, and I rolled my eyes at him.

He grabbed my chin and forced my face to his. "Don't be sassy," he said in a low tone. "I like it too much."

I bit my lip as an intense swelling filled my heart.

Sparks of light erupted between us, and he pulled his hand away, wincing.

"Can you two stop making eyes at each other and listen," Maev complained.

Brekt didn't look away from me. "The Ikhor is too powerful, Aethar. I have little control."

"As I was saying," Maev continued, ignoring us. "These maps show shrines all over the world. They are older than recent maps and show more shrines than what exists today. I want to go search them, see if there are ruins, and look for clues on where the gods might be hiding."

"Look, Erebrekt,"—Cal pointed to a new map he unrolled—"there are shrines of Night. Several of them. They no longer exist on modern maps."

"When did you find this one?" Maev drew closer, face lit with excitement.

Cal's smile was proud, yet his cheeks flushed when Maev was at his side. "You have been gone a long time, Maev. I've been on a few of my own adventures."

Brekt went to Cal's side and crossed his arms, studying the map. "I've never laid eyes on a shrine of Night. You said we can have this map?"

"I can make a copy for you. I only made one for Maev and Liv."

"I go with Liv," Brekt said, giving Maev a hard look, daring her to argue.

"What about the Guards?" I asked.

"They can have the second map."

There seemed no point arguing with him.

"Is it safe for you two to travel together?" Maev asked, fidgeting with papers.

"I go with Liv. End of discussion."

"We need a Sea-leg to go to Mayra's shrines. One of her children." Maev bit her lip.

"He's one," Brekt pointed out, nodding to Cal.

"Mayra wouldn't answer me," Cal said, studying his map, hair falling in his face. "I've never been dedicated to my legacy. I never prayed or worshipped my so-called mother. If she still lives, she will not come for me."

"I'll get Nuo on it then."

Maev made a sound in the back of her throat. "Like he'd help."

Brekt went stiff, and I stepped between him and Maev, holding a hand up. "Nuo's been ... he's not the same. Since you left."

The tension bracketing his mouth melted away. "I'm sorry to bring this to an abrupt end ..."

"But you feel the Aspis coming?" My heart sank when he nodded—I hadn't noticed before how strained he'd become.

Brekt's obsidian gaze warmed. "I will come back. Promise. Maybe I can catch up with the others before I see you again."

I hugged myself, watching him head out of Cal's door.

"Go," whispered Maev.

"What?" I spun to face her.

"Give him a better goodbye than that," she said, as if I were stupid.

I ran out of Cal's door and up the stone steps that led outside. "Brekt," I shouted, shielding my eyes from the daylight, finding him several feet in the trees.

"Couldn't even wait a day," he teased. "I promised I would come back."

I swallowed my growing nerves. "I wanted to—"

Shit. How was I supposed to be brave when I didn't know how to do this?

"I wanted to know if Nuo has been more himself since you're back."

He scratched the back of his head. "I know him well. I've seen him in his dark moments. Despite Nuo's casual behaviour, he feels things deeply. He was never shown love and was told it was a weakness. It might be the reason he has that poem on his back—because that's all he ever wanted."

"It was him that told me of soul-bonded lovers." My face heated, not daring to ask Brekt about the subject. "I knew that about him. He's a romantic, and he was a good friend."

Brekt was quiet for a moment. "Was he awful to you?"

I blew the hair from my face, my mood souring. "I'm not trying to get him in trouble. Did your dreams not warn you of what would happen when you died?"

Brekt ignored my clipped tone. "I only ever saw things I was present for."

"Oh, right."

"But I know him. I know what to expect. Nuo should have never become a Guard. He should never have grown up in the North. He excelled only because I forced him. He should have been like the Sea-leg inside there, your new friend. Nuo should have been a scholar. And he's suffered for it. Kept that suffering to himself. He's likely lost control of his own head."

"He could use an apology," I admitted. Perhaps I was ready to give him one.

"Sounds like he could use a kick in the ass."

I bit back my smile. "Be nice."

Brekt walked back to me. "I'm only nice to you, love. You take up all of my capacity."

I shoved a hand into my pocket and passed several glowing crystals to him, putting something between us before I forced him to stay. "For the others," I said.

He opened and closed his mouth.

They used to search caves and risk their lives for crystals. Now, I could make them without a thought.

"You'll come back soon?" I searched his face, looking for that hesitation, the signs that Brekt was hiding himself from me. But I didn't see it. He hid nothing, and it made me feel bolder. Could I say it?

"If you'll be here."

My heart thundered. "I will be. As well as the map of the shrines."

Brekt touched the side of my face, sending a thrill over every nerve ending. "The only reason I want to search those shrines is to get that magic out of you."

"So you can stop being forced into being the Aspis?"

He barked a laugh. "I love being the Aspis." He took a step back. Then another. His smile grew wolfish. "I just want to be able to touch you with my own hands. To not be struck by lightning when I fuck you."

My heart stopped.

My mind—everything just stopped. I forgot what I had wanted to say.

Shadows swirled around his feet, horns grew from his head, and fangs sprouted behind his wicked grin. No, Brekt was not hiding anymore. The Aspis burst from the smoke and took off into the sky, and I staggered back—the size of it was getting bigger still.

My chest rose and fell, my face heating. Hearing Brekt say those kinds of things—though I had berated him before, saying he was acting like a beast ... I liked it when he talked to me like that.

"Wow." I turned to find Maev standing at the door, facing skyward. "Your photo really didn't do him justice. Brekt is really hot," she said wistfully.

I laughed. "First Bastane, now Brekt? You like the whole enemies-to-lovers, don't you."

"I read a lot of romances." She played with the end of her braid as she walked closer. "I'm not thinking of the Shadow Guard that way, but I wouldn't mind running into the golden Day-leg again. He was actually sweet."

"You forgot how he betrayed me."

"I remember how he apologized. Took a hit for you in the canyons."

"You don't think I'm crazy? We are walking a fine line, Brekt and I. Half the time we are uncertain of the other." I leaned against a tree.

"No, you're not crazy. Not for the feelings you have. Crazy in many other ways. Others might say to stay away from him, to protect you. But I respect the Shadow Guard. He's fighting the Aspis for you."

I was surprised. "You've seen him when he has no control."

"Sounds like someone else I know." She put a finger to my forehead and pushed. "Yet you're fighting every day to survive and to return the magic."

I puffed the hair out of my face. "Neither of us is who we were before. What am I going to do?"

"You're going to take him to your room next time and get him into your bed." She pinned me with a look. "You need it."

CHAPTER
SIXTY-THREE

Nuo

"A map of shrines? That's their big idea? I always knew the Aethar weren't intelligent." I was pacing between the trees while Brekt explained what he'd seen in the Sea-leg's crypt of a home.

We were on enemy lands. With little warning, they loaded airships with Guardians, supplies and Deathmakers. We spent two weeks travelling over the massive sea between continents. The attacks from pirates were endless, yet we always held them back. When the Aethar wastelands came into view, the Guardians on board lined the top deck, gaping at a shore lined with green. Trees larger than our northern forests swayed from the salty breeze. The wind on board wasn't enough to drown out the whispers, the questions, the anger.

"The shrines on their map aren't shown on the ones we've seen," Brekt said. "There's a reason they aren't shown, I'm sure of it. I want you to call for Mayra. I want you to check the shrines for drawings, paintings, anything that might tell us how to find the gods."

That stopped me. "Me? Why would I do a thing like that?

Mayra's a god. She's not going to come for a legacy with weak blood like mine. She never has before."

"We need someone we trust to call her, ask her to help Liv and me. I will stress the *me* in that statement." Brekt watched me go back and forth, making a path in the dirt. "We can't tell just anyone the Ikhor and the Aspis are working together or that we are trying to find the gods."

Kazhi was climbing one of the tall Aethar trees to get a strange-coloured fruit growing up high. "Get your head out of your ass, Nuo, and help them."

I was restless. I was always restless lately, but if I stopped moving, the tension in my chest would set in. I rubbed at it, trying to stop the pain from building. Brekt noticed, and I shoved my hands in my pockets, ready to deck him if he made a comment.

"I will be given a copy of this map?" I asked.

Fruit dropped all around us, and Brekt reached out and caught a yellow one, peeling it. "Yes, they're making one as we speak. Or perhaps that was yesterday."

I continued wearing a path in the dirt. "Then you can tell that blue fucker to give back my other map. She stole it from me."

Bastane stood in my path, stopping me. "No more names. You stole what was hers, too."

I shoved him away. "Stop playing hero to every woman you see."

Brekt took Bastane's side. "They are helping us. And Liv is going to get an apology, too. You are going to make it up to her. Both of you. All of you."

Bastane was wise enough to look ashamed, but I was livid that this was the reunion I got after another three weeks of him being gone.

"*I* need to apologize? You're insane."

Brekt turned his anger away from Bastane. "I know you. I know who you are underneath your act. I can only imagine the apology she deserves."

Unbelievable. "You going to make me?"

Brekt drew up to his full height. "If I must."

I squeezed my fists, then let them go. Even though I was pissed, I never imagined we'd be able to fight again.

"And what do you want me to say? 'Sorry, I didn't kill you when I promised I would? Sorry that I trusted you and let you in, only for you to betray me and take off with my enemy like I meant nothing after you gained all the power in the world and you left me to mourn the closest and oldest friend I'd ever had?'. Is that the apology I am supposed to give her?"

Kazhi whistled from up in the tree, but Bastane had the good sense to stay quiet.

Brekt lifted a brow. "You don't have to be so wordy. Though I know you usually can't contain yourself."

"And will you demand from your one and only that she apologize to me?"

Brekt jabbed a finger at me. "I expect she already has an apology written and practiced. She cared for you. Be a man, say sorry, and makeup. I won't have either of you wasting time. We don't have guarantees about what will happen tomorrow."

"I don't make any promises." He always asked too much of me. This was one thing that might be impossible. Forgiveness was never my strength.

"Nuo doesn't always follow through with his promises," Kazhi said. "He promised to kill her and didn't. He saved Bones when you came back as a creatureman. So don't waste your time getting him to make commitments to an apology now. Bones is tougher than that anyway—she doesn't need words."

A fruit landed on my head. "Ow!"

"Smarten up." Kazhi was lost in the leaves, and I grabbed the fruit that had hit the ground and threw it back at her. There was a loud thud. "Dammit Nuo."

I grinned. "My aim never fails, Kaz."

Bastane was staring daggers at me. "I grew up with women, Nuo, and saw how badly they can be treated. Don't be an asshole."

"Enough," Brekt said, stopping the fight.

We were all on edge, Kazhi having warned us that Falizha would come snooping soon.

Brekt refused to reveal he'd returned and would be leaving shortly. "I will ask for your map, Nuo, and bring you the new one. We will look for clues on how to gather the gods and give the magic back. Liv wants us to leave Rem for last as Ouras warned her that Rem would kill the Ikhor on sight."

"Why would he do that? But Mayra won't?" Bastane stepped away from me, peeling his own fruit, and I continued my pacing.

"Liv thinks Rem is up to something. That he might be the cause of the Ikhor's creation."

Brekt had told us of the Aethar's theory, how she thought maybe the Ikhor was made by Rem and the Aspis made by Ouras. If that were true, it would mean Mayra was dead like Erabas.

"In the meantime,"—Brekt threw his peels away as he spoke, and my chest tightened, knowing he was about to leave—"figure out what the Ravins are planning, listen for any word of the Aethar's brother. And try to find out what's going on in the north. I want to know what they're up to."

"Kaz, did you get a count on the crates they've brought with them?" Bastane tilted his head up to her.

"I stopped counting after fifty."

Brekt popped a piece of fruit into his mouth. "You say this weapon shoots faster than an arrow or cannon?"

I ran a hand down my face. "Faster than your eyes can track. And the impact causes enough damage to rip a big hole in the chest." I massaged mine again, worrying.

"And you believe Liv's friend might have survived that?" Brekt frowned.

I shrugged. "I thought I saw him moving once he hit the ground. Kazhi thinks they were keeping him alive to get him to talk."

We were silent, unsure of what to do next.

"Can you use your magic to help us get more information, Kaz?" Brekt asked.

She jumped down, landing next to Bastane. "I can't use magic around the Ravins. I don't know if they are the purebloods setting Veydes on fire. If they can use magic, they can sense mine, remember? You could sense it, too, mighty Aspis. It was a power you were born with, not from the beast. Your shadows are a natural part of you."

"How do you know for sure my abilities are magic?"

"I feel it when you disappear from sight. You're heightened senses are part of being a Night-leg. But the shift into shadows is magic. I've met many Night-legs in my day, so I know what it feels like. It's a slippery feeling."

Brekt's jaw went tight. "You've met others? Killed them?"

Kazhi eyed each of us through her lashes. "I've killed many people, some who didn't deserve it. But I've snuck many more away from Veydes to safety. When I was hired by an unknown agency, I was asked to target Night-legs. I made it look like they died. Many are safe and are serving a better cause."

"This rebellion you spoke of." Brekt leaned against the tree, playing with the fruit in his hands.

"Correct. Which you are welcome to join at any time. All of you. As I know, we are done with the Council and are loyal to each other until the end."

"Loyal enough that you'd tell us of your past?" Brekt dared.

I stopped pacing. Kazhi had refused to tell us, but would she do the same for Brekt?

An agonized expression crossed her features, but she shook it off. "It was a long time ago. I lost those I loved. I turned rotten." She narrowed her eyes at me.

"I get your point," I muttered. "If we can keep you for years without holding your secret past against you, maybe you can get over that I went a little dark."

Kazhi tilted her head.

"Okay, I was a nightmare. Wasn't a hired assassin, though."

"No, you just killed for the joy of it," she said.

Brekt sighed. "We all have been shitheads, one time or another.

Even me, I kept everything from you two." Brekt spoke to Kazhi and Bas. "And we can't forget that Bastane went to Falizha for assistance in waking the Aspis."

Bastane groaned, "Thanks for bringing me into this. If I could go back in time, I would."

I snorted. "I hope they don't write in the history books about the biggest fuck ups in the long lineage of the Guards."

"They might," Bastane said, sighing.

"Whatever. I'll just find the books and rewrite them myself."

"If you live." Kazhi was picking seeds from her teeth. "Which, with the amount of people Falizha brought, you might not."

"Thanks, Kaz. But you forgot, my best friend is the Aspis. I can sic my big black-horned buddy on them."

"I don't do tricks." Brekt glared.

I waved a long strand of my fruit peel his way. "Come on, boy. You can beat them. I bet you'd sit and roll over if the Ikhor asked you." Seconds later, I dodged a fist going for my stomach, laughing. "You got slow floating around in the sky all those months."

"I don't need speed, idiot. I have claws and teeth." Brekt gave up, sitting on a rock across from Kazhi and Bastane. "Another thing, the Sea-leg, Cal, mentioned the Lost Lands. He was talking to Liv about them, and based on his study of maps, he thinks they are in the north, protected and hidden by magic."

Bastane scratched at his jaw, while Kazhi considered what Brekt had said.

"Come on, you two," I groaned. "Do I have to put everything together? The north? Like maybe where Aeden has been constantly setting off to?"

"You mean experiment on magycris and these weapons?" Bastane's brows knit in confusion. "Bones never mentioned anything like that. She didn't know of magic or anything of the outside world. How could someone hide airships going back and forth and a place where they tested weapons."

I was twirling my knife again, thinking. "We don't know how big the Lost Lands are. BB—"

I stopped, sucking in a breath, waiting for the others to taunt me. How did I make such a slip?

"The Ikh—" Fuck me. "*Liv* never went far past her own village." I kept my eyes on the ground as I paced. I didn't want them to see the rollercoaster that was my mind.

"I like your train of thought, Nuo." Kazhi broke the silence. "Let's use that as a working theory. Maybe these maps we'll be given will show more than just the shrines."

The others stayed silent as I paced, and I could sense Brekt itching to leave again. I didn't tell him to go. He was a grown-ass adult and could do what he liked.

"Tell Bones she better be practicing her swords," Kazhi said, her voice going soft. She shocked me by walking up to Brekt and patting him on the arm.

His face went slack at Kazhi's show of *affection*.

"I will," he replied.

Liv was aware of the rebellion Kazhi was part of. Brekt was aware now, too. We were all carrying secrets again, but this time, they weren't from each other.

"And tell her thanks for the crystals. I want more," she said.

CHAPTER

SIXTY-FOUR

Liv

Maev had dropped me off at the castle, saying my suite should have buckets of empty crystals to soothe me. She had gotten them from her professor, who had saved them after their alchemy labs. Over a dozen buckets sat near the door, filled with empty stones of all shapes and sizes, and I wondered how long it would take to fill them.

Maev was supposed to go out with Hanold tonight—their first official date. So I had to kill time and hopefully relax enough to get a good sleep before we left on our journey.

We were finally going to find the gods.

I brought the buckets of crystals to my bed and spread some around the room, then lit candles so everything glowed a warm yellow. The fire made the room pleasant and inviting.

I changed into a lightweight, green nightgown that showed enough skin to send me to prison back home and sat on the edge of my bed. For the first time in a very long time, I felt safe. Sure, so much could go wrong when Maev and I left the city to search for the forgotten shrines, but tonight, I could enjoy this.

I left the bedroom to explore the rest of the floor. Other rooms had been closed up and left dirty, but I inspected those, too. I found an office with empty bookshelves and a desk cleaned of any personal items, and a sitting room with chairs covered in linen cloth. There was a room with piles of furniture and belongings. I picked through a dirty pile of paintings stacked against a wall until I came to a portrait, buried under several frames and covered with a sheet. It was difficult to see in the candlelight, but there was no mistaking the image of the queen and her three sons.

I stared at the queen of Avenmae. She was beautiful with a severe face. She looked powerful. She looked like a mother … and she had been until she lost her three sons. Three men sat at her side—tall, proud, dark-haired princes. They reminded me of the Avenmae citizens. They were not warriors like the Guardians and wouldn't have stood a chance against an invasion of their city.

My heart pounded while I held the painting, lost to time. Did anyone remember the royals or what they looked like? Or was the Queen a forgotten ghost?

A pull in my chest startled me, and I dropped the sheet back over the portrait, determined to come and examine the other portraits at another time. But right now, I wanted to be at the end of the cord tugging on my chest. I closed the doors to the room of forgotten treasures and hurried back to my bedroom. And there, before the fire, next to the large, cushioned chairs, was Brekt. From the doorway, I could see out the window to the balcony—a starry sky shone above Avenmae.

Brekt was picking up crystals, holding them to the fire, testing their weight and dropping them. He found my swords by my bedside and slid one out of its leather case and inspected those glowing crystals, too.

He was beautiful.

He was cleaned up in fresh clothing. There were no holes in his shirt from wounds caused on the burning field, and he'd cut his hair too. It sat on his shoulders, worn down in dark waves and parted slightly off-centre.

I leaned against my doorframe, watching him.

The black shirt he wore was loose, unbuttoned at the top. His dark pants were for comfort, not for battle. He was more exotic tonight, less like a hardened warrior. And with the candlelight warming his skin, it gave him a sensual glow.

He set a crystal down, lifting his gaze to me. The corner of his mouth tilted up. "I would normally say it's rude to stare, but I enjoy hearing you sigh like that."

I jerked away from the doorframe. "I wasn't sighing."

"Panting?"

"I was just breathing."

Brekt's grin set my veins on fire, warming my face, and so did the temperature of the room. "You sound like an animal in heat, love. Get in here."

I tiptoed into the bedroom.

"You look like a dream," he purred. "Who's finding you these clothes? I must thank them. It will be a pleasure sleeping next to you tonight."

Shivers travelled over my body. "You're staying the night?"

He flopped down into one of the chairs by the fire. "If I'm welcome."

I held back my squeal of delight. However, I couldn't contain the smile, hearing he was mine to sleep next to. "And you are going to sit in that chair? That's your plan?"

Brekt leaned back, his legs spread, arms resting on the sides, head tilted. "I am just enjoying the view."

He was so different now, and I enjoyed the fact that he wasn't so reserved. Coming back from the dead looked good on him.

"Likewise." I padded across the room, stopping at the end of my bed, leaned against the frame and folded my arms to take him in. His attention snagged on my chest, where my nightgown sat low, and it lit up my confidence.

Brekt's gaze darkened when they landed on the scar on my shoulder. "You should be afraid of me. Look what I've done."

I rubbed the skin there, covering the scar. "This isn't over. It may get worse. And I scarred you first."

He traced a finger over his brow, where the scar began, and ran it down over his eye. "It's not a competition."

"Oh? Not a competitive man?" I bit my lip, holding onto the edge of my bed frame for support.

"Look at those bold words. Being evil becomes you."

I ignored the jab. "Being a beast becomes you. You used to hold back from me, hide from me. I hated it."

"Believe me, I hated it too. I was stupid to believe I could control what happened. I didn't want you to suffer as you did in my dreams."

"You never saw me use magic in those dreams?"

"No. Likely because when you do, I am the beast. I never dreamt of being the Aspis, either. Just knew it was there. I dreamt of myself fading away and then darkness."

"And you dreamt ... of us."

The darkness in his eyes changed, deepening until it was a sensual caress. "Many times. Often the same dream over and again. Eventually, I came to know you so well that I would dream of you on instinct and not as a glimpse of what would come. I would dream of you only because my heart wished you were real. Those dreams will never come to be, but what *will* come true will make you blush, just like you are now."

My thighs squeezed from the knowledge that what he dreamt of hadn't happened yet.

He played with the fabric on the chair. "What's with the buckets of crystals? You going to leave this city armed to the teeth? A little unfair for your old friends, don't you think?"

"I don't know what will happen to the crystals once I fill them. I just needed a lot. You can take some, as many as you like, when they are filled."

Brekt took in the number of buckets I had. "Why do you need so many? Is the magic hurting you that much?" He sat forward, leaning closer to inspect me.

Several feet separated us. It was too much.

"It doesn't hurt. More like it drains my energy when I don't use it—it makes my body feel tight. I become so wound up that it's difficult to breathe, so I need to release the magic into the crystals."

"Do it now. I know a thing or two about being wound up with no release." His eyes danced with mischief, and I couldn't stop my blood from roaring. But then concern etched the corners of his mouth. "I don't like hearing you have to go through that."

"I don't want to use the magic. You'll turn. I want you to stay. The crystals will eventually take what seeps out of me. The leaking of magic I can't control."

Brekt sat back but didn't relax as before. "Why haven't the gods replaced the magic in the crystals if they put it there in the first place."

"That's a question we have all been asking. I think because they don't have magic like they used to." I pointed to myself to explain why.

"It's not your duty to fill them for other people, Liv. Don't do that to yourself. When we return the magic to the gods, we will correct it for everyone."

"You are very quick to take my side after years of being taught to hate me."

He held my stare, looking into me, seeing me, and it was the most intimate appraisal anyone had ever fixed me with. "You know why I do."

My heart skipped.

"I wanted all these crystals in case you visited me."

Confusion flickered across his face.

"My plan wasn't as sweet as you sleeping over."

It was difficult to breathe around my pounding heart. I was back in his suite in the Guardian City—shy, unsure, inexperienced.

Understanding shone in the way his smile grew, and he put his hands behind his head, crossing his feet at the ankles. "You want me to kiss you again?"

I waited.

His brows went in the air. "You want more?"

I nodded, feeling unsure about it all.

Brekt scanned the room and surprised me when he laughed.

My face went red, embarrassed I had been so forward. Was it a ridiculous thought?

"That explains all the crystals. There's a lot." He rested his elbows on his knees. "As much as I love seeing the pink on your cheeks, wipe that look from your face. You didn't need to gather so many crystals to suck up your magic."

"And why is that?"

"All the magic in the world won't stop me from fucking you tonight."

Hearing those words in Brekt's timbre stopped my heart completely. I moved toward him with no thought, and he rose from the chair. We were two worlds colliding with enough force to rattle the stars.

He lifted me, and my legs went around his waist. When our lips met, everything disappeared but the fire building in me. It ravaged my body, sending heat to every place he touched. His tongue found mine and stroked deliciously, tasting. I moaned and dug my fingers into the back of his head.

The Ikhor and the Aspis were finally at war to see whose hands were faster. Whose lips were more brutal. Whose desperation leaked further into the other.

Brekt was shameless as he walked me to a wall. My back hit the solid surface, pushing my chest closer to him as he ground himself into me. I moaned, bit at his lip, and pulled at his hair. I caught sight of his devilish smile. The iridescence flashed as he looked down at the clothes we still wore.

He growled, pulling me away from the wall and taking me to the bed. He dropped me, not being gentle, and I bounced on the mattress before lying back, squeezing my legs together as he ripped his shirt over his head. His chest, covered in scars, was sculpted to perfection. The Aspis tattoo was visible on his neck, disappearing over his shoulder and reappearing again at his hip, covering half of the deep lines that cut past the top of his pants.

Watching him move, seeing the heat in his stare ... I slid a hand over my chest, playing with myself. "Brekt. I need you."

He knew my past, knew I had little experience with lovers. But with him? I could do anything.

He crawled onto the bed, his knees pressing into the mattress, encasing me on both sides. Hair fell in his face, nearly hiding the glowing yellow of his eyes.

Yellow eyes. *No.*

He was turning.

I could see it in his movements—predatory, a desperate gleam in the way he scanned my entire body.

I tried to sit up but was stopped when Brekt grabbed the top of my nightgown with both hands and ripped. The loud tearing blocked out my gasp as the fabric fell to the side, exposing me. The cool air peaked my nipples. I was bare for him. Brekt stopped, looking down at me. The beast faded just long enough to see it there—his wonder.

"I never thought this would be real," he whispered, running the back of his knuckles over my collarbone, lightly tracing them down my front.

I sunk into the mattress, turning to liquid as the warmth of his fingers caressed me. I didn't care that the Aspis was here, too. I needed more. "Make it more real. Touch me. I want to feel everything."

All the sweetness left him. He went feral, claiming my mouth once more. A hand tightened around my jaw, and then both hands followed a path down, over my shoulders, to my chest, and when they found my breasts, Brekt moaned his pleasure as he squeezed, kneading them.

Gods, nothing had ever turned me on so quickly. The sensation of his rough hands on the softer skin of my chest was unexplainable. I could let him touch me like that forever. I arched my hips beneath him. The rest of his body was too far away.

His knees dug into my hips, trapping me below him, and his

mouth wandered down my neck, kissing, licking. The wicked man took his time.

I cried out when his mouth found my nipple, and a new wave of pleasure went through me when he flicked his tongue over the hardened peak.

My magic vibrated.

"Crystals," I panted. I reached a hand to his hair and pulled. "I need the crystals closer."

Citrine eyes rose to meet mine.

Brekt was losing the battle with the Aspis. His pupils narrowed to slits, angered that I had stopped him, and phantom horns faded in and out of sight.

"Now," I demanded.

One knee left my side slowly. Then the other. His movements were animalistic, and the beast's eyes never left mine as he backed off the bed. But I wasn't afraid. This beast was mine.

Several heartbeats later, his sharp gaze finally left me, searching for the crystals. Brekt lifted a bucket and poured the crystals across the end of the bed. They flickered and pulsed with light, easing the building heat in my chest. I grabbed several in my fist and shrieked when my knees were gripped hard and forced wide.

He leaned over, holding my legs open as his eyes flared. He put a knee on the edge of the bed, trapping mine in place. His tongue travelled over his teeth, showing fangs as he gazed down at me. "I know how you taste, yet I have never tasted you," he said, his voice impossibly deeper. "Shall I run my tongue up your centre, love? Shall I fuck you with it and taste you at the same time."

Oh, my god. Brekt was *wild*. It set my core on fire.

"Yes. Everything," I begged.

Brekt lowered himself until he was kneeling at the side of the bed. He still held my legs, but grabbed me under the knees and yanked me toward the edge. My arms scraped over crystals, and the sting turned to pleasure.

Very slowly, so I had to watch the wicked gleam in his eyes, he lifted one of my legs over his shoulder. He bit his lower lip as he lifted the second. His hands slid up the outsides of my legs as he leaned closer, putting himself a breath away from where I craved him most.

I waited as he watched me, his pupils dilating.

"I've dreamt of you so many times. I've craved you more than anything. I know what you want. You have a wild heart, love. You like wild fucking."

I knew he was dangerous from the moment I met him. He was dark, the *cursed child*, the host of the Aspis, and now I could add— dirty and unashamed.

He was as much of a beast as the Aspis. And he loved it.

So did I.

His tongue flicked out. Once. Quick. And I erupted in pleasure.

His hands travelled across my stomach, and I gripped the crystals tighter as his tongue drew a line up my centre, stopping on the most sensitive spot and circling there.

"Oh my god!" I screamed. I couldn't take it. Two movements of his tongue, and I was so close.

"You remember the dream by the fireplace? The one you snuck into?"

He had used his mouth on me in that dream.

"You are so much wetter this time."

I threw the crystals in my hands away. They were full. I grabbed more and leaned my head to the side, practically crying when his tongue moved again, this time stroking in an even rhythm across my clit.

"You taste even better than my visions. So much flavour." He licked up my centre.

Shock rippled through me. I covered my face. I couldn't believe he said that. I couldn't believe how exposed I was.

Brekt *growled*, the sound half beast, and his hands tightened on my waist. "You're blushing."

Then his mouth was on me, and he was *devouring*.

The room pulsed with light as sparks ignited above me. The crystals on the bed filled as my magic poured into them, brought to life by the climax Brekt was pushing me toward. And when his hands came up and squeezed my breasts, and his fingers found my nipples and pinched as he sucked my clit into his mouth, I came.

My legs tightened, trapping his face while I rode it.

His hands didn't stop their painful tightening on my breasts as I was being torn apart, and the air cracked at the same time I called out his name.

When my body turned to liquid, Brekt stood above me and shoved all the crystals from the bed in one savage motion. They chimed as they hit the floor, a shower of stones. He grabbed another bucket, dumping it all around me, then threw it to the other end of the room.

The pants he still wore didn't hide a single inch of his desire. Shirtless, with his hair falling in his face, the wolfish smile that showed fang ... Brekt was sinful. How in the world had I come out of the Endless Forest and landed for him to find me? It seemed impossible that this man was here with me now.

The Aspis was just as much a part of him as my magic was me. Brekt's eyes were yellow, his horns were solid, and his skin crawled with shadows. He smiled down at me as he grabbed his pants and pushed them down.

I couldn't breathe when he sprung loose.

My stomach ached. I was so hungry. I needed him like a starved animal.

"Let go of the crystals, Liv."

"What?"

Brekt crawled over me like he had before, pinning me between his knees, and my attention snagged on how large he was. He lifted my hand, the one with working fingers, pulling my fist up to his face and inspecting it. Blood was dripping from between my knuckles. I hadn't even felt it.

"Let go, love." The softness with which he spoke didn't match the rock-hard beast towering over me, but it matched the concern he pinned me with.

When I didn't let go, he opened my fist himself, finger by finger. Blood spread to his hands as he removed the glowing red crystal from my grip, tossing it to the side. His eyes flicked down to me in hesitation and back to my palm. Then he lifted my hand to his mouth and kissed me there. His tongue wiped the blood from his lips, and he set my hand back down.

"You just tasted my blood."

He lifted a brow when he saw my shock. "I will have all of you." Brekt leaned over, a hand resting next to each side of my head. He caged me in beneath him. His hair fell, framing his face as he leaned closer until his lips were a breath away from mine. "And now I plan to fuck my woman."

I had called him a beast when he returned, claiming me as his. But I had lied. I hadn't been angry at him. I wanted it. I wanted more. I craved to be worshiped, but not by those who wanted my magic. I wanted Brekt to claim me as much as I had claimed him.

"I want to feel my man as he comes inside of me. Promise me," I said.

Brekt ran his fingers down my cheek as his eyes darkened. "I would do anything for you, Liv. *Anything*."

I bit my lip, and I lifted trembling fingers to his face, tracing them along his cheek and down the scar that ran from temple to jaw. Brekt closed his eyes, practically purring from my touch, and it amazed me how he let me be soft—that it was welcomed next to his primal desire. The moment was so gentle, even though my thoughts were anything but.

That's who we were. Two people from worlds apart, woman and man, soft and violent, magic and beast, shadow and light— and we brought it all into bed with us.

And he would deny me nothing.

"I don't want you to be gentle."

His smile spread, and his eyes opened to reveal snake-like slits.

He fisted my hair, making me cry out as his mouth came over mine. His tongue explored again, sucking mine into his mouth.

We were messy. We came together like a storm as I pulled him closer. He moved overtop me so my legs could wrap around his waist, and when his hips lowered, and I felt every hard inch of him, I knew I could die like this. The feeling could kill me. The need for this man could rip my soul from my body, and I wouldn't regret it. Because having all of him was all I wanted in life.

Gods and magic be damned.

The head of Brekt's cock played at my entrance as he kissed me. I had waited so long for this, denied pleasure and happiness for too many years.

I am done fucking waiting.

Reaching down between us, I grabbed him, earning a groan of pleasure that rattled in his chest. I guided him to where I needed him, arching my hips up. He understood what I wanted, and I cried out when, in one thrust, he pushed his cock to the hilt, filling me and driving me back on the bed. I screamed his name.

My life would never be the same after feeling this man fill me. He was big. He was hard. He was warm. He was everything.

Brekt didn't take me gently, didn't waste a moment of our time or wait for me to adjust to his size. He knew I chose pleasure over comfort, chose this war over safety.

Because, how I felt right now, it was dangerous. The two of us could bring the world to heel. We could topple mountains and carve canyons, and I would do it for him.

Brekt moved his hips, thrusting into me, holding me by the shoulders so I wouldn't slide any farther. He fucked me hard and with a steady pace that had my heart racing. He ground me into the mattress, and when his fangs scraped along the skin of my neck, I clawed at his back.

He clawed at the bed. Literally. Next to my ear, I heard the sound of sheets ripping. When I tilted my face to the side, I found long claws where nails should be, making a mess of my mattress, and the crystals pulsed with the same rhythm as Brekt's fucking.

It was so wild and raw.

I dug my nails into his back as I came again. Locking his hips into place, clamping down on him when he was seated all the way inside me, I rode wave after wave of pleasure, grinding myself against him.

Brekt fucked like I was the air he needed to survive.

He pushed himself up so he could look down at me. He watched me as he slowly pulled himself out, still hard and wanting more. He moved so that he was straddling my knees. "As much as I love seeing your face flushed—"

Brekt grabbed me by the hips and flipped me so fast I couldn't react. I was on my stomach, facing the main door, and I wanted to rebel against him. I wanted to look at him! Not the room.

But when he grabbed my hips and pressed into me, I stopped squirming and played along. I pushed myself back against him, and he drove in deep. So unbelievably deep. I thought I saw stars. It could have been my magic.

His arms swallowed me up, with one banded around my waist, another around my neck, as he pinned me to the bed. His mouth came to my neck, and he thrusted once. I swallowed back a cry.

He thrust again, and I moaned.

He thrust again, and my cheek grew wet with tears.

It was euphoric. Being in his arms. Him inside me. No barriers, no secrets and nothing to stop us.

I got an arm loose and pulled more crystals toward me. I was overheating. I was sparking. Igniting. Brekt had to be feeling it, too.

His arm around my waist loosened, and a hand landed near my head. Claws sank into the sheets. Fangs scraped my neck.

He was definitely feeling it, too.

Having the beast at my back should have been unnerving. Having the fangs at my neck should have been terrifying. I had toyed with the idea of meeting death so many times, and now I was playing a new game.

Death and sex were lovers, beast and magic. We weren't ending the world—Brekt and I were making a new one.

With a growl, he lifted himself, grabbed my hips, and pulled me back toward the edge of the bed, leaving me on all fours. He placed one knee beside mine, half standing, while he pounded into me.

The sounds he made would be seared into my mind until my last breath. They were pure, masculine pleasure, and I would worship him to hear those sounds every night. I would worship him like the legend he was.

"Nothing feels like you, Liv. Tight, hot, wet. Mine. I could fuck you like this forever."

I screamed into the mattress as he pounded harder, fucking me like he was desperate.

Suddenly, he stopped.

"Brekt?" I looked over my shoulder to see him hunched over.

Sparks of light ignited next to his face and he winced.

He stepped back, holding a hand up to me so I wouldn't move.

"Are you—"

His lips curled back, his fangs growing. His skin darkened as pieces flaked away. He staggered away from the bed and dropped into a chair. He leaned over, lowering his head into his hands.

I climbed off the bed and his head snapped up. He found another bucket of crystals and dumped them all around the chair.

I looked over my shoulder to find the bed full of glowing crystals. We were on the third bucket. Or was it the fourth?

Brekt was battling the Aspis and losing.

But when I looked back, what I found was a half-beast watching me with pure lust written all over his face. Brekt wasn't lying when he said he liked being the Aspis. He was pumping himself, sitting on the chair, smirking at me. His chest was rising and falling, his scars lit by the tiny bursts of light around the room. "Pain for pleasure, love. Now, get on my lap and ride." He held out a hand to bring me to him.

Crystals dug into my knees as I climbed the chair and settled into his lap. I grabbed his face, kissing him, and found he was hard and ready beneath me. I didn't know what I was doing. I had never been in this position before, had never ridden a man. With only one lover before him, one who hadn't shown me all that sex could be, I wasn't sure I would know how to do this, but my desire for him led the way.

I seated myself on him, and he reached a place inside me he hadn't before. My clit scraped against him as his cock hit that spot deep inside, and the power that surged through me was not from the magic but from pure feminine prowess. It was life-altering.

"You feel so good." I bit his lip, holding his stare. I lifted myself up and dropped back down, earning a pleasured moan from him.

He grabbed my hips, lifting me and holding me above him. When he had me in place, he thrusted upward, setting the pace, and taking control. I held onto him, watching the many faces he made as he took his pleasure. Pain and joy and ecstasy and need. Brekt's pace increased. Faster and faster and so much harder. He took me, hovering above him.

The fire behind him roared and outgrew the fireplace. The sparks crackled in my ear. The crystals around the room glowed and pulsed. Light enveloped the room as I became pure energy.

I came again, head thrown back, riding every inch of Brekt.

With him pumping inside me, I felt every vibration as he shuddered, his hands squeezing harder. He pulled me down on his lap, rolling his hips into me as he came. His hands gripped so hard it hurt, but I loved it. I loved how his body jerked underneath when he lost control and emptied himself inside me. He slowed, but continued moving, pumping several more times until spent.

I fell against him, burying my face in his neck, feeling his quickened pulse.

He pulled me closer, wrapping his arms around me, keeping me seated on his lap, right where I wanted to be.

We were both panting.

The room was much darker now—half the candles were out,

and the fire was nearly embers—the glow of the crystals provided most of the light.

I stayed there, melted against Brekt.

"I don't think I can move." My voice was husky.

Brekt kissed my temple, healing broken pieces of me that had been buried deep, parts that had been alone for too many years. A rush of emotions flooded my heart.

"Then don't, love. This is where you belong."

I was home.

I would never let him go.

CHAPTER
SIXTY-FIVE

Liv

Brekt had taken me again in front of the fireplace. Then again, against the wall. His strength was no surprise, but his creativity was. Eventually, we ran out of crystals and didn't wish to push our luck.

Deliciously sore, my body showed the evidence of our night together. Wrapped in a blanket, I tucked myself into Brekt's side on the balcony of my suite, star gazing.

The crown of Erabas shone in the southern sky. *A way forward.* We had a way forward. Tomorrow, Maev and I would leave for the first shrine of Mayra, one that didn't appear on current maps. I was excited and terrified.

I was terrified because the Guards were meeting us there.

"The whole world thinks we are enemies." My cheek was pressed against his bare chest, my legs wrapped around his. Skin to skin, I let my hand explore every inch of him, learning each muscle of his body.

His deep timbre vibrated through me when he replied. "Don't get caught up in the details."

"Those are big details."

His arm squeezed me tighter to him. "We should be used to big details by now. You're the Ikhor, I'm the Aspis. We can control the details. One is that you are mine, and I don't give a fuck what the world thinks of us."

I buried my smile against his warm skin. "Tonight ..." I wasn't sure how to ask what was on my mind. But I tried anyway. "Was that you or ... was part of it the Aspis?"

Brekt was silent, and I was too afraid to look up at him. Until I realized his chest was vibrating—he was laughing at me.

"Are you worried you were making love with the god's creation?"

"Yes, and I want to know for certain how much of it was real— how much was you."

Brekt kissed the top of my head. "All of it was real, Liv. Every moment. The Aspis may have invaded my body at times, but never my heart or my intentions. Everything I did tonight was out of my own desires. It would have been no different between us if I wasn't possessed. Of this, I am certain."

I thought of all the dirty things he'd said and done. "So you're always that ... creative?" I was happy he couldn't see my face. Heat rushed to my cheeks.

"Was it to your liking?"

I lifted my head, surprised to hear the worry in his tone. "Oh, yes. Completely."

A slow smile spread across his face, stretching the scar running down to his jaw. "Good. Because I have a strong feeling it will always be that way between us. It was in my dreams when I saw you. The Aspis has taken control of my body, but it doesn't stifle my heart. Tonight was just you and I, with our powers reacting to emotions we both felt."

He didn't say what that emotion was, and neither did I.

My head fell to his chest once more, and we were both silent for several long minutes.

His fingers trailed through my hair. "When did it begin to fade?" He spoke in a low voice.

A breeze tickled my feet, and I pulled my blanket closer. "One of the twins first noticed my eyes and hair was beginning to change. Maybe a few weeks after you died."

"Hmmm."

"What?"

"I knew I was the Aspis since I was a young man. I held the beast for many years more than you've been the Ikhor. I'm worried your magic hasn't settled yet."

I sat up. Brekt was laying with his arm behind his head, his legs crossed at the ankles. The light of the moon and stars set the balcony in greys and blues. The soft wind blew his hair into his face, and I pushed it back. "What if I become fully possessed?"

His muscles flexed with the heavy breath he took. "If you truly fade?"

I nodded.

"If you are no longer yourself ... what would you have me do?"

"You know what you *have* to do. The Aspis has to kill me. I don't know what the magic will do to the world when I no longer control it."

Brekt pulled me back down, and I closed my eyes while he held me tight. "I could say I will honour your wishes, but I don't know if I could."

"We don't have to talk about it. Until then, we have a good plan."

"It's a plan based on the hope we might find a better plan in a hidden shrine. If I were running the show, I would not be searching shrines for the answers on how to save you."

I smiled. "What would the Guard of the Aspis do?"

"I'd kill the gods and keep the magic."

"What?" I sat up again, this time crossing my legs and facing him. I wrapped the blanket around my shoulders, keeping a modest portion over his midsection. Not that he would mind lying naked in front of me. I had learned he wasn't ashamed, and he shouldn't be.

"They made this whole mess," he said. "Maybe with their deaths, the magic and the beast would disappear."

"Now, who's planning on a hunch?"

"I'd rather fight my way out of this than explore."

"What would the others do?"

He knew I meant the other Guards. Or, more specifically, a particular Guard. He gave me a knowing look. "Nuo would talk me out of fighting. He was the smart one. We're right to include him in our search of the shrines."

"Well, Maev is pretty smart too. She and her friend were the ones who thought of this plan in the first place." I paused a moment, hesitating. "Does Nuo know you're here?"

"Yes. He was pissy when I came back. And when I left."

"Isn't that a bit childish? By now, he should be over it … somewhat."

"That's Nuo when he's angry. He's not rational, but it's mostly talk. Did he do anything to hurt you?"

"He said things that hurt me." Would Brekt understand words were as hurtful as actions?

"I know that perhaps you don't want to consider his situation, but remember, he was raised without love or protection, and everything he has is thanks to his own hard work. He fought for who he is today. That's why you and him became such close friends so quickly."

"Oh yeah?"

Brekt's hand snuck under the blanket and made a delicious path up and down my leg. "You both fight to have the best of this world when you've been shown the worst. I didn't fight as Nuo did. He was the reason I survived this long. He doesn't handle his deeper emotions well, much like someone else I care for."

I searched the sky for the stars I knew as a child. My chest hurt as a weight pressed down on it, squeezing that box tight and threatening to set the emotions loose. I had grown up under pressure to act one way in front of others, while my mother pushed me to be so much more.

When she left—it was while watching her die that I learned how to hate people. I hated the Keepers so thoroughly that they would never receive pity or understanding from me. I lived for years alone, knowing weeks-long silence, hearing only the wind and the birds until my mind went crazy. Sometimes, the loneliness was so bad my vision blurred. I would scream so loud, and no one ever heard.

Would I have been different if I'd had someone like Brekt?

Those were thoughts I should have written in my journal. I needed to stop dwelling on the past.

"You were also the reason Nuo survived," I said around a lump in my throat. I missed my friend, and it hurt as much as the hate I felt for those who tried to push me down.

"Can you get past your anger with him for the things he said and did? He chased the Ikhor across the world. Not you."

"I've seen hate, in all forms, on the faces of many. Nuo's hate was one I understood—one born out of hurt. That kind of hate can be cured. With time."

"You will find that time. We all will." Brekt stroked the soft skin of my neck, giving me a look that scared me. I didn't want to know what he was thinking.

"You believe that." It wasn't a question.

"I'm making the rules now. My life will be my own. And I'll make the rules for you, too, if you ask it of me."

He was so open compared to before. I had only known him for a short time before his death, and it was not who was lying next to me.

"You were scared to touch me once. Was that because you knew you were the Aspis?"

He let out a long sigh. "I knew what would happen to me. And that I would be leaving you with nothing. I didn't want you to remember me that way—as someone selfish."

"I wouldn't have minded you being selfish. When I thought you were dead, all I could think of was how we didn't have more memories together."

"My death caused you pain. I could have saved you from that. Would it not have been better to have left you in the Last City after we first found you?"

"To become the Ikhor anyways?"

Brekt went silent. The moonlight set a strong contrast to his once-tanned skin and dark hair. It had been too long since he'd walked in the sun. He was looking more like the Night-legs from the cave paintings.

I played with the blanket around my shoulders. "What would you have done once we faced each other in battle? If you hadn't found me then. Would you have killed me?"

"I ... I don't know."

That stopped me. "You would have, wouldn't you." Of course, he would have. He wouldn't have known me. I would have been as bad as the Aethar.

"Liv, you're making hypotheticals."

"No, I'm asking if you regret getting to know me. That is the only reason I am alive, and we are here."

He sat up, grabbing my face between two hands. "I don't regret that I am here."

"I could be the reason you die. One of us may kill the other."

He stroked his thumbs along my wet cheeks. "You forget who you're sitting next to. What I am—a Guard. Have you ever seen me back down or cower in fear? I am not afraid of you, little evil, nor will I give in and take your life. Look at what we accomplished tonight."

The deep tone in his voice reminded me how powerful this man was. And at that moment, when I was afraid, he snapped me out of it with his strength.

He stroked the hair back from my face, leaning in slowly and kissing me softly. His hands found my arms over the blanket, and he held me tight while he ran kisses across my face. "Fate didn't stop me. The magic didn't stop me. The gods can't fucking stop me. I'll end this."

I looked him dead in the eye. "Promise?"

The iridescence flashed as he replied, "I promise you everything. For every life you ever live."

My chest tightened. I wanted to feel brave, to say the things I couldn't outside of Cal's home, but I was still afraid. "How can you feel that way about me? There's so much wrong with me."

He ran a hand down my arm, pushing the blanket from my shoulders and picking up my hand. He brought it to his mouth, kissing it, his gaze heating with my chest exposed to the night air. "Your flaws fit snugly next to mine. I don't know if this pull is ours or the magic, but I know you're mine, Liv. And if the fates haven't said so, then I do."

"Like soul bonded?" I whispered. Like Nuo's dream.

"Perhaps it's a bond we made ourselves." Brekt grabbed my cheek, pinching it. "You're blushing. We don't have enough crystals left."

I pushed him away, sitting back so I could watch him while he teased me. "I don't think I can handle any more of you tonight, anyways."

I was almost completely exposed to him, the blanket pooling around my waist, and Brekt groaned, running his hand along my thigh. He grabbed my leg and bit down on it.

I screeched and swatted the back of his head. "What are you doing?"

"Marking you as mine," he smiled up at me. "If I can't fuck you until you can't walk, this will have to do."

"I thought you were no longer a beast!"

"I am what I am. And I want you to display reminders that I was here." He scanned my body. "Where else should I leave a mark?"

I pushed him away with the little strength I had against him. "My shoulder is already heavily scarred by you. I can't use two fingers." I wiggled the working ones for him. "You don't need to leave marks. Everyone knows I'm yours." I didn't mask my face. I let him see how much I meant what I said, even when there was so much more I wanted to say. "Plus, it's not fair if I can't mark you."

He lifted a brow, turning, showing me his back.

"Oh my god!"

Red marks, evenly spaced, covered Brekt's shoulders. The Aspis, though tattooed down his entire back, didn't hide that I had drawn blood from digging my nails in too hard.

When he faced me, there were no signs of anger. "I like the sting, knowing the cause of it."

"Turn back around. Where did you get that big scar?"

He swung his legs off the lounger, giving me a glorious view of his muscled back. I got to my knees, running a finger down a long white scar. "This can't be the one from Bellum?"

His muscles bunched under my touch. "It is."

"But I put magycris on it. This scar is horrid."

"Magycris can prevent scars if applied well. You're no healer."

My nostrils flared and my anger rose when he glanced over his shoulder, giving me a mocking smile.

"Plus, having pieces of our time marked on my skin doesn't bother me. Aren't you sorry for the one you've put on my face? " He put a finger to the scar over his eye.

"Oh no, not that one." I wrapped my arms around his shoulders, leaning against his warm back. The night was getting cooler, and his body heat was heavenly.

"And why is that? You could have blinded me."

I leaned farther over his shoulder, kissing his cheek. "That one makes you look handsome."

His smile faltered. "Was I not already handsome?"

"Has no one told you that you are?"

"Not in a while. I haven't heard it from you."

"Yes, I have!" I swatted him, pulling away from his back. He turned to face me, and a shiver ran through me when I remembered he was gloriously nude, and I could see every large part of him on display.

"No. You called me devastating. I'm upset if this scar has reduced me to handsome."

"I'll correct myself." I rolled my eyes, giving him a Maev look. "You're *more* devastating."

He seemed satisfied with my answer and laid back, pulling me down with him once more. I put the blanket over us both and went back to running my hands along his body, this time searching for all the little battle scars marring his skin. "What do you think it means that the Aspis tried to absorb my magic? Did you know you were doing it?" I asked.

Brekt thought for a moment. "No. I can't remember it. Except it makes sense. If the Ikhor stole the magic from the gods and the Aspis was created as punishment, the story could be only incorrect by a single detail."

"What do you mean?"

"Perhaps the Aspis was created to get it back, and in the process, kills the host without meaning to. I don't think the Aspis is made of blind, killing rage. It doesn't feel like that. It's more desperate, hungry."

I thought about what he said, but felt no closer to understanding who we were or if our plans were taking us down the right path.

"I need to leave soon." Brekt ran kisses over my face. "Morning approaches. I need to prepare the others and sneak them away from the other Guardians so they can meet you at the shrine."

"Where are they now?"

"Farther north than the shrine. It's hard to say—when the Aspis travels, it sees the world as something smaller than itself."

"What does it feel like? To be the beast."

He rested his head on mine. "A multitude of things. I feel free, powerful, a king of this world. I appreciate and love what exists below me. But then I feel so desperate. I know only hunger and desperation. I feel pulled in one way and then another. And at the end of the strongest desire is you." I kissed his cheek, and Brekt went completely still. "In all my life, I don't think I will ever get used to being shown kindness so easily."

I understood what he meant. "I've never been free to show kindness."

Brekt got up to leave and gathered his clothing from the room before he came back out to the balcony where I waited. I stuffed my sadness away. After tonight, being without him would be even harder.

"Will I see you tomorrow?" I asked.

"I will meet you at the shrine if it's okay. I would like to spend some time with the others." He pulled his pants up around his waist, tucking himself in, snagging my attention.

"Of course. I didn't mean to keep you away."

He leaned over the lounge and kissed my head. "Not even being cursed by the gods kept me from coming back to you. The Guards won't stop me either."

Brekt turned to leave, skin darkening, eyes shifting, smoke rising. He was close to the edge of the balcony.

"Brekt!" I yelled, rising from the lounge.

Be brave. Fake it if you have to.

He turned, and my favourite sight hit me—iridescence shining in the dark. He was waiting.

"I—" I didn't know how to say it. After all this time, stepping out of my comfort zone remained difficult despite having been given so much power.

Brekt folded his arms, looking smug as if he knew.

I was trapped at the moment now, uncertainty bleeding into my self-doubt.

"I've got all the time in the world, Liv. I'll wait." The wind blew his hair around.

God, he was sexy.

"Bastard," I muttered, hugging the blanket around my shoulders and studying my bare toes.

"You can do it," he encouraged, waiting.

My anger simmered, warming my face. Had he known I wanted to tell him back at Cal's?

"Never mind." I returned to my room, wrapping the blanket

under my arms. Glowing crystals covered the room, and my bed was in shambles, ripped to shreds. There was nowhere I could sit and feel embarrassed.

"Still waiting." His deep voice carried in through the doors—he was a silhouette against the moon and early morning light.

I grabbed a pillow and threw it at him, hitting his head. "I love you! Idiot."

It was so much louder inside the room, bouncing off the tall ceilings. I finally got the words out, and I yelled it at him. I groaned—my emotions ruined everything.

Brekt stepped in between the doors, the crystals setting him aglow. "That's my girl. The fire in your veins was never from the Ikhor, love."

The pillow landed at my feet when he tossed it back. He looked at me in a way he'd never looked at me before. It was vulnerable, scared, and so full of emotion.

In the softest I had ever heard him speak, he replied, "I love you too, Olivia." He walked backwards, fading from the glow. "Since the first time I dreamt of you."

When I ran out to the balcony, all that remained of the Aspis was smoke soaring directly upward. I turned my smiling, tear-streaked face to the sky.

I had never been so happy.

SIXTY-SIX

Liv

Even with the relief of Brekt's return, the box in my chest grows heavier. How much happiness will it take to undo years of loneliness? I need to get rid of this box. I need to feel and live and not fight my past. I haven't had companionship since my mother died, but I have it now. I don't have to piece myself back together alone.

"What are you wearing?"

Maev wore a tight leather outfit that hugged her slim figure beautifully. It was made of varying shades of navy blue and grey. There were pockets and straps everywhere. She had goggles on her head and all sorts of gadgets attached to her hip.

"You look like a Guardian," I admired.

Maev tore through my room, ready to leave. "I may have taken some inspiration from the Guards. Their clothing was practical for travelling." She spun in a circle, showing me where she kept extra crystals, her prototype tracker and other gadgets we may need in our search for the shrines.

We were leaving, headed for a new adventure, and all I could think about was the dirty things Brekt had done and said to me last night.

Maev wore a belt around her waist with pockets attached to it. "You look like you copied Nuo," I noted.

"Yeah, well, he is the mapper, right? I am taking on that role for our team."

"The Guard of the Ikhor. I was right when I teased you about it the first time."

Maev busied herself with her bags, then stopped, glancing around the room, taking in the mess and the crystals full of magic.

I cut her off before she said anything. "What happened with your date last night?"

Her face fell. "It was ... not what I hoped. We will see what happens when I come back. Hanold and I are going out again. Livy, did you fill all these crystals?" Maev was standing over a bucket that had toppled over.

Actually, no bucket was left standing. It would require some cleaning to collect every crystal.

"Interesting diversion," I muttered, wondering what happened on her date.

I joined Maev in packing crystals for our trip. We filled every pocket in our bags that we could.

"I don't need to ask what happened here." She winked at me, nodding toward my shredded sheets.

When we had everything we needed, Maev passed me an outfit similar to hers. I dressed in soft leather pants and a tight fabric top secured with a leather vest. I pulled the strings at the sides, glancing down as the vest shoved everything up and together.

"It's a little revealing, Maev," I said, my face heating.

"If the Aspis is following us, you'll be thanking me later." She finished packing her bags and rushed us out the door. She planned to leave a few crystals for her professor before we departed Avenmae for the shrine.

Several hours later, and after a quick lunch aboard a new airship, we were away from Avenmae and approaching the western coast of Rydavas. The airship Maev had arranged for us was unlike the others I had seen before. It wasn't as large as Falizha's, but it was similarly built for a small crew to live comfortably during long-distance flights.

"You already updated this ship's maps?" I inspected the map displayed on a table in the navigation room.

The map hovered, a series of glowing lines and names projected with magic. If you spun the tabletop, the map spun with it. It wasn't easy to understand how it worked because I couldn't make sense of most of the terms she used.

Maev had brought several of her inventions, powered by crystals, including updating the ship's AO tech. She'd done other masterful things I couldn't understand, so I just nodded as she explained.

"As you know, I've been preparing for this trip, knowing what it was like on our last. We weren't ready for everything we faced before. Now I know to be ready for anything to go wrong at any time."

"That's reassuring," I muttered.

"That's using your head," she replied.

Maev was bouncing in the front seat, steering us toward the shrine. We were to meet the Guards there.

"If Ollo were piloting, I could be working on other updates and unfinished projects while we travel."

"Maybe the Guards will know more once we meet them," I said as the blue sky soared past the front window.

I stayed near the front, enjoying the view. Rydavas was much nicer to see from the sky when the magic wasn't consuming me. "Too bad Cal wouldn't come. He would have been useful."

"We will have fun this time," Maev said, spinning to face me. "We will make sure of it."

MAYRA'S SHRINE was visible from the airship even before we began our descent. I could imagine it once rising high in the sky with spiralling towers made of shining white. Those towers had now crumbled, a scattered heap of stones and shells littering the forest floor. The shrine's pearlescent glow had faded to dark blue near the base, resembling an ocean wave. Only a few large sheets of rippled glass remained intact in several windows to the left of the shrine. The other half was in ruins, pieces of the roof gone. It looked like it could crumble at any moment. Overgrowth consumed the area where gardens may have once been, and past the shrine, the forest gave way to rocky shores where the sea divided Veydes and Rydavas.

Maev steered us away from the shrine to find a place to land. It would be a long walk through the forest to get back to it.

I leaned on her chair at the narrow front of the airship. "You think the Guards are here already?"

"The Guardian's ship that was reported to the aerial units was a day's ride away. If they came on foot, they may not arrive until tomorrow." Maev performed a series of actions to land the ship smoothly.

I paid attention as best as I could in case I needed the information in the future. "The Guards would find a way to be here. They wouldn't waste time walking," I said.

Maev had our bags ready to go, having packed our things efficiently, and we headed west toward the shrine, listening for any signs we may not be alone. The forest was dense and full of life. Birds chirped, and the wind hummed through the trees.

"How can they not have this shrine on a map? It's obviously here. It's huge." I touched the trees as I passed, the bark smooth under my fingers.

Maev's hair was down today—she had braided a single strand to the side of her temple to keep the hair falling in her face. "It could be as simple as it's no longer in use, and mappers decided not to include it for travellers. It could be that someone doesn't want us snooping in there. There are no villages around here and no major roads, so it's not like many people would see it unless they were passing by sea."

I twirled around a tree. "There's the shrine, now." A blue reflection stole my breath away. "And if you wouldn't believe it, the Guards are already here."

Their voices carried through the forest. They were arguing as we inched closer.

"Nuo, you got branches caught in my hair," Kazhi complained.

"They've been there for hours." Nuo's reply was so casual it surprised me. I hadn't heard him talk like that in a very long time, like nothing was bothering him. Like normal.

Maev pulled on my arm before I could break out into a run. "I know you feel comfortable meeting them. But remember, when you walk us out there, I'm facing off with members of the most feared group of warriors our people have ever heard of. I have no defences against them nor guarantees they are on my side."

"Brekt won't allow anything to happen to you."

I was eager to get moving. Although it had only been several hours, I was excited to see him. We walked carefully out of the forest, trying not to make too much noise in case it was a trap. Maev's nerves were making me doubt my judgement.

Tall grass filled the clearing in front of the shrine, and from down below, the decaying structure seemed impossibly tall. The blue stones and shells sparkled in the afternoon sun.

The Guards, hidden up to their waist in the grass, went silent when Maev stepped on a twig and snapped it. Four apprehensive glares swivelled in our direction.

Brekt was first to relax, and my heart pounded in my chest. The shrine behind him disappeared as visions of what we'd done, the things he'd said, quickened my breath. If it weren't for the other wary glances my way, I would have run into his arms.

Our eyes locked. I tracked every small movement his body made.

"I love you too, Olivia. Since the first time I dreamt of you." I had replayed those words over and again before I fell asleep last night.

I had once envied the woman in Brekt's dreams—the version of me he saw before we met. But now I was thankful and wondered just how strongly he felt when we first travelled together.

Brekt stood in the shadows of the trees above, a breeze playing at the pieces of hair falling in his face. I melted at the sight of him, but was soon distracted by the others.

The other Guards' hands inched closer to their belts. They were all in black, loaded with weapons as if ready for battle. Bastane didn't have his typical fur-lined cloak. Instead, he had on a tight top, similar to Brekt's, with his bow wrapped around the front of his body. Kazhi had her high boots and leather skirt, with knives strapped in every possible location. Brekt had his sword at his side and a heated look on his face as he watched me approach. I suppose he'd never seen me wearing tight leather. Not that he had to use his imagination to know what was underneath.

Nuo ... I didn't notice what he wore because I was caught in how he stared at us. He was emotionless. His perfect mask was back on, hiding what he really felt.

I swallowed my fear. Maev was right. These were the fiercest warriors from across the sea, maybe in the entire world, and the two of us could barely fight.

Brekt caught my faltering step when Nuo shifted his weight, and he smacked Nuo in the gut with the back of his hand. "Stop it, dickhead."

Nuo lifted his palms skyward. "I'm doing nothing. I'm being civil, as you instructed."

"You know what you're doing. Say something. Stop staring like that."

Maev and I halted several feet away, and Bastane's attention roamed over her, nodding with a small smile.

Kazhi gazed into the distance, clearly not interested in the reunion, and Brekt took a long, tired breath but waited for Nuo to step up and be the first to address me.

"You're looking worse, Bones," Kazhi said as I tucked a near-white strand of hair behind my ear, suddenly self-conscious.

"The magic is getting stronger, harder to hold within."

Bastane was eyeing me, too, taking in all the changes since he last saw me. "Do you feel its presence? The Ikhor?"

I shook my head. "I am the Ikhor—the magic is in me, not some evil being. I just ... it's difficult to do, but I'm learning. I've learned to use my emotions to guide it."

Bastane gave me a slow, contemplative nod. "If you are having trouble with control, those exercises I taught you are a practical method of calming the mind. Could help you."

"Have you heard anything new on your travels, Bones?" Kazhi asked.

"Nothing that you'd find useful. The Elders in Avenmae gave no indication they were aware of the Council's plans."

Maev fidgeted next to me.

Kazhi didn't reply, so I cleared my throat. "Have you heard any more on Ollo? Maev's brother."

An air of discomfort settled over the Guards, while Kazhi shook her head. "I have been listening when I can. But I don't know anymore. My belief is that, if he lives, he is being held hostage by Aeden Ravin. Falizha won't be given authority over a prisoner like that."

"Where?" Maev stepped forward, her voice cracking. "Where do I have to go to find him?"

Kazhi tilted her head to the side, an animalistic movement that sent a shiver through me. "You will do no such thing. You would have your brother killed before you reached him. I plan to follow Aeden when he leaves Aethar lands. I will search for your brother then. In return, you two continue to do as you promised here."

"Am I the only one aware of what you asked me?" I wondered if she'd told the truth to the others. She wanted us to gather information to help the rebellion. But the Elders didn't seem to be involved in the disappearing of legacies or burning lands like the Council. So, what could I do in Rydavas when the biggest enemy was sitting in the Guardian City?

"The boys are aware that I ferry away unwanted citizens," Kazhi said. "And who I am working with. Who you are working with now, too."

"We are done with the Council. We only keep our title of Guard for the good it could do the people," Bastane added.

"Then it sounds like we are all on the same side." I gave a pointed look to Maev, so she understood, too—we were working together.

"So what are we searching for here?" Brekt nodded to the shrine behind him.

"The Elders and aerial units have been made aware of a Guardian airship on our western shores," Maev said, ignoring Brekt's question. "What is the purpose of such a large presence? If you are here, where are the others?"

"Are the people here in danger?" I asked.

"Falizha brought a large crew," Kazhi said. "With weapons for every Guardian. The Council must be aware of the citizens living here—otherwise, there would be no mission to a land void of life. We think it's another attack. But we have been shut out. No one speaks to us, even those we have once considered friends. We were told late last night that scouts are being sent out, and we will have new orders in two days' time."

Maev tensed. "I will need to make sure our units are close to the villages."

"You will outnumber her crew," Bastane said. "If the Council is aware of your people, they would know of your aerial units, as you call them. Which leads me to believe they have other plans."

I kept my attention on Brekt while they talked. He was growing more sour as time went on. "Enough," he finally said. "We can consider their motives all afternoon and waste the time we don't have before they question our absence. We came to help. What do you need of us."

"Are you really here to help Liv?" Maev asked, cutting Brekt off again.

"What do you mean?" Brekt's voice lowered.

"I am concerned for Liv's well-being. The Guards and the Aspis have chased her across the world. I want to know my friend is not entering that shrine to find danger."

Nuo grabbed Brekt by the shoulder, stepping forward, but I spoke to Maev before he could snap at her. "I appreciate your concern, Maev. They are here to help."

"I'm only thinking of you," she whispered. "They're standing before us armed to the teeth, staring you down like you're their enemy and expect you to march into the ruins alongside them. I don't like it."

I twirled my friendship necklace between two fingers, a warm feeling in my chest. "Thank you for being here with me today. I appreciate your concern. But the Shadow Guard won't let any harm come to me."

"You're godsdamned right I won't," Brekt growled.

"And what about the Interrogator?" Maev glowered at Nuo. "What do you have to say?"

"I have nothing to say." Nuo looked me straight in the eye. It was a dare.

I clenched my fists at my side. "I don't need to hear anything, anyways." I didn't care that I sounded miserable. *He* was the friend who was supposed to worry about my safety, and it pissed me off that I still felt that way. "Not from him," I lied.

Brekt faced the sky, already done with us.

Nuo studied the trees, giving me his profile. "And you won't hear anything from me because I have nothing to say."

I crossed my arms. "You mentioned. Don't need to repeat it."

Five seconds was all he lasted before whipping his attention back toward me. "And why should I apologize? You can apologize to me."

"Excuse me? I didn't ask for your apology." I took a step forward, remembering to keep my anger in check.

"You heard me." He pointed at me. "You're the one who fucked up."

"Haven't heard this argument before," Bastane muttered.

I shoved my hands in my pockets, where I had stuffed the crystals. I held onto one, easing the stress of magic. "How did I fuck up? I told you—I had no idea what was happening."

"You knew damn well what was happening when you turned. Brekt was dying. You took the first chance you could and ran away with the enemy."

"You were looking at me like I was the enemy. What was I supposed to do? Let you take me back to the Council?"

"I just expected you not to be a coward," he spat.

It was too close to home, just like what the Eagle said.

"Liv is not a coward," Maev interrupted.

I took the crystal from my pocket and chucked it at Nuo.

It landed with a thud in the middle of his forehead, and he hissed, clapping a hand to his head where it drew blood. "What the fuck was that."

"A crystal. Don't talk to me like that. And never call me a coward."

Kazhi elbowed Brekt. "Are you going to step in here?"

He shook his head. "She can manage him."

Nuo pulled his hand away, seeing red on his palm. "I'll say what I want, Ikhor."

My blood ran hot. "Shut up, you stupid idiot."

He gave me a mocking smile. "Stupid and idiot are the same things."

One of his dimples appeared, and I hated that the first time I got to see it after all these months was when he was mocking me.

Kazhi came to my side and grabbed a crystal from my pocket. She lifted it and threw. It landed right next to where mine hit.

"Owww-chuh. What the fuck, Kaz." Nuo's face fell, giving Kazhi a dumb look.

"You're acting like children," she said to both of us. "I'll throw a knife next."

Maev was to the right of me, just a few feet from where Bastane stood, and she peeked over at him. "Were they always like this?"

Bastane leaned down. "Welcome to the family reunion. We fight with each other more than with the enemy."

"Ollo and I didn't even fight this much."

Bastane held out a hand to lead Maev away. "I'm very sorry about your brother. We promise to do everything we can to find him."

They walked toward the shrine, and Kazhi took off, too, following Maev and Bastane, joining their conversation when it turned to the maps.

Brekt, Nuo and I were left staring.

Nuo's nostrils flared. "I don't need this shit right now," he said before turning and walking away.

Brekt whistled. "That went much better than I thought it would. Only a drop of blood."

CHAPTER

SIXTY-SEVEN

Liv

Brekt waited for me to do something. His casual stance told me he knew what I wanted, so instead of arguing with him, I ran after Nuo.

He was already reaching the bottom of the stairs leading up to the shrine, not waiting for anyone to enter. I caught up to him and pulled on his arm, forcing him to look at me.

His mask was in place, hiding his true feelings.

"Please," I said. "Just wait."

"What more is there to say? We clearly aren't interested in talking to each other."

The sea breeze blew his long hair across his face, and I caught sight of his gills before his hair fell back into place. "You know, you were the most honest with me."

Nuo reluctantly turned back, giving me a weary expression. "What do you mean?"

"You were keeping Brekt's secrets, but it was him that lied. Kazhi hid her identity from everyone, and Bastane betrayed me. But you, you never lied to me."

Nuo waited, and I latched onto the moment. "The only time you've hurt me was when you were angry."

"Hurt you?"

I raised my hands. "What you said hurt. Badly. You wouldn't have been able to protect me from the Aspis or the Council. I was scared of your anger, and I knew the twins would protect the Ikhor. I wanted to live."

A muscle in his jaw twitched. "Well, you lived."

"I did. And you've learned that it's still me in here."

Nuo was taking in my hair, my eyes, and the slight glow to my skin. His nostrils flared. "You look like the thing that has caused every problem in this world. The thing that carved out my future and took my chances at a normal, happy life. The thing next to the Aspis in every depiction of the final battle."

"Well, I don't want to look like this. Do you only make judgments with what you see? When we first met, you knew I wasn't a legacy like you, yet even with the suspicion I might be an Aethar, you became my friend."

Nuo leaned closer. "I did that for Brekt because he recognized you."

"So all of our talks, the nicknames, the time we drank on the deck of the airship, that was all for Brekt's sake?"

It took several long seconds before he said, "No."

"See? We were both handed this shitty situation. I was leaving the twins in Danuli to come find you when we ran into each other by the river."

Surprise flashed across his face. "So why did you run."

"Because you began to chase me."

Several emotions flashed across his face, each time hidden behind the mask, before shaking his head. He reached behind him, and for a moment, I thought he would pull out one of his sharp knives. Instead, he held something clear and shiny, waiting for me to grab it.

My heart skipped. He held my crystal brush I had left in the Guardian City. It was the brush found amongst the Aethar belongings while Nuo sat at my side—when our friendship blossomed.

"You brought it for me?" My voice broke over an emotion too strong to put away.

"Don't ask me why."

My vision blurred as I took my brush, nodding because I was too choked up to speak.

He'd kept it. He'd thought of me. He didn't hate me.

I moved to grab my bag, but before I could, Nuo grabbed my arm. "This doesn't change things between us."

I nodded, knowing that wasn't true, and when I tried to grab my pack again, he stopped me. "Don't do anything stupid from now on, okay? If you're searching the continents for shrines, watch your back. Don't trust the Aethar."

I pretended to be annoyed but couldn't help smiling. For the third time, as I tried to put my brush away, he stopped me. "I can't protect you forever. I told him I would, but you're on your own if you keep following the blue one."

"I'm not on my own. She's my friend, too."

Nuo's face fell. "Really? I'll ignore her lack of weapons for argument's sake. Just … watch your own back."

I nodded and was grabbed *again*. "I'm sorry for what I said when he died. This doesn't mean I forgive you for ditching me at the first sign of trouble."

"Trouble? I became the fucking Ikhor, Nuo. That's a little bigger than trouble."

He waved his hand. "Ya, ya. Just, I'm sorry for what I said about killing you and everything. I'm a Guard," he shrugged. "It's what I do."

My mouth popped open. Was he—"That's an apology."

He clapped my shoulder. "A good one, I thought. Now, your turn."

"That's the best you'll get from him," grumbled Brekt, coming to stand next to me. He eyed the brush in my hands.

I smiled at Nuo, showing my teeth. "Then I'm sorry I said you looked weak and haggard when we were in Danuli."

Nuo's back went straight. "And I'm sorry I said you're an evil, lying betrayer with creepy eyes."

"You didn't say that."

"I just did." He let go of the humour, turning serious. "Please, BB. Don't die. Not before we can fight this one out."

"Wait!" I said, reaching into my bag and pulling out a bracelet. I shoved it toward him.

"What is this?" He held it up, eyeing the small shells trapped in blue string.

"It's a friendship bracelet. I have a matching one. See?" I held up my wrist, where a blue and black string bracelet sat next to the crystals the Oracle gave me. "I thought it looked like the right kind for a Sea-leg."

Nuo kept it suspended in the air, his face twisting in confusion. "Bracelets are for women."

Brekt smacked him in the back of the head, and Nuo quickly stuffed the bracelet in his pocket, muttering a thank you. He walked away stiffly, removing the vines from the massive door at the entrance to the shrine, and disappeared inside.

"I got you one, too." I dropped the black one in Brekt's hand and raced up the stairs so that I wouldn't feel embarrassed. Yet, my heart was soaring because it felt like I was breaking down a wall with Nuo.

Brekt caught up to me atop the stairs and grabbed my wrist, dragging me in for a kiss. The memory of our night together came rushing back, and I wanted him all over again. He pulled away, cupping my cheek. "You care for my brother. He deserves the best in the world. I could love you just for being his friend."

Love. And he did love me. He told me last night.

"Don't get ahead of yourself." I patted his chest.

"You are a good person, Liv. You have a good heart."

I bit back my denial. "Can you tell that to the rest of the world?"

Brekt barked a laugh. "They wouldn't believe me. When you eventually show that temper, they'd call me a liar." I swatted him, and he caught my hand, kissing it. He tapped the bottom of my chin with a finger. "Keep your spirits up. You don't need approval from others to be good. You don't need them to know it, to see it. You just are."

His words wrapped a warm blanket around the box inside my chest.

I followed him through the crumbling entrance to the shrine. Light cascaded off every surface, reflecting an aqua blue—we were entering a new world. I lifted a hand and watched the eerie glow over my skin, it was like I was floating underwater. Above us, light poured through the rippled glass, making the floor resemble the bottom of a lake.

Maev stayed close as the Guards roamed ahead, moving debris so we had a path toward the central dais near the back. The right side of the shrine had no roof. Sunlight poured over the dirty walls and onto a second-story balcony that ran along both sides of the shrine, stairs leading up to it near the dais.

The room reminded me of the hall where I had met the Elders.

"It's beautiful in here." Maev pointed to the back wall lined with several doors. "Prayer chambers, I'm guessing."

Brekt stopped in the middle of the temple, where the sunlight shone down, turning his skin golden. When Nuo stepped to his side, the rippled light bathed him, turning his skin a pale blue from the glass above. Brekt regarded Nuo with concern, but I couldn't see what set him off when I searched the shrine.

"We should pray in the back chambers," Maev said loud enough for the others to hear. "To see if we can call Mayra."

"Nuo," I asked when we joined him in the middle of the temple. "I think the goddess would answer to you before anyone here. Do you mind trying?"

"I'm here, aren't I?" Nuo held up his hands before Brekt threw a fist at his gut. "Hey, I'm being nice."

Brekt's jaw clenched. "You know godsdamned well you are not. She's being nice. You're holding grudges."

Nuo dropped his hands to his side. "The fact that I am not holding my blade while in the same room with the Ikhor and an Aethar means I am being nice."

Maev slid me a weary look.

"Fine," Nuo admitted. "I'm not. But I am being cooperative. I'll pray. The goddess isn't likely to answer to the many Day-legs we're dragging around these days."

"We can split up." Brekt pointed to the four doors lining the back wall. "Liv and I can start on the left, looking for scrolls or anything of use left in the shrine."

Nuo studied the lines of Maev's leather clothing, narrowing his eyes at the pockets and her contraptions. His lip curled as if considering having to search the shrine alongside an Aethar was the worst thing ever to happen to him.

Maev removed her pack and squatted down next to it on the ground. Everyone stopped to watch her as she pulled out a bundle of rolled-up maps and stood. Her eyes darted from me to Nuo, and when she bit her lip, I knew what she had in her hand.

I held my breath—this interaction could decide the fate of the two nations. Nuo, who hated the Aethar more than most, and the Mechanist, who was no warrior but perhaps one of the brightest minds of her generation.

Nuo's mask slipped as his attention went from Maev to the maps in her hand.

She didn't move any closer. "The map of the old shrines— yours to keep—and the map I had taken from the Governor's daughter's ship. Your map."

Nuo opened his mouth, but Maev cut him off. "I will trade them for my device. I know you have it."

Nuo didn't blink. He reached into his vest, pulled it out, and inspected it. "I was surprised an Aethar had such a thing. Who did you steal it from?"

Maev went scarlet. "I made it myself. I am a Mechanist,

capable of much more than you can imagine. I don't steal ideas." Maev pointed the maps at Nuo. "Just give it back. It's not like you would know how to use the device anyway. The controls are too advanced for a brute like yourself."

Nuo's swagger was back, he gave Maev a charming smile. "You made this, Blue?" He tsked, waving the device in the air. "I can't say I believe it. I took it apart. I know how it works. "

Maev ran up to him, yanking it from his grasp to inspect it. When she realized she stood within reach of the Interrogator, she shoved the maps against his chest and put several paces between them.

Nuo didn't inspect the maps. Instead, he rested them on his shoulder, cocking a hip to the side. "You've wired it to detect the changing frequencies of the crystals. They react to power and vibrate on a level invisible to the naked eye. Your device picks up on the frequencies, and the map programmed in the device points in the direction of the strongest source of magic it detects."

Maev's mouth was hanging by the time Nuo finished.

When he knew he'd impressed her, his eyes crinkled, his stance full of ego. "I'm not just a handsome face, Blue."

I elbowed Maev. "I told you he was clever." But I dropped my smile when I noticed Nuo stiffen.

Maev put her device away. "How did you figure all that out? You aren't a Mechanist."

"I am many things, Aethar. I would say stick around and find out, but I don't want you to stick around."

Bastane wiped a hand down his face. "I apologize," he said to Maev. "He is usually not this rude."

"Yeah, he is," Kazhi shouted from across the room, where she was moving debris away from doorways. "No matter how hard I've tried to beat it out of him."

Nuo scoffed and walked away.

Bastane gave Maev a quick smile. "Nuo isn't the man the Aethar believe. You have seen this side of him only because of the history between him and Bones."

Bas nodded to Maev before following Kazhi through a prayer door on the right, bathed in sunlight.

"I will pray on my own," Nuo said over his shoulder, walking toward the back right of the shrine, aiming for the door next to where Bastane and Kazhi disappeared.

"I am going with Liv," Brekt said to Nuo, who lifted a hand in a dismissive wave.

Maev tugged on my arm, shaking her head, and I realized she was pleading not to be left alone without me.

"Go with Nuo," I said to Brekt, walking up to him so my voice didn't bounce around the room so loudly.

Brekt swallowed. "Perhaps I will. The blue lights in here are making me nervous."

I searched his face, missing his meaning.

"My dreams." He nodded toward Nuo, and then I remembered Brekt had dreamt of Nuo's death—in those dreams, he was blue and cold. I had seen him that way, too, when I was in the dream place.

I pushed Brekt. "Go. I'll take Maev with me to the other chamber. Keep her safe."

"And you? The gods may not be happy to see the Ikhor."

The feeling was mutual. "I can keep myself safe. Who knows, I may have more magic than them these days." I raised my voice as Nuo approached the back doors. "Plus, you need to keep Nuo safe."

He whipped his head around so fast I thought he might fall over. "I don't need Beastboy to babysit me."

Brekt crossed his arms, but this time, the tired look was directed at me.

"Look for paintings on the walls," Maev said, pulling my arm and leading me toward a chamber at the back of the shrine.

SIXTY-EIGHT

Liv

The prayer chamber resembled an underwater grotto—a large, circular room with thin beams of light filtering through horizontal cracks in the ceiling. The air was stuffy, and the back half of the room sunk into a low pit in the shape of a crescent moon. Moss-covered rocks filled the pit.

Maev crept close to the edge of the platform, looking down into the moon-shaped recess. "I bet this used to be a pool of water. The sea must have once touched the back of the shrine, and the Sea-legs could pray above or below."

I bent over the edge, eyeing the rocks. "You're always so clever. Why am I even here?"

"Haven't figured that out yet," she teased, turning back to the rest of the chamber. "There's no paintings on the walls like I hoped."

I ran my hands along the rough stone of the circular walls. "There could have been paintings here once. This shrine is ancient." I remembered all the places I had seen the painting of the two legends. "The image of the Aspis and the glowing Ikhor is depicted all over Veydes, but the painting in the Avenmae Palace was different. Have you seen the legends depicted in any other way?"

"I haven't, but I have never explored caves or shrines before. The texts I'm usually interested in are not about the legends, but rather alchemy."

Our voices echoed in the large chamber. The dark lighting comforted me, and I wondered about the Sea-legs coming here to pray to their goddess. How many centuries had this shrine stood? And when did it crumble?

"Not much to look at in here." Maev took out a notebook and scribbled in it. "I'll go to the next one and check that it's the same."

"You're okay going out there on your own?"

Maev put her notebook away. "The Interrogator is being babysat. I'm far less nervous. Plus,"—she played with the end of her braid—"I think Bastane would step in if anything were to happen."

She wasn't wrong. "What about the guy back home? You didn't tell me about your date—you only mentioned you have another one planned."

Maev's hands dropped to her sides, and her cheeks went scarlet. "I don't know. It was amazing at first, and then ... I don't know how to say it."

"Did something happen?" I stepped toward her.

"Nothing I didn't want to have happen," she hesitated, then added, "Only, it was disappointing when it did. And it was over really fast."

"Oh." Maev's discomfort had me unsure of what I could ask.

"It mostly ... um ... it wasn't as good as I thought it would be. That's all." She chewed the inside of her cheek, turning an even darker shade.

Ah. Now I felt awkward. "It's not your fault. You just had bad luck and found a partner that didn't know what he was doing."

"It seemed like he knew what he was doing. Then, afterward, I walked home alone, and I couldn't help feeling disappointed."

"I don't think you should go out with him again," I said.

Maev threw her hair over her shoulder, standing straight. "I told him I would when I got back. It will be better the second time."

"Maybe a certain Guard will keep your mind occupied until then."

Maev opened her mouth to say something and stopped. She looked past me and paled.

"What?" I looked over my shoulder, finding what had distracted her.

A light so bright it made my eyes water lit the prayer room, shining through the cracks above, blinding us in sharp beams of sunlight. More filtered in until it wasn't just coming in through the cracks, but through the *wall*. It seeped through the stone, collecting in a ball before us.

My feet froze in place as a glowing orb floated into the cavernous room, bathing me in golden light. The hair on my arm lifted as the buzzing of magic travelled through me. It was so familiar, had haunted me since I left the Endless Forest.

The light descended on us, tinkling like a bell.

"The talking Light," I whispered. This was the same thing that had found me by the river back home.

How? How had it found me here?

"What?" Maev clapped her hands over her ears.

The light, the similar sensation, and that high-pitched ringing in my ear—the same magical, talking Light that stole me from my homelands and told me to "Wake the Aspis".

"Go, Maev," I shouted, pushing her toward the door. "It's the Light that stole me from my lands and brought me here."

"No, Liv, what if it takes you back?" Her eyes went round with panic.

"Then I won't let it take you too. Warn the others. The Guards can help me."

She nodded, running from the room and slamming the door closed.

Was I wrong before, thinking the Light that found me was the magic of the Ikhor? What was going on?

A chilling cold swept through the room as every part of my soul screamed to run and hide, recognizing that humming sound. I had heard the same sound in the Guardian City.

It wasn't the talking Light.

It belonged to the golden god, Rem.

SIXTY-NINE

Nuo

The prayer chamber revealed nothing. "It's not going to work. I need to be underwater—every Sea-leg knows that."

"Try harder," Brekt groaned. "I've got a bad feeling about this place."

"No kidding. We flew to Aethar lands in Falizha's ship. There's a female Aethar out there who we are helping alongside the Ikhor."

"It's something else."

Brekt brought up the recurring dream he'd had of me. I wouldn't admit to him I was nervous, too. No one wanted to face death, but here? With the blue one being the most significant threat? Doubtful. "I will avoid those blue rippled lights for the rest of the search. Today will not be the day that I die. That would be too pathetic for someone as skilled as me."

"This isn't the time to joke," Brekt grumbled. He paced the room, scratching at his head. "Falizha brought nearly a hundred Guardians to the Aethar lands."

I clenched my teeth to prevent myself from cursing. How was I supposed to pray when Brekt was feeling chatty? "The Ravins have explained very little," I said. "Aeden's not open with his sister. Shocking, who would be? I can't stop thinking about Aeden possibly being connected to the Lost Lands. There was a piece of Falizha's journal I wrote down back when we first boarded her ship with Liv. Once I translated it, I thought it was useless. But now that I'm thinking about it ... fuck, I almost forgot!"

"What?" Brekt asked, pacing.

"The last line from the section I copied said, 'All the while, Aeden has not returned from the island, and I have not been told what he's doing there.' " I waited for Brekt to understand, and when he did, he turned my way. "See? I was right. Aeden is connected to the Lost Lands. They're experimenting up there with more than these Deathmakers."

Brekt nodded. "You could be right, but we may be missing something. What other experiments do you think they are doing?"

"Bastane told us of the liquid they used on Liv to knock her out cold when Falizha kidnapped her and took her to the burning field." I crossed my arms as I watched Brekt continue to walk in circles.

"So we know they are messing around with the magic in the crystals. On top of that, how did they produce so many Deathmakers without it being known? Why did they bring so many Guardians with them?"

"My guess? To end the Guards. They want an excuse to execute us."

Brekt stopped, gaping at me. "Then why the ship full of Guardians?"

"They need witnesses to confirm the stories. Or perhaps they plan to attack the big city the blue ones are from and take us out in the process."

Brekt chewed on that while I went back to praying, but it wasn't long before he broke my concentration again. "That Aethar is an interesting one," he said. "She knows her stuff. She'll be a big help to Liv."

I forgoed trying to call for Mayra, she wasn't coming. I eyed him, noticing no traces of the yellow eyes or swirling darkness under his skin, but something was off. "You are more worried than usual. Even when you used to go dark, it was never like this. You're not hiding it very well."

Brekt cursed, and it set my nerves alight. I'd seen him worry, but this was something more … he was scared.

"I used to go dark, fearing what I would become," he said. "Now I've become it and have learned there are worse things to fear."

"Listen, man," I began, but was cut off by loud shouts outside the room.

A loud bang rang out, accompanied by screams. We grabbed our weapons and rushed to the door. Maybe Brekt sensed more than he let on.

Before he threw open the door, I shoved him back. "If you want to remain unseen, then stay here."

I followed the yelling back into the main chamber and skidded to a halt, unable to understand what I was seeing.

SEVENTY

Liv

"Eyes down, Olivia. Don't react, Olivia. Blend in, Olivia." These were the lessons passed on from my sister Rebeka. For all her betrayals, her advice of blending in had kept me alive in the Endless Forest. Too bad I no longer had that option.

I backed away as the glowing orb floated toward the edge of the platform.

He was here.

Had it been Rem who had done this? Put the magic of the Ikhor inside me, telling me to wake the Aspis and giving me a death sentence?

"Ikhor," Rem commanded. The glowing light stretched and grew, forming into a tall golden figure, lithe like a dancer, standing over ten feet tall. "What is this, I hear? You wish to return our magic?"

The buzzing intensified as the bright light ebbed, leaving him standing solid before me, gazing in that unblinking manner that set me on edge. I reminded myself that his children claimed he was good. Ouras's warning that he would kill me may have been overly dramatic.

Rem's golden glow had once been so bright I could hardly look upon him. His presence had caused me pain. But no longer. My magic hummed in response to his presence, wild but not debilitating. Interesting.

Rem didn't move, yet his eyes narrowed a fraction, giving away his annoyance with me. "I know you. I've seen you before."

I didn't answer.

"*Don't speak your name to the gods, even if they ask,*" the Oracle had told me.

"The Guardian City," his layered voice echoed.

My heart skipped. I didn't dare breathe.

"You were with the Guards." Rem barked a laugh, reverberating in an array of tones, none of them pleasant. "I thought you were a pure-blooded child, carrying magic in you. There aren't many left, but I know when I meet them. How wonderful. The Ikhor was right there with me, and I had no idea. Clever girl. You have something that belongs to me."

"No," I whispered.

This was what I wanted, right? I had planned to return the magic, but some part of me screamed not to give it to Rem.

Run, Liv. A warm presence wrapped around my heart, and my mother's voice rang clear in my mind.

"You called for a god." Rem tilted his head like an animal, sizing up its prey.

"I came for Mayra. But I didn't call—"

"You call with your heart. Your intention was to speak with a god. I am here. Why are you looking for us? What do you need with my brethren?"

"I want to return the magic."

No, no, NO! It was a second voice in my head—not one I recognized.

"I was told to find the gods."

"You seek to find Erabas, then."

"You know where he is?"

Rem was like stone. Solid. Inhuman. "No one does. He is gone."

"Did you kill him?" I clapped a hand over my mouth—*wrong thing to ask.*

Rem's glow intensified. "You fail to understand why you are here. The Ikhor, full of rage and hate. Every time, it's the same, and the lessons are never learned. The mistakes of our children live on in you."

"How do I carry anyone else's mistakes? I am not bad or evil."

"Have you not destroyed? Killed? Hated? Things never change. Times were dark when four gods ruled. Four powerful beings who disagreed on how the lands should be controlled. The gods have done their duty to do better for their children, yet you all fight and cause so much destruction."

"You say times were dark. Was that because of Erabas?"

Rem tilted his head to the other side. "His world was anarchy. It was chaos. Mine is peace, where hate and war are brought to heel."

The Desert Eagle claimed that in a lawless land, the crimes were out in the open. But that was not how the Guardian lands were run.

"Peace? Doesn't look that way to me."

"And who are you to judge? A nameless legacy that harbours the magic brimming with the same chaos. You're an endless cycle, damning this world. Even now, you've brought war to the shrine of my beloved sister. The Guardians are here. They have met with your friends and are putting them in their place."

The Guardians. Not the Guards. Falizha and her crew were here?

"Maev—"

"Who are you, Ikhor? Why do I not sense the touch of a god on you? Unless ... unless you have escaped your little prison."

All the fear within me went still, focused on the god before me. "Prison?"

The door to the prayer chamber opened behind me, and I turned in time to see surprise flash across the face of someone I hated more than anyone else.

Falizha Ravin.

She ignored me, bowing to her god. "Father. I did not know you would be here today. You have blessed us. We have discovered the Guards have betrayed our people. I have come to reveal them as traitors and finish the Ikhor."

Rem held a hand to his heart. "My child, what has become of the Guards? I have been told of their intent to turn on the people and help the Ikhor."

Falizha's mocking smile drifted my way. "They are being rounded up. My brother's new weapons are proving useful in putting them in their place."

"I leave you to it, then. I will speak with the Ikhor. I wish to hear its excuses for mercy." Rem waved a hand, dismissing Falizha.

I needed to get to the others, to Maev, and I ran, but a strong wind kicked up. The door slammed before I could reach it, cutting off the screams coming from the main chamber. My heart seized.

It sounded like Nuo.

Leave. Run, the voices in me demanded, and I whipped around to find Rem leaning over me. I stumbled back, pressing myself against the door while he inspected my face. He stood toe to toe with me.

Do not falter. The dark voice said.

"It doesn't want to be returned," I whispered, sensing the magic raging against Rem's presence. "The magic is corrupted. It doesn't want to be given back anymore."

The blacks of Rem's eyes swam with stars, like the darkest parts of the night sky. "What do you know of the magic's intent?"

"It's not a part of you anymore." I gritted my teeth against the growing hum. The vibrations of Rem's magic pushed against me, rattling my bones and stealing my breath. "The magic is fighting me."

"Humans have not yet learned from their mistakes. The cycle of hate and war is their punishment for their greed." Rem stood straight. "The magic doesn't *think*. It doesn't want or need. It can't be returned to me because it's full of human hate. It is no longer compatible with my true, benevolent nature."

Rem's response surprised me. I was on Aethar lands. Did he think I still believed the Guardians' teachings that the Ikhor was evil? The tales of the Ikhor were a lie, so why did he believe them?

I fought against his presence, the cords on my neck pulling tight. "By coming here to speak to one of you, am I not proving that people have learned? I don't want power."

"Your reasons are selfish," he hissed. "You're trying to rid yourself of the curse. To save your own life. I feel the amount of hatred you harbour within your heart."

Curse? What curse?

I took a shallow breath, holding back my retort because Rem was right. I was selfish. I wasn't here to save the world—maybe a handful of people.

If I couldn't help myself, however, I had to help my friends. "The Guards. They aren't turning on their people. They are helping me to return the magic, not go against the Veydians."

The god took careful steps about the chamber, never taking his eyes off me. "If the Guards were innocent, they would not be questioning the nature of the Ikhor. They would be helping the Aspis defeat it."

"I am not evil! I am not possessed. They are innocent of the crimes Falizha claims."

Rem's mouth twitched, and he stopped pacing. "Are you not possessed? Look how you lose control around me. Look how you react to my presence. I am a god—you should bow before me, yet here you are, standing as if you are my equal. All these years and nothing has changed."

I lifted my hand to shield my eyes, catching a glimpse of my glowing bracelet. Next to Rem, the glow was so similar. The magic hummed as he hummed.

I sucked in a sharp breath—Ouras hadn't glowed like Rem.

My earlier theory came back to me. "Did you create the Ikhor?" I stared into the black abyss swirling around his inhumane, golden glare.

Rem was so still he became a statue—like Ouras had been. "What are you insinuating, girl?"

"I've seen images painted of the Ikhor—glowing, like you. The magic I possess came to me, glowing like you. I don't think the stories of the first child are true."

"I think you'll find yourself harmed if you keep talking."

Everything in me froze at the threat. Even the voices stayed silent, scared of the warning in Rem's voice.

I swallowed my fear. "Then answer me this—am I the first to try to return it?"

Rem's laugh was like ice cracking on a lake. "Of course, you're not. Mortals. Always trying to save each other. It's pathetic."

"Isn't that proof we are good?"

So much for being a benevolent god. He insulted his *children*—or at least the children of his brethren.

"Why haven't you taken it back? History says the gods haven't even tried."

"History is written by those who *win*, girl. It is what I say it is. I don't want the corrupted magic you carry."

I swallowed my surprise. Rem was admitting he'd altered the truth, that history was what he had made it. "You're the reason the cycle doesn't end. Not the hate in human hearts."

"And those that discover the truth find themselves meeting an untimely end. My children carry out my desires and erase the truth. There is no need to instil fear in those who remain. They shall continue to believe there is a chance the gods will take the magic back, and one day, this will all be over."

"You control the Council." I didn't understand his reasons, but I was piecing together that Rem was keeping everyone in the dark.

"That's why no one lives to tell the truth? The Guards, the Aspis, the Ikhor. You kill them."

"No. Not I. I barely lift a finger. I let them kill each other. Or my children—those who truly act in my image—do it in worship, carrying out my will. Whoever orchestrates it is of no interest to me. I just don't stop it."

The person Falizha mentioned in her journals, the one they took orders from, didn't sound like Rem because …

"The Council follows orders from someone higher up. Someone who answers directly to you."

"Someone with more intelligence than that fat oaf on his stolen throne. One of my first children. Ruthless and cunning, he has made me proud."

"But you're killing legacies. You're hurting people. Don't you care for the children of your brothers and sister?"

Rem's light flared, and I backed against the door, my bones aching. The blacks of his eyes darkened as his anger rose. "Did Mayra care for me when she hid her children below her seas? Did Erabas care for my children when he chose his favourites and protected them instead? Does Ouras care for my children while he keeps his docile—never to engage with others, never to join my own children in making the world a more structured place? I think not. We care for our own, and the best future for my children is one where they rule."

"They aren't ruling, they're massacring."

"Semantics, dear child. Now, I think I will take that magic from you after all. I don't like the look in your eye. Like you think you can do something about it."

The magic rebelled, spiralling and thrashing in my chest, burrowing itself down deep.

Rem's glow intensified as he reached for me. His magic pulled at mine, feeling like it had when the Aspis tried to take it from me, though it wasn't a match. Rem's face transformed into one of fury. Black swallowed the gold in his eyes until I stared into the ends of the night skies. Inhuman. Deadly. His anger leaked into the surrounding glow, pulsing. He couldn't take the magic. He was *struggling*.

My theories were right—the magic stolen from the gods had made them weaker.

I am stronger than the god of Day.

I buried my magic, imagining my box inside and slamming the lid closed.

"It won't go to you," I said.

"Give it to me!" The room shook with his anger.

I clapped my hands over my ears. Warm liquid pooled around my fingers, and I wondered if my ears were bleeding. I squinted against his light, bending over as I suffocated from the pain.

Until a shadow pulsed across the room.

Behind Rem, a swirling darkness loomed, pacing back and forth, agitated, much like the glowing god before me. The shadow monster was here. Taller than Rem, it soaked up the light in the room, swallowing everything that existed past the golden god. I watched it prowl silently, its movements filled with anger.

Rem caught my staring, and he, too, peered over his shoulder. "What are you looking at?" he asked.

I shook. "You can't see it."

If Rem couldn't see the shadow, it couldn't be a servant of Erabas or the missing god himself. What was this monster following me? Why could no one sense it, not even a god?

The shadow rose tall in the chamber, consuming Rem's light, towering over him. The humming from Rem's magic and the whooshing sound coming from the shadow behind him forced me to shout to be heard. "Make it stop!" I grabbed my ears. "End this!"

Rem pulled back, nearing the shadow that paced around him as claws grew from the shadow's hands. "End? There is no end to hate and cruelty. You'll see. Watch how everyone looks at you, Ikhor. Watch how they treat you. You'll burn the world in the end, just like the rest. And I won't have to even ask you to do it."

Tears streamed down my cheeks as my legs trembled violently, nearly buckling beneath me. For the first time since leaving the

Endless Forest, I almost wished I hadn't been found. Death would be so much better.

"You're a monster," I cried.

"Says the monster," he purred. "Erabas would be put out to know what happened to his world when he was defeated."

Defeated?

Erabas was gone. So then, how did I know the language of Night? Why was I haunted by shadows?

"Am I a child of night?" I asked, and the shadow went still, its faceless head swirling in my direction. The room grew darker.

"No. It makes me wonder how you got loose. How did you escape your little island? No one has since the conflict between the gods."

I didn't have time to register what Rem said because that was the moment the shadow monster ran in my direction. I screamed as it flew past Rem, colliding with me.

"What are you doing?" Rem's voice was small, the sight of him dimming.

The monster hadn't grabbed me like I had dreamt before. It didn't crowd me, choke me, or pin me down—it ran *into* me, absorbing me, or I absorbed it.

Inch by inch, that darkness disappeared, sinking into my skin. It reached into my body, my mind, my soul, and it took over. Then I finally realized why no one else saw it or sensed the monster when it was close.

"I know what it is." I had repressed it, denied it, and it grew into a monstrous thing.

"What?!" Rem screamed, "What is it."

The Oracle had warned me, had given me the answers. *"You were brought here by chaos and darkness."*

I was brought here by the magic, the shadow monster, the—

I looked into Rem's menacing black eyes. "It's the Ikhor."

Blackness clouded my vision, and I lost sight of Rem.

The shadow monster hadn't been following me. It had been within me, trying to get loose, trying to gain control. This whole time, I had been sensing the evil buried within me, manifesting it outside my body as if being haunted.

The shadow stopped struggling as the last of its essence latched onto me. Tiny wisps danced around my vision until the Ikhor fully consumed me.

Rem stared at me, his black eyes matching the monster crawling under my skin.

I looked out through eyes that no longer belonged to me.

"It has taken over," Rem whispered in fear before disappearing, taking the light with him and casting me into darkness.

CHAPTER
SEVENTY-ONE

Nuo

Aeden Ravin dragged Bastane out of the prayer chamber next to ours. Why the fuck was Aeden Ravin here?

"Bastane," I shouted, held back by Brekt when he saw the state of Bas's face. He was a bloody mess, and his body had gone limp from the beating he took. His feet dragged on the floor while Aeden stomped to the centre of the shrine.

It made no sense. How had Bastane been put in such a state while Brekt and I had been praying in the next room?

Brekt faded from sight, using his Night-leg magic to blend into the shadows cast by the balcony above.

Aeden glanced over his shoulder, not missing a step, his mouth forming a cruel smile, showing the man hidden behind the Guardian clothes. He was breathing heavily, the veins on his neck bulging. Aeden didn't have as much fighting knowledge as the Guards. He was never rewarded for battles won. How had he taken Bas down?

Kazhi sprung from the same chamber, running for Aeden with her knives out. She, too, was a mess, blood streaming from her temple. I snapped out of my bewildered state, following her.

Falizha stood in the centre of the large chamber, grinning at Bastane's battered form. "The Traitor will get what he deserves, as will the rest of you."

Light poured through the missing parts of the roof, setting the Day-legs alight.

Kazhi reached Aeden's back, knives poised to take him down. He spun, grabbing her and lifting her as if she weighed nothing. With strength I'd never seen, he flung her across the large room. She collided with a wall, and the impact rattled the stones loose. They crumbled around her as she collapsed to the ground.

Kazhi didn't get up.

"How—"

Brekt stopped me, though I couldn't see him. "Something is off about him. Look at his neck."

Sickly red veins pulsed in Aeden's neck. The sight reminded me of the rash I'd seen forming on his skin in the Guardian City. Something was wrong with him.

Aeden's roar of fury echoed in the shrine as he picked up Bastane and slammed him on the ground at Falizha's feet. Bastane groaned in pain, his head falling limp to the side.

"The Guards are done with, as of today!" Aeden screamed to the shrine. Movement from higher up caught my attention. The Guardians Falizha had brought to the Aethar lands lined the second level, wrapping around the entire shrine. Each held one of the weapons Aeden showcased back at the City. And they had them aimed at us.

"This is an execution," Brekt whispered from somewhere to my left. "Liv—"

"She can protect herself," I said in a low voice. "And they might not know she is here." I glanced toward the door Liv had gone through, past the dais separating the chamber doors, and caught a flash of blue behind the debris—the Aethar. She cowered behind a large stone slab that had fallen from the roof. Her eyes were wide with fear as they met mine. I tilted my palm to the ground to warn her to stay down.

"Come forward into the light, Nuo." Falizha stood over Bastane, casting a shadow over him while the sun lit her hair aglow. "The Guardians here want to know why you entered this shrine with the Ikhor."

Brekt swore, staying hidden.

"You were followed here!" a woman shouted from above. My head spun when I saw it was Lin, the woman I'd taken to bed back in Danuli. Her hateful glare was on me. "The scout saw you meet with the Ikhor. You're traitors!"

"The Council has always talked of replacing you because you refuse orders," another man shouted. "And now we find the truth. They were right about you!"

I stepped into the sunlight, letting them see me. "And did none of you question the Council's truths when you were brought to these lands? Did you not expect wastelands filled with scarred Aethar? The Guards have been asking the right questions for much longer. You are all being deceived."

"You're with the Ikhor, Nuo!" Lin shouted.

"The Ikhor isn't possessed!" Brekt stepped out of the shadows.

The Guardians all gasped. No one had seen him in months. Falizha had known Brekt was host of the Aspis, had seen him transform on the field, but she showed no surprise at seeing him alive again. Had the scout reported seeing him, and she kept it a secret from everyone else?

"Where have you been, Erebrekt? We were told you'd abandoned the Guards," a man shouted.

"The Council hid from you that I was the host of the Aspis." When the shrine stayed silent, Brekt continued, "It slumbered in me, and when the magic of the Ikhor woke, the transformation took place. I did not abandon the Guards."

"Why haven't you killed the Ikhor?" Lin questioned.

Brekt patted his chest. "I am proof the legends are lies. The Aspis is not chasing the Ikhor to save the people. It wants to steal the Ikhor's magic and possess it!"

The Guardians stayed silent, sending each other confused looks.

"The Ikhor isn't some evil creature," Brekt said desperately, "but a woman who can wield magic. Nothing more."

"The rumours are right, the Ikhor is your lover. You are protecting her," Lin said.

"Magic is for the gods, not their children. That alone is the threat we must protect ourselves from!" another Guardian shouted.

"Enough!" Aeden said. "You have been given your orders, Guardians. You have been trained on your new weapons. Aim to kill. The Ikhor is here. We will end this today and claim another era of peace for our descendants."

The Guardians aimed their weapons at Bastane, Brekt, myself, and Kazhi, still unconscious by the wall. My mind raced. What could I do? I knew how fast these Deathmakers could kill. We had no training for this type of scenario.

"Walk forward, Guards," Falizha said smugly next to her brother.

"Never listened to you before, not going to now." I held my killing blades, eyeing her throat.

Aeden, carrying his weapon in his other hand, pushed the tip of the Deathmaker against Bastane's temple. Both Brekt and I reacted, moving forward.

"Stop there," Aeden ordered.

I halted several feet from the golden siblings. Everything in me screamed not to listen, not to give him the power, but Bastane was so bloody that I doubted he could even see the threat standing above him.

"Kneel," Falizha said in a delighted tone.

"Do it," Brekt said next to me. And we did. It killed my ego to land on my knees before Falizha. She was going to die, and I wouldn't wait for Kazhi's okay.

"Good." Aeden kept the weapon pointed at Bastane. "Armel

comes with us," he said to Falizha. "I will use him to test my new weapons. His father will be told he died in battle."

"What about the others?" A Mount-leg asked from above.

"We told you all!" Falizha yelled. "The Guards betrayed you. You wouldn't believe us until we brought you here."

So this was it, why the Ravins brought all the Guardians. They knew they would catch us helping the Ikhor.

"I saw you in the Canyons, Nuo," Falizha went on. "I saw you standing with the Ikhor, talking, not fighting."

Aeden rested a boot on Bastane's chest, leaning his full weight on his knee, making Bas gasp for air. "The Guards haven't been so sneaky. We know you have been keeping secrets."

"This isn't right," a Guardian shouted from the balcony, looking around at his fellow warriors. "We are aiming at the *Guards*. At the Aspis! We know them. They wouldn't go against their own—this isn't right!"

Aeden's face transformed into one of rage, turning to the balcony. "Bring him here!"

Several Guardians snatched up the man who had argued against the Ravins' commands. They brought him down a large stone staircase off to my left and pushed him to his knees next to Brekt.

Aeden rose to his full height, keeping his Deathmaker trained on Bastane. "Falizha, this little Guardian has rebelled. Take care of him and show the others what happens when they don't listen to commands given by their superiors."

"What?" The man squirmed next to Brekt. "You can't shoot me for asking a question. What is this?"

The Guardians holding him didn't budge as the man fought for his life.

"Stop this!" Brekt yelled.

"Don't you move, Erebrekt." Aeden tilted his head, the red veins in his neck protruding. "Who will you save—the man disobeying orders? Or your fellow Guard at my feet?"

Brekt shook, his anger forcing his Night-leg magic to kick in.

He began to disappear from sight, but Aeden pushed his Deathmaker into Bastane's neck.

Brekt yelled, coming back into view. Bastane had betrayed him, giving his girl to the Ravins. Brekt hadn't forgiven him, and neither had I, but Brekt was loyal to those he called family—loyal to a fault. Bastane said he'd pay for his betrayal, but we wouldn't let him die.

"Falizha, take care of that one," Aeden barked, and the man next to us looked around the room for help, but he saw the same view as us—corrupted minds and fellow warriors who now saw us as the enemy.

Falizha's golden skin paled to a sickly yellow as she swallowed, lifted her Deathmaker, and slipped her brother a wide-eyed plea.

"And here I thought you wanted to look strong for Daddy," Aeden remarked.

Falizha's jaw went tight. She held the weapon to her shoulder and closed her eyes as she shot the man down.

Shocked silence followed the thud of his still body hitting the stone floor.

Coward. Murderer. My stomach rolled as the blood of one of our own pooled on the shrine of Mayra.

The Guardians above went silent as they all realized how corrupt the Ravins were.

Aeden faced the higher level, raising his free hand. "You will all be rewarded when you get home as long as you follow orders. If you don't ..." He gestured to the ground where the man lay dead. "I think you understand. Aim for your targets."

I noticed Lin's weapon pointed at me, and her face contorted in rage. "They won't let you return home after what you've seen," I warned them. "You will be next."

"Make sure your weapons are loaded to kill, not incapacitate."

"Yes, sir," Guardians shouted.

"Nuo," Brekt whispered, his voice strained.

"Don't even fucking start," I said through gritted teeth. "I've already said my goodbyes to you one time too many."

A woman screamed, and I turned for the doors behind me. *Liv.* She was fighting someone in her prayer chamber.

I caught a glimpse of the blue Aethar. She might be the only one of us who would make it out of here. The Aethar found me watching and shifted her attention behind me, nodding her head.

I followed her line of sight to where Kazhi had been lying. With the distraction of the Deathmakers, I had missed that she was no longer lying across the shrine room. I scanned the debris—Kazhi was inching around a large piece of stone wall, hidden in the shadows cast by the second level. She was limping, holding a knife in her free hand.

"I need to get to her," Brekt said. "I need to get to Liv."

"She can handle it." I met his wide stare. "She has the magic. We need to put these assholes down."

"Any last words, Guards?" Falizha asked.

"Stop putting on a fucking show," Aeden spat at her. "Or I'll put you on your knees with them."

Her face went red, but she stayed quiet.

My chest rose and fell from the adrenaline. I waited for Aeden's command and for those weapons to send metal flying through my chest.

But Aeden's command never came.

The room went dark. Murmurs echoed in the chamber as shadows stretched over every blue-stained surface. Both Brekt and I looked up to find the light disappearing. It came back and faded again.

"Is the fucking sun flickering on and off?" Aeden asked.

Falizha's answer made me go cold. "Rem is in the prayer chamber with the Ikhor. We are to continue here."

"And so we shall," Aeden replied.

The Ravins were proven wrong, however—Rem wasn't taking the light from the shrine. Just then, the door behind me burst open, crashing against the stone wall and splintering.

AN AGONIZED CRY tore through the room—the sound was out of my worst nightmares. Everyone turned for the door to the prayer chamber, eyes wide with fear.

A shape moved in the shadows cast by the balcony. The sounds of feet being dragged echoed, and when the figure entered the light cast down from the fading sun, I heard someone scream.

The embodiment of evil prowled from the doorway, carrying darkness with every step. It wasn't my old friend who walked from the prayer chamber. No, this was the Ikhor—as terrifying as every image painted in Veydes.

Every horrid thing I'd said to her. Every moment I wasted with anger. I wished to take it all back. Apologies would be too late now. She was ... Liv was gone.

The air left my lungs, and I turned to Brekt, who had paled from the horror stalking toward us. He, too, understood what he was seeing.

The Ikhor's skin glowed through its leather outfit. Black surrounded its enraged red eyes, and its lips pulled back in a snarl. This was the evil destined to rise. I had been wrong, thinking Liv could protect herself with her magic. She'd lost against it.

It dragged its feet as if fighting itself to move forward. It was the creepiest fucking thing I'd ever seen. The room continued to darken as if its magic ate up all the light. Its shoulders hunched, hands twitching as it grabbed its hair, pulling it, shaking its head. Another scream tore from its mouth, and the voice was both low and high.

"Guardians!" Aeden shouted. "New target!"

His command triggered the Ikhor's awareness. Its glowing, red gaze sliced across the room, and it stopped, colliding with mine. Pure blackness surrounding the iris—like a god's. Its head swivelled to face Brekt, and when it saw him, it choked itself. "No. No. No," it's many voices said as one.

"Fight it, Liv!" Brekt called out. He, too, was fighting the beast within. His skin turned to dust, replaced with black scales. Horns appeared on his head, and his eyes glowed a bright yellow, as if the presence of the Ikhor was making him shift.

"What do I do, Brekt?" I asked. The Guardians were no longer watching us. "What do I do?"

"I don't fucking know," he growled. "But whatever it is, she must be saved. Don't forget what you promised me."

Of all the promises I'd ever made in my lifetime, that one would cost me the most.

A dozen Guardians joined the Ravins behind us, having left their post on the second floor. "Which target?" an older male Sea-leg asked.

"We will let the Aspis deal with the Ikhor," Aeden replied.

"He won't. She's his lover," another said.

"Then we will make him."

"He's no longer the beast. He's just a man!"

Aeden appraised Brekt before he slid his gaze my way. "I think I know how to make the beast come forth."

I jumped at the loud boom of Aeden's weapon going off. Fear gripped my chest—I couldn't watch Brekt die a second time.

The pain in my chest intensified, feeling like a rib had cracked.

"Nuo!" the Ikhor shouted in its double voice.

I lowered my chin, seeing moisture leaving the side of my chest. It wasn't just fear causing the pain ... I had been shot.

"Fuck," I coughed. "That hurts." I met the glowing, hateful eyes of the Ikhor over my shoulder. "Kill the bastards," I moaned before I collapsed on the ground, landing in the rippling blue light of the temple—just like Brekt had seen.

"Sorry, man," I struggled to say to my brother, who was screaming next to me, fading to the beast. "I guess your dream was right."

"*This energy is an iron will. It surrounds you like the hardest metal and darkest storm. It is a beautiful essence and divine love. It is feminine energy. It will carry itself with you, Liv, into your darkest days. When you feel your heart is being ripped from your chest and your mind is split in two, don't let go. Do not rip away your shield. It will be all that can save you.*"

CHAPTER

SEVENTY-TWO

The Ikhor

This is my body!

The girl's presence in my head was a nuisance, but I would squash her shortly. I was finally gaining enough power to hold this body as my own.

Rem had vanished before I could punish him, but I sensed the dark beast's physical presence in the next room. It would be my next target. I would return to my full strength and claim the world, and then I would find Rem.

Don't you dare hurt Brekt.

I pushed open the chamber door, and she fought me the entire time, dragging her feet to hold us back. Her will was impressive, and I knew I had chosen the right body. Though it had taken months to find a weak spot in her will, I was proud of the little mortal I had chosen.

The girl had been dying when I found her in that faraway place, a perfect host to embed myself into. Her mind, her heart, was that of a warrior—and she could have been, had she shed her doubts. Her life had broken her, but not completely. She had learnt to remake herself—and what a fighter she had become.

It wasn't Rem who brought me to these lands?

Rem, I could laugh. Rem didn't have power like mine. Maybe once, for a moment in time.

No, mortal. I am the magic stolen. I am the definition of power.

I grew stronger with each rebirth, grew one step closer to becoming whole. I yearned to be more than incorporeal magic. I would become permanent. I only needed the right host to do my bidding, and I chose each host for their willpower. I believed the girl would be no different, but she had full control over her anger. It was through her fear I finally gained access when she had heard her little friend screaming. Her body and mind would serve me well, and I used her determination as my own—it powered me to stalk from the chamber and find my prey.

Her heart still controlled part of her body, and it ached when she saw two men on their knees. No matter—the one on the right was my target. She could only fight me for so long.

I used her anger to fuel me. She had built up so much of it over the years from the wrongdoing of others. I almost pitied her—such a bright soul beaten down by a cruel world.

She fought against every laboured step I took.

A man shouted, his voice ringing with magic. He stood in the middle of the room, a descendant of the god of Day. Another lay, near to death, at his feet. The one standing shouted an order, and a loud bang sent something flying and into the body of a kneeling man—a legacy of Sea.

Some of Mayra's children remained on land. Interesting.

He didn't feel it at first, but the blood running down the side of his chest made the spirit of the girl go wild.

"Nuo!" She took over our voice long enough to shout his name. Her spirit rebelled against me to go to him.

Stop it, mortal. Your time here is done.

No! They are my friends. You must save them, she demanded.

I have not waited thousands of years to save one man.

He is not one man. He is my friend!

No.

The bleeding child of Mayra's face contorted in pain, turning his anger on me. "Kill the bastards," he said, and I could not agree more.

He collapsed, sending a wave of agony through my body. But it was not my rage nor my revenge that took root. It was hers which powered me, bringing my magic to life. It washed through us, glowing, its power so strong it lifted us from the floor to hover in the air. We saw the mortals on the balconies and the ones on the ground below us. Light flared as we laughed.

Her rage was powerful and beautiful. She thought of strange things—*Keepers, Day-leg, Aethar, burning fields.* This mortal had dark memories that she wished to unleash on the world.

With our magic, our beautiful beast reacted. It sprung from the host, rising into the air and tearing apart what little roof remained of the sea shrine. It rose into the sky, sending debris raining down on those below.

Shots fired in my direction and bounced off my magic.

I tsked. "Witless mortals. You were not my target. But it seems you will pay. When you die, know it is her pain that killed you. You should have never touched her little friend."

Fire spread across the ground, and the vibrations in the air tickled me from her head to toe. "What is this?"

The magic was not mine, but a weak imitation. I searched for the source. There were so many legacies, but I found it. The golden man was conjuring fire. The son of Rem had power.

"Look! The Ikhor is attacking," he shouted. "It's setting fire to Mayra's shrine. Fire at will."

People in black yelled back and forth, and more weapons pointed at me.

I tilted her head—clever boy, blaming me so he could mask his treachery.

My host screamed, trying to gain control. *It was him! The fires— it was he who started them all! The burning fields, South Aspis, it was him! He must die first.*

We would show him what magic looked like. I closed her eyes, feeling the earth sing, and I called to the sea that sat so close to the crumbling shrine.

The strain this woman had let her body endure to withhold me was admirable. I had slept so long that I had forgotten what walking in a mortal body felt like. They were all so different, each one a novel experience.

I let my magic spread, pulling the power of the sea on land until it reached the shrine. Water pooled in from the prayer chambers. Eddies swirled around one another as the sea answered my call and came to deliver my wrath on those who meant me harm. The little Guardians ran for the second story. The water caught a few mortal specks in its rage, and they screamed as others ran. I would drown them all.

Kill them all, she repeated. *They hurt him. They hurt Nuo. Kill them all.*

Usually, the mortals feared my power, but not my host. This girl feared a cage, something I understood well. This time, we would both gain freedom. She was too young to be controlled and too stubborn to ever give up. She welcomed my power now. Together, we controlled her hands, sending a wall of unbreakable water to the balconies.

More screams tore through the shrine. The little mortals slipped and fell, unable to swim against the power of the sea.

My host had controlled the magic a handful of times, using her emotions as a conduit. She was clever, but now that I controlled things, we no longer relied on such tactics. I thought, and the earth responded—just as it had millennium past.

Fire battled the water, failing and hissing as the weak magic turned to steam. I caught frightened golden eyes and smiled. I enjoyed their fear.

The son of Rem had grabbed the beaten, bloodied man at his feet, shoving others out of his way to flee the torrent coming for him. I tried to catch him with my waves, but the girl's spirit concentrated on those below, those she cared for, making sure the water stayed far away from them.

They will not drown. Her compassion matched her fury.

Mayra's son, shot, pushed himself to his feet below me, yet I felt his life force ebbing.

Another child of Rem, the one with blue skin and markings across her face, hid behind a boulder in safety. My host was protecting her, too.

Don't you touch them!

I ignored her demands and found I had missed my chance to take down the magic-altered son of Rem, who commanded the Guardians. He was leaving the shrine, leaving his warriors to fight in his stead.

But I was not done.

I pulled her hands to make fists. *What is this?* Two fingers of her hand would not close. Our magic should heal.

The magic was too late. The Aspis got me.

How will I choke the life from their mortal bodies?

My hands are too small to choke anyone. Use our magic!

I lifted her hands to the forests beyond and commanded the earth. My host had such trouble with earth magic. She struggled to feel grounded, but no such insecurity held me back.

Vines sprung from the stone floors and reached for the mortals wearing black, tying them, holding them below water. I slung vines around their necks and lifted them to hang from the second story, cutting off their air.

I searched for my targets, her targets, the golden children of Rem. They were fleeing, and the girl's anger intensified as she narrowed our attention on a female screaming at the man leaving.

"Aeden, don't you leave without me!" the gold woman shouted.

Her brother turned, knocking others out of his way. "I will take care of Armel. You finish the other Guards off."

The son of Rem gave orders to those standing, some of whom hesitated. He shot them down and issued his orders to the next ones he found. He was killing his own—the ones trying to escape the shrine.

He blocked the main doors, and a blue figure inched closer to the son of Rem, hiding behind a pillar.

Maev! My host screamed. *She's going to follow Aeden, no! I have to stop her.*

No. I had more victims to deal with.

She thinks she'll find Ollo.

My host's voice grew smaller as I pushed her down.

I released the hold on the water, and it poured out of the doors and down the steps, leaving a dripping wet room.

The Guardians saw my smile and collectively held their breath in fear.

I changed the course of my thoughts and set fire to the walls, blocking their way to the doors. The legacies stopped, not daring to run past the fires, and spun to stare in horror. Some screamed for their leader to come help them. It was no use. The son of Rem was shooting at his own people.

I laughed, layered and wicked. The mortals would be finished by *me*, and I welcomed the challenge.

My host welcomed it and threw her anger in one direction— the golden woman left behind the wall of fire. This daughter of Rem's name was carved into a special place inside the girl's chest.

"Falizha."

She whipped her head my way when I called her name.

My vines spiralled toward her, blocking her escape and wrapped around her ankles, holding her in place as I floated on an invisible wind, creeping closer. "You will die, Falizha," we said, setting fire to the vines at her feet.

"You will have to use more than fire to harm me, Ikhor." Her fear was palpable, soaking the air.

Interesting. A first child. Fire magic would not work.

The girl's will took over, speaking through us. "You haven't been told Falizha?" Our head tilted at an unnatural angle, scaring the woman on the ground. "The Ikhor can do so much more than burn."

I lifted my hands, ready to take out my revenge, the girl's

revenge, and claim my place in the world once more, but we were stopped when a man stood between us blocking the daughter of Day from my sight.

One of Mayra's children dared to stop me. He held his side with a bloodied hand, leaning over in pain. He coughed, blood coming from the sides of his mouth.

Nuo. Her heart cried.

He was panting, holding a hand up to us. "Stop, Liv."

"Stop?" we said in unison. "You wished us to kill them all. We were aligned in our vengeance."

He nodded, hair falling in his face. "I did. And you have killed many. Falizha's life is mine. The others are pleading for mercy. You will regret this, believe me."

"You think to command the Ikhor?" My vines crept around his feet.

My host resisted—her screams were a nuisance, but her rage was young. Mine had existed for tens of thousands of years. Hundreds of thousands. I would find my revenge.

"I am not commanding the Ikhor," Mayra's son said, wincing from the pain in his side. "I am asking my friend Olivia to gain control and stop before she becomes something I can no longer protect."

Damn mortal. Whatever he was doing, it was working on my host.

He saw my hesitation and forged on. "Olivia, if you are in there, please do me a favour and stop. Brekt asked me to protect you. You're making that very hard for me right now."

Brekt. Brekt. Brekt. Brekt.

No!

My mortal's will flared, and I found that box inside her chest to shove her into.

You won't control me. Listen to Nuo, he is my friend.

I fought against her, sending her into the darkness so I could finally take control.

But something happened. Another force inside her body took

over, a willpower that was hers but not hers, strong as iron, seized a hold of our limbs. The power compelled us to stand tall.

This willpower was something I had not felt in a long time. It was soft, yet more powerful than any emotion she used to control the magic. It took hold of my host's spirit and put a shield around it, protecting her.

My mother ... she taught me to survive. I will survive you. The magic will be mine to control, as will my body!

With their combined will, they drove me to the ground. Our feet touched the stone, and I fought against their hold.

Mayra's son cut through the vines. "I will get our friends out of here, BB. Leave the rest up to me."

I screamed in my rage, shaking the foundation of the shrine. I would not let her take control.

But in my rage, I had forgotten the beast. The beast was physical prowess, something I should respect and be proud of. I was powerful, too, but my host's body was not.

The Aspis tore through the roof, coming for me. I sent a wave of magic to stop it, but I was not in control. The girl held some of the power back, and the Aspis sucked the magic in, absorbing it, and barrelled right into us. Its teeth tore into me, trapping me in its vicious jaw, taking away my power and flying us from the shrine.

We screamed as it carried us into the sky, thrashing against its hold and watching the ground disappear. I pushed at its teeth, larger than my host's body, but the Aspis did not relent.

And it did not kill us.

Its intent was being controlled. I could feel it. The man, the host, was leading us away. He was playing hero. He absorbed just enough of our power to weaken me, letting the girl's will take over.

I battled against her. But she had practiced forcing things down many times, and with the shield around her spirit, I could not gain control. She shoved me down, down, down until I could no longer see or feel. Caged once more.

Then she slammed the lid closed.

CHAPTER
SEVENTY-THREE

Nuo

My chest burned, my breathing ragged, but I had enough left in me to fight. I needed to get to Bas and find Kazhi, so I cut through the vines around my ankles, turning to find Falizha doing the same. She was less than ten feet away.

Brekt was in the air. He would be fine. He would save Liv. But, *Endless Night*, the Ikhor was worse than the paintings depicted it. It was fucking floating! Glowing, just like we'd been taught. I had just begun to believe the stories weren't true, that Liv was in full control, and then the Ikhor turned the shrine into a place of horror, killing everyone it laid eyes on.

Screams tore through the shrine as fire consumed the Guardians. Some had already drowned and several bodies hung from the second floor, swinging from vines that were holding them by the neck. The Ikhor targeted them one by one and then killed them all. I didn't count how many escaped.

Aeden stopped those who survived, turning on them when they didn't follow his command.

It was chaos—no one knew who to target. I caught several near the main doors, unsure who to point their Deathmakers at.

"Get out of the shrine! The Ikhor may come back."

If any of the Guardians heard, I couldn't tell. With the Ikhor gone, the remaining fires were out of control.

Where was Kazhi? The Aethar girl?

My desperation rose, and I coughed around the heat from the flames—dry air was a Sea-legs worse nightmare. I wiped at my mouth. Blood stained my hand. *Fuck.* I lifted the other hand I held tight to my rib. Blood poured through my fingers. I wouldn't make it long. I needed magycris.

In my time as a Guard I'd been stabbed, cut and badly bruised. But this wound—this was something else.

I pushed the pain aside. Guardians and a wall of fire surrounded Falizha, as she yelled at her brother over the roar of flames. Aeden had Bastane slung over his shoulder. I needed to stop them.

I ran for Falizha when a wind kicked up, stopping me.

"Nuo!" Through the flames, I spotted Kazhi against the far wall. She searched for a way to get to me. The wind rushed me again—she was trying to use her magic to put the fires out. "I'll get Bas," she said. "You get healed!"

She was right. I was losing energy.

Kazhi had a clear path to Aeden, which left Falizha for me. I took three pained steps before I was blocked. Falizha stood before me, sneering. How had she moved so fast? The shrine moved under my feet, and I realized I was losing too much blood.

Behind Falizha, her brother ran out of the shrine, carrying Bastane's limp body. He turned to his sister. "Surely you can take down a Guard who's nearly dead."

"Kazhi," I screamed over the smoke and flame. "Go after him!"

She nodded before disappearing, leaving Falizha and me alone.

"It's time, Falizha," I mocked, opening my arms as if to embrace her. Her body shook, backing away from me but stopping before the flames touched her. "I promised it would be me who did the honours of ending your life."

"I will not die by your hand. You are nobody! You're pathetic, a weak-blooded Sea-leg!"

"Are you trying to convince yourself? Cause no one else is listening, hun." I swaggered forward, dirt crunching under my boots. This would be easy, even bleeding out.

The shrine was bathed in an orange glow. "I was right, wasn't I? This was a slaughter. We didn't come here for the Aethar."

Falizha pulled her own knife, mouth set in determination. She was actually going to try and fight me.

I circled her, eager to get this death and claim it. "I promised your life was no longer your own."

"You kill me, and you can never go home again. You are an enemy to the Guardian City."

"Sounds like a fair trade to me. Besides,"—I pointed to the burning shrine—"odds don't look good for me anyways."

For the first time since I met the slimy bitch, she showed an ounce of bravery when she charged to strike me first. "You disgusting Sea-leg. I will gladly cut you up into pieces."

She was surprisingly skilled with her blade. Her long hair spun as she dodged my knives. Her cape whipped out as she moved.

My side was killing me, slowing me down, but it was like fighting a child.

Her golden face burned with rage as our weapons clashed. Over and over again.

I pushed her back, and she slammed against a crumbling pillar. Her chest rose and fell as fast as my own. She was putting up a decent fight.

"My brother was ordered to make sure none of you left here. The time of the Guards is done. The Ravin family will control the beast from now on."

"Is that so? You think Brekt will follow you? You think you can get through the Ikhor?"

Falizha smiled. "We only needed proof the Ikhor caused the transformation. Control the Ikhor, control the beast."

The breath left my lungs. "Control the Ikhor? Are you insane?" That was their plan?

Falizha rested a hand against the pillar, holding herself up. "Oh, Nuo, you are so clueless." She bit her lip, enjoying this. "Do you think it's normal for a man to be able to toss someone across the room as Aeden does?"

I waited to hear more, hating the delight that crossed her face. She loved having the upper hand.

She gave me a taunting grin. "We have been developing weapons in secret for a very long time. We have been controlling people in ways you could never imagine. And now, we will use those same methods to control the Ikhor."

Her brother. He had looked strange. What had he done to himself?

"Figuring it out?" she asked. "We've been testing magycris and finding other ways to use it. Aeden is much more powerful than any warrior who has ever lived. And as much as the magycris can give power, he has figured out how to take it away."

The shrine groaned, the fires spreading up the walls. It wouldn't be long before the entire thing collapsed.

"I'm talking to you, Nuo! Don't worry about this crumbling shithole. It's a fitting place for you to die. In a place that holds no meaning to the world anymore. A dead shrine for a dead goddess." Falizha charged, trying again to strike me.

Again and again, we parried. I was playing with her while she fought to find a weak spot on my side. There was no weak spot, even wounded. I barely had to try to keep her off me.

Guardians stumbled down from the second floor, so few left, fleeing from the fires.

Falizha saw me watching them. "Looking for a way out? There's no escaping through those flames."

"Why don't you put them out for me, sweetie?" I mocked. "Be a good girl and do as you're told."

Falizha screamed her wrath, and then it hit me.

"You can't? Can you?" I laughed as we battled. "That's why you are such a spiteful person. You can't use the magic. Not like big brother."

She became frenzied then, slashing at me, sloppy, powered by anger.

I needed to end this—there would be no drawing out her death. I had waited so long for this moment, but it would have to be quick. I needed to find the others.

Falizha's knife clashed with mine. She held on, blade to blade, her arms shaking against my strength. Her defence was strong, but she left her stomach exposed, and must have forgotten my other blade.

"You pathetic—"

She coughed, looking down.

My blade embedded to the hilt, blood streamed onto the metal and over my hand. I held onto it so that she wouldn't collapse and twisted it, earning a scream. I held her upright because I wanted her to look me in the eye as she died.

"Your brother is next," I said through gritted teeth, hardly satisfied with her death. "Then your father. I will take the entire Council down, member by member."

The blade she held raised against mine slid away, her strength draining. She wrapped her free hand around my arm, the one holding the knife in her gut. "Filthy, Sea-leg," she sputtered, her breathing laboured. "Your death will be as pitiful as mine."

I was about to laugh when a sharp pain in my neck stopped me.

Bastane always told me I was too quick to celebrate my victories.

I didn't think she had it in her to use the last of her strength to plunge her knife into my neck.

Into my fucking gills.

My second set of lungs opened, thinking I was breathing in

water. My chest spasmed when I inhaled my blood, choking myself. They expanded again, drawing in the warm liquid.

Bitch, I wanted to say, but blood slid out between my teeth.

Falizha fell to the ground when I could no longer hold her up. She was sprawled on her ridiculous purple cape. I collapsed on my side next to her. She watched the sky, the sun fading now, while I choked on my blood.

Her jaw worked around her last breaths. Her eyes shot upwards to a shadow standing over us. "Brother." Her hand rose and fell, trying to reach for Aeden, standing at my back.

"Well, this is not how I wanted to tell Father you died."

"Help—" she tried.

"Help? My hands are a little full putting out these fires. I need to collect the weapons. What I am taking back north is worth more than your life. Goodbye, little Lizha. I wish you could have seen how we won in the end. Then again, I could hardly care that you were part of it."

Aeden grunted commands to the Guardians left standing. He waved his hands toward the fires, and somehow, they were put *out*.

I choked on my laugh, knowing Falizha wasn't powerful enough to control magic like her brother. I could have pitied her in another life had she not made mine so miserable.

Falizha's nostrils flared, and then, with a final huff, her body shrunk, giving up.

She was dead.

Her vacant, open eyes stared past me to a quiet shrine.

I used the last of my strength to roll myself onto my back. The rippled blue glass from a remaining piece of the roof above me set the room aglow with beams of light like I was floating under the surface of a clear lake. I could hear the weak cries for help of those who survived the attack and the quiet footsteps of someone walking amongst the dead.

Bastane was captured. Kazhi might be dead, too. Brekt and Liv had likely taken the battle elsewhere, and who knew how that would end.

And I was going to die alone, under the rippling blue waters.

Time slowed as I stared above. The sound quieted to a breeze whistling between cracks in the walls, water dripping from the corpses hanging from the balcony.

I thought killing Falizha would feel like a victory. So why did it feel like the Ravins had won?

The Guards were broken. The Guardians had turned their backs on us. Liv lost her battle against the evil. What hope was there to end the cycle?

Footsteps grew louder as they approached. My vision blurred, and I could no longer see who stood around me, but I knew who it was.

Mother.

Creator.

The one who didn't come when I called but came to take me to her dark depths.

Mayra's shining blue aura floated over me, ready to take me back to her seas. She was a blur at first, coming into focus as she drifted closer. She was beautiful. My favourite colour of blue.

"I'm going to help you." Her voice was soft, high-pitched and feminine. Not layered and angry like her brother Rem.

I didn't move, rather concentrated on the voice keeping me tied to the living world. She spoke to me, saying things I didn't understand, leaning down overtop of me.

"And then you're going to help me. It just so happens I need a Sea-leg."

Mother. I couldn't get the words out. I couldn't speak to her.

After a moment of silence, Mayra spoke again. "I am going to regret this."

CHAPTER
SEVENTY-FOUR

Liv

In many stories, people look inside themselves for the kernel of magic, for their power, but this power isn't mine. I'm not even sure it's the gods. The Ikhor wants something, and it's not to be returned. In fact, it wants revenge. It's connected to the earth and uses the earth's power as its own, as if connected to all magic—I can feel it in every rock and tree, even more so in the crystals. This being that possessed me, I've made its voice my own and learned to speak its language with my heart—my emotions. Unfortunately for the world, my heart is broken, tainted and full of hate.

Nuo had once given me so much drink that I woke feeling like I had fallen from a great height and mashed every bone in my body. I discovered in the worst way what falling from a great height and breaking every bone actually felt like.

I had battled the Aspis, passing through clouds, fighting to be free of its sharp teeth, only to be thrown into the open sky. We had flown a great distance until the air turned cold, freezing me. Until the Aspis could no longer be controlled.

Brekt had tried for as long as he could to stay in command, but I paid for it when he faded away. The Aspis opened its mouth, roaring, and dropped me.

I plummeted to my death. The wind stole my breath while the beast chased me through the clouds, so I fought and sent a ball of fire to its face.

As I fell and fell and fell, it followed me, snapping its teeth, trying to catch me or end me—I couldn't tell.

Smoke churned around its long body, slithering through the sky. Arms formed from the smoke, with vicious claws tearing through the skin. I sent a bolt of lightning at it, catching it between the eyes and causing it to lose consciousness.

My hair whipped me in the face, but I didn't look away from the beast. The Aspis fell through the sky with me, and I spread my arms wide to slow myself, reaching its horns and grabbed on, pulling myself around. I held onto the black curling horn, wrapping myself around it as the ground rose to meet us.

Everything below was white. Ice cliffs rose to the sky. Until we were atop them. The icy rock scraped along the beast's side as I used the last of my energy to summon wind, slowing the Aspis down as it crashed through ice and snow. I gripped its horn, praying my magic could heal a body broken from such a fall.

We crashed against the rock and ice, sliding down a mountainside.

A sound boomed like the earth cracking in two, and then it went dark.

I drifted for a time in the nightmare place. I may have even seen Brekt there. We were connected in a place outside of the real world, and I didn't have an answer to the dreams, even after discovering what the shadow monster was, who was setting fires to the earth and what it was that took me from my lands. The dream place was a mystery.

But I didn't stay there for long, and when I came to, I groaned, writhing in pain as my magic stitched my body back together. I only prayed it went back together the right way.

I wasn't sure if I had lost my vision or if it was night. I blinked several times, making sure my eyes were open, and was met only with darkness.

The Aspis was alive. Its laboured breathing wasn't far from where I lay. By the rattling sound, it had been badly hurt, too. Served it right for trying to kill me high above the ground. I prayed Brekt felt none of it the next time he woke.

My fingers burned as I felt around me, meeting icy rock. I continued to writhe in pain, reminded of the time when Kazhi healed me in a tub. Magycris's healing was much the same. Of course, it was—magic healing didn't save you from feeling how your body stitched back together.

After an eternity of bones being repaired and pain stealing my breath, my mind went quiet, savouring the peace that returned with a healed body.

The Aspis's deep breathing gave off a slight echo, meaning we had to have walls around us. My right side absorbed the warmth it gave off.

"Ugh," I pushed myself up, sitting, thankful that I could. I didn't dare call out for help, not in the dark. I didn't want to know what might answer. Instead, I summoned a bit of fire. It burst to life, blinding me.

"I'm not angry," I said in a low voice. I felt no emotion, yet the fire came easily, resting as a tiny ball in my palm. It flickered, warm light shining off glistening scales a few feet to my right—I was controlling it with just a thought.

I blinked, and it was out. I summoned it again, and it exploded in my hand, burning my cheeks—*maybe not full control.*

I moved my hand to angle the light downward. My leather pants were scraped but not destroyed, and my swords remained attached to their belt. Curiously, my pack was lying several feet away, half-buried in snow.

I grabbed a strand of hair with my free hand—white. So, the magic healed my wounds but had not turned me back to my former self.

I stood, brushed the snow off my pants, swiped my hair from my face, and wrapped my free arm around myself, shaking from the cold. I willed the fire to grow, amazed when it obeyed, bathing in its warmth.

The Aspis's head was hidden in the dark.

I would need to find wood to set alight so I could stop using the magic; otherwise, Brekt would not be able to take control and return. And all alone in this darkness, I needed him more than ever.

I walked along the side of the Aspis until I reached its head. It was slanted to one side, and its eyes were closed, but it was alive. I rested my free hand against the scales of its massive jaw. "You'll live. I promise. I will get us out of here."

Frost gathered at the tips of its scales. I would need a big fire to keep the beast from freezing. Its breath was warm, easing the cold from my joints before I braved moving past it in the dark.

I tried to recall what happened. I remembered Rem, the shadow monster, and then ...

"Kill the bastards."

Nuo had been shot. Dying. My steps faltered as I remembered him lying on the ground, bleeding out.

But no, he had stood again. He had spoken to me, telling me to stop. Stop what?

My feet crunched on ice as I tried to remember. I recalled flashes of water, fire and bodies hanging from vines—I sucked in a breath. "What did I do?" My voice echoed.

I spun to find the Aspis still sleeping—images came back to me of death. So many people dead. Had I caused that?

The Aspis's breathing shook, as did my own. I watched its curled body rise and fall while I panicked. I needed to get out of here, get back to the shrine, and find the others.

I conjured more flames, lighting up a larger area, spinning to find a way out, only for the light to bounce back. We were in an ice cave. I couldn't see very high up, but the Aspis must have crashed through ice, taking us below ground. I ran through the glittering cavern, with hard, cold rock under my feet, until I came to a wall of stone.

I lifted my hand to find the stone going up and up. "There has to be a way out."

I followed the rock wall, farther away from the Aspis, until I discovered the massive painting spanning the entire facade. We couldn't be far from the outside. In every cave I visited with the Guards, the paintings were always near the entrance.

I summoned more fire until both hands were alight with it. For a moment, I was distracted by how easily the fire came, but I shook it off. Tilting my head up, I studied the images, which were so large that they disappeared into shadow. My muscles relaxed as the warmth of the fire spread, forcing the cold away.

I lifted my palms to further illuminate the painted image. I stepped to the right, then to the left. I jumped to see higher, my movements becoming more frantic as more of the painting was revealed.

"Oh my god."

I couldn't believe what I found in a pure, terrifyingly fortunate streak of luck.

"Oh my god!" I repeated.

Other caves I had visited in Veydes had paintings of the legacies, depicting them standing around their temples. It was much the same as this painting, only this time ...

"This is a map!"

Ouras's temple, depicted with his Mount-legs in Veydes,

settled in a forest above river lands, but Danuli wasn't painted. That had to mean this map was ancient.

In the southern desert land sat Rem's temple.

"The Temple of Day," I whispered, seeing not only the golden Day-legs around the building like they painted in Veydes, but blue and white too. Was this cave in Rydavas? Or was it hidden for so many years the truth hadn't been erased?

I lifted my hands to search north of Rem's temple, and sure enough, the South Aspis Guardian camp didn't exist.

Wherever the Aspis had flown us was far away from any modern-day settlements. No one was exploring these caves, looking for crystals. This cave was untouched. It had to be if these images were left intact.

The sea between Veydes and Rydavas differed from Nuo's map —larger, with rivers going through where the Eagle's canyon now sat, splitting the continents in two.

Each piece of this painting was perfectly intact.

"In the cave before the Oracle's village ... the cave painting Nuo and I inspected, pieces of it were missing as if *scraped* away," I muttered to myself. Was this another piece of history changed by Rem? Had he instructed his children to erase the truth?

My heart threatened to stop, it was pounding so fast. I needed to see higher. Something important had to be in the far north. I ran from the wall, fumbling in the snow and slipping on the ice. It took me far too long to find several stones small enough to carry back and make a pile to stand on. I stacked them, one on top of the other before climbing the stones and steadying my weight. Then, summoning the fire back to full strength, I reached my arms high, standing on my tiptoes.

Adrenaline pumped into my magic, brightening the flames and sending the light across the cave wall. I lit up the river lands, the plains, and the Oracle's jungle, which had been bare mountains long ago. Bellum didn't exist, but other small settlements I had never heard of scattered across the lands. I moved the flames again, scanning farther across the wall and—

"Oh my god."

There it was.

Dark and massive, a terrifying structure was shown surrounded by legacies, all with glowing eyes. Black spires rose high into the sky, so much larger than the people below.

Brekt had said there were no records left showing the locations of the missing temples, but he hadn't searched a cave like this one.

I had.

And I had found the lost Temple of Night.

Acknowledgments

First, I would like to apologize to my bèbè for constantly bugging you about my book. Every. Single. Day. Thinking about your unwavering belief in me from the start makes my heart all fuzzy.

To my homie, KP, for coming up with awesome ideas for fight scenes and a wicked back story for the Desert Eagle. The Eagle would only be a quarter as cool without you—but I'll take some credit since I wrote the damn book.

Thank you to my beta readers who started off with a super rough —and cringy—story and helped me polish it. Jocelyn, Breanna, Kelsey and Sam, you each have a unique way of critiquing the work. Having a variety of unique thinkers is a massive bonus to a writer.

I want to do the biggest, loudest and most obnoxious thank-you rant to my editors. Sam and Kelsey, you two could not be more different in the type of comments you return to me. Sam, with her bluntness and dislike of symmetrical men, and Kelsey, with her attention to detail and knack for finding unintended kinks, you both made my story amazing, even to me—you're wizards, or something equally magical and important!

To my sisters, Emily and Sam, thank you for supporting my career as an author and following me to every signing event in the past two years. Knowing I can count on you two makes it so much easier to show up and speak to real people in real life, something I am often averse to doing. I appreciate you, Sambo—who doesn't read fiction—for memorizing all my tropes to repeat to readers when they ask what my book is about. Emily, I appreciate how you refuse to read my book because of the world-building. If anyone has monster romances where they "get some" by page five, please send recs her way.

And of course, I want to thank anyone who has picked up my story and read it. Whether you read a page or the entire book, thank you for giving your time to the Guardians. Thank you to those who have given a review, made a post or even a video. Tiktokers, Instagrammers, Facebookers and Redditers—I appreciate you all. A special shout-out to the Reddit user who gave my book three-stars but still recommends it every other day. I don't know who you are, but I appreciate your tenacity—PS: Liv doesn't have amnesia, she's just out to lunch, but the rest of the tropes you've got right, and you're recommending it to the best threads. Unsarcastic two thumbs up! Keep up the good work!

I'm so thankful for every small interaction I have as an author. Please don't hesitate to reach out on social media or even the old-fashioned way with an email. I love getting messages, hearing your thoughts and gushing about the characters.

To Nuo's fans, have faith. The next book is for you ;)

ABOUT THE AUTHOR

Sarah was born and raised in rural Ontario, Canada, where she loved to explore her backyard in search of magical creatures and talking trees. In her twenties, she spent several years travelling the far reaches of the world. She eventually returned home with an imagination more vivid and overflowing with ideas. Stories began to sprout. Finally, in her early thirties, she began writing those stories down and discovered her real passion. In her spare time, she also enjoys playing music, drawing and practicing martial arts, in which she holds a first-degree black belt.

Curious about what comes next? Sign up for Sarah's newsletter to receive updates. www.sarahrosebooks.com

9 781738 845439